"I dived straight in, emerging a couple of days later – with a grin on my face... an engaging, fast paced cocktail of violence and intrigue that grabs you right from the outset and doesn't let go until you run out of pages."

My Favourite Books

"*Kell's Legend* is a rollercoaster ride of a book that grabbed me right from the first page and tore off at a rate of knots like I hadn't seen in a long time."

Graeme's Fantasy Book Review

"*Soul Stealers* is fast, brutal and above all unmissable, there is quite simply nothing out there that can currently compare to Andy Remic's unrelenting, unforgiving and unflinching style. The new King of Heroic Fantasy has arrived. 5*****"

SFBook.com

"Add to the mix a good dollop of battlefield humour... backed up with a stark descriptiveness and it's a tale that gives Remic a firm footing within the genre."

Falcata Times

"A rip-roaring beast of a novel, a whirlwind of frantic battles and fraught relationships against a bleak back-ground of invasion and enslavement. In other words, it takes all the vital ingredients for a good heroic fantasy novel and turns out something very pleasing indeed."

Speculative Horizons

"A fun ride... I give it four bloody axes out of five."

Gnostalgia

ALSO BY ANDY REMIC

The Clockwork Vampire Chronicles
Kell's Legend
Soul Stealers
Vampire Warlords

The Spiral Series
Spiral
Quake
Warhead

Combat-K
War Machine
Biohell
Hardcore
Cloneworld

ANDY REMIC

The Clockwork Vampire Chronicles

KELL'S LEGEND • SOUL STEALERS

VAMPIRE WARLORDS

ANGRY ROBOT

ANGRY ROBOT
A member of the Osprey Group

Lace Market House,
54-56 High Pavement,
Nottingham,
NG1 1HW, UK

www.angryrobotbooks.com
Blood for oil

This omnibus first published by Angry Robot 2012

Cover art by Kekai Kotaki.

Distributed in the United States by Random House, Inc., New York.

ISBN 978-0-85766-205-7
eBOOK ISBN 978-0-85766-206-4

Printed in the United States of America

9 8 7 6 5 4 3 2 1

THE CLOCKWORK
VAMPIRE CHRONICLES

Kell's Legend

Soul Stealers

Vampire Warlords

INTRODUCTION

Despite rumours to the contrary, the original spark of inspiration for Kell wasn't actually Druss the Legend from David Gemmell's fabulous fantasy novel, *Legend* (although there was no doubt some subconscious devil-trickery at play there). No. One winter afternoon, I was mountain biking across the Pennine Moors with my good buddy Jake, when we breached a high moorland rise and looked down over an ice-encrusted lake. For a split second, through the whipping snow and ice, through the cackles of a howling bitter wind, I envisioned a lighthouse on the edges of a choppy shore, and in the lighthouse lived an old, gnarled axe-man with grey beard, whiskey habit and a lust for battle. He was an old fisherman, a retired sailor. A hermit. A recluse. And a very bad man. The novel was to be called *Kell's Legend*, and recount his tales of the ocean. This old man would be a much darker anti-hero than Druss, with an evil bloody background of piracy and dark deeds. Sure, he had a beard and an axe – but hell, how many characters in *Lord of the Rings* carried an axe?

That evening I sketched out some ideas, and promptly shelved the novel. I was far from being published at the time, and working on a hard SF novel called *War Machine* (unrelated to the eventually published *War Machine*, some 10 years later).

Anyway, that would have been around... 1995. Long before I was published. And a good fourteen years before I actually sat down to write what became *Kell's Legend*.

After being asked by AR publisher Marc Gascoigne to write a

tasy trilogy for the new imprint, I knew I wanted to do something surrounding my *vachine* creation; about clockwork mpires. This was an image and idea that had haunted many a drunken night around the camp fire. And from the dredges of a twisted memory arose Kell, the perfect character to populate my new world of vachine and cankers and deviant blood-oil magick.

In retrospect, *yes*, maybe he was similar to Druss in the same way that David's *Legend* was similar to *Zulu*. But my intention was to start with the old grizzled warrior, honourable and strong and unwilling to take any grief – and then gradually make him my own, gradually shift him into the realm of an independent creation. To this end, I believe I was successful. But that's not to take away from the fact that David Gemmell's *Legend* was a formative novel of my reading years, and indeed, David Gemmell a larger-than-life hero to me – me, a man who doesn't believe in heroes.

Kell's Legend, *Soul Stealers* and *Vampire Warlords* were all published as single volumes, and the first two ended with roaring huge cliff-hangers. Many people cursed me for this, whilst at the same time praising the books and bemoaning how desperate they were to discover the fate of the heroes within. I found this quite amusing, in a cruel and evil cackling sort of way, because I, too, know how annoying a cliff-hanger can be. Which is why I use them. However, *now* with this single volume there will be no such teasing; I present the books here for your enjoyment, in one twisted whiskey barrel.

The reception to the three individual novels, *Kell's Legend*, *Soul Stealers* and *Vampire Warlords* has been phenomenal. I've had an endless stream of good reviews (barring one cracking negative review of *Kell's* over at Pornokitsch blog, a fantastically comic-written piece in its own right that made me laugh out loud with drools of snot and saliva, and simultaneously want to sink a chipped axe-blade into the writer's skull splitting him from crown to bollocks in one easy meat slice). Anyway. I've also had a barrage of mail from fans of the books, all positive I'm pleased to say. It would seem most people "got" what I was trying to do – which is to pay homage to David Gemmell, a great writer taken in his prime; and also an attempt to keep the spirit of Druss alive whilst trying to add my own dark twist.

In fact, now that *Vampire Warlords* (the third volume) is published, I have indeed had more letters and praise about this sequence of novels than any other I've written – and every single missive asks the same question: Will there be more stories of Kell and Saark?

I can say here that I've had ideas for another two "trilogies" in the same universe, effectively two more cycles in the Kell/Saark saga. I'm not sure how long they will take to write, or even when they will appear, but trust me that only an untimely death will stand between me writing more of Kell and Saark. As I'm sure you will appreciate upon reading these books, there is just too much joy and sparkle in the relationships of the characters to never revisit. The bond, bantering and bickering of Kell and Saark is a brilliant thing to write; these characters live for me, they simply flow from my fingers like magick...

I hope you enjoy the *Clockwork Vampire* chronicles as much as I enjoyed writing them. Believe me when I say each moment was a treasure.

Andy Remic
October 2011

I
KELL'S LEGEND

PROLOGUE
Slaughter

"I know you think me sadistic. You are incorrect. When I punish, I punish without pleasure. When I torture, I torture for knowledge, progression, and for truth. And when I kill..." General Graal placed both hands on the icy battlements, staring dream-like to the haze of distant Black Pike Mountains caught shimmering and unreal through the mist: huge, defiant, proud, unconquered. He grinned a narrow, skeletal grin. "Then I kill to feed."

Graal turned, and stared at the kneeling man. Command Colonel Yax-kulkain was forty-eight years old, a seasoned warrior and leader of the Garrison Regiment at Jalder, Falanor's major northern city and trading post connecting east, south and west military supply routes, also known as the Northern T.

Yax-kulkain was hunkered down, fists twitching uncontrollably, staring up into Graal's blue eyes. Pupil dilation told Graal the commander could still understand, despite his paralysis. Graal smiled, a thin-lipped smile with white lips that blended eerily into the near-albino skin of his soft, some would say feminine, face. Running a hand through alabaster hair Graal released a hiss and gave a heavy, pendulous nod. "I see you understand me, colonel."

Yax-kulkain murmured something, an animal sound deep in his throat. He trembled, in his frozen, kneeling position, and with ice crackling his beard, gradually, with incredible force of will, lifted his blue-hued face and snarled up at the conquering general. There came a crack as he forced frozen jaws apart. Ice fell, tinkling from his beard. In rage, the ice-chilled warrior spat, "You will... rot... in hell!"

General Graal turned, staring almost nostalgically across frosted battlements. He spun on his heel, a fast fluid motion, slim blade slamming to cut the command colonel's head from his body. The head rolled, hitting stone flags and cracking a platter of ice. It rocked, and came to a halt, eyes staring blank at the bleak, snow-filled sky.

"I think not," said Graal, staring down the long line of kneeling men, of rigid, frozen soldiers that stretched away down the considerable length of the ice-rimed battlements. "It would appear I am already there." His voice rose in volume to a bellow. "Soldiers of the Army of Iron!" He paused, voice dropping to a guttural growl. "Kill them all."

Like automatons, insects, albino soldiers stepped up with a synchronised rhythm behind the ranks of frozen infantry at Falanor's chief garrison; white hair whipped in the wind, and black armour cut a savage contrast to pale, waxen flesh. Black swords unsheathed, eight hundred oiled whispers of precision steel, and General Graal moved his hand with a casual flick as he turned away. Swords descended, sliced through flesh and fat and bone, and eight hundred heads toppled from twitching shoulders to thud and roll. Because of the frozen flesh, there was no blood. It was a clean slaughter.

Ice-smoke swirled, thickening, flowing in the air from a resplendent and unwary city below, beyond the smashed protection of the garrison stronghold. Buildings spread gracefully and economically up the steep hillside from the broad, half-frozen platter of the Selenau River; and as Graal's odd blue eyes narrowed to nothing more than slits, it was clear the ice-smoke was anything but natural: there were sinister elements at play.

Graal strode down the line of corpses, halting occasionally and stooping to force his finger into the icy stump of a soldier's neck. The swirling smoke thickened. Through this carnage, up the narrow steps to the battlements, glided–

The Harvesters.

They were tall, impossibly tall for men, and wore thin white robes embroidered with fine gold wire and draped over bony, elongated figures. Their faces were flat, oval, hairless, eyes small and black, their noses nothing more than twin vertical slits which hissed with a fast rhythm of palpitation. Their hands were hidden under flapping cuffs and they strode unhurriedly, heads bobbing as they stooped to survey the scene. The ranks of motionless albino soldiers took reverential steps back, and whilst faces did not show fear exactly, the albino warriors of Graal's army revealed a healthy respect. One did not cross the Harvesters. Not if a man valued his soul.

The first halted, peering myopically down at Graal, who folded his arms and smiled without humour. "You are late, Hestalt."

Hestalt nodded, and when he spoke his words were a lazy sigh of wind. "We were preparing the ice-smoke for the city. We had to commune with Nonterrazake. Now, however, the time has come. Are your men ready with their primitive weapons of iron?"

"My soldiers are always prepared," said Graal, unruffled, and he unsheathed his own slender sword. The Harvester did not flinch; instead, a hand appeared from folds of white robe. Each finger was ten or twelve inches long, narrowing to a tapered point of gleaming ivory. The Harvester turned, bent, and plunged all five bone fingers into the corpse of Command Colonel Yaxkulkain. There came a gentle resonance of suction, and Graal watched, mouth tight-lipped, as the body began to deflate, shrivelling, flesh shrinking across the bones beneath.

Hestalt withdrew bone fingers, and leaving a tiny, shrivelled husk in his wake, moved to the next dead soldier of Falanor. Again, his fingers invaded the man's chest, deep into his heart, and the Harvester reaped the Harvest.

Unable to watch this desecration of flesh, General Graal shouted a command which rang down the mist-filled battlements. Ice-smoke eddied around his knees, now, expanding and billowing in exaggerated bursts as he strode towards the steps leading down to the cobbled courtyard. His albino regiment followed in silence, swords unsheathed and ready, and like a tide, with Graal at its spearhead, moved to mammoth oak gates that opened onto a cobbled central thoroughfare, which in turn led down the steep hillside into Jalder's central city – into the city's heart.

Two albinos ran forward, slim figures, well balanced and athletic, graceful and moving with care on ice-slick cobbles. The oak portals were heaved apart, iron hinges groaning, and Graal turned glancing back at the tall stooping figures that moved methodically along the battlements, draining the dead Falanor garrison of life-force. Like insects, he thought, and made distant eye contact with Hestalt. The Harvester gave a single nod: a command. He pointed towards the city… and his instruction was clear.

Prepare a path.

Ice-smoke gathered in the courtyard, a huge pulsing globe which spun and built and coalesced with flickers of dancing silver; suddenly, it surged out through the gates to flow like airborne mercury into the city beyond, still expanding, still growing, a flood of eerie silence and cotton-wool death, a plague of drifting ice-smoke shifting to encompass the unwary city in a tomb-shroud of blood-oil magick.

ONE
Death-Ice

Kell stood by the window in his low-ceilinged second-storey apartment, and stared with a twinge of melancholy towards the distant mountains. Behind him a fire crackled in the hearth, flames consuming pine, and a pan of thick vegetable broth bubbled on a cast-iron tripod. Kell lifted a stubby mug to his lips and sipped neat liquor with a sigh, feeling alcohol-resin tease down his throat and into his belly, warming him through. He shivered despite the drink, and thought about snow and ice, and the dead cold places of the mountains; the vast canyons, the high lonely ledges, the slopes leading to rocky falls and instant death. Chill memories pierced the winter of his soul, if not his flesh. Sometimes, thought Kell, he would never banish the ice of his past... and those dark days of hunting in the realm of the Black Pikes. Ice lay in his heart. Trapped, like a diamond.

Outside, snow drifted on a gentle breeze, swirling down cobbled streets and dancing patterns into the air. From his vantage point, Kell could watch the market traders by the Selenau River, and to the right, make out the black-brick bulks of huge tanneries, warehouses and the riverside slaughter-houses. Kell remembered with a shudder how dregside stunk to heaven in high summer – that's why he'd got the place cheap. But now... now the claws of winter had closed, they kept the stench at bay.

Kell shivered again, the vision of dancing snow chilling old bones. He turned back to his soup and the fire, and stirred the pan's contents, before leaning forward, hand thumping against the sturdy beam of the mantel. Outside, on the steps, he heard a clatter of boots and swiftly placed his mug on a high shelf beside an ancient clock and beneath the terrifying butterfly blades of Ilanna. Inside the clock, he could see tiny whirring clockwork components; so fine and intricate, a pinnacle of miniature engineering.

The thick plank door shuddered open and Nienna stood in silhouette, beaming, kicking snow from her boots.

"Hello, Grandpa!"

"Nienna." He moved to her and she hugged him, the snow in her long brown hair damping his grey beard. He took a step back, holding her at arm's length. "My, you grow taller by the day, I swear!"

"It's all that fine broth." She peered over his shoulder, inquisitively. "Keeps me fit and strong. What have you cooked today?"

"Come on, take off your coat and you can have a bowl. It's vegetable; beef is still too expensive after the cattle-plague in the summer, although I'm guaranteed a side in two or three weeks. From a friend of a friend, no?" He gave a broad wink.

Removing her coat, Nienna edged to the oak table and cocked one leg over the bench, straddling it. Kell placed a hand-carved wooden bowl before her, and she reached eagerly for the spoon as Kell sliced a loaf of black nut-bread with a long, curved knife.

"It's good!"

"Might need some more salt."

"No, it's perfect!" She spooned greedily, wolfing her broth with the eagerness of hunger.

"Well," said Kell, sitting opposite his granddaughter with a smile which split his wrinkled, bearded face, making him appear younger than his sixty-two years. "You shouldn't be so surprised. I *am* the best cook in Jalder."

"Hmm, maybe, but I think it could do with some beef," said Nienna, pausing, spoon half raised as she affected a frown.

Kell grinned. "Ach, but I'm just a poor old soldier. Couldn't possibly afford that."

"Poor? With a fortune stashed under the floor?" said Nienna, head down, eyes looking up and glinting mischievously. "That's what mother says. Mother says you're a miser and a skinflint, and you hide money in a secret stash wrapped in your stinky socks under the boards."

Kell gave a tight smile, some of his humour evaporating. "Your mother always was one for compliments." He brightened. "Anyway, my girl, you're the cheeky monkey here! With your tricks and cheeky words."

"I'm a bit old for you to keep calling me that, grandpa."

"No, lass, you're still a little girl." He leant forward, and ruffled her hair. She scowled in distaste.

"Grandpa! I am not a girl anymore! I'm nearly seventeen!"

"You'll always be a little girl to me. Now eat your broth."

They ate in silence, the only sound that of fire crackling through logs as the wind outside increased in ferocity, kicking up eddies of snow and howling mournfully along frosted, cobbled streets. Nienna finished her broth, and circled her bowl with the last of the black bread. She sat back, sighing. "Good! Too much salt, but good all the same."

"As I said, the best cook in Jalder."

"Have you ever seen a monkey? Really?" she asked suddenly, displaying a subtle hint of youth.

"Yes. In the deep jungles of the south. It's too cold up here for monkeys; I suppose they're fond of their bananas."

"What's a banana?"

"A soft, yellow fruit."

"Do I really look like one?"

"A fruit, or a monkey?"

She smacked his arm. "You know what I mean!"

"A little," said Kell, finishing his own broth and chewing thoughtfully. His teeth were paining him again. "There is a likeness: the hairy face, the fleas, the fat bottom."

"Grandpa! You don't speak to a lady like that! There's this thing we learnt in school, it's called eti... ettick..."

"Etiquette." He ruffled her hair again. "And when you're grown up, Nienna, then I'll treat you like a grown-up." His smile was infectious. Nienna helped to clean away the bowls. She stood by the window for a few moments, staring out and down towards the distant factories and the market.

"You fought in the south jungles, didn't you, Grandpa?"

Kell felt his mood instantly sour, and he bit his tongue against an angry retort. *The girl doesn't realise,* he chided himself. He took a deep breath. "Yes. That was a long time ago. I was a different person back then."

"What was it like? Fighting, in the army, with King Searlan? It must have been so... romantic!"

Kell snorted. "Romantic? The dung they fill your head with in school these days. There's nothing romantic about watching your friends slaughtered. Nothing heroic about seeing crows on a battlefield squabbling over corpse eyes. No." His voice dropped to a whisper. "Battles are for fools."

"But still," persisted Nienna, "I think I'd like to join the army. My friend Kat says they take women now; or you can join as a nurse, to help with battlefield casualties. They give you good training. We had a command sergeant, he came to the school trying to sign us up. Kat wanted to sign, but I thought I'd talk to you first."

Kell moved across the room, so fast he was a blur. Nienna was shocked. He moved too quickly for a big man, for an old man; it was unreal. He took her shoulders in bear paws with surprising gentleness. And he shook her. "Now you listen to me, Nienna, you have a gift, a rare talent like I've not seen in a long while. The music's in your blood, girl, and I'm sure when the angels hear you sing they'll be green with envy." He took a deep breath, gazing with unconditional love into her eyes. "Listen good, Nienna, and understand an old man. An unknown benefactor has paid your university fees. That person has spared you a lifetime of hardship in the tanneries, or in the factories working weaving machinery so treacherous it'll cut your damn fingers off; and the bastards will let it, rather than stop production. So, girl, you go to your university, and you work like you've never worked before, or I'll kick you so hard from behind, my boot will come out of your mouth."

Nienna lowered her head. "Yes, Grandpa. I'm sorry. It's just..."

"What?" His eyes were dark glowing coals.

"It's just – I'm bored! I'd like some excitement, an adventure! All I ever see is home, and here, and school. And I know I can sing, I know that, but it's not a future filled with excitement, is it? It's not something that's going to boil my blood!"

"Excitement is overrated," growled Kell, turning and moving with a wince to his low leather chair. He slumped, grimacing at the pain in his lower back which nagged more frequently these days, despite the thick, green, stinking unguent applied by old Mrs Graham. "Excitement is the sort of thing that gets a person killed."

"You're such a grump!" Nienna skipped across the room, and

tugged on her boots. "I've got to get going. We're having a tour of the university this afternoon. It's a shame the snow has come down so thick; the gardens are said to be awesomely pretty."

"Yes, the winter has come early. Such is the legacy of the Black Pike Mountains." He gazed off, through the wide low window, to a far-distant haze of black and white teeth. The Black Pikes called to him. They always would. They had a splinter of his soul.

"Some of my friends are going to explore the Black Pikes this summer; when they finish their studies, of course."

"Fools," snapped Kell. "The Pikes are more dangerous than anything you could ever imagine."

"You've been there?"

"Three times. And three times I believed I was never coming back." His voice grew quiet, drifting, lost. "I knew I would die, up there. On those dark rocky slopes. It is a miracle I still live, girl!"

"Was that when you were in the army?" She was fishing for stories, again, and he waved her away.

"Go on! Get to your friends; go, enjoy your university tour. And make sure you sing for them! Show them your angel's voice! They will have never heard anything like it."

"I will, Grandpa." Nienna tugged on her coat, and brushed out her long brown hair. "Grandpa?"

"Yes, monkey?"

"I... I nearly told mam, about you, this morning. About coming here, I mean. I do so want to tell her... I hate keeping secrets."

Kell shook his head, face stern. "If you tell her, girl, she will make doubly sure you never see me again. She hates me. Can you understand that?" Nienna nodded, but Kell could see in her eyes she did not have the life experience to truly comprehend the hate his daughter carried for him – like a bad egg in her womb. But one day, he thought savagely, one day she'll learn. We all do.

"Yes, Grandpa. I'll try my best." She opened the door, and a bitter chill swept in on a tide of fresh, tumbling snow. She stepped forward, then paused, and gave a half-turn so he couldn't quite see her face. "Kell?"

"Yes, granddaughter?" He blinked, unused to her calling him by name.

"Thanks for paying my university fees." She leant back, and kissed his cheek, and was gone in a whirl of coat and scarf leaving him standing blushing at the top of the steps. He shook his head, watching her footprints crunch through a fresh fall towards a gentle mist drifting in off the Selenau River.

How had she guessed? he thought. He closed the door, which struggled to fit the frame. He thumped it shut with a bear's fist, and absently slid the heavy bar into place. He moved back to the fireplace, reclaiming his abandoned resin-liquor and taking a heavy slug. Alcohol eased into his veins like an old friend, and wrapped his brain in honey. Kell took a deep breath, moving back to the wide window and sitting on a low bench to watch the bartering traders across a field of flapping stalls. The mist was creeping into the market now, swirling around boots and timber stanchions. Kell gazed at the mountains, the Black Pike Mountains, his eyes distant, remembering the hunt there; as he did, many times in a day.

"Join the army – ha!" he muttered, scowling, and refilled his mug from a clay jug.

Kell awoke, senses tingling, mouth sour, head fuzzy, and wondered not just what had awoken him, but how in Hell's Teeth he'd fallen asleep? "Damn the grog," he muttered, cursing himself for his weakness and age, and swearing he'd stop the liquor; though knowing, deep in his heart, it was a vow he'd never uphold.

Kell sat up from the window-bench, rubbing his eyes and yawning. He glanced right, but all he saw through the long, low window was mist, thick and white, swirling and coalescing through the streets. He could determine a few muffled stone walls, some snow-slick cobbles, but that was all. A terrible white had expanded to fill the world.

Kell moved to his water barrel and gulped three full flagons, with streams running through his grey beard and staining his cotton shirt. He rubbed his eyes again, head spinning, and turned to watch the mist creeping under his door. Odd, he thought. He glanced up to Ilanna, his axe, hanging over the fireplace. She gleamed, dull black reflecting firelight. Kell turned again, and with a crack the window, nearly the width of the entire room, sheared with a metallic crackling as if it had been placed under great pressure. Mist drifted into the apartment.

In reflex, Kell grabbed a towel, soaked it in his water barrel, and wrapped it over his mouth and nose, tying it behind his head. What are you doing, you crazy old fool? screamed his mind. This is no fire smoke! It will do you no harm! But some deep instinct, some primal intuition guided him and he reached up to tug the long-hafted battle-axe from her restraining brackets. Bolts snapped, and the brackets clattered into the fire...

Ice-smoke swirled across his boots, roved across the room, and smothered the fire. It crackled viciously, then died. Outside, a woman gave a muffled scream; the scream ended in a gurgle.

Kell's eyes narrowed, and he strode to his door – as outside, footsteps moved fast up the ice-slick ascent. Kell twisted to one side. The door rattled, and soundlessly Kell slid the bar out of place. The door was kicked open and two soldiers eased into his apartment carrying black swords; their faces were pale and white, their hair long, braided, and as white as the ice-smoke which had smothered Kell's fire.

Kell grinned at the two men, who separated, spreading apart as Kell backed away several steps. The first man rushed him, sword slashing for his throat but Kell twisted, rolling, his axe thundering in a backhand sweep that caught the albino across the head with blade slicing a two-inch slab from the soldier's unprotected skull. The man stumbled back, white blood spraying through clawing fingers, as the second soldier leapt at Kell. But Kell was ready, and his boot hooked under the bench, lifting it hard and fast into the attacker's path. The soldier stumbled over oak and, double-handed, Kell slammed his axe overhead into the fallen man's back, pinning him to the bench. He writhed, gurgling for a while, then spasmed and lay still. A large pool of white blood spread beneath him. Kell placed his boot on the man's armour and tugged free his axe, frowning. *White blood?* He glanced right, to where the injured soldier, with a quarter of his head missing, lay on a pile of rugs, panting fast.

Kell strode to him. "What's going on, lad?"

"Go to hell," snarled the soldier, strings of saliva and blood drooling from his teeth.

"So, an attack is it?" Kell hefted his axe thoughtfully. Then, his face paled, and his hand came to the water-soaked towel. "What dark magick is this? Who leads you, boy? Tell me now, and I'll spare you." It was a lie, and it felt bad on Kell's tongue. He had no intentions of letting the soldier live.

"I'd rather fucking die, old man!"

"So be it."

The axe struck the albino's head from his shoulders, and Kell turned his back on the twitching corpse showing a cross-section of spine and gristle, his mind sour, mood dropping fast into a brooding bitter pit. This wasn't supposed to be his life. No more killing! He was a retired soldier. An old warrior. He no longer walked the mountains, battle-axe in hand, coated in the blood and gore of the slain. Kell shook his head, mouth grim. But then, the gods mocked him, yes? The gods were fickle; they would see to it any retirement Kell sought was blighted with misery.

Nienna!

"Damn them." Kell moved to the steps, peering out into ice-smoke. He nodded to himself. It had to be blood-oil magick. No natural mist moved like this: organic, like coils of snakes in a bucket. Shivering, Kell moved swiftly down the steps and ice-smoke bit his hands, making him yelp. He ran back up to his apartment and pulled on heavy layers of clothing, a thick hat with fur-lined ear-flaps, and a bulky, bear-skin jerkin which broadened Kell's already considerable width of chest. Finally, Kell pulled on high-quality leather gloves and stepped back into the mist. He moved down wooden stairs and stood on a mixture of snow and cobbles, his face tingling. All around, the mist shrouded him in silence; it was a padded world. The air was muffled. Reduced. Shrunk. Kell strode to a nearby wall, and was reassured by the rough reality of black stone. So, he thought. I'm not a victim of a savage, drunken night-mare after all! He laughed at that. It felt like it.

Head pounding, Kell moved warily down the street towards the market. The cobbled road dropped towards the Selenau River, then curved east in a broad arc and wound up the hill towards rows of expensive villas and Jalder University beyond. Kell reached the edge of the market, and stopped. There was a body on the ground, mist curling around withered, ancient limbs. Frowning, Kell dropped to one knee and reached out. He touched dry, crisp flesh, and cried out, shocked—

Boots thudded at him from the white, and a sword slashed for his head. His axe came up at the last moment, and there was clash of steel. Kell rammed his left fist into the soldier's midriff, heard the woosh of expelled air as the man doubled over. Kell stood, and stamped on the man's head, his heavy boot crushing the al-bino's skull as more came from the mist and Kell, shock and realisation slamming through him, recognition that he was outnumbered, and his brow furrowed and dark thoughts shot through his brain and his blood was pumping, fired now, a deep pulsing rhythm, and he hadn't wanted this, he'd left this behind and it was back again, drawing him in, drawing him onto the knife edge of–

Murder.

Another sword whistled towards his head, and Kell ducked one shoulder, rolling left, axe whirring fast to embed in flesh. His right elbow shot back into a soldier's face and they were around him, swords and knives gleaming but that made life easier. He grinned. They were all enemy. Kell's mind took a step back and coolness washed his aura. His brain calmed, and he changed with an almost imperceptible *click*. Years fell away like abandoned confetti. He felt the old, dark magick flowing through blood like narcotic honey. He'd fought it. Now it was back. And he welcomed it.

Smoothly, Kell whirled and his axe thundered in an arc trailing white blood droplets. An albino soldier was beheaded, the axe continuing, then reversing suddenly to slam through another's breast-plate, cleaving through steel to shatter the sternum and pierce the pumping white heart within. Kell's fist clubbed a soldier to the ground; he ducked a sword slash, which whistled by his ear, and Ilanna slammed a third albino between the eyes, splitting his head like a fruit. Kell's thick fingers curled around another soldier's throat, and he lifted the lithe albino, legs dangling, and brought him close to his own serene and deadly calm features. He headbutted the soldier, spreading nose across pale white skin, and allowed the figure to flop uselessly to the cobbles. Then Kell was running, pounding through the market dodging husks of dried corpses, his own mouth dry, not with fear, but a terrible and ancient understanding as the extent of the slaughter dawned on him. This wasn't a few rogue brigands. This was a full-scale attack!

And the enemy, with matching armour, were professional, skilled, disciplined, ruthless. Throughout Kell's recent economic slaughter there had been no panic, no retreat. These were a people bred for war. And yet, even so, Kell had a premonition that he had met only the untrained – the frontliners, the new recruits. The expendable.

Sourly, Kell ran on, and stopped by the edge of the market, leaning against the stall of Brask the Baker to regain his breath. The smell of fresh bread twitched Kell's nostrils, and reaching out, he realised the racks of loaves were frozen solid. And so was Brask, down on his knees, hands on the edge of his stall, flesh blue and rigid.

"The bastards," snarled Kell, and calmed his breathing. Unused to running, and suffering the effects of excessive liquor and pipe-smoking, a decade out of the army, ten years sat watching the mountains and the snow, well, Kell was far from battle-fit. He waited for pain to subside, and ignored the flaring twinges of hot knives in his lower-back and knees, in his right elbow and shoulder, an arthritis-legacy from decades wielding a heavy battle-axe and carving lumps of flesh with solid, jarring bone-impact.

The Days of Blood, whispered a corner of his imagination, then cackled at him.

Go to hell!

Kell glanced up, into the mist. No, he corrected himself. Into the smoke. The ice-smoke.

He wasn't far from Jalder University. But it was uphill, and a damn steep hill at that. Gritting his teeth, face coursing with sweat under his thick hat and heavy clothing, Kell began a fast walk, holding his ribs as he prayed fervently to any gods willing to listen that Nienna was still present in the university grounds... and still alive.

Saark gazed down at her beautiful face, skin soft and coolly radiant in the glow from the snow-piled window-ledge. He lifted his hand and ran it through his long, curled black hair, shining with aromatic oils and the woman smiled up at him, love in her eyes, mouth parting, tongue teasing moist lips. Saark dropped his head, unable to contain himself any longer, unable to hold back the hard hot fiery lust and he kissed her with a passion, tasted sweet honey, sank into her warm depths, savoured her gift, inhaled her scent, imbibed her perfume, fell deep down into the soft lullaby of their kissing, their cradling, their connection, their joining. His hand moved down her flank and she pressed eagerly against him, moaning deep in her throat, in her chest, an eager, primal animal sound. Saark kissed her harder, more ferociously, feeling the beast inside him rear from the pit of his belly to his throat to encompass his mind and drown everything of reason in a pounding drive of hot blood and lust and the desperate need to fuck.

She stepped from her dress, and from glossy, silken underwear. Saark watched as if in a dream. He removed his jacket, careful not to let the jewels – so recently stolen from this beautiful lady's jewellery box – tinkle, as he draped it over a gold-embroidered chair.

"You are a real man, at last," she breathed, voice husky, and Saark kissed her breasts, tasting her nipples, tongue toying, his voice lost, his mind scattered; how could anybody keep such a gorgeous creature locked in a high cold crenellated tower? But then, her husband was ancient, this woman his prize, a beautiful peasant bought like any other object with favours from an outlying nobleman's villa. He kept her secreted here, a creature denied liberty and sexual congress.

Saark kissed her neck, her throat and her breasts which rose to meet him as she panted in need. He bit her nipples and she groaned, thrusting her naked body onto him. "Why does he keep you locked away, sweetie?" mumbled Saark, and as he murmured his fingers dropped to her cunt, which pressed against his cupping hand, warm, slick, firm, inviting him, urging him to take her... to take her hard...

Both her hands ran through Saark's long, curled black hair. "Because," she hissed, "he knows what a wild cat I'd be if he let me out to play!" She threw Saark to the floor and dropped, straddling him. Saark glanced up as she towered over him, aggressive, powerful, dominant, totally in charge, her jewelled hands on naked, swaying, circling hips, the smile of the jailer etched on her face as she eyed him like a cat eyes a cornered mouse. Saark's gaze slowly strayed, from the sexual cunt-honey dripping from her quivering vulva, to the large rubies on the rings that circled her fingers. He licked his lips, dry now at the excitement of gems and gold. "I think," he said in all honesty, and without any trace of the subtle cynicism which commanded him and in which he prided himself, "I think this is my lucky day."

It was later. Much later. Weak light sloped through the ice-patterned window. Saark propped himself on one elbow and gazed down at the sultry vixen beside him. She was breathing deep, lost in sleep and a totality of contentment. Gods, thought Saark, with a wry grin, I'm fucking good. In fact, I must be the best.

He ran long fingers from her throat and the gentle hollow there, down her sternum, over her rhythmically heaving breasts, and further down to curl in the rich mound of her pubis. She groaned, lifting her hips to him in unconscious response, and Saark eased his hand away. No. Not now. Not *again*. After all, there was business to attend to. He couldn't afford to get her excited; although, he considered, it was extremely tempting. However. Business was business. Gold was gold. And Saark took his business very seriously.

He stood, and slowly, easily, silently dressed. Finally, he pulled on his long leather cavalry boots, and gazed longingly at the beautiful woman, head thrown back on the bed. Oh, to have stayed there for a whole day and night! They would have enjoyed so many sexual adventures together! But... no.

Saark moved to the mahogany sideboard, and eased open the top drawer. There was money, a small sack of thick gold coins, and these Saark tempted into his pocket. The next drawer held nothing but silken underwear – Saark considered helping himself, but greed for wealth over trophies got the better of him; he didn't want to be too much of a pervert. The third drawer held papers tied together by string. Saark rifled them, looking for bonds, shares or agreements; he found only letters, and cursed. On top of the sideboard he found a long, jewelled dagger, used, he presumed, to open correspondence. It had fine emeralds set in a heavy gold hilt. He pocketed the dagger, and moved to the wardrobe, opening the door with a slow, wary gesture, seeking to avoid the groan of aged wood and tarnished hinges. Swiftly he searched the contents, and at the back he found a satchel. It was locked. Dropping to his knees, he pulled free the jewelled dagger and swiftly sawed through leather straps. Inside, there was a sheath of bonds and Saark whistled silently to himself. He held a small fortune. His smile broadened, for these were Secken & Jalberg; he could cash them at any city in Falanor. Today, Saark realised, was not just a good day. It was probably the first day of a new retirement–

"You... bastard." The words were low, barely more than a growl. Slowly, and still on his knees, Saark turned to see the wavering point of his own slender rapier.

"Now don't be like that, sweetie." He wanted to use her name, but for the life of him, he couldn't remember. Was it Mary-Anne? Karyanne? Hell.

"Don't sweetie me, you pile of horse-shit *thief*."

"Hey, I'm not a thief!"

"And a rapist," she said, eyes gleaming, lips wet with hatred, as they had so very recently been wet with lust.

"Whoa!" Saark held up his hands, and went as if to stand. The rapier stabbed at him, nearly skewering his eye. "What the hell do you mean, Darienne?"

"It's Marianne, idiot! And do you know what the Royal Guard do to rapists when apprehended?" She glanced at his groin, and made a horizontal cutting motion with her free hand.

"Marianne! We had such sweet sex! How can you do this to me? It's despicable!"

"Despicable?" she screeched. "You take advantage of me, then seek to clean me out of every penny I've squirreled away from that old vinegar bastard I call a husband! Do you know what I've had to put up with, marrying the stinking toothless old goat? His acid sour breath? His pawing, hairy hands on my tits? His unwashed, fucking rancid feet!"

Saark managed to get to his feet without losing an eye, and with both hands held in supplication, his voice a soothing lullaby, he searched frantically for a way of escape. "Now, now, listen Marianne, we can both still come out of this smelling of roses…"

"No," she hissed, "I can come out of this smelling of expensive perfume, and satisfied, but you," she jabbed at him again, drawing a shallow line of blood down his cheekbone, "you're coming out of this without your *balls*."

In a swift movement Saark slid free the jewelled dagger, lifted his arm – and froze. The door behind Marianne had opened revealing a tall, lithe warrior with shoulder-length white hair and crimson eyes. The albino stepped forward in a sudden violent movement, and his sword-tip burst from Marianne's chest in a blossom of spurting blood. Marianne's eyes met Saark's. They were filled with confusion and pain and for a moment there was a connection, a symbiosis deeper than words, deeper than souls… she opened her mouth to speak, but a spurt of rich arterial blood flooded out and ran down her breasts, stained her flat toned belly, and dripped with a spattering of rainfall to the warped uneven floor. Marianne toppled over, trapping the albino's sword.

Saark's hand slammed forward, and the jewelled dagger entered the soldier's eye. The albino stumbled back, sitting down heavily. Incredibly, he lifted his hand and pulled free the blade with a *slurp*, letting it tumble to the wooden planks with a deafening clatter.

Saark leapt forward, kicking the soldier in the face and scooped his rapier from Marianne's dead grip. The soldier grappled for his own sword, milk-like blood running from his ruined eye-socket; Saark slammed his sword hard into the soldier's neck, half-severing the head. Saark staggered back, watching milk-blood pump from the limp corpse, and he tripped over Marianne's body, slipping in her blood, hitting the ground hard. His eyes met her glassy orbs. Her face was still, and awesomely beautiful, like frozen china. "Damn you!"

Saark stood, slick with Marianne's warm blood, and moved across the room and, ever the thief, retrieved the jewelled dagger that had saved his life. With rapier tight in his fist, he stepped onto the stairwell and glanced down where ice-smoke drifted lazily. Frowning, Saark descended, and felt the bite of savage cold on his legs. He retreated, and rummaged through the wardrobe, finding heavy furs and leathers. Wrapping himself up, Saark descended again, and stepped warily out onto the cobbled road.

Here, property displayed affluence with open vulgarity, the houses, villas and towers wearing wealth and privilege like jewels. The street was deserted. Even through thick clothing Saark could feel the cold nipping at him, stinging his skin, and he hurried down the street and towards the river – stopping only to gaze at a small child lying face down on the cobbles. Saark moved forward and knelt gingerly by the boy. He prodded the child, then rolled the boy, who was only four or five years old, onto his back and drew back with a gasp. The face and limbs were shrivelled, shrunken, the shirt opened over the boy's heart and deep puncture wounds showing clearly, gleaming under drifting ice-smoke. Saark reached forward and counted five holes, his hand hovering above the wounds. "What did this to you, child?" he whispered, horror suffusing his mind. Then his jaw clenched, his eyes hardened, and he stood, hefting his rapier. "Whatever did this, I'm going to find them, and kill them." Rage swam with his blood. Anger burned his brain. Hatred became his fuel, and death his mistress.

Saark, the outcast.

Saark, the jewel thief!

Once proud, once honourable. No! He had stooped low. He had traded his honour and pride and manhood for a handful of worthless baubles. Saark laughed, his laughter brittle and hollow... like his self-esteem. Yes, he was beautiful; powerful and muscular and dazzlingly handsome. The women fell over themselves to bed him. But deep down... deep down, Saark realised he despised himself.

"Kill them? You will not have to look far, little man," came a soft, ululating voice from the ice-smoke. Saark turned, and there towering over him and wearing snakes of smoke like drifting charms stood the stooped, white-robed figure of a Harvester.

The Harvester's tiny black eyes glowed, and it lifted its hand allowing the sleeve to fall back, revealing five long, bony fingers... pointing at Saark, gesturing to the man's unprotected chest, and the heart, and the pumping blood-sugar within...

Saark took an involuntary step back. A sudden fear ate him.

"Come to me, little one," smiled the Harvester, black eyes glowing. "Come and enjoy your reward."

TWO
A Dark Shroud Falls

Kell reached Jalder University's huge iron gates and stopped, panting, wiping sweat from his eyes. He listened, eyes darting left and right. Screams echoed, distant, muffled by ice-smoke. And more, off to the right, down the hill from where he'd emerged. Kell's teeth clamped tight, muscles standing out along the ridge of his jaw-line; the bastards were murdering everybody! And for what? What petty purpose of slaughter? Invasion? Wealth? Greed? Power? Kell spat, and wiped his mouth with the back of his hand.

I thought I'd left the Days of Blood behind?

I thought my soldiering was done. He smiled, a grim bloodless smile with coffee-stained teeth. Well, laddie, it seems somebody has a different plan for you!

Hoisting his matt-black axe, Kell glanced momentarily at the twin butterfly-shaped blades, like curved wings. It would have been a very dark butterfly: poisonous, deadly, utterly without mercy. This was Kell's bloodbond. The *Ilanna*. Sister of the Soul, a connection wrenched from him by ancient rites and dark blood-oil magick, flowing with his lifeblood, his very essence. Ilanna had many tales to tell. But then, the horror stories of the axe were for another day.

Kell moved warily up a well-kept path. He could barely see past low bushes and winter flowers which lined the walkway beyond neatly trimmed grass. He stopped, as something loomed from the mist: it was a circle of corpses, young women, each a shrivelled dry husk with faces stretched like horror masks, skin brittle like glass. Kell's heart-rate increased and his grip tightened.

If they've hurt Nienna, he thought. If they've hurt Nienna...

He reached the entrance, past more corpses from which he averted his eyes. Up stone steps, he rattled the large oak doors. Locked. Kell's gaze swept the mist, his senses singing to him; they were out there, the soldiers, he could feel them, sense them, smell them. But... Kell frowned. There was something else. Something ancient, stalking the mist.

Shivering with premonition, Kell moved warily around the edges of the building. He found a low window, and using his axe-blade, prised the jamb and struggled inside. It was cool and dark. Ice-smoke swirled around the floor. No candles were lit, and Kell's boots padded across thick rich carpets, taking him past fine displays of silverware and ceiling-high shelving containing an orgy of books. Kell seemed to be in some kind of office, and he reached the door – with its ornate arched frame – and eased out into a carpeted corridor lined with small statues. He listened. Nothing... then a scream, so loud and close-by it rammed Kell's heart into his mouth. He whirled around the nearest corner, to see a young woman on her knees, hands above her face, palms out, skin blue with cold. An albino soldier stood over her, a short knife in his hand. He turned as Kell's eyes fell on him... despite Kell making no sound.

The albino smiled.

Kell launched his axe, which sang across the short expanse and thudded through armour and breast-bone, punching the soldier from his feet to sit, stunned, a huge butterfly cleaving his heart. His mouth opened, and milk-blood ran over pale lips and down his chin. Kell strode forward and crouched before the albino.

"But... you should be powerless against us," whispered the man, eyes blinking rapidly.

"Yeah, laddie?" Kell grasped the axe-haft, put his boot against the soldier's chest, and ripped the weapon free in a shower of waxy blood. "I think you'll find I'm a little different." He bared his teeth in a skull smile. "A little more... *experienced*, shall we say."

Kell turned and crouched by the woman, but she was dead, skin blue, eyes ringed purple. Her tongue protruded, and Kell touched it; it was frozen solid, and he could feel the chill through his gloves.

A distant memory tugged at Kell, then. It was the ice-smoke. He'd seen it, once before, as a young soldier on the Selenau Plains. His unit had come across an old garrison barracks housing King Drefan's men; only they were dead, frozen, eyes glassy, flesh stuck to the stone. As the cavalry squad dismounted and entered the barracks, so tiny wisps of mist had dissipated, despite sunlight shining bright outside. Kell's sergeant, a wide brutal man called Heljar, made the sign of the Protective Wolf, and the inexperienced men amongst the squad imitated him, aware it could do no harm. "Blood-oil magick," Heljar had whispered, and they'd backed from the garrison barracks with boots crunching ice.

Kell rubbed at his beard through leather gloves, and glanced down at his axe. Ilanna. Blessed in blood-oil, she would protect him against ice-smoke, he knew. She would allow him to kill these magick-cursed men. Allow? Kell smiled a bitter smile. Hell, she would encourage it.

Now. Where would Nienna be? The dormitories?

If under attack, where would she run?

Kell, following instinct, following a call of blood, strode through the long corridors and halls of the university building, past corpses and several times past soldiers intent on their search. Up to the second floor, Kell found piles of bodies, all frozen, all arranged as if awaiting... what? What the hell do they want? wondered his confused mind.

A scream. Above.

Kell broke into a run, past lines of bodies laid out with arms by sides, faces serene in cold and death. His hands were tight on Ilanna, his breathing ragged and harsh, and he could sense his granddaughter close by. Up more steps, growing reckless the more he grew frantic with rising fear. Through a dormitory, beds neatly made, wooden chests unopened, and up another tight spiral staircase, taking the steps two at a time, his old legs groaning at him, muscles on fire, joints stabbing him with pain, but all this was washed aside by a surge of adrenalin as Kell slammed into the room–

There were four dead girls, lying on the floor, with long hair seeming to float behind pale chilled faces. Nienna and two others stood, armed with ornamental pikes they'd dragged from the walls during their flight. Before them stood three albino warriors with long white hair, all carrying short swords, their black armour a gleaming contrast to porcelain skin.

The soldiers turned as one, as Kell burst in. With a scream he leapt at them, axe slamming left in a whirr that severed one soldier's sword-arm and left him kneeling, stump spewing milk blood. Nienna leapt forward, thrusting her commandeered pike into an albino's throat but he moved fast, grabbing the weapon and twisting it viciously from Nienna's grip. She stumbled back nursing injured wrists, and watched with mouth open as the skewered albino stubbornly refused to die.

"Magick!" she hissed.

The albino nodded, smiling a smile which disintegrated as Kell's axe cleaved down the centre of his skull and dropped him in an instant. The third soldier turned to flee, but Ilanna sang, smashing through his clavicle. The second strike severed his head with a savage diagonal stroke.

The world froze in sudden impact.

Kell, chest heaving, moved forward. "Are you hurt?"

"Grandpa!" She fell into his arms, her friends coming up close behind, their faces drawn in fear, etched with terror. "It's awful! They stormed the university, started to kill everybody with swords and... and..."

"And magick," whispered a young woman, with short red hair and topaz eyes. "I'm Katrina. Kat to my friends. You are Kell. I've read everything about you, sir, your history, your exploits... your adventures! You are a hero! The hero of Kell's Legend!"

"We've not time for this," growled Kell. "We have to get out of the city. The soldiers are killing everyone!"

Katrina stooped, and hoisted one of the albino's swords. "Normal weapons won't kill them, right?"

Kell nodded. "You catch on fast, girl. The soldiers are blessed – or maybe cursed – with blood-oil magick. Only a suitably blessed and holy weapon can slay them. Either that, or remove their heads."

"Will this kill them?"

"There's only one way to find out."

Nienna and the third young woman, Yolga, armed themselves with the dead soldiers' swords. Kell led them to the spiral stairs, moving cat-like, wary, his senses alert, his aches and pains, arthritis and lumbago all gone. He could sense the women's fear, and that was bad; something dark flitted across his soul, something pure evil settling in Kell's mind. He didn't want the responsibility of these women. They were nothing to him. An inconvenience.

He wanted simply to save Nienna. The other two? The other two women could…

I can kill them, if you like.

The thought came not so much as words, but as primitive, primal images, drifting like a shroud across his thoughts. For a decade she had remained silent. But with fresh blood, fresh magick, fresh death, Ilanna had found new life…

"No!"

They halted, and Nienna touched his arm gingerly. "Are you well, Grandpa?"

"Yes," came his strangled reply; and for a moment he gazed at his bloodbond axe with unfathomable horror. The Ilanna was powerful, and evil, and yet – yet he knew without her he would not survive this day. Would not survive this hour. He owed her – *it*, damn it! – owed it his life. He owed it everything…

"I am well," he forced himself to say, words grinding through gritted teeth. "Come. We need to reach the river. We can steal a boat there, attempt to get away from this… horror."

"I think you will find the river frozen," said a low, gentle voice.

The group had emerged like maggots from a wound, spilling from stairs into a long, low hall lined with richly polished furniture gleaming under ice-light from high arched windows. The whole scene appeared grey and silver; a portrait delicately carved in ice.

Kell stopped, mouth a line, mind whirring mechanically. The man was tall, lithe, wearing black armour without insignia. He was albino, like the other soldiers, with long white hair and ashen skin; and yet, yet – Kell frowned, for there was authority there, integral, a part of his core; and something not quite right. This was the leader. Kell did not need to be told. And his eyes were blue. They glittered like sapphires.

"You are?"

"General Graal. This is my army, the Army of Iron, which has forcibly taken and now controls the city of Jalder. We have overrun the garrison, stormed the Summer Palace, subdued the soldiers and population. All with very little loss to my own men. And yet–" He smiled then, teeth bared, and took a step forward, the two soldiers flanking Graal remaining in position so the general was fore-grounded, set apart by his natural authority. "And yet you, old man, are fast becoming a thorn in my side."

Kell, who had been eyeing other corridors which fed the hall in the hope of an easy escape route, eased to his right and checked for enemies. The corridor was empty. He turned, fixing a steel gaze on the general who seemed to be observing Kell with private amusement; or at least, the disdain a piranha reserves for an injured fish.

"I apologise," growled Kell, eyes narrowed, "that I haven't rolled over to die like so many other puppies." His eyes flashed dangerously with a new and concentrated form of hate. "It would seem you caught many of the city-folk by surprise, Graal, with the benefit of blood-oil magick at your disposal. I'm sure this makes you feel like a big cock bastard down at the barracks, Graal, the whoremaster, joking about how he killed babes in their beds and soldiers in their sleep. The work of a coward."

Graal was unfazed by insult. He tilted his head, watching Kell, feminine face laced with good humour. "What is your name, soldier?" His words were a lullaby; soft and enticing. *Come to me*, that voice whispered. *Join with me.*

"I am Kell. Remember it well, laddie, 'cause I'm going to carve it on your arse."

"But not today, I fear. Men? Kill them. Kill them all."

The two albino soldiers eased forward, bodies rolling with athletic grace. Kell's eyes narrowed. These men were special, he could tell. They were professional, and deadly. He knew; he'd killed enough during his long, savage lifetime.

The two soldiers split, one moving for Kell, the other for Nienna, Kat and Yolga. They accelerated smoothly, leaping forward and Kell leapt to meet his man, axe slamming down, but the albino had gone, rolling, sword flickering out to score a line across Kell's bearskin-clad bicep that saw the big man stagger back, face like thunder, teeth gritted and axe clamped in both hands.

"A pretty trick, boy."

The albino said nothing, but attacked again, swift, deadly, sword slamming up then twisting, cutting left, right, to be battered aside by the butterfly-blades of Kell's axe. The albino spun, his blade hammering at Kell's neck. Kell's axe slammed the blade aside with a clatter. A reverse thrust sent the bloodbond axe towards the albino's chest, but the man rolled fast and came up, grinning a full-teeth grin.

"You're fast, old man." His voice was like silver.

"Not fast enough," snapped Kell, irate. He was starting to pant, and pain flickered in his chest. Too old, taunted that pain. Far too old for this kind of dance...

The albino leapt, sword slamming at Kell's throat. Kell leant back, steel an inch from his windpipe, and brought his axe up hard. There was a discordant clash. The soldier's sword sailed across the room, clattering from the wall.

"Kell!" came the scream. He whirled, saw instantly Nienna's danger. The three young women were backing away, swords raised, the second albino warrior bearing down on them, toying with them. But his stance changed; now, he meant business. Even as Kell watched, the man's sword flickered out and Nienna, face contorted, lashed out clumsily with her commandeered sword; it was batted aside, and on the reverse sweep the albino's blade cut deep across Yolga's belly. Cloth parted, skin and muscle opened, and the young woman's intestines spilled out. She fell to her knees, face white, lips mouthing wordless, her guts in her hands. Blood spilled across complex-patterned carpet. "No!" screamed Nienna, and attacked with a savage ferocity that belied her size and age. And as the albino's sword slashed at her throat, in slow-motion, an unnervingly accurate killing stroke, Kell heaved his axe with all his might. The weapon flew, end over end making a deep thrumming sound. It embedded so far through the albino that both blades appeared through his chest. With spine severed, he dropped instantly, flopping spastically on the ground where he began to leak.

Kell whirled back, eyes sweeping the room. The first soldier had regained his sword. Of Graal, there was no sign. The man, eyes locked on his dead comrade, fixed his gaze on Kell. The look was not comforting, and the arrogant smile was gone. He stalked towards the old warrior who realised–

Bastard, he thought. He'd thrown his axe.

Kell backed away.

You should never throw your axe.

"Graal said nothing about a swift death," snapped the albino, and Kell read in those crimson eyes a need for cruelty and torture. Here was a man with medical instruments in his pack; here was a man who enjoyed watching life-light die like the fall of a deviant sun.

Kell held up his hands, bearded face smiling easily. "I have no weapon." Although this was a lie: he had his Svian sheathed beneath his left arm, a narrow blade, but little use against a sword.

The albino drew square, and Kell, backing away, kept his hands held in supplication.

"Your point is?"

"It's hardly a fair fight, laddie. I thought you were a soldier, not a butcher?"

"We all have our hobbies," said the albino with a delicate smile.

Nienna's sword entered his neck, clumsily but effectively, from behind, finally embedding in his right lung. The albino coughed, twisted, and went down on one knee all at the same time. His sword lashed out in a reverse sweep, but Nienna skipped back, bloodied steel slipping from her fingers.

The albino coughed again, a heavy gurgling cough, and felt blood bubbling and frothing in his damaged lung. He felt the world swim. There was no pain. No, he thought. This wasn't how it should end. He felt tingling blood-magick in his veins, and his fingers twitched at the intercourse. He dropped to his other knee. Blood welled in his throat, filled his mouth like vomit, and spilled down his black armour making it gleam. His head swam, as if he'd imbibed alcohol, injected blood-oil, merged with the vachine. He tried to speak, as he toppled to the carpet, and his eyes traced the complex patterns he found there. Darkness was coming. And weight. It was pressing down on him. He glanced up, unable to move, to see boots. He strained, more white blood pooling like strands of thick saliva from his open maw. Kell was standing, his axe, blades stained with blood and tiny flutters of torn flesh, held loose in one hand, resting on the carpet. Kell's head was lowered, and to the albino his eyes looked darker than dark; they appeared as pools of ink falling away into infinity. Kell lifted his axe. The albino soldier tried to shout, and he squirmed on the carpet in some final primitive instinct; a testament to an organism's need to survive.

Ilanna swept down. The albino was still.

Kell turned, glanced at Nienna. She was cradling Yolga's head and the girl was mumbling, face ashen, clothes ruined by her own arterial gore. The other girl, Kat, was standing to one side, eyes wide, mouth hung loose. As Kell watched, Yolga spasmed and died in Nienna's arms.

"Why?" screamed Nienna, head snapping up, anger burning in the glare she threw at Kell.

Kell shrugged wearily, and gathered up one of the albino's swords. This one was different. The steel was black, and intricately inlaid with fine crimson runes. He had seen this sort of work before. It was said the metal was etched with blood-oil; blessed, in fact, by the darkness: by vachine religion. Kell ripped free the albino's leather sheath, and looped it over his shoulders. He sheathed the sword smoothly and moved to Nienna.

"Get your sword. We need to move."

"I asked you – *why*?"

"And my answer is *because*. I don't know, girl. Maybe the gods mock us. The world is evil. Men are evil. Yolga was in the wrong place at the wrong damn time, but you are alive, and Kat is alive, so pick up your sword and follow me. That is," he smiled a nasty smile, "if you still want to live."

Nienna moved to the fallen soldier. She took hold of her embedded sword, and tugged at it until it finally gave; it squelched from the corpse. She shuddered, tears running down her cheeks, and followed Kell to the corridor. Kat put her hand on Nienna's shoulder, but the young woman shrugged off the intimacy, displacing friendship.

"How do you feel?"

Nienna snorted a laugh. "I think I've lost my faith in the gods."

"I lost mine a long time ago," said Kat, eyes tortured. Nienna stared at her friend.

"Why?"

"Now is not the time." Kat hoisted her own stolen sword. "You did well, Nienna. I froze. Seeing Yolga like that…" She took a deep breath, and patted her friend once more. "Honest. You did brilliant. You… saved us all."

"How so?"

"That soldier would have killed your grandpa. Without a weapon, he was just meat."

Nienna looked at her friend oddly, then transferred her gaze back to Kell, whose eyes were sweeping the long, majestic hall. He glanced back, bloodied axe in his great huge paws. And with his thick grey beard and the bulk of his bearskin, for a moment in time, a sliver of half-glimpsed reality, he appeared to be natural in that skin. A warrior. No, more. A bestial and primitive ghost.

"Follow me," he said, breaking the spell. "And stay silent. Or we'll all be dead."

Nienna nodded, and with Kat in tow, they followed Kell out to the hall.

Saark stared, transfixed, as the Harvester stooped and bobbed, striding forward with a rhythmical, swinging gait, ice-smoke trailing from its robes, black eyes like glossy coals drawing Saark into a world of sweetness and joy and uplifting mercy–

> *Come to me, angel.*
> *Come to me, holy one.*
> *Let me savour your blood.*
> *Let me take you on the final journey.*
> *Let me taste your life…*

The long, bony fingers reached for Saark, who stood with every muscle tense, his body thrumming like the string on a mandolin. Saark's eyes flickered, saw the hooded man creeping up behind the Harvester even as those long points of white reached for Saark's chest and his shirt seemed to peel away and five white-hot needles scorched his skin and he opened his mouth to scream as he felt flesh melt but there was no sound and no words and no control and pain slapped Saark like a helve to the skull, stunning him, his legs going weak as an ice-wind whipped across his soul–

The hooded man screamed a battle-cry and charged, a large meat-cleaver held clear above his head, his bearded face, red and bitten savagely by the ice-smoke, contorted into a mask of frenzy.

The Harvester turned, smooth, unhurried, and as the cleaver lashed down the Harvester's arm lifted in a sudden acceleration, and the cleaver bounced from bone with a clack and spun off, lost from the man's flexing hands. The Harvester's finger slammed out, puncturing the man's chest above his heart. He screamed.

Saark fell to his knees, choking, coughing, and released from the spell, grappled wildly at his burning, melting chest. He glanced down, at five deep welts in his skin, deep purple sores surrounded by concentric circles of heavy bruising. Saark continued to cough, as if slammed in the heart by a sledgehammer, and he watched helpless as the Harvester lifted the brave attacker high into the air kicking and screaming, impaled by the heart on five spears of bone.

Body thrashing, the man screamed and screamed and Saark's eyes widened as he watched the man sucked and shrivelled, arms and legs cracking, contorting, snapping at impossible angles as the skin of his face was drawn and shrivelled until it was a dry, useless, eyeless, husk.

The corpse hit the ground with a rattle; like bones in a paper bag.

The Harvester turned back to Saark, flat oval face leering at him. Thin lips opened revealing a black interior ringed with row after row of tiny teeth.

Saark grunted, rolled onto his hands and knees and accelerated into a sprint faster than any man had a right to. He powered away, chest on fire, heart pounding a tattoo in his ears, mouth Harmattan dry, bladder leaking piss in squirts down his legs. Down long alleys he fled, with no sounds of pursuit. He turned, and almost choked. The Harvester was pounding after him, so close and silent Saark almost fell on his face with shock. He slammed right, twisting down a narrow alleyway, dropping ever downwards towards the river. He skidded on icy cobbles, turned again, and again, ducking into narrow spaces between carts and stalls and wagons, squeezing past boxes, and suddenly shoulder-charging a door to his left and barging through a deserted house, past still bubbling pans and up narrow stairs to the roof–

He halted, listening.

Nothing.

His terrified eyes roved the staircase below, and he moved to the window and stared down into the street. Had he lost it? He tried to calm his breathing, and climbing out of the window, he reached up to the eaves of the house and with frozen fingers, ice-smoke swirling around his boots, he grunted, hoisting himself up onto slick slate tiles. Carefully, Saark climbed to the ridge-line and without waiting moved swiftly along the house apex, leaping a narrow alleyway with a glimpse of dark cobbled streets encased in ice below. Scary, yes, but not as heart-wrenchingly terrifying as the creature that pursued him; the monster that sucked life and blood and fluid from bodies, the beast that drank out people's souls. Saark shuddered.

What hell has overtaken the world? he thought. What law did I break, to be so cursed?

From house to house, from roof to roof, Saark leapt and slithered, many times nearly falling to cobbles and stalls far below.

Through drifting mist he ran, a rooftop ghost, a midnight vagabond; only this time he was on no simple errand of theft.

This time, Saark ran for his life. And for his soul.

"Wait."

Kell's hushed whisper, despite its low tone, carried with surprising clarity. Nienna and Kat froze instantly in place. Both young women were walking a high-rope, skating thin ice, breathing the tension of the besieged and sundered city. Again and again they passed corpses, shrivelled husks, sometimes piles of men, women, heaps of disjointed child corpses, huddled together as if for warmth; in reality, all they craved was a chance at life.

Kell lowered his hand, half-turned, gestured for the girls to join him. They scampered down the cobbled road, gloved hands holding cloth over the freezing skin of their faces, swords sheathed at waists more as tokens than real weapons. Both girls understood that in real world combat, their lives hung by a thread. And the thread was named Kell.

"See," he hissed, gesturing towards the Selenau River, flowing like ink beneath swirling tendrils of ice-smoke. "The enemy have a foothold here; now it'll be damn impossible to steal a boat."

Nienna watched the albino soldiers, streams of them in their hundreds, marching down the waterfront. Many dragged prisoners, some kicking and screaming. These, they locked in huge iron cages which had been erected beside the sluggish wide river. Many dragged corpses, and these they piled in heaps as if… Nienna frowned. As if they were waiting for something?

Nienna's eyes searched as far as the false horizon. Sometimes, ice-smoke parted and she got a good glimpse down a length of the river. Huge black and red brick factories lined the water; they were mainly dye-works, slaughterhouses and tanneries. The sort of place which Nienna had been destined to work before her "nameless benefactor" stepped in with university fees. Huge iron cranes stretched across the river for loading and unloading cargo. Wide pipes disgorged chemical effluence, dyes and slaughterhouse blood and offal into the river. Even in winter, the place stank to high heaven; in summer, vomit lined the waterfront from unwary travellers.

Kat edged forward, and crouched beside Kell. She met the old warrior's gaze and he had to admire her edge. "What about another way out of the city? There's too many of the bastards here." She spat on the ground.

"They will have the gates covered. This whole situation stinks, Kat. I've seen this sort of... slaughter, before. The Army of Iron don't want anybody getting out; they don't want anybody to spoil their master plan. If somebody was to get word to King Leanoric, for example..."

"That is our mission!" said Katrina.

"No, girl. Our mission is to stay alive. Anything else – that comes later."

In truth, Kell still felt deeply uneasy. What sort of conquering army simply committed murder and atrocity? It didn't make sense. Slaughter all the bakers, who would bake bread for the soldiers? Murder the whores and dancers, who then to provide entertainment? Soldiers marched on their stomachs, and fought best when happy. Only an insane general went on a pointless rampage. Kell had seen it once before, during the Days of Blood. Bad days. Bad months. Kell's mouth was dry at the thought. Bitter, like the plague.

The Days of Blood...

A dark whisper. In his soul.

A splinter. Of hatred. Of remorse.

You took part, Kell. You killed them all, Kell.

Visions echoed. Slashes of flashback. Crimson and shimmering. Diagonal slices, echoes of a time of horror. Screams. Writhing. Slaughter. Whimpering. Steel sawing methodically through flesh and bone. Worms eating skin. Eating eyes. Blood running in streams down stone gutters. Running in rivers. And soldiers, faces twisted with bloodlust, insanity, naked and smeared with blood, with piss and shit, with vomit, capering down streets with swords and knives, adorning their bodies with trophies from victims... hands, eyes, ears, genitalia...

Kell swooned, felt sick. He forced away the terrible visions and rubbed a gloved hand through his thick beard. "Damn you all to hell," he muttered, a terrible heaviness sinking through him, from brain to stomach, a heavy metal weight dragging his soul down to his boots and leaking out with the piss and the blood.

"You look ill." Kat placed a hand on his broad, bear-clad shoulder.

"No, girl, I am fine," he breathed, shuddering. And added, under his breath, "on the day that I die." Then louder, "Come. I can see a tunnel under the tannery."

"That's an evil place," said Kat, pulling back. "My little brother used to collect the piss-pots used in the tannery; he caught a terrible disease from there; he died. I swore I would never go inside such a place."

"It's that, or die yourself," said Kell, not unkindly.

Kat nodded, and followed Kell and Nienna down the street, all three crouching low, moving slowly, weapons at the ready and eyes alert. As they approached the tunnel, an incredible stench eased out to meet them: a mixture of gore and fat, dog-shit, piss, and the slop-solution of animal brains used in the bating process. Kell forced his way inside, treading through a thick sludge and coming up grooved and worn brick steps into a room hung with hides still to be stripped of hair, gore and fat. They swung, eerily, on blood-dried hooks. There were perhaps a hundred skins waiting for the treatment that would eventually lead to water-skins, armour, scabbards and boots. Kell stepped over channels running thick with disgorged brains.

"What is that?" gagged Nienna.

"When the skins arrive, they need to be scraped free of dried fat and flesh. The tanners then soak skins in vats mixed with animal brains, and knead it with dog-shit to make it soft." He grinned at Nienna, face demonic in the gloomy light where shadows from gently swinging skins cast eerie shapes over his bearded features. "Now you can see why you were so lucky to be accepted into the university, girl. This is not a place for children."

"Yet a place where children work," said Kat, voice icy.

"As you say."

They moved warily between swinging skins, the two women flinching at the brush of hairy hides still strung with black flesh and long flaps of thick yellow fat. At one point Kat slipped, and Nienna grabbed her, hoisting her away from a channel filled with oozing mashed animal brains and coagulated blood.

"This is purgatory," said Nienna, voice soft.

Kat turned away, and was sick.

As Kell emerged from the wall of hung skins, so he froze, eyes narrowing, head turning left and right. Before him stood perhaps twenty large vats, four with fires still burning beneath their copper bases. This was where excess flesh and hide strips were left to rot for months on end in water, before being boiled to make hide glue. If nothing else, this place stunk the worst of all and Kell was glad of the cloth he held over his mouth.

Then Kell turned, frowning, and strode towards a vat containing the foul-smelling broth and hoisted his axe. "Are you coming out, or do I come in axe-first?"

"Whoa, hold yourself there, old fellow," came an educated voice, and from the shadows slipped a tall, athletic man. Nienna watched him, and found herself immediately attracted; something the dandy was no-doubt used to. His face was very finely chiselled, his hair black, curled, oiled back, neat above a trimmed moustache and long sideburns that were currently the height of fashion amongst nobles. He wore a rich blue shirt, dark trews, high cavalry boots and a short, expensive, fur-lined leather cloak. He had expensive rings on his fingers, a clash of diamonds and rubies. His eyes were a dazzling blue, even in this gloomy, murky, hellish place. He had what Nienna liked to call a smiling face.

Kat snorted. Nienna was about to laugh as well, so ridiculous did the nobleman look in this evil-smelling tannery from hell; until she saw his sword. This, too, had a faint air of the ridiculous, until she married it to his posture. Only then did she consider the broad shoulders, the narrow hips, the subtle stance of an experienced warrior. Nienna chided herself. This man, she realised, had been underestimated many times.

"Why are you skulking back there, fool?"

"Skulking? *Skulking*? Old horse, my name is Saark, and Saark does not skulk. And as for fool, I take such a jibe as I presume you intend; in utter good humour and jest at such a sorry situation and predicament in which we find ourselves cursed."

"Pretty words," snorted Kell, turning back to Nienna and Kat. He turned back, and realised Saark was close. Too close. The rapier touched Kell's throat and there was a long, frozen moment of tension.

"Pretty enough to get me inside your guard," said Saark, voice soft, containing a hint of menace.

"I think we fight the same enemy," said Kell, eyes locked to Saark.

"Me also!" Saark stepped back and sheathed his blade. He held out his hand. "I am Saark."

"You already said."

"I believe it's such a fine name, it deserves saying twice."

Kell grunted. "I am Kell. This is Nienna, my granddaughter, and her friend Kat. We were thinking of stealing a boat. Getting the hell away from this invaded charnel house of a city."

Saark nodded, moving close to Nienna and Kat. "Well, hello there, ladies." Both young women blushed, and Saark laughed, a tinkling of music, his eyes roving up and down their young frames.

"Saark!" snapped Kell. "There are more important things at play, here. Like the impending threat on our lives, for one."

Saark made a tutting sound in the back of his throat, and surveyed his surroundings. And yet, despite his smile, his fine clothes, his finer words, Nienna could see the tension in this man; like an actor on the stage, playing a part he'd rehearsed a thousand times before, Saark was enjoying his performance. But he was hampered, by an emotion which chipped away at the edges of his mask.

Fear.

It lurked in his eyes, in his stance, in a delicate trembling of his hand. Nienna noticed. She enjoyed people-watching. She was good at it.

Saark took a deep breath. "How did you know I was here?"

"I could smell you."

"*Smell me*?" Saark grinned then, shaking his head. His face was pained. "I cannot believe you could smell me amidst this stench. I like to think I have better grooming habits."

Kell had moved to a window, was standing back from the wooden shutters and watching soldiers down by the river. He turned and eyed Saark warily. "It was your perfume."

"Aaah! Eau du Petale. The very finest, the most excitingly exquisite…"

"Save it. We're moving. We can escape via the pipe which dumps tannin and slop out into the river. If we head down into the cellars, I'm sure…"

"Wait." Saark brushed past Kell and stood, one manicured hand on the shutters, the other on the hilt of his rapier. Suddenly, Saark's foppish appearance didn't seem quite so ridiculous.

"What is it?"

"The carriage. I know it."

Kell gazed out. A carriage had drawn alongside a cage full of weeping prisoners; all women. The carriage was black, glossy, and had an intricate crest painted on the door. The horses stomped and chewed at their bits, disturbed either by the stench of the tanneries or the moans of the women. The driver fought to keep the four beasts under control and their hooves clattered on ice-rimed cobbles.

"Well, I know *him*," snarled Kell, as General Graal stalked towards the carriage and folded his arms. His armour gleamed. He ran a hand through his long white hair, an animal preening. "He's the bastard in charge of this army. He called it the Army of Iron."

"You know that one?" Saark met Kell's gaze.

"The bastard sent a couple of his soldiers to kill me and the girls."

"He was far from successful, I see."

"I don't die easy," said Kell.

"I'm sure you don't, old horse." Saark smiled, and turned back to the distant performance. The carriage door was opened by a lackey, and a man stepped down. He was dressed in furs, and held a cloth over his face against the chill of ice-smoke, which was dissipating even as they watched – its job now done. The man had shoulder length black hair, which gleamed.

"Who is he?" said Kell.

"That," said Saark, staring hard at Kell, "is Dagon Trelltongue."

"The king's advisor?"

Saark nodded. "King Leanoric's most trusted man. He is, shall we say, the king's regent when the king is away on business."

"What about Alloria?"

"The queen?" Saark smiled. "I see, Kell, you have little schooling in nobility, or in royalty. It would be unseemly for a woman to rule in the king's absence; you would have her meeting with common-folk? Doing business with captains and generals? I think not."

"Why," said Kell, ruffled, "would Trelltongue be here? Now?"

Saark transferred his gaze back to the two men beside the carriage. "A good question, my new and aged and ragged friend. However, much as I would love to make his acquaintance at this moment in time, I fear your escape plan to be sound – and immediately necessary. Would you like to lead the way, Kell, to this pipe of disgorging effluence?"

Kell hoisted his axe, looked at Nienna and Kat, then tensed, crouching a little, at what appeared behind the two women.

"What is it?" hissed Nienna, and turned…

From the hanging wall of skins, moving leisurely, gracefully, came a Harvester. Its flat oval face seemed emotionless, but the small black eyes, coals in a snowman's face, searched across the room. Vertical slits hissed with air, and the creature seemed to be… sniffing. The Harvester gave a grimace that may have been a smile.

"I followed you. Across the city." The voice was a dawdling, lazy roll, like big ocean waves on a fused beach.

Saark drew his rapier, and gestured to the two women to move. He took a deep breath, and watched as the Harvester lifted a hand. The embroidered robe fell away leaving five long, pointed fingers of bone…

"I thought I explained, sweetie. You're just not my type." But terror lay beyond Saark's words, and as he and Kell separated, Kell loosening his shoulders, axe swinging gently, Saark muttered from the corner of his mouth, "Watch the fingers. That's how they suck the life from your body."

Kell nodded, as the blast of terror hit him. He stood, stunned by the ferocity of fear which wormed through his mind. He saw himself, lying in a hole in the ground, worms eating his eyes, his skin, his lungs, his heart.

Come to me, came the words in his head. A song. A lullaby. A call stronger than life itself.

Come to me, little one.

I will make the pain go away.

The Harvester drifted forward, and with a scream Saark attacked, rapier moving with incredible speed; a lazy backward gesture slapped Saark a full twenty feet across the tannery, where he landed, rolling fast, to slam against a vat with a groan.

Five bone fingers lifted.

Moved, towards Kell's heart.

And with tears on his cheeks, the old soldier seemed to welcome them…

THREE
A Taste of Clockwork

Anukis awoke feeling drowsy; but then, the ever-present tiredness, like a lead-weight in her heart, in her soul, was something she had grown to endure over the years, something which she knew would never leave her because... because of what she was. She stretched languorously under thick goose-down covers, her long, curled, yellow hair cascading across plump pillows, her slender white limbs reaching out as if calling silently across the centuries for forgiveness.

Anukis glanced at the clock on the far wall. It was long, smooth, black like granite. Through a glass pane she could see tiny intricate cogs and wheels, spinning, turning, teeth mating neatly as microgears clicked into place. A pendulum swung, and a soft *tick tick tick* echoed through the room. Anukis's eyes stared at the clock, loving it and hating it at the same time. She loved it because her father, Kradek-ka, had made the clock; and just like his father before him, he had been one of the finest Watchmakers in Silva Valley, his hands steady, precise, incredibly accurate with machining and assembly; his eye had been keen, not just with the precision of his trade, but with the delicate understanding of materials and what was perfect for any machine job. But it had been his mind that set him apart, indeed, highlighted him as a genius. Anu's grandfather had accelerated and pioneered the art of watch-making, turning what had once been a relatively simple art of mechanical time-keeping into something more... advanced. This way, Kradek-ka had upheld the family traditions, and helped to save, to prolong, and to advance their race. The vachine.

Anukis rubbed at her eyes, then stood, gasping a little at the cool air in the room. Naked, goose-bumps ran up and down her arms and she hurried into a thick silk gown which fell to her ankles. She moved to a porcelain bowl and washed, her long, dainty fingers, easing water into her eyes, then carefully, into her mouth. She rubbed at her teeth, cold water stinging, then moved to the window of her high tower, gazing out over Silva Valley, eyes scanning the high mountain ridges which enclosed the huge tiered city like predator wings around a victim.

Anukis smiled. A victim. How apt.

Maybe they'll come for me today, she thought. Maybe not.

A prisoner of the High Engineer Episcopate since her father had died (had been murdered, she thought hollowly), she was not allowed out from a small collection of rooms in this high tower suite. However, what the high-ranking religious Engineers and Major Cardinals did not realise, was that Anukis was not a pure *oil-blood* like the majority of the city population lying under a fresh fall of snow below, pretty and crystalline, a pastel portrait from her high window.

The smile faded from Anukis's face.

No. She was far from pure. She carried the impurity seed within her. Which meant she could not drink blood-oil. Could not mate with the magick. Could not... feed, as a normal vachine would feed.

Anu could never enjoy the thrill of the hunt.

There came a knock at the door, and a maid entered carrying a small silver bowl which she placed by Anukis's bed. With head bent low, she retreated, closing the door on silent hinges, hinges Anukis herself had oiled for the purpose of freedom. Anu moved to the bowl, glanced down at the tiny, coin-sized pool of blood-oil that floated there, crimson, and yet at the same time streaked with rainbow oils. This was the food of the vachine. Their fuel. That which made them unholy.

Anukis could not drink blood-oil. In its refined state, such as this, it poisoned her, and made her violently sick. She would be ill for weeks. To the Watchmakers, the Major Bishops, the Engineers, this was heresy, a mockery of their machine religion; punishable by exile, or more probably, death. Anu's father had gone to great pains to protect his daughter for long years, hiding her away, dealing with the amoral Blacklippers of the south and their illegal import of Karakan Red, as it was known. Only this unrefined, common source – fresh from the vein – would, or could, sustain Anukis. And, she was sure, it was this subterfuge which had led to her father's untimely death...

A face flashed in her mind. Vashell! Tall, athletic, powerful, tiny brass fangs poking over his lower lip. He was prodigal, a power-house of physical perfection and one of the youngest ever Engineer Priests to have achieved such a rank. Destined for great-ness. Destined for leadership! One day, he would achieve the exalted rank of Major Cardinal; maybe even Watchmaker itself!

He had asked Anukis to marry him on two occasions, and both times her father had rejected Vashell's advances, fearing that for Anukis to marry was for Anukis to die. But she saw the way Vashell looked at her. When he smiled, she glimpsed the tiny cogs and wheels inside his head, saw the glint of molten gold swirling in his eyes. He was true and pure vachine; a wholesome, blood-oil ser-vant to the Vachine Religion. Vashell, a spoilt prince, an upstart royal, had got everything he ever wanted. And, she knew with a shudder, he would never stop until he possessed Anukis.

And... then that happens? She smiled sadly to herself.

Well, she would have to kill him. Or failing that, kill herself.

Far better death than what the Engineers would do to her if they discovered her tainted flesh.

Anukis opened the window and a cold wind gusted in, chilling her with a gasp and a smile. Far below, the sweeping granite roads shone under fresh snow, most of which had been swept into piles along the edges of the neat, gleaming thoroughfares. Buildings staggered away, maybe six or seven storeys in height, and all built from smooth white marble mined from the Black Pike Mountains. The architecture was stunning to behold, every joint precise. Arches and flutes, carvings and ornate buttresses, many inlaid with precious stones to decorate even the most bare of Silva Val-ley's buildings – gifts from the all-giving Pikes. And the city itself was huge; it drifted away down the valley, mountains rearing like guardians to either side, for as far as Anukis could see. And her eyesight was brilliant. Her father had made sure of that.

The scent of snow came in to her, and she inhaled, savouring the cold. The vachine had a love affair with cold, but Anukis, being impure and contaminated, preferred a little warmth. This, again, was a secret she had to jealously guard. If the Engineers discovered what she was... and the things she did when darkness fell...

Despite its well-oiled silence, Anukis caught the sound of the door opening. She also sensed the change in pressure within the room. Her eyes shone silver with tears and still gazing out over her beloved city, the one which her grandfather, and father, had given so much to advance, she said without turning, her voice a monotone, "What can I do for you, Vashell?"

"Anukis, I would speak with you." His voice was soft, simple, almost submissive in its tone. But Anukis was not fooled; she had heard him chastise servants on many occasions, watched in horror as he beat them to death, or kicked them till they bled from savage wounds. He could change at the flick of a brass switch. He could turn to murder like a metal hawk drops on its prey...

"I am still in mourning. There is little to say."

"Look at me, Anu. Please?"

Anukis turned, and wiped away a tear which had run down one cheek. With the tiniest of clicking sounds, she forced a smile to her face. Ultimately, her father would want her to live. Not sacrifice herself needlessly for the sake of sadness, or misery, or impurity. She took a deep breath. "I'm looking, Vashell. You have picked a bad time to intrude on my thoughts. And I am barely dressed. This is an unfortunate time to receive company. But then, if the High Engineer Episcopate keeps me a prisoner, I suppose my body is theirs to do with as they please..."

"Hush!" Vashell stepped forward, but stopped as Anukis shrank back, cowering almost, on the window-seat. "If anybody hears you speak so, your life will be forfeit! They will drain your blood-oil. You will be husked!" For a vachine, there was no greater shame.

"Why would you care?" Her voice turned harsh, all the bitterness at her father's death, all the poison at being kept prisoner rising to bubble like venom on her tongue. "You are a party to all this, Vashell! You said, twice, that you loved me. And twice you asked my father for the gift of marriage. Yet you stand by the Engineers whilst they keep me locked here," and now her eyes darkened, the gold swirling in their pupils turning almost crimson in her flush of anger, "and you collude in the capture of my sister."

Vashell swallowed, and despite his mighty physical prowess, he edged uneasily from one polished boot to the next. "Shabis is fine, Anu. You know that. The Engineers are taking care of her. She is well."

"She is a young girl, Vashell, whose father has just died and whose sister has been imprisoned. When can I see her?"

"It will be arranged."

Anukis jumped down from the window-seat and strode to Vashell, gazing up at him. He was more than a head taller than the slender female, and she herself was nearly six feet in height. "You said that a week ago," she snarled, staring up into his eyes. Vashell squirmed.

"It is not easy to arrange."

"You are an Engineer Priest! You can do anything!"

"Not this." His voice dropped an octave. "You have no idea what you ask. So many in the High Council outrank me." He took a deep breath. "But... I will see what I can do. I promise."

"On your blood-oil soul?"

"Yes, on my eternal soul."

Anukis turned her back on him, moved to the window. She gazed across the city, but the beauty was now lost on her; decayed. A sudden wave of hate slammed through her, like a tsunami of ice against a frozen, volcanic beach. She would see it destroyed! She would see the Silva Valley decimated, and laid to a terrible waste...

"You came here to ask me, didn't you?"

"I can help you, Anu."

"By marrying me?"

"Yes! If you become the wife of an Engineer Priest, you will be sacrosanct. The Engineers cannot keep you prisoner! It would go against the Oak Testament. You know that."

"And yet, still I choose to say no."

Anukis felt Vashell stiffen, without turning to look. She allowed herself a small smile. This was one thing she could deny him. But when he spoke again, the smile slowly drained from her face like bronze from a melting pot.

"Listen carefully, pretty one, when I say this. For I will speak only once. Your father was found guilty of heresy by the Patriarch; I do not know what happened to him, but we both know, without seeing the corpse, that he is dead. The Engineers wanted you and your sister dead, also; I am all that stands between the two of you, and the Eternal Pyre. So, think very carefully before offering a facetious answer... because, if I choose to withdraw favour, the last of your worries will be your separation from your sister."

Vashell swept from the apartment, door slamming in his wake so hard it rattled the oak frame. Dust trickled from between well-machined stones. Echoes bounced down the stairwell.

Shivering, Anukis turned and stared at the elegantly carved portal, then back out over the city. She shivered again, and this time it was nothing to do with the cold. Above her, her father's clock ticked, every second reminding her of a melting life.

Anukis licked ice-cold lips.

She thought about blood.

And that which was denied her.

Tonight. Tonight, she would visit the Blacklippers.

The sun set over the mountains casting long crimson shadows against granite walkways. Anukis listened, acute hearing placing guards down in the tower entry. She could hear muted conversation, the flare of a lit pipe, the laughter of a crude rude joke. Anukis pulled on her ankle-length black gown, belted the waist, and lifted the hood to obscure her golden hair and pastel features.

She moved to a heavy cabinet beside the door, lifted it with ease, carrying it across a thick rug and tilting it to wedge under the door handle. Moving back to the window, she watched the sun's weak, crimson rays finally die like spread fingers over the jagged peaks of the Black Pikes; then she leapt lightly onto the window seat and prised open the portal.

An ice wind whipped inside. Anukis climbed out, finding narrow handholds in the marble and stone, and easing herself over the awesome drop. "Don't look down," she murmured, but just couldn't help herself. It was a long fall to hard granite ruts polished smooth by brass wheels. Anukis eased herself along the narrow crack, moving only one hand, or one boot, at a time, so she always had three points of contact. The wind snapped at her with teeth. Away from the window, darkness fell like molten velvet. Anukis felt totally isolated. Alone.

For perilous minutes she eased herself around the flank of the tower, to where she'd discovered a worn vertical rut. Above, tiles converged into a marble trough which had grown a leak, probably a hundred or more years previous. This in turn had allowed water to groove the marble facade, giving slightly deeper handholds, almost like steps, down which Anukis could climb several storeys to a sloping ridge of tiles.

Several times she almost slipped; once, gasping, she swung away from the wall and her boots scrabbled on marble as sweat stung her eyes, and she felt a fingernail crack. But she calmed her breathing, stopped her panicked kicking, and hauled herself up on bloody fingertips, regaining her handhold, saving her life.

Down, she eased, an inch at a time, as the wind mocked her with brutal laughter.

Below, Silva Valley spread away, some sections well lit, others deep dark pits of intimidation. Despite Watchmaker rule, not every vachine was equal; a complex religious hierarchy existed which sometimes led to murder and civil unrest. Royal torture was delivered for gross acts of sacrilege, but the vachine were powerful, proud, and physically superior. The illegals took some ruling. Only the Machine God kept them sane.

Anukis hit the tiles lightly and dropped to a crouch. Her eyes scanned, swirling with gold, finding the patrolling Engineer Deacons and their minions and watching them as she had watched from her cell window. With care, she eased across sloping tiles on her carefully plotted route, and dropped down to a second storey balcony. She knocked a plant-pot, which clattered, and swiftly she scaled the rails, hung, and dropped to a lower balcony as light emerged above her, muttering voices casting curses on the wind.

Anukis landed on the smooth granite road, and checked herself. Tugging her hood tight, she hurried down the dark street, winding downhill to the Brass Docks.

Silva Valley was just that, a valley; but at its heart, a dissection, lay the Silva River, which emerged from a complex core of caves and vast subterranean tunnel systems beneath the Black Pike Mountains, and named the Deshi Caves. In his youth, Anukis's father Kradek-ka had explored the tunnels in detail, had been part of several professional vachine expeditions to map the labyrinth beneath the mountains. But something odd had occurred which the more religious of the vachine called *bo-adesh*. Occasionally, the tunnels moved, altered, shifted within the infrastructure of the mountain vaults. Some said it was down to blood-oil magick; some said the Black Pike Mountains were alive, had been alive longer than Man, and were in contempt of vachine deviation and intrusion. Whatever, many of the under-mountain routes were mapped and used for travel on long brass barges, or even to reach other distant valleys; but some were prohibited. Dangerous. Death to those who travelled...

In those early days of exploration, many had been lost to the Deshi Caves. Anukis remembered long cold evenings, sitting on her father's knee, staring into dancing flames as he recounted some of his travels, how they used blood-oil markers on the stone, ropes under the water, magick fires by which to see. And still many had died; hundreds had died, lost, drowned, or simply vanished. Sometimes, an empty brass barge would drift from the mist of an early morning, a single bell chiming. Empty. No signs of struggle. It had been Kradek-ka's view that terrible beasts lived under the Black Pike Mountains; creatures nobody had ever before seen... or at least, seen and lived thereof to speak.

Anukis shivered; and not just with the cold.

She stopped at an intersection, easing into shadows beyond the pooled light from a swinging brass lamp. Two guards passed and stopped beneath the yellow orb, lighting long pipes and exchanging pleasantries. Anu watched them carefully; these weren't real Engineer Deacons; they didn't have the shaved heads and facial tattoos of the Royal; but they were as near as damn it. And certainly authorised to kill Anukis beyond curfew. She smiled, her smile a crescent in a bloodless face. And the reason for curfew?

The vachine were running out of blood-oil.

The vachine had bled the cattle dry...

Oh, the irony!

The guards moved on, and so did Anukis, loping across the road and delving into more darkness. Down she strode, cloak pulled tight, breath emerging in short gasps of dragon smoke.

She rounded a corner, and the Silva River opened before her, vast, wide, and glass-still at the base of the Silva Valley. Buildings staggered in staccato leaps far down the steep descent before her, right to the ebony water's edge. Anukis hurried on, down narrow back-streets of this vast and beautiful city, down ill-advised routes. Three times she spotted thieves before they spotted her, and circumnavigated their positions. Even so, she knew, she would have needed no weapon to deal with their kind. Outcast. Impure...

Like me, she realised.

But then, despite her disabilities, she was... special.

Her father had made sure of that.

Anukis reached the long flanks of the Brass Docks and halted, a few feet from the water, listening to the lilting slap against brass jetties. She waited patiently, searching out more guards; finally, she moved down a wide curving walkway which followed the crescent of the Silva River towards... The Black Pikes. And the Mouth, which disgorged ice-pure mineral-rich waters from deep beneath echoing mountain halls. She felt the Breath before she saw the river's ominous exit; it emerged, hissing and singing sometimes, to wash cool mineral-scented air over those who stood within five hundred yards. Anukis walked into the breeze, which tugged annoyingly at her hood, and stopped by the Brass Docks warehouse block. She glanced right, where huge brass and bronze freighters bobbed at anchor, trade vessels and smaller navy vehicles, many unmanned and silent, some showing tiny yellow glows from fat-oil lamps. Carefully, she stepped down a narrow alley and entered a maze, skilfully negotiating a complex route which led her to a steep, dark stairwell.

From the depths, a cold breeze blew, and Anu skipped down slick granite, slowing as she reached the bottom. The crossbow appeared before the Blacklipper, strung and tensioned, and his teeth gleamed behind the black-tainted scarring of his lips.

"Going somewhere, my pretty?"

"I have business with Preyshan."

The Blacklipper moved from the shadows, and she saw he was what they called a Deep Blood; not only his lips were stained black from the powerful narcotic, even the veins beneath his skin had taken the taint, showing a diffused map of web-strands beneath his pale white skin. Anukis shuddered inside; he had to be close to death to look like this. Ready for the Voyage of the Soul.

Seeing the shudder, the man smiled. "Don't you be worrying about me, pretty one. I've had a good life. My Paradise awaits."

"One filled with blood-oil?"

The crossbow jerked towards her, and his eyes narrowed. "One such as you shouldn't readily condemn, pretty, outcast vachine."

Only she wasn't an outcast.

Because – they didn't know... yet.

And if the Watchmakers discovered her impurity?

She heard they had special chambers for just such occurrences.

Anukis shuddered, and squeezed past the leering Blacklipper, feeling his fetid rigor-mortis breath on her face, his body pressed close to her own, its muscles surprisingly iron-hard beneath his web-traced skin. She hurried on, down more and more steps, and deep into a maze of brass-walled corridors which eventually gave out to smooth-hewn tunnels, some flooded. Several times Blacklippers challenged her, and several times Anukis used her magick card. The name: Preyshan. One of the three kings of the Blacklippers.

As she entered the maze beneath the Silva River, so she could discern a distant booming sound. It was said to be the noise made by the souls of the drowned, banging on the river bed for spiritual release. Anukis moved on, hand touching the smooth wall where lode-veins of crystals and blood-red mineral deposits could be traced, glittering, in the glow of irregularly placed fat-lamps.

The corridor ended in an iron gate. She gave her name, and the gate swung open revealing a long, low chamber filled with perhaps fifty men, and only a handful of women. Many were Blacklippers, some from the south, over the mountains; Falanor couriers who had sworn an oath to keep from using blood-oil and its deviants in order to turn huge profits smuggling. Money, not blood-oil, was their own particular narcotic.

"Anu!" boomed Preyshan, striding forward, towering over the vachine and beaming her a generous smile. His lips were jet black, riddled with blood-oil, his eyes blue and wide. He wore a bushy black beard, and his size was prodigious beneath cheap market clothing. "So long since you last visited! How is your father?"

"My father is dead," said Anukis, voice soft, her eyes lowered to the ground lest she fill with tears and betray her weakness here, of all places. "I think the Engineers murdered him." Preyshan reached out, a huge, black-nailed hand cupping her chin and lifting her eyes to his, where there came a spark of connection.

"Truly, Anukis, I am sorry. He was a great man."

"And now he's a dead man."

"You have escaped their machinations?"

"For now. But I must return. I have come for..." She did not say it. Could not say it. But Preyshan understood; after all, the only vachine who visited Preyshan and his underground minions were those in need of the impure, and the illegal, Karakan Red. Smuggled in from beyond Black Pike. Fresh blood.

Preyshan gestured, and could sense the need in Anukis. A man ran forward with a small brass cylinder. He passed it to Anukis, who took it gratefully and unscrewed the top. Carefully, she consumed a small amount of the contents, and the Red glistened on her lips. As Preyshan watched, the blood shone against tiny, elongated canines of the female vachine before him, and he caught a sense of movement deep within her mouth; of whirring wheels, tiny cogs meshing and integrating, balancer shafts lifting, rotating cylinders and pumping pistons. He smiled, and it was a dry smile.

Paradoxical, thought the large Blacklipper, that as the vachine feed from man, so here, and now, in an ironic twist of fate and science, so men feed from the vachine to become Blacklipper. A twisted symbiosis? Ha! He could debate the philosophy all night.

Anukis gave a deep, drawn-out breath. Gold clouds, like golden oil, swirled in her eyes. She glanced up, a swift movement, lethargy gone as energy infused her, as blood infused her. "I'll need to take more," she said, quietly.

Preyshan nodded. "Why not stay here, with us? You will be safe here, Anu. You know that."

For an instant she saw the longing in the big man's eyes, but then it was gone, a neat mask replaced, the portcullis gate closed. Anukis licked her lips, tracing the last of the Red and swallowing. Inside, she felt greased. Oiled. Whole again.

"I cannot. The Engineers have Shabis…"

Preyshan nodded, and taking the woman's elbow, guided her to one side of the low chamber. Here, where a breeze blew in from deep subterranean mountain tunnels, where they could not be overheard, Preyshan leant against the wall and interlaced his fingers.

"If you stay, Anukis, I will fetch Shabis for you."

"How–"

He reached out, placed a finger against her lips. "You vachine are powerful, yes. But you do not understand my heritage; or my history." His eyes glittered. "The Engineers hold no fear, for me. Nor does Vashell."

Anukis shook her head. "If I allowed you to do this, I would place you all in great jeopardy. Your whole world…"

"I know this. We know this. Our existence is a dangerous one at best. But still…" He touched her arm. "You know I would do this for you. For your father, the great man, but mainly… for you."

"I understand." Anukis stepped forward, reached up on tip-toe, and kissed him on his black necrotic lips. "You are a great man, Preyshan. I am lucky to be… loved, by such as you."

Preyshan opened his mouth to speak, but his eyes narrowed, shifting over Anukis's shoulder.

"Breach!" screamed a voice, followed by a metallic screech and a twanging sound as five crossbows disgorged industrial quarrels. Three vachine, tall, athletic, hands curved into gleaming metal claws, skin peeled back from faces revealing long, curved steel fangs bared and growling, screaming, leapt from the tunnel. Crossbow bolts riddled them, and one vachine was punched back, slamming the wall, body a torn and twitching marionette of tattered flesh and twisted, bent gears; savaged clockwork. The others leapt amongst the men in great bounds, claws slashing left and right sending severed limbs flying, and long fangs descending on throats, ripping out windpipes in a sudden harsh attack. Swords hissed from sheaths as the two vachine paused, hunkered on all fours like beasts, heads rotating, eyes glittering, tiny cogs and wheels humming in their skulls. The Blacklippers converged, sword and axes drawn, spears held in clammy hands, faces grim with a need to kill these invaders–

Preyshan ran forward, his own sword held in one great paw, his face merciless in the cold glow of brass lamps. The vachine leapt, fangs tearing at arms and throats in a mad flurry of ripping flesh and savagery and inhuman speed; swords slammed, spears stabbed, and Preyshan, as if with some primeval instinct, turned back towards the iron gates – open, now, with this sudden breach of violence.

His soul fell from his world.

In the tunnel, more vachine eyes glittered. And with a roar they flooded the chamber, ten, twenty, fifty of the clockwork vampires, bowling over and through the Blacklippers ripping at flesh tearing heads from bodies steel fangs and brass claws tearing easily through unprotected flesh and succulent raw bone...

Preyshan skidded, turned, sprinted back towards Anukis who stood, shocked, mind not registering what her eyes could see. "We've got to get out of here!" he screamed at her, pounding across stone, but as he reached her he faltered, and his eyes met hers, and there was confusion there, and sudden pain, and he glanced down at the brass blade emerging from his chest. Blood bubbled around the wound, and his mouth opened allowing blood to roll through his thick beard. He reached out towards Anukis, and their fingers met, but Preyshan carried on falling to the floor and hit with a heavy slap. He lay still.

Anukis fell to her knees amidst the sounds of slaughter, tears on her pale cheeks, and she stroked Preyshan's beard. Gradually, a presence drifted through her confusion, and into her consciousness. Sobbing, she glanced up.

Vashell smiled, placed his boot on Preyshan's back, and pulled free his short brass sword, weighing the weapon thoughtfully.

"What a surprise, finding you here in this den of iniquity. And I see, you've drank your fill of Karakan Red. And left none for me? Tut tut, sweetheart." He shook his head, eyes mocking. "No wonder you could never marry me, Anukis." He squared his shoulders. Took a deep breath through fangs stuck with torn flesh. "I see now, with your impurity, with your taint, with your fucking sacrilege, how we could never be compatible."

"Damn you, Vashell! What brought you here? Why kill these–"

"Blacklippers? Why? You ask me why?" He pressed the heavy brass blade against Anukis's throat and lifted her, panting, from her knees using the point. "Because, my darling, they are illegal smugglers. Because, sweetheart, they undermine our core vachine society. And because, my beautiful little Anukis, they are the unholy, the impure, and the damned."

He glanced over his shoulder, to where savage vachine warriors had finished off the last of the Blacklippers in a bout of savagery that had sprayed the walls with blood. The chamber was littered with mangled corpses. The vachine started a low, metallic keening, and with fangs prominent, savoured the kill.

Vashell leant close. His breath was sweet. "Just like you," he said.

FOUR
Canker

Kell drifted in a world of darkness, a sea of dark oil, lantern oil, fish oil, blood-oil, unrefined, a tar mess like offal and the thick syrup from which butchers fashioned their tasty black puddings... and his eyes closed, and opened, in a languid breath for this was a dream and he knew it was a dream, and as a dream it could not be real. But if it was not real, why the hell was Ilanna so damned cold in his hands?

You must let me in, she said.

Her voice was cool, a metallic sigh, the voice of bees in their hive, the voice of ants in their nest, and Kell shivered and felt fear, not the adrenalin fear of a sudden bar brawl, nor the terrifying heart-gripping fear of hanging from high places, boots trying to scrabble on ice-slippery rock, sure as hell that when you fell the rocks and jagged natural spikes and the mountain herself would have no mercy, no pity, just a hard fast cold death. No, this fear was different, strange, an educated fear; this was the fear of knowledge; this was the fear of loss. This was Ilanna, the bloodbond axe, and she was in control. But more than that. She knew she was in control, and that she would always win the battle.

No, said Kell, scowling, fists clenching hard. He breathed her in; breathed in her metal, the musk of her iron-oil, the stench of old blood clinging like a parasite to her haft, her blades, her edge. He breathed in the perfume of the axe. The aroma of death. The corpse-breath of Ilanna.

But you must, she pleaded, *I am Ilanna, I am the honey in your soul, I am the butter on your bread, the sugar in your apple. I make you whole, Kell. I bring out the best in you, I bring out the warrior in you.*

No, he snarled. You bring out the killer in me.

That's what you always wanted, she said.

I never wanted what you had to offer.

You lie! If I was flesh and blood and bone you would have been in my bed quicker than a drunk husband after a whore. But I am steel, with sharp blades and a taste for blood. And you took what I had to offer, Kell, my sweet, you took my gift of darkness, my gift of violence, and you saved your own life. But there is a price, a price for everything, and you know you must let me free, out into the world again.

Kell laughed. "Must?" Words like "must" ring sour in my head like corked wine; they crack my skull with their... he savoured the word, instruction. What if I climbed the highest Black Pike peak, Ilanna? Dropped you into a crevasse, one of the mile deep pits guaranteed never to see anybody but the most foolhardy explorers? You'd be fucked then, my lass, would you not? Kell grinned to himself. Never again a taste of blood. Never again the splinter of bone. Just darkness, ice, the drip of water, the passing of centuries.

So you wish to die, Kell? Her voice was a beautiful lullaby, so musical in better times happier times it would have lulled Kell to his bed. Often Kell had pictured the woman behind the voice. He corrected himself. The demon behind the voice, for Ilanna was anything but human, a thousand leagues from mortal. He pictured her as tall, beautiful, elegant; but also haughty, arrogant, filled with a self-love that made her despise all others. A cruel woman, then. And a deadly foe.

I do not wish to die, he said, and the words shamed him.

The Harvester is a terrible, deadly enemy, Ilanna said, and Kell felt the axe vibrating in his fingers, growing hot *with a million tiny judders. You cannot kill it, so do not ever try. Even I could not sever his head, crush his bones. The best you can do is slow him down, for every cell in his alien body is infused with blood-oil magick. He is a creature of blood, and nothing mortal can break him.*

How do I slow him?

He is tall, off-balance; a creature of mechanical motion. Aim for his knees, strike his knees and ankles with all your might. You may buy yourself a minute at best. But be quick, Kell. Her voice rose to a shriek as their sliver of time, their slice of twisted reality started to accelerate in sudden violence into the real–

World.

The bone tubes slammed for Kell's heart and he rolled, fast, slamming the ground and coming up, teeth bared in a grimace, axe clenched tight to his breast. The Harvester chuckled, frame bobbing as he turned on Kell who charged, axe swinging for the Harvester's chest. The creature made no move to protect itself, but instead attacked, clawed hands lashing out at Kell who altered his strike at the last moment, his charge turning into a low roll as the axe swept for the Harvester's knees… there came a crunch, a compression of bone, and the Harvester shrieked and buckled, toppling like a sack of dry twigs and Kell was up and running, pushing Nienna and Kat along towards the stunned figure of Saark, who was crawling to his knees, clutching his head. Blood tricked from a cut at his temple, and he looked ashen, about to be sick.

"Is it dead?" breathed Nienna, and they all glanced back.

Across the gloom of the tannery, the Harvester rose to its feet and turned to face them. Its eyes burned like tiny black holes of hatred. It pointed at Kell, and started forward, and the group ran between huge tankers, rusted and smeared with shit, making the girls gag and vomit. Down a brick slope they ran, and Kell pointed with his axe, in silence, almost afraid to speak. There was a wide tunnel, which led out and down…

"I can't crawl in there!" wailed Nienna.

"You'll have to, chipmunk," said Saark, flashing Nienna a smile she did not understand, and jumped in, shit and chemicals splashing up his leggings, staining his silk shirt, mixing with blood, and vomit and rendering his dandy imagery a bad comedy. The opening wasn't as wide as it first looked, and Kell leapt in, splashing forward, with the girls following reluctantly. They stooped, squeezing into the waste pipe, Kell leading and Saark taking up the rear, his rapier out, his eyes dark.

The Harvester stopped, making a soft keening sound. Ice-smoke drifted from the cuffs of its robe, and it watched the four people vanish. In silence it turned and stalked from the tannery.

The waste pipe led down, beneath the tannery and into a narrow black-brick sewer filled with waste. Kell dropped in, scratching the skin of his hands and shins and belly, then helped Nienna and Kat to climb down the rugged, crumbling brickwork. He turned, squinting at distant light, as a cursing Saark dropped down beside him.

"Thanks for the help," he said, tone openly sardonic.

"Don't mention it."

"Damn! Would you look at this silk shirt? I'll never be able to get it clean. Do you know how much it cost? It's the finest weave, from the Silk-Blenders of Vor... they wear these in Leanoric's Court!"

"There are more important things than silk shirts, Saark."

"Don't be ridiculous. Do you know how many women this shirt has wooed? How many tapered fingers have stroked its flank? It's like a magick key. First it unlocks the heart; then it unlocks the chastity belt."

"Grandpa, what's a chastity belt?" came Nienna's voice from the gloom.

Kell threw Saark a dark look. "Nothing, don't listen to the pampered shit-streaked fool. Follow me. We need to move fast."

They splashed through thick, swirling waste, trying hard not to think about the guts and offal, dyes and dogshit which made up the slurry. At one point Nienna brushed against a dead cat, half-submerged, and she screamed, her hand coming up to cover her mouth. Her body heaved, frail frame wracking with disgust, and Kat comforted her, holding her close, as they continued to wade forward. There wasn't time to stop; no time for weakness. The Harvester might be waiting at the other end of the tunnel.

The tunnel was long, dropping at several stages on its way down to the Selenau River. Occasionally vertical venting tunnels, narrow fist-wide apertures, rose up through brick and stone and promised tantalising glimpses of the outside world.

Kat screamed, suddenly going down on one knee. Slop rose up to her chin and she spluttered, eyes closed, face twisted in disgust. "Nienna," she wailed, but Kell surged back to her, pushing Nienna up ahead to Saark, who was muttering dark oaths, his face smeared with guts and old blood. It was even stronger than Saark's perfume.

"What's wrong?" snapped Kell.

"I twisted my ankle."

"Can you walk?"

"I don't know."

"Walk or die," said Kell, voice low, eyes glittering.

Kat forced herself up, wincing, and leaning on Kell's shoulder she limped after Nienna and Saark. She was stunned by the iron in the old man's muscles, but equally stunned by the icy turn of his attitude.

Would he have left me? she thought.

The Hero of Jangir Field?

The Black Axeman of Drennach?

She ground her teeth, thinking of her life, of the bitterness, of the failures, of the people who had left, and more importantly, the people who had returned. Of course he would leave her, she thought, and a particular lode of bitterness ran through her heart. That's why he came back, instead of letting Nienna help her friend. If she'd broken her ankle, slowed them down, made excessive noise... she looked up at his grey beard, the wide, stocky set of his shoulders, the huge bearskin which made him seem more animal than human. Well, she thought. She was pretty sure his long knife would have slid through her ribs, ending the problem, negating the threat.

She shivered, as a chill breeze caressed her soul.

And for the first time she looked at Kell not as an old man; but as a killer.

Saark had stopped, hand held out towards the others. He turned, eyes meeting Kell's. "It's the river," he said.

Kell nodded, pushing to the front. The noise of fast flowing water invaded the tunnel egress, and he watched the circle of light, drifting with ice-smoke, for quite some time. He edged forward, took a good grip on his axe, and peered outside.

Slop and effluence dropped down through a series of concrete channels, and fell under a timber platform and into the Selenau River. Here, the river took a tight turn, narrowing between two rock walls and raging over several clumps of stone, white and frothing, and charging off through the city. The timber platform was based on rock, then edged out on stilts over the river, the wood dark and oil-slick with preservative. Several drums and barrels stood at one end, and a small, calm off-shoot of concrete-hemmed water housed five small boats on a simulated canal.

Saark was beside him. "We take a boat?"

"Seems like a good idea, lad."

"Let's do it."

"Wait." Kell placed a hand on Saark's chest. "That... thing, a Harvester it's called; it was keen to suck our blood, yes?"

Saark nodded.

"Chances are, it's out there. We need to move fast, Saark. No mistakes. Be ready with that pretty little sword."

Again, Saark nodded, and the group waded out into grey light, the sky filled with wisps and curls of ice-smoke, thinner now, but still reducing visibility over a hundred yard range. Kell was scanning left and right as they scrambled down icy concrete ramps, past where the sludge from the tannery pipes fell. Then his boots hit the wooden platform with a thud, and he stood, a huge bear, arms high, axe held before his chest as his gaze swept the world.

Nienna and Kat slid down the concrete ramps on their bottoms, followed by Saark, his poise perfect, fine clothing ruined by dyes and shit. His sword was in his fist, and his eyes were narrowed, focused, searching...

Kell moved to a boat, and hacked through the knot with his axe blade. Taking the rope in one fist, he ushered the girls and Saark, who had turned, towards the end of the timber platform lost in mist – from which drifted the Harvester, eyes glowing, five bony fingers pointing towards the group.

"Get in," growled Kell.

Saark took the girls, and they leapt into the boat, cracking ice around the vessel in the still-water channel. The currents tugged, and Saark leaned forward, grasping the platform. "Get in, Kell," he snapped. But Kell had turned, and rolled his mighty shoulders as the Harvester accelerated, frame bobbing as it moved fast towards him, a high-pitched keening coming from its flat, oval nostrils. Kell sprinted, and leapt, axe lashing out but the Harvester moved, fast, rolling away from the blades, bony fingers lashing out. Kell's axe cut back on a reverse stroke, slamming the arm away, and he skidded on icy wood, righting himself. The Harvester lowered its head towards him.

"You will die a long, painful death, little man."

"Show me, laddie," snarled Kell, head low, shoulders lifted, powerful, as the Harvester attacked. His axe lashed out, was knocked aside but he ducked, whirled a low circle with Ilanna singing through cold air to slam fast at the Harvester's legs... it stepped back and the axe turned, coming up over Kell's head in a glittering arc as he stepped in, and the blades smashed down at the Harvester's shoulders. There came a sound, like snapping wood, the blades were savagely deflected to the right dragging Kell off-balance. A fist hit Kell in the ribs, and he hit the ground on the way down. The Harvester's fingers slammed at his heart, but he rolled, Ilanna cutting an arc to smash the extended fingers, trapping them in the wood, embedding both bony fingers and axe in the platform.

Kell climbed to his feet, clutching his ribs, and the Harvester tugged at its trapped fingers, making a low but high-pitched growling sound. Its head snapped up, black eyes scowling at Kell who reached under his jerkin and pulled out his Svian knife. He leapt forward, knife slashing for the Harvester's throat, blade cutting white flesh that parted like fish-meat, but no blood came out no scream emerged and the Harvester slapped a back-handed blow against Kell sending him rolling across the platform.

"Get in the boat!" screamed Saark. The current was pulling at them more viciously, and ice crackled in a flurry of shots.

Kell climbed to his feet, bearded face filled with a dark, controlled fury. He watched the Harvester rip its fingers free with a splintering of torn wood, and Ilanna fell to the platform with a slap. The Harvester stood tall, flexing its undamaged fingers. Kell swallowed. The blades should have amputated; instead, there was no mark. His gaze lifted to the slit throat, but the fish-flesh had knitted together, and was whole again.

Kell knew, now. There was blood-oil magick here; he could not kill this creature. Ilanna had been right, and this sickened him.

He ran, and the Harvester leapt at him with a hiss, fingers slashing for his heart. But Kell ducked, turned his run into a slide on icy wood, under the Harvester's flashing bone talons to grasp his axe. Arms pumping, he sprinted for the boat even as Saark's grip finally lost its battle and the boat slid out along the still water, crackling ice, to join the flow of the raging torrent. Kell leapt, landing heavily in the boat which rocked madly for a moment. Then he stood, staring back at the Harvester as he replaced his Svian in its sheath beneath his left arm, and they were whisked away into thickening mist.

"A good effort," said Saark, smiling kindly at Kell. "If the bastard had been human, it'd now be dead."

"But it's not," growled Kell, slumping down and taking the boat's oars. "And that makes me want to puke. Come on, let's get out of this godsforsaken city. It gives me the shits."

General Graal led the way to the elevated tower room, presenting the broad target of his back to Dagon Trelltongue.

Dagon, a tall but slender man with shoulder-length grey hair and small eyes, wearing the finest silk and wool fashion-clothing of the south, felt keenly the presence of the delicate sword at his waist, the jewelled knife under his arm and the poison in the vial at his hip-belt. He swallowed, dry spit in a dry mouth. He could kill Graal, a swift piercing of sword through lungs, watch the general's blood bubble onto the rich carpets they now walked. Dagon could send the Army of Iron back north, with no leader, no hope, no fire; he could save the coming war, save his friend, lord, and King, Leanoric – and indeed, all the people of Falanor.

Dagon's eyes narrowed. Bastards!

No. They would pay. They would suffer.

Damn them all.

They entered a large chamber, once one of Jalder's finest council offices. Thick carpets kept chill from stone flags, the walls were plastered and painted white, and the whole room was decorated with dark wood, inlaid with gold. Fine works of art hung at intervals around the chamber; discreet. Many comfort couches were set apart, amidst desks and stone pedestals showing several of Falanor's heroes. Dagon had been here before, on many occasions, usually on business for King Leanoric. Now, there was a more sombre, and chilling, atmosphere.

Graal reached a long, lacquered desk and turned, suddenly, a swift movement. His long white hair drifted around his face for a moment, bright blue eyes fixing on Dagon who swallowed, seeing the smile on Graal's face, knowing that Graal had read his thoughts, had presented his broad back as a test, a free shot, a target; and Dagon also knew this man was a mighty warrior. If he'd dared to attack, to try and save his people… well, he would now be dead.

"A brandy?"

"No, I shouldn't," came Dagon's rich voice. He was a born orator, but here, in this company, he felt like a child. All his richly rehearsed speeches crumbled in the air like the stench of warm cabbage.

"I appreciate the, ah, ice-smoke is not to everybody's liking. It chills the bones. Go on, Dagon, you have made a long journey to visit, a long journey to –" he laughed softly – "save your life. A little brandy cannot hurt. It is distilled from peaches from King Leanoric's own orchards, I believe."

Dagon took a glass, and his eyes reflected in Leanoric's crest carved skilfully into the faceted crystal surface. He drank deep, and observed Graal watching his trembling fingers, his nervous tongue, and he finished the brandy, felt warmth flood him, felt alcohol tingle his brain giving him just a little courage.

"So you will tell me everything?" said Graal, sipping at his own drink. Dagon saw the man's fingers were long, tapered, even the finger-nails white. His gaze moved up to blue eyes fixed on him. Strange, that they were blue, thought Dagon. He watched. Graal did not blink.

"Yes," croaked Dagon, eventually, feeling weak at the knees, full in the bladder, frightened to his very core.

"Numbers of infantry, cavalry, archers, pikemen? Where the divisions are stationed? The names of their division generals? Brigadier generals? Numbers of horses, supply chains, military routes through Falanor, everything?"

"Yes."

"And of course," said Graal, moving to Dagon, stooping a little to peer closer into the official's eyes, "Leanoric. They say he is a great battle king. That he cannot be beaten on the field. He has shown, endlessly, that he has a brilliant mind, a tactician without compare. He is strong, handsome, commands respect and honour from his soldiers. Is all this correct?"

"It is… my lord."

"I am a general, not a lord," snapped Graal, crushing his crystal glass. It shattered, long jagged shards slicing Graal's hand, thick brandy flowing over the wounds and dripping, mixed with normal red blood into the carpet. Graal did not flinch, did not even look at the wound, but retained his connection with Dagon.

"Yes, general," whispered Dagon.

"There is one more thing."

"General?" Dagon's voice was little more than a whisper.

"Alloria. Leanoric's queen. The mother of his two boys. She is his backbone, is she not? His love, his life, his strength. I want to know where she is, where she travels in the winter, who her maids of honour are, and which hand she uses to wipe her arse."

"Alloria? But… I agreed to instruct you in armies, military strategy, and to speak of Leanoric…"

Graal's hand snapped out, taking Dagon by the throat. Shards of crystal, embedded in Graal's flesh, pierced Dagon's skin and he squealed, legs kicking as Graal lifted him off the ground. "You will tell me everything. Leanoric is a worthy adversary; but if I remove his reason for life, diverge his thoughts by taking his queen then I have a powerful bartering tool, I have, shall we say, a strategy our tactician will appreciate. I cannot afford to lose time on this… " he smiled, almost sardonically, "invasion. You understand, Trelltongue?"

"Ye-es," he managed, throat weeping blood.

Graal dropped Dagon to the carpet, turned, and languorously poured himself another brandy. His head came up as something drifted through the doorway, and Dagon's breath caught in his throat as he watched the Harvester approach. He had seen them at work, seen them drain the corpses of women, and children. These creatures filled him with a terror straight from a deep primeval pit; a terror so awesome he could barely vocalise.

"Hestalt. There is a problem?"

The Harvester nodded, black eyes turning on Dagon and burning through the king's advisor. Graal waved his lacerated hand, "Don't mind him, he is of no consequence." Graal began picking shards from his flesh, some as long as two inches. He did not wince. "What's wrong?"

"The man. The *hero*. Kell."

"He still lives?"

"More than that. He has been a… thorn, in my side. He has escaped."

"Send a squad. They'll catch up with one old man."

"No, Graal. He is more dangerous than you could comprehend… and it stems from his axe. I know a bloodbond weapon when I see one. Graal, he must be dealt with immediately. You understand?"

Graal rubbed at his chin, eyes distant. "He was there? During the Days of Blood? If he is in possession of a bloodbond weapon he must surely have experienced those days; one way or another." Graal's eyes glittered. His splintered hand was forgotten. "There is immense power in such a weapon. Power we can use, yes?"

The Harvester nodded. "Send a canker."

Graal frowned. "A little excessive, my friend."

"I want him stopped. His life extinguished. Now!"

Graal gave a single nod. It was rare he'd seen a Harvester so ruffled. He walked to the window, wondering if there was some unwritten bond here; some information to which he was not privy. Graal signalled to an albino soldier, who disappeared. Dagon Trelltongue used the time to pull himself to his feet, removing a tissue from one pocket and dabbing at his bleeding throat. He could feel the flesh, bruised, swollen, punctured, and he knew he would struggle to speak for the next few days.

Distantly, there came a sound, savage, brutal, a snarling like a big cat only this noise was twisted, and merged with metal. Dagon shivered involuntarily, and found General Graal's eyes locked to him again. The general was smiling, and gestured idly to the doorway. "A canker," he said, by way of explanation, as six soldiers pushed a cage through high, ornately-carved double-doors.

Dagon felt piss running down his legs as his eyes fastened on the cage, and he was unable to tear his gaze free from the vision.

It was big, the size of a lion, but there the resemblance ended. Once, it had been human. Now it raged on all fours, pale white skin bulging with muscle and tufts of white and grey fur. Its forehead stretched right back, mouth five times the size of a human maw, the skull opened right up, split horizontal like a melon and with huge curved fangs dropping down below the chin like razor-spikes. Everywhere across the creature's body lay open wounds, crimson, rimmed with yellow fat, like the open, frozen flesh of the necrotic, and inside Dagon could see tiny wheels spinning, gears meshing, shafts moving and shifting like, like...

Like clockwork, he realised.

Dagon blinked, and tried to swallow. He could not.

The creature snarled, shrieked and launched at the cage wall. Huge bars squealed, one rattling, and the creature sat back on its haunches with its strange open head, its twisted high-set eyes, one higher than the other, staring at Dagon for a moment and sending a spear of ice straight to his heart. Inside that skull he saw more clockwork, gears and levers stepping up and down, tiny wheels spinning. He fancied, if he listened carefully, he could hear the gentle, background *tick tick tick* of a clock.

"What is it?" he whispered.

"A canker," repeated Graal, moving over to the cage and putting his hand inside. Dagon wanted to scream *Don't do that, it'll rip your fucking hand off!* But he did not. He stared, in a terrible, dazed silence. "When vachine are young, little more than babes, they go to the Engineer's Palace for certain, necessary, modifications. However, the vachine flesh is occasionally temperamental, and suffers, shall we say, a setback. The muscle, bone and clockwork do not meld, do not integrate, and as the vachine grows so it loses humanity, loses emotions, loses empathy, and becomes something less than vachine. It twists, its body corrupting, its growth becoming an eternal battle between flesh and clockwork, each component vying for supremacy, each internal war filling the new-grown canker with awesome pain, and hatred, and, sadly, insanity. Eventually, one or the other – the flesh, or the clockwork – will win the battle and the canker will die. Until that point, we use them for hunting impure vachine. The Heretics, the Blasphemers, and the Blacklippers."

Graal turned, then. His words had been soft, a recounting of Engineer Council Lore, the Oak Testament, and he blinked as if awaking from a dream. "This is Zalherion. Once, he was my brother. The vachine process was good to me. But not, I fear, to him."

The canker moved forward, and licked at Graal's hand like a dog would its master. The canker growled, then, head turning, its eyes fixed again on Dagon and Graal gave a laugh, a sweet sound, his blue eyes sparkling. "No, not him, Zal. We have another one for you." The canker growled, a distorted lion-sound, and with a squeal of bolts Graal opened the cage.

The canker leapt out, brass claws gouging rich carpets. It moved with an awesome power and feline grace despite its twisted frame and open wounds, towering over the men, even the Harvester, and gazing down at Graal with something akin to love.

Graal's head turned, and the Harvester moved forward, eyes closing, five bone fingers reaching out towards the canker. It growled, backed away a step, hunkered down. Then a moment later, it stood and sprinted from the room leaving grooves in the stone.

"What did you do?" whispered Dagon, aware that if he survived this encounter, and the one soon to follow, it would be a miracle of life over insanity; of luck over probability.

"The Harvester imprinted an image of Kell inside the canker's mind. Now, Zal will not stop until Kell is dead."

Dagon lowered his head. Tears ran down his cheeks.

• • • •

The small boat sped down the river, but eventually the banks widened and the urgency and violent rocking slowed. Nienna sat, stunned, huddled close to Kat for warmth, and also the mental strength of friendship. She had watched her grandpa, Old Kell, fight the Harvester in something like a dream state, aware at any moment that the creature might smash him from existence, suck the life from his shell with those long razor bone fingers... and yet it was like she was watching a play on a stage, because, to see her grandpa fight was unreal, surreal, something that just wasn't right. He was an old man. He cooked soup. He told her stories. He moaned about his back. He moaned about the price of fish at the market. It wasn't right.

"Are you well?" asked Kat, hugging her briefly.

Nienna looked up into Kat's blood-spattered, toxin-splashed face, and nodded, giving a little smile. She took a deep breath. "Yes, Kat. I think. Just. Everything has been crazy. Wild! I can't believe Grandpa is so... deadly."

Kat, remembering her companion's perceived savagery back in the tunnel, her cold realisation that Kell would leave her to die, said nothing, simply nodded. An ice-veil dropped over her heart, smothering another little piece of her humanity with bitter cynicism.

"We'll be all right," said Nienna, mistaking Kat's inner turmoil and total fear – not at the world outside, but at the man in the boat. "We'll get through this, you'll see. We'll go to university. Everything will be all right."

Kat gave a small, bitter laugh. "Yeah, Nienna? You, with your sheltered upbringing, your loving mother, your doting grandpa, all caring for you and holding you and being there for you. I never had any of that." Her voice was astringent. Filled with acid. "I've been alone in this world, alone, for such a very long time, sweet little pampered Nienna. I fought every step of the way just to gain entry to Jalder University; I lied, I cheated, I stole, in order to try and crawl up from the stinking gutter, to make a better life for myself, a better future. Nobody has ever been there for me, Nienna."

"What about your aunt? The one who raised you after you parents died? The one who baked you bread, and washed your clothes, and braided your hair with beads?"

Kat gave another laugh, and gazed off along the frozen river banks. The trees were full of snow, the air full of mist from the fields, and they were leaving the city fast behind, the Selanau River carrying them south. "My aunt? She never existed. I used to live in taverns, haylofts, anywhere I could find. I would sneak into merchant's houses and use their baths, steal clothes from servants, steal bread from the ovens and soup from bubbling pans. I was a ghost. A thief. An expert thief." She laughed again, tears running down her cheeks. "I've always been alone, Nienna. Always been a fighter. Now… it's gone, isn't it? The university? Life in Jalder? All I fought to build, it has been taken away with a click of some dictator's scabby fingers."

"I'm there for you, now," said Nienna, voice small, and hugged Kat.

"Everybody leaves me in the end," she said.

"No! I will be there for you. Forever! Until we die."

"Until we die?"

Nienna squeezed her friend, took her hands, pressed her cold skin, her frozen fingers, and hugged her like the sister she'd never had. "I swear on my soul," she whispered.

The boat ride had slowed, and within a couple of hours they finally left the clinging veils of ice-smoke and mist behind. A new world opened before them, fresh and bright as they drifted from wreaths of haze into a landscape of rolling fields crisp with frost and patches of snow. Large hills lined the horizon, many thick with great scars of conifer forest, junipers, yews and blue spruce, great green and white swathes that stretched in crescents across the undulating hillsides peppered with teeth of rock and littered with pink and magenta winter heather giving bright splashes of colour.

Eventually Kell guided the boat to the banks of the river lined with towering silver fir, and they cruised for a while in silence, each huddled in their own damp clothing, stinking from the tannery, lost in thought at the recent, savage events that had overtaken Jalder.

"There," said Saark, pointing.

Kell nodded, spotting the small stone cottage backed by yews, and guided the boat towards a shingle beach where he leapt out into the shallows and dragged the boat up the shingle with a grunt. He stood, axe in pink chilled hands, as the others jumped free and Saark joined him, rapier out, searching for any possible enemy.

"You think they'll follow us here?" said Saark.

"Have you *ever* seen a creature like that Harvester?"

"No."

"Me neither. I've no idea what they'll do, my friend. But for now, at least, we've put a good twenty miles between us and the... madness in Jalder." At his words, he saw Nienna shudder and he moved to her, placing his arm around her shoulders. "Come on, Nienna. We'll build a fire." He hugged her.

"I was thinking. Of mam."

Kell frowned. "She'd gone to work at Keenan's Farm, yes? To work on the pottery?"

Nienna nodded, face frightened.

"That's eight miles out of the city," said Kell, soothingly. "She'll be fine. Trust me. The enemy want the garrison; it's not worth their effort scouring the countryside for every little farmstead."

Nienna gave another nod, but Kell could see she wasn't convinced.

They approached the stone cottage warily. It was single storey, simple in construction with a thatched roof. No smoke came from the chimney, and no livestock scattered in the yard as was normal for these modest but cosy dwellings.

"It's deserted," said Saark, kicking a bucket which clattered across the mud.

Kell threw him a dark scowl, and moved to the entrance. "What's the matter? You sorry there are no serving wenches at hand to see to your every petty whim?"

Saark shrugged, and stood, a hand on one hip, his rapier pointing at the ground. He plucked at a tattered, stained cuff. "Well, I'm sorry there are no serving wenches sat on my hand, Kell old horse. It's been commented in social circles how I can supply the most exquisite of pleasures to even the most buxom pigs with a face like a horse arse." He smiled, showing neat teeth. "I have a certain way with female flesh. And with male flesh, come to think of it."

"Keep your thoughts to yourself," said Kell darkly, "or you'll have a way with my fist," and he entered the cottage. He emerged a moment later, and gestured them inside. They stepped in. The floor was flagged with stone, and a table and several chairs, old, battered but expertly crafted, stood in one room. A kitchen bench ran down one entire wall containing wooden plates and cups, and a large jug. The second room contained a huge bed, still scattered with old blankets. Saark peered in, and tutted.

"What's the matter now?" snapped Kell.

"No silk sheets," smiled Saark, and rubbed at weary eyes. He yawned, and stretched. "Still, it's good enough for tonight. I'm going to take a nap."

"No you're not," said Kell, turning to face him across the long table.

"Excuse me?"

"I said," growled Kell, "you're not going to put down your head and leave all the work to us. We need wood for the fire, water for the pot, and I spied a vegetable patch outside with cabbages and potatoes. They need to be pulled from the frozen soil and scrubbed clean."

"I'm sure you'll get on just wonderfully with such menial labour," smiled Saark, Kell's anger apparently lost on him. "It is, of course, no job for a nobleman and dandy of such high repute."

"Are you hungry?"

"Of course! But alas, I cannot cook, have never chopped wood, and my lower back is a tad sore from all my romantic endeavours. Alas, your jobs, valiant and necessary as they are, are beyond a simple coxcomb like myself." Saark turned, as if to enter the mouldy bedroom.

"If you don't work, you don't eat," said Kell, voice low.

"Excuse me?"

"Is there a problem with your hearing? Something, perhaps, that needs cleaning out with the blade of my axe?"

Saark scowled. "I may be a sexual athlete, and I may dress in silks so expensive the likes of you could not afford them even if you worked a thousand years; but I will not be threatened, Kell, and don't you ever doubt my skill with a blade."

"I don't doubt your skill with a blade, boy, just the skill with your brain. Get out there, and chop some wood, or I swear I'll kick you down to the river like an old stinking dog and drown you."

There was a moment of tension, then Saark relaxed, and smiled. He crossed to the doorway, both young women watching him in silence, and he turned and gave Kell a nod. "As you wish, old man. But I'd do something about that sexual tension; it's eating you up, and alas, turning you into a cantankerous ill-tempered bore." His eyes flickered to Kat, lingered for a moment, then he gave a narrow smile and left.

Within moments, they heard the chopping of wood. Saark had obviously found the wood shed.

Nienna crossed to her grandpa, and touched his arm. "He means no harm," she said. "It's just his way."

"Pah!" snapped Kell. "I know his sort; I saw plenty of them in Vor and Fawkrin. He takes, like a parasite, and never gives. There are too many like him, even in Jalder. They have spread north like a plague."

"Not any longer," said Kat, eyes haunted. "The albino soldiers killed them all." She took the jug from the long bench and left, heading down to the river for water. Kell sighed, and placed Ilanna on the table with a gentle motion. He took Nienna by both shoulders, and looked into her eyes, deep into her eyes, until she blushed and turned away.

"You did well, girl."

"In the university?"

"All of it," said Kell. "You were strong, brave, fearless. You haven't been moaning and whining," he glanced outside, his insinuation obvious, "and you have proved yourself in battle." He smiled then, a kindly smile, and Nienna's old grandpa returned. "Funny, you said you wanted an adventure. Well, you've brought us that, little Nienna." He ruffled her hair, and she gave a laugh, but it faded, twisted, and ended awkwardly.

This was not a day for laughter.

Kat washed herself as best she could, then filled her jug at the river, and carrying it back towards the stone cottage she stopped, observing Saark work. He had tied back his long, dark curls, and stripped off his shirt revealing a lean and well-muscled torso. He had broad shoulders tapering to narrow hips, and although he claimed never to chop wood, he did so with an expert stroke, his balance perfect, every swing striking true to split logs into halves, quarters and eighths ready for the fire.

Kat watched him for a while, the sway of his body, the squirming of muscles under pale white skin, and the serenity of his handsome face in its focus, and concentration. No, she decided; not a handsome face, but a beautiful face. Saark was stunning. Almost feminine in his delicacy, his symmetry. Kat licked her lips.

He turned, then, sweat glistening on his body despite the chill, and he waved her towards him. Slowly, she approached, eyes down now, feeling suddenly shy and not understanding why.

"Hello, my pretty," he said with a wide friendly smile. "Would it be possible to quench my thirst?"

"Sir?"

"The water," he laughed, "can I have a drink?"

Kat nodded, and Saark took the jug, taking great gulps, water running down his chest through shining sweat. She saw his chest had the same curled, dark hair as his head, and as he lowered the jug he grinned at her, eyes glittering.

"Do you like what you see?"

"What do you mean?"

"You were watching me. Whilst I chopped wood."

"I was not!"

"How old are you, girl?"

"I'm eighteen. I'm a woman, not a girl."

Saark looked her up and down, eyes widening. "Well, I can see that, my pretty." His voice deepened. "You are all woman."

"Have you finished with the jug?"

Grinning again, Saark handed it back and Kat turned to leave.

"You can sleep with me tonight, if you like? I'll keep you warm against the ice and the snow; keep you safe against the bad men in the dark."

"The only bad man in the dark would be you," snapped Kat, without turning, and stalked back towards the cottage, her cheeks flushed red. But she was smiling as she walked.

Kell lit a fire, and within an hour warmth had filled the cottage. Darkness fell outside, and night brought with it a storm of snow and hail, which rattled off the windows as a mournful wind howled through the yew trees out back.

Nienna and Kat cooked a large pot of stew, thick with cabbage and potatoes, and plenty of salt which Kell found in a cupboard along with dried herbs, thyme and rosemary, which they added for flavour. They sat around the table, eating. All had cleaned themselves as best they could in the ice-cold river, and Nienna found some old clothes in a chest in the bedroom. Despite being cold, and smelling mildly of damp, they were far superior to the stained items which had suffered the tannery. Each in turn changed, burning old clothes on the fire and pulling on woollen trews and rough cotton shirts. Saark went last, and when Nienna handed him the thick trousers and shirt he held them at arm's length, his distaste apparent.

"What would you like me to do with these?" he asked Nienna. She gave a short laugh. "Put them on, idiot!"

"Are you sure? I thought they were for cleaning out the pigs." He glanced over at Kell and grimaced. "I see you've settled comfortably into your new wardrobe, old horse."

"These clothes are fine," Kell said gruffly, not looking up.

"Not itchy at all?"

Kell glanced up from his stew. "Not for me," he said. "But you may find them a little rough, what with your baby-soft skin, manicured hands and cream-softened arse."

"Ha! These are the clothes of the peasant. I'll not wear them."

"Then you'll stink of dog-shit, old brains and cattle-fat for the next week."

Saark considered this. "You sure they don't itch?" he asked. "There's nothing worse than a peasant's fleas. Except, maybe, a whore's syphilis!" He laughed at his joke, and carried the clothes through to the bedroom with Kell staring after him, eyes glowing embers.

The door closed, then opened again. "Any chance one of you young ladies could help me dress? You know how tiresome this can be for us fine noble types."

"I'll do it," said Kell, pushing back his chair which scraped against the stone floor.

"Ach, that's all right, big man. I… I think I can manage."

Saark disappeared, and Kell returned to his stew, complementing Nienna and Kat on their cooking.

When they'd finished eating, Nienna said, "Grandpa?"

"Yes, monkey?"

"Will the…" she seemed to be fighting with her thoughts, "will those albino soldiers come after us? This far from Jalder?"

"No, girl," said Kell. "They took the garrison, then the city. If they do intend to invade Falanor further, then the logical route is to head south down the Great North Road. After all, King Leanoric built it for transporting his troops." He smiled, and it was grim. "It's ironic, however, that I think he envisioned his own soldiers using it. Not the enemy."

"Where did those albino men come from?" said Kat. She was leaning back, hands stretched towards the fire, belly full and at least savouring a little contentment.

"From the north, past the Black Pike Mountains. I saw them once; they have a huge civilisation there."

"Why does nobody in Jalder speak of them? Why is there no trade?"

Kell shrugged. "The paths across the mountains are treacherous indeed. For most of the year impassable, even; certainly impossible for an army to travel. This Army of Iron must have found a new route, something to which I am not privy."

"Is it true there are tunnels under the Black Pikes?"

Kell nodded. "Many. And more treacherous than the mountain trails, of that I am certain." His eyes were distant, now, as if reliving ancient days. "I've seen many a man die in the Black Pikes. The mountains take no prisoners."

"You speak as if they live?"

"Maybe they do," said Kell, rubbing wearily at his eyes. "Maybe they do."

Saark chose that moment to make his grand entrance, and he grinned, giving a twirl by the bedroom door. "I look like you people, now," he said, tying back his long curls.

"You said they were clothes for a peasant," pointed out Kell.

"Exactly," smiled Saark. "Is there any more stew? I'm famished."

"You've already had two bowls," said Kat.

"I'm a growing lad who needs his energy." He winked at her, and sat down, ladling more stew into his bowl. "By all the gods, this stinks of cabbage."

"You can always go hungry, lad," said Kell.

"No, no, I'm starting to enjoy the... ahh, cabbage flavour. It's certainly an acquired taste, but I think, in maybe a year or two, I might just get used to it."

After the girls were asleep, Saark waved a small flask at Kell. "Drink, old horse?"

"Stop calling me old horse. I ain't that old."

"Ach, so you won't be wanting this whisky, aged fifteen years in oak vats, will you?"

"Maybe just a drop," conceded Kell. "To warm against the winter chill." He took the flask, drank deeply, and handed it back to Saark, smacking his lips. "By all the gods, that's a fine drop." He eyed Saark. "Must have cost a pretty penny."

"Stolen by my own fair hand."

"'The World despises a thief, leste he undermyne Mighty Kings'," quoted Kell, staring hard at Saark. "I kind of echo that sentiment, laddie."

"All fine and well, when you have money in your purse. Ask those without. The merchant who shared his produce won't be needing it; the albino soldiers killed him and his wife."

"And I suppose you had just... ravished her?"

Saark snorted laughter, and took another drink. "Ravished? Come come, Kell, we are both men of the world. You can speak to me as one man to another. Yes, I fucked her. And what a pretty piece of quim she was, too. Never have I tasted such succulent honey."

Kell's eyes hardened, fists clenching. "You have very little respect for women, lad."

Saark considered this. "Well, they have very little respect for me. Now, listen Kell." He leant forward, firelight dancing in his dark eyes. "We need to decide what we're going to do next. You know, as I, the Army of Iron will head south. We have but a few days; they will consolidate their position, leave their own garrison in command of Jalder, and travel the Great North Road. We need to be gone from here by then; their scouts will spread out, and will certainly find us. We are easy to spot." He thought. "Well, you are."

Kell nodded, and when he replied his voice was cool. He found it hard to hide his distaste for the popinjay. Kell was a simple man who wore emotions on his face, and on his fists. He told it like it was. "What do you have in mind, Saark?"

"Much as it pains me to say this, for there is little actual personal profit in it for me, but... we should ride south. We should warn King Leanoric. It is the right thing to do."

Kell picked up a sharp bread knife, toyed with it between his fingers. He seemed uneasy. "Surely, the king already knows? His northern capital has been sundered."

"Maybe. Maybe not. If the Army of Iron surprises Leanoric... well, they can plough through Falanor like a knife through a sleeping man's eyeball. Our armies would topple. People enslaved. All that kind of tiresome business of Empire. Could you live with that on your conscience, Kell?"

"You're a fine one to speak of conscience."

"For a cuckolded husband? No. For the slaughter of an entire population? Use your head, Kell. And anyway... there may be a warm spot in the Hall of Heroes for somebody who does the Heroic Thing." He winked. "One must always try and please the gods. Just in case."

"You're a worm, Saark."

"Maybe. But a man needs all the help he can get. We must warn Leanoric. He will need to gather the Eagle Divisions; if surprised, he could be sorely routed. What life then for a dandy on a mission?"

Kell nodded, and his eyes met Saark's. "You are from the south, aren't you lad?"

"Yes. Hard to hide the Iopian burr."

"Have you met the king?"

"Once," said Saark, his voice dropping soft, eyes becoming dreamy. "Many moons ago, old horse."

The fire was burning low. Outside, the wind howled and hail rattled in bursts against the windows like a smash of arrows. Kell came awake, one arm cold, head foggy. The whisky had done him few favours. It rarely did.

What had woken him?

Kell sat up, from where he lay before the fire. He could hear Nienna's rhythmical snoring in the bedroom. Across from him, Saark turned in his sleep, but did not wake. Kell stood, and reached for his axe, then crouched beside Saark and shook him.

"Mmm?"

"Shh. I heard something."

"Probably a rat."

"There are no rats. I checked."

"Probably a chicken." He shook off Kell's grip. "Let me go back to sleep."

"Might be an albino soldier with a dagger for your throat," whispered Kell in Saark's ear.

Saark rolled over, pulled on his boots, and drew his rapier. "You are the fun soul of any party, Kell, you know that? Shit then. Let's go check it out."

"Wake the girls."

"Why? Women are best left asleep after the night's work is done, in my opinion."

"We may need to leave fast."

Saark moved to the bedroom, woke the girls and watched without embarrassment as they dressed in the gloom, leaning against the doorway, his eyes lingering on breasts. Kell moved to the front door and stopped. He stared at the wooden planks, which rattled in the wind; outside, hail bombarded the world and Kell tilted his head, frowning, eyes narrowing, then was suddenly moving, twisting, diving aside at high speed as the door – including torn hinges and wrenched locks – imploded with a squeal and crash, the whole thing slamming across the room and missing Kell by inches, to crash into the far wall where it exploded into chunks and splinters. Kell lifted his axe, Saark whirled around, face drawn, sword high, and there in the entrance stood... the canker, Zalherion. It growled, a low metallic sound underlain with a thrashing of delicate brass gears.

"What the hell–" hissed Saark.

The canker leapt, its bulk smashing stones from the door surround as Kell rolled right, axe thundering in an arc to slam flesh with a thump and spray of bright blood; Saark's rapier slashed the creature's flank, carving a long razor-line down bulging muscle and the creature roared, head thrashing as it turned, bulky and huge in the room as it stomped chairs to tinder. Saark whirled. To Nienna and Kat, he hissed, "Out the window! Run down to the boat, now, as if your lives depend on it!"

He leapt as the canker turned on him, and a great paw on the end of a bent, angled, barely human arm snapped at him. Talons tore three shallow jagged lines across his clothing, hurling him across the room upside down to thud the wall and hit the floor, tangled and groaning. Kell's axe, Ilanna, slammed at the creature's spine, blades embedding in flesh. He tore his axe free as the canker screamed, rearing up, head smashing the ceiling and bringing down thick plaster and several cracked wooden beams. Grimly, Kell wrenched free his axe, took a step back for balance and weighting, and hammered it again as if chopping wood. Blades bit flesh, muscle, and several small brass gears were flung free of the canker, tinkling as they scattered across the stone floor.

The creature turned on Kell, huge open maw filled with gnashing clockwork and drooling thick crimson pus. It howled, and charged at him in the confined space, and Kell scrambled back, twisting to avoid the swipe of massive talons at the end of a human arm, his axe coming up to deflect a second blow, ducking a third swipe which hit the fireplace behind him, cracking stones with sheer force of impact.

Kell looked deep into the canker's eyes. The rage there was indescribable... the pain, the suffering, the anguish, the hatred. He swallowed hard as its shoulders tensed, and Kell realised it was going to crush him against the stone of the cottage wall with sheer bulk and weight – and he didn't have room to swing Ilanna! There was nothing he could do.

FIVE
The Church of Blessed Engineers

Anukis awoke slowly, as if from a long, bad dream. She could taste blood, and two of her teeth were smashed. She reached into her mouth and plucked the tiny pieces of bone free, wincing, wanting to cry, but forcing back the piercing pain and ignoring the fire. She had more urgent matters to consider.

Coughing, Anukis sat up and opened her eyes. She was naked, wrists chained, and the room was illuminated by a dim light. However, her superior vachine eyes kicked in with a tiny background whirr of clockwork, and her eyes enhanced the ambient light. She was in a cell. It was a good cell, a clean cell; precise, and fashioned totally from metal.

Anukis looked about. The floor was steel, ridged for grip, and sporting channels no-doubt to carry away blood and the water used to sluice out the honey from the tortured. The walls were black iron, rusted in patches, the ceiling brass and set with tiny squares to allow entry for distant daylight.

Anukis stood, testing her body, checking how much damage had been done. The vachine had beat her; oh, how they enjoyed their sport, slamming the impure with fists and boots, but no teeth – no, Vashell had not allowed them to rip her apart with fangs and claws.

Not yet, anyway.

Anukis endured her savage beating; it lasted maybe an hour. She recognised it had gone on long after she had lost consciousness. Slowly, now, she checked her way through her bones, searching for breaks; there was a mild fracture in her left shoulder blade, and she winced as she rolled it, ignoring the torn and protesting muscles, the impact bruises, but going deep, analysing the pain within. One finger was snapped, on her left hand – ironically, her wedding ring finger. I suppose Vashell won't be asking me to marry him anymore, she thought, and felt a hysterical giggle welling in her breast which she quashed savagely. No. Not here. You cannot lose your mind here. Because to lose your mind is to...

Die.

Such a simple word. An effortless concept. The natural order of all things: to live, and to die. Only the vachine were different, for they had introduced a third state with their hybrid watchmaking technology... as created by her grandfather, and refined, accelerated and implemented by her father Kradek-ka. It was a state of life which was partially removed from life; not death, no, not exactly. But only a side-step away from the long dark journey.

Anukis realised two ribs were cracked, and she bit her tongue against the pain as she shifted her weight. She ran her hands over her naked, pale skin, up and down her legs, over her hips and belly, stroking her flanks, searching for tears in flesh and damage to muscle and tendon within. Finally, satisfied, Anukis walked around her cell, hands tracing contours on the walls and pausing, occasionally, at odd-shaped slots and sockets. These were for the mobile torture devices of the Engineers and Cardinals. She had heard of such things; but never witnessed. With a cold chill she grasped her position, and understood with clarity that her opportunity might come sooner than she realised.

Anukis moved to the cell door for analysis. It was brass, thick and very, very heavy, a solid slab with only a hand-sized portal through which to feed prisoners. Anu's fingers traced the join between door and the metal wall – it was precise, as befitted a religion and culture of engineers and metal craftsmen.

As she stood, she heard a lock mechanism whirr and took a hurried step back. The door swung inwards, silently, and a figure was outlined. It was the athletic figure of Vashell, the light source behind him, his features hidden in darkness and shadow.

"Have you come to gloat, bastard?"

His fist lashed out, slamming Anukis's face and dropping her to the floor. He stepped forward, and his boot smashed her face, stamped on her chest, and as she lay, stunned, bleeding, he stamped on her head.

Vashell pulled off a pair of gloves and moved, sitting on her bed, reclining a little, hands clasped around one armoured knee. He smiled, his brass fangs poking over his lower lip, and his eyes were dark, oil-filled, glittering first with resentment, then with amusement at Anukis's pain.

She lay, wheezing, head spinning, and it took many minutes for the effects of the blows to subside. Finally, she sat up, coughed up blood which ran down her breasts and pooled in her lap, in her crotch, an ersatz moon-bleeding.

"Ten years ago we played in my father's garden," he said. "We ran through the long grass, and you giggled, and your hair shone in the winter sun. We walked down to the river, sat watching the savage fast waters filled with ice-melt from beneath the Black Pikes; and I held you, and you told me you loved me, and that one day we would be together."

"No."

"Yes."

"Your memories are twisted, Vashell. It didn't happen like that." She coughed, holding her breast, blood staining her chin like a horror puppet. "You chased me. I struggled. I asked for you to leave me alone!"

"Liar!" he surged to his feet, face contorted into a vachine snarl. Inside his mouth, gears stepped and wheels spun.

Anu was crying as she looked up at him. "Vashell," she said, gently, "I never said I loved you, I never loved you. You saw what you wanted to see. You pursued me for a decade, and never once did I give you reason to believe I returned your love; I was careful, because you were an Engineer Priest, and I knew to anger you would be fatal."

Vashell subsided, and sat again, staring at her, his expression unreadable. "I loved you," he said, simply.

"You captured me, had me beaten. Just now, you kicked me like a dog. How can you sit there and say you loved me?"

"You betrayed me!" he snarled, spittle flying from his fangs. "You made me a fucking mockery amongst the Engineers; you have undermined my authority, lowered my rank, and you sit there and wonder why I strike you? That is my *right*, fucker. You have earned the beating, and much, much more. You are impure. Bad blood. A Heretic. No true vachine would have led an Engineer Priest on such a pretty dance."

"I led you nowhere! You are a fool, Vashell. Weak and stupid, brutal and savage. What could I possibly see in you to love? And you know what the worst thing is?" Her voice dropped, her face lowered, and her eyes were dark, staring up at him, submissive, subservient, and yet totally in control at the same time. "If I, a simple ill-blood, would not join you as your wife, would not mother your children, then what pure-blood vachine would ever touch your corrupt and deviated shell?"

Vashell did not reply in words, only in actions. He knelt by her, looking down at her pale white flesh, her slender limbs, her feminine curves, and with his clenched fist, claws curled tight, he pounded her face again and again, and took her head in his hands and rammed it against the floor, and even as she lay, bleeding, head spinning, not even understanding what hit her so mercilessly, so he suddenly halted and rocked back on his heels, crying a little, tears on his cheeks. He leant forward, low, and kissed her smashed lips, her blood running into his mouth like the finest Karakan import; he kissed her, his tongue sliding between her lips and his hand moving down her throat, over her breasts, stroking her belly, dipping between her legs to play for a while as she lay, panting, chest rising and falling in rapid beats, and she finally coughed, eyes flickering open...

"Get *off* me!" she screamed, and Vashell rocked back, stood and swiftly left the cell. The door slammed shut, and Anukis was left, crying and alone, battered and bleeding, abused and frightened, on the cell floor.

Kill me now, she thought. For I am nothing more than a slave.

A female vachine entered after a day of bad dreams, and with a bowl of water and a rag, cleaned the blood from Anukis's body with gentle strokes and soothing clucks. Anu opened her eyes, watched the vachine, an ugly specimen where the clockwork had become mildly disjointed, misaligned, and merged with the flesh of her face so that gears and cogs were openly visible against her cheeks, on her tongue, inside her bone-twisted forehead; whilst she was still vachine, it was considered vulgar to have such a show. And yet like any disease, this was totally uncontrollable.

"There you go, little lady," said the woman.

"Thank you," said Anukis.

"Soon have you good as new."

"What's your name?"

The vachine smiled. "I am Perella. I've been assigned by Torto, one of the five Watchmakers, to tend you during your stay."

"Where am I?"

"The Engineer's Palace, of course."

Anukis groaned. When you entered the Engineer's Palace, as one such as she, it was a rarity you left. At least, not with the same number of limbs, cogs or brain platters.

"Do not fret," said Perella, kindly. "I'm sure everything will be all right."

"You are kind." Anu's voice was stiff. "But can I ask, do you know why I'm here? I am impure. I cannot take blood-oil. I am a Heretic." She bowed her head, accepting her shame.

"To me, you are just another vachine." Perella smiled. "It is my understanding that your... condition, comes through no fault of your own. It's a simple unmeshing, something over which you have no control – despite what religious fanatics might believe. Shh. Someone approaches."

Footsteps slapped the metal walkway, and Vashell appeared. He smiled warmly at Anukis. "It is good to see you well."

"What?" she snarled. "You beat me unconscious and arrive to make pleasantries? Go to your grave, Vashell, and enjoy the worms eating your eyes."

Vashell made a gesture, and Perella hurried from the room. Vashell's face darkened, and only then did she see the collar and lead he carried. He moved forward, fastened the collar around her throat and wound twin clanking chains around his gloved gauntlet. "Come with me. We're going for a walk."

"You would parade me naked?"

"Heretics deserve no dignity," he said.

Anu snarled then, a vachine sound, and her fangs lengthened showing the gleam of brass. Vashell laughed, and tugged on the chains making Anukis stumble; she righted herself with difficulty, through her broken bruised frame, and he dragged her out into the corridor where the metal grille walkway dug viciously into her naked feet.

Anu's face burned red as Vashell led her like a dog, tugging occasionally as if for his own amusement. They moved away from the prison block, and back to the hub of the Engineer's Palace. As they approached from the prison arm so they passed more and more vachine, and several Engineers and Cardinals who stared at Anukis with distaste, some with open hatred, baring fangs in a show of aggressive challenge. Anu kept her head high, meeting the gaze of every pureblood, challenging them, snarling back with her own hatred and loathing.

At the hub central there was a high domed ceiling of brass, and a huge circular desk fashioned from a single mammoth block of silver-quartz and polished into smooth perfection, gleaming, beautiful, and sculpted with fine chisels into a thousand different scenes of vachine history, and vachine victory. Behind this circular symbol sat the bulk of the Engineers and their subordinates, Engineer Priests, working on intricate machinery, individual workstations full of delicate hand tools and machine tools, some powered by burning oil, some by the energy and pulse of silver-quartz which was mined, with great loss of life, by the albinos deep beneath the Black Pike Mountains. Silver-quartz was one of the three fabled ingredients of the vachine. The timing mechanism of a vachine's heart; and indeed, his soul.

Vashell stopped before the huge silver bank, and grinned at the other Engineers, obviously displaying his prize with pride. The sentiment was clear; what he had failed to dominate by love and marriage, he now dominated by fear and violence. This would gain him respect after his perceived darkening at Anu's newly discovered impure status. He had been right. She had made a fool of him.

The Engineers to a man – for they were all male – set down delicate tools with care and stood. There were nearly three hundred of them; the core of vachine society trained highly in the arts of clockwork and the magick of blood-oil. Anu's eyes swept along the ranks, ranging across short and tall Engineers and Engineer Priests alike, all wearing silver religious insignia on their shoulders, all focused with looks of hatred at this woman, this half-pure, the daughter of one who had, once, been great. Kradek-ka. The Watchmaker.

"See?" bellowed Vashell, pulling the chains tight so his superior height caused Anu to stand up on tiptoe, straining, the veins and muscles of her throat standing out. "The one who shamed me! Now, she walks as my slave. Until I see fit to dispose of her."

The Engineers were staring, eyes narrowed, and began to hiss, the noise filling the domed chamber as steel and brass fangs slid from jaw sheaths and they narrowed eyes at the impure; but more than that. A high-ranking impure who had shamed an Engineer Priest. This was not done.

And then, standing there, naked and chained before the Engineers, Anukis realised the full extent of her slavery. Desolation swamped her. This was not going to be a simple case of torture and execution. No. Not only Vashell's pride and vachine honour were on trial here; the whole of the Engineer culture felt cheated, abused, despoiled, and Anu realised with a lead heart that they would force her to live as long as possible... and make her suffer humiliation, degradation, and pain greater than any impure had ever suffered.

Anu shivered, goose-bumps running along her flesh, and Vashell pulled her tight before his Engineer brethren and his fangs grew long, and suddenly a hushed silence flowed through the chamber and Vashell's head dropped, his fangs plunging into Anu's neck, into her artery, and he sucked out her blood and lifted her, like a ragdoll in his powerful arms as he drank her, drank her impurity, and Anu grew limp, dizzy, and lying naked in Vashell's abusive embrace she slipped away into welcome darkness.

The rhythm danced through her. It pumped through every blood vessel, every vein, every artery, to her heart. It pumped, an echo to her own heart, a heartbeat doppelganger chasing through haemoglobin and the rainbow thick mix of blood-oil and alien blood and her mind was transfused with confusion, like a spider spinning a web over glass, and as she awoke her mouth was full of fur, her eyes sticky with blood, her ears pounding with an ocean, waves crashing a bone beach of despair and she coughed, and choked, spluttered, her eyes forced open through stickiness and she stared down at silk sheets.

Anukis coughed again, phlegm spattering the fine white silk, and she groaned, pain slamming her from every angle. She stared straight ahead, at the rock wall filled with lodes of minor silver-quartz thread, and realised with a start she was *in* the mountain...

She rolled, and sat up, her golden curls cascading down her back. She had been washed, shampooed, scrubbed of blood and dirt, and now she wore a light cotton gown that did little to protect her vulnerability. Her hand came up, touched her neck, caressed the dual puncture marks.

He bit me, she thought, eyes narrowing.

The ultimate disgust, from one vachine to another.

The ultimate rape. An implied and direct insult; of superior blood over toxic blood. No vachine bit another. It was not done.

Winter sunlight sleeted through long, low windows at the edge of the room, and Anukis eased her feet over the edge of the bed, feeling tender, feeling sore, feeling battered and bruised and weak. She filled up with self loathing and spat on the fine thick red carpets. "The bastard."

She stood, trembling, limbs frail, and tottered across to a marble stand containing a brass jug. She poured herself a little water, and drank. It made her feel sick.

Before her, through the window, she could see the spread of Silva Valley. It was beautiful, serene, a pastel painting of perfect civilisation, vast and finely sculpted, a culture at its peak. Where am I? she thought, and the answer came easily enough. This was a mountain villa, and obviously belonged to Vashell's parents. They were rich. They were Engineers. They were royalty.

The mountain villas were built at the summit of the rising city, up at the head of the valley in premium sites for exaggerated architecture, and using the mountain itself as a base. These villas overlooked the vachine world, and commanded the greatest views one could buy in Silva Valley.

Anukis stood for a while, watching the view. It was morning, and the vachine world was coming awake. She could see thousands of vachine on the streets below, buying, selling, transporting goods. If she stretched, she could just determine the bulk of the Engineer's Palace to the left, and a curved walkway leading to a dark mouth. A steady stream of vachine queued along the snake of the path, many carrying bundles in their arms. These were inventions, or broken mechanisms they wished fixing. Some came with requests for the Engineers. Some came with information.

Anukis smoothed her hands down her cotton flanks, and thought of Shabis, her younger sister. Shabis was true vachine, no impure blood ran through her veins, greasing her cogs and wheels, and Anukis knew that even her own sister knew not of her impure nature. Only Kradek-ka had been party to the secret; and they both guarded it fervently. After all, if word got out, she would forfeit with her life.

Anukis smiled, for what felt the first time in a century. She thought of Shabis, young Shabis, only sixteen years old, long beautiful golden curls, taller than Anukis, more slender, her limbs delicate and regal. Her eyes were dark, her face a little more pointed; she was a stunning Vachine Goddess!

The smile fell from Anu's face. If Shabis still lived…

There came the tiniest of clicks. Vashell stood there. He wore full battle armour, and a dazzling array of weapons. His boots were polished, his head held high, his face and eyes unreadable. Then he smiled, and moved forward, standing beside Anukis to stare out over Silva Valley and the jewelled contents of the vachine empire.

"I cannot believe it came to this," said Vashell. His voice sounded, genuinely, hurt.

"Go away, and die quietly," whispered Anukis.

Vashell turned, and took her hands in his own. He held her gently, but there was no illusion there for Anukis; she knew damn well how brutal he could be. His gentility was an affectation. His humbleness a façade.

"If you had asked me our futures three months ago, I would have been so sure, so adamant, that we would be wed, and living a life of rich royalty. We were the perfect match, Anukis."

"You abused me," she hissed, looking at him then, her eyes flashing dark. "In front of the Engineers and Priests! You took my blood, you humiliated me, you beat me. You are a canker, Vashell; maybe not visibly so, not in the open flesh, but deep in your heart your clockwork has deformed and twisted, and even now has eaten that part of you which was human."

Vashell stood, stunned by the insult. To call a vachine a canker was… unthinkable.

He took a deep breath, and Anukis watched him master his anger; his fury.

"I can make this right," he said.

"An utter impossibility."

"I still love you."

Anukis stood, and turned back to face the Silva Valley. Still, Vashell held her hands and she felt his grip grow tight, holding her, refusing to allow her a simple freedom.

"The only person you love is yourself," said Anukis.

"Listen to me." There was urgency in his voice. "You were caught red-handed with the Blacklipper king himself. You were witnessed drinking Karakan Red. We had been staking out the lair for months, tracing Preyshan's suppliers – and then you stumbled in screaming out your impure status. It was all I could do to stop the Engineers slaughtering you where you stood… and believe me, I put my own life on the line in those few moments out there under the Brass Docks. Since then, I have been observed, closely watched by the Watchmakers to see how I'd react, to see how I treated you. Don't you understand, Anukis? If I had not behaved the way I did, both our lives would have been forfeit! We would never have escaped the claws of Silva Valley! But now… now I have a *plan*."

"Explain to me your plan." Her voice was low. Still she did not face Vashell. Her anger went beyond speech.

"Since the humiliation inside the Engineer's Palace, it is believed I have broken you, and brought you here as my sexual plaything, until I grow tired, until I murder you and send your corpse back to the Engineer's Palace for dissection. Now, their watch has grown lax. I feel the trails of blood-oil magick weaken with every passing second, every heartbeat. Within a few days we will be free, and can leave this place. Together. If you so wish."

"What of Shabis?"

"She will come with us! You must believe me, Anukis. It has all been an act! I love you dearly; more than life itself. I have been working to secure our freedom, to sneak us from under the vachine net."

Anukis turned, and looked into his eyes, and chewed her lip.

"You mean this?"

"Yes," he said. "Kiss me."

"What?"

"Kiss me. Show me what I am missing."

Anukis frowned, and it felt wrong, Vashell's words felt wrong and they came crashing down inside her brain. Why would a High Born Royal, an Engineer Priest with all the makings of earning a future rank of Watchmaker give up everything for her? Her own lack of self-esteem bit her, and bit her hard.

"I don't know whether to trust you," she said, her voice low, trembling. "You did terrible things to me, Vashell. You tore out my heart, you humiliated me; you took away what vestiges of pride still remained!"

"No." He shook his head. "Your pride was already gone. I saved your life. It's that simple. You know I speak the truth. You know how we are watched. And now, I can save both you, and your sister, if you only trust me. You took that physical beating from me; and I was observed. It was an evil necessity. Now I have only love for you." He moved close, shushing her, lips tickling her ear, and slowly his mouth moved around and he kissed her and his kiss was gentle, loving, his hands running through her hair, gently, over her body and she squirmed under his grip, a mixture of lust, and love, and confusion, and hatred, all running and combining with her fear and uncertainty and he kissed her, and she kissed him back, and she fell into him, fell into his world and he hugged her, his face over her shoulder, and his fangs eased free of brass jaw sheaths and Vashell closed his eyes, face a rapture of love and contentment.

He came to her that night, and in the darkness and the glow of molten lanterns she loosened her cotton robe which slipped from perfect, bruised shoulders. Vashell stood, his eyes wide, basking in her beauty, basking in her slender vachine warmth, and he stepped forward and his hands moved out, rested lightly on her lips and she smiled up at him, and he smiled back, and love was in his eyes as he gave a low growl of lust and pushed her back to the bed. He kissed her, his hands on her flesh, his claws tracing grooves down her curves, and Anukis moaned as she gave herself to him, fucked him, partially from want, partially to save her life, and to save her sister, and confusion raged through her and only later did she wonder about the love in his eyes. Was it his, or simply the reflection of her own?

Anukis had a dream. She dreamt of Kradek-ka. He was tall, and powerful, a noble Watchmaker in full vachine battledress. He stood over her, then sat down, cross-legged before her, his swords scraping the floor. A fire burned, an old wood fire, traditional, smoke trailing embers into the air. Flames glittered in his swirling gold eyes.

"Anukis?" he said gently.

"Father!" She fell into his arms and he held her, his powerful arms encircled her and she cried, cried tears of gold and blood, and she knew then that everything would be fine, the world would be good, and Anukis would not have to face the horrors of the world alone. "I've missed you so much, Daddy. I've been so alone and so terrified without you."

"You need to listen to me, girl." His voice was gentle, despite his size. "I am in… a curious place. I think I may be dead."

"How did you come to my dreams?"

"I do not know, girl. What I do know is your position. They have found out, yes?"

"It was horrible," she wept.

He wiped away her tears. Firelight glinted on his silver fangs. Out of all the vachine, every single one of the eighty thousand strong population in Silva Valley, Kradek-ka was the only creature who could take pure silver. Normally, silver would disrupt every other element of clockwork, twist every ounce of silver-quartz, dislocate every heartbeat rhythm; but not with Kradek-ka. He was a mystery to the Engineers. A conundrum to other Watchmakers, and even to the Patriarch Himself.

"I have advice for you."

"Tell me what to do."

"Marry Vashell."

"What?"

"It is your greatest chance of survival. And I want to see you live, Anukis. I want to see you live so very, very much."

She awoke, and the room was warm; it smelt of oil. It smelt of the narcotic, blood-oil.

Vashell was there, naked beside the bed. His erection was magnificent to behold, his balls inset with tiny gears, the smallest of spinning toothed cogs which ground and whirred, and all reflecting the light from a hundred burning candles.

Anukis lay back, panting, her golden curls highlighting her pale frame.

"I wanted you so much," he said.

"I love you, Vashell," she said, remembering the fear in her father's eyes. The lie tripped easily from her tongue. It was a lie of existence. A lie of endurance. A lie of survival; for if she survived, she could find her father, and save her sister.

"And I you." He touched her, his hands on her breasts, her hips, sliding smooth into her slick cunt, and she closed her eyes and allowed him to take her, again, and again, and again, the only sound his panting, and the tiny *tick tick tick* of his clockwork inside her.

"Shabis!"

Shabis ran across the room, bare feet curling in thick carpets, and fell into Anu's arms. "Nuky," she said, nuzzling her older sister, and they held each other, breathing one another's natural scent, feeling the flow of sisterly love, of a bond greater than all else.

Shabis pulled back, tears coursing her cheeks. "How are you?"

Anu glanced to Vashell over her shoulder. "I am well. I am in love! How are you? Have the Engineers harmed you? Are you well?"

"I am fine," laughed Shabis. "I have been treated like royalty. Spoilt, really. You look happy, Anukis; although battered a little." She glanced over her shoulder at Vashell. "He told me about you, kept me informed about your health. I am so glad you two are in love! It will be a marriage made perfect, and your children will be beautiful!" She giggled, pulling Anukis to the bed. She turned, and waved Vashell away. He departed.

"Truly, have they looked after you?"

"They have," said Shabis, and kissed Anu's cheek. "And you?"

Anu's face went hard. "I have been condemned, Shabis. I have been treated worse than any dog, worse than any canker." She pulled away, stood, walked to the splendid view. It had begun to snow in Silva Valley, and a thick fall muffled the world.

"What do you mean?"

Shabis was behind her. Holding her. Concern shone in her eyes.

"Vashell beat me. He hurt me, Shabis. He hurt me bad. He paraded me like a slave before the Engineers. Then he… he took my blood." She heard a hiss of intaken breath. "He drank from me, Shabis. He drank from my veins, made my impurity whole, for all to see. Then he… he took me. Physically. Carnally. I had little choice if I wanted to save both of us."

She fell silent, brooding, watching the snow. Somehow, Silva Valley had again lost its beauty, its charm. It was a perfect pastel painting, framed by silver-quartz and yet to Anukis, now, after everything that had happened, it was a vision of hell. Worse. Of a canker-riddled cancer hell.

"What will you do?" Shabis's voice was barely more than a whisper.

"I have a plan!" Anu took Shabis, and shook her with passion. "I will kill Vashell. And we will flee. We will leave Silva Valley, we will leave this world for good. Cross the Black Pike Mountains; make a new life."

"But what of the vachine?" said Shabis, softly. "What if the clockwork becomes faulty? Who will fix us?"

"I have some skill," said Anu, eyeing her sister, sensing the fear, the lode of cowardice that ran through her like an earthquake fault in the world mantle. "Don't you understand, Shabis, they killed our father! We are alone now. Alone in the world."

"Killed... no! They did not! He still lives! He is on a journey under Black Pike, he will be back in a few months."

"And you believe them?"

"Why should I not?"

"What else have they told you?"

"Nothing! Anu, you're frightening me. Stop it!"

"I'm sorry, little one. Sweet Shabis, we must leave this place. I want you to be ready. Do you understand?"

"Yes. I understand."

Anu shook her, and Shabis's hair fell, tousled. "You're hurting me!"

"This is serious, Little One. Do you understand?"

"Yes! Anu, yes!"

"Good."

There came a hiatus. Shabis played with her hair, and they both watched the snow. Eventually, Shabis said, "Anu?"

"Sister?"

"How will you kill him? Vashell, I mean?"

"I have a secret weapon."

"What is that?"

Anu's eyes glowed dark. "You will see."

Night had fallen. Anu was awoken by a savage blow across her face, which broke her nose and left her choking on a gush of blood down her throat. She rolled instinctively, momentarily blinded, covering her face, her claws out and slashing a wild vicious arc, but connecting with nothing. After a few moments she could see, and she stood, naked, blood covering her breasts, to see Vashell holding a pick-axe helve. It was stained with her blood. His eyes shone.

"What is this?" she snarled, fear touching the edges of her heart.

"Show me your secret weapon! Come on, Anukis, show me how you intend to kill me! Show me now."

Anu backed away, and Vashell moved around the bed.

"Where's Shabis? What have you done with my sister?"

"Shabis?" Vashell smiled, and from the gloom, in the glow of the candles, Shabis appeared. She was smiling, a broad smile. Her hands came up, rested, interlacing over Vashell's shoulder. Her hips were staggered, her stance commanding.

"What are you doing?" said Anu. She felt understanding flood from her soul.

"Vashell is mine, bitch. He will marry me. He told me what you did to him; how you tried to poison him with your impure blood. You are a canker, Anu, diseased, toxic, not a true vachine. You will rot in hell."

Anu stood, mouth open, pain pounding through her head, her crushed nose stinging, and stared with utter, total disbelief at the scene before her. Her jaws clacked shut, and she watched Vashell turn, kiss Shabis, sliding his tongue into her mouth.

"He will never marry you," said Anu, eventually.

"Liar! We are betrothed. The Watchmakers will conduct the ceremony in three weeks' time. You lied about him taking you; you lied to make him more evil in my mind, so when the time came for you to kill him I would help. Vashell is filled with honour; he would never stoop to fuck an impure." She snarled the word, fangs ejecting a little. Her dark eyes were narrowed, and Anu could not believe what she was seeing. She could not comprehend the hatred emanating from her sister. She did not understand.

Vashell ran his hand down Shabis's flank, stroking her, and said, softly, "Kill her, Shabis. Kill Anukis."

Growling, Shabis ejected claws and fangs with tiny slithers of steel and brass. She dropped to a crouch, and moved around the bed, eyes narrowed and fixed on her sister, face full of hatred, her tongue licking lips in the anticipation of fresh blood...

"No," said Anu, voice near hysteria. "Shabis! Don't do this! Vashell lies!"

"Spoken just like an impure," snapped Shabis, and with a feral vachine snarl, leapt at her lifeblood.

SIX
Toxic Blood

Kell tensed as the canker lowered its head, muscles rigid, a low metal buzzing growl coming from its wide open head and loose flapping jaws; and he stared into that gaping maw, stared into those eyes and shuddered as his past life – and more importantly, more hauntingly, the Days of Blood – flashed through his mind and he felt regret and self-loathing, and a despair that he hadn't put things right, hadn't found forgiveness and sanctuary from others, and more importantly, for himself…

The canker howled, rearing up. More dust and stones poured from the destroyed ceiling. A huge cross-member dropped, clunking against the canker which hit the ground under huge weight, snarling and snapping, and through the falling dust Kell saw Saark, his blade buried deep in the canker's flank and Saark screamed, "The roof's coming down! We've got to get out!"

Kell nodded, slammed his axe into the canker's head with a thud which brought another bout of thrashing and snarling, then he squeezed around the edges of the wall and sprinted, as more stones and timber toppled around him, diving out of the doorway and hitting the snow on his belly with a violent exhalation of air. Behind, the cottage screamed like a wounded beast, shaking its head in agony; and the roof caved in.

Saark was there, black with dust, dragging Kell to his feet. "I don't think it will stop the bastard."

Kell took a deep breath. Snow drifted around him, like ash in the night. He turned, staring at the cottage which seemed to rise, then settle, a great dying bear. For a second it was still, then somewhere deep within started to shift and stones, rubble, timber, all started to move and rise and Saark was already running towards the shingle beach and the boat, where Nienna and Kat urged them on. Kell followed, wincing at pains in his ribs, his shoulder, his head, his knees, and he felt suddenly old, and weary, battered and bettered, and he stumbled down onto the shingle as behind them, with a terrible sadistic roar the canker emerged from the detritus in a shower of stones.

The heavens grumbled, and distantly lightning flickered a web. Thunder growled, a beast in a storm cage behind bars of ignition, and heavy hail pounded the shingle around Kell as he heaved the boat down the beach, axe cleaving the securing rope, and leapt in, rocking the vessel.

They moved away from the bank, as the canker orientated.

"It can't see us," whispered Saark. "Shh." He placed a finger on lips.

As they drifted away, they watched the canker, seemingly confused; then its head lifted, huge open maw searching the skies, and it turned and its head lowered and it charged across cobbles and mud and snow straight in their direction...

Nienna gave a gasp.

"It's fine," breathed Saark, throat dry with fear. "The river will stop the bastard."

The canker reached the edge of the rampant water and without breaking stride leapt, body elongating into an almost elegant, feline dive. It hit the black river, rippled by hailstones, and went under the surface. It was gone immediately.

Kell stood, rocking the boat, and hefted his axe.

"Surely not," snapped Saark, lifting his own blade and peering wildly about their totally vulnerable position.

"It's under there," snarled Kell. "Be ready."

Silence fell, like a veil. Hail scattered across the river like pebbles. More thunder rumbled, mountains fighting, and lighting lit the scene through storm clouds and sleet.

"It was sent, wasn't it?" said Saark, gazing at the dark river.

"Yes," said Kell, eyes searching.

"How did it find us?"

"It followed your petal-stench perfume, lad."

"Hah! More like the stench from your fish-laden pants."

Calm descended.

They waited, tense.

The boat suddenly rocked and there came a slam from beneath; it swayed violently, turning around in the current. Something glided beneath them, snapping the oars with easy cracks; broken toothpicks.

"I don't like this!" wailed Nienna.

"Shut up," growled Kell. "Take out your swords. If you see anything at all, stab it in the eyes."

The boat was slammed with tremendous force from beneath, lifting out of the water, then slapping down again and spinning, turning, all sense of direction lost now, gone now, in the turbulent storm. The boat was hammered again, and it shuddered, timbers creaked, and a long crack appeared across the stern.

"We need to get back on land!" shouted Saark.

"We have no oars," said Kell, voice calm, axe rigid in steel-steady hands. "We will have to kill it."

Abruptly the canker emerged, mighty jaws ripping free the prow of the boat and Saark ran with a scream, sword raised, as the canker released the boat and lunged, grabbing his leg and dragging him backwards, his body thumping from the boat's prow and disappearing suddenly over the edge...

Everything was still.

The river surged, and the water levelled.

"Saark!" screamed Katrina. But the man was gone.

With a curse Kell dropped his axe to the floor of the boat, and leapt into the black river. He was encompassed immediately, swamped by darkness, by a raging thunder, merging with the gathered filth of Falanor's major northern city. Down he plunged, unable to see Saark, unable to find the canker. He swam down with powerful strokes, and withdrew his Svian from beneath his arm; down here, Ilanna would be useless. What a warrior needed was a short sharp stabbing weapon...

Where is he? screamed Kell's mind.

His lungs began to burn.

He thrashed, turning, round and around, but everything was black. He felt panic creep into him like crawling ivy; he had scant seconds before the canker drowned Saark, and that was providing the beast hadn't ripped him apart with tooth and claw.

Kell was saved by the lightning. It crackled overhead, above the boat, and for an instant the churning river was lit by incandescent flashes. Kell saw the canker, dragging Saark down, and powered after them, Svian between his teeth, straggled hair and beard flowing behind him. He found them in the darkness, and his blade slashed down, he felt it enter flesh, grind in cogs, felt the canker lashing out and he was knocked back, and everything was a confusion of bubbles and madness and darkness and something was beside him, huge and cold, a wall of smoothness that slid past and Kell felt, more than saw, Saark slide up beside him. He grabbed the unconscious man, his very lungs filled with molten lava as he kicked out, boots striking the smooth, gliding wall and propelling him to the surface...

Lighting crackled again, a maze of angular arcs transforming the sky into a circuit. Kell looked down, and saw a battle raging beneath the river, between the canker, all claws and disjointed fangs, and a huge, silent, black eel. It must have been fifty yards long, its body the diameter of three men, its head a huge triangular wedge with row after row of sharp teeth. It had encircled the canker, was crushing the thrashing beast, its head snapping down, teeth tearing flesh repeatedly. Kell thought he saw trails of blood like confetti streamers in the black; then he burst from the surface, lungs heaving in air, Saark limp under one arm, and looked for the boat.

It had gone, slammed down the river without oars on powerful currents and a rage of mountain snow-melt.

Kell cursed, and half swam, half dragged Saark through the water, angling towards the high banks. He stopped, shivering now, teeth chattering, bobbing under the high earth walls too high to climb. He moved on, still dragging Saark's leaden weight through the darkness, through ice-filled waters, until the banks dropped and wearily Kell rolled onto a frozen, muddy slope, dragging Saark up behind him, and he lay for a while, breath panting like dragon smoke, head dizzy with flashing lights.

Eventually, the cold bit him and Kell roused himself. He shook Saark, who groaned as he came awake, coughing out streamers of black water. Eventually, he stared around, confused.

"What happened?"

"The creature dragged you under. I dove in after you. I'm pretty damn sure you're not worth it."

"Charming, Kell. You would whisk away the pants from any farmer's daughter without hindrance. Where's the boat?"

"Gone."

"Where are we?"

"Do I look like a fucking mapmaker?"

"Actually, old horse, you do, rather."

Something surged from the river nearby, a huge black coil, then submerged with a mighty splash. In its wake, the canker, or more precisely, half of the canker, floated for a few moments, bobbing, torn, trailing strings of tendon and jagged gristle, before gradually sinking out of sight.

"At least that's one problem sorted," said Saark, voice strangled. He reached down, rolling up his trews. Puncture holes lined his shins and knees, bleeding, and he prodded them with a wince. "I hope I'm not poisoned."

"It's dead. For now." Kell climbed to his feet. He sheathed his Svian and cursed. His axe, Ilanna, was on the boat. Gone. Kell ran hands through his wet hair and shivered again. Snow began to fall, just to add to his chilled and frozen mood.

Saark had found something in one of the puncture wounds, and with a tiny schlup pulled free a fang. "Ugh!" he said, staring at the brass tooth. "The dirty, dirty bastard." He flung it out into the river. "Ugh."

"We need to find Nienna," said Kell.

"And Kat," said Saark, glancing up at the old man.

"And Kat," agreed Kell. "Come on."

"Whoa! Wait up, maybe you're in the mood for running cross-country in the dark, covered in ice; I'm going to die if I stay out here much longer. And you too, by the looks of it. You're turning blue!"

"I've crossed the Black Pike Mountains," growled Kell. "It takes more than the fucking cold to kill me."

"And that was... how many years ago? Look at you, man, you're shivering harder than a pirate ship in a squall. We need fire, and we need dry clothes. Come on. These lowlands are populated; we'll find somewhere."

They walked, Saark limping, roughly following the course of the river until a thick evergreen woodland of Jack Pine and Red Cedar forced them inland. Trudging across snow and frozen tufts of grass, they circled the woods and eventually came upon a small crofter's hut, barely four walls and a roof, six feet by six feet, to be used during emergencies. With thanks they fell inside, forcing the door shut against wind and snow. As was the woodland way, a fire had already been laid by the last occupant and Kell found a flint and tinder on a high shelf. His shaking hands lit a fire, and both men huddled round the flames as they grew from baby demons. Eventually, what seemed an age, the small hut filled with heat and they peeled off wet clothing, hanging items on hooks around the walls to dry, until they sat in pants and boots, hands outstretched to the flames, faces grim.

"What I'd give for a large whisky," said Kell, watching steam rise from their clothes.

"What I'd give for a fat whore."

"Do you ever think about anything other than sex?"

"Sometimes," said Saark, and turned, staring into the flames. "Sometimes, in distant dreams, I think of honour, of loyalty, and of friendship; I think of love, of family, of happy children, a doting wife. All the good things in life, my friend. And then I remember who I am, and the things I did, and I am simply thankful for a fat whore sitting on my face. You?"

"Me what?"

"I gave you a potted history. Now it's your turn. You're a hero, right?"

"You make the word 'hero' sound like 'arsehole'."

"Not at all." Saark grinned, then, his melancholy dropping like a hawk from the heavens. "I heard a poem about you, once. 'Kell's Legend', it was called. That's you, right? You're the character of legend?"

"You make 'character' sound like 'arsehole'."

"Very droll. Come on, Kell. It was a good poem."

"Ha! A curse on all poets! May they catch the pox and have ugly children."

"This poem was a good one," persisted Saark. "Proper hero stuff. Had a decent rhyme as well. Foot-tapping stuff, when recited in a tavern by men with harps and honey-beer and the glint of wonder in their eyes."

Kell drew his Svian blade. His eyes glowed and he pointed at Saark in the close proximity. "Don't even fucking think about it. All poets should be gutted like fish, their entrails strung out to dry, then made to compose ballads about how they feel with the bastard suffering. A curse on them!"

Saark sang, voice soft, hand held out to ward off Kell's knife should he make a strike:

"Kell waded through life on a river of blood,
His axe in his hands, dreams misunderstood,
In Moonlake and Skulkra he fought with the best
This hero of old, this hero obsessed,
This hero turned champion of King Searlan
Defiant and worthy a merciless man."

Kell snorted. "Poets make a joy out of slaughter, the academic smug self-satisfying bastards. I am ashamed to be a part of that song! Bah!" Kell frowned darkly. "And you! You sing like a drunkard. I can sing better than that, and I sound like a fart from a donkey's arse... and I'm proud of it! A man should only sing when he's a belly full of whisky, a fist full of money, and the idea of a fight in his head. You can keep your cursed poetry, Saark, you idiot. A bad case of gonorrhoea on you all! Death to all poets!"

"Death to all poets?" chuckled Saark, and relaxed as Kell sheathed his long, silver-bladed Svian. "A little harsh, I find, for simply extending the oral tradition and entertaining fellow man. But was it true? The stuff in the poem? The Saga?"

"No."

"Not even some of it?"

"Well, the bastards spelt my name right. Listen, Saark, we need to go after Nienna and Kat. They could end up miles away. Leagues! They could be in danger even as we sit here, wasting our breath like a whore wastes her hard-earned coin."

"We'll die if we go back to the storm." Saark's voice was soft.

"Where's your courage, man?"

"Hiding behind my need to stay alive. Kell, you're no use to her dead. Wait till the sun's up; then we'll search."

"No. I am going now!" He stood and reached for his wet clothes. Saark sang:

"And brave Kell marched out through the snow,
His dullard brain he left behind,
He took with him a mighty bow,
His thumb up his arse and shit in his mind."

Kell paused. Stared hard at Saark, who shrugged, and threw another chunk of wood on the fire. "You're being irrational, my friend. I may dress like an idiot, but I know when to live, and when to die. Now is not the time to die."

Kell sighed, a deep sigh of resignation, and returned to the fire. He sat, staring into flickering flames.

"Say it," said Saark.

"What?"

"Admit that I'm right."

"You're right."

"See, that wasn't too painful, eh, old horse?"

"But I'll tell you something, Saark. If anything happens to Nienna, then I'll blame you; and it'll take more than fucking poetry to remove my axe from your fat split head."

Saark laughed, and slapped Kell on the back. "What a truly grumpy old bastard you are, eh? You remind me of my dad."

"If I was your dad, I'd kill myself."

"And if I was your son, I'd help you. Listen, enough of this banter; we need to get some sleep. I have a strange feeling tomorrow's going to be a hard day. Call me extreme, but it can't get any worse."

"A hard day?" scoffed Kell. "Harder than yesterday? That seems unlikely. However, young man, I will take your advice, even though it pains me to listen to somebody with the wardrobe sense of a travelling chicken."

"At least that beast... at least it was dead, in the river. It was dead, wasn't it?"

"It was a canker."

"A what?"

"A canker. That's what it was."

"How do you know that?"

"I saw one. Once. Halfway up a mountain in the Black Pikes; it tried to kill us."

"What happened?"

"It slipped on ice. Fell six thousand feet onto rocks like spears." Kell's eyes gleamed, misted, distant, unreadable. He coughed. "So put that Dog Gemdog gem in your poem, laddie. Because the canker, well, it's a vachine creation. And there are more of the bastards where that one came from."

Saark shivered, and scowled hard at Kell. "Well, thanks for that cheerful nocturnal nugget, just before I try and sleep. Sweet dreams to you as well, you old goat!"

• • • •

The boat spun out of control through the blackness and Nienna screamed, clinging to Kat. "What do we do?"

"We row!"

"The oars were smashed!"

The two girls looked frantically for something to use as a paddle, but only Kell's axe caught Nienna's eye and she stooped, picking up the weapon. She expected a dead-weight, impossible to lift, but it was surprisingly light despite its size. She hefted the weapon, and it glowed, warm for a moment, in her hands. Or had she imagined that?

"You can't paddle with that," snapped Kat.

"I was thinking more of hitting it into the beast's head."

"If it comes back," said Kat.

They both thought of Saark, and Kell, under the freezing river, fighting the huge beast. They shivered, and neither dared to wonder what the outcome would be.

The boat spun around again, and bounced from a rotting tree-trunk, invisible in the darkness. The river grew wider, more shallow, and they found themselves rushing through a minefield of rocks, the river gushing and pounding all around.

"What do we do?" shouted Kat over the torrent.

"I don't know!"

Both girls moved to the boat's stern, and with four hands on the tiller, tried to steer the boat in towards the shore. Amazingly, it began to work, and they bounced and skimmed down the fast flow and towards an overhanging shoreline in the gloom... with a crunch, the boat beached on ice and stones, and Nienna leapt out as she had seen Kell do, holding his axe, and tried to drag the boat up the beach. She did not have the strength. Kat jumped out and they both tried, but the boat was dragged backwards by wild currents and within seconds was lost in the raging darkness.

Snow fell.

The girls retreated a short distance into the woods, but stopped, spooked by the complete and utter darkness. A carpet of pine needles were soft underfoot, and the heady smell of resin filled the air.

"This is creepy," whispered Nienna.

Kat nodded, but Nienna couldn't discern the movement; by mutual consent, their hands found one another and they walked deeper into the forest, pushed on by a fear of the canker that outweighed a fear of the dark. They stared up at the massive boles of towering Silver Firs, and a violent darkness above which signified the sky. Random flakes drifted down through the trees, but at least here there was no wind; only a still calm.

"Will that creature come back, do you think?" asked Kat.

"I have Kell's axe," said Nienna, by way of reply.

"Kell and Saark couldn't kill it," said Kat.

Nienna did not answer.

They stopped, their footsteps crunching pine needles. All around lay the broken carcass shapes of dead-wood; ahead, a criss-crossing of fallen trees blocked their path, and cursing and moaning, they dragged themselves beneath the low barricade to stand, again, in a tiny clearing.

"Look," said Nienna. "There was a fire."

They ran forward, to where a ring of stones surrounded glowing embers. Kat searched about, finding dead wood to get the blaze going, and they fed twigs into the embers, waiting for them to ignite before piling on thicker branches. Soon they had the fire roaring, and they warmed their hands and feet by the flames, revelling in their good fortune.

"Who do you think was here?" asked Nienna.

"Woodsmen, I should think," said Kat. "But they'll be long gone. A fire can burn low like that for a couple of days." She took a stick, and poked around in the fire. Flames crackled, and sparks flew out, like tiny fireflies, sparkling into the air. Around them, the chill of the forest, the smell of cold and rotting vegetation, filled their senses.

"What are we going to do, Kat?" said Nienna eventually, voicing that which they were both thinking.

"I don't know. Kell will find us."

"Maybe he..." She left it unsaid.

"I've read about your grandfather," said Kat, staring into the fire. "He's a survivor. He's a... killer."

"No he's not. He's my grandpa." Nienna scowled, then glanced at Kat. "What do you mean? A killer?"

"His legend," said Kat, avoiding Nienna's gaze. "You'll see. He'll come looking for us. For you, I mean."

"He'll come for both of us!" snapped Nienna, frowning at the tone Kat employed. "He's an honourable man! An old soldier! He would always do the right thing."

Kat said nothing.

"Well well well," came a strange voice from the trees. It was a twisted voice, full of friendly humour and yet mocking at the same time. "What have we got here?"

Both girls leapt up, and Nienna lifted the axe. From the gloom of the forest emerged six men, drifting slowly from the black. They were a rag-tag bunch, dressed in little more than rags and stained, matted furs. They wore heavy scuffed boots and carried tarnished swords; two men hefted fine yew longbows.

"What do you want?" snarled Kat.

The man who spoke was tall and lean, his face pock-marked, his eyes large and innocent. His hair was long and dark, tied back beneath a deerstalker hat with furred edges. He was grinning at the two young women, showing a missing tooth.

"We don't want anything, me sweets. You've made yourself comfortable in our camp, is all."

"Are you robbers?"

The man held his hands apart, and he carried no weapons. "Tsch, just because I lives in the forest, me sweets, doesn't make me a robber. Has been a hard time for us all I think. This winter is a harsh one, for sure. Only now, we were out hunting for meat." He gestured, to where one of the forest-men carried a pole containing two dead hares. "Pickings are lean," he said, eyes narrowing, but then he smiled again. "Don't let us worry you. You got the fire going; that's got to be worth a mouthful of rabbit meat."

Kat nodded, and the men moved around easily, leaning weapons against trees with two of them sitting by the fire, holding out chilled hands. The leader seated himself and gestured to Nienna and Kat, still standing, to have a seat.

"I won't bite, me sweets. Honest. Come and sit yourself down here. Keep yourself warm. You both looks like you'll die from the cold! I'm Barras, and I'd wager you're a long way from your homes. City girls, are ye?"

"From Jalder," said Nienna, and Kat kicked her on the ankle. Nienna threw her a dark look.

"Jalder's a fine city," said Barras, smiling broadly, friendly, as one of his companions began to skin and gut the rabbits. "I have a lot of good friends who live there. Well, people I owe money to, anyways."

"It was overrun! By an army. An army of albinos!" hissed Nienna, her eyes wide.

112

Barras rubbed at his chin with a rasping sound. "Is that so ways? That would be bad news, if I hadn't owed so much silver to the Hatchet Man."

"Who's the Hatchet Man?" asked Kat, intrigued.

"Runs the gambling dens. When you don't pay, he cuts off your hands with a hatchet. Chop!" He roared with laughter, as one of his men brought a large pan of water and set it on the fire. Barras leaned forward, then, his lips pouting as he considered a question. Almost instinctively, Kat leaned forward to listen; but Nienna found her hands tightening on Ilanna. Something wasn't right. The atmosphere felt... just wrong.

Nienna glanced about. And it hit her. All of the men still wore weapons. They had removed some for show; but they still wore short swords. They were behaving like they were winding down, making camp, but nobody skinned a rabbit with a sword sheathed at his side. Or was she simply looking for trouble where none should be found? She stared at Barras. His face was filthy, yes, but honest. Why not trust him? He was a simple woodsman enduring a harsh winter... surely they would have a house or cottage nearby. A wife? Three children to feed?

Barras edged a little closer. He licked his lips. "What's your name, me sweets?"

"Kat."

"I was a-wondering, Kat, if you taste as good as you look?"

There came a moment of silence, and both Nienna and Kat surged to their feet but one of the woodsmen had circled behind and a club cracked Nienna's skull, sending her sprawling sideways, fingers losing grip on Ilanna, and two men grabbed Kat, bearing her to the ground where she screamed, until one punched her, a heavy blow that silenced her in an instant.

Nienna's last sight was of Barras, lifting Ilanna and frowning a little as his eyes scanned the delicate faded runes along the black haft. He shook his head, then stared at Nienna in a curious way; before a second vicious blow from behind rendered her unconscious.

Nienna awoke to pain, pain in her fingers, hands, and running like fiery trails along her forearms and biceps, to end like pits of coal deep within her shoulders. She moaned, and her eyes flickered open. Her head pounded. A sour taste filled her mouth, and she realised she had vomited down her shirt.

She was moving, swaying, and at first she thought it a reaction to being hit over the back of the head. Then she realised the awful truth; she was tied up, and hung from the branch of a tree. She scowled, anger charging to the front of her mind. Bastards, trussing her up like a chicken! She heard laughter, and shouting, the crackle of the fire, and as she gently moved around on her length of rope she saw Kat. She was in a state of undress. Six men had ripped free her shirt and trousers, and she stood in her underwear and boots, a long stick in her hands, face a curious mix of hatred and fear as the men spread out, surrounding her, and she jabbed at them with a stick.

"Watching them, me sweets?"

Nienna looked down, saw Barras standing close to her, not looking at her, but watching the spectacle with Kat.

"Let us go," she said.

"Why? We're going to have a pretty fun with you two for, oh, I'd say the next month. You can get a lot of use out of a young woman like yourself; you have so much stamina, so much passion, so much anger. But, finally, when we've fucked you, and beaten you, and broken your spirit worse than any high-bred stallion, when you no longer scream during orgasm, when you no longer scratch at faces and pull at hair... when your spirit is gone, me sweet little doll, then, and only then, do we slit your throats."

Nienna stared down at the man, tasting vomit, and wondering how she could kill him. His words frightened her more than anything she had had ever heard, or ever seen; worse than the albino army, worse than any canker. For here, and now, this was personal, not just an invasion, and this man was evil, a total corruption of the human shell. She was still stunned that she had not been able to see it. To smell it. It was a sobering life experience.

"How could you do that to us?" she asked, in a small voice.

Barras glanced up, then reached out, his hand creeping up the inside of her trouser leg. His fingers were rough on her skin. She squirmed, but he was stronger than he looked; he grinned as his fingers groped her inner thigh, her soft flesh, her young flesh, and his eyes were old and dark and deeply malevolent.

"Not everybody in this world has the same morals as you, little honey. You little rich girls; well, you deserve every fucking you get."

The men, laughing, got the stick from Kat and bore her to the ground. One kissed her, and when she bit his tongue in a spurt of bright blood he slapped her hard, across the face, then again with the back of his hand. Blood trickled from her nose and she lay, stunned, fingers clenching and unclenching. The man pulled free her vest revealing small, firm, breasts. He squeezed them, one in each hand, to the cackling of his companions...

"Call them off," said Nienna, voice so dry she could hardly speak.

"Why, me sweets?"

"You saw the axe," said Nienna, voice turning hard. "It's Ilanna."

Barras narrowed his eyes then, scowling at her. "Where did you hear such a name?"

"It's true," she hissed. "It's my grandfather's axe. He's coming. Soon. He will kill you all."

"What's his name?"

"You know his name, you heap of horse-shit."

"Speak his *name*!" snarled the woodsman.

"He is Kell, and he will eat your heart," said Nienna.

This impelled Barras to move, and cursing (cursing himself, he knew he had seen the axe before), he stepped forward to talk to the woodsmen; but something happened, a blur of action so fast he blinked, and only as a splatter of blood slapped across his face and dirt-streaked stubble did he leap into action...

The creature slammed across the clearing from the darkness of the trees in an instant, picking one man up in huge jaws, lifting the man high at the waist and crunching through him through his muscle and bones and spinal column and he screamed, gods he screamed so hard, so bad, as the canker shook him and gears spun and wheels clicked and turned and gears made tiny *click click tick tock* noises, and it threw him away like a bone into the forest.

Barras ran forward, screaming, his sword raised...

The canker whipped around, a blur, and leapt, biting off the woodsman's head in a single giant snap.

His body stood for a moment, still holding a tarnished sword, an arc of blood painting a streak across the forest in a gradually decreasing spiral. Then a knee buckled; the fountain of blood soaked the pine needle carpet, and the body crumpled like a deflated balloon.

Nienna struggled against her ropes, and she could see Kat crying, pulling on her vest and trews.

"Kat! Over here! Get the axe!"

The remaining four woodsmen had grouped together, pooling weapons. With a scream, and as a unit that displayed previous military experience, they charged across the fire at the canker which growled, hunkering down, crimson eyes watching the charge with interest, as a cat watches a disembowelled mouse squirm.

Kat grabbed the axe and, still sobbing, half crawled, half ran towards Nienna. She swung at the rope, missed, then swung again and the sharp blades of Ilanna sliced through with consummate ease. Nienna hit the ground, and Kat helped her get the ropes from her wrists to the backing track of screams, thuds, gurgles, and most disturbingly, the solid crunches of impact, of gristle, of snapping bones.

The girls half hoped the woodsmen had won; but then, they'd have to face the prospect of rape and murder.

But what would happen with the canker?

Kat pulled on her boots, and something smashed off into the forest, a woodsman, picked up by the canker, slamming an axe into its back again and again and again as it charged through the forest with his legs in its jaws. There came the smash and crack of breaking wood. A gurgle. Another crack; this time of bone.

Nienna and Kat stood, shivering, wondering what to do.

Slowly, the canker emerged from the gloom, lit only by the flames of the fire. Blood soaked its white fur, and congealed gore interfered with fine cogs and gears, splashed up its uneven, distended eyes. Skin and torn bowel were caught in long streamers between its claws, and it made a low churning sound as if about to be violently sick…

"Back away," mumbled Kat, as Nienna hefted the axe and they started to retreat into the forest.

Nienna stood on a branch, which snapped.

The canker turned, slowly, red eyes watching them.

"Is it going to charge?"

"I don't know."

"Don't move!"

"It's already seen us!"

"Stop talking!"

"You're talking as well!"

They stopped. The canker stopped. They eyed each other, over perhaps fifty yards. Then, with a wide grin – which looked like the creature had peeled the top of its head right off – it let out a howl, a howl to the fire, to the forest, to the moon, and lowered its head with a grinding snarl and with a shift of gears, a mechanical grind of cogs, the canker leapt at the girls…

SEVEN
The Watchmakers

"Don't do this," said Anu, backing away, her face an image of horror as Shabis's fangs gleamed, her claws flexed and she leapt. Anu somersaulted backwards, away from the attack, landed lightly, and as Shabis leapt again, claws tearing the carpet, oil gleaming in her eyes, so Anu leapt, kicked off from the wall and flipped over Shabis's head. She landed in a crouch, unwilling to reveal her own killing tools, unwilling to fight her sister.

"Shabis!"

Shabis whirled, mad now. "You will die, bitch!"

"With what poison has he filled your head? What lies?"

Shabis charged, claws swiping for Anu's throat. Anu swayed back, brass and steel a hair's-breadth from her windpipe, then punched her sister in the chest, slamming her back almost horizontally where she hit the carpet on her face and coughed, clutching her chest, pain slamming violent through heart and gears and clockwork...

Anu's eyes lifted to Vashell. "Call her off."

Vashell backed away, tongue wetting his lips. She could see the bulge in his armoured pants. He was getting a thrill out of this: out of watching two sisters fight to the death.

"Stop her!" shrieked Anu, as Shabis crawled to her feet, the corners of her mouth blood-flecked.

"No," he said, voice barely more than a growl. "This is the final trial. Don't you see? This is the final... entertainment. A repayment, if you like, for all the pain and suffering you have caused.

117

Shabis." Shabis looked at him, the rage in her eyes flickering to love. "If you kill her, then we will marry, we will spend a glorious eternity together; you will never have to work again, we will languish in a blood-oil rapture; just you and I, my love."

Shabis turned to Anu, head low, eyes dark. She let out a snarl and charged at Anukis who was crying, great tears flowing down her cheeks, soaking her golden curls, and Shabis leapt like a tiger, both sets of vachine claws coming together to crush Anu's head and Anu swayed, ejecting a single claw which swiped down, sideways, as Shabis sailed past. There came a tiny *flash*, an almost unheard grinding sound, and Shabis hit the ground hard, rolling, wailing, her clawed fingers coming up to her face where blood and blood-oil mingled, leaking from her severed... fangs.

Anu had cut out Shabis's fangs. The ultimate symbol of the vachine.

"No!" wailed Shabis, blood-oil pumping as the cogs in her head, in her heart, ejected precious blood-oil. "What have you done to me, Anukis?" She climbed to her feet, ran to Vashell, who put out his arms to comfort her as she sobbed, her blood-oil leaking into his clothing and his eyes lifted to read Anukis who stood, face bleak, as she retracted her single claw.

"Now you need another assassin," said Anu, triumph in her eyes.

Vashell nodded. "You are correct." With a savage shove, he pushed Shabis away, drew his brass sword, and with a swift hard horizontal swipe, cut Shabis's head from her body. Blood and blood-oil spurted, hitting the ceiling, drenching the walls and bed in a twisting shower of sudden ferocity. Shabis's head hit the sodden carpet, eyes wide, mouth open in shock, pretty features stained. Anu could see the clockwork in her severed neck, between the fat and the muscle, the veins and the bone, nestled and intricate, bonded, and it was all still spinning happily, now slowing, as cogs could not mesh and a primary shaft failed in its delicate spin. Shabis's eyes closed, and her separated body folded slowly to the carpet, as if deflating. Her vachine aborted. Shabis died.

"No!" screamed Anu, running forward, dropping to her knees beside the corpse of her sister. Her head snapped up. "You will die for this!" she raged.

"Show me." Vashell still held his sword; it was a special blade, specifically designed for slaying vachine; for the killing of their own kind. It had a multi-layered blade, and carried a disruptive charge. It wasn't so much sharp as... created to cut through clockwork.

Anu's eyes narrowed. "You are a V Hunter?" she said.

"Yes." He smiled. It was a sickly smile, half pride, half... something else. Amongst the vachine, the V Hunters were despised; it was a rank handed out by the Watchmakers, and a V Hunter's sole role was to hunt down and exterminate rogue vachine... to cleanse and, essentially, betray their own. Amongst the population they were feared and loathed. Their identities were kept secret, so they could work undercover throughout Silva Valley. They reported directly back to the Watchmakers, and indeed the Patriarch, and answered to no Engineer.

"You have been hunting me all this time?"

Vashell laughed, and sheathed his sword. He turned, running hands through his hair drenched in the blood-oil of Shabis. He turned back, and stared down at Anu. "Don't be so naive. What would I want with you, pretty little plaything?"

"What *do* you want, then?"

"I want something much more precious. I want your father, Anukis. I want Kradek-ka. He has gone; fled. Left you to suffer, along with... that." He stared, a snarl, at Shabis's corpse. "Now, you will take me to him. By all that is holy, by all the relics of our ancestors, you will take me to Kradek-ka."

Anukis overcame her fear, and snarled with fangs ejecting, and leapt; Vashell dropped his shoulder, and with an awesome blow backhanded Anukis across the room where she hit the wall, cracking plaster, and hit the floor on her head, crumpling into a heap. She groaned, broken, and her eyes flickered open.

"I'll leave you to clean up the corpse," said Vashell, and leaving footprints in Shabis's blood, he stalked from the room.

Anu stared for long, agonising moments, her eyes seeming to meet those of her dead sister. Tears rolled down her cheeks, her body slumped to the ground, and her eyes closed as she welcomed the oblivion of pain and darkness.

It began as a ball. A tight ball; white, pure, hot like a sun. And that ball was anger, and hatred, and rage so pure, so hot, that it engulfed everything, it engulfed her concept of family and name and honour and duty and love and spread, covering the city and the valley and the Black Pike Mountains; finally it overtook the world, and the sun, and the stars, and the galaxy and everything broiled in that tiny hot plasma of rage and Anu's eyes flickered open and it was dark, and cool, and she was thankful.

She lay on a steel bench. She was dressed in plain clothes, and boots. She looked down, and started, and started to weep. Her vachine claws had been removed, the ends of her bloody fingers blunt stumps. She reached up, and winced as she felt the holes where her fangs should have been. Inside her, she felt the heavy *tick tick tick* of clockwork, in her head and in her breast; and she cursed Vashell, and cursed the Engineers, for they had taken away her weapons and she would rather be dead. It was what they once did to criminals before the Justice Laws, and just before a death-sentence was meted out. It was the lowest form of aberration. The lowest form of dishonour; beyond, even, the transformation to canker. Even a canker had fangs.

Winter sunshine bled in through a high window, and Vashell emerged smugly through a door. He wore subtle vachine battle-dress, skin-armour, they called it, beneath woollen trousers and a thick shirt and cloak. His weapons, also, were hidden. His eyes shone.

"Get up."

"No."

"Get up!" He ejected a claw, and held it to her eye. "Anukis, I will take you apart limb by limb, orb by orb, tooth by tooth. I will massacre you, but your clockwork, your mongrel vachine status, will keep you alive. We know Kradek-ka made you special; you think us fools? You think the Engineers haven't been inside you? Examined every cog, every wheel, every tiny shaft and pump? Kradek-ka did some very special things to you, Anukis, technology we didn't even know existed. First, we were going to kill you. It was fitting. You are an abomination. But then a specialist discovered… the advanced technology, inside of you. You will help me find Kradek-ka. I promise you this."

"I don't know where to look," she said, voice low, staring at the razor tip of Vashell's claw.

"I have a start point. But first, I want to show you something."

Vashell tugged on a thin golden lead, almost transparent, and scaled with a strange quartz mesh; sometimes, it could be seen, rippling like liquid stone; other times it was completely invisible, depending on how it caught the light. Anukis felt the jolt, and realised it was connected to her throat. Another humiliation. Another vachine slight.

Vashell tugged, and Anukis was forced to stand. She growled, tried to eject her fangs by instinct but only pain flowed through her jaws. She wept then, standing there on the leash. She wept for her freedom; but more, she wept for her dead sister, wept for her lost father.

"Follow me."

Anukis had little choice.

"Where is this?"

"Deep. Within the Engineer's Palace."

"I did not know these corridors, and these rooms, existed."

"Why should you? Even Kradek-ka would not tell you everything. After all," he smiled, eyes dark, filled with an inner humour, "you are female."

The corridors were long, and the more they delved into the Engineer's Palace, the deeper they penetrated, conversely, the more bare and more undecorated it became. Gone were carpets, silk hangings, works of oil-art. Instead, bare metal, rusted in places, became the norm. Deeper they travelled, Anukis trotting a little to keep up with Vashell's long stride.

They walked for an hour. Behind some doors they heard grinding noises, deep and penetrating; behind others jolts of enormous power like strikes of lightning. Behind others, they heard rhythmical thumping, or the squeal of metal on metal. Yet more were deadly silent beyond, and for some reason, these were the worst for Anukis. Her imagination could create Engineer horrors worse than anything they could show her.

Vashell stopped, and Anukis nearly ran into him. She was lost in thought, drowning in dreams. She pulled up tight, and he looked down, his look arrogant, his eyes mocking, and she thought:

One day, I will see you weep.

One day, I will watch you beg, and squirm, in the dirt, like a maggot.

One day, Vashell. You will see.

"We are here," he said.

"Where?"

"The Maternity Hall. Your father's creation."

"Maternity Hall? I have never heard of this." A cold dread

began to rise slowly through her, and Vashell pushed at the solid metal door, grey and unmarked, and Anukis found herself led into a huge, vacuous chamber which stretched off further than the eye could see. It was filled with booths and benches, and the air was infused with the cries of babes.

Goose-bumps ran up and down Anu's spine. She stood, stock still, her eyes taking in the bleak, grey place.

She walked forward, as far as her leash would allow, and Vashell tugged her to a halt. Obedience. She stared at benches, where babes lay, squirming, their cries ignored as Engineers worked on them. In the booths which drifted away she could see what looked like medical operations taking place. Many of the babes were silent, obviously drugged. Around some, a cluster of Engineers worked frantically. Every now and again, a buzz filled the air, or a click, or a whine.

Anu stared up at Vashell. "What are they doing?" she whispered.

"Welcome to Birth," said Vashell. "You don't think the vachine create themselves, do you? Every single vachine is a work of art, a sculpture of science and engineering; every vachine is created from a baby template, the fresh meat brought here shortly after birth to have the correct clockwork construct grafted, added, injected, implanted, and from thence the true vachine can grow and meld and begin to function."

"So… we all begin as human?"

"Yes."

"But we feed from human blood! The refined mix of blood-oil! That makes us… little more than cannibals!"

Vashell shrugged, and smiled. "Blood of my blood," he said, sardonically. "I find it hard to believe Kradek-ka never explained it to you. He kept you in a bubble, Anukis. He created this; this structure, this schedule, he elevated the systems of clockwork integration to make us better, superior, to elevate us above a normal impure flesh. With vachine integration we are the perfect species. Can you not see this, Anukis? This is your family's life work. This is the creation of the vachine."

Anu sagged, leaning against Vashell, her mind spinning as she watched a thousand babies undergoing vachine integration. She saw scalpels carving through flesh, through baby chests and into hearts, replacing organic components with clockwork, replacing valves and arteries with gears and tubes. Babies cried, squealed, and their wails were hushed by pads held over mouths until they lost consciousness. Blood trickled into slots and was carried away to be further refined and fed back into Blood Refineries in order to create the blood-oil pool.

"We are vampires," said Vashell, staring down at Anu who was pale and grey, a shadow of her former self. "Machine vampires. We feed on the human shell; revel, in our total superiority."

"What we're doing is *wrong*," snarled Anu.

"Why? The creation of a superior species?" Vashell laughed. "Your naivety both astounds and amuses me. Here, the rich noble daughter, blood-line of our very own vachine creators – and you do not even understand the basics?"

A babe squealed and there was a chopping sound. Anu saw the flash of a silver blade. The tiny head rolled into a chute and was sucked away. The corpse was thrown into a bag, and an Engineer moved to a distant cart and slung the body aboard, along with all the other medical waste.

"So," said Anu, fighting for air, "every babe that is born, here in Silva Valley, it comes here? It comes to be formed into vachine?"

"Yes. But more than Silva; the vachine have spread, Anu. We are breeding soldiers in other valleys. We are growing strong! We grow mighty! Our time for domination, for expansion, for Empire, is close."

"But–" said Anu.

Vashell frowned. "What do you mean?"

"Something is wrong," said Anu, with primitive intuition. "What's going on, Vashell? What's happening here?"

"We need to find Kradek-ka." He scowled. He would say no more.

For an hour Vashell dragged Anukis through the Maternity Hall, and she saw things so barbaric she wouldn't have believed them possible. The babies were operated on, implanted with clockwork technology – in their hearts, in their brains, in their jaws, in their hands. Even at such a young age they were given weapons of death, using blood-oil magic, clockwork, and liquid brass and gold, silver-quartz and polonium, in order to control and power and time the mechanisms of the vachine.

"How many work?" she said, at last, exhausted.

"I do not understand?"

"How many babes... become vachine? Successfully?"

"Fifty five in a hundred successfully make it through the – shall we say, medical procedures. Fifty five in a hundred accept the clockwork, accept the fangs, and can grow and meld and adapt and think of themselves as true machine."

"What about the others?"

"Most die," said Vashell, sadly. "This is a great loss; if we could improve the rate of melding, our army would be much larger; we could advance so much more quickly."

"And?"

"The cankers?" Vashell laughed. "They have their uses."

"Take me away from this place," said Anu, tears on her cheeks, fire in her part-clockwork heart.

"As you wish. I thought you needed to know, to understand, before we set out on our quest."

"Quest?"

"To find your father. He was working on a refined technology. In trials he had pushed acceptance from fifty-five to ninety-five in a hundred; we barely lost any babes. You see, Anu, why we need to find him? If you help me, if we pull this off for the Watchmakers, for the whole of vachine-kind, then you will be saving hundreds, thousands of lives, every year. You understand?"

"You bastard."

"Why so?"

"You have played me like a jaralga hand. I must help you. I must help end this atrocity."

"Your father's atrocity," corrected Vashell.

"Yes," she said, face ashen, voice like the tomb.

Anukis walked down long corridors of stone. She walked down long tunnels of metal. She became disorientated by it all; by the directions, the elevations, the dips and curves and banks, the smells of hot oil and cold metal. In weakness, she resigned herself. She was a puppet now, a creature to be controlled by Vashell. He had taken away her gifts, taken away her special gifts. She felt hollow. Abused. In pain. But more… she felt less than vachine, less than human, a limbo creature of neither one world or the next. She was a shadow; a shadow, mocked by shadows. Tears welled within her, but she would not let them come. No, she thought. I will be strong. Despite everything, despite my weakness, despite my abuse, I will be strong. I need my strength. I will need it as I hunt down my… father.

"Good girl," soothed Vashell, misunderstanding her compliance, and keeping her leash tight in his gloved fist. Anukis did not struggle, did not pull, did not fight her taming.

She smiled inwardly, although her face was stone. She was beyond the displaying of hatred. And when she killed him, when she massacred Vashell, as she knew, coldly, deep down in her breast and heart and soul that she would, it would be a long and painful death. It would be an absolution. A penance. An act of purifying like nothing the Engineers had before witnessed.

They walked, boots padding.

"Where are we going?" she asked, eventually.

"You will see."

Gradually, the stone and metal walls started to show signs of the Engineers; symbols replaced numbers, and decorations became evident as the wall design became not just more opulent, but more instructive. Anukis found herself staring at the designs on the wall, the artwork, the very shape of the stones. Many were fashioned into toothed cogs, gears of stone, and the whole corridor began to twist with design as the stone gave way to metal, gave way to brass and gold, laced with silver-quartz mortar. Slowly, the walls changed, became more than walls, became machines, mechanisms, clockwork, and Anukis recognised that this was no longer a corridor, but a living breathing working machine and the Engineer's Palace was more than just a building: it was a live thing, with a pulse of quartz and a heart of gold.

"Stop."

Vashell held something, what looked like a tiny circle of bone, up to a mechanism beside a blank metal door. There came several hisses, of oiled metal on metal, as the object in his hand slid out pins and integrated with the machine. The portal opened, but in the manner of nothing Anukis had ever seen; it was a series of curves, oiled and gleaming, which curled around one another, twisted like coils as the door didn't just open, it unpeeled.

They stepped through, into a working engine.

The room was crammed with a giant mechanism of clockwork, a machine made up of thousands and thousands of smaller machines. Brass and gold gleamed everywhere. Cogs turned, integrated, shafts spun, steam hissed from tiny nozzles, brass pistons beat vertically, horizontally, diagonally, and everywhere Anukis looked there were a hundred movements, of rockers and cams, valves and pistons, and she shivered for it reminded her of the clockwork she had watched inserted into babies... only on a much, much larger scale; a vast scale. A terrible scale.

Vashell led her forward, through a natural tunnel amidst the heart of the vast machine which stretched above them for as far as the eye could see, away into darkness. She could smell hot oil, and the sweet narcoleptic essence of blood-oil. And another smell... a metallic undertone, acidic, insectile, the metal perfume of a million moving parts.

Vashell's boots stamped to a halt, muffled against the brass floor, and Anukis looked up, blinking in the poor golden light. There was a simple metal bench, and behind it sat a woman. Her hands toyed with a complex mechanism, which moved and spun and gyrated and morphed, even as her hands moved endlessly around and within the machine. It was like watching a doctor performing high-speed surgery inside an organism, a living, beating, functioning organism. Anu looked to the woman's face. It was perfect and distorted at the same time. She seemed to wear a brass mask, which glittered dully.

"Hello, Daughter of Vachine," said the woman, smiling, her eyes shining, her hands still constantly merging and integrating with the almost organic clockwork. "My name is Sa. I am Watchmaker."

Anukis could not hide her amazement; nor her distaste.

The Watchmakers were clinically paranoid, in Anu's opinion. They never walked amongst the people, instead hiding away in the Engineer's Palace and issuing orders many of the vachine population found detached from the real world, divorced from the society in which a modern vachine lived, operated, ate and drank.

"You have abused me," said Anu, simply.

"We have strengthened you," said Sa.

"What do you want of me?" said Anu.

"We have a problem," smiled Sa, her golden brass eyes kindly, her fangs peeking just a little above the lip of her mask. She was beautiful, Anu realised, in a vachine way. Despite her lack of stature, despite an athletic and powerful appearance, Anu realised this small dark-skinned woman exuded energy and she noted Vashell's subservient stance. An ironic reversal, considering the behaviour she'd witnessed back in her cell: it had been a stage-act, just for her benefit. Anukis scowled. She was a pawn. Manipulated. Played for a fool. A tool in somebody else's workbox.

"You need my father," said Anu, voice now cold, eyes hardening.

"Our problem goes far, far deeper than your father," said Sa, head tilting to one side. Still her hands played, sinking into a mist of spinning gears and wheels. "It is the blood-oil."

"What about it?"

"We are running dry," said Sa, watching Anukis carefully. "As you know, to the north we have the Fields, out past the Organic Flatlands. But the cattle are dying, have ceased to breed, and our refined blood-oil supplies are nearly exhausted. We have sent a scouting force south, beyond the Black Pike Mountains; they are searching out new possibilities for fresh cattle."

Anu gave a single nod.

"Do you understand the implications of what I am saying?"

"If the blood runs out, it cannot be refined into blood-oil; then the vachine will begin to seize. And die."

"Yes. This is a threat to our civilisation, Anukis. But more than that, the Blood Refineries your father helped build... to develop and engineer. They have contracted, shall we say, a fault. Something endemic to his math, his engineering, his blood-oil magick, and subsequently an element only he can put right. Kradek-ka was a genius." She said it low; with ultimate respect. "He was Watchmaker."

"What happens if the Refineries fail?"

Sa smiled, but there was no humour there. "We will return to a state of hunting and savagery. But how can eighty thousand vachine satiate their blood-oil lust? We will devolve, Anukis. Our society will become decadent, will crumble, will fade as we turn on one another, revert back to clans and tribes. It does not even bear thinking about. The dark ages of our civilisation were a bloody, evil time, where we fed upon ourselves, upon each other. Now, we are fed by the blood of others. Our population is fed by cattle, bred for the purpose. The age-old war with the albinos from under the mountain, all that is in the past. We conquered, we dominated, they became our slaves – and all because of our culture, our civilisation, our evolution! I cannot allow this be taken away. I cannot let this hierarchy, this religion, fail."

"I am impure-blood," said Anukis, voice low. Her eyes were fixed on Sa. "You have cast me out from your vachine world. Why should I care if you perish? Vashell has abused me, humiliated me, murdered my sister, and I am cast out by my own people

127

because of a twist of genetics over which I had no control. I hate to be crude, Sa, but you meat-fuckers can suffer and die for all I care."

Sa smiled. Her eyes glittered behind her mask. "Did your father ever tell you about the origin of the cankers, sweet Anukis?"

"What do you mean?"

"Cankers are... Kradek-ka's greatest achievement. They are, shall we say, a method of utilising waste product. They are bred, and nurtured, deformities; a mish-mash of twisted clockwork and flesh, and put simply, the insane end-product of when a vachine goes bad. We keep them apart from vachine society; so you know the term, I am sure, as insult. But you have never seen the end product." She took a deep breath. "However..."

The pause hurt Anukis. She could not describe why she felt such a sudden, indescribable terror, but she did. Her eyes grew wide. Palpitations riddled her clockwork breast. Her hands clenched together, and fear tasted like bad oil in her mouth.

"What are you saying?" she said.

Sa stood, and placed her fluid clockwork machine on the bench. She walked around its outskirts, hand trailing a sparkle of clockwork slivers, gold dust, blood-oil. She stood before Anukis, looking up into the pretty woman's beaten face, deformed now by the removal of vachine fangs. She stood on tip-toe and kissed Anukis, her tongue slipping into her mouth, fangs ejecting and biting Anukis's lower lip, a vampire bite, a tasting, a savouring, a gentle taking of blood...

Sa stood down. Anukis's blood sat on her lips, in her fangs, and their eyes were connected and Anukis, finally, understood. Her hate fell, crushed. Her anger was crumpled like a paper ball. Her sense of revenge lay, stabbed and bleeding, dying, dead.

"You will help us find Kradek-ka. You will help us repair the Blood Refineries."

Anukis nodded, weakly. "Yes," she said.

"There are some things far worse than death," Sa said. Then turned to Vashell. "Show her the Canker-Pits on your way out. Only then will she truly understand the limits of her... future potential. And the extremes of her father's twisted genius."

"Yes, Watchmaker." Vashell bowed, and dragged Anukis on her leash.

• • • •

Alloria, Queen of Falanor, sat in the Autumn Palace looking out over the staggered flower fields. Colours blazed, and the trees were filled with angry orange and russet browns, the bright fire of summer's betrayal by autumn and a final fiery challenge to the approaching winter.

She sighed, and walked along a low wall, pulling her silk shawl a little tighter about her shoulders as her eyes swept the riot of colours stretching out, and down, in a huge two-league drop from the Autumn Palace to the floodfields beyond. Distantly, she could see workers tending the fields; and to the left, woodsmen cleared a section of forest using ox to drag log-laden carts back to the palace in readiness for the harsh snows which always troubled this part of the country.

"There you are!"

Mary ran along the neatly paved walkway and gave a low curtsy to her queen. Alloria grinned, and the two women embraced, the young woman – Alloria's hand-maiden for the past year – nuzzling the older woman and drinking in her rich perfume, and the more subtle, underlying scent of soap-scrubbed skin and expensive moisturiser.

Mary pulled back, and gazed at the Queen of Falanor. Thirty years old, tall, elegant, athletic, with a shock mane of black hair like a rich waterfall, now tied back tightly, but wild and untamed when allowed to run free without a savage and vigorous brushing. Her skin was flawless, and very pale; beautiful in its sculpture as well as translucency. Her eyes were green, and sparkled green fire when she laughed. When Alloria moved, it was with the natural grace of nobility, of birth, of breeding, and yet her character flowed with kindness, a lack of arrogance, and a generosity which ennobled her to the Falanor population. She was not just a queen, but a champion of the poor. She was not just queen by birth or marriage, but by popular consent; she was a woman of the people.

"You are cold," said Mary. "Let me bring you a thicker shawl."

"No, Mary, I am fine."

Mary gazed out over the splendour of fire ranged before them. It was getting late, the sun sinking low, and most of the workers were finalising their work and walking in groups along pathways through distant crops. "The winter is coming," she said, and gave an almost exaggerated shudder.

"I forgot," smiled Alloria, touching Mary's shoulder. "You hate the ice."

"Yes. It reminds me too much of childhood."

"Never fear. In a week Leanoric will have finished his training, and the volunteer regiments will be standing down for winter leave; he will meet us back at Iopia Palace and there will be a great feast. Fires and fireworks will burn and sparkle for a week; then, then you will feel warm, my Mary."

Mary nodded, still very close to Alloria. "I will never be as warm as when I am with you, my queen," she said, voice little more than a whisper.

Alloria smiled, and placed a finger on Mary's lips. "Shh, little one. This is not the place for such conversation. Come, walk with me back to my chambers; I've had a wonderful blue frall-silk dress delivered, and was wondering how well it will fit."

They walked, arm in arm, along stone and marble paved walkways, between sculpted stone pillars and under roof-trellises filled with roses and winter honeysuckle. Scents filled the air, and Alloria closed her eyes, wishing she was back with her husband, her king, her lover, her hero. She smiled, picturing his smile, feeling his hands on her body. She shivered, then, as a ghost walked over her grave.

"What's the matter?"

"Nothing. I am just thinking of Leanoric. I miss him."

"He is a fine husband," said Mary. "Such strength! One day, perhaps, I will find such a man."

"Erran has been watching you, I think."

"My lady!" Mary blushed furiously and lowered her eyes. "I fear you are mistaken."

"Not so. I have seen him watching you, watching the way you walk, the sway of your hips, the rising of your breast when you have run an errand. I think he is in love."

Erran was the Captain of the Guard at the Autumn Palace, thirty-two years old, single, muscular, attractive in a dark, flashing way. He was gallant, noble, and one of the finest swordsmen in Leanoric's Legions; hence his placement of trust in protecting Queen Alloria.

"You jest," Mary said, eventually.

"Come, let us ask him!"

"No, Alloria!" gasped Mary, and Alloria let out a giggle, breaking away from the younger woman and running up a flight of marble steps. At the summit two guards stood to attention carrying long spears tipped by savage barbs. They stared, eyes ahead, as Alloria approached and swept between them, skirts hissing over inlaid gems in the gold-banded floor.

"Erran! Erran!"

He arrived in a few heartbeats, at a run, hand on sword-hilt. "Yes, my queen?"

"Do not worry, there is no alarm. I have a simple question for you."

Mary arrived, panting a little, and Alloria saw Erran's eyes drift longingly over Mary, then flicker back to her face, a question in his eyes, a sense of duty restored. "I will do my best, my queen."

"No," whispered Mary.

"I wondered if you'd found replacement guards for the two men taken sick last week? It leaves us with a force of only eighteen in the palace grounds."

"Word has been sent to the nearest town, my queen. Replacements are riding even as we speak from the local garrison. I have the captain's personal guarantee that he sent two of his finest men."

"Good! When will they arrive?"

"Later this evening, I believe," said Erran, with a smile of reassurance. "Have faith in those who serve you, my queen."

"I do, Erran. I do." Her smile was dazzling and she moved towards her chambers beneath arches of alabaster, steel and marble. Behind, the bloated shimmering sun was sinking over the horizon, and near-horizontal beams cast a rich ruby ambience throughout the Autumn Palace. Mary followed, a hand on Alloria's arm, her face flushed red.

Erran stood stiffly to attention. "My queen," he said.

"Oh, one more thing." She turned, suddenly. "Mary here is feeling a little flushed, a little tired. I wondered if you might walk with her, out in the gardens? Give her maybe an hour of your time? She would greatly appreciate it."

"I would… be honoured, my queen. But I am on duty."

"I am taking you off duty."

Erran gave a crooked smile. "And who would do my job whilst I walk in the gardens?"

"Oh hush, there are guards everywhere, man, and I am but a few heartbeats away. I have lungs, do I not? And I was trained by Elias, Leanoric's Sword-Champion. I am not as fragile as many people assume." She grinned, her eyes twinkling. "I could beat you, I'd wager."

Erran smiled broadly. "I know this, my queen," he said. "I have seen you best three of my men with a blade. The humiliation stung my pride like a horse-whip! But–"

"No buts. This is a direct order," said the queen. "And I would hate to inform Leanoric you disobeyed a direct order."

Erran snapped a salute. "As you wish, Queen Alloria." He turned, and smiled at Mary, who seemed suddenly incapable of speech. "If you would like to follow me, my lady? I will escort you for fresh air."

Mary nodded, threw a scowl at Alloria, and departed, her silk slippers silent on marble steps.

Alone now, Alloria entered her chambers and closed the doors. She loved to be alone, without guards or hand-maidens, without servants or lackeys. She knew attendance came with her position, and this made her crave solitude even more... except at night, in the cold dark hours, when she would cry out for Leanoric, missing him terribly, missing their two sons, Oliver and Alexander, aged twelve and fourteen, who were travelling with their father learning the Art of Warcraft.

No. In the darkness, Mary would come and climb into bed with Alloria, and they would hold each other, sharing warmth, sharing the simple comfort of human contact, and Alloria knew that Mary loved her, knew that Mary loved her in a way slightly accelerated from the contact and comfort Alloria craved, and that Mary treasured those nights they spent, only thin layers of silk and cotton between their firm, sleep-warmed bodies. But Alloria belonged to Leanoric, her king, her one true love, her hero and soldier and lover and father and husband, a man, a real true strong man, who...

The image flashed like lightning, piercing in her mind.

The Betrayal.

She stumbled a little, righted herself, and gasping ran to a stand and poured water into a goblet. She drank, greedily, then slapped the cup down, panting, cursing herself for having a memory, or at least, having a memory of those terrible days and weeks when she had–

No, don't say it, don't even think of it...

it did not happen; it was a dream, a bad dream.

Why had she done such a terrible thing to the man she loved? Her husband? The father of her children?

And he had forgiven her. Her smile was cracked as she looked at herself in the silver mirror. Her eyes had lost their green fire. She blinked away tears, found inner strength, and reached towards a tiny stone jar. Her hand paused over the jar, which was intricately decorated with ancient battle scenes and heroes from Falanor's long turbulent history.

"No." Her word seemed loud, and cracked, in the echoing empty chamber, despite the proliferation of hanging silks and furs and the many tapestries which adorned walls, again depicting the history of Falanor.

Her hand moved away from the jar and hovered, uncertainly, for a moment; she felt weakness flood her, rising from her toes to her brain like the sweep of an Elder wand, and her hand snaked out, knocked the lid clumsily from the jar which clattered to the marble table-top. Alloria refrained from cursing, and didn't look inside the jar, simply wetting her finger and dipping it into the dark blue powder therein. She stared at her green eyes in the mirror as she rubbed the powder under her tongue, instantly enjoying the relaxing honey of blue karissia entering her blood, entering her mind, and she knew it was weakness and a certain specific horror from her past that made her indulge in this rare drug, and that was no excuse, but it was something she had come to rely on during the old days and the bad days when things had seemed so unclear and seemed to go so wrong. Blue karissia pulsed in her, flowed with her heartbeat, and the world swayed and quickly Alloria slipped from her shawl and dress and climbed into bed to fall instantly asleep, her dreams filled with colour and beauty and an enveloping blue.

Alloria woke to darkness, and the world felt wrong. She could taste the bitter after-effects of the narcotic, and wondered how long she had been under its spell. An hour? Three hours? She sat up, disorientated and feeling mildly nauseous. She shivered, and stepping from her bed pulled on a long silk gown, kicked her feet into thick slippers and found the water jug. She drank greedily, the dehydrated drink of the blue, and only then did a flood of questions tumble into her gradually awakening mind...

Why had the lanterns not been lit? In her chambers, and also outside, on the paved walkways? Normally the garden would be filled with globes of light. Alloria found it hard to believe the lightsmiths had been remiss in their duty.

Warily, she moved to the doors of her chamber and opened one a crack. Outside, a velvet silence rolled through the Autumn Palace. Alloria listened for the familiar footsteps of guards, the distant clink of armour. She heard nothing. She opened her mouth to call out, and closed it again, changing her mind.

Where was Erran? And the other guards? During the hours of darkness she usually had two men posted outside her sleep chambers. Where were they? It was unthinkable they would be away from their post.

Her eyes scanned the black, and goosebumps ran up and down her flesh. Something was wrong; deeply wrong. She could feel it in her blood and bones. Slowly, she eased the door shut. She had a short sword, nicknamed a glade blade, back by the bed. She crept away, back, and padded across the floor. She winced as she drew the blade, for it whispered, oiled steel on leather, but she felt better with the sword in her hands. She knew how to use it; how to defend herself; although she had never been called upon, in reality, to kill, and somewhere deep in her subconscious she wondered how she would respond to the necessity.

She stood, in the darkness, uncertain of what to do.

Then a voice broke the silence; it was cool, clear, and way too arrogant. "What are you going to do with the sword, sweet little Queen Alloria?"

She tensed, poised for attack, tracing the voice that was *in the room, gods, he was in the room and with her and where was Erran, where were the guards? Would she have to fight the intruder alone?*

Fear flooded her.

"Who are you?" Her voice was stone. Ice.

Something moved in the darkness, and Alloria lifted her sword, a swift movement, or so she thought. In retrospect, it was probably hampered by the drugs she'd taken to help her sleep; to help alleviate the nightmares.

"I am here to help."

"Who are you?"

"My name is Graal. I have travelled a long way for you, my queen." He stepped into a pool of light filtering through high windows; he was tall, athletic, and moved with grace. He had long white hair and blue eyes blackened by the night. His face was beautiful, and Queen Alloria found herself paralysed by the effect. He carried no weapon.

"My guards are nearby," she said, voice quieter than she would have liked.

"Your guards are all dead," sighed General Graal. As if emphasising his point, and with perfect timing, something huge moved outside, crunching wood, gouging marble, and settled with a grunt. It was big, Alloria could sense that; and primitive. It grunted when it breathed, its shadow a crazy dance on a far wall.

What are you? she thought, with a shudder.

What is happening here?

Graal approached, and the sword flickered up with a hiss, but he carried on moving and stepped within her reach, batting the blade aside with a consummate ease that shamed her. She tried to withdraw the weapon, to stab at him, but he held the blade and then he held her jaw, and fear flushed through her like an emetic.

"Where is Mary?" she said.

"Alas, nearly everyone is dead."

"No!"

"All dead."

"Erran?"

"All dead, my sweetness. It is you we have come for; and your... drug taking has made it so easy. So sweet." Alloria fell from the world, then, fell and fell and only recovered when she realised Graal was removing her clothes.

"What are you doing?" she shrieked. Outside, the huge creature shifted again, cracking timber.

"Alas, this is a necessary consequence of war."

She started to fight, but Graal was too strong, and he punched her, suddenly, viciously, and she lay stunned half on the bed, her gown hitched high, her cold pale loins exposed in the gloom.

Without passion Graal fucked her, raped her, and she cried and her tears soaked into the bed sheets and as Graal rose to ejaculation so his head lowered, incisors ejecting, and he bit her neck and she screamed and he tasted her blood, drank her as with a grunt he came, and she felt warmth inside her and blood pumping from her, and everything made her sick and weak and weeping; she turned, and vomited on the bed, and conversely, this seemed to give Graal some pleasure; some form of satisfaction.

He pulled up his breeches, his childmaker pale and thin and glittering with complex gold and brass wires in the spilling light from the moon. Emphatically, he licked Alloria's blood from his vachine fangs.

"My husband will hunt you down for this," snarled Alloria, eyes narrowed, fingers plugging the twin wounds in her neck. Hatred was a real thing in her core, a toxic scorpion wild in her breast.

"I hope so," said Graal, and gestured, to where Mary was held in a tight embrace by an albino warrior. She was bound, gagged, her eyes wide. She had seen everything. Graal smiled, a crooked smile full of malice. "See she is released near to Leanoric's camp. It will provide... interesting results, I feel."

"What are you doing?" hissed Alloria.

A sword pressed against her throat, and she whimpered, and Graal leant in close. He kissed her lips, passionately, with love, and she was too frightened to pull away. She could still feel his seed, warm inside her, and with shame she feared him, but more, with guilt she feared the cold darkness of death.

"I am laying a trail," he said, and gestured. Mary, the sweet little one who had attended Alloria so honourably, was dragged by her hair from the room. Blood streaked her face, her breast and her loins. She had not been treated well.

"He will kill you," hissed Alloria. "He will kill you all!"

"We will see," said Graal, and struck a savage blow which knocked her to the bed; then to the floor. Darkness flooded in, and she remembered no more.

EIGHT
Stone Lion Woods

The canker leapt with a howl, and the girls hunkered in terror. It landed, and with a blink they realised they weren't the target. One of the woodsmen was still alive, groaning softly, and had lifted his sword and rolled, groan turning to a snarl at the sight of the canker... which stooped, suddenly, and with a crunch, bit off his head.

Kat eased through dead pine needles, through the rotting forest underlay as the canker ate the corpse noisily. It tore long strips of meat from his thighs and bones with crunches and rips, and then from the man's broad arse, huge lumps which glistened. It swallowed them down in a fast, slick gobble.

They both crouched, watching the canker. Nienna felt herself shivering, and they scavenged around for what torn items lay at their feet. As they dressed in rags, so Kat stood on a dead branch, which cracked. The canker lifted its head from its feast, blood rimed around the massive open jaws, and stringing from its twisted teeth. Nienna saw, suddenly, that this was a different creature from back at the cottage. The mouth was smaller, more lop-sided to the left, the teeth like blackened steel stumps, which bludgeoned meat rather than sliced it. It was also slimmer, less bulky than the first canker they'd witnessed, and with a start, Nienna saw it had breasts, small and rounded, hanging down between its stumpy front legs; the nipples gleaming like polished iron, aureoles of copper, and within the frighteningly thin translucent skin tiny pistons worked.

It was a woman, Nienna realised, and this, somehow, made the cankers a thousand times worse. One thing to be a monster; but to be a monster created from a human shell? To think that through a series of twisted decisions, of incorrect choices, of random bad luck, one could end up... like *that*?

"Gods," she hissed, and the canker tilted its head, focusing on her and Kat as if for the first time. Its tiny gold-flecked eyes narrowed, and raising its head, it bellowed up into the dark night forest in something akin to pain...

Not waiting to see if it attacked, Nienna and Kat turned and ran, sprinting as fast as they could, tearing down forest lanes and leaping fallen trunks, ducking under thick branches, as all around the snow continued to pepper the forest innards and the cold stillness invaded them, their bodies and their minds, threatening with icy chill...

Breaking branches told them they were being pursued. Nienna glanced back to see the canker wedge between two boles of trees that must have been a hundred years old apiece; it roared again, a terrifying squealing bass sound that echoed off through the forest, through the trees which swayed high up as if in hissing appreciation of the gladiatorial hunt taking place within.

With a grunt, and the cracking of wood, the canker broke through the trees. They fell, toppling from high above, crashing through branches and other smaller trees and bringing a whole mass of forest down in a howling crunching terrifying clump.

Nienna and Kat were running, pine needles peppering their hair from above as trees fell and whipped. The canker howled again, and continued to crash after them, clumsy in its passion.

"Thick woods," panted Nienna, face streaked with sweat and covered by numerous tiny scratches.

"What?"

"Head for thick woods; the trees will stop the canker. Slow it down!"

Kat nodded, and they veered left. The canker altered its course, crashing and smashing, thumping and tearing its way through the forest like a whirlwind. Soon, the trees grew more closely placed, but this plan didn't work as well as Nienna and Kat anticipated; for one thing, the more dense sections of forest were the younger sections of forest. The older, thicker trunks were more widely spaced; they had conquered their territory, their particular arena of forest floor, and at their bases where little sunlight reached were simple carpets of pine and discarded branches. Here, now, in the midst of entanglements was where new trees fought for supremacy, for height, for sunlight, and Nienna realised with a pang of horror that the canker ploughed through such trees with ease. There was no halting it…

"I've got to stop!" wailed Kat.

"What is it?"

"My feet, they're cut to ribbons!"

Darkness poured into the thick forest, like from a jug. That was the second downside, Nienna realised, acknowledging her own error of judgement with a sour grimace. The thicker the woods, the more dark and terrifyingly cloying it was. With bigger trees, at least some light, and snow, crept through. Here it was just icy and dark, with little ambient light

Kat stopped, and Nienna stopped beside her. They stood still, listening to the canker falter, and halt; a bellow rent the air, and they heard the deformed beast sniffing.

"Maybe it won't see us," said Kat, voice trembling. She shuffled closer to Nienna, and they held each other in the caliginous interior. They could not even make out one another's faces.

"Yes."

The canker, snuffling and grunting, came closer. Now they could hear the tiny, metallic undercurrent of vachine noise; the click of gears, the whistle of pistons, the spinning of cogs.

"What the hell is it?" said Kat.

"Shh."

Even now, it came closer, and closer, and both girls held in screams and prayed, prayed for a miracle as their feet bled and they shivered, sweat turning to ice on their trembling flesh…

Something huge moved above them and Nienna felt a great presence in the trees, as if a giant stalked the forest and the canker growled, screamed, and leapt, and there were sounds of scuffling, of claws scrabbling wood and jaws clashing with metallic crunches and then a mammoth, deafening, final *thud*. The forest shook, as if by a giant's fist.

Silence curled like smoke.

Nienna and Kat, both trembling, looked at one another.

What happened?

To the canker, but also… out there?

There came a series of sudden hisses, and clanks, and then silence again. Whatever had happened to the canker it had been immediate, and final. Some giant predator? A bear, maybe? Nienna shook her head at her internal monologue. No. A bear couldn't have killed the – thing – that pursued them. So what, then?

"Come on, let's move," whispered Kat.

Something huge and terrible reared above them in the darkness, smashing branches and whole trunks in its ascent and making Kat scream out loud, all sense of self-preservation vanished as primeval terror took over and the dark shadow reared above, and roared, suddenly, violently, a deep and massive bass roar without the twisted undercurrents of the canker…

"I know where we are," hissed Nienna, clutching Kat in the shade.

"Where?" she wept.

"Stone Lion Woods," whispered Nienna, her mind filled with horror.

"I'm telling you," said Saark, "it's crazy to head out into the snow!"

"Well, I'm going, aren't I."

Kell opened the door, and stepped out into the storm. It had lessened now, and small flakes tumbled turning the forest clearing into a haze. Kell's eyes swept the dark trees.

"Get your sword."

Saark reappeared in his damp clothes, grumbling, and stood beside the immobile form of Kell in the snow. "What's the matter now, you old goat? Forgot your gold teeth? Left your hernia cushion? Maybe you need a good hard shit?"

Kell turned on him, eyes wide, flared in anger. "Shut up, idiot! There's something in the trees."

Saark was about to offer further sarcastic comment, but then he, too, sensed more than heard the movement. He turned his back on the small hut and faced the trees, rapier lifting, eyes narrowing.

Kell drew his Svian from under his arm, and cursed the loss of his axe. He felt it deeply; not just because it was a weapon, and he needed such a weapon now. But because the axe was… his. Ilanna. His.

"Hell's teeth," muttered Saark, as the albino soldiers edged carefully from the trees, gliding like pale ghosts, their armour shining in shafts of moonlight tumbling between snow-clouds.

"I count ten," said Kell, delicately.

"Eight," said Saark.

"Two archers, just inside the trees, off to the right."

"By the gods, you have good eyesight! I see them!"

"Horse-shit. I wish I had my axe."

"I wish I had a fast horse."

"Very heroic."

"Not much use for dead heroes in these parts."

The albino soldiers spread out, crimson eyes locked on the two men. Kell stepped away from Saark, mind settling into a zone for combat; and yet, deep down, Kell knew he would have struggled even with his axe. With a long knife? Even one as deadly as the Svian? And with his bad knees, and cracked ribs, and god only knew what other arthritic agonies were waiting to trip him up?

He grimaced, without humour. Damn. It wasn't looking good.

"Drop your weapons," said the albino lieutenant.

"Kiss my arse," snarled Kell.

"Superb: weaponless *and* an idiot," said Saark, eyes fixed on the soldiers.

"You can always run back through the woods and jump in the river."

"Now that is a good idea."

They stood, tense, waiting for an attack. The lieutenant of the albino soldiers was wary; Kell could see it in his eyes. He wasn't fooled by an old man and a dandy dressed in villager's clothing. He could see Saark's hair, the cut of his stance, the quality of his rapier. There were too many factors of contrast, and the albino was cautious. This showed experience.

"Ready?" muttered Kell... as something huge, and hissing, with gears crunching and hot breath steaming slammed from the trees and into the midst of the albino soldiers, rending and tearing, ripping and smashing, causing an instant sudden confusion and panic, and the albinos wheeled in perfect formation, swords rising, attacking without battle cries but with a superb efficiency, a cold and calculating precision which spoke more of butchery than sol-diering... swords slammed the canker, and two sets of arrows flashed from the trees, embedding in the canker's flanks. Rather than wound the creature, or slow it, it sent the canker into a vio-lent rage and it whirled, grabbing an albino and ripping him apart to scatter torn legs spewing milk blood in one direction, and a still screaming torso and head in the other. More arrows thudded the canker's flanks, and it reared, pawing the air with deformed arms, hands ending in glinting metal claws, and fangs slid from its jaws as its vampire vachine side emerged and it leapt on a soldier, fangs sinking in, drinking up milky blood and then choking, sitting backwards as swords hacked at its cogs and heavily muscled flesh and it spat out the milk, reached out and grasped an albino by the head, to pull his head clean off trailing spinal column and clinging tendons which *pop pop popped* as they dangled and swung like ripped cloth.

"This is our invitation to leave, I feel," muttered Saark.

"Into the woods," said Kell. "I'll wager they've got horses nearby."

As the savage battle raged, so Kell and Saark edged for the trees, then ran for it, tense and awaiting the slam of sudden arrows in backs. They made the tree-line, cold, snow-filled, silent, and behind them howls and grunts bellowed, and swords clanged from clockwork as the canker spun and danced in a twisted spastic fury.

"There." Kell pointed.

They moved through the trees, the sounds of battle fading behind; within minutes the noises were muffled, like a dream from another world.

A group of horses were tethered to a tree by a small circle of logs. Kell untied the reins, and taking four mounts they spurred the remaining creatures and mounted two black geldings, leading the other two along a narrow forest deer-trail.

"Which way?" said Saark.

"Away from the canker."

"A good choice of direction, I feel."

"Seems the wisest, at the moment."

"A thought occurs, Kell."

"What's that?"

"That creature back there. It was different to the last, the one ripped apart in the river. There are… two of the beasts, at least. Yes?"

"Observant, aren't you, laddie?"

"I try," grinned Saark, in the dark of the snow-locked forest. "What I'm trying to say is that, if there are two, maybe you were right, maybe there will be more. And they are not the sort of beasts we can fight with peasant's sword and axe."

"Under the Black Pike Mountains, Saark," Kell's voice was a grim monotone, "there are thousands of these creatures. I saw them. A long, long time ago."

They rode in silence.

Eventually, Saark said, "So, to all intents and purposes, there could be an essentially endless supply of these ugly bastards?"

"Yes."

"Well. That's put a dampener on things, old horse." He followed as Kell switched direction, heading deeper into the forest. Now, the sounds of battle, all sounds in fact, had vanished. Only a woolly silence greeted them. Above, the trees swayed, whispering, false promises murmured in dreams. "By the way, which way are we going?"

"Towards Nienna."

"And you know this because?"

"Trust me."

"Seriously, Kell. How can you know?"

"She has my axe. I can feel it. I am drawn to it."

Saark stared at Kell in the murk. One of the geldings whinnied, and Kell leaned forward, stroking his head, calming him. "There, boy. Shh," he said.

"He's not a dog, Kell."

"Do you ever stop yakking?"

"What's that supposed to mean?"

"Back in Jalder, a neighbour of mind had a shitty yakking little bastard of a dog. All damn night, yak yak yak, with barely a word from the woman to chastise the beast. Many times, the little bastard yakked all night; so one summer, fatigued by lack of sleep, and in a temper I admit, I took down my axe, went around to my neighbour, and cut off her dog's head."

"Is this a sophisticated parable?"

"The moral of my story," growled Kell, "is that dogs that yak all night tend towards decapitation. When I'm annoyed."

"Proving you are no animal lover, I'd wager. What happened to the neighbour?"

"I broke her nose."

"You're an unfriendly sort, aren't you, Kell?"

"I have my moments."

"Was the yakking dog some veiled reference to my own delicate tongue?"

"Not so much your tongue, more your over-use of said appendage."

"Ahh. I will seek to be quiet, then."

"A good move, I feel."

They eased through the night, listening with care for the canker, or even a squad of albino soldiers; neither men were sure who would be victorious, only that the battle would be vicious and long and bloody, and could not end without some form of death.

Suddenly, Saark started to laugh, and quelled his guffaws. Silence rolled back in, like oily smoke.

"Something amuse you, my friend?"

"Yes."

"Like to share it?"

"That damn canker, attacking its own men. I thought they were on the same side? What a deficient brainless bastard! Laid into them as if they were the enemy; as if it had a personal vendetta."

"Maybe it did," said Kell, voice low. "What I saw of them, they had few morals or intelligence as to who or what they slaughtered. They were basic, primitive, feral; humans who had devolved, been twisted back by blood-oil magick."

"Humans?" said Saark, stunned. "They were once men?"

"A savage end, is it not?"

"As savage as it gets," said Saark, shivering. "Listen, old man – how do you know all this?"

"I was in the army. A long time ago. Things… happened. We ended up, stranded, in the Black Pike Mountains and had to find our way home. It was a long, treacherous march over high ice-filled pathways no wider than a man's waist. Only three survived the journey."

"Out of how many?"

Kell's eyes gleamed in darkness. "We started with a full company," he said.

"Gods! A hundred men? What did you eat out there?"

"You wouldn't want to know."

"Trust me, I would."

"You're like an over-eager puppy, sticking your snout into everything. One day, you'll do it to something sharp, and end up without a nose."

"I still want to know. A nose has limited use, in my opinion."

Kell chuckled. "I think you are a little insane, my friend."

"In this world, aren't we all?"

Kell shrugged.

"Go on then; the suspense is killing me."

"We ate each other," said Kell, simply.

Saark rode in silence for a while, digesting this information. Eventually, he said, "Which bit?"

"Which bit what?"

"Which bit did you eat?"

Kell stared at Saark, who was leaning forward over the pommel of his stolen horse, keen for information, eager for the tale. "Why would you need to know? Writing another stanza for the Saga of Kell's Legend?"

"Maybe. Go on. I'm interested." He sighed. "And in this short, brutal, sexually absent existence, your stories are about the best thing I can get."

"Charming. Well, we'd start off with his arse, the rump – largest piece of meat there is on a man. Then thighs, calves, biceps. Cut off the meat, cook it if you have fire; eat it raw if you don't."

"Wasn't it... just... utterly disgusting?"

"Yes."

"I think I'd rather starve," said Saark, primly, leaning back in his saddle, as if he'd gleaned every atom of information required.

"You've never been in that situation," said Kell, voice an exhalation. "You don't know what it's like, dying, chipped at by the howling wind, men sliding from ledges and screaming to their deaths; or worse, falling hundreds of feet, breaking legs and spines, then calling out to us for help for hours and hours, screaming out names, their voices following us through the passes, first begging, then angry and cursing, hurling abuse, threatening us and our families; and gradually, over a period of hours as their words drifted like smoke after us down long, long valleys, they would become subdued, feeble, eaten by the cold. It was an awful way to die."

"Is there a good one?"

"There are better ways."

"I disagree, old horse. When you're dead, you're dead."

"I knew a man, they called him the Weasel, worked for Leanoric in the, shall we say, torturing business. I got drunk with him one night in a tavern to the south of here, in the port-city of Hagersberg, to the west of Gollothrim. He reckoned he could keep a man alive, in exquisite pain, for over a month. He reckoned he could make a man plead for death; cry like a baby, curse and beg and promise with only the sweet release of death his reward. This Weasel reckoned, aye, that he could break a man – mentally. He said it was a game, played between torturer and victim, a bit like a cat chasing a mouse, only the cat was using information and observation and the nuances of psychology to determine how best to torture his victims. The Weasel said he could turn men insane."

"You didn't like him much, then?"

"Nah," said Kell, as they finally broke from the trees and stood the geldings under the light of a yellow moon. Clouds whipped overhead, carrying their loads of snow and hail. A chill wind mocked them. "I cut off his head, out in the mud."

"So you were taking a moral standpoint? I applaud that, in this diseased and violent age. Men like the Weasel don't deserve to breathe our sweet, pure air, the torturing bastard villainous scum. You did the right thing, mark my words. You did the honourable thing."

"It was nothing like that," said Kell. He looked at Saark then, and appeared younger; infinitely more dangerous. "I was simply drunk," he said, and tugged at the gelding's reins, and headed towards another copse of trees over the brow of a hill.

Saark kicked his own mount after Kell, muttering under his breath.

The sun crept over the horizon, as if afraid. Tendrils of light pierced the dense woodland, and Kell and Saark had a break, tethering horses and searching through saddlebags confident, at least for the moment, that they had shaken their pursuers. More snow was falling, thick flakes tumbling lazy, and Kell grunted in appreciation. "It will help hide our tracks," he said, fighting with the tight leather straps on a saddlebag.

"I thought the canker hunted by smell? Lions in the far south hunt by smell; by all accounts, they're impossible to shake."

Kell said nothing. Opening the saddlebags, the two men searched the albinos' equipment, finding tinder and flint, dry rations, some kind of dried red-brown meat, probably horse or pig, herbs and salt, and even a little whisky. Saark took a long draught, and smacked his lips. "By the balls of the gods, that's a fine dram."

Kell took a long drink, and the whisky felt good in his throat, warm in his belly, honey in his mind. "Too good," he said. "Take it away before I quaff the lot." He gazed back, at the thickly falling snow.

"The question is," said Saark, drinking another mouthful of whisky, "do we make camp?"

"No. Nienna is in danger. If the albino soldiers find her, they'll kill her. We can eat as we ride."

"You're a hard taskmaster, Kell."

"I am no master of yours. You are free to ride away at any moment."

"Your gratitude overwhelms me."

"I wasn't the one pissing about on the bed of a river, flapping like an injured fish."

"I acknowledge you saved my life, and for that I am eternally grateful; but Kell, we have been through some savage times, surely my friendship means something? For me, it's erudite honour to ride with the Legend, to perhaps, in the future, have my own exploits recounted by skilled bards on flute and mandolin, tales spun high with ungulas of perfume as Kell and Saark fill in the last few chapters of high adventure in the mighty Saga!" He grinned.

"Horse-shit." Kell glared at Saark. "I ain't allowing no more chapters of any damn bard's exaggerated tales. I just want my granddaughter back. You understand, little man?"

Saark held up his hands. "Hey, hey, I was only trying to impress on you the importance of your celebrity, and how a happy helper like myself, if incorporated into said story, would obviously become incredibly celebrated, wealthy, and desired by more loose women than his thighs could cope with."

Kell mounted his horse, ripped a piece of dried meat in his teeth. He set off down a narrow trail, ducking under snow-laden branches. "Is that all you want from life, Saark? Money and a woman's open legs?"

"There is little more of worth. Unless you count whisky, and maybe a refined tobacco."

"You are vermin, Saark. What about the glint of sunlight in a child's hair? The gurgle of a newborn babe? The thrill of riding an unbroken stallion? The brittle glow of a newly forged sword?"

"What of them? I prefer ten bottles of grog, a plump pair of dangling breasts on a willing, screaming, slick, hot wench, a winning bet on some fighting dogs, and maybe a second woman, for when the first wench grows happily exhausted. One woman was never enough! Not for this feisty sexual adventurer."

Kell looked back, into Saark's eyes. "You lie," he said.

"How so?"

"I can read you. You have behaved like that, in the past, giving in to your base needs, your carnal lusts; but there is a core of honour in your soul, Saark. I can see it there. Read it, as a monk reads a vellum scroll. That's why you're still with me." He smiled, his humour dry, bitter like amaranth. "It's not about women, wet and willing, nor the drink. You wish to warn King Leanoric; you wish to do the right thing."

Saark stared hard at Kell, for what seemed like minutes, then snapped, "You're wrong, old man." His humour evaporated. His banter dissolved. "The only thing left in my core is a maggot, gorging on the rotten remains. I drink, I fuck, I gamble, and that's all I do. Don't think you can see into my soul; my soul is more black and twisted than you could ever believe."

"As you wish," said Kell, and kicked his horse ahead, scouting the trail, his Svian drawn, a short albino sword by his hip on the saddle sheath. And ahead, Kell smiled to himself; finally, he had got to Saark. Finally, he had shut the dandy popinjay's mouth!

Saark rode in sullen silence, analysing his exchange with Kell. And in bitterness he knew, knew Kell was close to the bone with his analysis and he hated himself for it. How he wished he had no honour, no desire to do the right thing. Yes, he drank, but always to a certain limit. He was careful. And yes, he would be the first to admit he was weak to the point of village idiot by a flash of moist lips, or the glimpse of smooth thigh on a pretty girl. Or even an ugly girl. Thin, fat, short, tall, red, brown, black or blonde, light skinned, freckled, huge breasts or flat; twice he'd slept with buxom black wenches from the far west, across Traitor's Sea, pirate stock with thick braided hair and odd accents and smeared with coconut oil... he grew hard just thinking of them, their rich laughter, strong hands, their sheer unadulterated willingness... he shivered. Focused. On snow. Trees. Finding Nienna. Reaching Leanoric.

Up ahead, Kell had stopped. The gelding stamped snow.

Saark reined behind, slowing the other two horses, and loosened his rapier. "Problem?"

"This fellow doesn't want to proceed."

Saark looked closer in the gloom of the silent woods. The gelding had ears laid back flat against its head. The beast's eyes were wide, and it stamped again, skittish. Kell leaned forward, stroking ears and muzzle, and making soothing noises.

"Maybe there's a canker nearby."

"Not even funny," said Kell.

"He can sense *something*."

"I think," said Kell, eyes narrowing, "this is Stone Lion Woods."

Saark considered this. "That's bad," he said. "I've heard ghastly things about this place. That it's... haunted."

"Dung. It's dense woodland full of ancient trees. Nothing more."

"I heard stories. Of monsters."

"Tales told by frightened drunks!"

"Yes, but look at the horses." Now, all four had begun to shiver, and with coaxing words they managed another twenty hoof-beats before Kell and Saark were forced to dismount and stroke muzzles, attempting to calm them.

"Something's really spooking the animals."

"Yes. Come on, we'll walk awhile."

They moved on, perhaps a hundred yards before Kell suddenly stopped. Saark could read by his body language something was wrong: he had seen something up ahead. And he didn't like it...

"What is it... oh." Saark stared at the statue, and his jaw dropped. It was thirty feet high, towering up between the trees. It was old, older than the woodland, pitted and battered by the elements of a thousand years, sections covered in moss and weeds, lichens and fungi; and yet still it stared down with a menacing air, a violent dominance.

"What's it supposed to be?" questioned Saark, tilting his head.

"A stone lion, perhaps?" muttered Kell. "Hence, Stone Lion Woods."

"I've never seen a lion look like that," said Saark. "In fact, I've never seen a lion. Not in the flesh. Apparently, they are terrifying, and stink like the sulphur arse-breath of a cess-pit."

"It is a lion," said Kell, voice low, filled with respect. "Only it's twisted, deformed, reared up on hind legs. Look at the mane. Look at the craftsmanship in the sculpted stonework."

"I'm more interested in whether it'll topple on us. Look at those cracks!"

The two men watched the statue, a hint of awe in their eyes, hands stroking the skittish horses, calming the beasts with soothing murmurs. A little snow had filtered through the canopy of Stone Lion Woods, and sat on the statue, shining almost silver in the gloom. The effect was ghostly, ethereal, and Saark shivered.

"I don't like it here. The rumours speak of terrible beasts. Ghosts. Hobgoblins. Were-dragons."

"Horse-shit. Come on. I feel my axe; she's getting close."

Saark looked oddly at Kell. "You can really sense the weapon?"

"Aye. We are linked. She's a bloodbond weapon, and that means we are joined, in some strange way I cannot explain, nor understand."

"A bloodbond. I have heard of such things." Saark closed his mouth, reluctant to speak more. The tales and legends of bloodbond magick were dark and fearful indeed: stories used to frighten little children. Like the Legend of Dake the Axeman; he was huge and shaggy, with the grey skin of a corpse and glowing red eyes. Dake would creep down the chimney of bad little boys and cut off their hands and feet in the night. If they were really bad, Dake would take the child with him, back to the Tower of Corpses where he'd hang the child in a cage from the outside wall and let Grey Eagles eat their flesh. Even now, Saark remembered his father scaring him with such stories when he'd been a bad boy: when he'd slapped his sister, or stolen one of his mother's fresh-baked pastries.

For years, such nightmares had been erased from Saark's memory. Now, especially in this caliginous and eerie place, watched over by a twisted stone statue, the horror of those dark tales from childhood crept back into Saark's sparking imagination. He remembered all too clear huddling under thick blankets watching the twitching shadows on the walls... waiting for Dake the Axeman to come for him.

"Are you all right?" said Kell.

"I was just... thinking of my childhood."

"Were they happy times, aye?" said Kell.

Saark pictured running into the house holding a kite he'd made to find his father swinging from a high rafter by the neck, his face purple, one eye hanging on his cheek. There was dried blood around his mouth, his tongue stuck out like some obscene cardboard imitation. Taking a bread knife, he'd cut down the dead man and sat with him, rocking his head, holding his stiffening hands until his mother arrived home... with the city bailiffs, ready to repossess their family home. There had been no sympathy. A day later, they were walking the streets.

"Happy, yes," said Saark, banishing the memories like extinguishing a candle. Strange, he thought. To resurrect them here,

150

now. He'd locked them away in a deep, hidden place for decades. Saark coughed, and tugged at the horses. "Come on. Let's move. This place gives me the shits."

"You sure you're well?" asked Kell. He appeared concerned. "You looked, for a moment there, like you'd seen a ghost."

Saark pictured his father, swinging. "Maybe I did," he said, voice little more than a whisper; then he was gone, striding down a wide, twisting trail and Kell tugged his own mount forward. The gelding gave a small whinny of protest, and moved reluctantly.

"That's not good," muttered Kell, sensing a change in Saark's mood. "Not good at all."

They moved through the woods, deep into gloom for an hour, gradually picking a route over roots and branches, through a mixture of junipers, Jack Pine and Tsugas, through rotting leaves from towering twisted oaks and thick needle carpets from clusters of Red Cedar. The woods were old here, ancient, gnarled and crooked, and huge beyond anything Saark had ever witnessed.

Reaching a natural clearing, Saark halted and gazed at the array of statues, his mouth dropping open. There were seven, arranged in a weird natural circle as if the trees themselves were wary to set root and branch near these twisted effigies.

"What," he said, "are those?"

"The Seven Demons," said Kell, quietly. He placed a hand on Saark's shoulder. "Best move quietly, lad. We don't want to upset them."

"What do you mean by that?"

"Blood-magick is an old beast, no matter what the vachine think. It goes back thousands of years. When you've travelled as much as I, you learn a few things, you see a few things; and you begin to understand when to keep your head down."

"You've been here before?"

"Yes."

"So, is this place haunted, then?"

"Worse, laddie, so let's just be quiet, move quickly, get to Nienna and hope we don't upset anything."

"That sounds ominous."

"It can only get worse, trust me. The Stone Lion Woods didn't garner their savage reputation through idle banter, drunken discourse or the loose tongue of a happy mistress." Kell grinned at

Saark, and at his contradiction. He could see it in Saark's eyes... you've conned me, thought Saark. Kell shrugged. "Follow me close, lad. And keep your puppy yelps to yourself."

They moved through the circle of statues. Some were big, incredibly old, unrecognisable in their shape or form, weathered, battered, broken, and covered in fungus and moss. Two of the statues were man-sized, a stone representation of twisted, unfathomable monsters; a third was a man, tall and proud, regal almost; another was a lion, and another... something else entirely. A final statue was small, only knee high, and reminded Saark of a deformed embryo, only a touch bigger, and stood on hind legs with joints reversed like those of a dog. He shivered. He felt curiously sick.

They plunged back into the woods, Kell following his senses, although Saark wondered if Kell was crazy and simply navigating a random path. Regularly Saark checked his back-trail, for albino soldiers, or worse, the cankers which seemed to be hunting them. They walked all day, sometimes slowing to squeeze through narrow sections of tangled branches, and leading the skittish horses with care.

The night fell early, and again the two warriors came upon a circle of seven statues at dusk. Saark began to get twitchy, jumping at lengthening shadows as the trees crowded in, gnarled and crooked, limbs reaching over them, towards them, brushing at faces and clothing, dropping their lodes of snow to the woodland carpet.

Kell stopped. "We'll leave the horses here," he said. They were beside a narrow cross-roads, trails probably formed by wild deer, badgers and boars.

Saark nodded. "Is Nienna close?"

"Ilanna is close. I'm hoping the girl is with her."

"You mean your granddaughter."

Kell stared at Saark. "That's what I said."

They carried on, on foot, until they came to a long corridor in the thick woodland; it was almost rectangular and walled with evergreen leaves and pine branches, holly and juniper and hemlock entwined with honeysuckle and creepers. The air was thick with resin and woodland perfume, cloying, a heady aroma, and Nienna and Kat were both seated on a thick fallen log.

"Nienna," said Kell, his voice low, barely more than a growl. His eyes fixed on Ilanna, resting beside the girl; and then transferred back as she turned. Her face was frightened, skin tight, eyes wide; she mouthed at Kell, and he frowned, trying to make out the words.

Saark crept up beside Kell, crouched at the edge of the leaf corridor. He frowned. "What's she trying to say?"

His words, although quiet, reverberated down the natural sound channel. Nienna stood up suddenly and grasped Kell's axe in tiny hands, turning away from the men towards a distant clearing, rich in its greenery. Something began to click, like pebbles dropped on boulders, and Kell stood and launched himself down the corridor towards the two girls... beyond, almost out of sight but hinted at, it rose hugely from the ground, earth and dead leaves and brown pine needles tumbling around the *thing* as it detached from the woodland floor and huge grey limbs unfolded to reveal fists, each the size of a man, and twisted limbs only barely reminiscent of the lion it had once represented...

"It's a Stone Lion," shrieked Nienna as Kell reached her, took her in his hands, shook her.

"Are you injured?"

"No! It saved us! Saved me and Kat from the canker!"

A noise began to *thrum* through the woods. It was ancient, if a noise could be such a thing, primeval, not really words but music, a song, a song made from stone and wood and fire, and it rose in pitch and volume until it was a roar and Kell glanced back, saw the fear in Saark's eyes, could hear the whinny of their tied horses struggling at tethers and he took his axe, his Ilanna, and she melted into his hands like warm soft female flesh, and she was there with him and his agitation and fear fled and Kell was whole again, a total being and he realised, in that crazy snapshot of time how his addiction and his need was rooted deep down in his skull, his bones, his blood, his soul, and Ilanna was his saviour; and more, also his curse.

"It said it would kill you," hissed Nienna, her eyes not on Kell but the creature still rising from the earth at the end of the tunnel. "It said we were protected by the forest, because of our... innocence. But it knew you would come, you and Saark; it said you were defiled. Abused. You were not creatures of the Stone Lion Woods. It said it would eat you, like it ate the canker..."

"Go to Saark," said Kell, his face grim, and grabbed Kat, pushing her after Nienna and both girls fled along the green corridor. A cold wind blew, filled with the smell of ice and leaves, of rotting branches, of sap, of mouldy pines and wild mushrooms and onions.

Kell grasped Ilanna, and faced the Stone Lion.

Its roar died down, and it stooped low, stepping into the corridor. It was five times the height of a man, twisted, a merged and joined creation of stone and wood, earth and trees, and primal quartz; it was a carved thing, a live thing, a demon of the deep woods, a spirit of the darkness, and its face, despite being a worn weathered blur of stone and wood, looked down at Kell and he could have sworn it was grinning.

He glanced back. Tightened his grip on his axe. "Saark!" he roared. "Get to the horses! Get the girls out of here!"

Saark nodded, and they fled.

Kell turned back, faced the Stone Lion. It growled, a long, low, permanently mewling sound, and took a few tentative steps, as if testing its legs worked. It lowered its head then, spine crackling, and roared at Kell with a hot blast scream which stank of rotting wood, sulphur, onions and death.

Kell's beard whipped about him, and he ground his teeth, face dropping into a snarl.

Give me your blood, said Ilanna. Her voice was sweet music in his mind, but Kell steeled himself, for he knew the deception, knew how this thing worked; he had been tricked before, had been used before by Ilanna... and it had led to terrifying results.

"You know I cannot."

You will *not!*

"I remember the last time," he muttered, as the Stone Lion took another step forward on twisted legs, sizing him up, its eyes falling on the axe in his hands, its head tilting to one side, almost... inquisitive.

It's going to crush me, he thought.

How can I fight something that... big?

It will be different this time, promised Ilanna. *I will be good. I promise you. I will smash this puny creature of blood-oil magick, of the forest and the soil. I will not... abuse you, Kell. I know I injured your mind, and your pride. It will be different this time!*

"No."

The Stone Lion charged, the ground thundering, and Kell stood his ground, axe raised, eyes narrowed, mouth a grim, sour, dry line and it smashed towards him, and at the last moment he rolled, felt the Stone Lion's huge bulk slam past and the axe sliced one leg, a butterfly blade exiting with chunks of stone and wood splinters. Kell's shoulder hit the earth, he rammed the wall of the green lane, was spun around by the incredible force, and with a grunt he gained his feet, watched the Stone Lion stumble, skid, turn, and lower its head towards him. He hefted Ilanna, moving to the centre of the trail, studying the way the Stone Lion carried itself; he'd injured it, damaged it in some way, but it had not screamed. There was no blood. Now, in silence, it advanced, more slowly, and its huge long arms came thumping towards Kell and he swayed back, fast, a stone-like fist whirring a hand's-breadth from his face and his axe slammed the arm but glanced off, nearly wrenching Kell's arms from sockets. He skipped back avoiding another blow, then the Stone Lion surged forward and Kell was backing away, his axe ringing from arms and fists as he deflected blow after blow, his own arms jarring with every strike of the axe-blade, but the Stone Lion was tough, its skin like stone and Kell realised its legs were its weakness; he ducked a whirling appendage, then rolled under its reach towards the thick trunk-like legs. Ilanna sang in his scarred hands as he cut chunks from the Stone Lion's twisted timber shins, embedded one butterfly blade in a thigh with a clunk and wrested it free as the Stone Lion caught him in the chest with a blow, accelerating him down the green lane to tumble, and lie on his chest, panting, before scrambling to his feet and lifting his axe with a grimace.

The Stone Lion was gazing down at itself, at its damaged legs. It looked up, glared at him, and let out a high-pitched roar that made Kell shudder. But he stood his ground, and glimpsed a thick yellow liquid oozing from the cuts and slices he'd inflicted. The Stone Lion took a step forward, then went down on one knee. It stood again, grasping the lane to heave itself up.

Kell decided this was the right moment.

He turned and ran, stampeding through leaves and dead pine, listening for pursuit from the massive creature of legend. As he reached a thick section of woodland he risked a glance back, but the Stone Lion still stood its ground, glaring at him, its chest... heaving? Heaving, or laughing. Kell was unsure which. Then he blinked, and realised the wounds he had so skilfully inflicted were healing, the thick yellow liquid had hardened, formed a shell over the cuts like hardening sap.

Kell fell into the woodland; only then did he hear the pursuit, the thump thump thump of a heavy pendulous charge, and the ground was shaking beneath him and fear filled him up like a jug. He realised he could not kill it… unless he gave control to Ilanna. He scowled. That would only happen over his dead body.

Run! If he could reach the horses, he could outrun the Stone Lion. Perhaps.

He charged on, branches slamming his face and arms, the Stone Lion in pursuit. He reached the cross-roads where they'd tethered the horses, and for a second was flooded with relief, for Saark and the young women were nowhere to be seen; they had fled, were gone, were safe. His sacrifice had bought them time. Only, now… he frowned. All the horses were gone. Which meant he was… on foot.

"Saark, you dandy bastard!"

A roar echoed through the trees behind, and Kell cast about; Saark had headed south, as they'd discussed, to reach King Leanoric, warn him of events in Jalder. Kell sprinted down the trail but the recent fighting, lack of sleep, and the curse of age and in-activity hit him like a cobble. He faltered within a hundred yards, was streaming with sweat after two. The Stone Lion still pursued. It ceased its bestial roar, but Kell could hear the thump of heavy steps… how could he not? He grimaced.

"Horse-dung," he muttered. He was going to die here.

Ahead, through heavy snow, the trees grew thinner and a fantasy entertained Kell; maybe he was by the edge of Stone Lion Woods? Maybe there was a boundary to the Stone Lion's territory, beyond which it could not pursue? Blood-oil magick worked like that, sometimes…

But there was no guarantee.

Kell laboured on, and could hear the Stone Lion growing closer, and closer, a dark shadow behind, a black ghost in the trees. Kell stopped, wheezing, red lights dancing in his brain. He hawked, and spat a lump of phlegm to the woodland floor.

A high roar, bestial, like a choking woman, made him jump and surge forward… as growls up ahead made him skid to a halt, confused. Through the trees, Kell saw the shape of a canker. Something died inside him. He was trapped. By all the gods! Trapped!

"Not good."

His eyes narrowed, as the first canker was joined by two more, all three different shapes and sizes, but each with a wide-open head showing cogs and gears clicking and moving. Kell glanced back. The Stone Lion was there, advancing on him. He could see its legs now, and no wounds were visible... it had completely healed.

Kell sprinted, axe tight in sweat-slippery hands, and the cankers saw him; with spastic jerks of deformed and bloated heads, they let out vicious, triumphant growls and howls and thuds of accelerating, deviated twisted clockwork with bunched muscles run through with lodes of silver-quartz, and with snarls they leapt to the attack... and in a whirling chaos of confusion, with the Stone Lion roaring behind, and the smell of hot canker oil in his nostrils, Kell narrowed his eyes and lifted his axe in the eerie snow-brightened woodland where snow flurries drifted and swirled, and as panic detonated around him he leapt at the cankers and brought the singing, glinting blades of Ilanna around in a savage downward sweep...

NINE
Army North

Leanoric sat his charger on the hill just outside the ruins of Old Valantrium, and thought about his father. To the northeast, he could see the distant gleaming spires of Valantrium, one of Falanor's richest, most awe-inspiring cities, constructed by the finest architects and builders in the land, its streets paved with marble painstakingly hewn from the Black Pike Mines in the south-west of the staggering and awe-inspiring mountain range.

What would your father do? he thought, and despair settled over him like a cloak.

Leanoric turned his charger, gazing west. He could just make out the gleaming cobbles of the Great North Road, which some called his finest creation. A single, wide avenue, it ran for nearly sixty leagues through hills and valleys, through forests and moorland, dissecting the country and linking Falanor's capital city Vor in the south, with the major northern university city of Jalder. The Great North Road was an artery of trade and guaranteed protection, patrolled by Leanoric's soldiers. It had been successful in banishing thieves, solitary highwaymen and outlaw brigands, sending them either further north into the savage inhospitable hell of the Black Pike Mountains, or south, across the seas to worry other lands.

What would your father do?

Leanoric rubbed his stubble, evidence of three days in the saddle, and turned his charger again, scanning for his own scouts due back from Old Skulkra and Corleth.

The rumour, delivered by an old merchant on a half-dead horse, had sent prickles of fear lacerating Leanoric's spine and scalp.

Invasion!

Jalder, invaded!

Leanoric smiled, a bitter careful smile, and placed his Eagle Divisions in his mind; he had twin regiments of eight hundred men each camped on Corlath Moor, three days march from Jalder; he had a further battalion of four hundred men stationed at the Black Pike Mines at the west of the range, maybe a week's march, longer if the coming snows were heavy. Further north, he had a brigade of sixteen hundred infantry near Old Skulkra, and close to them a division of five thousand led by the wily old Division General, Terrakon. And another brigade to the east of Valantrium Moor, on manoeuvres.

Within two weeks he could muster another four brigades from the south of Vor, and descend on Jalder with nearly twenty thousand men – the entire Army of Falanor. Twenty thousand heavily armed, battle-trained soldiers, infantry, cavalry, pikemen. But... but what if this was nothing more than the ravings of some drunken, insane old merchant? Some bastard high on blue karissia, frothing at mouth and veins, and with his speculative fear putting into action the slow mechanical wheels of an entire army's mobilisation?

It had not escaped Leanoric that winter was coming, and thousands of soldiers were looking to return to their homesteads. Leanoric had already delayed leave by three days; every hour, he felt their frustration growing, accelerating. If he didn't release his northern armies soon, they could become trapped by snow as the Great North Road became more and more impassable. Then, Leanoric risked insubordination, desertion, and worse.

Leanoric ground his teeth, sighed, and tried to relax.

If only his scouts would bring news!

It was a bad joke, nothing more, he told himself. The garrison at Jalder was more than able to cope with raiding brigands from the Black Pike Mountains; with outlaws, rogue Blacklippers and the occasional band of forest thugs.

Leanoric considered the old merchant, who even now was being tended by Leanoric's physicians in his own royal tent. The man could no longer speak, his skin burned and peeling as if half cooked over a fire. Eyes wide, the man – they still had not established a name – had ridden in on a horse which promptly collapsed and died, ridden to death, iron-shoes down to the hoof, foam ripe on mouth and nostrils. The tortured merchant had babbled, incoherently at first, then delivered his news in fits and starts between wails for mercy and cries for the king to spare his life. It had been... Leanoric searched for a word... he sighed, and ran a hand through his short, curled golden hair. It had been distressing, he thought.

So. What would his father have done?

Leanoric considered the former king, dead now the last fifteen years. After a lifetime as Battle King, a warrior without peer, huge and fast and fearless, a man to walk the mountains with, a man with whom to hunt lions, Searlan, King of Falanor, at the age of fifty six had been thrown from his horse and broke his neck and lower spine. He'd hung on grimly for three days as specialist physicians and the skilled University Surgeon, Malen-sa, tended him; but eventually the life-light, the will to live, had faded from his eyes as his paralysed limbs lay limp, unmoving, and understanding sank as if through a sponge to penetrate his brain. He would never walk again, never ride a horse, never hunt, dance, make love, fight. In those last few days, as realisation dawned, Searlan had lost the will to live; and had died. The physicians said, eventually, after much consultation, that death had occurred through internal bleeding. Leanoric knew this to be untrue; it had been his own blade that pierced his father's heart, at Searlan's request, one stormy night as Leanoric sat by the bedside holding back tears.

"Son, I will never walk again."

"You will, father," said Leanoric, taking the old man's hands.

"No. I understand my fate. I understand the reality of the situation; I have seen these injuries on the battlefield so many, many times. Now my turn has come." He smiled, but the smile shifted to a wince, then a gritting of teeth as he fought the pain.

"Can you still not feel your toes?"

"I can feel my heart beating, and move my lips, but my fingers, my toes and my cock all remain out of my control." He laughed again, although he struggled to perform even that simple function. "I am lucky I can still talk to you, my son. Lucky indeed."

Leanoric squeezed his fingers, although there was no movement there, no return pressure.

"I love you, father."

Searlan smiled. "You've been a good boy, Leanoric. You've made me proud, every single day of my life. From the moment the midwife brought you squealing from your mother's cut womb, covered in blood and mucus, your tiny face scrunched up in a ball and your piss carving an arc across the room – to this moment, here and now, there has been nothing but joy."

"There will be more joy," said Leanoric. Tears filled his eyes. His throat hurt with unspent sorrow.

"No. My time in this world is done."

"Let me fetch mother."

"No!" The word was like a stinging slap, and stopped Leanoric as he rose from the stool. "No." More gentle, this time. "I cannot say my farewell to her; it would break my heart, and hers too. It must be this way. It must be death in sleep."

Leanoric stared hard into his father's eyes.

"I cannot."

"You will."

"I cannot, father."

"You will, boy. Because I love you, and you love me, and you know this is the thing that must be done. I would ruffle your hair, if I could; even that simple pleasure is denied me."

"I cannot!" Now, he allowed tears to roll down his cheeks. Leanoric, rarely bested in battle, the son of the great Battle King who had led a charge against the Western Gradillians, suffering a short-sword blow to the head which cracked his skull allowing shards to poke free – and never uttered a whimper. Now, he allowed his fear and anguish to roll down cheeks from eyes far too unused to crying.

"Let it out, son," said Searlan, kindly. "Never be afraid to cry. I know I used to tell you the opposite," he coughed a laugh, "but I was making you strong, preparing your for kingship. You understand, boy, what I ask of you? It is not just for me; it is for all of you, and for Falanor. The land needs a strong king, a leader of men. Not a dribbling old fool in a chair, unable to wipe his arse, unable to ride into battle."

Leanoric looked into his father's eyes. He could find no words.

"Take the thin dagger, from the chest behind you. I have a wound, here on my chest, from fencing with Elias a few days ago; by gods, that man is fast, he will be a Sword-Champion one day!

I want you to pierce my heart, through the wound. Then plug it using cotton, don't let blood spray anywhere. It will look like I died in my sleep; that my heart stopped beating."

"I cannot do that to you, father. I cannot..." he tasted the word, "I cannot murder you."

"Foolish pup!" he raged. "Have you not listened to a single word I said? Be strong, damn you, or I will get one of the serving maids to do it, if you have not the mettle."

Leanoric stood, unable to speak, and took the dagger as instructed. He took a cotton cloth, and placed it over his father's heart. Then, looking down into the old man's eyes, he watched Searlan smile, and mouth the words, "Do it," and he pressed down, his teeth grinding, his jaw locked, his muscles tensed as Searlan spasmed, gritted his teeth, and with a massive force of will did not cry out, did not weep, did not make any other sound than a whispered... "Thank you."

Leanoric cleaned the blade, replaced it on the chest, cleaned his father's wound using a sponge and water, and replaced the old bandage over Elias's original sword strike. Then, slowly, his hands refusing to work properly, he pulled the covers back over Searlan's body. Gently, he reached down and closed his father's eyes, silently thanking him for being a hero, a great king – but most of all, the perfect father.

Now, sitting atop his charger with the weight of the country across his own bowed shoulders, Leanoric took a deep breath and wiped away a tear at the memory. I hope, he thought, I will have such courage at the time of my own death.

A horse galloped towards him. It was Elias, Sword-Champion of Falanor and Leanoric's right-hand man, general, tactician and adviser. Elias saluted, and rode in close. "One of your scouts is approaching, yonder."

"From Jalder?"

"No, he wears the livery of the Autumn Palace."

"Alloria?" Leanoric frowned; it was rare Alloria troubled him when out with the army. She would only send a rider if there was... an emergency. Coldness and dread swept through him.

The horse, heavily lathered, ran into camp and Leanoric, with Elias close behind, spurred his mount towards the rider. Soldiers helped the rider dismount, and as the person practically fell from the saddle it was with shock they realised it was a woman, in a tattered, torn, bloodstained dress. She wore the livery colours of the Autumn Palace; but beneath that, she wore defeat and desolation.

"Gods, it's Mary, Alloria's maid!" She looked up, and dirt and despair were ingrained in her skin, and in her eyes. She saluted the king, and dropped to one knee, head bowed, weeping, although no tears flowed. The horror of past hours had bled her dry.

"King," she said, words burbling, body shaking, "I bring bad news."

Leanoric leapt from his horse, and turned to the nearest soldier. "Man, go and get a physician! And you man," he pointed to another, "bring her water." He rushed forward, caught Mary as she went to topple, and found himself cradling the pretty young woman, her face filthy, blood in her eyelashes.

"Who did this to you?"

"The soldiers came," she sobbed, "oh, sire, it was terrible, and Alloria…"

The soldier returned with water, and Leanoric forced down his panic, despite the look in Mary's eyes which made him falter, made a splinter of ice drive straight through his heart. In a strangled voice, he said, "Go on, Mary, what of Alloria?"

"Great king, there has been… an attack. On the Autumn Palace."

"By the gods," growled Elias.

"What of Alloria?" repeated Leanoric, voice quiet, a strange calm fluttering over his heart, his soul. He knew it could not be good. He knew, intrinsically, that his life was about to change for ever.

"She has been taken," said Mary, averting her eyes, staring at the ground.

"By whom?"

"He had white, pale skin. Long white hair. Bright blue eyes that mocked us. He said he was part of the Army of Iron. He said his men had taken the garrison at Jalder… And…"

"Go on, woman!" Leanoric's eyes were burning with fury.

"He has taken Alloria with him."

"What was his name?" said Leanoric, voice emotionless.

"Graal. General Graal."

Leanoric turned to Elias, but the man shook his head. He returned to the shivering form of Mary, and she glanced up at him, pain in her face, in her eyes, then looked away.

"There is more?" said Leanoric, softly.

"Yes. But for you alone. Can we go to your tent?"

Leanoric stood, picking up Mary in his arms and bearing her swiftly through the camp. Fires burned, and he could smell soup, and stew. Men were laughing, bantering, and leapt to their feet saluting at his rapid approach. He ignored them all.

Elias pulled back the tent flaps, and Leanoric laid Mary on a low bed of furs and silk. She coughed, and Elias closed the tent flaps, offering the woman another mug of water which she thankfully accepted.

"Can we speak in private?" said Mary.

Leanoric nodded, their eyes met, and Elias departed. Alone now, with shadows lengthening outside, Mary reached up to Leanoric, put her hand on his shoulder, her eyes haunted in a curious reversal, from subject to monarch, from young to old, from naïve to wise.

"Did they hurt her?" snapped Leanoric. "Tell me! What did they do to her?"

Mary opened her mouth, and some tiny intuition made her close it again. What if, she wondered, Graal's abuse of the queen made her a less than valuable commodity? Maybe, and as she looked into Leanoric's eyes she felt a terrible guilt at her thoughts, but maybe if she told him the truth, told the king of the violent rape by General Graal, maybe he would not want her back at all. After all, it was only a few short years since Alloria's betrayal...

"He... bit her," said Mary, finally.

Leanoric stared at her, without understanding. "What do you mean? He *bit* her?"

"I know it sounds... strange. Metal teeth came out from his mouth, long metal teeth, and he bit Alloria in the throat and drank her blood." Mary closed her mouth, confused now, aware she sounded like a mad woman. She risked a glance at Leanoric. "Graal said he had taken Jalder, he had taken Jangir, and would march on the capital, on Vor. He said if you stood in his way, he would kill Alloria."

"Do you know where he has taken her?" Leanoric's voice was frighteningly soft.

"Yes. She has been sent to a place called Silva Valley, in the heart of the Black Pike Mountains. Graal said it was the home of the Army of Iron. What are you going to do, Leanoric? Will you rescue Alloria? Will you stand against this man who drinks blood?"

Leanoric stood, and turned his back on Mary, his soul cold. He opened the tent flap, ushered in a physician and stepped out into fast-falling dusk. Around the camp laughter still fluttered, and Leanoric had a terrible premonition. Soon, there would be little to laugh about.

"What is it?" said Elias, stepping close.

"Walk with me."

They strode through the camp, past the outlying ruins of Old Valantrium and up a nearby hill on which a beacon fire had been lit. Leanoric pushed a fast pace, and reaching the top, he finally turned to Elias, his face streaked with sweat, his eyes hard now as events tumbled around him, fluttering like ashes, and he set a rigid course through his confused mind. He knew what he had to do.

Jangir had a garrison brigade posting of sixteen hundred men. If Mary was right, if it had been taken... and if Graal had infiltrated as far as the Autumn Palace, and therefore had men in Vorgeth Forest, and could even now be marching with his army on Vorgeth, Fawkrin, or further east to Skulkra and Old Skulkra... Leanoric's mind spun.

How could he not know?

How could he not realise his country was under attack? Infested, even.

"What are we going to do?" said Elias.

Leanoric gave a grim smile that had nothing to do with humour. He pulled on his battle-greaves. In a voice resonant of his father, he said, "Old friend, we are going to war."

Standing there, as the sky streaked with red and violet, as he watched his world, his country, his beloved Falanor die under a blanket of darkness, Leanoric outlined his plan to his general, and his friend.

"These bastards have come from the north, taken Jalder, and taken Jangir. So their forces amass to the west of the Great North Road, somewhere around Corleth Moor, maybe Northern Vorgeth; this makes sense, these damn places are desolate, haunted, and people try not to go there because of the twisted history of Jangir Field. A good place to hide an army, is what I'm thinking."

"What then?"

"I have a brigade at Gollothrim, and a division here at Valantrium. We can pull our battalion down from the Black Pike Mines, and we have a brigade near Old Skulkra. If we can surround the bastards, hit them from each flank and make sure the

Black Pike infantry emerge from the north... well, we can rout them, Elias. They'll think the whole damn world has descended on them."

"We need more information," said Elias, warily. "The size of the enemy force. Exact locations. Does this Graal have heavy cavalry, spears, archers? Are his men disciplined, and do they bring siege weapons?"

"There is little time, Elias. If we don't act immediately I guarantee we will be too late. This Graal is a snake; he is striking hard and fast, and taking no prisoners. We did not see him coming. It is a perfect invasion."

"Still, I advise despatching scouts. Three to each camp with your plans following separate routes, in case any rider is captured; we can code the messages, and pick hardy men for the task. I'll also arrange for local spies to scour Corleth Moor; we can send message by pigeon. I have a trusted network in the north."

Leanoric nodded. "With a little more information, and time, we can encompass them. I still only half believe Mary! Who would dare such an outrage? Who would dare the wrath of my entire army?" With twenty thousand men at his disposal, this made Leanoric perhaps the most powerful warlord between the four Mountain Worlds.

Elias considered their plan, rubbing his stubbled chin, his lined face focused with concentration. Internally, he analysed different angles, considered different options; he could see what King Leanoric said made sense, made complete sense; yet still it sat bad with him, an uneasy ally, a false lover, a cuckolded husband, a friend behind his back with a knife in his trembling fist.

"Consider," said Elias, voice as quiet as ever, and as he spoke his hand came to rest on the hilt of his scabbarded sword – a blade no other man alive had touched. "This General Graal cannot be a foolish man. And yet he marches halfway across Falanor to steal the queen; why? What does he gain?"

"He makes me chase him."

Elias nodded. "Possible. Either chase him, or to undermine your confidence. Maybe both. And yet he has already, so we believe, conquered two major cities with substantial garrisons. So he either has a mighty force to be reckoned with, or..."

"He's using blood-oil magick," said Leanoric, uneasy.

"Yes. You must seek counsel on this."

"There is little time. If I do not muster the Eagle Divisions immediately, the entrapment may not work. Then we'd be forced to fall back..." his mind worked fast. "To Old Skulkra. It is a perfect battleground. And I have a... tactic my father spoke of, decades ago."

"But if Graal uses the old magick, your plan will not work anyway," said Elias. "You know what I'm thinking?"

"The Graverobber," said Leanoric, voice sober, voice filled with dread. "I fear he will kill me on sight."

"I will go," said Elias.

"No, I have another job for you."

Elias raised his eyebrows, but said nothing. He knew his king would speak in good time.

Leanoric pursed his lips, lifted his hands to his face, fingers steepled, pressed against his chin. Then he sighed, and it was a sigh of sadness, of somebody who was lost. He spoke, but he would not meet his friend's gaze.

"What I ask of you, Elias, I have no right to ask."

"You have every right. You are king."

"No. I ask this on a personal level. Let us put aside rank, and nobility, for just one moment. What I ask of you, is... almost certain death. But I must ask anyway."

Elias bowed his head. "Anything, my king," he said, voice gentle.

"I would ask you to travel to the Silva Valley." Leanoric paused, as if by leaving the words unspoken, he would not have to condemn his general, would not have to murder his friend. He sighed. He met Elias's gaze, and their eyes locked, in honour and truth and friendship and brotherhood. "I would ask to you find and rescue Alloria."

"It would be my honour," said Elias, without pause for breath.

"I recognise–"

"No." Elias held up a hand. Leanoric stopped. "Do not say it. I am a man of the world, and if I may point out, far more seasoned a warrior than you." He smiled to take the sting from his words. "I trained with your father, and I admired your father; but I love his son more. And I love my queen. I will do this, Leanoric, but feel no burden of guilt. I do it gladly, of my own free will."

Leanoric grasped Elias, a warrior's grip, wrist to wrist, and beamed him a smile; a grim smile, but a smile nonetheless.

"I will save the country; but you must save my heart-blood. You must find my wife."

"It will be an honour, my friend."

"Bring her back to me, Elias."

Elias smiled. "That, or die trying," he said.

After thirty minutes, Elias was ready to depart. He had a swift black stallion, compact saddlebags and his trusted sword by his hip. He looked down at Leanoric, and the few men gathered.

"Ride swift," said Leanoric.

"Die young," replied Elias.

"Not this time, Elias."

"As you wish."

"Bring her back to me."

"I'll see what I can do, my liege."

He touched heels to flanks. The stallion, a fine, proud, unbroken beast of nineteen hands, needed little encouragement, and with a snort of violence galloped off down a wide cart track, and towards the distance snake of grey: the Great North Road.

Leanoric watched for long, long minutes, long after Elias, his Sword-Champion, had vanished from view. He listened to the night air, to the hiss of the wind, and fancied he could smell snow approaching.

Grayfell, one of Leanoric's trusted brigadier generals, glanced off into the gloom. "There's a storm coming," said the short, gruff soldier, rubbing at his neatly trimmed grey beard. His eyes of piercing yellow met Leanoric's, and the king gave a curt nod.

"That's what I am afraid of," he said.

As dawn broke, Elias stopped by a fringe of woodland and surveyed the Great North Road. It glittered in weak dawn light, wreathed with curls of mist, cobbles gleaming like grey and black pearls. For long minutes the king's Sword-Champion watched, listening, observing, analysing, wondering. He eased out from cover, and within minutes allowed the stallion his lead so that he galloped along the cobbles, hoof-beats clattering through the early morning air.

Elias rode hard, all day, pausing only in the early afternoon to allow his horse a long cool drink by a still lake. As he stood, stretching his back and working through a variety of stretching exercises taught to cavalry riders, which he usually reserved for before battle, a few eddies of snow drifted around him and he gazed off to the distant northern hills, and saw the white gathering

eagerly like icing on a cake. Cursing, Elias continued north, sometimes running the stallion on smooth grass alongside the hard
cobbles, sometimes dismounting and walking the beast. He knew
in his heart this was going to be a long journey; a test of stamina,
and endurance, as well as strength and bravery. Still, Elias thought
grimly, he was up for the task.

That night, camping beneath a stand of Blue Spruce, wrapped
in his thick fur roll, Elias came awake as snow brushed his face.
His eyes stared up at thick tree boughs ensconced in needles, interlaced above him, rich perfume filling his senses, and beyond at
an inky, violet sky. Snowfall increased, and with it a sinking in
Elias's breast. The enemy, with Alloria as prisoner, had a good head
start. Snow would slow them down; but it would also slow him.
He could only pray they were travelling by cart, or on foot; but he
doubted it. They'd kidnapped the Queen of Falanor; they would
be riding fast horses, hard, to put as much distance between
Falanor's Eagle Divisions and their reckless prize. Once they hit
the Black Pike Mountains, Elias knew he was doomed. The range
was treacherous, the valleys and narrow passes a labyrinth, and
once inside their enclosing wings Elias would have lost the
queen... and even if he did manage to navigate to this Silva Valley,
what would he find there? A waiting army? A division of grinning
soldiers? Damn, he thought. He had to catch up with them before
the Black Pikes. He had to rescue his queen before she entered the
death-maze...

He started before dawn, filled with a rising panic, and an increased level of frustration.

Elias pushed the stallion hard, too hard he knew, and just after
noon as more snow fell muffling hoof-beats on the Great North
Road, he spied a village and guided his mount from the cobbles,
bearing east down a frozen, rutted track. However, a hundred
yards from the collection of rag-tag huddled cottages, he halted.
His stallion snorted, stamping the snow.

Something was wrong, he could feel it, and a cold wind blew,
ruffling his high collar and making him shiver. Unconsciously, he
loosened his sword in its scabbard as his gaze scanned from left
to right, then back.

Nothing moved. No chickens clucked in the yards, no children
squealed, no people walked the street, or stood on corners with
pipes and gossip. Elias narrowed his eyes, and dismounted. Feeling

foolish, and yet at the same time fuelling his sense of necessity, he drew his sword and dropped his mount's reins. He advanced on the deserted village, sword at waist-height, head scanning for enemy…

And who are the enemy, mocked his subconscious?

The Army of Iron? Halting in its mighty conquest of Falanor to annihilate one tiny, insignificant village?

The answer was yes.

Elias stopped at the head of the main street, and gazed out, and down, across frozen mud and fresh new drifts of snow, at the corpses which littered the thoroughfare. Elias squinted. He'd thought of them as corpses, but as he peered closer, now that he thought about it, they seemed more like…

"Gods!" he hissed, skin freezing on his bones, blood chilling in his veins, eyes wide, lips narrow, sword gripped unnaturally tight. "What in the Nine Hells has caused this?"

He stopped by an old man, face down, frame shrivelled, skin little more than parchment shell over brittle narrow bones. Elias dropped to one knee, crunching fresh snow, and rolled the old man onto his back… only to cry out, stumbling back as he realised it wasn't the corpse of an old man at all, but a young woman, her flesh melted away, skin pulled back over her grinning skull like some parody of decrepitude and death.

Elias stalked down the street, his horror rising, his hatred rising, his rage and anger fuelled to a white-hot furnace by what he saw. And he knew; knew without truly understanding the intricacies of blood-oil magick that this this was a result of the dark art; the old art.

"Bastards," he said, shaking his head, gazing down at children, shrivelled husks, still holding hands. Their faces were far from platters of serenity; they had died in terrible pain, without honour, without dignity, and Elias stared and stared and cursed and spat to one side of the street.

"Is this what Graal has in store for us?" he muttered, considering this Army of Iron and its white-haired general.

Back down the street, a scream rent the air, and it took Elias long slack moments to realise it was his horse. He turned and ran, skidding on ice as he rounded two low-walled cottages, their doors barely high enough to allow a child entry.

The horse was on its side, in the street, quivering as if in the throes of epilepsy. Mist curled in tendrils at boot-height and

Elias narrowed his eyes, approaching warily, searching left and right for signs of the enemy. Had it been struck by an arrow? Or something more sinister? He was ashamed to notice that his hands shook.

"A fine beast," came a soft, lilting voice, mature and yet... deranged, to Elias's ears. "Such a shame the source is poor, toxic you understand, for purposes of refinement. Otherwise, we might not have to harvest you."

Elias whirled, sword flashing up, to see a tall creature in thin white robes, delicately embroidered in gold and blue. But it was the face that sent shivers down Elias's spine, and had the hairs on his neck crackling like thin ice over a deep pond. The face was flat, oval, hairless, and incredibly pale. Small black eyes watched Elias with what he considered to be intelligence, and the nose was little more than slits in pale skin. The creature, for this was no man, breathed fast, hissing and hissing and sending more shudders to wrack Elias's body as it suddenly moved towards him, bobbing as it walked, a display which would have been almost comical if it wasn't for the aura of death and the stench of putrefaction which seemed to pervade the creature and its surroundings with every living, breathing pore...

"What are you?" breathed Elias, words barely more than a whisper.

The creature came close. "I am a Harvester, boy. And you are Elias."

"How could you know that?"

"I know many things," said the Harvester, and lifted its hand, the sleeve of its robe falling back to reveal long, bony fingers. "I know you are the friend of King Leanoric. I know you seek his Queen, Alloria, taken by the vile Watchmaker Graal... but all in time, my son, all in time, for you are prime fodder, are you not? And you have information which may aid our cause. Come, come to me..."

Elias leapt, but even as he leapt ice-smoke poured from the Harvester, from its tiny black eyes and open mouth, from its fingers and very core and it slammed Elias, dropping him in a moment, sword frozen to the skin of his fingers, body convulsing and juddering, spastic fits wracking him with a violence he could not have believed possible...

"Let's take away your pretty toy," said the Harvester, stepping close, and Elias saw the skin stripped from his fingers leaving several with nothing more than bone and a few strips of dangling, pink flesh. And as Elias dropped into a descent of terror and disbelief, and pain and raw burning agony, he could still hear the Harvester talking as it worked, and remembered those five bony fingers hovering over his heart... "Come to me now, boy, come to the Harvester, we'll look after you, we'll take you to the Watchmaker and you'll have such a pretty time, you'll have the time of your life..."

Elias opened his eyes. It was dark, and cold, and wooden walls surrounded him. For a terrible long moment he thought he was in a coffin, buried alive beneath fetid soil with worms struggling to ease through cracks and eat his eyes as he still breathed... a scream welled in his throat, bubbling through phlegm as his hands slapped out, thudding against wood...

"Where am I?" he croaked, realising he was terribly dehydrated, blinking, coughing, and he sat up and realised he wasn't in a box, but a cart, and it bumped over rough ground and he stared down at his hand where two fingers were nothing more than torn and shattered bone, and he screamed, even though there was no pain, he screamed and his screams echoed out through the darkness...

"Quiet!" snapped a soldier, his sword prodding Elias in the chest and forcing him back to his rump in the cart.

Elias said nothing, but cradled his wounded hand and gazed around through veils of red sweet nausea. Darkness and mist filled his vision, and through the vapour like ghosts walked soldiers, ten, a hundred, a thousand, and each one had a pale face and crimson eyes and white hair; their armour was black, and Elias leant forward and vomited into his own lap, and stared for a long time at strings of saliva and puke as he rewound his brain and played through the meeting with... the Harvester? So. He had found the army. But how long had he been unconscious? How far from Leanoric was he now? He could have travelled a hundred miles, or a thousand. No, he thought to himself, staring again at his flesh-stripped fingers. Realisation struck him worse than any axe blow to the back of the head.

His hand was crippled; a deformed relic.

He could no longer hold a sword.

Tears ran down his face then, and all dignity and pride fled him. He knew, deep down, that all men feared something more than all else; each man had a breaking point, whether it be cancer, loss of sight, the death of children or parents. But for Elias, Sword-Champion of Falanor, it was a loss of his right to swordsmanship.

Random images flickered through his mind, and he realised he was delirious.

He was a boy again, practising with a wooden blade...

He was a man, teaching his own children the art of the sword...

He was standing, shivering, behind the curtains as Leanoric killed his father, King Searlan...

Time flowed like black honey; with no meaning. The cart stopped and he was given bread and water, but did nothing more than vomit when it hit his stomach. A harsh voice snapped, "Leave him, if he dies, he dies."

"No. Graal will have the entire fucking army flogged!"

"Damn that Harvester; if he'd done his job a'right, we wouldn't be having these problems." There came a curse in another, guttural, almost mechanical language, and harsh hands with smooth skin forced more water down his throat. This, Elias managed to retain, and after another few miles bouncing in the cart, which he now realised was drawn by two pale, milk-skinned geldings, they halted and Elias was dragged from the platform, his hands bound tight behind his back with thin gold wire which bit his skin and made him cry out... it felt like he was being eaten by insects. Glancing back, he watched the wire moving constantly, with tiny blades, like tiny teeth, all made of copper and brass and continually sawing.

Elias was forced through the camp. They were on high moorland. Trees formed a solid black wall to the north. Above, the stars were obscured by bunching snow-clouds. Mist swirled around his boots. His hand throbbed, fingers stinging him like nothing on earth; and tears still flowed like acid down his cheeks. How had he been taken so easily?

Elias grimaced. If this was the sort of magick they were using, if an icy blast could take out the best Sword-Champion of Falanor in a few seconds of confusion, of utter cold, then this new threat, this new menace, this terrible foe was going to roll over Leanoric's Eagle Divisions like a hot knife through butter.

We're doomed, he realised.

I must get to the king. I must warn the king!

Elias was dropped to the ground, and he realised he was prostrate within a circle of men. He looked up, around at their faces which showed no empathy, no emotion, and then a black armoured warrior, tall and elegant, wearing a black helm obscuring his long, flowing white hair, turned and gazed at him.

"You are Elias," he said. "The Sword-Champion of Falanor."

"I am!" Pride flared in his breast. They could torture him, but he would not talk. He spat at the soldier. "Damn you, what do you horse-fuckers want?"

"I know you think me sadistic," spoke the soldier, looking up at the sky. "You are incorrect. When I punish, I punish without pleasure. When I torture, I torture for knowledge, progression, and for truth. And when I kill... I kill to feed."

"Then kill me, and be done with it!" snarled Elias, fury rising. He tried to surge up, to attack this arrogant albino, but only then did he realise hands pinned his soldiers, holding him to the ground.

"No," said Graal, dropping to one knee and staring into Elias's face. "Today is not your day. This time, it is not your time." He half-turned. "Bring her."

Queen Alloria was dragged, kicking and struggling, to the centre of the circle. She was beaten, her face bloodied, her arms tied behind her back with wire, blood covering her bare arms and wrists and hands. But she did not cry. She held her head high, eyes fierce, and she spat at Graal as she was thrown to the heather. She struggled to her knees and glared at her captors, glared at the albino soldiers around.

"Elias?" she hissed, almost disbelievingly, voice filled with an agony of recognition.

"I came to find you," smiled Elias. "Leanoric sent me. Even now he musters the Army of Falanor. We will wipe this pale-skinned scum from the face of the world!"

"You don't understand," said Alloria, eyes filled with tears.

"Hush now," said Graal, and kicked her in the head, a movement of gentle contrast as he sent her spinning violently to the heather, stunned, blood leaking from smashed lips, mouth opening and closing from the sudden shock of the blow.

Elias looked up. "I'll kill you, fucker," he said.

"Later, later," said Graal, waving the Sword-Champion into silence. "I had bad news this morning. It would appear my... brother, is dead." Graal's crimson eyes were locked to Elias. Elias smiled.

"Good. I hope the maggot suffered."

"He suffered, my boy. He was a twisted vachine, you see. A canker. A creature who could not absorb the clockwork, whose body betrayed his heritage, a living rejection constantly at war with his own internal machinery." Graal sighed. "But I see you don't understand; I see you need... an education."

Graal stood, and waved beyond the circle of soldiers. A handcart was dragged by four men, and aboard it lay... Elias, knelt, was stunned by the vision, his eyes wide, failing to recognise, or at least comprehend, what they saw. It was big, a twisted lion-shape, with pale white skin, tufts of white and grey fur, a huge head split wide with long curved fangs of razor-brass. The body was torn open in places, and Elias could see fine machinery moving inside, tiny wheels, miniature pistons. Elias coughed, and tilted his head, failing to comprehend.

The stench washed over him. Elias vomited on the heather.

Graal moved to the carcass, in two pieces, and placed a hand on bloated flesh. He looked almost fondly into small dark eyes, lifeless now, despite the moving machinery inside the canker's flesh. "Dead, but not dead. Alive, but not alive. Poor Zalherion. Poor Zal. You never thought it would be this way, did you? You never thought it would be like this."

Graal turned, and pointed at the ground. The flat of a blade slammed Elias's head, and he went down with a grunt. Stars spun. He opened his eyes, and heard a sound of hammering as stakes were driven deep into the frozen earth. His hands and legs were staked out, and as he came round he began to struggle. "What are you doing?" he screamed, voice rimed with panic. "What the hell is going on?"

"You will help us," said Graal, voice cool.

"What do you want to know?" panted Elias.

"Not that way. You see," Graal turned, and moved back to the cart. Drawing his sword, he slit the dead canker, his brother, from groin to throat. Skin and muscle peeled back as if the carcass had been unzipped, intestines and organs tumbled out, most merged with tiny intricate machinery, still moving pistons, still spinning gears. Some parts had tiny legs, and they began to walk rhythmically, like the ticking of clockwork, across the heather... "You see," continued Graal, "when a canker dies, then usually the machine within him dies at the same time. But at times a phenomenon occurs which we do not understand; the machinery becomes

175

parasitical and self sustaining... it lives on after the death of the host, and can be transferred to another living creature. Watch."

"No!" hissed Elias, voice barely a whisper.

"Watch this, it's unique," said Graal, smiling, stepping back as machinery moved across the heather towards Elias's staked out figure.

Pistons whirred, accelerating, as if sensing new blood, new flesh. Gears clicked in quick succession. Wheels spun and golden wires writhed like snakes, flowing through the heather until they reached Elias and crawled up his body as he began to scream, and shout, struggle and kick and thrash but the wires edged up his skin, up his hands and feet and arms and legs, worming under his clothing and dragging behind them small intricate units, machine devices, all clicking and whirring and stepping gears. Wire crawled over his face like a mask, and Elias screamed like a woman, but the wires wriggled into his mouth and wormed up his nose, they squirmed into his eyes making him thrash all the more, screams suddenly halting, a cold silence echoing across the moors as the first machinery unit arrived, scampered up his cheek and wedged into his mouth amidst muffled cries. It forced itself into him, down his throat, cutting off his airways and, subsequently, noises of pain. More machinery arrived, and tiny sharp scalpels sliced the flesh of Elias's belly, opening his stomach wide and amidst spurts of blood and coils of bowel, with tiny brass limbs and pincers they dragged themselves inside him to feed and to merge and to join with his flesh in a union of muscle and artery and machine...

"They're so independent," said Graal, unable to disguise his wonder. "Even as Watchmaker, I do not understand. It is a miracle! A true and awe-inspiring sight, to stand here, mortal, bowed, subservient, and observe this sentience! This metal life! It is a privilege not bestowed by the Oak Testament."

Around him in the mist, albino soldiers stood uneasily, eyes wide, watching the staked out figure of Elias squirm, their faces forced into neutrality as the metal-wreathed man, now seemingly more machine than human, thrashed and struggled, kicking and wriggling, and thrashing with such violence they thought he might tear off his own arms and legs...

Alloria opened her eyes, face-down on the heather, and turned, watching Elias consumed by metal, by wire and pistons, by gears and cogs. The clockwork ate into Elias, severing and savouring his flesh like ripe fruit, entering him, raping him, melding him, joining him, and Alloria watched with all blood flushed from pale cheeks, unable to speak, unable to scream, unable to vomit, as Graal stood amiably by and revelled in the clockwork creating a second-hand vachine.

TEN
Jajor Falls

Kell met the canker head on, both snarling, both leaping through witch-light on the snow-laden woodland. They hammered together, canker claws clashing a hair's-breadth from Kell's face as his axe slammed the beast's neck, and he felt blades bite through thick corded muscle and into whirling clockwork deep within; their bodies thumped together and all was madness; even as they collided, Kell's free hand grasping a huge claw-spiked canker paw, something huge and dark sailed over their heads and the Stone Lion landed snarling, elongated face stretching to roar and with fangs clashing, it collided with the two cankers, and the three figures smashed together, claws raking, teeth gnashing, and blood and wheels went spinning off into the undergrowth. One canker kicked back, crouched, then leapt atop the Stone Lion, fangs fastening on its head. With a massive crunch it bit the Stone Lion's head in two, pulling back, claws fixed in the Stone Lion's torso as it shook its prize like a dog with a bone and the Stone Lion went down on one knee; but even as the canker chewed, spitting out chunks of wood and stone, so the Stone Lion's fist whirred up, over, and down with a *whump* that shook the woodland and crushed the canker into a mewling heap, spine broken, and claws flexed and ripped out its lungs in a bloody spray of mechanical parts and still pumping organs. The Stone Lion smacked the second canker against a tree, as Kell hit the ground, Ilanna embedded in the canker's neck, but a high shriek filled the woodland and the canker turned from Kell, leaping on the Stone Lion's back as its companion attacked the Stone Lion from the front, and both fastened huge jaws on the Stone Lion which spun in a fast circle, long arms flailing, trying to dislodge the beasts from its body.

Kell sat down heavily with a grunt, all energy flushed from him. He pulled out his Svian half-heartedly and watched the raging battle as the Stone Lion charged trees, crushing the cankers against ancient oaks, and the feral twisted vachine deviants retaliated with brass claws, opening holes in the Stone Lion's belly to allow molten fungus to pour free...

Wearily, drained, saddened, Kell rolled his shoulders and neck, only now realising the muscles he had strained, the joints impacted, the huge bruises and many lacerations to his skin. He felt like a pit-fighter after twelve bouts, each one knocking another chunk from his prowess, as well as his sanity. He laughed a little, then, as the roaring went on, and for a few minutes Kell had a ringside seat in the most savage battle he had ever seen.

The two remaining cankers were gradually chewing the Stone Lion to death, cutting chunks from it, attempting to get another premium hold for that final, terminal great bite. Even with half its head missing, the Stone Lion was putting up a good fight, pounding huge fists and claws into the cankers to accompanying shrieks of mis-meshed gears and the thump of compressing flesh. All the time, the wounded canker with no lungs and a broken spine paddled aimlessly in the dead leaves, making a strange mewling sound, not so much expelled air but the pathetic squeaking of a winding-down clock. Kell saw dark blood-oil pump out in a few savage spurts, and eventually the wounded canker was still.

"At least they fucking *die*," murmured Kell, eyes narrow, wary, observing the final performance.

The Stone Lion accelerated backwards, hammering a tree and finally dislodging the clinging canker. It stamped down on the canker's head, pushing it deep under the earth as the remainder of heavily muscled body flopped like a rag-doll, and it turned, searching out the final beast... which bounded to the attack, ducking low under a swipe and catching the Stone Lion in the throat with its fangs, ripping out a huge section of stone- and wood-flesh to reveal narrow tubes, like vines, within. The Stone Lion dropped to one knee, and slammed the canker with a fist, a blow that propelled it into a tree where it snapped a rear leg with a brittle loud crack that echoed through the woodland.

The Stone Lion settled slowly to the ground, forming almost a heap of what now appeared nothing more than an outcropping of stone and ancient wood. It seemed to give a huge sigh, and Kell watched the great, ancient creature die on the woodland carpet. Despite its savagery, he felt almost sad.

The canker trapped under the earth by Stone Lion finally stopped struggling, with Kell's axe poking from the rigid, corded muscles of its throat. Kell stood, walking numbly through the carnage, to place his boot on the carcass and tug free Ilanna.

He turned, staring at the final canker. It growled at him, a feral sound of hatred, and tried to stand. Instead, it fell back in pain and whimpering. Something metallic squeaked in a rhythmical manner.

Kell hefted his axe, and strode to the canker which glared. It lunged, and he dodged back, then planted his axe blade in its neck. He rocked the blade free and blood-oil spurted, along with several coils of wire. Kell hefted Ilanna again, dodged another swipe of canker claws, and with the second strike decapitated the beast.

Blood gushed for a while, then slowed to a trickle. Kell could see the gleam of parts inside the neck, but each cog and wheel was curiously formed, as if kinked, and each piston was bowed or bent, each gear buckled. Kell shook his head; he didn't understand such things. Looking around, he grasped a handful of dead leaves and started cleaning the twin axe blades.

"Old horse! Why didn't you wait for us? You've had all the fun!"

Kell glanced up, gradually, to see Saark leading his horse amidst the flesh and clockwork debris. The clearing – the creatures had smashed the trees into a clearing – appeared as a minor battlefield. Blood gleamed everywhere. The ground was littered with brass and steel clockwork mechanisms.

Kell said nothing.

"It's fine," Saark called back through the trees. "Kell's heroically battled three cankers and the Stone Lion, and managed to kill them all!"

Saark stopped before Kell, who watched Nienna and Kat appear, faces shocked by the carnage. The horses were skittish, and they tied them to a tree by the edge of the battle and moved to Kell. Nienna hugged him, and he smiled then, but his eyes never left Saark.

"I injured the Stone Lion," he said. "Then I ran. But there was no horse for me." There was a dark gleam in Kell's eye, a suggestion of violence in his stance, and Saark noticed Kell did not lower his axe.

"We left a horse for you, old boy," said Saark, voice lowering, humour evaporating. "Didn't we, girls?"

"We left your horse," said Kat, smiling uncertainly, not understanding the tension in the air.

"We did, grandfather," said Nienna, putting her hand on Kell's torn bearskin. "I saw Saark tie the creature myself. He is not to blame if it escaped."

Saark held his hands wide. "An accident, Kell. What, you think I'd leave you to die back there?"

Kell shrugged, and turned his back on the three, gazing off through the trees. His emotions raged, but he took a deep breath, calming himself.

Once, said Ilanna, in his mind, in his soul, *you would have killed him for that.*

I would have questioned him.

No. He would already be dead.

That was in the bad days! he stormed. When I was so drunk on the whisky I didn't know what I was doing. Those were evil days, Ilanna, and you used to fuel me, used to feed me, used to push me towards violence every step of the way, only so you could taste blood yourself, you depraved fucking whore!

Kell turned and faced Saark, and forced a smile. "I apologise," he said, as their eyes locked. "I mistrust too easily. There is a thing called a Fool's Knot – the slightest pressure, and it slips. But of course, you would never use such a thing on me."

Saark grinned. "Of course not, Kell! In fact, I have only now just heard of such a knot, this very moment you mentioned it. Now. We are all exhausted, the girls are frightened, hungry, in a fiery agony of chafing from riding, and I fancy I saw evidence of civilisation only a few short leagues from this very spot."

"What kind of evidence?"

"Traps. Trappers never stray too far from home. Come on, Kell! Think of it! Comfy beds, whisky, hot beef stew, and if we're lucky," he lowered his voice, leaning in close, "a couple of willing buxom wenches apiece!"

"Show me the way," said Kell, and frowned. Saark confused him; he wanted to believe the man, but his intuition told him to plant his axe in Saark's head the first chance that arose. "If it was just me and you, I'd say no. I have a feeling the albino army is moving south; chasing us, effectively. It will destroy every damn town and village it hits, raiding for supplies and destroying buildings in the army's wake so their enemies can't make use. I have seen this before."

"But think of the girls," said Saark, voice lower, playing to Kell's weakness. "Think of Nienna. Frightened half to death, chased by horrible creatures, forced to fight for her life; she told me she and Kat were captured by evil woodsmen, who proceeded to–"

"Tell me they didn't!" Kell gripped his axe tight, eyes slamming over to Nienna.

"No, no, calm down, Kell. The girls have their integrity. But it was only a matter of time; that Stone Lion you so effectively slew… " Saark peered at the dead creature, frowning, "Gods, did you cut off half its head? Anyway, that Stone Lion rescued them. The woodsmen were attacked by a canker, and the Stone Lion killed the canker. Saved their lives, but damn near frightened them to death! They need time to relax, Kell. They need normality."

"And you need an ale," said Kell, staring hard at Saark.

"I admit, I am a man of simple pleasures."

"Let's move, then."

Kell and Saark walked to where Nienna knelt, examining an intricate piece of machinery. "I don't understand," she said, looking up at the two men. "Are they just monsters? They have… this thing inside them. At school once the teacher took an old clock apart, and it looked like this, with wheels and cogs and spinning parts; only this looks… bigger, stronger, as if it would power a much larger clock."

"It powered something more dangerous than a clock," said Kell, rolling his neck with cracks of released tension.

I can tell you what it is, said Ilanna.

Go on.

It is an Insanity Engine, invented by the forefathers of Leerdek-ka and Kradek-ka, then further refined by those Engineers. We saw creatures powered by these machines under the Black Pike Mountains.

Kell's face coloured, and he ground his teeth. Never mention that, he snarled. Understand? If you ever bring up Pike Halls again, I will cast you into the river! Do you understand me, bitch?

You are still ashamed, then? Ilanna's voice, so beautiful and musical, was little more than a whisper.

Aye. I am still ashamed. Now leave me be; I have two frightened girls to attend to.

They rode in silence through the remainder of the day until evening drew close, and finally emerged from the dense woodland of Stone Lion Woods. Saark scouted ahead, checking for signs of the Army of Iron; or indeed, cankers or any other creature that might take a fancy to the small travelling party.

Kell, Nienna and Kat stood by the edge of the woods, looking out over snowy fields and hills. Saark had been right: distant, a few lights shone, lanterns lit against the fast encroaching darkness.

"I'm sorry," said Kell, at last, facing them.

"What for?" asked Kat, eyes wide.

"For leaving you, on the boat. It was foolish. I should have stayed with you. I should have known when I jumped that you'd be swept away and have to fend for yourselves. That was... foolish of me."

"But Saark would have died," said Kat.

Kell gave a little shrug. "And you two nearly died... and worse, according to Saark. Those woodsmen; I knew them. They were savage creatures indeed, and if the canker hadn't come you would still be there, singing a high sweet tune with skin hanging in strips from your backs and arses." He saw their eyes, wide and pale, and coughed, taking a deep breath. "Sorry. Listen. You stay with me from now on. You understand?"

"Saark will look after us, as well," said Kat, face round and innocent in the failing light. The moon had risen, a pale orb the colour of dead flesh, as the sun painted the low western horizon a dazzling violet.

"Be careful with Saark," warned Kell.

"Don't you trust him?" asked Nienna, surprised.

"I do not know the man," said Kell, simply. "He joined us in the tannery; aye, I saved his life, but that was just me being... human. Instinct. I curse it!" He gave a bitter laugh. "They write poems about you for less, so it would seem."

"He is totally trustworthy," said Kat, nodding to herself, eyes distant. "I know it. In my heart."

"In your heart, lass?" Kell smiled a knowing smile. "I've seen the way he looks at you. And you have, too. But I warn you; don't trust Saark, and especially not like that. He has enjoyed a hundred women before you, and he'll have a hundred women after."

Kat flushed red. "I am waiting for the right man to marry! I am not... for sale, Kell. Saark can look all he wants, I know his ilk, and I know what I want in a man. Yes, Saark is handsome; never have I seen such hair on a man! And he has the gift of the silver tongue, in more ways than one, I'd wager..." Nienna giggled, "but I am proud of my virtue. I know a good man is out there, waiting for me. I do not need your... fatherhood." She narrowed her eyes. "I can look after myself."

"As you wish," said Kell curtly, returning his sweeping gaze to the snowy fields. "But know this. Saark is not a man of honour. He will come for your flesh."

"A man of honour? And I suppose you are as well–"

"What's that supposed to mean?" snapped Nienna, glaring at Kat. "That's my grandpa you're speaking to. The hero of Kell's Legend! Don't you know your contemporary history? Your battle-lore? He saved the battle at Crake's Wall, turned the tide of savages in the Southern Jungles!" Anger flushed her cheeks red. Her fists were clenched.

Kat looked sideways at Kell, who continued to stare across the fields. "It's fine, Nienna," he said, voice little more than a whisper. Then, to Kat, "You're talking about back at the tannery, aren't you lass?"

Kat nodded.

Kell continued, "Yes. I was brutal, brutal and merciless towards you, and I shocked you into movement, into action! If you'd lingered on your injuries, on your fear, you could have killed us all. I could not allow you, even as a friend of Nienna, to be responsible for her death. I would not allow it!" He turned, stared at his granddaughter with a mix of love, regret, and nostalgia. He smiled then. "I would cross the world for you, my little monkey. I would fight an army for you. I would kill an entire city for you. Nobody will get close to you again, this I swear, by the blood-oil of Ilanna."

Nienna moved forward, took his hand, snuggled in close to him. "You don't have to do all that, grandfather." Her voice was small, a child again, nestling against the only father figure she had ever known.

"But I would," he growled. "No canker will get close. I'll cut out the bastard's throat."

"Saark's coming."

They watched him approach, walking his horse with care over snowy undulations. He was smiling, which was a good sign; at least the Army of Iron hadn't rolled through destroying everything in its path. For a long, hopeful moment Kell prayed he was mistaken, prayed to any gods that would listen that he was wrong; but a sourness overtook his soul, and he fell into a bitter brooding.

"There's an inn, with rooms. I've booked us three." He glanced at Kell. "Wouldn't like to put up with your snoring again, old horse. No offence meant."

"None taken; I am equally horrified by the stench of your feet."

"My feet! I am aghast with horror! Oh the ignominy! And to think, we risked mutilation and death to come back for you with a horse. Old boy, we should have left you to eat fried canker steaks for the next week; maybe then you would have learnt manners."

Kell pushed past Saark, leading his own horse. "That's an impossibility, lad. A man like me... well, I'm too honest. A farmer. A peasant. Manners are the reserve of gentry; those with money, those born with silver on their tongue..." Saark smiled, inclining his head to the compliment, "... and equally those with a brush up their arse, shit in their brains, a decadent stench of bad perfume on their crotch, and a sister who's really their cousin, their mother and their daughter all rolled into one. Inbreeding?" He growled a laugh. "I blame it on the parents."

He stalked off, down the hill, and Saark turned to the young women. "Who rattled his chain and collar?"

"He rattled it himself," said Nienna, stepping forward, touching Saark's arm. "Don't be too offended; back in Jalder, he made few friends."

"How many friends?"

"None," admitted Nienna, and laughed. "But he was a wonderful cook!"

"So wonderful he poisoned them all?"

"You are full of charm," said Nienna, breathing a sigh as Saark took her arm. They started down the hill, leaving Kat with two horses, and she scowled after them, eyes narrowing, watching the sway of Saark's noble swagger as he walked, one hand on his hip. He was going home; or at least, to a place of modest civility.

"We'll see who's full of charm," she muttered.

• • • •

Darkness had fallen as they entered the outskirts of the town, which Saark identified as Jajor Falls. Six cobbled roads ran out from a central square which acted as a hub and market, and there was an ornate stone bridge containing six small gargoyles over a narrow, churning, river. A fresh fall of snow began, as if heralding the travellers' arrival, and they walked tired horses up the snow-laden street, hoof-strikes muffled, looking left and right in the darkness. Some houses showed lantern light in windows; but most were black.

"A sombre place," remarked Kell.

"The inn's livelier."

"What's it called?"

"The Slaughtered Piglet."

"You have to be joking?"

"Apparently, there is a long archaic story of magick and mayhem behind the title. They'll tell us over a tankard of ale." He winked. "You have to admire these peasant types; they tell it like it is."

"Sounds grand."

They heard music before they saw the inn; it came into view, a long, low, black-stone building. Smoke pumped from a stubby chimney, and light showed from behind slatted shutters. Kell led the horses to stables behind the inn, handing them over to a skinny old man who introduced himself as Tom the Ostler. He wore nothing but a thin shirt against the snow, and his limbs were narrow, wiry, his biceps like buds on a branch. He grinned at Kell in a friendly manner, taking the horses, stroking muzzles, staring into eyes, blowing into nostrils. "Come with me, my beauties," he said, and Kell could sense the old man's love for the beasts.

Kell strode back to the inn's door, entered slowly, eyes scanning the busy main room. Tables were crammed in, and full, mainly, of men drinking tankards of ale and talking Falanor politics. A few women sat around the outskirts of the main room, mostly in groups, talking and laughing. Some wore bright dresses, but most wore thick woollen market skirts. Smoke filled the inn, and a general hubbub of noise made Kell gradually relax. Sometimes, it was nice to be anonymous amidst strangers. He looped a long leather thong through the haft of his axe, then over his shoulder, drawing the weapon to his back. Then, he strode to the bar, searching for Saark, Nienna and Kat.

The barman waved at Kell. "What'll it be, squire?" he asked.

"My friend's booked three rooms for the night."

"Ach yes, I just gave him the keys. Up the stairs," he pointed, "rooms twelve, thirteen and fourteen."

Kell grunted thanks, strode up the stairs, and turned on the landing to survey the common room. He made out the gambling table in the corner. Near it were three women, dressed in high stockings, their lips rouged with ink, feathers in their hair. Whores. Kell grunted, eyes narrowing, thinking of Saark and his eagerness. He moved into a smoke-filled corridor and searched for the rooms. Floorboards squeaked under his boots, and this was good. It would be hard to creep down such a passageway.

Locating the first room, he tapped. "Grandfather?" came Nienna's voice, and Kell pushed open the portal, stepping inside, scanning the sparse furnished space. There was a large bed, with ancient carved headboard depicting a raging battle. Thick rugs covered dusty boards, and drawers and two stools lined the far wall. The windows were shuttered. A lantern burned on a table with honey light.

"Cosy," he said, setting down a pack he'd taken from the albino soldier's horse. Then he removed his axe, and stretched broad shoulders. "I hope there's a bath in this place, because I stink, and I hate it when I stink."

"You look like you've had a beating," said Nienna, moving over to him. "I could ask the landlord for some cold cream, to take down the swellings." She reached out, tenderly touched his bruised cheek.

Kell cursed.

"Does it hurt?" said Nienna, concern in her eyes.

"No. It's just people remember a beaten face. I stand out. That's not good."

Nienna nodded. "Shall I go and see if the bathing room is free?"

Kell looked around, then. He frowned. "Where's Kat?"

Nienna shrugged. "I don't know."

Kell moved back to the corridor, walked to the next door with a surprisingly light step, and opened it. Both Saark and Kat were sat on the bed, side by side, just a little bit too close. Kat's laughter tinkled like falling crystals.

Saark looked around, up into Kell's face, and the smile dropped from his features.

"Saark. A word, if you please."

Saark coughed, stood up; Kell saw he had removed his boots. He stepped out. "There a problem, old horse?"

Kell reached past, closed the door, smiling at Kat, then grabbed Saark by the throat and rammed him up against the wall with a thud. Saark's feet kicked for a moment, and Kell lowered him until their faces were inches apart.

"She's not to be touched," growled Kell.

"I don't know what you mean!"

"The girl, Saark. Kat. And my granddaughter, as well, whilst we're having this little man-to-man discussion. Both are not to be... *molested* by you. Do you understand, boy?"

"They're grown women, Kell. They are intelligent, and intuitive. They make their own choices." Saark's smile was stiff.

"And I'm a grown man, telling another grown man that they're little more than children, and if you touch them, I'll break every fucking bone in your spine." His voice was low, but deadly, deathly serious. Saark met his stare with a neutral expression.

"You need to open your eyes, old man. They're far from children. They are roses, blossoming into beauty. They are river currents, flowing out to sea."

Kell snorted, and dropped Saark to the floorboards. "Save your pretty words for the whores downstairs," said Kell. "There was enough good coin in the soldiers' saddlebags to entertain you for a week; take it. But I warn you. Keep away from the girls."

Saark nodded, and brushed down his roughed clothing. He coughed. Stared at Kell, tilting his head. "You finished now, Grandfather? Can I go and get some ale, and a bite to eat? Or would you like to offer a sermon on further corruption and impurity in the world?"

Kell nodded, and Saark moved back to the room. Kell stood, waiting, and Kat emerged, eyes lowered, and hurried into Nienna's room. Kell followed her, retrieving his pack and axe. "I'll meet you down in the common room for food, in about twenty minutes. Aye?"

"Yes, Grandfather," said Nienna. Kat said nothing.

Kell grunted and left.

"How dare he!" raged Kat, a few moments later.

"Shh, he might hear!"

"Damn him, damn him to hell, I don't care! I don't need his

protection! I don't need him treating me like his granddaughter, because I'm not, and I've looked after myself far too long to begin adopting an over-zealous guardian now!"

"He… only means well," said Nienna.

"Rubbish! He's jealous! He sees my young limbs, my hips, my ripe breasts, and he wishes he could have a slice of my rich fruit pie. Well, he can't."

Nienna stared at Kat, then. She shook her head. "That's horse-shit, Katrina."

"Maybe so. But Saark says I'm beautiful, and I could take my pick of Jevaiden, Salakarr, Yuill or Anvaresh; and I could make money, lots of money, with my beauty."

"By doing what?"

"I could be a dancer, or escort rich men to the theatre. Saark said they pay a lot of good money to have a beautiful young woman on their arm."

"And in their bed," snapped Nienna. "Are you really that fool-ish? You'd be little more than a whore!"

"Maybe that's what I want!" stormed Kat, her temper escalat-ing, her fists clenching. "At least it'd be my choice!"

At that moment Saark entered, and stood, smiling at the two women. He was transformed. He wore a fine silk shirt of yellow, with ruffled collar and cuffs of white cotton; he wore rich green trousers made from panels of velvet, high black leather boots, and his long curled hair had been oiled and was scraped back into a loose ponytail. He looked every inch the ravishing dandy, the court noble fop, the friend of royalty. He smiled, and a rich per-fume invaded the room, a musky scent of flowers and herbs.

Kat whirled, and her temper died. She smiled at Saark. "You look… ravishing!" she said.

"Where did you get the clothes?" asked Nienna.

"I bought them. From a clothes merchant. I make contacts fast, especially when I enter a new town looking like a diseased cesspit cleaner."

"Kell said for us to keep a low profile."

Saark grinned. "This *is* me keeping a low profile."

"But," said Nienna, choosing her words tactfully, "you look ex-tremely, um, wealthy. And the smell! What is that smell?"

"The perfume of gentry," said Saark. "Popinjay's Musk. It's ex-pensive. Well, ladies, I'm waiting to eat."

"We need to change," said Nienna. "Or at least, to beat the dust from our clothes."

"Wait there," said Saark.

He disappeared, with Nienna and Kat frowning at one another. When he returned, he carried two dresses, one of yellow, one of blue. Both were silk, richly embroidered, and Nienna and Kat clasped their hands together in wonder.

"Saark!" said Nienna. "I don't believe it!"

"They're beautiful," beamed Kat, walking around Saark, her hand reaching out, almost timidly, to touch the silk.

"Only the finest clothes, for such beauty," he said, grinning, his eyes shining, lips moist.

"But we can't wear them," said Nienna, suddenly, smile dropping, lip coming out a little. "Kell wouldn't approve."

"To hell with the old goat. You've been to the Pits of Daragan and back; you deserve a little pampering. I surely couldn't let you go downstairs to eat wearing those tattered rags. It would be... indecent!"

"Thank you, thank you," said Kat, eyes shining.

"Get dressed. I'll meet you down there."

"Did you get anything for Kell?"

"No. If he wishes to look like a beggar in a sack, so be it. He wishes to blend in? Let the old sourpuss blend in. I'm going to have a fine time. We nearly died back there, in Jalder, and on the journey. And I may be dead tomorrow. But tonight! Tonight, ladies, we dance!"

Kat giggled, and Nienna swirled, holding the dress to herself. Saark turned to leave, then whirled about suddenly. He peered out, down the corridor, checking Kell wasn't about to inflict damage on his body again. Then he pulled a vial from his cuff, and handed it to Kat.

"What is it?"

"Perfume. To make you smell as good as you look."

Kat uncorked the vial, and sniffed, and her eyes widened. "But," she said, shrugging, "where do I put it? I've never had perfume before. Old Gran used to say it was the trademark of the whore."

"Pah! Sour words uttered by every damn woman who couldn't afford it. It's called Flowers of Winter Sunset. I once knew a queen who wore it... so trust me, it's special."

"It must have cost a fortune," said Nienna, eyes narrowing. "Or you're full of horse-dung."

"No, it cost a pretty penny," said Saark. "Let's just say the horse I took from the soldier had enough gold coin to sink one of Leanoric's Titan Battleships. So, I cannot take full credit. But enjoy, ladies! Enjoy! I will go and see what paltry food is served on these premises." He stepped forward, took the vial from Kat, tipped the vial to the cork, then dabbed some behind her ears. "Here, princess," he said, smiling into her face. He repeated the action, reached forward, and drew a vertical line down her breastbone, to the dip in her cleavage. "And here," he said, eyes locked to hers. She took the vial from him, then he was gone with a swirl of oiled hair, his rapier flat by his side.

Kat turned to Nienna. Her face was flushed.

"Kell is going to be pissed," said Nienna.

"Saark was right. We've been through *hell* the past couple of days. We deserve a good time."

Nienna shrugged, and sighed. Then she nodded. "Yes," she agreed, and took the perfume bottle from Kat. Mimicking Saark, she dabbed it between her breasts, "And let's put lots here, *you sexy little vixen.*"

Both girls erupted into laughter at her mimicry, and felt tension lift from their shoulders. It was good to laugh. It was good to joke. And for a few hours, at least, ever since the invasion of Jalder, it was good to relax in a safe and secure environment.

Saark caused a stir as he entered the main room, mainly because of his dress, but then because in a loud bellow he announced a round of free drinks for everyone in the room. A cheer went up, and Saark found himself a corner table, the oak planks warped with age. Around the walls were a variety of stuffed creatures, from weasels and foxes to a particularly annoyed looking polecat. Saark sat, sinking a long draught of snow-chilled ale, and allowing his mind to ease.

The second stir occurred when Nienna and Kat entered, in their fine silk dresses, and drew the attention of every man and woman in the room. They moved to Saark, seated themselves, and Saark ordered them each a small glass of port from a bustling server.

"Kell doesn't let me drink," said Nienna, as the server returned holding two glasses. Saark shrugged.

"Well, you're old enough to do what you like."

"What do you think of the dresses?" asked Kat.

Saark gave her a broad smile. "I was stunned upon your entry to the premises; for it was as if two angels, holidaying from the gods, had stowed their wings and glided through gilded windows of pure crystal. The room was diffused with light and effervescence, my nostrils incarcerated by perfume – not just the ravishing scent of wild flowers under moonlight, but the sweet and heady aroma of gorgeous ladies acquiring a friend. You stunned me, ladies. Truly, you stunned me."

Kat was left speechless, whilst Nienna tilted her head, searching Saark's face for traces of mockery. He met her stare with an honest smile, and she realised then he had switched, reverted to a former self, like an actor on the stage. Here, he was at home; revelling in his natural environment. He was a chameleon, he shifted depending on his surroundings. Now he was playing Lord of the Clan, and preening with a perceivable, educated superiority.

Kat laughed out loud, and placed her hand on Saark's knee, leaning forward to say, "You have a beautiful way with words, sir."

"And you have the face of an angel," he replied, voice a little husky.

Kell entered, stalking down the stairs at the far end of the room, and Kat hurriedly removed her hand. Kell eased through the crowded common room, searching, and only spied the group when Saark waved his arm high in the air. Kell strode to them and stood, hands on hips, face full of raw thunder.

"What's this?" he growled.

"A table," said Saark, feigning surprise. "I'm agog with amazement that you failed to recognise such a basic appliance of carpentry."

"The clothes," he raged, "you brightly coloured horse-cock! What do you think you're doing?"

"You would rather the ladies dressed in rags? Showed tits and arses through threadbare holes for every punter to see?"

"No, but... something less... *colourful* would have been appropriate." He lowered his voice, eyes narrowing. "Couldn't you have bought some cotton shirts and trews? We'll be travelling in the snow later; what good are silk dresses then?"

"I have purchased a few normal items, and fur-lined cloaks, Kell, even for you; although I'll wager you'll be as grateful as a rutting dog after a savage castration. Listen, these were all the merchant had. What was I supposed to do? Let them come here with knife rips in their shirts? For I know what would have been the more suspicious."

"Hmph," muttered Kell, slumping to a stool.

Saark turned, and winked at the girls. Kat covered her mouth, and giggled. "Anyway," said Saark, twirling his wrists to allow puffed cotton to flower. "Don't you like my noble attire, good sir? I find it serves when attracting the attention of sophisticated ladies."

"Saark, you're a buffoon, a clown, a macaroni and a peacock! I thought we were travelling to King Leanoric carrying urgent news? Instead, you strut about like a dog with three dicks."

"We are," snapped Saark, "but we can at least have a little fun along the way! Life is shit, Kell, and you have to grasp every moment, every jewel. You go out back and eat with the pigs from their slop-trough if you like; me and the ladies, we are going to dine on meat and sup fine wines."

"No drink," said Kell.

"Why not?"

"We may have to leave fast."

"Bah! You are a killjoy, a grump and a… a damn killjoy! We will drink, the ladies are my guests, and if you have any sense, man, you'll at least have an ale. You look like a horse danced on your face. Admittedly, it improves your savage and ugly looks, but it must hurt a little, surely? A whisky would do no harm, against the pain of injury and winter chill."

"An ale, then," conceded Kell.

The server arrived, a young woman, slightly overlarge and with rosy cheeks. Saark ordered the finest food on the menu – gammon, with eggs and garnished potatoes. He also ordered a flagon of wine, and two whiskies.

Kell muttered something unheard.

They talked, and Kell surveyed the room. They had attracted a certain amount of attention with their fancy clothes, and the act of Saark buying the inn's population a drink. He was showing he had perhaps a little too much money; they were certainly marked as strangers to the Falls.

Little happened before the food arrived. When plates were delivered, Saark expressed his delight and tucked in heartily, knife and fork cutting and rising like a man possessed. The girls ate more sparingly, as befitted their new image as ladies, and Kell sat, picking like a buzzard worrying a corpse, despite his hunger, one eye on the crowd and the door, wondering uneasily at the back of his mind if the albino army was marching south. And if they were, how far had they traversed across the Great Nòrth Road? Did Leanoric know of the invasion of Falanor? Did he have intelligence as to the taking of Jalder? Surely he must know... but only if somebody had escaped the massacre, and managed to get word to him.

Uneasily, Kell ate his eggs and gammon, allowing juices from the meat to run down his throat. Kell always ate slowly, always savoured his food; there had been times in his life when he could not afford such luxuries. Indeed, times in his life when there was no food to be had, camping in high caves in windy passes, the snow building outside, no way of making a fire, no food in his pack... but worst of all, there had been times far too miserable and brutal to recollect, times

running through dark streets, the only light from fires consuming buildings as citizens cowered indoors screaming flames consuming flesh hot fat running over stone steps and into gutters; charging through streets, blood smeared flesh gleaming in the light of the burning city, axe in hands and blades covered in gore and glory in his mind violence in his soul and dancing along a blade of madness as the Days of Blood consumed him...

Kell snapped out of it. Saark was looking at him. Nienna and Kat were looking at him. He frowned. "What?"

"I said," repeated Saark, rolling his eyes, "are you going to drink that whisky, or stare at it all night?"

Remembering his vision, Kell took the whisky. It was amber, a good half tumbler full – these tiny outpost villages always provided generous measures – and he could see his face distorted in the reflection. He knocked it back in one, then closed his eyes, as if savouring the moment; in reality, he was dreading the moment, for he knew deep down in his heart and deep down in his soul that when the whisky took him, consumed him, he could and would become a very, very bad man...

But not any more, right? He grinned weakly. Those days were dead and gone. Buried, like the burned corpses, the mutilated women, the hacked up pigs...

"Order another," he said, slapping the glass on the oak planks.

"That's my boy!" cheered Saark. He eyed Kell's plate. "Are you going to eat those potatoes?"

"No. Suddenly, I don't feel hungry." He wanted to add, the minute I begin drinking I cannot eat, for all that I want is more whisky. But he did not. Saark reached over and speared a potato, gobbling it down.

"Can't be wasting good food," he said, grinning through mash. "There's village idiots in Falanor starving!"

"You've eaten enough to feed a platoon," said Kell.

Saark pouted. "I'm a growing lad! Need to keep up my strength for tonight, right?"

"Why?" said Kell, as his second whisky arrived. "What's happening tonight?"

"Oh, you know," said Saark, stealing a second unwanted potato. "I feel like a hermit, locked up for a whole month! It's been days since I had a good time. I'm a hedonist at heart, you realise."

"What's a hedonist?" asked Kat.

"A skunk's arsehole," said Kell.

"Funny," snapped Saark, raising his glass. "Here's to getting out of Jalder alive."

Kell lowered his glass. "I don't need to toast that. It's the past. What we should think about is the future."

"No problem," grinned Saark. "Well, let's toast these fine young ravishing women beside us. They are the future!"

Warily, Kell toasted, and Nienna and Kat drank their own glasses of port. Nienna, who had never before experienced alcohol, felt her senses spin. The room was a pond of swimming colours, and warbled sounds and fluctuating smells. Suddenly, her belly flipped, felt queasy, but she fought the sensation for her mind was filled with liquid honey, and Saark was looking surprisingly handsome, now she really thought about it, he was tall and dashing, witty and charming, and when his eyes fell on Nienna she felt her heartbeat quicken and her legs go weak at the knees. She glanced over at Kat, but Kat's topaz eyes were fixed on Saark.

One of the innkeeper's daughters arrived. "You ordered hot water for a bath, sir?" she enquired.

Kell nodded, and stood, feeling the whisky bite him. Damn, he thought. I should never have drunk it so fast! But then, two little whiskies couldn't hurt him, could they? He was a big man, an experienced man, and Saark – damn his fancy ways – was right. It was a miracle they were alive. They deserved at least some normality...

He nodded to Saark. "I need this bath. Don't get in any trouble when I'm away."

"You're right, you do need the bath," agreed Saark. "And don't worry about a thing. I'll look after the ladies. We were considering dessert; some kind of sugared sponge cake, covered in cream. How about it, ladies?"

Kat nodded, licking lips in anticipation. It was rare she got such a treat.

Kell followed the innkeeper's daughter across the crowded room, aware that eyes were on him, curious but somehow... disconcerting. He hated being any centre of attention; the gods only knew, it had happened enough in his life. Usually during combat.

Halting by the stairs, he called the girl back, and checking to see Saark and Nienna weren't watching, told her to bring a bottle of whisky to the bathing room.

"We don't usually..." began the woman.

"I'll pay you double."

"I'm sure it can be arranged, sir," she said, and Kell was gone, stomping up the steps, days of sweat and blood itching him now that a promise of hot water and soap were reality.

After their cake, Saark reclined, patting his belly. "By the gods, I think I've put on a few pounds there."

"Me too," laughed Kat.

"Does port always make you feel like this?" said Nienna.

Saark nodded, and grinned. "How does it feel?"

"I feel like the room is moving. Spinning!"

Saark shrugged. "You'll get used to it. Listen, I have a fancy to go out back to the stables, to check on the horses. Will you two young ladies be fine by yourselves? Feel free to order anything you like to eat or drink."

"We'll be fine," said Nienna, waving her hand.

Saark stood, checked his sword, and left the inn. Nienna missed the meaningful look between him and Kat, and so a minute later, when Kat whispered, "I need to pee, I'm going to the ladies room,"

Nienna simple smiled, and nodded, and reclined in her own little world of honey and swirling sweet thoughts.

Kat stepped into the snow, but felt no chill. Excitement was fire in her blood, raging in her mind, and she crept around the outer wall of the inn, hearing the noise and banter inside as a muffled backdrop, a blur of sounds rolling into one strange, ululating whole.

She reached the corner, which led to a short opening and the stable-square beyond. She could see nothing.

"Saark?" she whispered. Then louder, "Saark!"

"Yes, princess?" He was behind her, close, and she felt his breath on her neck and a quiver of raw energy rampaged through her veins. She did not turn, instead standing stock still, now she was here, out in the darkness with this beautiful man, and suddenly unsure of what to do.

"I thought you really had gone to see to the horses," she said.

"Maybe I did," he said, and kissed her neck, a gentle tease of lips and tongue, leaving a trail which chilled to ice in the cold air.

Kat shivered. A thrill ran down her spine.

"Did that tickle?"

"It was wonderful."

"Shall I do it again?"

Kat turned, looked up into his eyes. They were wide and pretty and trustworthy. They shone with love. They shone with understanding. She felt her heart melt; again. "Do you really think I'm beautiful?'

"More beautiful than the stars, princess, more beautiful than a snowflake, or a newborn babe." He reached forward, until his lips were a whisper from her own. She felt his hands come to rest lightly on her hips, and again a thrill raged through her, pulsing like energy with every beat of her heart. Her head spun, and she wanted him, wanted him so badly she would risk anything to be with Saark right now, here, in this cold place of snow and ice...

He kissed her.

He was gentle, teasing, his tongue darting into her mouth and she grasped his head in eagerness and pressed her face into his, kissing him with passion, kissing him with a raw ferocity; his arms encircled her waist and she felt his hardness press against the front of her silk dress and it thrilled her like nothing in the world had ever thrilled her before...

He pulled away.

"Don't stop," she panted.

"You're an eager little fox," he said.

"Kiss me," she said. "Kiss me everywhere! Touch me everywhere! *Please*..."

"Oh, my princess," whispered Saark, eyes glinting in the darkness, "believe me, I will."

Kell sank into hot water. It slammed him with a violence he welcomed. He poured a huge glass of whisky, balanced it on the rim of the old, ceramic bath, and allowed the oils in the water to fill his senses with pleasure.

You cannot drink it, said Ilanna.

Go fuck yourself, mused Kell, and sloshed in the bathwater. I'll do what I damn well please. You're not my mother!

You cannot return there!

I can return to whatever piss-hole I like. I am Kell. They wrote poems about me, you know? You were in them as well, but I was the hero, I was the legend. Kell's Legend they called it – sour crock of deformed and lying shit it really was.

Please don't drink it, Kell.

Why do you care? Because I won't perform? Because I won't kill as efficiently for you? To supply your blood fantasy? Your blood-oil craving?

You misunderstand.

What are you? My gran? Kell was mocking, his laughter slurred. He took the whisky. He drank the large glass in one, felt it swim through him like tiny fishes in vinegar. His mind reeled and he welcomed the feeling; glorified in the abandon.

It had been a long time.

Too long.

Nienna is feeling ill, said Ilanna, playing to the one emotional fulcrum she knew.

Kell cursed, and stood, water and oils dripping from his old, scarred, but mightily impressive frame. Most men grew stringy as they aged, their muscles becoming stretched out, their strength gradually diminishing. Not so Kell. Yes, his joints ached, yes arthritis troubled him, but he knew he was as strong as when he was twenty. Strength was something which had never failed him; he was proud of his prodigy.

Damn you. You lie!

I do not.

What's going on?

Three men are talking to her. They can see she is drunk on the port Saark bought. They seek to bed her, in sobriety, or not.

Kell surged from the bath, knocking the bottle of whisky over. It glugged amber heaven to the rugs and Kell ignored it. He wrenched on his trews, boots and shirt, grasped his axe, and stormed out and down the stairs.

Ilanna had been right. The inn was even more crowded, now, noisier, rowdier, no longer a place for a genial meal; now this was a pit in which to drink, get drunk, and flirt with whores.

Nienna sat, back to the wall, face a little slack. Three men sat around her in a semi-circle; even as Kell strode down the stairs one pushed a glass to Nienna, feeding her drunken state, and she giggled, throwing back the liquor as she swayed. The men were young, late twenties, in rough labourers clothing and with shadows of stubble.

Kell stopped behind them, and placed his hands on hips. Nienna could barely focus.

"Grappa?" she said, and grinned.

The three men turned.

"I suggest," said Kell, face dark like an approaching storm, "you move away. I wouldn't like to cause a nasty scene in the inn where I sleep; it often increases my lodging bill. And if there's one thing I don't like, it's an extortionate bill for broken furniture."

"Fuck off, grandad, this girl's up for some fun," laughed one young man , turning back to Nienna, and thrusting another drink at her. This meant he'd turned his back on Kell. Later, he would realise his mistake.

Kell's fist struck him on the top of the head so hard his stool broke, and as he keeled over and his head bounced from floorboards, it left a dent. He did not move. Kell glared at the other two men, who half stood, hands on knives.

Kell drew Ilanna, and glared at them. "I dare you," he said, voice little more than a whisper. Both men released knives, and Kell grinned. "I'd like to say this wouldn't hurt. But I'd be lying." He slammed a straight right, which broke the second man's nose, dropping him with a crash, and a powerful left hook broke the third man's cheekbone, rendering him unconscious. It took less than a second.

The innkeeper stepped in, holding a helve, but took one look at Kell and lowered the weapon. "We don't want no trouble," he said.

"I intend to give none. You should allow a better class of scum into your establishment," he said, and gave a sickly smile. "However, I am a fair man, who has not yet lost his temper. Get your daughters to escort my granddaughter to her room, and tend her a while, and I won't seek compensation."

"What do you mean?" asked the innkeeper, touched by fear.

"My name is Kell," he said, eyes glowering coals, "and I kill those who stand in my way. I'm going outside for fresh air. To cool off. To calm down. When I return, I expect these three piglets to have vanished."

At the name, the innkeeper had paled even more. There were few who had not heard of Kell; or indeed, the bad things he had done.

"Whatever you say, sir," muttered the innkeeper.

Still furious, more with himself than anybody else, and especially at invoking the vile magick of his own name, Kell strode to the door and out, away from the smoke and noise now rumbling back into existence after the fight. He took several deep lungfuls, and cursed the whisky and cursed the snow and cursed Saark… why hadn't the damn dandy kept an eye on Nienna as he'd promised? And where was Kat?

"The useless, feckless bastard."

Kell glanced up and down the street, then moved to the corner of the inn. Snow fell thickly, muffling the world. Kell stepped towards the stables and thought he heard a soft moan, little more than a whisper, but carrying vaguely across the quiet stillness and reminding him of one thing, and one thing only…

Sex.

With rising fury and a clinical intuition, Kell stomped through the snow towards the nearest stall. He stopped. Saark was lying back on a pile of hay, fully clothed, his face in rapture. Kat stood, naked before him, stepping from her dress even as he watched. Kell was treated to a full view of her powerful, round buttocks.

"You fucking scum," snarled Kell, and slapped open the stable door.

"Wait!" said Saark.

Kell lurched forward, kicking Saark in the head, stunning the man who fell back to the hay. He turned to Kat, face sour. "Get your clothes on, bitch. You'll be having no fun tonight."

"Oh yes? Why? Haven't you a hard enough cock yourself?"

Kell raised his hand to strike her, then stared hard, glancing at his huge splayed fingers; like the claws of a rabid bear. He lowered his hand, instead grabbing Saark by the collar and dragging him through the hay, back out onto the street and throwing him down.

"What did I tell you?" he snarled, and kicked Saark in the ribs. Saark rolled through the snow, grunting, to lie still, staring at snowfall. He gave a deep, wracking cough.

"Wait," Saark managed, lifting his hand.

Kell strode forward, rage rushing through him, an uncontrollable drug. Deep down, he knew it was fuelled by whisky. Whisky was the product of the devil, and it made him behave in savage, evil ways, ways he could not control...

"You would abuse a young, innocent girl?" he screamed, and swung a boot at Saark's face. Saark rolled, catching Kell's leg and twisting it; Kell stumbled back, and Saark crawled to his feet, still stunned by the blows, his face twisted as he spat out blood.

"Kell, what are you doing?" he shouted.

"You went too far," raged Kell, squaring up to Saark. "I'm going to give you a thrashing you'll never forget."

"Don't be ridiculous, old man."

"Don't call me *old man*!" Kell charged, and Saark side-stepped but a whirring fist cracked the side of his head. He spun, and returned two punches which Kell blocked easily, as if fending off a child. Kell charged again, and the men clashed violently, punches hammering at one another in a blur of pounding. They staggered apart, both with bloodied faces, and every atom of Saark's good humour disintegrated.

"This is crazy," he yelled, dabbing at his broken lips. "She's eighteen years old! She knows what she wants!"

"No. She knows what you tell her! You're a womaniser and a cur, and I swear I'm going to beat it out of you."

They clashed again, and Kell clubbed a right hook to Saark's head, stunning him. Saark ducked a second blow, smashed a straight to Kell's jaw, a second to his nose, a hook to his temple, and a straight to his chin. Kell took a step back, eyes narrowed, and Saark realised a lesser man would have fallen. In fact, a great man would have been out in the mud. Saark may have come across as an effeminate dandy, with a poison tongue and love of female sport and hedonism, but once, long ago, he had been a warrior; he knew he could punch harder than most men. Kell should have gone down. Kell should have been out.

Kell coughed, spat on the snow with a splatter of blood, and lifted his fists, eyes raging. "Come on, you dandy bastard. Is that all you've got?" He grinned, and Saark suddenly realised Kell was playing with him. He had allowed Saark the advantage. But Kell's face turned dark. "Let's see what you're fucking made of," he said.

Saark started to retreat, his head pounding, his face numb from the blows, but Kell charged, was on him and he ducked a punch, spun away from a second, leapt back from a third. He held out his hands. "I apologise!" he said, eyes pleading.

"Too late," growled Kell, and slammed a hook that twisted Saark into the air, spinning him up and over, to land with a grunt on the snow, tangled. He coughed, and decided it was wise to stay down for a few moments.

"Get up," said Kell.

"I'm fine just here," said Saark.

"Grandfather!" Nienna was standing in the inn's doorway, sobered by the spectacle, and surrounded by others from the inn who jostled to watch. She ran down the steps, silk shoes flapping, and placed herself before the fallen Saark and the enraged figure of Kell.

"What are you doing?" she shrieked.

"He was trying to rape Kat," said Kell, eyes refusing to meet his granddaughter's.

"I was doing no such thing," snapped Saark, crawling to his knees, then climbing to his feet. "She needed no persuasion, Kell, you old fool. Have you no eyes in your head? She was lusting after me, even back in the tannery. You just can't stand the thought of a young woman desiring a man like me…"

Kell growled something, not words, just primal sounds of anger, and a continually rising rage, and Nienna stepped forward, slapping both hands against his chest. "No!" she yelled, voice strong, eyes boring into her grandfather. "I said NO!"

Viciously, Kell grabbed Nienna and threw her to one side. She stumbled, went down in the snow with a gasp, then rolled over to stare in disbelief at the man she had known for seventeen years, from babe to womanhood, a man she irrefutably knew would never lay a hand on her, would never pluck a hair from her head.

"That's it!" laughed Saark, voice rising a little as he saw the inevitability of battle, of destruction, of death rising towards him like a tidal wave. "Take it out on a young girl, go on Kell, what a fucking man you are." His voice rose in volume, tinged by panic. "Is this really the hero of Jangir Field? Is this truly the mighty warrior who battled Dake the Axeman, for two days and two nights and took his decapitated head back to the king? Go on Kell, why don't you just kick the girl whilst she's on the ground... after all, you wouldn't like her to fight back now, would you, bloody coward? You're a fucking lie, old man... the Black Axeman of Drennach?" Saark laughed, blood drooling down his chin as Kell stopped, and unloosed his axe from his back. The old man's eyes were hard, harder than granite Saark realised as a terrifying certainty flooded his heart. "I spit on you! I bet you cowered in the cellars during the Siege of Drennach, listened to the War Lions raging above tearing men limb from limb... whilst the real men did the fighting."

Kell lifted his axe. His face was terror. His eyes black holes. His visage the bleakness of corpse-strewn battlefields. He was no longer an aged, retired warrior with arthritis. He was Kell. The Legend.

"Go on," snarled Saark, hatred fuelling him now, spittle riming his lips, "do it, kill me, end my fucking suffering, you think I don't hate myself a thousand times more than you ever could? Go on, bastard... kill me, you spineless gutless cowering heap of horse-cock."

"No!" screamed Nienna.

"You speak too much," said Kell, his voice terribly, dangerously low. "Here, let me help you." He hefted Ilanna, huge muscles bunching, and only then did Saark glimpse, from the corner of his eye, a tendril of white mist drifting across the street. His head twitched, turned, and he watched ice-smoke pour from a narrow alleyway, to be joined by another from a different alley, and yet another from a third... like questing tendrils, wavering tentacles of some great, solidifying mist-monster...

"The albino soldiers!" hissed Nienna, eyes wide as Kat skidded around the corner, face flustered, dress hitched up in her hands.

"They're here! Kell, they're *here!*"

Kell lifted Ilanna, face impassive. His body flexed, and twisted, and the mighty axe sang as she slammed in a glittering arc towards Saark's head.

ELEVEN
A Secret Rage

Anu revelled in the cold air gusting from mountain passes as Vashell led her on her chain through the town. As they walked down metal cobbles towards the Engineer's Docks, many vachine stopped to stare, eyes wide at this utterly humiliating and degrading treatment. Anu grinned at them, sometimes hissed, and once, when a young man protruded his fangs she snarled, "Stare as much as you like, bastard, I'll be back to rip out your throat!"

Vashell tugged her tight, then, and she fought the chain for a few moments until Vashell back-handed her across the face, and she hit the ground. She looked up, eyes narrowed in hatred, and Vashell lifted his fist to strike another blow...

"Stop!" It was a little girl, a baby vachine, who ran across the metal cobbles, clogs clattering, long blonde hair fluttering, and she placed herself between Anu and the enraged Engineer. "Have you no shame, Engineer Priest?" she said in her tiny child's voice.

Vashell glowered at the girl, no more than eight or nine years old, in a rage born of arrogance. She turned her back on him, reached down, and took Anukis's hand. She smiled, a sweet smile, and her eyes were full of love. Inside her, Anu heard the *tick tick* of clockwork. Inside the girl, the vampire machine was growing.

"Thank you." Anu stood. She reached out, ruffled the girl's hair. "Thank you for being the only one in the whole valley to show me kindness."

"Everybody is scared of you," said the girl. "They're scared you'll bring down the wrath of the Engineers."

"And we call this a free society?" mocked Anu, casting a sideways glance at Vashell. He snarled something, tugged her lead, and Anu followed obediently... but strange thoughts of her father flowed through her blood and flashed in her mind, and she felt, deep inside her own twisted and failed clockwork, the very thing which made her impure, the very thing which made her different to the vachine around her and unable to take in the gift of blood-oil which kept them alive and fed their cravings and lubricated their clockwork... she felt a tiny, subtle *twist*. Something clicked in her breast, and she felt nauseous, the world spinning violently, and she glanced back and saw the little girl watching her, a curious look on her face, and Anu tilted her head unable to place that look, unable to decipher what it actually meant...

A cold wind blew, peppered with snow.

Huge, perfectly sculpted buildings flowed past, and the vachine population continued to stare as Vashell strode proudly down the centre of the street with his dominated, subdued prize. Above, beyond, to either side, the devastatingly huge Black Pike Mountains reared, black and grey and capped with white, and splashed down low on their mighty flanks with occasional scatterings of colourful green pine forest.

I know what that look meant, realised Anu. Snow whipped her, and she shivered.

It was a look of friendship, of memory, of a link. She knows me, thought Anu, but I do not know her. How is this possible? What does it mean? Where does she come from?

The cobbled street was immensely steep, down to the Engineer's Docks. Distantly, she heard the Silva River slapping the dockside, and Vashell unconsciously accelerated due to the gradient. Anu moved faster, to keep up with the cruel Engineer's long stride, still puzzling over the golden haired child and her curious recognition...

Another puzzle, she thought.

Another conundrum.

Inside her, her clockwork continued to do strange things. She felt odd whirring sensations, the spinning and stepping of gears, like nothing she had ever before felt. Maybe I'm dying, she laughed to herself. Maybe I've been booby-trapped? Whatever, the process made her sick to her vachine core.

They reached the dockside, which was bustling with activity. Brass barges were being loaded and unloaded up and down the river, and Vashell led Anu to a long, sleek vessel. They climbed a narrow plank, went aboard, stood on deck for a moment and then dropped into a plush cabin as befit an Engineer. Vashell tied Anu's lead to a hook, and locked a clasp in place with a *click*. Anu felt a bubble of rage flood her; she felt like a dog.

"Don't want you attempting escape," said Vashell, voice low.

"Go to hell."

Vashell shrugged, and moved away, into the front of the brass barge. After a few moments Anu felt the rhythmical, pendulous hum of the clockwork engine and the barge slid away from the Engineer's Docks, away onto the smooth platform of the Silva River.

Anu sighed, and looked out of a circular portal, watching the Silva River drift by, glinting with ice as Vashell guided them through chunks and small, choppy waves. The noises of the docks drifted away behind them, until only the hum of the engine could be heard and the barge turned north, then northeast, past the opening for the Deshi Caves which seemed to tug at them with unseen currents, with honeyed promises. Come to me, the caves seemed to call. Come and explore my long, winding tunnels. I promise you riches, and glory, and immortality. That, and death, thought Anu.

Vashell picked up a narrow tributary, and guided the barge between silent mountain sentinels. Sheer walls of rock scrolled past, black and rugged grey, with a few sparse and twisted trees clinging for survival. It seemed cold, and gloomy, and snow whipped through the air. The barge hummed on, rocking, and Anu, exhausted with pain, fear, humiliation, and the still-present nagging sensation in her body core, felt sleep creep upon her and she leaned to the side, eyes closing, and for once she truly welcomed the deep dark oblivion of sleep.

"Wake up."

Vashell was shaking her. Anu yawned, and sat up. Her mouth tasted of metal, of copper, and brass, and something else.

"Where are we?"

"We've stopped at the Ranger Barracks. I've been waved ashore; you will come with me, but no trouble, Anu – or I'll cut the head from your body. Understand?"

"Why don't you leave me here? I am exhausted."

Vashell grinned, eyes twinkling. "What? And have you pull

some clever trick, and the next moment the barge is cruising into the Black Pikes without me? No. You never leave my sight... not until the day I die."

Anu was too tired to argue. Conversely, she was more weary than before her sleep, and checking the barge's clock, she saw she'd had six hours. What was the matter with her? Again, she tasted metal... almost a liquid metal, and her tongue explored the weird interior of her mouth. She was not right. Something was changing inside her.

Vashell unlocked her chain, took it in his fist and climbed the steps into cold, bleak sunlight. A bitter wind blew scattered snow from surrounding cliffs, causing the weird effect of sunlight filtering through a snowstorm. Anu followed, shading her eyes, and saw a rough wooden jetty and barracks beyond, with enough accommodation for perhaps two hundred soldiers. The barracks seemed deserted, although she could have been wrong. There was a long, low building, also constructed from rough timber, and a door opened and three albino warriors stepped out, their matt black armour gleaming in the sunlight as they shaded eyes. They hated sunlight, she knew; as did the vachine. It caused them a certain amount of pain, and in really strong light caused their clockwork to slow down, overheat, and in some extreme cases even kill the host through mechanical failure. No. Vachine preferred the cold, and the dark; their albino slaves even more so.

Anu stared at the warriors, and behind them saw a woman, tousled and battered, blood dried on her face and arms, her clothing rimed in filth. She looked little more than a vagabond and Anu's heart went out to her immediately; here was somebody mistreated, beaten, abused, as was she. There was a common link: the humiliation of the victim.

Anu studied the woman carefully, and her gaze was met by a proud, green-eyed stare, returned with a ferocity and attitude which had no doubt earned her endless pain. And, despite her recent beating, and old beatings by the look of her; despite torn clothing, naked feet covered in scabs and sores, despite her matted mane of hair, Anu saw through the agony and attitude, saw a strong woman, tall, elegant, it was in her bearing, in her manner, in her very spirit. And that had not been broken.

"The bitch is a hard one to crack," laughed one of the albino soldiers, gesturing to the woman.

"You have been instructed to treat her thus?" Vashell seemed... vexed. Anu considered his deviated sense of righteousness.

"Yes," replied a second soldier. "By Graal himself. He told us the more we beat and raped her, the more we abused her, the more we broke her – as long as we didn't kill the royal bitch, then it would be a good tool in subjugating her husband."

"Any news on Leanoric's military progress?"

"I will leave those matters for discussion between you and General Graal," said the soldier, who Anu realised was a captain of some sort, although she didn't understand the complexities of the Army of Iron's ranking system. "I was simply instructed to bring her here and await an Engineer's Barge. We thought that was why you had come."

"Coincidence," said Vashel. "I have... another mission."

Vashell tugged the chain, and Anu stumbled, and uttered a guttural growl. The three albino soldiers looked on, amused, laughter smiles touching their lips.

"A wild one, is she?"

Vashell looked back. "One of the wildest," he said, licking his lips, and smiling with narrowed eyes.

"Isn't she Anukis, Kradek-ka's daughter?" said one soldier, peering a little closer, his humour evaporating.

Vashell changed, his manner becoming more professional – more superior – in an instant. "Mind your own business, captain. We are on direct orders from the Watchmakers; I suggest you return to your... little lady, there, and continue with your petty sport. She's looking at you with the longing eyes of a bitch on heat... and trust me well when I say my business does not concern you."

Anu and Alloria's eyes met. Understanding flowed between. This was the Queen of Falanor. A bartering tool for the Engineers, and for The Army of Iron in the fast escalating conflict, the accelerating invasion. "Help me," mouthed Alloria, and Anu saw then, saw the swirl of madness deep at Alloria's core. She was putting on a proud front; but they had nearly destroyed her. There was only so much a human mind could endure.

Anu coughed, and again something *changed* inside her. She felt as if about to vomit, and instead, heard a heavy thunk. Part of her machinery changed. What was wrong with her? What had the bastards *done* to her?

She looked up. The world seemed… different. Almost black and white, and diffused, as if seen through a fine shattered mirror. She felt strength flood her system, like nothing she had felt before. She felt iron wires merge through her muscles, felt her heart swell, felt new claws springs from her fingertips, delicate and gleaming with silver. Silver fangs flowed through her hollow jaws, molten at first but solidifying, and new vampire fangs sprouted from her teeth, replacing the holes where her fake vachine fangs had been forcibly removed. Everything became acute; she could hear the snowfall, the distant flutter of birds in pine, the creak of rock in the Black Pike Mountains, distant avalanche falls, and she could smell the albinos, a certain metallic stink like that of insects, and Vashell reeked of sweat and shit and piss, and Queen Alloria even more so, and she could smell the resin in the timber jetty and the oil on the albino soldier's swords, she could see the hairs in their nostrils, taste their sweat oils in the air… and Anu *smiled*.

She lifted herself to her full height, and took a deep breath, aware her new vachine fangs gleamed silver… an impossibility, for pure silver was a poison to vachine. But now she knew. She knew her father had made her different, created something… unique, when compared to every other vachine in Silva Valley. He had been experimenting with advanced vachine technology. And she had been the template, the upgrade, using the finest clockwork in a non-parasitic fashion… and that's why she could not imbibe the blood-oil narcotic; she did not need it. All Anukis needed to survive was…

Blood. Pure blood.

Ironically, the sign of the impure.

But in this context, a technological advancement.

Her eyes glowed, and she sensed Vashell move and he gathered the chain, his movements slow and bulky, lethargic almost, and Anu lifted her own end of the chain and she pulled. Vashell was jerked from his feet and Anu leapt, a blur of speed, her claws slamming through the chain with a tinkling like ice chimes. Vashell stumbled back, going for his sword, but Anu whirled the length of chain around her head and it slammed Vashell's face, knocking him from his feet with a grunt. She took the collar in her hands and wrenched it apart, bolts pinging across snow.

The albinos tensed, drew their own swords and Anu walked towards them. She heard Vashell lift his weapon, could smell his bloodlust rising and mission or no mission, instructions or no instructions, he was going to kill her and to hell with the consequences.

The soldiers, elite warriors of the Army of Iron, charged.

Anu leapt amongst them, swayed back as a blade hummed over her, and her fist lashed out, talons smashing *through* black iron breast plate and through the albino's chest, exiting with his heart in her fist. She tugged him in close, as her claws shredded his heart in a blur, and she withdrew her fist with a *schlup* sound. Even as he fell, she flicked sideways, rolling in snow, grabbing the second albino by the head and twisting violently. His neck snapped with a crunch, and she took his sword, hurling it across the clearing where it speared the third albino through the throat, pinning him to the barrack wall. He struggled, gurgling, refusing to die, his hands scrabbling at the blood-slippery blade.

Anu turned, ignoring the cowering blood-spattered form of Alloria. She stared at Vashell, who was approaching with the fluid grace of a perfect vachine warrior. She smiled, and ejected claws and fangs.

"You're going to taste death, bitch."

"After you," invited Anu, with a smile, and they leapt at one another, clashing in mid-air, bouncing from each other as Anu twisted, avoiding Vashell's claws and her own cut a line down his flank, through armour and clothing and flesh, and a bloody spray spattered across the snow. They landed ten feet apart, crouched like animals.

Vashell touched his own wounded side. His eyes narrowed. "You'll pay for that."

"Too long I have heard your pretty words," said Anu, her voice quiet, eyes lowered. "You don't understand, do you, poor Vashell? That which alienated me from the rest of the vachine, that which made you call me impure, outcast, illegal, is twisted, reversed, for I was bred by my father to be a superior vachine, an advanced vachine lifeform... not addicted to your blood-oil concoctions... but independent of your controlling Watchmaker and Engineer pseudo-religious culture. Is that why you fear me so? Because you know I am special?"

"Kradek-ka is Heretic!" spat Vashell. "That is why he must help us; and then die."

"He seeks to improve our race using clockwork science," said Anu.

"He seeks to overthrow the Engineers," snapped Vashell, the edge of pain making his words come out fast.

"And the irony! Your Blood Refineries are breaking down; without him, you cannot fix them. You will revert to old savagery; old ways."

"Shut up and die." He snarled and leapt, and this time Anu stood rock still, eyes fixed on him, sunlight glinting from her silver fangs... at the last, split second, she twisted, and his claws slashed past her throat; his fangs slammed for her artery but she was moving, rolling away, to come up with her own claws extended, a curious calm on her face as Vashell growled, and they circled, and he leapt again with a scream of anger and Anu swayed, faster than a blur, and slammed a blow which removed Vashell's face. The skin came off in Anu's claws, removed like a mask, to leave him stood, muscle-masked skull gaping at her in utter disbelief. His face was now a red, pulsing orb from hairline to jaw, and Anu stood up straight, holding his face in her hands, watching his blood drip to the floor and he glanced up, eyes full of pain, eyes full of staggered understanding...

"That's for betraying me," she whispered.

With a growl, he launched at her and she delivered a side-kick to his chest, knocking him back, then leapt high, coming down with both claws extended to slam Vashell to the ground. She landed, kneeling atop his chest, claws locked around his throat.

"Don't kill me," he said, and she looked down at his new, bloody, destroyed face.

"Why not?"

His claws flexed behind her, and without moving her own vachine claws slammed out, cutting them from his fingers, then again to his other hand. Vashell howled in fresh agony, blood-oil spurting from all ten mangled stumps, and Anu leant close to him, mastery flooding her, along with a cold metallic hate. She leaned forward, and her fangs sank into his throat, and he writhed for a while, legs kicking, clawless hands slapping at her in an attempt to dislodge this vachine parasite from feeding. She appreciated the irony of reversal as he screamed and struggled, flapping uselessly, weakly, and Anu finally pulled away, her mouth wearing a beard of blood-oil, and she smiled down at him, reached down, and with a savage wrench, plucked out his fangs.

• • • •

Anu sat on the jetty, kicking her legs, as Alloria approached to crouch beside her. Tentatively, the woman's hand touched Anu's shoulder and she turned, their eyes meeting, Anu's face coated in slick blood. Some way off, Vashell lay, curled into a ball, weeping salt tears onto the open muscles of his face.

"Are you in pain?"

"No." Anu shook her head, forced a smile. "Come. We must leave this place. It will attract more soldiers like moths to a lantern." She stood, stretched, and her fangs slid away. She walked over to Vashell with Alloria trailing her, uncertain, her green eyes filled with a curious mix of fear and wonder.

"Wait," said Queen Alloria.

"Yes?"

"Where am I? What am I doing here?"

"This is the Silva Valley – where the vachine live."

"I have never... heard of such a place. And yet we are in the mountains, yes? The Black Pike Mountains?"

"Yes. In their heart."

"I thought the Black Pikes were impassable. That is what the people of Falanor believe."

Anu shook her head. "Many of your, shall we say respectable citizens, think like that. But there is a roaring blood trade by Blacklippers. They have no morals. They have no... empathy. No fear."

"What is a Blacklipper?"

"The Halfway People. Illegal to the vachine of Silva Valley, and ostracised by the good men and women of Falanor. They are your illegals, your freaks and vagabonds, the army deserters destined to die, the deformed left to perish in low mountain passes. That is your tradition, isn't it? With the babes who have no arms? Those of twisted limb? Those are the Blacklippers, they are not the pretty people of a good, noble society. They are the weak. The cripples. The diseased. The underlings who you would rather imagine did not exist." Anu took a deep breath, then looked away up the cold, flowing river. Like me, she thought. And smiled. "I'm sorry. I'm bitter. I have recently been... abused, as an outcast, something different. It's not a pleasant feeling to be hated by those who once accepted you." She met Alloria's gaze. "Once, your outcasts ran to us; but the vachine, also, are filled with a primitive superiority and they turned on the Blacklippers. Now, illegally, the Blacklippers gradually feed your nation to ours. They think of it as a kind of justice. Of payback."

"Feed?"

Anu smiled. "We have a currency in blood," she said, and Alloria gasped, hands coming to her mouth.

"Is that why your army invaded?"

Anu nodded. "Our civilisation expands, and our needs multiply. We are losing the war in an ability to satiate our own needs. And so…" her voice trailed off, as her eyes alighted on the now silent form of Vashell. "So we must spread out, move south; to where there are many ripe, succulent pickings."

"You talk about my people, the good people of Falanor, as if they are cattle!" snapped Alloria, eyes hard.

"They soon will be," said Anu, her head tilting to one side. "Once the vachine roll in the Blood Refineries."

"I don't understand. My husband, the king, is a great warrior. He has thousands of soldiers at his disposal; an army of unconquerable might! He will oppose any invasion with savage force, and chase your vachine people back to the mountains like the savages you undoubtedly are. Either that, or slaughter them without mercy."

Across the clearing, Vashell started to laugh. He sat, bloody face leering at them, mangled hands in his lap, laughing in an obscene gurgle.

Anu strode to him. "Something funny, you faceless bastard?"

Vashell reclined a little, looking up at her. "My. Kradek-ka really did a fine job on you, my twisted, sweet little deformity. His technology, I admit, is superb, for never have I been bested in battle. Not by human, not by vachine." He took a deep breath, and Anu could see the pain in his eyes; not just a physical pain, but a mental scarring. He was trying to mask this with bravado; but she knew him too well.

"I threw your face in the river," she said, leaning close. "I didn't think you'd be needing it again."

Vashell shrugged. "You may do what you wish to me; but you do know they will come."

"Who?"

"The Harvesters. I am linked. They have sensed my pain. As you sit there, on your arse, squabbling with prime succulent Falanor Queen-meat, they have already decided your fate. No longer is Kradek-ka to be brought back. I'd wager they simply need your extermination, for your threat is great; your threat, now, is terrible. If you are lucky, little Anu, you little twisted vachine experiment Anu, they will send the cankers. But if you are unlucky..."

"They will never catch us," said Anu, and there was a tinge of panic to her voice. She feared the Harvesters. Everybody feared the Harvesters.

"If you're unlucky, they will come themselves."

Anu's claws slid free. She glared down at Vashell, and even in his pain, now over the sudden shock of his ripped-off face, he mocked her. His arrogance, and loathing, had returned. "I will kill you," she growled, her own hatred swelling.

"No," said Alloria, grasping Anu's arm. Anu threw Alloria to the ground, where she lay, staring up at these two alien creatures.

"I will kill you," repeated Anu, and moved in close...

"That would be foolish. How, then, would you find your father?"

Snow was falling, and the rearing mountains were diffused. Light had started to fail, and the sky held that curious grey brightness, a cold tranquillity, only found in the mountains. A slow unrolling of mist eased in from around the barracks, and Anu caught the silent approach from the corner of her eye. Ice prickled up and down her spine.

"Where is he?" she snapped.

"You need me," said Vashell, his eyes burning. "Only I know where he was last seen. I have my reports. If you kill me, and believe me, I am willing to die, then he will be gone from you forever." He snarled at her, through torn and ragged lips, from a face of rancid horror, from a face that was no longer a face.

"I will cut out your eyes," said Anu.

"Then do it! And stop yapping like a clockwork puppy."

The mist, cold and brilliantly white, spread across the ground, rolling out onto the river and masking the currents. It covered the corpses of the slain albino soldiers, and Vashell pushed himself up onto elbows as it rolled around him, and he sighed, and his eyes alighted on Anu and there was a glint of triumph there...

"The Harvesters move quickly," he said, voice a lullaby, and filled with the honey of blood-oil narcotic; his system was overloading on the substance, in lieu of his savage beating. "There must have been one close by."

Anu felt panic slam her breast. "No," she said whirling around, eyes scanning the open spaces. She pointed at Alloria. "Get into the barge!" she snapped, and then turned back to Vashell, her claws and vampiric fangs emerging. "It is simply mountain mist!" she hissed, but her voice was cracked, there was a splinter in her heart. They both knew how savage the Harvesters were; and how strange, even to the vachine whom they deigned to help. They were creatures of the Black Pike Mountains, creatures from far beneath the stone; and they had their own esoteric agenda.

When the Harvesters drained corpses for Blood Refinement, it was suspected that they themselves received something by way of a bonus. When they husked a human, they took a little part of the soul. But no vachine ever voiced these theories; not if they valued their own life. The Harvesters were above the gods, as far as the vachine society were concerned; and even though Anu would never voice this sentiment, she felt they were the Puppet Masters, and the vachine simply actors on another creature's stage.

Vashell shrugged, and watched Anu closely.

"You have grown strong," he said, voice slurring a little, so infused was his damaged system with blood-oil. "But do you think you have grown strong enough?"

There came a hiss, like snow on a forest canopy, and from the swirled ice-smoke came the Harvester. The oval face stared at Anu as it seemed to glide over the ground, and it stopped for a moment by the slain albino warriors.

"Sacrilege?" it said, voice high-pitched, merging in an odd way with its fast-paced breathing. Then it looked at Vashell, who shrugged, almost dreamily, and returned its gaze to Anu. "So. The daughter of Kradek-ka. You have discovered your gift, I see."

"He would have killed me," said Anu, pointing to Vashell, her finger shaking.

The Harvester drifted a little closer, head bobbing, tiny black eyes without emotion fixing hard on Anu's soul. She felt like she was being eaten, from the inside out, by a tiny swarm of parasites. She shivered, as a feeling passed through her, and she was sure the Harvester could read her thoughts.

"I see," said the Harvester, and she could not read the black eyes. Fear tasted copper on her tongue. She felt urine dribble between her legs. She pictured the husks of the slaughtered; men, women, vachine, children, dogs. The Harvester had no empathy, no remorse, no understanding. It could not be negotiated with. It would do what it wanted, protected by vachine law, and practically indestructible…

"I am going to look for my father," she said, voice trembling.

"You are going nowhere, child."

Anu hardened her resolve, through her blanket of fear. More ice-smoke swirled around her ankles, with a biting, icy chill. This fuelled her strength. The Harvesters controlled everything...

"I will find my father," she said, again.

"You disobey me?" said the Harvester.

She considered this, and knew she had embarked upon a path of mystery, a journey she could never have foreseen, understood, nor prophesised. She had stepped sideways from the vachine of Silva Valley; she was an outlaw, yes, and she was totally alone. She realised in a flash of understanding that things would never, could never, be the same. And if she defied this Harvester, she broke every law of the Mountain. Of the Valley. Of the Oak Testament.

"Yes," she said, meeting the Harvester's gaze and holding it.

Long bony fingers emerged from the robe, and the Harvester lifted its arms in a gesture at the same time a little bizarre, a little ridiculous, but containing a thrill of raw terror.

"Then you must die," it said, voice a monotone.

Anu felt strength flood her. Confidence bit through fear. Pride and necessity ate her horror. She smiled at the Harvester, and flexed her claws, and lowered her head, and snarled, "Come and take me, then, you bone-headed freak," as she leapt to the attack.

TWELVE
The Jailers

Saark watched the axe, Ilanna, in Kell's mighty hands; watched her sing in dark prophecy as she rushed towards his skull. And as he observed that crescent razor approach, an utter calm descended on him and he reflected on his life, his early goals, his mistakes, and on his current self-loathing; and he knew, knew life was unfair and the world took no prisoners, but that ultimately he had made his own choices, and he deserved death. He deserved the cold dark earth, the sombre tomb, worms eating his organs. He deserved to be forgotten, for in his life he had done bad things, *terrible things*, and for these he had never been punished. With his death, his end, then the world would be a cleaner place. His scourge would be removed. He smiled. It was a fitting end to be slain by a hero such as Kell; poetic, almost. Despite the irony.

The blade sliced frozen earth a hair's-breadth from his ear, scraped the ice with a metallic shriek, then lifted into the air again and for a horrible moment Saark thought to himself, the old bastard missed! He's pissed on whisky, and he damn well fucking *missed*!

But Kell glared at him, face sour, eyes raging, and held out his hand. "Up, lad. It's not your time. We have a job to do."

Saark turned, rolled, and sprang lightly to his feet, his injuries pushed aside as he watched, with Kell, Nienna, Kat and the others; watched the albino soldiers drifting from wreaths of ice-smoke.

Kell whirled on the gathered crowd. "You must run!" he bellowed. "The ice-smoke will freeze you where you stand, then they

218

will drain you of blood. Stop standing like village idiots, run for your lives!"

A knife flashed from the darkness, and Ilanna leapt up, clattering the blade aside in a show of such consummate skill Saark found his mouth once again dry. The old boy hadn't missed with his strike; nobody that good missed, despite half a bottle of whisky. If Kell wanted Saark dead, by the gods, he'd be dead.

Saark sidled to Kell. The advancing albinos had halted. They seemed to be waiting for something. The mist swirled, huge coils like ghostly snakes, as if gathering strength.

"What do we do, old horse?"

"We run," said Kell. "Tell Nienna and Kat to get the horses."

Kell stood, huge and impassable in the street as the albinos arrayed themselves before him; yet more drifted from the shadows between cottages. They wore black armour, and their crimson eyes were emotionless, insectile.

Like ants, thought Kell. Simply following their programmed instructions...

There were fifty of them, now. Off to the right a platoon of soldiers emerged, and a group of villagers attacked with swords and pitchforks. Their screams sang through the night to a musical accompaniment of steel on steel; they were butchered in less than a minute.

"Come on, come on," muttered Kell, aware that some spell was at work here, and he growled at the albino warriors and then, realised with a jump, that they watched his axe, eyes, as one, fixed on Ilanna. He lifted the great weapon, and their eyes followed it, tracking the terrible butterfly blades.

So, he thought. You understand her, now.

"Come and enjoy her gift," he snarled, and from their midst emerged a Harvester, and Kell nodded to himself. So. That was why they waited. For the hardcore magick to arrive...

Iron-shod hooves clattered on ice and cobbles, and Nienna and Kat rode free of the stables, the geldings sliding as they cornered and Saark whirled, leapt up behind Kat, taking the reins from her shaking fingers.

"Kell!" he bellowed.

Kell, staring at the Harvester, snarled something incomprehensible, then turned and vaulted into the saddle behind Nienna – hardly the action of an old man with rheumatism. "Yah!" he snarled and the horses galloped through the streets, churning snow and frozen mud, slamming through milling people and over the bridge and away...

Behind, the screams began.

"Soldiers ahead!" yelled Saark as they charged down a narrow street of two-storey cottages with well-tended gardens, and there were ten albino warriors standing in the road, swords free, heads lowered, and as Saark dragged violently on reins the gelding whinnied in protest. Kell did not slow, charging his own horse forward, Nienna gasping between his mighty arms as Ilanna sang, a high pitched song of desolation as she cleaved left, then right, leaving two carved and collapsing corpses in sprays of iridescent white blood. Kell wheeled the horse, and it reared, hooves smashing the lower jaw from the face of an albino who shrieked, grabbing at where his mouth had been. Behind, Saark cursed, and urging his own gelding forward, charged in with his sword drawn. Steel rang upon steel as he clashed, and to his right Kell leapt from the saddle as Nienna drew her own sword from its saddle-sheath. Kell carved a route through the soldiers, his face grim, eyes glowing, whisky on his breath and axe moving as if possessed; which it surely was.

Nienna sat atop the horse, stunned by events; from fine dresses and heady drinks to sitting in the street, sword in hand, petrified to her core. Again. She shook her head, feeling groggy and slow, mouth tasting bad, head light, and watched almost detached as a soldier stepped from his comrades, focused on her, and charged with sword raised...

Panic tore through Nienna. The soldier was there in the blink of an eye, crimson eyes fixed, sword whistling towards her in a high horizontal slash; she stabbed out with her own short blade, and the swords clashed, noise ringing out. Kell's head slammed left, as Ilanna cut the head from a warrior's shoulders. Kell sprinted, then knelt in the snow, sliding, as Ilanna slammed end over end to smash through the albino's spine, curved blade appearing before Nienna's startled gaze on a spray of blood.

Saark finished the last of the soldiers, slitting a man's throat with a dazzling pirouette and shower of horizontal blood droplets. The corpse crumpled, blood settled like rain, and behind them, on the road, ice-smoke crept out and curled like questing fingers.

"We need to get out of Jajor Falls," panted Saark.

"Yes. Let's go."

"How do you do that?"

"Do what?" Kell took the reins, smiling grimly up at Nienna who rubbed her tired face.

"You're not even out of breath, old boy."

"Economy of movement," said Kell, and forced a smile. "I'll teach you, one day."

There came an awkward hiatus. Saark gazed into Kell's eyes.

"I thought you were going to kill me, back there."

"No, laddie. I like you. I wouldn't do that."

Saark let the lie go, and they mounted the geldings. As they rode from Jajor Falls, out into the gloom under heavy falling snow, down a narrow winding lane which led to thick woodland and ten different tracks they could choose at random, behind them, in the now frozen village, the Harvesters moved through the rigid population with a slow, cold, frightening efficiency.

As day broke, so the trail they followed joined with the cobbled splendour of the Great North Road, winding and black, shining under frost and the pink daubs of a low-slung newly-risen sun. The horses cantered, steam ejecting from nostrils, and all four travellers were exhausted in saddles, not just from lack of sleep, but from emotional distress.

"How far to the king?" said Kell, as they rode.

"It's hard to say; depends with which Eagle Division he's camped, or if we have to travel all the damn way to Vor. Best thing is stop the first soldier we see and ask; the army has good communications. The squads should be informed."

"You know a lot about King Leanoric," said Kat, turning to gaze up at Saark. She was aware of his powerful arms around her, his body pressed close to her through silk and furs, which he'd wrapped around her shoulders in the middle of the night to keep her warm. It had been a touching moment.

"I... used to be a soldier," said Saark, slowly.

"Which regiment, laddie?"

"The Swords," said Saark, eyes watching Kell.

"The King's Own, eh?" Kell grinned at him, and rubbed his weary face. The smell of whisky still hung about him like a toxic shawl.

"Yes."

"But you left?"

"Aye."

Kell caught the tension in Saark's voice, and let it go. Kat, however, did not.

"So you fought with the King's Men? The Sword-Champions?"

Saark nodded, squirming uneasily in the saddle. To their left, in the trees, a burst of bird song caught his attention. It seemed at odds with the frost, and the recent slaughter. He shivered as a premonition overtook him.

"Listen, Kell, it occurs to me the Army of Iron is moving south."

"Occurred to me as well, laddie."

"And they're moving fast."

"Fast for an army, aye. They're taking every village as they go, sweeping down through Falanor and leaving nobody behind to oppose them. If the king already knows, he will be mustering his divisions. If he does not…"

"Then Falanor lies wide open."

Kell nodded.

"He must know," said Saark, considering, eyes observing the road ahead. They were moving between rolling hills now, low and rimed with a light scattering of snow, patches of green peeping through patches of white like a winter forest patchwork.

"Why must he?"

"Falanor is riddled with his troops, sergeants, scouts, spies. Even now, Leanoric will be summoning divisions, and they will march on this upstart aggressor. We can be of no further use."

Kell looked sideways at Saark. "You think so, do you?" he murmured.

Saark looked at him. "Don't you?"

"What do you have in mind?"

"We could head west, for the Salarl Ocean. Book passage on a ship, head across the waves to a new land. We are both adept with weapons; we'll find work, there's no question of that."

"Or you could steal a few Dog Gemdog gems, that'd keep you in bread, cheese and fine perfume."

Saark paused. He sighed. "You despise me, don't you? You hate my puking guts."

"Not at all," said Kell, and reined in his mount. "We need to make camp. The girls are freezing. We've put a good twelve leagues between us and the bastards. If we don't get some warmth we'll freeze to death; and my arse feels like a blacksmith's anvil."

"Here's a spot," said Kat, and they dismounted. Kell sent the young women to a nearby woodland to gather fallen branches, as he rummaged in the mount's saddlebags, pulling free two onions, salt and a few strips of jerked beef. "Hell's teeth. Is this all there is? I suppose we left in a hurry."

"We were brawling in the street," said Saark. "We had little warning to gather provisions."

Kell looked at Saark, then placed a hand on his shoulder. "I'm sorry. About that." His face twisted. He was unused to apology. "I... listen, I over-reacted. Kat is a beautiful young woman, but I know your sort, out to take what you want, then you'd leave her behind, weeping and broken, heart smashed into ice fragments."

"Your opinion of me is pure flattery," said Saark, coldly.

"Listen. I lost my temper. There. I said it." He looked into Saark's eyes. "I wouldn't have killed you, lad."

"I think you would," said Saark, carefully. "I've seen that look before."

Kell grinned. "Damn. You're right. I would have killed you."

"What stopped you?"

"The arrival of the soldiers," said Kell, hissing in honesty. "You were the one who brought up this poem, right? This Saga of Kell's Legend. But have you heard the last verse? It's rare the bards remember it; either that, or they choose easily to forget, lest it ruin their night of entertainment."

"The one about Moonlake and Skulkra? Kell fought with the best?"

"No. There is another verse."

"I did not realise."

Kell's voice was a low rumble as he recited, unevenly, more poetry than song; he would be the first to admit he was no bard. Kell quoted:

"*And Kell now stood with axe in hand,*
The sea raged before him, time torn into strands,
He pondered his legend and screamed at the stars,
Death open beneath him to heal all the scars
Of the hatred he'd felt, and the murders he'd done
And the people he'd killed all the pleasure and life
He'd destroyed.

"Kell stared melancholy into great rolling waves of
a Dark Green World,
And knew he could blame no other but himself for
The long Days of Blood, the long Days of Shame,
The worst times flowing through evil years of pain,
And the Legend dispersed and the honour was gone
And all savagery fucked in a world ripped undone
And the answer was clear as the stars in the sky
All the bright stars the white stars the time was to die,
Kell took up Ilanna and bade world farewell,
The demons tore through him as he ended the spell
And closed his eyes."

Kell glanced at Saark. There were tears in his eyes. "I was a bad man, Saark. An evil man. I blame the whisky, for so long I blamed the whisky, but one day I came to realise that it simply masked that which I was. I eventually married, reared two daughters... who came to hate me. Only Nienna has time for me, and for her love I am eternally grateful. Do you know why?"

"Why?" said Saark, voice barely more than a croak.

"Because she is the only thing that calms the savage beast in my soul," said Kell, grasping Ilanna tight. "I try, Saark. I try so hard to be a good man. I try so hard to do the right thing. But it doesn't always work. Deep down inside, at a basic level, I'm simply not a good person."

"Why so glum?" said Nienna, dumping a pile of wood on the ground. She glanced from Saark to Kell, and back, and Kat came up behind with her arms also laden with firewood. "Have you two been arguing again?"

"No," said Saark, and gave a broad, beaming smile. "We were just... going over a few things. Here, let me build a fire, Nienna. You help your grandfather with the soup. I think he needs a few warm words from the granddaughter he loves so dearly."

Kell threw him a dark look, then smiled down at Nienna, and ruffled her hair. "Hello monkey. You did well with the wood."

"Come on, we're both starving." And in torn silk dresses and ragged furs and blankets salvaged from dead soldiers' saddlebags, the group worked together to make a pan of broth.

• • • •

It was an hour later as they came across a straggled line of refugees, who turned, fear on faces at the sound of striking hoof-beats. Several ran across the fields to the side of the Great North Road, until they saw the young girls who rode with Kell and Saark. They rode to the head of the column, and Kell dismounted beside a burly, gruff-looking man with massive arms and shoulders like a bull.

"Where are you riding?" asked Kell.

"Who wants to know?"

"I am Kell. I ride to warn the king of the invading army."

The man relaxed a little, and eyed Kell's axe and Svian nervously. "I am Brall, I was the smithy back at Tell's Fold. Not any more. The bastard albinos took us in the night, two nights back, magick freezing people in the street. I can still hear their screams. A group of us," he gestured with his eyes, "ran through the woods. And we'll keep on running. Right to the sea if we have to."

A woman approached. "It was horrible," she said, and her eyes were haunted. "They killed everybody. Men, women, little ones. Then these... ghosts, they drifted through the streets and drank the blood of the children." She shuddered, and for a moment Kell thought she was going to be sick. "Turned them into sacks of skin and bone. You'll kill me, won't you, Brall? Before you let that happen?"

"Aye, lass," he said, and his thick arm encircled her shoulder.

"Have you seen any Falanor men on the road?" asked Saark, dismounting.

"No." Brall shook his head. "Not for the last two weeks. Most of the battalions are south."

"Do you know where King Leanoric camps?"

Brall shrugged. "I am only a smithy," he said. "I would not be entrusted with such things."

"Thank you." Saark turned to Kell. "I know what's happening."

"What's that?"

"More than half of Leanoric's men are paid volunteers; summer men. They go home for the winter. The Black Pike Mountains, much of Leanoric's past angst, are now impassable with snow. So as winter heightens, spreads south, so he stands down most of the volunteers and they return to families. He's been travelling through his divisions, reorganising command structures, deciding who can go home for the winter, that sort of thing."

"So as we stand here, he might even now be disbanding the very army he's going to need?"

"Precisely."

"That's not good," said Kell. "Let's move out."

They cantered on, leaving behind the straggling line of survivors from Tell's Fold.

They rode all day, and as more snow fell and the light failed, so they headed away from the Great North Road, searching for a road shelter, as they were known. In previous decades, following work begun by his father, Leanoric had had shelters built at intervals up and down the huge highway to aid travellers and soldiers in times of need. The snow fell, heavier now, and Saark pointed to the distance where a long, low, timber building nestled in the lee of a hill, surrounded by a thick stand of pine.

"Hard to defend," muttered Kell.

"We need to recharge," said Saark, his cloak pulled tight, his eyes weary. "You might be as strong as an ox, but me and the girls... we need to eat, to sleep. And the horses are dead on their feet."

"Lead the way," said Kell, and they walked through the ankle-deep fall.

Saark opened the door on creaking hinges, allowing snow to blow in, and Kell led the horses behind the road shelter and tied them up in a lean-to stable, at least secluded from the worst of the weather. He found a couple of old, dusty horse blankets and covered the beasts, and filled their nose-bags with oats from the dwindling remains of their saddlebag stores. Saark was right. They needed to rest and recharge; but more, they needed supplies, or soon the wilderness of Falanor would kill them.

"It's bare," said Nienna, moving over and sitting on the first bed. The room had a low roof, and was long, containing perhaps sixteen beds. It was like a small barracks, and was chilled, smelling of damp. A fire had been laid at the far end, but the logs were damp.

"It'll save our life," shivered Saark, and struggled from his cloak. In the gloomy light, his frilled clothes, splattered with dried blood, no longer looked so fine. "How are you two?"

"Exhausted," said Kat, and flashed Saark a smile. "It's been... a strange few days, hasn't it?"

"We need to get a fire going. Nienna, will you go and find some wood?"

Sensing they needed to be alone, Nienna left and the door slammed shut. Saark approached Kat.

"What happened back there..."

"It's all right," she said, smiling and placing a finger against his lips. "We both got carried away in the moment..."

"No. What I meant to say was, I think you're special. I am trying to be different. A reformed character." His smile was twisted, self-mocking. "In my past life, I have been a bad man; in many ways. But I feel for you, Katrina." He stared into her topaz eyes, and ran his hands through her short, red hair, still stuck with bits of straw from back at the village stables.

She reached up, and kissed him, and for a long moment their lips lingered. "Let's take it one step at a time. Let's reach the king. Let's save Falanor. Then we can play at holding hands."

Saark grinned. "You're a wicked wench, that's for sure."

She stroked his moustache, winked, then turned her back on him. "You better believe it, mister."

Nienna returned with firewood, followed by Kell, shivering and brushing snow from the shoulders of his mighty bear-skin jerkin. "Let's get a fire lit," he rumbled, "I could do with a pan of soup."

"You and your soup," said Saark.

"It's good for the ancient teeth," said Kell, but whereas once Saark would have bantered, now a gloomy silence fell on the group and they worked quietly, their humour a thing of the past.

Once the fire was lit, and a little warmth built inside the road shelter, Kell used the last of their supplies to make a thin, watery soup. He also discovered he'd used the last of the salt. He cursed. What was life without a little salt?

Outside, darkness fell, and the snowfall increased in intensity.

"Winter's finally come," said Saark, gesturing out of the small windows.

"Good," grunted Kell. "It'll slow the invading army."

"Don't you find it odd," said Saark, playing with his dagger on the thick-planks of the table.

"What do you mean?"

"The Army of Iron, invading at the start of winter. Guaranteed a slow advance, men freezing to death, supply problems, lowered morale. There's nothing like standing all night in the damn snow to sap a man's morale; it's like spreading syphilis. I know, I've done it. I thought my feet would never get warm again. It was two whole days before I felt life in my little toes! So, a strange choice then, yes?"

"Yes," grunted Kell, finishing the last of his broth. He had made better, but the girls didn't complain. He'd expected a few jibes from Saark, along the lines of his soup being the watery consistency of old goat piss; but Saark had remained silent, moody. Since their fight in the street, Saark had retreated into himself, into his shell, and whilst a part of Kell was glad of the change in character, another part of him, a part he did not recognise, actually missed the banter. With a jolt like a shock of lightning, Kell realised he liked the dandy; although he was damned if he could figure out why.

Nienna and Kat moved away to sort out the sleeping arrangements, and check for extra blankets. They'd found some, which they laid out on the floor before the fire to banish vestiges of damp. Now they searched the cupboards and drawers at the back of the shelter.

"Look," said Kell, staring at Saark across the table. "I… I wanted to apologise. Again. For what happened back at the tavern. It rests uneasy with me, laddie. It shouldn't have happened. I am ashamed of what I did."

"Don't worry about it."

"No," said Kell. "I feel bad. And it wasn't totally your fault; when I drink whisky, it twists my brain. Turns me into the bad man from the poem." He smiled wryly. "Yes, the stanza they never repeat, lest it sour my legend. Ha!" He turned, stared into the fire for a while. Then he reached across the table. "Take my hand."

"Why? You want to read my palm?"

"No, I want to crush your fingers, idiot. Take my damn hand."

Saark took the old man's grizzled paws, felt the massive strength contained therein. He looked up into Kell's eyes, and swallowed. There was power there, true power, charisma, strength and an awesome resolve.

"That will never happen again, Saark, I promise you. I count you as a friend. You have saved my granddaughter's life, and you have fought with great courage on my behalf. If you ever see me touch a whisky bottle to my lips, please, smash me over the head with the fucking bottle. I will understand. And… I owe you, my friend. I owe you with my life. I will give my life to protect you."

Saark blinked, as Kell released him, and sat back a little. He grinned. "You could have just blown me a kiss."

"Don't get smart."

"Or sent some flowers."

"I might not kill you," snarled Kell, "but I'll slap your arse, for sure. Now be a good lad, and go and find some candles... the dark outside, well, it's getting kind of eerie; what with these Harvesters and cankers and damned albino bastards roaming the land."

"Candles won't stop the horrors of the dark, my friend."

"*I know that*! Just find some."

As Saark was rummaging around in the bottom of an old cupboard, the door to the road shelter opened and three figures were illuminated by firelight. They stood for a moment, surveying the interior, and then stepped in, leading another four refugees, presumably from recent slaughter in a local village.

Kell stood, taking up his axe, and stared at the newcomers. The villagers he dismissed immediately from his mind, for they were obviously refugees in tatters, half dead with cold. But the first three; they were warriors, vagabonds, and very, very dangerous. Kell could tell from the glint in their eyes, the wary way they moved, the cynical snarls ingrained on weary, stone-carved expressions.

"We saw your fire," said one of the newcomers, stepping forward. She was tall, taller than Kell even, her limbs wiry and strong, her fingers long, tapered, the nails of her right hand blackened from constant use of the longbow strapped to her back. She had short black hair, cropped rough, and gaunt features, her eyes sunken, her flesh stretched and almost yellow. "My name is Myriam."

"Welcome, Myriam," said Kell, watching as the other newcomers spread out. The four villagers cowered behind them, staring longingly at the fire. "Do you bring any supplies?"

"We have potatoes, meat, a little salt. The villagers here also have food between them. Are those your horses out back?"

"So what if they are?" said Saark, smoothly, standing beside Kell. "They are not for sale."

"I didn't say I wanted to buy them," said Myriam, and stalked forward, taking up a chair, reversing it, and sitting down, her arms leaning over the solid back. The two men approached, standing behind her; she was obviously the leader.

Kell eyed the men carefully. One was of average height, squat, and inexorably ugly. He had pockmarked skin, narrow dark eyes, or eye, as the left was a lifeless socket, red and inflamed, and his cubic head sported tufts of hair as if shaved with a blunt razor.

Worst of all, his lips were black, the black of the smuggler, the black of the outlawed Blacklipper, and it gave his countenance a brooding, menacing air. Kell instinctively decided never to turn his back on the man.

"This is Styx," said Myriam, following Kell's gaze. She gave a narrow smile. "Don't lend him any money."

The second man was small and angry-looking, as so often small men were. He wore a thin vest, bloodstained and tattered, and scant protection against the cold. He was heavily muscled in chest, arm and shoulder, but what set him apart more than anything were his tattoos which writhed up hands, arms and shoulders, onto his neck and scampered across his face. His heavy tattooing denoted him as a tribesman from the eastern New Model Tribes, weeks of travel over treacherous swamps and land-pits, as the quicksand plains were known; even past Drennach.

"This is Jex," said Myriam, and Kell nodded to both men, who grunted at him, eyes appraising, noting his manner and his axe. They were gauging him for battle, and it made Kell uneasy. This was not the time, nor place.

"I am Kell. This is Saark. The two girls are Nienna and Kat."

Myriam nodded, and seemed to relax a little now introductions had been made. Styx and Jex pulled up chairs, scraping them across the boards, and sat behind Myriam as if deferring to her to speak.

"I've heard of you, Saark."

"You have?" he said, eyes glittering.

"You were the King's Sword-Champion. I saw you fight, in Vor, about five years ago. You were stunning, if a little arrogant."

"Well, I'll, admit I'm ever more arrogant now," he said, hand on hilt, "and happy to give a display of violence to any who beg."

"Styx here, despite being a Blacklipper and getting the shakes, is adept with a blade. Maybe in the morning we could have a tourney; spin a little coin?"

"I'd feel he was disadvantaged, having only one eye. It makes a devil of defence on that side. But you, my pretty, I'm sure you're adept with your little metal prick…"

Myriam flushed red, frowning, and started to rise.

"Enough!" boomed Kell, and Myriam settled back. Kell glared at Saark, then returned to the woman. "There are enough of the enemy out there to satisfy your bloodlust for a century. So let's just roast that nice bacon joint the villagers brought in, boil a few potatoes, and enjoy a bit of civilised company."

"I'm going to check on the horses," said Saark, and left the cabin, allowing cold air to swirl in.

Myriam shivered, and started to cough. The cough was harsh, savage, and Kell watched as the two men attended her, almost tenderly, despite their vagabond appearances. She coughed for a while, and Kell thought he saw blood. He looked again at her gaunt face, the sunken eyes, the shape of her skull beneath parched skin. He had seen such afflictions before; men, and women, riddled with cancers. He would wager Myriam was getting perilously close to death. It spooked him with a sense of his own mortality.

Give me an enemy to fight with my axe any day, he thought sourly, rather than some nasty sneaky little bastard growing deep down inside. Kell's eyes burned. He felt a stab of pity for the woman. Nobody should die like that.

Kell stood, poured a cup of water and carried it to Myriam. She drank, and smiled her thanks. Through her pain, and gaunt features, and harsh cropped hair, Kell saw a glimmer of prettiness. Once, she would have been beautiful, he thought. But not just cancer had eaten her; bitterness and a world-weary cynicism had removed what beauty lines remained.

"I suggest you sit nearer the fire."

"She'll sit where she damn well pleases," snarled Jex, voice heavy with an eastern burr.

"As you wish."

"Wait," said Myriam, and met Kell's gaze. "Can I speak with you?"

"You're speaking with me."

"In private."

"There is no privacy." He smiled, coldly.

"Outside. In the snow."

"If you like."

They walked from the long cabin, boots crunching snow, Kell following Myriam a good distance until she stopped, leaning against a tree, wheezing a little. She gazed up at the falling snow, then turned, smiling at Kell. "It's the cold. It affects my lungs."

"I thought it was the cancer."

"That as well. What pains me most are the things I can no longer do, actions I remember performing with ease. Like running. Gods!

Once I could run like the wind, all bloody day, up and down mountains. Nothing stopped me. Now, I'm lucky to run to the privy."

"You wanted to speak?" Kell stared at her, and felt a strange twinge of recognition. He leaned close, and she leaned away. "Do I know you?" he said, finally, his memory tugging at him.

"No. But I know of you. The Saga of Kell's Legend, a tale to frighten and inspire, a tale to breed heroes and soldiers, don't let the little ones leave the safety of the fire." She laughed, but Kell did not. "You're a hero through these parts," she said.

"According to some, aye," he sighed, and leant his own back against a pine. The wind howled mournfully through the trees, a low song, a desolate song. Somewhere, an owl hooted. "What's it to you?"

"I just… I heard stories of you. From my father. When I was a child."

"A child?" said Kell, disbelieving. "How old are you, girl?"

"Twenty-nine winters, round about now." She blushed. "I know. I look a lot older. It's because I'm dying, Kell. And… I know some of your past. Some of your history."

"Oh yes?" He did not sound thrilled.

"You could help me."

"I'm busy. There's an invasion going on, or hadn't you noticed?"

"You could save me from dying," she said, and her eyes were pleading. "You've been through the Black Pike Mountains. I know this. I've talked to an old soldier who swears he went there with you. He said you know all the secret trails, the hidden passes; and ways past the deadly Deep Song Valley, the Wall of Kraktos, and the Passage of Dragons. Well," she took a deep breath, "I need to go there; I need to walk the high passes. I need to reach…"

"Where do you need to reach?" said Kell, voice impossibly soft.

"The hidden valley," breathed Myriam, looking Kell straight in the eye. "Silva Valley."

"And what would you do there, lady?"

"You can see what is happening to me," said Myriam. Tears shone in her eyes. "For the past three years I have grown steadily weaker. Meat has fallen from my bones. I get terrible pains, in my sides, in my hips, in my head. I spent a fortune in gold on fat physicians in Vor; they told me I had tumours, parasitical growths inside, each the size of a fist. The physicians said I would die within the year, that there was nothing I could do… damn them all! But, three years later, I am still here, hanging on by a thread, still searching for a cure. But sometimes, Kell, sometimes the pain is so bad I wish I were dead." She started to cough again, and covered her mouth, turning away, staring into the night-blackened trees. Snow swirled on eddies of breeze. Kell could smell ice.

"You didn't answer the question," he said, when the fit had passed.

"What would I do in Silva Valley? They have… machines there. Machines that could heal me."

"They would change you," said Kell. "I have seen the result of their experiments. It was not good."

Myriam was closer, now, had edged closer so that Kell could smell the musk of her body. She pressed herself in to him, and he felt something he had not felt for a long time; a rising lust, surging from a deep dark pool he had thought long vanished with age. It had been a long time. Perhaps too long.

Kell's eyes shone, and he licked his lips, which gleamed, and calmed his breathing.

"I would make it worth your while. I would do anything to live," she said, her gaunt face inches from Kell's, her arms lifting to drape over his shoulders. Her body was lean against his, her small breasts hard, nipples pressing against him.

"You don't understand," Kell said, voice low, arms unconsciously circling her waist. "They are called the vachine. They would change you. They would… kill every part of you that is human. It is better, I think, to die like you are, than to suffer their clockwork indignities."

Myriam was silent for a while. She was crying.

"I'm sorry," said Kell. "The answer is no."

Myriam kissed him.

Back in the cabin, Saark sat back, aloof, watching the two men with open distaste. They were exactly the opposite of Saark; whereas he was beautiful, they were ugly; whereas he was elegant, they were clumsy. He dressed like a noble, Styx and Jex dressed like walking shit.

"Can I get you a drink?" said Kat, approaching the two men.

"You can sit on my lap, pretty one," said Jex, grinning through his tattoos.

"Ahh, no, just…"

"She's with me," said Saark, eyes cold.

"Is that so, dandy man?" Jex smiled at Saark, and he knew, then, knew violence was impending. These were dangerous, rough outlaws. They knew no rules, no laws, and yet by the scars on their arms they had survived battle and war for a considerable time. They were good, despite their savage looks and lack of dress-code. If they weren't good, they'd be long dead.

"It's simply a fact," said Saark, eyes flicking left to where the four refugees were unpacking meagre belongings. There were two men, two women, the youngest woman only sixteen or seventeen years old, hair braided in pigtails, pink skirts soiled from her forest escape. His eyes flickered to the two men. They were plump, hands ink-stained: town workers and bureaucrats, not warriors.

Styx leant forward a little, and drummed his fingers on the table. Saark saw they were near to Kell's Svian, and he blinked. It was unlike Kell to leave behind this weapon; it was his last blade, what he used when parted from his axe. A Svian, so the unwritten rule went, was also used in times of desperation for suicide. For Kell to have left it was… foolish, and meant that something had touched him; had rattled his cage. Did he know these people?

"You're a pretty little man, aren't you?" said Styx. He smiled through blackened stumps of teeth, which merged nauseatingly with the stained lips of the Blacklipper. I bet his breath stinks like a skunk, thought Saark.

"What, you mean in contrast to your own obviously handsome facial properties?"

Anger flared in Styx's good eye, but he controlled it with skill. Saark became wary. There was something more at stake here than a simple trading of insults. This was too controlled, too planned. What did they want?

"What I meant to say," said Styx, tongue moistening his black lips, "is that you're a pretty boy."

"Meaning?"

"Well, it's like this. I love fucking pretty boys, so I do. In more ways than one."

Jex laughed, and Saark caught a glimpse of steel beneath clothing. A hidden blade. Saark's hand strayed towards his own sword, a tentative crawl of edging fingers, eyes never leaving the two men exuding hate and arrogance and dark violent energy.

"I like to hear them squeal, you understand," smiled Styx, "only because pretty boys take so much better to the knives, to the scars. They scream, high and long, like a woman, and when you fuck them, later on as they're bent over a log or table, oh that feeling, so tight, so much resistance," he laughed, a low grumble of mirth, "what I like to call a good tight virgin-fuck, well man, that brings tears to old Styx's eye. But not as much as flowing tears to the weeping eyes of a pretty boy."

Saark smiled easily. "Well then, gentlemen, you seem to have me mixed up with somebody else. Because I fuck women, I fuck men, I fuck anything that moves. I'm used to taking it, so would offer little sport as your... how do you say? Virgin-fuck? But what I will offer..." He launched up, sword out, a movement so quick it brought the room to a sudden standstill and caught Styx and Jex with their mouths open... "Well, if it's a little sword-sport you want, I'm all yours, gentlemen."

Slowly, Jex pulled a weapon from beneath his clothing and pointed it at Saark. It was small, little bigger than his hand, and made from polished oak. Saark tilted his head, frowning. He had never seen such a weapon. There came a tiny *click*.

"You are familiar, of course," said Jex, "with the workings of a crossbow? This is similar. It can punch a fist sized-hole through a man at a hundred metres. It works on clockwork, was created by the very enemy who now advance through our land." He stood, chair scraping, and Saark licked suddenly dry lips. Styx stood as well, beside Jex, and pulled free a similar weapon.

"We call it a Widowmaker," said Styx, single eye gleaming. "But rather than cause unnecessary bloodshed, I see you need a demonstration." His arm moved, there came a *click* and a *whump* as the clockwork-powered mini-crossbow discharged. The sixteen year-old villager was picked up and slammed across her bed, an impact of red at her breast, a funnel of flesh exploding from her back and splattering up the wooden wall with strips of torn heart and tiny shards of bone shrapnel.

"No!" screamed the older woman, and ran to the dead teenager, sobbing, mauling at her corpse which rolled, slack and useless and dead, to the floor. The room fell still; cold and terrifying.

"Damn you, you could have fired at a target!" raged Saark.

Styx nodded, gaze fixed to Saark. "Aye, I did. I find the horrors of the flesh have more immediate impact."

235

Kat stalked forward, eyes furious, hands clenching and un-clenching. "You cheap dirty stinking bastards! She was an innocent villager, she meant no harm to you; why the hell would you do that? Why the hell would you kill an unarmed girl?"

Styx smiled, showing blackened stumps. "Because," he said, eye narrowing, all humour leaving his face to be replaced by an innate cruelty, the natural evil of the predator, the natural amorality of the shark, "I am a Jailer," he said, "and I thrive on the pleasure of killing sport."

"The Jailers," said Saark, voice barely above a whisper, sword still poised.

Styx nodded. "I see you have heard of us."

"What the hell are Jailers?" snapped Kat, eyes moving fast be-tween Jex, Styx and Saark. She willed Saark to attack. She had seen him in battle, seen him kill with his pretty little rapier; she knew he could get to them in time, could slaughter them like the walking offal they were...

"They spent five years in Yelket Jail," said Saark, speaking to Kat but not moving his eyes from the two men with their clockwork crossbows. "They are very, very dangerous. They were put inside because of Kell. And six months ago, they escaped, and have been terrorising travellers on the Great North Road, killing Leanoric's soldiers and innocent people up and down the land... they are des-tined to be hanged."

"See, you do know us," smiled Styx, and his weapon settled on Kat. "Now, Saark, my queer little friend, I want you to place your sword *very slowly* on the ground. One wrong move, and I blow a ragged hole through Kat's pretty, pouting face."

Saark tensed... and from outside, heard a shout–

Myriam kissed Kell, and he allowed himself to be kissed, but his thoughts flowed back to his long dead wife, so long ago, so distant and yet so real and images flickered through his mind... getting married under the Crooked Oak, Ehlana with flowers in her hair and she kissed him and it was sweet and they were young and carefree, not knowing what troubles would face them over the coming years... and here, and now, this kiss felt like a betrayal even though she was dead, and so long ago gone, and cold, and dust under the ground. Kell pulled away. "No," he said.

"Help me," breathed Myriam.

"I cannot."

"You *will* not."

"Yes." He looked into her torture-riddled eyes. "I will not."

"I think you will," she said, and pushed the brass needle into his neck. Kell grunted in pain, taking a step back as he slammed a right hook to Myriam's head, making her yell out as she was punched into a roll, coming up fast, athletically, on her feet with a dagger out, eyes gleaming, triumphant, a sneer on her lips.

Kell staggered back, fingers touching at the brass needle poking from his flesh like a tiny dagger. "Bitch. What have you done to me?"

"It's a poison," said Myriam, licking her lips, her eyes wide and triumphant. "Very slow acting. Comes from a brace of Trickla flowers, from way across the Salarl Ocean." She tilted her head. "I'm sure you've heard of it?"

Kell nodded, and with a hiss, pulled the needle free, stared down at it, glinting in his palm, covered in his blood.

"You have killed me, then," he said, eyes narrow, face filled with a dark controlled fury.

"Wait!" Myriam snapped, and seemed to be listening for something. Then she stared up at the night sky. "There is an antidote." She grinned at him, head like a skull by starlight. "I have hidden it. Far to the north. Take me to the Black Pike Mountains, Kell, and you will live!"

"How long do I have?"

"A few weeks, at most. But you will grow weak, Kell. You will suffer, even as I suffer. We will be linked, lovers in pain, suffering together in dark throes of an accelerating agony, both searching for a cure."

"I could kill you now, bitch, and take my chances."

Myriam stood up straight, and sheathed her dagger. She held her head high. Her hair was peppered with snow. "Then do it," she said, eyes locked to Kell, "and let's be finished with this fucking business."

Kell took his axe from his back, loosened his shoulder with a rolling motion, and strode towards Myriam with a look of pure and focused evil.

Inside the cabin, Saark leapt, sword slashing down. Styx and Jex moved fast, slamming apart in a heartbeat and Styx's Widowmaker gave another click and whump and something unseen blurred across the open space hitting Katrina in the throat and smacking her back against the wall, pinned her to the boards as her legs kicked and her topaz eyes grew impossibly bright with collected tears and she gurgled and choked and spewed blood, and her fingers scrabbled at her chest and neck and the huge open wound and the dark glinting coil of brass and copper at her throat and quite suddenly...

She died.

Kat slumped, hung there, limp and bloodied, a pinned ragdoll, her legs twisted at odd angles.

"No!" screamed Nienna, dragging free her own sword in a clumsy, obstructed action. "No!" She charged.

THIRTEEN
Insanity Engine

General Graal, Engineer and Watchmaker of the vachine, stood on the hilltop and surveyed the two divisions below him, each comprising 4,800 albino soldiers, mainly infantry; they glittered like dark insects in the moonlight, nearly ten thousand armoured men, one half of the Army of Iron, standing silent and disciplined in ranks awaiting his command. The second half of his army were north, pitched to the southwest of Jalder, different battalions guarding northern passes and other routes leading through the Black Pike Mountains; in effect, guarding the route back to the Silva Valley, home of the vachine. Graal did not want the enemy, despite their apparent ignorance, mounting a counter-attack on his homeland whilst he invaded. But... was Graal making a mistake, taking only half his army south? He smiled, knowing in his heart it was not arrogance that fuelled his decision, but a trust in technology. With the Harvesters, and the power of blood-oil magick, the Army of Iron were... invincible! Even against a foe of far greater numbers; and Falanor barely had that.

Invincible!

And he also had his cankers.

A noise echoed across the valley, and Graal turned, and with acute eyesight aided by clockwork picked out the many canker cages used for more volatile beasts. The less insane were tied up like horses; seemingly docile for the moment. Until they smelt blood. Until they felt the thrill of the kill. Graal watched, licking thin lips, eyes fixing on the huge, stocky beasts which he knew linked so very closely to the vachine soul...

Occasionally, claws would eject and slash at the belly of another canker with snarls and hisses; but other than this, they could be safely tethered. Graal was in possession of just over a thousand cankers; the rejects of vachine society. But more were coming. Many more. Graal went cold inside, as he considered their tenuous position with the Blood Refineries. He thought of Kradek-ka, and his heart went colder still, the gears in his heart stepping up, cogs *whirring* as he grimaced and in a moment of rare anger bared his teeth and swept his gaze over the land before him. Moonlight glittered on armour. Beyond, lay Vorgeth Forest, and angling down he would march on Vor.

Mine! he snarled, an internal diatribe of hate. These people would suffer, they would fall, and his army would *feed!*

Graal calmed himself, for it was not seemly to show temper – an effective loss of control. And especially not before the inferior albino clans from under the mountain. No. Graal took a deep breath. No. A Watchmaker should have charm, and stability, cold logic and control. They were the superior race. Superior by birth, genetics and ultimately, superior by clockwork.

Frangeth was a platoon lieutenant, and with sword drawn he led his twenty men through the trees under moonlight. An entire battalion had divided, spread out, and from different points north were advancing as scouting parties, ahead of the great General Graal himself. Frangeth was proud to be a part of this operation, and would happily give his life. For too long he had felt the hate of the southerners, their irrational ill-educated fear, and how their culture and art depicted his albino race as monsters, little more than insect workers worthy of nothing more than a swift execution. He had read many Falanor texts, with titles like *Northern Ethics, On Execution*, and the hate-fuelled *Black Pike Diaries* about a group of hardcore mercenaries who had travelled the aforementioned mountains, searching out "rogue albino scum" and slaughtering them without mercy.

Frangeth had been part of an elite squad under the command of the legendary Darius Deall, and they had infiltrated Falanor – a decade gone, now – to the far western city of Gollothrim. There, under cover of darkness, they had found the remains of the mercenary squad, and in particular, the authors of the *Black Pike Diaries*. Drunk, and rutting in whorehouses on the proceeds of their hateful tome, the five men had been captured, harshly beaten, and driven by ox-cart to the outskirts of Vorgeth Forest where lawlessness was a given. Here, in an abandoned barn previously scouted, old, deserted, with cracked timbers and wild rats, the authors of the *Black Pike Diaries* had been pegged out, cut and sliced and diced, and then left for the rats whilst the albino squad watched from a balcony, eating, drinking, talking quietly. The wild rats, free from a fear of man, took their time with their feast. The authors of the *Black Pike Diaries* had died a horrible but fitting death for their crime.

Frangeth shook his head, smiling at the memories. Ten years. Ten long years! He had raised a family back in his tunnel since then: two daughters, one of them only three years old and even more pretty than her mother, her eyes a deeper red, her skin so perfectly translucent veins stood out like a river map.

Frangeth pushed the images away. No. Not now. This was a time of invasion, a time of war. And here he was, back in the province of the southerners, with their hate and unrivalled prejudice; here he was, travelling the darkest reaches of Vorgeth Forest, searching for the enemy. Any enemy. He smiled. All southern blood tasted the same.

Frangeth and the soldiers were angling south-east, at the same time as a similar battalion crossed Valantrium Moor to the east and angled south-west, the idea being they would link as a forward host to the main force of Graal's army on the Great North Road. That way, it would be difficult for Leanoric's battalions to circle and hit them from behind. That way, it would be a straight fight, with the blood-oil magick chilling ice from the earth, and chilling the enemy... to their very bones.

Frangeth halted, and held up his hand, which gleamed, pale and waxen in the moonlight filtering through firs. Behind, the other nineteen members of the platoon dropped to one knee and waited his instruction. Frangeth heard several whispers of iron on leather, and his eyes narrowed. Such noise was unprofessional.

He focused. It had been a shout, of surprise, more than pain, that alerted him. He took in the scene with an experienced glance, watched the huge man, bear-like in his stance, pluck something from his neck and stare at his great paws. He spoke with... a woman, but a woman who appeared as nothing Frangeth had ever seen. She was skeletal, and quite obviously close to death. Frangeth watched the huge man un-sling a battle-axe from his back and march on the woman and a thrill coursed his veins, for the warrior's demeanour was quite obvious, his intention to kill...

The woman's head snapped right, and her eyes fixed on the darkness where Frangeth and his albino soldiers crouched. Impossible! They were shrouded by blood-oil magick; they were invisible! She drew a small weapon and her arm extended towards the group, she snarled something at the huge warrior as suddenly, there came an explosion of glass and through the window of the timber building accelerated a small, powerful man, to land with a grunt on the snow.

Frangeth glanced back. He blinked. They were waiting.

"Take them," he said, and from the close nigritude of the forest streamed twenty albino warriors...

Myriam fired her Widowmaker with a *whump*, and one of the charging albino soldiers was smacked from his feet with a gurgle and wide spray of blood. Kell loosened his shoulder and lifted his axe, waiting coolly for the rush of men. Saark leapt from the window of the building, landed lightly in the snow behind the stunned figure of Styx, and lifted his rapier to deliver a killing blow – as his eyes focused on the stream of albino soldiers and Kell bellowed, "Saark, to me!" and the albino soldiers were on them, swords slamming down, flashing with moonlight. Steel rang on steel as Myriam dragged free her own sword, the Widowmaker useless at such close quarters. Kell's axe whirred, decapitating a soldier then twisted, huge blades cleaving another's arm from his body. Kell ducked a whistling sword, but a boot struck his chest and he staggered back. Saark leapt into battle, and as the forest clearing was filled with savage fighting, the clash of steel on steel, grunts of combat, a shout from Myriam echoed.

"Styx! Jex! To me! I need you!"

Styx rolled from the snow, and came up fighting. Jex staggered from the building with a sword-wound to his upper arm, face grim, and lifting his blade he leapt into battle. At the doorway appeared Nienna, face drawn grey in fear, her short-sword clasped in one hand, the blade edged with Jex's blood. With a gasp, she turned and ran back to check on Kat...

Almost unconsciously, Kell, Saark, Myriam, Jex and Styx formed a fighting unit, a battle square upon which the albinos hurled themselves. Swords and Kell's axe rose and fell, and they covered one another's backs, pushing forward deeper into the forest as the albinos swarmed at them, and were cut down with a savagery not just of desperation, but born from a need to live.

Eight albinos lay dead, and the rest backed away a little, then split without word, six men moving off to each side for an attack against both flanks.

"Kell, what the hell's going on?" snarled Saark.

"Long story," growled Kell. "I'll tell you when we've killed these bastards."

"When?"

"Listen, just don't trust this bunch of cut-throats!"

"I already discovered that," snarled Saark. "Styx killed Katrina."

"What?"

In eerie silence the albinos attacked, and again the clearing was filled with steel on steel. Then a sword-blow cleaved Styx's shoulder with a crunch, and shower of blood. Styx drew out a short knife, and rammed it into the albino's belly, just under the edge of his black breast-plate. He pushed again, harder, and the albino slumped forward onto him. Myriam broke from the group, whirling and dancing, dazzlingly fast as she took up a second sword from a fallen soldier and leapt amongst the men, blades clashing and whirring, then in quick succession killing three albino soldiers who hit the ground in a burst. Saark killed two, and Kell waded into the remaining group with a roar that shook the forest, Ilanna slamming left, then right, a glittering figure of eight which impacted with jarring force leaving body-parts littering the clearing. Kell ducked a sword-strike, front kicked the soldier who stumbled, falling back onto his rump. Kell's axe glittered high, and came down as if chopping a log to cut the albino soldier straight through, from the crown of his head down to his arsehole. His body split in two, peeling away like parted sides of pork revealing brain and skull and fat and meat, and a slither of departing internal organs and bowel. A stench filled the clearing, and Kell turned, face a bloody mask, chest heaving, rage rampant in his eyes and frame. He realised the soldiers were all dead, and he lifted his axe, staring hard at Myriam. Styx sat on the floor, nursing his injured shoulder as Jex tried to stem the flow of blood.

Nienna ran out from the barracks, crying, and fell into Kell despite his coating of gore.

"Styx killed Katrina!" she wailed, then looked up into her grandfather's eyes. "Kill him, please, for me," she turned and pointed at Styx and wailed, "Kill him! Kill him now!"

Kell nodded, pushed Nienna aside, and started forward hefting his axe. Myriam leapt between them, head high, eyes bright, and she lifted a hand. "Wait. To kill him, you must go through me. And if you do that, you'll never find the antidote."

"A chance I'm willing to take," growled Kell. "Move, or I'll cut you in half."

"Nienna has also been poisoned."

Kell stopped, then, and his head lowered. When he lifted his face, his eyes were dark pools of evil in a face so contorted with rage it was inhuman; a writhing demon. Myriam took a step back.

Kell turned to Nienna. "Did he stick a needle in you?"

Nienna nodded, pointing at Jex. "That's why I was able to hit him. With my sword. He was too busy playing with his little brass dagger... his needle? What have they done to me?"

"They've poisoned us," snarled Kell.

"But there's an antidote?" said Saark.

"Yes. To the north. If I take this whore to the Black Pike Mountains. She wishes," he gave a nasty grin, "to explore the vachine technology. She wishes to live."

Saark stood alongside Kell, and Nienna. "We should kill them now. We will find this antidote."

"You do not have time," said Myriam, voice soft. "It takes between two and three weeks for the poison to kill. It would be more than that to sail across the Great Salarl." She transferred her gaze to Nienna, and gave a narrow, cruel smile. Without looking at Kell, she said, "I understand your willingness to condemn yourself, old man. But what of this sweet child? So young, pretty, and with so much to look forward to. So much to *live* for."

"We need to warn Leanoric," said Saark, hand on Kell's arm.

Kell felt himself fold, internally; but outside he kept his iron glare, and turned to Nienna. "Do you understand what is happening?"

Nienna nodded, and wiped away her tears. "I understand there are many evil people in the world," she said, voice little more than a whisper. "But we must warn King Leanoric that the enemy approach. Or thousands more will die!"

Kell nodded, glancing at Myriam. "You hear that, bitch? I will take you to the mountains. But first, we ride south."

"You would gamble with your life? And that of the girl?" Myriam looked aghast, and she shook her head, staring down at Styx and Jex. Styx had his shoulder bound tight, and stood, flexing the limb.

Kell scowled at him. "Know this, Blacklipper. When we are done, I will come looking for you."

"I will be waiting," said Styx.

Ilanna beat a tattoo of warning in Kell's mind, and he gazed off between the trees. "I think there are more," he said, voice low. "We need to get the horses. We need to ride south now."

Saark and Jex went for the mounts, as snow tumbled from bleak dark skies above the edges of Vorgeth Forest. Within a few minutes they had mounted, Nienna behind Saark, and as the forest whispered with ancient leaves and branches and needles, so more platoons of albino soldiers, drawn by distant sounds of battle, emerged warily from the foliage. There were two platoons – forty soldiers, and their cautious advance turned swiftly into a run with weapons drawn as they spotted fallen comrades...

"Ride!" shouted Saark, and his horse reared. Myriam led the way, thundering out of the clearing down a narrow dark path, her sword in her fist, head lowered over her mount. The rest of the group followed, with Jex bringing up the rear firing bolts from his Widowmaker with metallic winding *thumps*, and smashing several soldiers from their feet.

Then they were gone, lost to the sinister forest.

King Leanoric calmed his horse, a magnificent eighteen-hand stallion, and peered off through the gloom. A curious mist had risen, giving the moorland plateau a curious, cut-off feeling, a sidestep from reality, a different level of existence.

He had left his personal guard behind, a mile hence, aware that the Graverobber would never agree to meet him with soldiers present. The Graverobber was a fickle creature at the best of times, but add in a heady mix of weapons, armour and soldierly sarcasm... well, claws were ejected and the Graverobber would begin to kill without question.

Leanoric walked over springy heather, and stopped by the towering circle of stones. *Le'annath Moorkelth*, they were called in the Old Tongue. Or simply the Passing Place in every contemporary

Falanor lexicon. Whatever the origins of the stones, it was said they were over ten thousand years old, and evidence of an earlier race wiped from existence by an angry god. Leanoric peered into the space between the stones, where the Graverobber dwelled, and again felt that curious sensation of light-headedness, as if colours were twisting into something... else. Leanoric rubbed his beard, then stepped into the circle and heard a hiss, a growl, and the patter of fast footfalls on heather...

The Graverobber leapt at him, and Leanoric forced his eyes to remain open, forced himself to stare at the twisted, corrugated body of the deformed creature, once human but deviated by toxins, poisons, its skin a shiny, ceramic black, tinkling as it moved, tinkling as if it might shatter. It, or he, was thin-limbed, his head perfectly round and bald with narrow-slitted eyes and a face not a thousand miles from that of a feline. He had whiskers, and sharp black teeth, and a small red tongue, and as he leapt for Leanoric with claws extending and powerful, corded muscles bunched for the kill, so Leanoric spoke his name, and in doing so, tamed the savage beast–

"Jageraw!"

The Graverobber hit the ground lightly, and turned, spinning around on himself on all fours before rearing into an upright walking position. Leanoric heard the crinkle of ceramic spine, and pretended he hadn't.

"What want you here, human?"

"I have questions."

"What makes you think I answer?"

"I have a gift."

"A gift? For me? How pretty. What is it?" Jageraw's demeanour changed, and he dropped to all fours again, black skin gleaming unnaturally. Leanoric opened the sack he was carrying, and steeling himself, put in his hand. He pulled out a raw liver. It glistened in the gloom, and the muscles on Leanoric's jaw went tight.

Jageraw sniffed, and edged closer, eyes watching Leanoric suspiciously. He swayed, peering past Leanoric into the gloom, then focused on the liver. "Human or animal?"

"Human," said Leanoric, voice little more than a whisper. "Just the way you like it."

Jageraw lashed out, taking the liver, then went through an elaborate sequence where he sniffed, and licked, and tasted, and sampled. When finally happy, the shiny black creature, glistening as if coated with oil, moved to the centre of the stone circle, dug up a little earth and buried the organ.

"You bring me more, human man?"

"Answers."

"To questions? Ask questions. You bring me more?"

"I have two hearts, two kidneys and another liver."

Jageraw's eyes went wide, as if offered the finest feast of his life. He licked his thin shiny lips, and his sharp teeth clattered for a moment as if in unadulterated excitement.

"Ask your questions."

"There is an army advancing on my land. It is said they use blood-oil magick." Jageraw twitched, as if stung, and a crafty look stole over his face. "I want to know if it is true."

"Who leads the army?"

"General Graal. He is a… vachine."

Jageraw hunkered down, and hissed. "They are not good. They are bad. They are not pretty. They are far from pretty. You want to avoid these men, they have blood-oil magick. Yes."

"How do I fight them?"

"Hmm. The food smells nice. Smells pretty. Smells succulent. Jageraw would like another sample."

Leanoric threw the bag, which thudded as it hit the ground. Jageraw leapt forward, excitement thrumming through his taut muscled body, and Leanoric watched the Graverobber chewing and tasting, head in the bag, then emerging, blood dribbling down his chin as his dark eyes surveyed King Leanoric.

"You are very generous, *sire*." He chuckled, as if at some great jest. His head tilted, and not for the first time Leanoric thought to himself, what the hell kind of creature are you? What happened to you? Why do you eat human remains – hence earning the title of Graverobber, from earlier days? Days when you robbed graves for your food. And, ultimately, why can you no longer leave this ancient circle of stones? Others had asked such questions, and several eminent professors from Jalder University had been sent to research the Old Ways and the Blood-oil Magick Legacy for purposes of scholarly study. All were dead. Jageraw might seem an oddity, but he was powerful beyond belief, and had the ability to… fade away when threatened.

Once, three mercenaries had been hired to bring back the

Graverobber's carcass, with or without a head. One entered the circle with a bag of goodies, and enticed Jageraw out as his comrades waited in the gloom of falling night with powerful longbows. They peppered Jageraw with savage, barbed, poisoned arrows, six or seven of which thudded home to sprays of bubbling blood in slick black flesh. In squealing agony, Jageraw grabbed the first mercenary within the circle and they... vanished. Or so the story went. The man's companions waited for three nights for their friend, and one evening emerged to discover him lying in the circle, his body peeled but still, incredibly, alive. He'd whimpered pitifully, pleading and begging for help. His companions on impulse rushed into the circle, and Jageraw pounced from nowhere, his body perfectly healed, his claws cutting through swords and shields to sever heads from bodies. That night, Jageraw ate well.

Now, people left the Graverobber to himself.

"You want to fight Army of Iron, you say? Yes. Their blood-oil magick is powerful, very powerful, and they walk the Old Ways with Harvesters of Legend. That is where their power comes from. Freeze your men with horror," he chuckled, "they will."

"I never said it was the Army of Iron," said Leanoric, eyes narrowing.

"That is who Graal commands. Kill him, you must." Jageraw took a bite from a human heart, and chewed thoughtfully, staring down at his food. "Their magick takes time to cast, that is your strength. They attack at night, yes, pretty pretty night. You must think of a way to circle them, or draw them out. Once they unleash their magick, for a little while, it is out of their control. Now I must go. Now I must eat. Told you too much, I have."

Jageraw grinned, dark eyes glinting malevolently.

"Thank you... Jageraw."

"Come back any time," said the slick black creature, backing away from King Leanoric with ceramic tinklings. "Bring gifts, bring feast, pretty meat from still warm human bodies is what I prefer." His eyes blinked, and he started to fade. "If you survive, little king," he chuckled, and was gone.

Leanoric realised he was kneeling, and stood up. He backed hurriedly from the ancient circle of stones, and realised his sword was half drawn. He shivered, aware there were some things he would never understand; and acknowledging there were things he did not want to understand. Jageraw could rot, for all he now cared.

Leanoric turned, mounted his horse, and set off across the mist-laden moors as fast as he dared.

Behind, at the edge of the circle, unseen and rocking rhythmically sat Jageraw, gnawing on fresh liver, and waving with crinkled, blood-stained claws.

Kell, Saark, Nienna, Myriam, Styx and Jex rode hard through the rest of the night, exhausting their horses and breaking out onto the Great North Road just north of Old Skulkra, a deserted ghost-city which sat three leagues north of the relatively new, modern, and relocated city of Skulkra.

They reined in mounts on a low hill, gazing down the old, overgrown, frost-crusted road which led from the Great North Road to distant, crumbling spires, smashed domes, detonated towers, fragmented buildings and fractured defensive walls. On the flat plain before Old Skulkra Leanoric had two divisions camped after moving north from Valantrium Moor, 9,600 men plus a few cavalry, lancers and archers stationed to the north of the infantry to provide covering fire in case of surprise attack. In the dawn light their fires had burned low, but there was activity.

"Remember," said Myriam, leaning forward over the pommel of her saddle. "Any tricks or signals, and the girl dies in two weeks time. A terrible, painful death."

"How could I forget?" said Kell, and went as if to ride for Leanoric's camp.

"Wait," said Saark, and Kell turned on him. There was pain there, in Saark's face, in his eyes, and he smiled a diluted smile at Kell, then gazed off, towards the camp. "I cannot come," he said.

"Why the hell not?" snapped Kell. "It was your damn fool idea to warn the king in the first place!"

"To travel to that camp would mean death," said Saark, voice gentle.

"What are you muttering about, lad? Come on, we need to warn Leanoric. Those bastards might only be a few hours behind us. What if they hit the army now, like this, camped and scratching its arse? It will be a rout, and they'll flood into the south like a plague."

"If I go down there," said Saark, quietly, "King Leanoric will have me executed."

"Why the hell would he do that, lad?"

Saark looked down, and when he looked up, there were tears in his eyes. "I... betrayed him. Betrayed his trust. And he sentenced me to death. I... ran. Yes. I stand before you filled with shame."

"And still you have come back to warn him?" sneered Styx. "What a fucking fool you are, Saark. As I said. A pretty boy."

"If you do not close your stinking, horse-arse mouth, I'll shove my sword so far up your belly it'll come out the top of your head! Understand, *Blacklipper*?"

Kell held up his hand, glaring at Myriam. "What did you do, Saark?" His voice was soft, eyes understanding.

Saark took a deep breath. "I was Leanoric's Sword-Champion. I was entrusted with guarding the queen. Alloria. We... I, fell in love with her. We committed a great sin, both of us betraying the great King Leanoric." He fell silent, unable to look at Kell. Finally, he glanced up. He met Kell's gaze. "I have been running away ever since. I have been a coward. I knew, when the army invaded Jalder, that even though I might die I had to come here. I had to try and help, even though they would slaughter me as a base criminal, a rapist, a murderer. Now... I cannot face it. Although I should."

Kell nudged his horse forward, and patted Saark on the back. "Don't worry lad. You stay here. I'll go and speak to the king. I know him from... way back. I'll let him know what is happening to his realm."

Saark nodded, and Kell gestured to Nienna. "Come with me, girl. It is important to meet nobility, even in times such as these. I will teach you how to speak with a king."

"I am coming with you," said Myriam.

"No," said Kell.

"I don't trust you."

Kell laughed, then waved his hand. "So be it. You think I would risk my only chance of beating your pathetic little poison for my granddaughter? Come, then, Myriam; come and frighten the little children with your skull face." Myriam flushed crimson with fury, but bit her tongue and said nothing, eyes narrowed, hand on sword-hilt. If Kell had to endure her poison, he reasoned, then she, too, would have to endure his. They were symbiotic, now; but that didn't mean Kell had to enjoy it.

"You see the stand of trees? Over yonder?"

"Aye," said Kell.

"We'll wait for you there," said Saark, eyes hooded, face filled with melancholy.

Kell nodded, reading Saark's face. "Play nice, now," he said, and kicked his horse forward alongside Nienna. A moment later, Myriam followed leaving the three men on the low hill. They watched the small group descend, where they were quickly intercepted by scouts and a small, armoured cavalry squad. Weapons were taken from them, and they were escorted towards the shadowy, crumbling walls of a leering, eerie Old Skulkra.

"You leading the way, pretty boy?" grinned Styx. Saark glanced at him, and saw the Widowmaker held casual in one fist, wound and giving an occasional tick. Saark nodded, and guided his horse south, down the hill and towards nearby woodland. As he rode, his thoughts turned violent.

"Kell! By all the gods, it is good to see you!"

King Leanoric's tent was filled with incense, rich silks and furs, and he was seated in full armour around a narrow table containing maps, alongside Terrakon and Lazaluth, his Division Generals. They had cups of water clasped in gnarled hands, and Lazaluth smoked a pipe, dark eyes narrowed, ancient white whiskers yellowed from the pipe smoke he so loved.

The men stood, and Kell grinned, embracing first Leanoric, then Terrakon and Lazaluth, both of whom Kell knew well, for they had fought alongside one another in ancient, half-forgotten campaigns. The four men stood apart, smiling sombrely.

"I hope, by all that's holy, you've come to fight," said Leanoric.

"So my journey is wasted? You know of the events in Jalder?"

"Only that is has been taken. We have no specifics. It would seem," Leanoric's face turned dark, brooding, "that few survived."

Myriam and Nienna were taken outside, and seated with a group of women awaiting a meal of stew and bread. They accepted this food thankfully, and Myriam found Nienna watching her strangely; there was a hint of hate, there, but also a deep thread of needful revenge. Myriam smiled. Nienna's bitterness, growing cynicism and fast rise to adulthood started to remind her of herself.

Inside the war-tent, Kell hurriedly outlined his recent exploits in Jalder, from the ice-smoke invasion and the incursion of heartless, slaughtering albino soldiers, murdering men, women and children without mercy, down to accounts of the cankers and Harvesters, and the subsequent battles as they travelled south.

"Have you seen this Army of Iron?" said Lazaluth, puffing on his pipe and churning out a cloud of blue smoke.

Kell shook his head. "Only platoons of albino soldiers. But they fight like bastards, and use the ice-smoke blood-oil magick – freezing everybody in their path. And they have the cankers. I know in my heart they have more of these beasts; they are savage indeed."

"How far behind you lies this albino army?"

"The vanguard? No more than a few hours."

"Really," said Leanoric, voice low. His eyes narrowed. "My scouts, to a man, tell me three days. We have another two divisions on the march; they will arrive tomorrow, just ahead of the enemy."

"No," said Kell, shaking his head. "Your scouts are… lying. Or misinformed. Graal is closer than you believe, I swear this by every bone in my body."

"That's impossible!" roared Terrakon. "I have known Angerak since he was a pup! He is a fine scout, and would never betray his king, nor his country! Get the lad in here, we'll question him. You must be mistaken, Kell. It is not in this boy's nature."

Kell waited uneasily as Angerak was summoned, and he felt the eyes of the old Division Generals on him. He grinned at them, a broad-teeth grin. "You can cut out that shit, gentlemen; I no longer serve under your iron principles. You can stick your polished breastplates up your arse!"

"You always were a cheeky young bear," growled Terrakon. "But fight! Gods, I have never seen a man fight like you. It's good to have you here, Kell. It is a good omen. We're going to give this Graal a kicking he won't forget, send him running back to the Black Pikes squeaking with his shitty piglet tail between his legs. Aye?"

Angerak was shown in, and he bowed before Leanoric. He cast a sideways glance at Kell, displaying a narrowed frown, then returned his eyes to the king. "Majesty, you sent for me?"

"Tell me again what you saw of the enemy on your journey north."

"I filed a full report already, sire. I–"

"Again, Angerak."

Angerak looked left and right, at the old Division Generals, then coughed behind the back of his hand. "I travelled up over Corleth

Moor; it was bathed in a heavy mist, and I dismounted, moved further in on foot. There, in the Valley of Crakken Fell, I saw the Army of Iron, camped out with perhaps three to four thousand soldiers. They were disorganised, like children playing at war; like idiots in a village carnival. We will slaughter them with ease, sire. Do not worry."

"So," Leanoric chose his words with infinite care, "there is... no chance they could be closer?"

"No, sire. I would have passed them on my journey. I have been a scout for many years; I do not make mistakes. There were no other battalions nearby, and their skills at subterfuge were, shall we say, lacking."

"It's funny, laddie," interjected Kell, drawing all eyes in the war-tent to him, "but, you know, I've just been chased here through Vorgeth Forest with at least sixty albino soldiers right behind me. Their army is close behind, I'd wager. What would you say to that?"

Angerak placed his hand on his sword-hilt. "I would say you are mistaken, sir." A cool and frosted silence descended on those in the tent. Terrakon and Lazaluth exchanged meaningful glances. Angerak looked around, eyes hooded. "I would also suggest I do not like your tone."

"What are they paying you, boy? What did General Graal offer?"

Angerak said nothing. His eyes remained fixed on Leanoric. He shook his head. Finally, he said, "You are mistaken in your beliefs. I have been a faithful scout for the past–" The dagger appeared from nowhere, and in a quick lunge he leapt at Leanoric... but never made the strike. In his back appeared Ilanna, with a sickening *thutch*, and Angerak crashed to floor on his face. Kell stepped forward, placed his boot on Angerak's arse and wrenched free the weapon, dripping molten flesh. He looked around at those present.

"Get your scouts in here," he said. "It would seem Graal has already infiltrated your army." Kell threw Leanoric a thunderous frown. "I hope your strategy is in place, gentlemen."

"We have two divisions coming from the north-east," said Leanoric. "They will be here by the morning."

Kell rubbed his beard. "So you have just under ten thousand men? Let us hope the enemy is weak..."

"We must draw the Army of Iron back, into the city wasteland of Old Skulkra. I will have archers placed in ancient towers – a thousand archers! If we can do this, fake a retreat, draw them in, then we will slaughter them." Leanoric stepped forward, sighing. "Kell, will you stay? Will you help us?"

"You have your generals here," said Kell, voice grave, looking to Terrakon and Lazaluth. "I have my granddaughter to consider... but I will help, where I can." He stepped swiftly from the tent... just as a scream rent the air...

"Attack! We're under attack!"

The camp exploded into action, with men scrambling into armour and strapping on weapons. Fires flared. Distant over the plain, before Old Skulkra, the enemy could be seen: the Army of Iron, formed into squares, a huge and terrifying, perfectly organised mass. They marched down from the hills in clockwork unity, boots stomping frozen grass and snow, the gentle rattle of accoutrements the only indication they were marching into battle. Leanoric strode out behind Kell, his strong face lined with anxiety. Quickly, he surveyed the enemy, and something went dead inside as he realised the two armies were equally matched. This was not to be his finely trained troops routing invading, poorly fed brigands from the mountains. This was two advanced armies meeting on a flat plain for a tactical battle...

Draw them back into the city.

Break away from the ice-smoke, from the blood-oil magick...

His troops had been warned; they knew what to do if General Graal attempted underhand tactics. But would this be enough? With a skilled eye Leanoric read the albino discipline like a text. They were tight. Impossibly so.

Over the horizon, dawn light crept like a frightened child.

"Generals!" bellowed Leanoric, taking a deep breath and stepping forward. "To me! Captains – organise your companies, now!" Leanoric's men quickly fell into ranks, reorganised into battle squares, as they had done so many times on the training field. Leanoric felt pride swell his chest in the freezing dawn chill, for the men of Falanor showed no fear, and moved with a practised agility and professionalism.

Then his eyes fell to the enemy.

The Army of Iron had halted, weapons bristling. They looked formidable, and eerily silent, pale faces hazy through distance, and through a light mist that curled across the ground.

"They look invincible," said Leanoric, voice quiet.

"They die like any other bastard," growled Kell. "I have seen this. I have done this." He turned, and grasped Leanoric's arm. "So you're going to draw them back into the city? That is your strategy?"

"If it starts to go badly, aye," said Leanoric. He gave a crooked smile. "If they try to use blood-oil magick. I have a few surprises in store in Old Skulkra."

The enemy ranks across the virgin battlefield parted, and several figures drifted forward between heavily armoured troops, even as Leanoric's captains organised battle squares before the fragmented walls of Old Skulkra. The figures were impossibly tall for men, and wore white robes embroidered in fine gold. They had flat, oval, hairless faces, small black eyes, and slits where the nose should have been. As they advanced before the Army of Iron, they stopped and surveyed Leanoric's divisions.

"Harvesters," said Kell, his voice soft, eyes hard.

And then a howling rent the air, followed by snarls and growls and the enemy ranks parted further as cankers were brought forward, devoid of protective cages, all now on leashes and many held by five, or even ten soldiers. They pulled at their leashes, twisted open faces drawn back, saliva and blood pooling around savage fangs as they snapped and growled, whined and roared, slashing at one another and squabbling as they arraigned their mighty, heavily-muscled, leonine bodies before the infantry squares in a huge, ragged, barely-controlled line.

Leanoric paled, and swallowed. He felt a chill fear sweep his soldiers. "Angerak never spoke of these beasts," he said, voice impossibly low, eyes fixed on the living nightmare cohort of the snarling, thrashing cankers…

They heard a distant command echo over the brittle, chill plain.

The cankers were suddenly unleashed with a jerk of chains, and with cacophonous howls of unbidden joy and bloodlust, a thousand heavily muscled beasts, of deviated flesh and perverted clockwork, charged and surged and galloped forward with snarls and rampant glee… towards the fear-filled ranks of Leanoric's barely organised army.

FOURTEEN
Inner Sanctum

Anu snarled, leaping at the Harvester which made an almost lazy, slow-motion gesture which nevertheless swept Anu aside with an invisible blow. She rolled fast, came up snarling, and circled the Harvester with more care. The Harvester flexed bone fingers, and lowered its head, black eyes glowing, as behind the creature, Alloria backed away, towards the crumpled figure of Vashell and some strangely perceived safety.

More ice-smoke swirled.

Anu attacked, and the Harvester moved fast, arms coming up as Anu's claws slashed down. The Harvester swiped at her, but she ducked, rolled fast, and her claws cut its robe and the pale flesh within. Skin and muscle parted, but no blood emerged.

Anu rolled free, and her eyes were gleaming, feral now, all humanity, even vachine intelligence gone as something else took over her soul and she reverted to the primitive.

"She cut it," whispered Vashell, his eyes wide. Never had he seen such a thing.

The Harvester shrugged off its robe, to reveal a naked, sexless, pale white body sporting occasional clumps of thick black hairs, like a spider's. Its legs were long and jointed the wrong way, like a goat's, and narrow taut muscles writhed under translucent flesh.

The Harvester moved fast, attacking Anu in loping strides, bone fingers slashing the air with a whistle. Anu rolled back, came up with her fangs hissing, then leapt again to be punched from her feet, sliding along frozen grass and almost pitching into the sluggish flow of the Silva River. Immediately she was up, charging, and rolled under swiping bone fingers, reversing her charge to leap on the Harvester's back. It swung around, trying to dislodge her, and savagely Anu's claws gouged the Harvester's throat, ripping free a handful of flesh, of windpipe, of muscle. She landed lightly, back-flipping away as the Harvester staggered.

It turned, and glared at her, eyes glowing, face now snarling. It did not speak. It could not speak. Anu held its windpipe in her fist. Amazingly, instead of dying, the Harvester attacked and Anu deflected a quick succession of blows with her forearms, and bone fingers clattered against her claws and the Harvester looked surprised... Anu's vachine claws should have been cut free. They were not. It snarled at her with a curious hissing gurgle, launched forward and grabbed her, picking her up above its head and moving as if to throw her... but Anu twisted, and there came a savage crack. The Harvester's arm broke, bone poking free through pale skin, again with no blood, just torn straggles of fish-flesh. Anu landed, and her claws slashed the Harvester's belly, then she leapt and her fangs fastened on its head, bearing it to the ground like a dwarf riding a giant. She savaged the Harvester's eyes, biting them out and spitting them free, then staggered back, strips of pale flesh hanging from her fangs, her face stunned as the mangled form of the Harvester rose and orientated on her. The mangled face smiled, and with a scream Anu ran at the creature, both feet slamming its head and driving it staggering backwards. It toppled, into the river, went under, and was immediately swept away. *Gone.*

Anu knelt, panting, staring at the cold surging waters, which calmed, flowing back into position with chunks of bobbing ice. She stood, smoothed her clothing, then turned on Vashell. His eyes were wide in his bloodied mask.

"That is... impossible," he said, softly.

"I killed it!" snarled Anu, face writhing with hatred and a strange light of triumph, of victory, conquering her fear.

"No," said Vashell, shaking his head. "You *hurt* it. And now, it simply needs a little time to..." He gave a soft smile, a caricature of the vachine in his demonic, faceless face. "Regenerate."

Anu stared at him, then back to the river. "Get on the boat."

Vashell eased himself to his feet, huge frame towering over Alloria. Unconsciously, Alloria reached out to help him, to steady him, and he stared at her, surprise in his eyes. She said nothing, but aided him hobbling to the jetty, and then down onto the long Engineer's Barge. Vashell slumped to a seat, blood tears running down his neck, and Alloria stared at her hands – also gore-stained – and then into Vashell's eyes.

"Thank... you," he managed. He licked at the broken stumps of his vachine fangs. They leaked precious blood-oil. He was growing weak. He laughed at this, a musical sound. Maybe he would die, after all.

Anu leapt into the boat, and as they moved away from the jetty, the frozen ground sliding away, five more Harvesters emerged from the mist. They drifted to the edge of the river, staring silently at the boat.

Anu stared back, unspeaking.

"We will hunt you to the ends of the earth," said one, voice a sibilant whisper, and then they were gone, swallowed by towering walls of black rock, the Engineer's Barge sucked further away and further into the desolate, brutal realm of the Black Pike Mountains.

The brass barge journeyed up the river, clockwork engine humming, nose pushing through chunks of ice. A cold wind howled, desolate and mournful like a lost spirit, and eventually they came to a river junction, where two wide fast flowing sections split, each heading off up a particular steep canyon of leering mountains. Anu's eyes followed each route, then she turned to Vashell who was sat, head resting on the barge rail, clawless fingers flexing.

"Which way?" she said.

"You really want to know?"

"Yes." She scowled. "Take me to my father."

"You won't like what you find."

"I will be the judge of that, vachine."

Vashell chuckled, and sighed. His fingers touched his ruined face, tenderly, and he glanced up, and over, at the raging waters, pointing. "That way."

"Are you sure?"

"Of course I am sure, girl!"

"Where does it lead?"

"Why," Vashell smiled, a demonic vision on his tortured face. "It leads to the Vrekken. And to Nonterrazake beyond."

Anu stared at him for a while, holding the brass barge steady in a gentle equilibrium against the current. "That cannot be," she said, finally.

"Why not?"

"Nonterrazake is a myth."

"It is a reality," said Vashell, smugly.

"You have been there?"

"It is something I do not wish to discuss, child." His eyes became hooded.

"I can cause you much pain, and bring you a savage death," said Anu, face ugly with anger in the snow-laden gloom.

Vashell shrugged. "There are some things far worse than death, Anu. That, you will learn. You want me to take you to Kradek-ka, then I will take you to Kradek-ka, although I promise you, you will not thank me for it, nor like the things you learn. But such is the nature of humanity, is it not?" He laughed, then, at his own private joke. "And that of the twisted vampire machines."

Anu guided the Engineer's Barge up the river, and as night fell, and the raging torrents grew calm again, she moored the craft in the centre of the wide river in order to gain a few hours' sleep.

She moved to central chambers below deck, and watched as Alloria made herself comfortable on a narrow bunk. "How do you feel?" asked Anu, and saw the way Alloria looked at her. As if she was a lethal, unpredictable, uncontrollable wild animal. Anu sighed.

"I will be fine once I leave this country," said Alloria, voice gentle, eyes red-rimmed. Only then did Anu realise she had been crying. "Once I travel home."

"You are upset?"

"My country is besieged by a savage clockwork race, and my husband must risk his life in battle. Yes, I am upset. I fear my children will be slaughtered. I fear my husband will have his throat cut. But most of all," she stared hard at Anu, "I fear your people will conquer."

"I am not part of their war," said Anu.

"You are one of them."

"They cast me aside!"

Alloria shrugged, her fear a tangible thing, and Anu realised with great sadness that she had lost Alloria. Alloria had seen the beast raging in Anu's soul; it had shocked her to the core.

"You are still vachine," said Alloria, and turned her back on Anu, snuggling under a heavy blanket.

Anu moved back to the upper deck, and checked the bindings on Vashell. With his vachine claws, he would have easily escaped; but now, neutered as he was, a machine vampire gelding, he could do little harm.

"You should let me go," said Vashell, looking into Anu's eyes.

"No."

"I will tell you the way. Draw you a map... in my own blood." He laughed, and Anu met his gaze. "I do love you, Anu. You know that?"

"You would kill me! You saw me disgraced. You revelled in your power and violent abuse."

"I have many faults," said Vashell. Then he gestured to his face, and chuckled again. "You have taught me humility." His voice grew more serious, emerging as a low growl. "But I do love you. I will always love you. Until the day I die. Until the day you kill me. You thought, back in Silva Valley, I was full of arrogance and hatred and superiority. You were right. I was despicable, and I understand why you spurned my offers of marriage; it wasn't just your fear at being different, Anu, it was deeper, in your soul, under lock and key." He sighed, and looked up at the heavy, cloud-filled sky. More snow began to tumble, and it drifted like ash. "We are destined, you and I. To live in a world of mixed love and hate, each strand intertwining around our hearts, our cores."

He gazed at Anu, eyes filled with tears.

"I will still kill you," said Anu, with tombstone voice.

"Good! I would not have it any other way. Go to sleep now. I will try nothing, do nothing. Trust me. After all... you took away my claws, you took away my fangs. Don't you realise? I am like you, Anu. I am neutered. I am an outcast. You turned me into yourself. I can never go back."

Anu walked down to her cabin, a narrow affair with nothing more than a bunk and brass walls. She locked the door, and realised with horror that Vashell was right. By removing his vachine tools, she had destroyed his rank, his standing, his nobility. She had deformed him from a beautiful vachine. There would be no repair by the Engineers; only terminal condemnation for his very great weakness.

So where would he go? What would he do?

No. Anu had attached Vashell to herself, to her mission, with chains much stronger than love. She had condemned him with a force of exile; an extradition of country, but more importantly, also of race.

The morning was bright and crisp, and snow had fallen lightly during the night, covering the brass barge with a light peppering of white. Vashell uncurled from slumber as Anu crept up the steps, and he stared at her with a bleak smile. Already, his face was healing, skin growing back over his destroyed features; but he would never look the same again. Despite his advanced vachine healing powers, he would be savagely scarred. Anu had, effectively, taken away his handsomeness. Removed his nobility.

Within a few minutes the brass barge was nosing up river, and for the course of the day they came upon more and more tributaries where a decision had to be made on which path to follow. Unfalteringly, Vashell would point, sometimes with a smart comment, other times in brooding silence as his moods swung from savage brutality to almost joyous abandon, as if high on a natural heady cocktail, where he would joke about his ruined features, and mock Anu, saying she was now the only girl for him, and they could breed twisted canker babies together.

As night fell, Anu sat on the deck for a while, huddled in a cloak. Vashell revelled in the cold. Alloria, who had been brooding and silent for the day, returned to her small brass room and huddled under blankets, crying softly to herself. Anu attempted to comfort her, but Alloria had taken to ignoring the young vachine.

"Tell me about Nonterrazake," said Anu.

"No."

"Tell me!"

"No!" He laughed. "There are some secrets a man must keep. Some dark truths he must hold to his heart, like spirals of soul; I could tell you, but it would melt your sweet little mind, curl the edges of your heart into blackened wisps of hatred, burn your soul with an eternity of hell-fire."

Anu shrugged. "Will the Harvesters really come?"

"Yes." Vashell's tone turned serious. "You should not have done what you did; you have angered the Harvesters beyond reprise. They will never, ever, stop the hunt."

"Then I will kill them!" Anu snapped, annoyed at Vashell's negativity.

Vashell shrugged. "When they send five? Ten? A hundred?"

"There are that many?"

"You do not understand what they are," he said, voice gentle.

"Well, they will have to catch me, first," snapped Anu, eyes narrowed.

"That shouldn't be a problem," said Vashell, scratching at his wounded face and the itching, repairing skin.

"Meaning?"

"You travel to Nonterrazake. For your father. Well, that is their homeland. It is the Harvesters who hold Kradek-ka."

Anu sat in stunned silence, unable to speak, unable to think. She had assumed they were fleeing the Harvesters. Now, it seemed, to rescue her father she would have to travel into the belly of the beast.

She gazed up at the stars. They twinkled, impossibly distant. And for a long time, Anu felt her soul melt, felt all hope vanish, and realised that her strength had gone.

In despondency, she went below deck for an endless, troubled, twisting sleep.

Anu slept late, and Alloria awoke her.

"He's gone."

"What? Who?"

"Vashell. The man whose face you removed with your claws."

Groggy, and feeling as if she'd been drugged, Anu stumbled on deck and stared hopelessly at the place where Vashell had been tied. His bonds lay, broken on the deck. He was nowhere to be seen.

Anu ran to the barge's rail. "Vashell!" she shouted. "Vashell!" Her words echoed out across mountain stone, and bounced back wreathed in early morning mist. There came no reply.

"What do we do now?" asked Alloria, softly.

"We continue without him."

For the morning they travelled, clockwork engine humming, up the ice-filled river. Deep into the maze of the Black Pike Mountains they navigated, were *absorbed*, and Anu realised that there was no life this far in. No animals, no birds; nothing. It was desolate, barren, as bleak as another world. Even the vegetation was dreary, white and pale green, grey and black. There were few, or no trees, the heady rich evergreens had vanished leagues behind. Only tufted grass remained, mostly ensnared by snow and ice. And yet the mountains... spoke to Anu. Rock-falls boomed. Ice cracked. Rock walls shifted. Boulders fell, crackling with menace to be swallowed by the Silva River. High up, occasionally, out of sight, they heard the terrifying roar of avalanche.

With every sound, the Black Pike Mountains screamed their dominance.

After a short break for a lunch of dried meat from the brass barge's hold, they continued, until Alloria, who was leaning at the craft's prow allowing breeze to stream through her hair, gasped.

"What is it?"

"There! That narrow river. To the left. Follow it!"

"What did you see?"

"Just follow it! Maybe I am going insane."

Anu nudged the brass barge up the narrow river, and they travelled for maybe a quarter of a league; the water grew deep, channelled between two towering four thousand feet walls of sheer black granite, polished and gleaming with ice, and they emerged into...

Into a lush, green clearing.

The water ended in a circular flat pool, and beyond the water's edge stood a proliferation of trees, plants and flowers. Colours and perfumes raged through the clearing, and Anu brought the barge to a halt, bumping against a natural sloped jetty of rock.

Alloria jumped out onto the jetty, and stood with hands on hips, smiling. The sun was shining, beaming down, warming her face, and she turned back to Anu and laughed. "What is this place?"

Anu climbed from the boat, wary, aware that when on the boat she had some small sanctuary from the Harvesters. She shook her head. "I do not know."

"Vashell talked of such a place," said Alloria.

"He did?"

"Yes, he said it led to... the Vrekken? Whatever that is. He said there would be green trees and flowers; and there would be a tunnel. Follow the tunnel, and the foolish traveller would find the Vrekken."

Anu turned, and her eyes narrowed. In the far wall there indeed was a tunnel opening. It was too perfect, so obviously man-made as opposed to a natural occurrence. This made Anu even more suspicious.

"Did he say anything else?"

"No. Look! Fruit!" Alloria ran to a tree and pulled down an apple. She took a bite, and laughed through juice. "It's wonderful! Fresh and clean. I can't believe this little... garden exists amongst the mountains. And can you smell the flowers?"

"I can."

Alloria tossed Anu an apple, which she caught and bit. Juice ran down her chin, and she felt her mood lighten a little. Alloria was right; this place, with the winter sun shining down between towering walls of rock, was a serious uplift to the soul.

"We cannot stay. We must stock up with supplies. We must continue."

Alloria sighed, and waded through flowers to look deep into Anu's eyes. "What are you searching for, Anu?"

"My father. You know this."

"Truly? And to what end?"

Anu opened her mouth to reply, then closed it again. What she wanted more than anything was to be accepted in the Silva Valley; to be accepted as pure vachine. But that had gone, now. Denied her from an early age by the very same father she sought to save; but he'd had his reasons, hadn't he? For forcing her to become outcast? And, she realised suddenly, what she wanted more than anything was for Kradek-ka, the great inventor, to make her whole again. To put right that which he had twisted. But it was too late for that. Her chance had gone.

"I would seek acceptance," she said, finally.

Alloria nodded, and gazed off through the trees. Birds sang in the distance. It was an uplifting sound. "Vashell said there was a path, here; a path that leads south, away, out from the embrace of the Black Pike Mountains."

Anu stared at her. She licked her lips. "You wish to leave?"

"Yes. I would return to my husband. I would return to my children. You understand this, surely?"

Anu sighed. "Yes. I understand you. But it will be a harsh and terrible journey. I believe the paths are... treacherous."

Alloria nodded. "I would suffer anything to see my family again."

"Then go. With my blessing."

"You could come with me," said Alloria. "I heard what Vashell said; about this place, this Nonterrazake. And the Harvesters who reside there. You don't even know if your father still lives! It is insanity to go on."

"You listen well," said Anu, a little stiffly. "No. I will travel there. If nothing else, I will discover the truth."

Queen Alloria moved forward, and gazed into Anu's eyes. "I know I have been... distant." She licked her lips. "but... thank you, for saving me, from the soldiers. I find it hard to comprehend your ways, but hopefully, one day, if you arrive at my lands in Falanor, I will be able to extend you some form of courtesy; some help." She paused, awkward, not really sure what she wanted to say, her mind awash with conflicting thoughts.

Anu smiled, leant forward and hugged Alloria.

"It will be as you say."

Anu stepped back onto the Engineer's Barge, the scents of rich flowers in her nostrils, in her golden curls, and she nosed the boat away from this inner sanctum, this temporary Eden, and towards the ominous cave which seemed to beckon her with a tiny, sibilant whisper.

Come to me, the cave seemed to say.

Come to the Vrekken.

The brass barge glided across still waters, and entered the darkness of the tunnel.

Within seconds, Anu was swallowed. Was gone.

For hours the brass barge eased through blackness. Occasionally, it would bump against jagged rock walls, and Anukis found herself praying. She did not want to drown. Even worse, she did not want to drown in a tomb-world beneath the Black Pike Mountains!

The wind whistled eerily down tunnels, and it was with a start Anu realised she was in a maze. The tenebrosity obscured the nature of the labyrinth, and it only came with time, with context, as Anu realised she was being drawn along by powerful currents, and no longer the hum of the clockwork engine. For a while she set the engine to full power, heard it clonking, gears stepping, straining against the pull. Then she realised it was futile; whatever pulled the brass barge seemed almost sentient, and she would simply burn out the engine if she continued.

Anu cut the power, and sat in eerie silence made more deafening by the stillness of the barge. She realised, then, she had grown used to the sound of the clockwork engine; it had been a comfort, like mother's heartbeat in the womb.

Now, only the wind sang her to sleep.

Minutes passed into hours passed into days, and Anu lost all concept of time. She slept when she was tired, and ate what meagre rations remained in the hold of the barge, mainly hard bread, salted fish and a little dried pork. Or at least, animal flesh of some kind.

Eventually, veins of crystal ran through the black rock over Anu's head; faintly at first, no more than occasional threads, strands of orange and green to break up the monotony of the terminal black. Then the threads grew more proliferous and thicker in banding, and it provided an eerie, underground light of sorts. Anu could make out the backs of her hands, and a vague outline of the barge. That was all.

The noise came after... she did not know. It could have been two days, could have been five. It was a blur, a blur of time, of memory, of identity. The noise began as a tiny crackling sound, which had Anu scampering down to the engine to see if there was a fault. But the clockwork engine was dead; killed by her own pretty, vachine-clawed hands.

Then, after hours, the noise increased and Anu realised it was the sound of gushing water, like that of a waterfall, or fast rapids over rocks. It echoed through the tunnels, strange acoustics summoned and distributed by the very nature of the environment.

More hours passed, and Anu grew increasingly agitated as she realised the source of the increasingly raging noise. It was the Vrekken, a natural whirlpool talked about with reverence in adventurer circles, around camp fires in the middle of the night, by hushed bards in rush-strewn taverns; and by the Blacklippers, who were said to have some unholy alliance with the great whirlpool. Nowhere, however, had Anu ever heard tales that the Vrekken was beneath the Black Pike Mountains – effectively entombed.

She shivered, now, and was drawn along in the darkness.

She realised that forces beyond her controlled her fate.

And she accepted this fate with a great, heartfelt sigh.

It was said her father, Kradek-ka, was down there, in the mythical land of Nonterrazake, down through the Vrekken, down through the mingled salt and fresh waters of the curious rivers which joined and flowed between savage towers of rock. Either that, or a simple death awaited.

The noise grew with every passing minute, and Anu realised the brass barge was moving subtly faster. The noise increased until it was no longer a noise, but a roar, a roar of anger and bestial hatred, a roar to be feared, a roar to instil pure hot terror. Anu grabbed the barge rail, knuckles white, as it began to rock and she wished, for a fleeting moment, that she had stayed with Alloria, travelled the high mountain passes, faced the threat of the hunting Harvesters. But then her jaw muscles tightened, her eyes narrowed, and she conjured a single word.

No.

She would not fear death. She would search out her father. Or she would die in the process.

The roaring grew and grew until it was so loud Anu could have screamed at full pitch and not heard herself. The river was dangerously agitated, rocking the barge from left to right, and slapping it abusively against rock walls.

And then…

A world opened before Anu, at once incredibly beautiful, and awesomely dangerous. It was stunning like a shark up close is stunning, dazzling like black-magick fire, and it held her gaze and she knew, if she survived this ordeal, nothing, ever, would compare to this moment…

The Vrekken was nearly half a league across, and filling a cavern of such incredible scale she never would have believed it could fit inside a mountain. The arena was lit by wrist-thick skeins of mineral deposits in rock walls, swirling, twining bands of orange and green that put Anu in mind of a carnival or festival; only here, there was very little to celebrate. Unless one wanted to celebrate death.

The Vrekken roared, a mammoth circular portal, a frothing juggernaut of churning river water all spiralling down, down, down into huge sweeping circles and further, into a savage cone depth. Anu's eyes were fixed. Her mouth so dry she could not eject her tongue to moisten lips. The Engineer's Barge was tugged, then flung into the Vrekken and caught like the tiniest of toys, powering along on surges of current, nose in the air leaving a wide wake through circular waters and Anu spun down, and down, and round and down and she realised the mighty whirlpool consisted of layers and she passed down, through layer after layer of this oceanic macrocosm, of whirling dark energy, of raw power and screaming detonation and mighty primordial compression, and she thought…

There is no fabled Nonterrazake.

I am going to die, here.

I am going to die.

And the Vrekken roared in terrible appreciation.

FIFTEEN
End Game

The cankers charged, howling, and the brave soldiers of Falanor marched in armoured squares to meet the attack head on. In ranks, they advanced across the plain, shields locked, a full division of 4,800 men arranged in twelve battalions of four hundred, with six in the centre two battalions deep, and three battalion squares to either side of the main square, like horns, the intention being to sweep round and enclose the enemy on three sides.

As the two forces closed, so the soldiers let out war cries and increased their pace, and the cankers accelerated to crash into shields with terrifying force, snarling and biting and clawing, a thousand feral clockwork twisted deviants slamming the battalions with rage... for a moment there was deadlock, then the Falanor soldiers were forced back, their swords hammering out, hacking at heads and claws, at shoulders and bellies, but the cankers were resilient, awesomely tough, incredibly powerful, and their claws raked shields bending steel. With screams of metal, they leapt, fastening on heads and ripping them free of bodies and the armoured shield wall broke within only a few short minutes, panic sweeping through Falanor ranks like rampant wildfire...

Kell crouched beside Nienna, whose face was ghostly pale, watching the carnage below. Terrakon and Lazaluth had rushed away to command their troops, now only Leanoric remained, eyes fixed on the battle, face ashen, nausea pounding him.

"Find a horse," said Kell, softly, forcing Nienna to tear her gaze from the battle. He took her chin in his hand, made her look at him. "Steal one if you have to. Ride for Saark. You understand?"

"No, I can't leave you... what will you do?"

"I must help Leanoric."

"No, Kell! You'll die!"

He smiled, a grim smile. "I have my Legend to uphold!" he said, and pushed Nienna away. "Now go! You hear me?" She shook her head. "Go!" he roared, and saw Myriam there beside her, and Myriam locked eyes with Kell and a silent exchange, an understanding, passed between them. Myriam placed a hand on Nienna's shoulder, and nodded. Then they took off through the camp, towards the towering, fractured walls of Old Skulkra, and tethered horses beyond.

Kell strode to Leanoric. "Sire. It's time we went into battle." He lifted his axe and began to loosen his shoulder. He turned, and saw the main block of infantry being forced back yet again. The battalion horns had swung around to enclose the cankers, on Terrakon and Lazaluth's command, and cankers were falling under sword blows... but they were slaughtering the soldiers of Falanor in their hundreds.

Below came the snarl and thud of canker carnage. Claws through flesh. Swords through muscle. Kell mounted his horse, and clicked his tongue. In silence, Leanoric followed and the two men rode down from the camp and onto the flat plain, hooves drumming the icy grassland as they both broke into a gallop and readied weapons, and the armoured ranks flowed past and Kell felt the thrill of adrenaline course his blood, and it was like the old times, like the best times and Ilanna spoke to him, her voice metallic and cool...

I can help you.

I can help you win this. No ties. No conditions.

Just let me in.

Kell flowed past the infantry, could see pale faces peering at him as he screamed an ancient war cry and in his calm internal monologue he said, "Do it, Ilanna" and he felt the surge of new power new blood-oil magick flood through him and his mind seemed to accelerate, to run in stop-motion, those around him slow and weak and pitiful flesh and meat and bone and he connected with Ilanna, connected with a force more ancient than feeble vachine clockwork deviation – Kell slammed into the cankers, his axe cleaving left and cutting a beast clean in half, and in the same sweep cutting right to remove a head, the blades thudded and sparkled with drops of blood as Kell's mount pushed gamely on, the axe returning to complete a figure of eight, each blow crunching through bone and muscle and twisted clockwork, and the cankers fell beneath him, crushed before him, and he was laughing, face demonic and splattered with their blood, and a huge canker reared, a massive black-skinned twisted beast twice the height of a man and heavily muscled. Its first swipe broke the horse's neck, and Kell's mount went down and he leapt free, the huge canker rearing above him screaming and the whole battle seemed to pause, held in a timeless moment with thousands of eyes fixed on this crazy old man who'd ridden deep into canker ranks ahead of the retreating units of infantry and the canker screamed and howled and lunged and Kell's axe glittered in a tiny black arc and cut the canker from skull to quivering groin in one massive blow that seemed to shake the battlefield. Thunder rumbled. The canker peeled in two parts and a roar went up from the Falanor men and their armoured squares heaved forward, with vigour renewed, swords rising and falling and cankers were cut down left and right, bludgeoned into the churned mud of the battlefield, arms and legs cut from torsos, heads cut from weeping clockwork necks. The main body of infantry found new hope in Kell, and they surged forward hacking and cutting, smashing blades into skulls and Kell roared from the centre of the battlefield, his axe slamming left and right with consummate ease, every single mighty blow killing with engineered precision, every single strike removing a canker from the battlefield and they converged on him, roaring and snarling, rearing above him and dwarfing him from sight and Kell laughed like a maniac, drenched in blood, his entire visage one of gory crimson with bits of torn clockwork in his hair and beard and he spun like a demon, Ilanna lashing out, cutting legs from bodies, and a pulse emanated from the axe and he held it above his head and the cankers, squealing and limping and blood-shod fell back for a moment, stumbling away in hurried leaps from this bloodied gore-strewn man, and a roar went up from the Falanor men and the cankers covered their ears which pissed blood and tiny mechanical units, whirring clockwork devices that seemed to be trying to get away from unheard noise and the Falanor soldiers charged, breaking ranks and hammering into the disabled cankers as blood pissed from ears and throats and eyes and they writhed in agony, and swords and axes smashed down without mercy. The rest of the cankers fled, stumbling back towards the waiting, silent Army of Iron, almost blind in their pain and panic and Kell stood in the midst of the final butchery, Ilanna in one hand, hair soaked with blood, his entire visage one of butcher in the midst of a murder frenzy, and when the killing was done a cheer went up and soldiers crowded around Kell, chanting his name, "Kell Kell Kell Kell KELL KELL KELL KELL!" and someone shouted, "The Legend, he lives!" and the chant changed, roaring across the battlefield to the silent, motionless albino ranks, "Legend Legend Legend Legend LEGEND LEGEND LEGEND LEGEND!" before the captains, command sergeants and division generals managed to restore order and the soldiers of Falanor reassembled in their units and ranks.

Kell strode back to Terrakon and Lazaluth. Terrakon had a nasty slash from his temple to his chin, his whole face sliced in half, but he was grinning. "That was incredible, man! I have never seen anything like it! You turned the entire tide of the battle!"

Kell grinned at him, face a savage demon mask. "Horse-shit, man! I did no such thing. I simply gave the cankers something nasty to think about; the infantry charged in and did the rest."

"Such modesty should never be trusted."

"Such bitterness should never be concealed."

"You're a vile, moaning goat, Kell."

Kell rolled his shoulders. "That's a nasty gash to your face, Kon. Might need a few stitches." He grinned again.

"Fuck you, you old bastard."

"Old? I'm ten years younger than you!"

"Ha, well it's all about condition, Kell, and I look ten years younger than you."

Around the two men soldiers were chuckling, but the sounds soon dissipated.

"Here come the infantry," said Terrakon, humour dropping like a stone down a well. He switched his blade from one hand to the other, rolling his wrist to loosen it. "Damn arthritis to hell!"

"Now's a good time to bring in those archers," said Kell, prodding Lazaluth. "Go and tell the king."

The albinos marched out, in perfect formation. Their black armour gleamed. It began to snow from towering iron-bruise clouds, and the battlefield became a slurry of blurred men. A pall of fear seemed to fall across the soldiers of Falanor; they realised they had lost hundreds due to slaughter at the claws of the cankers; they were now at the disadvantage. It would be a hard fight.

"Chins up, lads!" roared Kell, striding forward to the head of the centre battalions. They had reformed, most with shields, all grasping their short swords in powerful hands. These were the veterans, the skilled soldiers, the hardcore. Hard to kill, thought Kell with a grim smile, and he bared his teeth at the men.

"Who's going to kill some bastard albinos with me?" he roared, and a noise went up from the Falanor men.

"WE!" screamed the soldiers, blood-lust rising, and slammed swords on shields as behind Kell the albino battalions spread out into a straight line. Kell turned, and laughed at their advancing ranks.

"BRING IT ON, YOU HORSE-FUCKING NORTHERNERS!" he roared, and behind him the Falanor men cheered and roared and banged their swords, as Kell moved back and slipped neatly into the front ranks at the centre, taking up his position alongside other hardy men. He looked left, then looked right, and grinned at the soldiers. "Let's kill us some albino," he said, as the enemy broke into a charge in perfectly formed squares, their boots pounding across churned mud. They did not carry shields, only short black swords, and each had white hair, many wearing it long and tied back. None wore helmets, only ancient black armour inscribed with swirling runes.

The snow increased, filling the battlefield with thick flurries. I hope them extra divisions arrive soon, thought Kell sourly to himself; the snow would be superb cover to hit the enemy from behind, to crush them between sea and mountains, hammer and anvil. But then, nothing in life was ever that easy, or convenient; was it?

The albinos charged in eerie silence, and Kell again felt fear washing through the ranks. This was no normal battle, and every man could sense a swirling essence of underlying magick; as if the very ground was cursed.

Distant drums slammed out a complicated beat. Kell tried to remember his old military training, but realised it would be useless. They would change the codes before any battle in order to confuse the enemy, and hopefully negate any information passed on by spies. But Kell realised what was going to happen; Leanoric had explained. They were going to fight, then retreat; draw the albino army back into the ruined city of Old Skulkra, fake a panicked break of ranks and charge through the ancient abandoned streets where nearly a thousand archers waited, hidden in high buildings and towers to rain down slaughter from above.

Kell smiled, dark eyes locked to the charging albinos.

It was a good plan. It could work. At first, it had been a plan nearly devastated by the unexpected cankers and their attack. The panicked breaking of ranks had very nearly been a reality; if that had happened too early, before archers took their positions, the battle would have been lost...

Kell could see the charging men, now, and picked out his first four targets. His butterfly blades would soon taste blood, and he licked his lips, adrenaline and... something else pulsing through his veins. It was Ilanna, like an old drug, a bad disease, her essence flowing through his veins and mingling in his brain and heart and his sister of the soul, his bloodbond axe strengthened him beyond mortality and he laughed out loud, at the savage irony, for he would suffer for this betrayal of his own code.

A roar went up from the Falanor men, but still the Army of Iron charged in silence. Kell could see their eyes now, could see their bared teeth, the jewelled rings they wore on pale-flesh fingers, the shine of their boots, the gleam of their dark swords and he tensed, ready for the awesome massive impact which came from any slam of charging armies...

The albinos suddenly stopped, to a man, and dropped to one knee. The charging ranks of soldiers, in their entirety and with perfect clockwork precision, halted. A surge of warning sluiced through Kell's system, and he realised with a sudden fast-rising horror that it was a trick; they had no intention of infantry attack, it was a stalling tactic to allow...

The ice-smoke.

It poured from the Harvesters in the midst of the albino ranks, and within seconds flooded out towards the Falanor army. "Back!" screamed Kell, "Back!" but the battalions were too tightly packed, their lack of understanding a hindrance, and they began to stumble, to turn and retreat but ice-smoke poured over the men, slowing them instantly, making many fall to knees choking as lungs froze and Kell roared, unable to retreat, and surged forward alone cleaving into the albino ranks who remained, immobile, eyes fixed with glowing red hate on the soldiers of Falanor as Kell's axe thumped left and right, scattering bodies and limbs and heads, and he screamed at the albino soldiers, screamed at the Harvesters but ice-smoke flowed and froze swords to hands, shields to arms, sent crackling ice-hair in shards to the ground, and men toppled over in agony, many dying, but most locked in a dark magick embrace...

Kell's axe slammed left, embedding in a soldier's eyes. He tugged it free, sent another head rolling, and saw the Harvesters converging on him. "Come on, you bastards," he roared with the surge of Ilanna through his veins and he realised, realised that Ilanna kept him pure from the dark magick, as she had done all those days ago during the attack on Jalder, and he revelled in the freedom and whirled, beard-flecked with crimson, blood-soaked snow, and stared in horror at the falling ranks of Falanor men. The ice-smoke had spread, through the main division and the reserves before the walls of Old Skulkra. Even as he watched, tendrils crept like oiled tentacles into the city. And Kell thought about Nienna. And his face curled into a snarl. He turned back as the Harvesters, heads tilted to one side, surrounded him and he blinked, saw General Graal marching towards him to smile, a knowing smile, as his eyes locked to Kell.

Kell placed the blades of his axe on the ground, surrounded by dismembered corpses, and leant on the haft, his dark eyes fixing on Graal. Graal stopped, and smiled a narrow smile without humour.

"We should stop meeting like this, Kell."

Kell laughed, a brittle hollow sound. "Well well, Graal the Coward, Graal the Whoremaster, using his petty little magick to win the day. It's nice to see some things will never change."

"This is a means to an end," said Graal, eyes locked.

"Remember what I said to you, laddie? Back in Jalder?" Graal said nothing, but his eyes glittered. "I told you to remember my name, because I was going to carve it on your arse. Well, it seems now's a good time—"

He leapt into action so fast he was a blur and Graal stumbled back as Harvesters closed in, and a blast of concentrated ice-smoke smashed Kell and he was blinded in an instant and chill magick soaked his flesh and heart and bones and everything went bright white and he was stunned and falling, and he fell down an amazing sparkling white tunnel which seemed to go on...

Forever.

Nienna urged the horse on, hooves galloping across snow, steam rising from the beast's flanks as it laboured uphill towards the woods where Saark, Styx and Jex waited. Myriam was close behind, her own horse lathered with sweat, and the two women flashed through early morning mist as snow swirled about them, obscuring the world.

Nienna reined her horse into a canter as she neared the woods, then stopped, stooping to stare under the trees. She could see nothing. "Saark?" she hissed, then louder, "Saark?"

A little way up, Styx emerged, smiled and waved. Nienna cantered over to him and dismounted, her eyes never leaving the mark of the Blacklipper, his stained dark lips.

"Where's Saark?"

"Further in the woods. We've set up camp. Come on, before enemy scouts see you."

Myriam dismounted behind, and they led their horses into the gloom of the Silver Fir forest. Pigeons cooed in the distance, then all was silent, their footfalls muffled by fallen pine needles.

"Up here." Styx led them along an old deer trail, and they emerged in a small clearing where an ancient, fallen pine acted as a natural bench. Jex was cooking stew over a small fire, and Nienna looked around.

"Where is he?"

The blow slammed the back of Nienna's head, and she felt her face pushed into needles and loam, and there was no pain. She remembered scents, pine resin, soil, old mud and woodland mould. When she blinked, groggy, and came back into a world of gloomy consciousness, she realised she was tied, her back leant against the fallen pine. She groaned.

"We have a live one," grinned Styx, crouching before her. Nienna spat in his face, and his grin fell, his hand lifting to strike her.

"Enough," snapped Myriam, voice harsh. "Go and help Jex pack the horses." Styx departed in silence, and Nienna ran her tongue around a mouth more stale than woodland debris.

"Why?" said Nienna, eventually, looking up at Myriam.

"You are my best bartering tool. When Kell has finished playing battleground hero, he will come looking for you. By taking you north, I guarantee he will follow."

"Is it not enough to poison us?" snapped Nienna, eyes narrowed and full of hate.

"It is not enough," said Myriam, gaunt face hollow, eyes hard.

Nienna's gaze transferred to Saark, seated, slumped forward, face heavily beaten. He lifted himself up a little, drool and blood spilling from his mouth, and smiled at her through the massive swellings on his face. One eye was swollen shut, and blood glistened in his dark curls. His hands were tied behind his back, but even as he shifted he winced, in great pain.

"Saark, what happened to you?"

"Bastards jumped me." He grinned at her, though it looked wrong through his battered features. "Hey, Nienna, fancy a kiss?"

She snorted a laugh, then shook her head. "How can you joke, Saark?"

"It's either that or let them break me." His eyes went serious. "And I'd rather die. Or at least, rather die than be ugly." He glanced up at Myriam, and winked at her with his one good eye. "Like this distorted bitch."

Myriam said nothing, and Styx and Jex returned with their horses. Styx grabbed Nienna roughly, and she kicked and struggled. He punched her, hard, in the face and she went down on her knees gasping, blinded. He dragged her back up again. "We can do this awake, or unconscious. I know which one I'd rather choose," growled the Blacklipper.

Nienna was helped into the saddle, and Styx mounted behind her. His hands rested on her hips, and he grinned, leaning close to her ear. "This is intimate, my sweet. The first of many adventures between us, I think."

"You wave your maggot near me, and I'll bite it off," she snarled.

Styx's grin widened, and he squeezed her flesh with strong fingers. "Like I said. We can do this awake, or unconscious."

Myriam crossed to Saark, and crouched before him. "Look at me."

"I'd rather not. The cancer has eaten your face. There's nothing the vachine can do for you now, my love."

"Bastard! Listen, and listen good. We're taking Nienna north, to the Cailleach Pass. The poison will take three weeks to kill Kell. The ride is around fifteen days. He can meet us by the Cailleach Pass northwest of Jalder; there, I have a partial antidote that will extend his – and Nienna's – lives. Enough to get us through the mountains at least. You understand all this?"

"I understand, bitch."

"Good." She smiled with tombstone teeth. "And here's a little present to remember me by." She pulled free a dagger, and slammed it between Saark's ribs. He grunted, feeling warm blood spread from the embedded blade, and as Myriam pulled it free he gasped, toppling onto his side where he lay, winded, as if struck by a sledge hammer. "Nothing fatal, I assure you. Unless you choose not to move your arse, and lie there like a stuck pig. It'll be a while before you use that pretty sword again, dandy man; Sword-Champion." She knelt and cut Saark's bonds, then turned and leapt with agility into her horse's saddle.

The group wheeled, and galloped from the forest clearing.

Silence fell like ash.

Saark lay, panting, bleeding. There was no pain, and that scared him. Then the lights went out.

King Leanoric knelt in the mud, heavily chained. Beside him were his Division Generals and various captains who hadn't died in either the battle, or from the savage effects of the invasive ice-smoke. Despair slammed through Leanoric, and he looked up, tears in his eyes, across the battlefield of the frozen, the ranks of the dead. His army had been annihilated, as if they were stalks of wheat under the scythes of bad men.

Distantly, the remaining cankers growled and snarled, but the albinos were curiously silent despite their easy victory. There were no battle songs, no drunken revelry; they went about building their camp in total silence, like androgynous workers; like insects.

Tears rolled down Leanoric's cheeks. He had failed, unless his divisions further north surprised Graal's Army of Iron and destroyed them in the night; they were commanded by Retger and Strauz, two wily old Division Generals, strategic experts, and Strauz had never lost a battle. Leanoric's heart lifted a little. If their scouts realised what had happened, that the king's men had been routed, frozen, and slaughtered like cattle...

Maybe then he would see his sweet Alloria again.

His tears returned, and he cast away feelings of shame. There was nothing wrong with a man crying. He was on the brink of losing his wife, his realm, his army, his people. How then did simple tears pale into comparison when so much was at stake?

King Leanoric needed a miracle.

Instead, he got General Graal.

Graal walked through the camp and stopped before the group of men. He drew a short black sword, gazed lovingly at the ornate rune-worked blade for a moment, then cut the head from Terrakon's shoulders. The old Division General's head lay there on frozen mud, grey whiskers tainted by droplets of blood, and Leanoric looked up with hate in his eyes. "My people will kill you," he snarled. "That's a promise."

"Really?" said Graal, almost idly, wandering over to Lazaluth and throwing Leanoric a cold, narrow-lipped smile. He reached up, ran a hand through his white hair, then fixed his eyes on the king. "So often I hear these threats, from the Blacklippers I slaughter, from the smugglers of Dog Gemdog gems, from the kings of conquered peoples."

His sword lashed out, and Lazaluth's head rolled to the mud, a look of shock on the death-impact expression. The body slumped down, blood pumping sluggishly from chilled neck arteries, and Leanoric watched with fury and cold detachment and he knew, he realised, he would be next but at least death would be swift... but hell, it wasn't about death, it was about his people, and their impending slavery. And it was a bad thing to die, knowing you had utterly failed.

Leanoric prayed then. He prayed for a miracle. For surely only a god could stop General Graal?

Graal moved to him, and hunkered down, slamming the black blade into the frozen mud. "How does it feel?" he asked, voice almost nonchalant. "Your army is destroyed, your queen sent north to my Engineers, your people about to become..." he laughed, a tinkling of wind chimes, "our supper."

"You will burn in Hell," said Leanoric, voice a flatline. He tried to estimate how long it would be before his returning battalions marched over the hill; for example, now would be a most opportune moment. A surprise attack? Rescued at the final second? Just like in a bard's tale.

Graal watched the king's eyes. Finally, their gazes locked.

"You are thinking of your army, your divisions, your battalions, your cavalry and archers who at this very moment march south, towards this very location in order to hook up with your army and smash the enemy invaders."

Leanoric said nothing.

Graal stood, and stretched his back. He glanced down at King Leanoric, as one would a naughty child. "They are dead, Leanoric. They are all dead. Frozen by the Harvesters blood-oil magick; slaughtered and sucked dry as they knelt. You have no army left, King Leanoric. Face facts. You are a conquered, and an enslaved race."

"No!" screamed Leanoric, surging to his feet despite the weight of chains and around him unseen albino soldiers in the mist drew swords as one, the hiss of metal on oiled scabbard, but Graal lifted one hand, smiled, then stepped in close, lifting Leanoric from his feet, and Leanoric kicked and saw a mad light in the General's eyes and he dragged Leanoric into an embrace and fangs ejected with a crunch and he bit down deep, pushing his fangs into Leanoric's neck, into his flesh, feeling the skin part, the muscle tear, rooting out that precious pump of blood, injecting the meat the vein the artery, closing his eyes as he sucked, and drained, and drew in the king's royal blood.

Leanoric screamed, and kicked, and fought but Graal was strong, so much stronger than he looked; chains jangled and Graal held Leanoric almost horizontal, mouth fastened over his neck, eyes closed in a final revelation; a final gratification.

Graal grunted, and allowed a limp and bloodied Leanoric to topple to the soil. Blood streaked his mouth and armour, and he lifted his open fangs to the sky, to the mist, to the magick, and he exhaled a soft howl which rose on high through clouds and spread out across the Valantrium Moor beyond Old Skulkra, across the Great North Road, across Vorgeth Forest and that howl said, This country is mine, that howl said, These people are mine, that guttural primal noise from a creature older than Falanor itself said, This world is mine.

Saark awoke. He was terribly cold.

He stared up at towering Silver Firs with his one good eye, and tried to remember what had happened in the world, tried to focus on recent events. Then reality and events flooded in and cracked him on the jaw, and he blinked rapidly, and his hand dropped to his ribs – and came away sticky.

"Bastards."

With a grunt, he levered himself up. He was incredibly thirsty. The world swayed, as if he was drunk, his brain caught in a grasp of vertigo. Saark crawled to his knees, and saw his horse, the tall chestnut gelding, still tied where he'd left him. Saark crawled slowly to the gelding, feeling fresh blood pump from the dagger wound and flow down his flank, soaking into his groin. It was warm, and wet, and frightening.

"Hey, boy, how the hell are you?" Saark use the stirrups to lever himself up, and grasping the saddle, he pulled himself to his feet with gritted teeth. Pain washed over him, and he yelped, dizziness swamping him, and he nearly toppled back.

"No," he said, and the gelding turned a little, nuzzling at his hand. "No oats today, boy." Saark struggled with the straps of his saddlebags, his fumbling fingers refusing to work properly, and finally he found his canteen and drank, he drank greedily, water soaking his moustache and flowing down his battered chin. He winced. He face felt like a sack of shit. He probed tenderly at his split lip, cracked nose, cracked cheekbone, swollen eye. He shook his head. When I catch up with them, he thought. When I catch up with them...

Saark laughed, then. Ridiculous! When he caught them? Gods, he could hardly stand.

He stood for a while holding the saddle, swaying, watching the falling snow, listening to the rustle of firs. The air, the world outside, seemed muffled, gloomy, a perpetual dawn or dusk.

Focus. Find Kell. Rescue Nienna. Kill bad people.

He smiled, grabbed the pommel of the saddle, and with a grunt heaved himself up on the third attempt. He slouched forward, and realised he hadn't untethered the gelding. He muttered, drew his rapier from behind the saddle, and slashed at the rope, missing. He blinked. He slashed down again, and the rope parted.

"Come on, boy." He clicked his tongue, turned the horse, and set off at a gentle canter through the trees.

The whole world spun around him, and he felt sick. He was rocking, an unwilling passenger on a galleon in a storm. His felt as if his brain was spinning around inside his skull, and he slowed the horse to a walk, took in deep breaths, but it did not help. His mouth was dry again. Pain came in waves.

After what seemed an eternity of effort, Saark reached the edge of the woodland. He gazed out, over grass now effectively blanketed by snow. Slowly, he rode through the gloom, across several fields and to the top of the nearest hill. He stared out across a decimated battlefield. His eyes searched, and all he could see was the black armour of the Army of Iron.

Cursing, Saark kicked the horse into a canter and removed himself from the skyline. He dismounted, leaning against the horse for support, his mind spinning. What, was the battle over already? But then, how long had he lain unconscious? The Army of Iron had won?

Holy mother of the gods, he thought, and drew his rapier.

That would mean scouts, patrols – and where was Kell? Had he been captured? Worse. Was he dead?

Saark turned his horse and slapped the gelding's rump; with a whinny, he trotted off down the hill and Saark crawled back to the top on his belly, leaving a smear of blood on the snow, but thankful at least that from this position the world wasn't rolling, his eyes spinning, the ground lurching as if he was drunk on a bottle of thirty year-old whisky. Saark peered out over the enemy camp, spread out now before the battered city walls of Old Skulkra. To Saark's right, the ancient deserted city spread away as far as the eye could see, with crumbling towers, leaning spires, and many buildings having crumbled to the ground after... Saark smiled, sardonically. After the troubles. He fixed his gaze on what was, effectively, a merging of two war camps. The corpses of Falanor's soldiers had been laid out in neat lines away from the new camp and, with a bitter, grim, experienced eye, Saark looked along row after row after row of bodies.

What are they doing? he thought, idly. Why aren't they burning the bodies? Or burying them? What are they waiting for? Why risk disease and vermin? The image sat uneasy with Saark, and he changed tactic, moving his gaze back to the camp. If Kell was alive, and with a sinking feeling Saark realised it was improbable, then he was down there.

Saark scanned the tents, and eventually his gaze was drawn to a group of men, mist curling between them. They were a group of albino soldiers with swords unsheathed, and Saark squinted, trying to make out detail through the haze of distance, gloom and patches of mist. There came some violent activity, and Saark watched a man picked up kicking, struggling, then dropped back to the frozen mud. Saark's mouth formed a narrow line. He recognised Graal, more by his arrogant stance than armour or looks. There was something about the way the general moved; an ancient agility; an age-old arrogance, deeper than royalty, as if the world and all its wonders should move aside when he approached.

Saark watched Graal walk away from the small hill, walking down towards... Saark's breath caught in his throat. There were cages. Lots of cages. *Cankers*. Shit. Saark's good eye moved left, and he saw a huge pile of canker bodies – a huge pile. His heart swelled in pride. At least we got some of the fuckers, he thought bitterly. He tried to spot Graal again, but the general had disappeared in the maze of cages and tents. Where had he gone? Damn. Saark searched, methodically, up and down the rows where cankers snarled and hissed and slept; eventually, he caught sight of Graal. The general was observing... a man. A man, in a cage. Saark grinned. It had to be! Who else needed caging like a canker? There was only one grumpy sour old goat he could think of. Then Saark's heart sank. What else had they done to Kell? Was he tortured? Maimed? Dismembered? Saark knew all too well, and from first-hand experience, the horrors of battle; the insanity of war.

At least he is alive, thought Saark.

He lay back. Closed his eyes against the spinning world, although even then the feeling did not leave him. He moved a little down the hill, then searched in his pockets, finding his tiny medical kit, and as he waited the long, long hours until nightfall, he busied himself with a tiny brass needle and a length of thread made from pig-gut. He sewed himself back together again. And afterwards, after vomiting, he slept.

Kell came back into a world of consciousness slowly, as if swimming through a sea of black honey. He was lying on a metal floor, and a cold wind caressed him. He was deeply cold, and his eyes opened, staring at the old pitted metal, at the floor, and at the mud beyond streaked with swirls of snow. He coughed, and placed both hands beneath him, heaving himself up, then slumping back, head spinning, senses reeling. And he felt... loss. The loss of Ilanna. The loss of his bloodbond axe.

Kell flexed his fingers, and gazed around. He was in a cage with thick metal bars, and outside, all around him, were similar cages containing twisted, desecrated cankers. Most slept, but a few sat back on their haunches, evil yellow eyes watching him, their hearts ticking unevenly with bent clockwork.

Kell rolled his shoulders, then crawled to his knees and to the corner of the cage, peering out. He was back in Leanoric's camp, only now there were no soldiers of Falanor to be seen; only albino guards, eyes watchful, hands on sword-hilts. Kell frowned, and searched, and realised that the two camps had been made to blend, just like a canker and its clockwork. The Army of Iron had usurped the Falanor camp.

Darkness had fallen, and Kell realised he must have been out of the game for at least a day. He peered out from behind his bars, could just make out the edges of Old Skulkra, with her toothed domes and crumbling walls. Beyond lay Valantrium Moor, and a cold wind blew down from high moorland passes carrying a fresh promise of snow.

Kell shivered. What now? He was a prisoner. Caged, like the barely controllable cankers around him. "Hey?" growled Kell to the nearest canker. "Can you hear me?" The beast gave no response, just stared with the baleful eyes of a lion. "Do you realise you have a face like a horse's arse?" he said. The canker blinked, and its long tongue protruded, licking at lips pulled back over half its head. Inside, tiny gears made click click click noises. Kell shivered again, and this time it was nothing to do with the cold.

"Kell." The voice was low, barely above a whisper. Kell squinted into the darkness.

"Yeah?"

"It's Saark. Wait there."

"I'm not going anywhere, laddie."

There came several grunting sounds, and a squeal of rusted metal. The side of the cage opened, and Saark, skin pale, sweat on his brow, leant against the opened door.

Kell strode out, stood with his hands on his hips, looking around, then turned to Saark. "I thought you would have come sooner."

Saark gave a nasty grin. "A 'thank you' would have sufficed."

"Thank you. I thought you would have come sooner. And by the way, you look like a horse trampled your face."

"I ran into a bit of trouble, with Myriam and her friends."

Kell's brows darkened; his eyes dropped to the bloodstains on Saark's clothing. He softened. "Are you injured?"

"Myriam stabbed me."

"She had Nienna with her."

"She still does. I'm sorry, Kell. She's taken Nienna north, to the Black Pike Mountains. She said to tell you she will wait at the Cailleach Pass. She knows you will come. I'm sorry, Kell; I could do nothing."

The huge warrior remained silent, but rolled his neck and shoulders. His hand leapt to where his Svian was sheathed; to find the weapon gone. "Bastards," he muttered, looked around, then turned and started off between the cages.

"Wait," said Saark, hobbling after him. "You're going the wrong way. We can head out through Old Skulkra; I think even the albinos won't travel there. It's still a poisoned hellhole; stinks like a pig's entrails."

"I'm going to find Graal."

"What?" snapped Saark. He grabbed Kell, stopping him. "What are you talking about, man?" he hissed. "We're surrounded by ten thousand bloody soldiers! You want to march in there and kill him?"

"I don't want to kill him," snapped Kell, eyes glittering. "I want Ilanna."

Saark gave a brittle laugh. "We can buy you another axe, old man," he said.

"She's... not just an axe. She is my bloodbond. I cannot leave her. It is hard to explain."

"You're damn right it's hard to explain. You'd risk your life now? We can escape, Kell. We can go after Nienna."

Kell paused, then, his back to Saark. When his words came, they were low, tainted by uncertainty. "No. I must have Ilanna; then I find Nienna. Then I kill Myriam and her twisted scum-bastard friends."

"You're insane," said Saark.

"Maybe. You wait here if you like. I'll be back."

"No." Saark caught him up, his rapier glittering in the darkness. "I may be stuck like a pig, but I can still fight. And if we split up now, we're sure to be caught and tortured. Damn you and your stupid fool quest!"

"Be quiet."

They eased through the nightshade.

It watched them. It crept low along the ground, and watched them. When they looked towards it, it hid its face, in shame, great tears rolling down its tortured cheeks as it hunkered to the ground, and its body shook in spasms of grief. Then they were gone, and it rose again, jaws crunching, and paced them through the army of tents...

Only once did Kell meet two albino guards, and the old man moved so fast they didn't see him coming. He broke a jaw, then a neck, then knelt on the first fallen guard, took his face between great paws, and wrenched the guard's head sideways with a sickening crunch. Kell stood, took one of the albino's short black swords, and looked over at Saark.

"Help me hide the bodies."

Saark nodded, and realised Kell danced along a line of brittle madness. He had changed. Something had changed inside the old warrior. He had... hardened. Become far more savage, more brutal; infinitely merciless.

They eased along through black tents, past the glowing embers of fires, and Kell pointed. It had been Leanoric's tent, in which Kell had stood only a few short hours before. Now, Kell knew, Graal's arrogance would make him take residence there. It was something about generals Kell had learned in his early days as a soldier. Most thought they were gods.

Kell stopped, and held up a blood-encrusted hand. Saark paused, crouched, glancing behind him. Slowly, Kell eased into the tent and was gone. Saark felt goose-bumps crawl up and down his arms and neck and went to follow Kell into the tent but froze. He glanced back again, and as if through ice-smoke General Graal materialised. Behind him marched a squad of albino soldiers, heavily armed and armoured, this time wearing black helmets decorated with swirling runes. Graal stopped, and smiled at Saark, and a chill fear ran through the dandy's heart like a splinter.

"Kell?" he whispered. Then, louder, eyes never leaving Graal, "Kell!"

"What is it?" snapped Kell, emerging, and looking at Graal with glittering eyes. "Oh, it's you, laddie."

"Looking for this?" said Graal, lifting Ilanna so moonlight shimmered from her black butterfly blades.

"Give her to me."

Graal rammed the axe into the ground. Behind him, the albino soldiers drew their blades. "Tell me how to make her mine, and you will live. Tell me how to talk with the bloodbond."

"No," snapped Kell.

Graal stepped forward, head lowered for a moment, then glanced up at Kell, blue eyes glittering. "I will grow unhappy," he said, voice low.

"I have been pondering a strange puzzle for some time," said Kell, placing his hands on his hips and meeting Graal's gaze. "How is it, lad, that you have the face and skin and hair of these albino bastards around you... and yet your eyes are blue?" Kell scratched at his whiskers. "I see you have the fangs of the vachine, and yet the vachine are tall, most dark haired, not like these effeminate soldiers behind you. What are you, Graal? Some kind of half-breed?"

"On the contrary," said Graal, taking another step closer. His eyes had gone hard, the mocking humour dropped from his face, and Saark realised Kell had touched some deep nerve with his words. "I am pureblood," said Graal. "I am Engineer. I am Watchmaker. But more than this–" He leapt, arms smashing down, but Kell moved fast and blocked the blow, taking a step back. "I am one of the first vachine; the three from which all others stem."

Kell grinned. "I thought I could smell something rotten."

Graal snarled, and lashed out again, but Kell ducked the blow, moving inhumanly fast, and delivered a right hook that shook Graal. The general whirled, rolling with the blow, taking Kell's arm and slamming him over to smash the ground. Kell rolled, as Graal's boots hit the frozen earth where his face had been. Kell rose into a crouch and launched himself, grappling Graal around the waist and powering him to the soil. Atop Graal, Kell slammed his fists down with power, speed, accuracy, three blows, four five six seven, his knuckles lacerated and bleeding and Graal twisted, suddenly, throwing Kell to the ground where he grunted, and came up. They leapt at one another with a *crunch*, and suddenly locked, heaving, a match for one another in strength, heads clashing, and Saark who had been eyeing the five albino soldiers uneasily saw long fangs eject from Graal's mouth and screamed, "Kell, his teeth!" and Kell twisted, following Graal's head with a mighty blow that sent Graal reeling to the ground. Kell stood, chest heaving, blood on his face and his fists.

Graal climbed to his feet and stood, and smiled through his blood. "Your strength is prodigious," he said, eyes narrowing. "Too prodigious. Nothing human can stand before me; and yet you have done so."

"I've had lots of practise," said Kell, fists clenching, head lowering. "Once, I worked in the Black Pike Mountains. I was part of a squad sent there by King Searlan to hunt down the vachine; to kill your kind. We did well. We were there for four years... four long, bitter, hard years... it was hard learning, Graal, but we learnt well. I think, even now, I am referred to as Legend by your perverse kind."

"You!" snarled Graal, eyes widening. "The Vachine Hunter! It cannot be! He was slaughtered in the Fires of Karrakesh!"

"It is I," said Kell, "and that is why you could never speak with my bloodbond axe, my Ilanna... for she is anathema to your kind; she is poison to your blood: she is the sworn vachine nemesis."

There came a snarl, high-pitched and terrible, and something cannoned from the darkness, hitting Graal in a flurry of slashing claws and frothing fangs. It was big, a cross between human and lion, obviously a canker and yet twisted strangely, different from the other cankers under Graal's command. The head was long and narrow, and wrapped around with hundreds of strands of fine golden wire so that only glimpses of eyes and nose and mouth could be seen. Slashes covered the tufted, half-furred muscular body, but again muscles, biceps and thighs and abdomen were all wound about with tight golden wire, and sections of clockwork could be seen outside the flesh, half embedded, clicking and whirring furiously, as if this body, this canker, was having some kind of furious internal battle with the very machinery which now, undoubtedly, kept it alive...

They fought in the gloom of the usurped camp, Graal and this twisted canker nightmare, a flurry of insane blows, writhing and wrestling and twisting in the mud, thumps echoing out, claws and teeth slashing. Graal had exposed his full vachine toolset; was biting and rending, face lost in a mask of raw primal savagery that had nothing to do with the human. They spun and punched and slashed in the mud, both opening huge wounds down the other's flanks, sparks flying from crumpled clockwork, grunting and growling and the canker's fist punched Graal's face, slamming his head back into the mud and the canker glanced up, eyes masked by the wires circling its head but they fixed, fixed on Saark with recognition, then on Kell, and the canker seemed to smile, a lopsided stringing of tattered lips and saliva and blood-oil drool...

Saark gasped. "Elias?" he hissed, in disbelief.

"Go – now," forced the canker between corrupted flesh, and Graal's hands grasped Elias's arm, twisted savagely with a popping of tendons and the canker was flung to one side, where it rolled fast and reversed the trajectory with a savage snarl, leaping on Graal's back and burying him and slamming the general into the mud.

Kell walked to his axe, Ilanna, and took her in his great hands. His head came up, eyeing the albino soldiers, who stood uncertainly, swords drawn. He attacked in a blur, each strike cutting bodies in half, and stood back with a grunt, covered in fresh gore, bits of intestines, slivers of heart, chunks of albino bone, to stare bitterly at the ten chunks of corpse.

Saark grabbed his arm. His voice was low. 'We have to move! Now, soldier!' Saark pointed. More enemy were gathering down in the main camp. They were strapping on swords and armour. Kell nodded, and then started to run with Saark beside him.

Saark suddenly stopped. Turned. He wanted to thank the twisted, corrupted shell of Elias; thank him for their lives. But the battle was a savagery of blows and scattered flesh.

They ran.

Through tents and paddocks of horses. Saark motioned, and they unlatched a gate, grabbing two tall chestnut geldings and leaping across them bareback. They kicked heels, and grabbing manes trotted from the paddock, then galloped through the rest of the camp towards the teetering walls of Old Skulkra... which loomed before them, vast, ancient, foreboding.

Old Skulkra was haunted, it was said. One of the oldest cities in Falanor, it had been built over a thousand years before, a majestic and towering series of vast architectural wonders, immense towers and bridges, spires and temples, domes and parapets, many in black marble shipped from the far east over treacherous marshes. It had been a fortified city, with towering walls easily defendable against enemies, each wall forty feet thick. It had vast engine-houses and factories, once home to massive machines which, scholars claimed, were able to carry out complex tasks but were now huge, silent, rusted iron hulks full of evil black oil and arms and pistons and levers that would never move again. Now, the city was century-deserted, its secrets lost in time, its reputation harsh enough to keep any but the most fearless of adventurers away. It was said the city carried plague close to its heart, and that to walk there killed a man within days. It was said ghosts drifted through the mist-filled streets, and that dark blood-oil creatures lived in the abandoned machinery, awaiting fresh prey.

Kell and Saark had little option. Either ride through a camp of ten thousand soldiers intent on their annihilation; or brave the deserted streets of Old Skulkra. It was hardly a choice.

They passed the forty-foot defensive walls, corners and carved pillars crumbling under the ravages of time. Huge green and grey stains ran down what had once been elegantly carved pillars. Despite their flight, Saark looked around in wonder. "By the gods, this place is huge."

"And dangerous," growled Kell.

"You've been here before?"

"Not by choice," said Kell, and left it at that.

They swept down a wide central avenue, lined by blackened, twisted trees, arms skeletal and vast. Beyond were enormous palaces and huge temples, every wall cracked and jigged and displaced. Even the flagstones were cracked and buckled, as if the city of Old Skulkra had been victim of violent earth upheavals and storms.

The horses' hooves rang on black steel cobbles. The world seemed to drift down into silence. Mist coagulated on street corners. Saark shivered, and turned to look back at the broken gates through which they'd entered. The mist made the vision hazy, obscure. But he could have sworn he saw at least a hundred albino soldiers, clustering there, swords drawn but... refusing to step past the threshold.

They're frightened, he thought.

Or they know something we don't.

"They won't follow us here," said Saark, and his voice rang out, echoing around the ancient, damp place. It echoed back from crumbling buildings, from towers once majestic, now decayed.

"Good," snapped Kell. "Listen. If we can get through the city, we can head northeast, up through Stone Lion Woods. Then we can follow the Selenau River up to Jalder, then further up towards the Black Pike Mountains..."

"She's safe," said Saark, staring at Kell. "They won't harm her. Myriam has too much to lose by angering you further. She knows Nienna is the only bartering tool she has."

Kell nodded, but his eyes were dark, hooded, brooding. He could feel the sluggish pulse of poison in his system, running alongside the bloodbond of Ilanna. It was a curious feeling, and even now made his head clouded, his thoughts unclear. Weakness swept over him. Kell gritted his teeth, and pushed on.

They rode for a half hour at speed, the horses nervous, ears laid back against skulls, eyes rolling. It took great horsemanship to calm them; especially without reins.

And then, they heard the growls.

Kell cursed.

Saark frowned. "What is it?"

"The bastards wouldn't come in on their own. Oh no."

"So what is it?" urged Saark.

"The cankers. They've unleashed the cankers."

Saark paled, and he allowed a breath to ease from his panicked, pain-wracked frame. "That's not good, my friend," he said, finally.

Kell urged his horse on, and they galloped down wide streets, angling north and east. The mist thickened, and the streets became more narrow, more industrial. The buildings changed to factories and stone tower blocks, vast and cold, all windows gone, all doors rotted and vanished an age past. The horses became increasingly agitated, and the occasional growls and snarls of pursuing cankers grew louder, echoing, more pronounced.

"We're not going to make it," said Saark, eyes wide, his tension building.

"Shut up."

They slowed the horses, which were verging on the uncontrollable, until Kell's mount reared, whinnying in terror, and threw him. He landed with a *thud*, rolling on steel cobbles, and came up with his axe in huge hands, eyes glowering, but there was nothing there. Darkness seemed to creep in. Mist swirled. The horse galloped off, and was lost in shadows.

There came a distant *slunch*, a whinny of agony; then silence.

Kell spun around, looking up at the towering stone walls surrounding him. It was cold. His breath streamed. Icicles mixed with the old blood of battle frozen in his beard.

"Get up behind me," said Saark, reaching forward to take Kell's arm. But his own horse reared at that moment, and he somersaulted backwards from the creature, landing in a crouch, rapier drawn, face white with pain. The horse bolted, was gone in seconds between the towering walls of ancient stone.

"Neat trick," growled Kell, rubbing at his own bruised elbow and shoulder.

"I'll show you sometime," Saark grimaced.

The sounds of pursuing cankers grew louder.

"This is bad," said Saark, battered face full of fear, eyes haunted.

"We need somewhere to defend. A stairwell, somewhere narrow." Kell pointed with Ilanna. "There. That tower block."

The edifice was huge, the walls jigged and displaced, full of cracks and mis-aligned stones. A cold wind howled through the block, bringing with it a sour, sulphuric stench.

"I'm not going in there," said Saark.

"Well die out here, then," snapped Kell and started forward.

The cankers rounded a corner. There were a hundred of them, snarling, slashing at one another with claws, and they came in a horde down the narrow street, pushing and jostling, fighting to be first to feed on fresh, sweet meat. Kell ran for the tower, beneath an empty doorway and through a sweeping entrance hall littered with debris, old fires, stones and twisted sections of iron rusted out of shape and purpose; he stopped, looking hurriedly about. "There," he snapped. Saark was close behind him. Too close.

"We're going to die," said Saark, ever the voice of doom.

"Shut up, laddie, or I'll kill you myself."

They ran, skidding to a halt by a narrow sweep of steps. Kell looked up, and could see the sky far far above, perhaps twenty storeys, straight up. The tower block had no roof, and snow-clouds swirled. The steps spiralled up, wide enough for two men, and with a shaky, flaked, mostly rotted iron handrail the only barrier between the steps and a long fall to hard impact. Kell started up, thankful the stairwell was built from stone. Saark followed. They powered up in grim silence, followed by cackles and growls. It was only when Kell ventured too close to the edge that there came a crack, and stones tumbled away taking a quarter section of the staircase with it. Kell leapt back, almost sucked away in the sudden fall.

Saark stared at Kell, sweat on his swollen face, but said nothing.

"Keep to the wall," advised Kell.

"I'd already worked that one out, old horse."

Below, the cankers found the stairwell. They started up, jostling and snarling. Saark glanced down, but Kell powered ahead, face grim, beard frozen with ice-blood, eyes dark, mind working furiously.

The cankers ascended fast, claws scrabbling on icy steps. Panting and drenched with sweat, the two men reached a landing halfway up – ten storeys in height, halfway to the tower block's summit – before the first canker appeared, a huge shaggy beast with tufts of reddish fur and green eyes. Kell's axe clove into its head and Saark's rapier sliced into its belly, and the beast fell back, spitting lumps of clockwork and spewing blood. The two men ran across the landing and onto the next set of steps, as a crowd of cankers surged onto the narrow platform and Kell screamed, 'Run!' to Saark, and stopped on the steps, turning with his axe, the snarling heaving mass only a few feet away as cracks and booms filled the tower. Kell lifted his axe, and struck at the landing, again and again, and the whole floor was shaking under the weight of the cankers and the impact from the axe, and they were there, in his face, fetid breath in his throat as a huge crack echoed through the tower block and the landing fell away, with a whole storey section of steps, fell and tumbled away carrying twenty cankers scrabbling and clawing down the centre of the spiralling stairwell and leaving Kell teetering on the edge of oblivion. He swayed for a moment, and something grabbed him, pulled him back and he fell to his arse, turned, and grinned at Saark.

"Thanks, lad."

"No problem, Kell. Shall we ascend?"

"After you."

They started up, hearing growls and snarls fall away behind as two cankers attempted to leap the chasm, and bounced from walls, dropping away clawing and snarling to be lost in dust and ice and debris. There were *booms* as they impacted with the floor far below, and merged component limbs with ancient lengths of rusted iron.

The two men ran, muscles screaming, sweat staining their skin, limbs burning, fatigue eating them like acid. Eventually, they reached the final set of steps, and burst out into snowy daylight, great iron-bruise clouds filling the sky. A cold wind slammed them. Old Skulkra spread out in all directions, vast, decaying, frightening.

The top of the tower block was a treacherous rat-run of stone beams and channels. Ancient woodwork had long gone, meaning the entire floor was a criss-cross network where one incorrect step meant a long fall to unwelcome stone beneath. The whole tower block seemed to sway in violent gusts of wind. The wind gave long, mournful groans. Kell stepped across various beams to the low wall encircling the top floor of this vast tower. He stared off, across the ancient city, to the Valantrium Moor beyond, distant, enticing, ensconced in a snow shroud.

Saark came up beside him. He peered at another, nearby structure. "Can we make the jump?"

"I'll let you try first," said Kell.

"We can't go back."

Kell nodded. "You can see the Stone Lion Woods from here," he said, pointing.

"We need a plan," said Saark, eyes narrowing. "How do we get down from this shit-hole? Come on Kell, you're the man with all the answers!"

"I have no answers!" he thundered, rage in his face for a moment; then he calmed himself. "I'm just trying to keep us alive long enough to think." He rubbed at his beard, fingers rimed in filth and old blood. Only then did he look down at himself, and he gave a bitter laugh. "Look at the state of me, Saark." His eyes were dark, glittering, feral. "Just like the old days. The Days of Blood."

Saark said nothing. His mind worked fast. Kell was losing it. Kell was going slowly... insane.

"There must be a way off here," said Saark, voice calm. "You wait here, guard the steps. I'll see if I can find a ramp, or gantry, or some other way to the roof of another building."

Saark moved around the outside wall of the tower block, each footstep chosen with care, with precision; below, the tower interior was like a huge, sour-smelling throat. Growls echoed up to meet him.

Saark stopped. He looked across the vast, rotting decadence of Old Skulkra. Beyond the walls he could see the enemy: the Army of Iron. A great sorrow took his heart, then, and crushed it in his fist. He realised with bitterness that General Graal had won. He had crushed Falanor's armies as if they were children. He had obliterated their soldiers, and... now what?

Saark frowned. From this vantage point he could see the Great North Road, snaking north and south, a meandering black ribbon through hills and woodland, all peppered with snow. To the west he could make out the sprawl of Vorgeth Forest, stretching off for as far as the eye could see. But there, on the road, he could see...

Saark rubbed his eyes. His swollen eye had opened a little, but still he could not understand what he witnessed. Huge, black, angular objects seemed to fill the Great North Road; from the ancient connecting roads of Old Skulkra heading north, for as far as the eye could see. Saark stroked his moustache, mouth dry, fear an ever-present and unwelcome friend.

"The Blood Refineries," said Kell, making Saark jump.

"What?"

"On the road. That's what you can see. The vachine need them to refine blood; and they need blood-oil to survive."

Saark considered this. "They have brought their machinery with them?"

"Yes." Kell nodded. He was sombre. Below, they heard a fresh growl, a snarl, and the scrabble of slashing claws. The cankers had found a way past the collapsed stairwell. They were on their way up.

"So they've won?" said Saark.

"No!" snarled Kell. "We will fight them. We will fight them to the bitter end!"

"They will massacre our people," said Saark, tears in his eyes.

"Aye, lad."

"The men, the women, the children of Falanor."

"Aye. Now take out your sword. There's work to be done." Kell strode to the opening leading to the stairwell. The cankers were growing louder. There were many, and their snarls were terrifying.

Saark stood beside Kell, his rapier out, his eyes fixed on the black maw of the opening.

"Kell?"

"Yes, Saark?"

"We're going to die up here, aren't we?"

Kell laughed, and it contained genuine humour, genuine warmth. He slapped Saark on the back, then rubbed thoughtfully at his bloodied beard, and with glittering eyes said, "We all die sometime, laddie," as the first of the cankers burst from the opening in a flurry of claws and fangs and screwed up faces of pure hatred.

With a roar, Kell leapt to meet them.

The Saga of Kell's Legend

The mighty Kell stood proud upon sandy shores,
He'd willingly cast out a palace of bores,
He pondered on glory of merciless days,
As lounged by his feet decadent poets sang praise,
But now his axe of old lay down by his side,
A weapon of terror and worthy genocide,
As the sea sweet her whisper carried o'er to him,
Her voice a bright loving invitation to swim,
Eternal bed, quoth she, I bring long soothing sleep,
Come to me my darling, now please don't you
    weep;

Our hero of old, he felt not the dread,
Of the battles gone by, of the children now dead,
He dreamt of the slaughter at Valantrium Moor,
A thousand dead foes, there could not be a cure
Of low evil ways and bright terrible deeds,
Of men turned bad, he'd harvest the weeds,
His mighty axe hummed, Ilanna by name,
Twin sharp blades of steel, without any shame
For the deeds she did do, the men she did slay,
Every living bright-eyed creature was legitimate
    prey;
Kell waded through life on a river of blood,
His axe in his hands, dreams misunderstood,

In Moonlake and Skulkra he fought with the best
This hero of old, this hero obsessed,
This hero turned champion of King Searlan
Defiant and worthy a merciless man,
Through Jangir and Black Pike Kell slaughtered
    the foe,
Each battle was empty, each moment gone slow,
And with each bloody murder Kell felt more the
    pain,
Reversal and angst brought home his heart bane.

[Rarely sung final verse:]
And Kell now stood with axe in hand,
The sea raged before him time torn into strands,
He pondered his legend and screamed at the stars,
Death open beneath him to heal all the scars
Of the hatred he'd felt, and the murders he'd done
And the people he'd killed all the pleasure and life
He'd destroyed.

Kell stared melancholy into great rolling waves of
    a Dark Green World,
And knew he could blame no other but himself
    for
The long Days of Blood, the long Days of Shame,
The worst times flowing through evil years of
    pain,
And the Legend dispersed and the honour was gone
And all savagery fucked in a world ripped undone
And the answer was clear as the stars in the sky
All the bright stars the white stars the time was to
    die,
Kell took up Ilanna and bade the world farewell,
The demons tore through him as he ended the spell
And closed his eyes.

II
SOUL STEALERS

PROLOGUE
Soul Stealers

It was an ink-dark dream. A razor flashback. A frozen splinter of
time piercing his mind like a sterile needle. Nienna, beautiful Nienna, his sweet young granddaughter; they stood by the edge of a
wide, sweeping river, spring sunshine warming upturned faces and
glinting like diamonds amongst swaying reeds. Kell was teaching
her how to fish, and he guided her hands, her long tapered fingers
a contrast to his wrinkled, scarred old bear paws, hooking the bait
(at which she pulled a screwed-up face) then casting out the line.
They sat, then, in companionable silence, and Kell realised Nienna
was watching him intently. He turned, scratching his grizzled grey
beard, eyes meeting her bright gaze, and she smiled, face radiant.

"Grandfather?"

"Yes, little monkey?"

"Isn't fishing... you know, unfair?"

"What do you mean?"

"Well, it's like a trap, isn't it? You dangle the worm on a hook,
and the fish swims along, unsuspecting, and you whip him out
and eat him for supper. It's really not fair on the fish."

"Well, how else would I catch him?" said Kell, frowning a little.
He chuckled. "I could always throw *you* in – you could *swim* after
all the little fishes, catch them in your teeth like a pike!" He moved
as if to grab her, to toss her into the deep waters, and she squealed,
backing away fast up the bank and getting mud on her hands
and clothes.

Nienna tutted. "Grandfather!"

"Ach, it's only a little mud. It'll wash off."

What Kell had wanted to say was that *all life* is a trap, a deceit, a bad con trick from a clever con artist. Life leads you on, life dangles tantalising bait on a dulled hook of iron – the bait being happiness, good health, wealth, joy – and you reach with both hands, mouth gaping like a slack-brained jester in the King's Court, but Life is a *bitch* and just when you think you've found it, found your dream, the line snags and you're yanked by your balls, guts and brain. Hooked, and slaughtered. That was Life. That was *Reality*. That was *Sobriety*. But Kell kept his mouth shut. Kept it shut tight. He didn't want to spoil the moment, this simple joy of fishing with his talented, optimistic granddaughter beside the Selenau River.

Now, Kell and Saark stood on the high rooftop of the shattered, teetering tower block in Old Skulkra. This was their trap. The bait had been laid by General Graal, his Army of Iron, his disgusting twisted *cankers*, and they had been snagged like fools, like naïve hatchlings, cornering themselves in Old Skulkra with an impossible task and a terrible fight.

Kell clutched his black axe Ilanna to his chest, gore-spattered knuckles white, face iron thunder, and Saark was tense, slim rapier wavering before him, his face a shattered silhouette of half-broken fear.

Below, in the bowels of the old stone block, something ululated, high-pitched and keening and far too feral to be human. It was followed immediately by a flurry of snarls, and growls, and heavy thuds and a scrabbling of brass claws clattering and booming through velvet black.

It was the cankers... and they were coming for fresh blood.

Kell's face was a thunderstorm filled with bruised clouds. Saark's face was hard to read, battered from a beating at the hands of Myriam's men, and his blood seeped through a torn and dirt-smeared shirt from a recent stab wound. Kell took a deep breath, nose twitching at fire from distant funeral pyres in the wake of the recent battle; he lifted Ilanna, and seemed, for a moment at least, to commune with the battered axe.

The cankers drew close. The two men could hear the beasts' heavy breathing on the stairwell.

Suddenly, a *pulse* seemed to pound through the ancient,

deserted city; through the world. It was subsonic, an esoteric rumble; almost an earthquake. Almost.

Saark allowed breath to hiss free between clenched teeth. His fear was a tangible thing, a stain, like ink. He glanced at Kell.

"We're going to die up here, aren't we?"

Kell laughed, and it contained genuine humour, genuine warmth. He slapped Saark on the back, then rubbed thoughtfully at his bloodied beard, and with glittering eyes said, "We all die sometime, laddie," as the first of the cankers burst from the opening in a flurry of claws and fangs and screwed up faces of pure hate.

With a roar, Kell leapt to meet them…

As the first canker leapt, so Kell's mighty axe slammed down in a savage overhead blow, splitting the head in two, right down to the twisted spine-top. Flesh, brain and skull exploded outwards, and mixed in there with muscle and bone shards were tiny, battered clockwork machines, wheels and cogs twisting and turning, clicking and shifting, clockwork gears clacking, and in a blur Kell stepped back, dragging his axe with him as the first canker corpse hit the ground and he swayed from a swipe of huge claws from the second snarling beast, Ilanna *singing* as she hammered left now, butterfly blades horizontal, cutting free the canker's arm with a jarring *thud* and a shower of flowering blood petals. The beast howled, but a third heaved and shouldered past, huge and bulky, the size of a lion, a disjointed, twisted lion with pale white skin bulging with muscle, like overfull bowels pressing against maggot flesh in an attempt to break free of a pus-filled abdomen. The canker was covered with a plague of grey fur, tufted and irregular, and its forehead was stretched right back, its huge maw five times the size of the human mouth which had formed its template, skull open like an axe-chopped pumpkin showing huge brass fangs which curled down from rancid gleaming jaws and were decorated with knurled swirls, like fine etchings in copper. The canker's body was covered in open wounds, and within each wound thrashed clockwork, a myriad of tiny, spinning wheels, gyrating spindles, meshing gears, but whereas the *pure* vachine was perfect, and noble, and secure in its Engineer-created arrogance, this canker – this deviation, this *corruption* – showed bent gears and levers and unmeshed cogs, and in a blur Kell leapt sideways, Ilanna carving a parting line of muscle across the canker's neck, like an unzipping of flesh. Despite pain and squirming, unreleased muscle, its sheer weight and bulk carried it forward across the scattered concrete beams of the tower block's flat roof, where it slammed into Saark as his rapier stabbed frantically, slashing open more huge curved wounds. They both staggered back, fell back, and Kell turned from Saark allowing the wounded man to deal with the dying canker in a hiss of steel opening flesh and a *gush* of severed arteries.

A fresh flood of cankers burst through the opening, forcing Kell towards a grim-faced Saark, and the two men stood side by side, shoulder to shoulder, faces grim and splattered with gore, weapons flickering skilfully to open savage wounds as the cankers formed an expanding wall of flesh, an arc of solid muscle, as more and more surged through the opening to reinforce their ranks until there were ten, fifteen, *twenty* of the huge beasts ranged against them, hissing and grunting.

Kell gave a sardonic snarl, teeth grinding, and rubbed his grey beard. At his feet lay five dead cankers, a feat for any mortal man – for each canker was a terrible foe. Kell's eyes glittered, dark and feral, and his gore-slippery axe lowered a little as he realised – realised with a *bark* of laughter – that they were waiting.

"What's the matter, lads?" he boomed. "Left your bollocks at home with your pus-ugly wives?"

The cankers growled, huge puddles of drool descending from wide stretched maws where brass fangs curled like scimitar blades. Behind Kell, Saark was panting, long curly hair in lank strips filled with bits of bone and flesh, his beautiful face now a tapestry of agony.

"What are they waiting for?" he whispered, as if afraid his voice would accelerate them into action.

Kell shrugged. "I reckon we'll find out soon enough."

Within seconds, the line of quivering flesh, of tufted fur and deviant clockwork was heaved aside, and a massive canker forced its way through the throng. Kell could smell hot oil, and fancied he could hear the steady, tiny *tick tick tick* of off-beat clockwork.

"Now we die," muttered Saark.

"No," snapped Kell, "for if we die, then Nienna dies, if we die, then we cannot hunt down her kidnappers, we cannot seek justice and revenge! So, Saark, will you *shut up* and focus!" Kell fixed his gaze on this new creature, this towering beast, eight feet tall, heavily muscled, with glowering red eyes and an accompanying stench like desecration. Its skin was terribly pale, corpse-flesh waxy and entirely without hair. Kell's eyes narrowed. It was almost like... almost like this *beast* was merged with the albino soldiers from Graal's Army of Iron. Kell's glittering gaze scanned the wounds in the canker's flanks and chest, where deep inside brass clockwork spun and meshed. He grinned, but his eyes were dark and unfriendly. "Gods, lad, you stink like a ten-week corpse after dysentery and plague. What the hell's *wrong* with you beasts? Don't answer that. It's nothing my axe can't put right." He gestured flippantly with Ilanna, eyes watching, and perceived the canker's understanding.

Snarls and growls echoed up and down the line, and Kell knew these unholy beasts could comprehend. They were intelligent, and that frightened Kell more than any display of corruption. It was when this huge, dominant creature suddenly spoke that Kell took a step back, boots thumping the concrete beams, surprised despite himself; although he fought well not to show it.

"I am Nesh," said the canker, forming its words with care; despite impedance from curved fangs, its accent was Iopian, and that shouldn't have been possible. The whole mass of corrupted flesh and clockwork shouldn't have been possible. It was nightmare made real. "My General, the Warlord Graal, requires the honour of your presence. Indeed, he grants you *life* in exchange for your cooperation. You may agree now, little man." The canker grinned, more saliva pooling to the shattered, ancient beams of the high roof.

Kell took another step back. Saark was beside him, and Kell glanced at his friend with hooded eyes. He muttered, "Have you found an escape route yet?"

"There's no way off this roof!" said Saark. "We're trapped!"

"We're going to have to fight our way free, then."

Saark eyed the twenty or so cankers, and could see the shadows and hear the snarls of more on the stairwell below. He shuddered, fear a dry dead rat in his throat, a snake of lard in his intestines, a fist of iron in his belly. Saark, ever the dandy, a lover of life, women, wine and any narcotic that could swell the hedonistic experience of all three, knew deep down in his darkest most terrible nightmares that he was going to die here, knew he was to be ripped apart by those huge fangs, torn into flesh shreds, into streamers of muscle and skin spaghetti, and there was nothing he could do to avert this fate.

"You're joking, right?"

Kell threw him a dark glance, and growled, "I never joke when it comes to killing. Now! Follow my lead! You understand, boy?"

Saark nodded, sweating, hands gripping his rapier tight.

Nesh, growing impatient, moved its angry red gaze from one warrior to the other, then back. Kell moved his own eyes over the waxy, pale flesh; he shivered. The creature had hints of humanity in its twisted corruption of skin and bone, but there, any similarity ended. It was a distortion, not just of humanity, but of albino and vachine; a creature of no place, despised by all. Strangely, a thread of sympathy wormed into Kell's mind. He cut it savagely with a mental blade. This beast would show no mercy, nor compassion. It was here to kill.

"So, man? Will you come?" growled Nesh, and Kell could see other cankers straining at the leash; they could smell blood, and fear, and even remnants of Saark's distant flowery perfume. Kell grinned, baring his teeth as his face screwed into a ball of hostility.

"Tell Graal he can shove my axe up his arse!"

Saark groaned… and readied himself for attack…

Winter had finally come to Falanor.

Snow fell in blankets from iron clouds beneath a pale, albino sun. Violent storms flung folds of white to cover Falanor's valleys and rolling hills, her forests and rivers and ragged, towering mountains. From the savage flanks of the Black Pikes to the north, down through recently conquered cities, from Jalder to Skulkra, Vorgeth, Fawkrin and the southern capital of Vor, winter knew no obstacle and arrived early, with a ferocity not seen in the world for two centuries.

Within three days all northern passes were blocked; an ideal situation in the normal running of the country, for it meant many of the brigands, deviants and Blacklipper smugglers who oft troubled northern towns were trapped like bears in their mountain hideouts until the following spring.

It also meant General Graal, and his albino Army of Iron, were trapped in Falanor, blockaded far from their homeland in the heart of the Black Pike Mountains, severed from the vachine civilisation occupying Silva Valley, seat of power for the High Engineer Episcopate and Engineer Council, the Engineer's Palace and revered resting place for the Oak Testament.

Graal had successfully brought his vachine-sponsored army of albino subordinates south, seizing the cities of Falanor, kidnapping Queen Alloria, murdering the heroic Battle King, Leanoric, and routing his armies, including the previously unconquered Eagle Divisions. He had done this using cunning and a merciless swift descent. And by utilising blood-oil magick.

In the wake of the successful invasion, and within hours of snow blocking the Black Pike Mountain passes, Graal's Harvesters had brought forth the Blood Refineries: huge angular machines not unlike siege engines, pulled by teams of horses and cankers and using, in a twist of final irony, of calculated mockery, the fine, wide roads built by King Leanoric for transportation of his own military divisions. Graal camped his army outside Old Skulkra, and the great blood refineries had come to rest on the plain before the deserted city just hours before heavy falls of snow rendered further transport from the north impossible.

Graal sat in his war tent, cross-legged before a low table of ivory and marble, a scatter of parchments laid out before his weary eyes. The tent flap opened allowing a swirl of snow to intrude, and a Harvester stooped low to enter. For a moment Graal stared, the uniqueness of this race never failing to occupy and twist his curious mind; he watched the tall, heavily robed figure of the Harvester with its flat, oval, hairless face, nose nothing more than vertical slits, fingers not so much fingers as long slender needles of bone used for the delicate extraction of blood from a human carcass... he watched the Harvester settle down in a complicated ritual. Satisfied, the Harvester finally lifted tiny, black eyes to focus on Graal.

"The roads are closed. We are severed from the vachine," spoke the Harvester, voice a sibilant hissing.

Graal nodded, and returned his gaze to his parchments, reports detailing the final military approach on Vor by three of his albino *Divisions*. "Then we have months before they discover the... *reality* of the situation. Yes?"

"Yes, general."

"Has the vachine-bred Engineer Princess Jaranis managed to cross the mountains south in order to inspect our situation? Although, what she expects to find other than a jewelled dagger in her guts I have no idea."

"She arrived, general. An hour ago, in fact, with her military entourage. That is why I am here."

"Entourage?" He showed interest, now. "How many?"

The Harvester chuckled, a disturbing noise deep in its long, quivering throat. "As I previously made clear, the vachine in all their pious arrogance are wholly trusting of your endeavour. Jaranis, damn her clockwork, travelled with ten men only, a unit commanded by a lowly engineer-priest. I have taken the liberty of immediate slaughter, and even now their corpses have been added to the frozen pyres of recent battle. Even now," he paused, black eyes glinting, "their clockwork halts. However. With regard to Jaranis herself... I thought it wise to allow you counsel with this twisted princess. After all, despite her pretty skin and innocent ways, she may have an inkling of our plans."

"Summon her," said Graal, without looking up from his papers.

After a few minutes there came a sudden commotion outside the war tent, and two albino warriors dragged a shackled woman into the cosy interior. Although, upon closer inspection, it was clear she was not entirely human for she sported the tiny brass fangs of the vachine – the machine vampires of Silva Valley. The vachine were a blending of human and advanced miniature clockwork, a technological advancement of watchmaking skills evolved and developed and refined over the centuries until flesh and clockwork merged into a beautiful, superior whole. The vachine relied on the narcotic of blood-oil, a concoction of refined blood, in order to keep their internal clockwork mechanisms running smoothly. Without blood, and more importantly, blood-*oil*, a vachine's clockwork would seize; and they would die. Hence the necessity of vampiric feeding.

Jaranis was thrown to the ground, where she spat up at Graal, eyes blazing with fury and shocked disbelief. Her fangs ejected with a tiny pneumatic *hissing*. She climbed smoothly to her feet. She was tall, elegant, with a shower of golden curls. She was beautiful beyond the human, and as she spoke Graal could see the tiny clockwork mechanisms in her throat, miniature gears and cogs and pistons working in a harmony of flesh and clockwork. Like a well-timed vampire machine. A vachine.

Graal smiled, some curious emotion not unlike lust passing through his mind; through his soul.

"Graal, you excel yourself with stupidity and arrogance!" snapped Princess Jaranis. "What, in the name of the Oak Testament, are you *doing*?"

Graal smiled, slowly, and stood. He stretched himself and gave an exaggerated, almost theatrical, yawn. Then his cold eyes focused on Jaranis and she could see there was anything but pantomime in that shadowed, brutal gaze.

"I admit, O *princess*, that it has been considerable time since I sought to pride myself on the baser concept of... *stupidity*," said Graal, handling the word like an abortion, and as he spoke he moved smoothly to a rack of armour and began to buckle on breastplate and forearm greaves fashioned from dull black steel. "Rather, my sweetness, I seek to pride myself on the twin lusts of *betrayal* and *dominion*."

"You would betray the vachine?" whispered Jaranis, stunned. "A society you helped build from a mewling wreckage of primal carnage and bestial evolution?"

Graal smiled, and halted midway through buckling a greave. His eyes seemed distant, and as he spoke his voice was lilting, a low growl, almost musical in its harmony. "Allow your mind to drift back, like drug-smoke, for a millennium, my sweet; there were once three Vampire Warlords, maybe you have heard of them? Their names are written in iron on the Core Stone of Silva Valley, carved into the back cover of the Oak Testament with a knife used to slit the throats of babes." His eyes grew hard, like cobalt. "They are Kuradek, Meshwar, Bhu Vanesh – Kuradek, the Unholy. Meshwar, the Violent. And Bhu Vanesh, the Eater in the Dark." He glanced at Jaranis, then, head tilting. With tight lips Jaranis shook her head, and frowned, seeking to understand Graal's direction.

"These warlords," continued Graal, "were, shall we say, all powerful. I am surprised you have limited knowledge of their prowess, for they are a pivotal part of baseline vachine history." He smiled. "That is, *your* vachine history. For as we all know, the Engineer Council seek to strongly enforce a true vachine culture in which nobody strays from a pure and holy path. Is that not so?"

"That is so," said Jaranis, voice little more than a whisper. She was trembling now, and Graal felt a trickle of lust ease through his veins like a honey narcotic. Sex, fear and death, he thought, went hand in hand, and were *always* a turn-on.

"The warlords, they had clockwork *souls*," said Graal, eyes blazing with a sudden fury. He calmed himself with intricate self-control, and finished strapping on his armour with tight, sudden little jerks.

"But then, you may not know this, for the High Engineer Episcopate practice and preach rewritten histories and a fictional past."

Jaranis shook her head, and Graal gestured to the two albino soldiers, who stepped forward, grabbing the young vachine woman and dragging her out into the freshly falling snow. All through the war camp tumbled jarring sounds, the snort and stamp of horse, cankers snarling, the clatter of arms, the low-level talk of soldiers around braziers. Jaranis was thrown to her knees, her fine silk robes stained with saliva, and just a little blood.

Graal emerged, striding with an arrogant air that made Jaranis want to rip out his throat. Her fangs ejected fully, eyes narrowing and claws hissing from fingertips. They gleamed, razor-sharpened brass. She considered leaping, but caught something in her peripheral vision: two figures, both female, both albino subordinates. She snarled in disgust, and turned to stare at these... soldiers.

They were tall, lithe, athletic, and wore light armour of polished steel unlike the usual black armour of the albino Army of Iron. Both women wore sleek longswords at their hips, and one had her long white hair braided into twin, wrist-thick ponytails, whilst the second had her hair cropped short. It was spiked by the snow. Their skin was white, almost translucent, and they had high cheekbones, gaunt faces, and crimson eyes. When they smiled, their beauty was stunning but deadly, like a newborn sun. And when they smiled, they had the fangs of the vachine.

Princess Jaranis hissed in shock. Albinos could not be vachine! It was not permitted. It was illegal. It was *unholy*.

Graal stepped forward, and touched one woman behind her elbow. She smiled at him. "This is Shanna, and this is Tashmaniok. Daughters, I would like to introduce the vachine princess, Jaranis." The two albino vachine warriors gave short bows and moved to stand erect, one at either side of Graal. They took his arms, as if enjoying a stroll down some theatre-lined thoroughfare in one of Silva Valley's more respectable cultured communities, and their eyes glowed with vampire hate.

"You will not get away with this... *blasphemy*!" snarled Jaranis, voice dripping poison and fury. "Not for giving White Warriors the clockwork, nor for betraying the vachine!"

"But, my sweetness, I think I already have," said Graal. He smiled down at Jaranis. "You vachine are so trusting, and so beautifully naïve. These girls, they are not some simple blending. Some back-street black-market clockwork abortion!" His voice rose, a little in anger, blue eyes glinting as his focus drilled into the vachine princess. "Don't you understand to whom you speak? Don't you recognise the birth of your death?"

"The Soul Stealers?" whispered Jaranis, in horror.

Graal smiled. He gave a slight, sideways nod, and Shanna detached from his linked arm and in one smooth movement, drew her sword and decapitated the vachine princess.

Jaranis's head rolled into the snow and blood, and blood-oil, spurted from the ragged neck stump. The body paused for a moment, rigid, then toppled like a puppet with cut strings. As blood-oil ran free, so clockwork machinery grew noisy, it rattled and spluttered until it finally faltered, and came to a premature clattering halt with a discordant note like the clashing of swords in battle.

Graal knelt in the snow, ignoring the vachine blood which stained his leather trews. He stared into the severed clockwork face of the murdered vachine; in death, she was even more beautiful.

He glanced back. The Soul Stealers were poised motionless, beautiful, deadly.

"I had a mind-pulse from Nesh," he said, voice low and terrible. "He says Kell and that puppet, Saark, are cornered in the maze of Old Skulkra."

"Yes, father," said Tashmaniok.

"Bring them to me," he said, and shifted his gaze to the Soul Stealers' bright, focused eyes, "It is the Soul Gem that matters, now. You understand?"

"We serve," they said, voices in harmony.

With the stealth of the vampire the Soul Stealers vanished, like ghosts, through the snow.

ONE
Ankarok

Kell grinned. "Tell Graal he can shove my axe up his arse!"

Saark groaned... and readied for attack...

"As you wish," said Nesh, lowering its strange, bestial, wrenched clockwork head, red eyes shining, mouth full of juices in anticipation of the feed to come. Muscles bunched like steel-weave cables, fangs jutted free with crunches, and behind it the other cankers growled and the growl rose into a unified howl which mingled and merged forming one perfectly balanced single note that held on the air, perfect, and signified their reward.

Kell's eyes were fixed on the lead canker, his body a tense bow-string, senses heightened into something more than human. He was the delicate trigger of a crossbow. The impact reflex of a striking snake.

It was going to be a damn hard fight.

But then... the incredible happened. Nesh settled back on its haunches, eyes meeting Kell's, and the old warrior was sure he saw a corrupt smile touch the beast's lips like a tracing of icing sugar on horse-shit. Nesh stood, turned, and pushed through the cankers. The howling subsided into an awkward silence; then the cankers slowly filed after their leader, one by one, until only their rotten oil stink remained – alongside five canker corpses, bleeding slow-congealing lifeblood onto the stone roof.

"What happened?" breathed Saark, his whole body relaxing, slumping almost, into the cage of his bones. Kell shrugged, and turned, and fastened his gaze on the small boy standing perhaps twenty feet away, by the low wall overlooking Old Skulkra's ancient, crumbling remains.

Kell pointed, and Saark noticed the boy for the first time. He was young, only five or six years old, his skin pale, his limbs thin, his clothing ragged like many an abandoned street urchin easily found in the shit-pits of Falanor's major cities. The boy turned, and looked up at Kell and Saark, and smiled, head tilting.

It's in his eyes, thought Kell, his cool gaze locked to the boy. His eyes are old. They sparkled like diseased Dog Gems, those rarest of dull jewels left over from another age, another civilisation.

Kell stepped forward, and crouched. "You scared them off, lad?" It was half question, half statement. The air felt suddenly fuzzy, as if raw magick was discharging languorously through the breeze.

The boy nodded, but did not move. He shifted slightly, and something small and black ran down the sleeve of his threadbare jacket. It was a scorpion, and it ran onto the boy's hand and sat there for a while, as if observing the two men.

Saark let out a hiss, hand tightening on rapier hilt. "The insect of the devil!" he snapped.

"Look," said Kell, slowly. "It has two tails." And indeed, the scorpion – small, shiny, black – had two corrugated tails, each with a barbed sting.

Saark shivered. "Throw it down, lad," he called. "Our boots will finish the little bastard."

Ignoring Saark, the boy stepped across loose stone joists, moving forward with a delicate grace which belied his narrow, starved limbs. He halted before Kell, looked up with dark eyes twinkling, then slowly plucked the twin-tailed scorpion from his hand and secreted the arachnid beneath his shirt.

"My name is Skanda," said the boy, voice little more than a husky whisper. "And the scorpion, it is a scorpion of time."

"What does that mean?" whispered Kell.

The boy shrugged, eyes hooded, smile mysterious.

"You scared away the cankers!" blurted Saark. "How did you do that?"

Skanda turned to Saark, and again his head tilted, as if reading the dandy's thoughts. "They fear me, and they fear my race," said Skanda, and when he smiled they saw his teeth were black. Not the black of decay, but the black of insect chitin.

"Your race?" said Kell, voice gentle.

"I am Ankarok," said Skanda, looking out over Old Skulkra, over its ancient, deserted palaces and temples, tenements and warehouses, towers and cathedrals. All crumbling, and cracked, all savaged by time and erosion and fear. "This was our city. Once." He looked again at Kell, and smiled the shiny black smile. "This was our country. Our world."

Saark moved to the edge of the crumbling tenement, staring over the low wall. Below, he could see the retreated cankers had gathered; there were more than fifty, some sitting on the ancient stone paving slabs, some pacing in impatient circles. Many snarled, lashing out at others. At their core was Nesh, seated on powerful haunches, almost like a lion, regal composure immaculate.

"They're waiting below," said Saark, moving back to Kell. He glanced at Skanda. "Seems their fear only extends so far."

"I will show you a way out of this building," said Skanda, and started to move across the roof, dodging holes and loose joists.

Saark stared at Kell. "I don't trust him. I think we should head off alone."

Ignoring Saark, Kell followed the boy, and heard the battered dandy curse and follow. "Wait," said Kell, as they reached a segment of wall where a part of the floor had appeared to crumble away revealing, in fact, a tunnel, leading *down* through the wall. Kell could just see the gleam of slick, black steps. It dispersed his fears of magick, a little. "Wait. Why would you do this for us? I have heard of the Ankarok. By all accounts, they were not, shall we say, a charitable race."

Skanda smiled his unnerving smile. Despite his stature, and his feeble appearance of vagrancy, he exuded a dark energy, a power Saark was only just beginning to comprehend; and with a jump, Saark recognised that Kell had not been fooled. Kell had seen through the – *disguise* – immediately. Saark snorted. Ha! he thought. Kell was just too damned smart for an old fat man.

"Why?" Skanda gave a small laugh. "Kell, for you we would attack the world," said the little boy, watching Kell closely. His dark eyes shone. "For you are Kell, the Black Axeman of Drennach – and it is written you shall help save the Ankarok," he said.

His name was Jage, and they left him to die when he was six years old. He couldn't blame them. He would have done the same. The blow from an iron-shod hoof left his spine damn near snapped in two, discs crushed in several places, his bent and broken body crippled beyond repair – or at least, beyond the repair of a simple farming people. Nobody in the village of Crennan could bring themselves to kill the child; and yet Jage's mother and father could not afford to feed a cripple. They could barely afford to feed themselves.

His father, a slim man named Parellion, carried the boy to the banks of the Hentack River where, in the summer months when the water level was low, the flow turned yellow, sometimes orange, and was highly poisonous if drank. It was completely safe, so it was said, in the winter months when the flow was fast, fresh, clear with pure mountain melt from the Black Pikes; then, then the water could be safely supped, although few trusted its turncoat nature. Most villagers from Crennan had seen the effects of the toxins on a human body: the writhing, the screaming, flesh tumbling from a bubbling skeleton. Such agony was not something easily forgotten.

Jage's father placed him gently on the bank, and Jage looked up into his kindly face, ravaged by years of working the fields and creased like old leather. He did not understand, then, the tears that fell from his father's eyes and landed in his own. He smiled, for the herbs old Merryach gave him had taken away the savage pain in his spine. Maybe they thought they'd given him enough herbs to end his life? However, they had not.

Parellion kissed him tenderly; he smelt strongly of earth. Beyond, Jage could see his mother weeping into a red handkerchief. Parellion knelt and stroked the boy's brow, then stood, and turned, and left.

In innocence, naivety, misunderstanding, Jage watched them go and he was happy for a while because the sun shone on his face and the pain had receded to nothing more than a dull throb. The sunshine was pleasant and he was surrounded by flowers and could hear the summer trickle of the river. He frowned. That was the poisonous river, yes? He strained to move, to turn, to see if the waters ran orange and yellow; but he could not. His spine was broken. He was crippled beyond repair.

For a long time Jage lay amongst the flowers, his thirst growing with more and more intensity. The herbs had left a strange tingling sensation and a bitter taste on his tongue. I wonder when father will come back for me? he thought. Soon, soon, answered his own mind. He will bring you water, and more medicine, and it will heal your broken back and the world will be well again. You'll see. It will be fine. It will be good.

But Parellion did not return, and Jage's thirst grew immeasurably, and with it came Jage's pain beating like a caged salamander deep down within, in his body core, white-hot punches running up and down his spine like the hooves of the horse that kicked him.

Stupid! His mother told him never to walk behind a horse. The eighteen-hand great horse, or draught horse as they were also known, was a huge and stocky, docile, glossy creature, bay with white stockings, prodigious in strength and used predominantly for pulling the iron-tipped plough. Jage had been concentrating on little Megan, flying a kite made from an old shirt and yew twigs, and her running, her giggling, the way sunlight glinted in her amber curls... He ran across the field to speak to her, to ask if he, too, could fly the kite and *impact* threw him across the field like a ragdoll, and for a long time only colours and blackness swirled in his mind. Everything was fuzzy, unfocused, but he remembered Megan's screams. Oh how he remembered those!

Now, the copper coin of the sun sank, and bright fear began to creep around the edges of the young boy's reason. What if, he decided, mother and father did not return? What if they were never going to return? How would he drink? How would he crawl to the river? He could not *move*. Tears wetted his cheeks, and the bitter taste of the herb was strong, and bad, in his desiccated mouth. But more, the bitter taste of a growing realisation festered in his heart. Why had they brought him here? He thought it was to enjoy the sunshine after the cramped interior of their hut, with its smell of herbs and vomit and stale earth.

And as the moon rose, and stars glimmered, and the river rushed and Jage could hear the stealthy footfalls of creatures in the night, he knew, knew they had left him here to *die* and he wept for betrayal, body shuddering, tears rolling down his face and tickling him and pitifully he tried to move, teeth gritted, more pain flaring *flaring* so bad he screamed and writhed a little, twitching in agony and impotence amongst the starlit flowers, their colours bleached, their tiny heads bobbing.

Suddenly, somewhere nearby, a wolf howled. Jage froze, fear crawling into his brain like an insect, and his eyes grew wide and he bit his tongue, tasting blood. Wolves. This far south of the Black Pike Mountains? It wasn't unheard, although the people of Crennan were keen to hunt down and massacre any wolves sighted in the vicinity. The mountain wolves were savage indeed, and never stopped at killing a single animal. Their frenzies were legendary. As was their hunger.

The howl, long and lingering and drifting to silence like smoke, was answered by another howl, off to the east, then a third, to the west. Jage remained frozen, eyes moving from left to right, his immobility a torture in itself, which at this moment in time far outweighed the physical pain of his broken spine.

If they found him, they would eat him, of this he was sure.

Eat him alive.

Jage waited, in the darkness, in the silence, with pain growing inside him, his severed spine pricking him with hot-iron brands of agony, his heart thumping in his ears. I will be safe, he told himself. I will be safe. He repeated the phrase, over and over and over, like a mantra, a prayer-song, and part of him, the childish part, knew that if danger truly approached then his father, brave strong Parellion, would be waiting just out of sight with his mighty wood-cutting axe and he would smash those wolves in two, for surely the village was near enough for them to hear the howls? The villagers would not tolerate such an intrusion by a natural predator! But another part of Jage, a part that was quickly growing up, an accelerated maturity and a consideration to *survive* told him with savage slaps that he was completely alone, abandoned, and if he did *nothing* then he would surely die. But what can I do? he thought, fighting against the urge to cry. I cannot move!

He wanted to scream, then. To release his frustration and pain in one long howl, just like the wolves; but he bit his tongue, for he knew to do so would be to draw them like moth to candle flame.

Jage waited, tense and filled with an exhaustive fear; he eventually drifted into a fitful sleep. When his eyes opened, slowly, he knew something was immediately wrong despite his sensory apparatus unable to detect any direct threat.

Then, grass hissed, and Jage's eyes moved to the left and into his field of vision stepped the wolf. It was old, big, heavy, fur ragged and torn in strips from one flank; its fur was a deep grey and black, matted and twisted, and its eyes were yellow, baleful, and glittered with an ancient intelligence. This creature wasn't like the yelping puppies in the village; this wolf was a killer, a survivor, and it knew fresh, stranded meat when it saw it.

"Oh no," whispered Jage, eyes transfixed. Like a snake before a charmer, Jage watched the wolf pad close, then look left and right as if expecting a trap and humans waiting with pitchfork and axe. Other wolves edged into Jage's vision, growing in confidence and spreading in a wide arc. The young boy shuddered involuntarily.

They were going to eat him. Eat him alive. And there was nothing he could do.

A snarl came, low and malevolent, and those eyes never left Jage's. There was a connection between the two, between victim and killer, and Jage wasn't sure what it meant, only that he felt like a bound sacrifice on an altar; and felt suddenly, violently sick.

The wolf lowered its head, fangs baring, and the snarl elongated into a continuous threatening growl. A paw edged forward, and at the same time Jage felt a tickling across his legs which twitched as if in automatic response, and the tickling moved up over his belly and onto his chest and Jage gaped at the spider there, small, glossy, black, about the size of his hand, so close he could see the many hairs that covered its legs and thorax and he blinked, for this was the highly toxic and very, very deadly Hexel Spider, otherwise known – sweetly, ironically – as a *Lupus* Spider. Jage allowed a slow breath to escape his fear-frozen throat, and watched the spider turn to face the wolf – which had stopped, one paw extended, eyes narrowed as if in consideration.

The spider's two front legs came up, then, poised in the air, and Jage could see long curved chelicerae which he knew, even at this young age, were linked to glands carrying venom.

The wolf halted, but the growl remained, and the old creature was wise enough to recognise danger in this tiny creature. More growls echoed, and then with a shiver Jage felt more tickles spread across his body like rainfall, and his vision was *flooded* by a swathe of Hexel Spiders as they ran up him, over him, and poised, a glossy mass of legs and exoskeletons, almost covering his body entirely and certainly covering the ground around him in a bristling carpet. The wolf snarled, turned, and loped away; was gone.

Jage, however, could not breathe a sigh of relief, and his eyes roved frantically over the spiders which slowly lowered their legs from attack posture and began to move across him, down onto the ground and he was waiting, waiting for that painful bite which would bring about oblivion and this must have been why his parents left him here by a spider nest – certain of a quick, venomous end.

Jage blinked. One spider remained, on his chest, and he could see its tiny black eyes watching. Then it moved forward, and crawled up his face and he could feel each tiny footfall pressing his flesh and he wanted so desperately to scream but knew any sudden noise would bring about the bite.

The spider stopped, suspended over his mouth, and Jage gave the tiniest of whimpers.

From somewhere in the spider, whether it be chelicerae, gland or spinneret, a tiny droplet detached and fell into Jage's throat. It was warm, and slick. More drops followed, and a bitter taste flooded through him, and darkness came in a violent rage and he thought, I have been poisoned, I am dying, I was left for this, and a black swell of raging pain rushed up to meet him and he fell into and through a bottomless pit, and remembered no more.

Jage awoke face down, staring at rock. An incredible thirst still raged through him, and he had distant memories of motion but everything was blurred and his face felt sticky and he realised his skin was covered, covered with a sheen of silk honey web.

So they want to eat me, he thought, miserably. They've brought me back to their cave, so that they can eat me one piece at a time. I am a prisoner. I am food.

He struggled to move, but could not. However, there was no pain, and Jage frowned. Then he spied a flood of spiders undulating across the rocky floor towards him, each the size of his hand, many with chelicerae clicking. Some carried sacks of eggs, encased in silk, some held them in jaws but others carried their precious cargo on their backs. Jage watched, fascinated for a few moments, until he realised they had come to feed; had come to feed their young. He shuddered, and fresh tears fell, and the surging carpet of spiders stopped and several clambered over him, delicate footfalls teasing his flesh with a terrible, mocking agony. He felt the bite, directly over his broken spine, and he screamed then and would have thrashed if he could have moved... another bite came, and another, and Jage was sobbing uncontrollably as the spiders clicked and injected him with venom, and he waited for the pain to smash through him.

Instead, only euphoria eased into his veins, and thankfully he slipped into a welcome unconsciousness.

• • • •

Jage awoke, propped against rock, seated in the dark, in the cold. A breeze blew, which soothed his feverish skin. He licked dry lips, and his throat throbbed raw from excessive screaming. He turned his head, surveyed the narrow tunnels which led to this small, cramped space. On a rock near his foot, to the right, there was fruit; small berries, some strawberries, several mushrooms and a potato. Jage felt an incredible hunger rush through him, and he reached out, lifting the fruit and eating it, and berry juice ran down his face staining his chin red and he laughed, and his feeding increased in frenzy until the fruit and raw vegetables were gone.

He felt stiff, and sore, and only then did realisation dawn.

He could move! He could move again.

The young boy twisted, and his back felt strange, tight and odd and *not quite part of him*. He frowned, and reached behind himself, his hand groping for his spine. What he found there made him freeze, for there was some kind of thick cord on the outside of his skin, stretching from the base of his spine all the way up to the base of his skull. His fingers traced the strange, smooth, hard substance, and as he moved, and explored, he realised the thick cord was moving with him, flexing with him. It seemed to be integral to his flesh.

What have they done to me? Jage thought, dreamlike, drifting, and he saw the spiders moving slowly into his cramped cave, only this time there was something else, another spider, much bigger this time but with exactly the same markings and appearance as the tiny Hexels. Jage fixed on this large arachnid, and its graceful movement of all eight legs in choreographed coordination; it was the same size as Jage, and he realised, at least, that answered the question of how he had been moved to the cave. What was this? A queen? A king? How did it work with spiders?

The spider eased forward, ducking a little, each leg movement a forced hydraulic step, and it stopped before Jage and he looked into the four black orbs – its eyes – and the spider was watching him and he had absolutely no idea what it *wanted*. Was it going to eat him? Was it going to poison him? Did it want to be friends?

"Hello," said Jage, head tilting. His spine gave a tiny, tiny *crackle*. "Thank you, for saving me, from the wolves."

The gathering of worker spiders did not move. They were a carpet of black, all eyes on him. The large one (which he later discovered *was* the queen) stepped even closer, and Jage's nostrils twitched, for he could smell acid and hemolymph. He kept his face perfectly straight as chelicerae the size of daggers moved to his face and the spider seemed to be… sniffing him? It moved yet closer, all eight legs surrounding him, encompassing him in a strange spider-limb cocoon, and then against all odds the spider started to sing, a song without words, a high-pitched croon, a lullaby, and Jage sat there, ensnared, and she sang to him and he felt strangely at ease, a part of this family hiding under the ground and inside the rock, feared and reviled and his face formed into a strange grimace which should have had no place on a human mask and he found *acceptance* for he had been abandoned and left to die but here, here and now, with the spider queen's song soothing through his skull and veins he realised he was a part of this new family; they would look after him, and protect him, and love him, and make him *strong* again.

Deep in the caves, there was a river. The water was black, but Jage drank from it often and never suffered ill effects. He moved around the tunnels freely for a while, exploring winding tunnels and caves and caverns, many littered with bones and long, ancient drifts of web. Most of the Hexel Spiders did their hunting outside, and fed mainly on other insects, although sometimes the three larger queens who inhabited the central caves would head out into the night and return, often with rabbits or snakes, once a weasel spitting and snarling in its sack of silk; and once, even, a wolf.

Jage watched as the three queens brought the cocooned wolf into the hub of caves and tunnels; it no longer struggled, and Jage reasoned it had been given a moderate bite to sedate it. The massive shaggy beast was wrapped heavily in thick cords of restraining silk, and Jage crawled forward, curious, head tilting to one side as he realised with a start the creature was the wolf that had threatened him all those months earlier, as he lay paralysed and abandoned beside the Hentack River. On hands and knees Jage crawled until his face was only inches from the wolf, and he stared into those old, baleful yellow eyes and the wolf seemed to grin at him, panting in short bursts, and Jage felt some kind of victory and he wondered if this was sheer coincidence, or if his new family had hunted down the wolf and brought it to him.

Jage turned, and at that moment the wolf lunged, jaws snapping, slicing through his shoulder and making the young boy scream. The wolf locked jaws, and shook him, and Jage flopped to the rock and the spiders rushed over the wolf and the queen was there, small black eyes emotionless as chelicerae swept down and there came a terrible *cracking*; she snapped the wolf's muzzle in two, then a leg punched out, entering the old creature's skull with pile-driver force and skewering the brain within.

Jage fell back, weeping, pain flooding him. Gently, the queen gathered him up and a honey liquid oozed from her fangs and into his mouth and the pain eased away, closely followed by wakefulness.

Jage awoke. His shoulder felt good. It felt more than good. It felt *strong*. He looked down, and from the mid-point of his chest across his shoulder and down to his elbow, there were panels of black chitin, glossy like spider armour, and woven deep into his flesh, indeed, deep into his very muscle and bone.

The queen entered, and settled down before him. Then a fore-leg reached out and touched Jage's face, and he closed his eyes and he could... *he could flow with her thoughts and feel her desperation for she was a Soulkeeper of Species and they were at war and hunted and reviled and the battle had raged for thousands of years with the Trallisk, who came with fire and poison to burn them and sting them, and battles had been fought, huge underground wars in tunnel and cave systems ranging for thousands of leagues to destroy the Sacred, and the Soulkeepers had finally been defeated in a huge bloody scourge, and since that day they moved from cave system to cave system, always running, always hiding, taking the Sacred with them, but one day they would conquer for it was their way, they were a warrior species descended from a warrior species and Jage, Jage was a human exception, a conundrum for he had shown them kindness and a form of understanding and she knew he was different and unique and they needed something unique to beat the Trallisk in war and this, this meant acceptance, for he was young and in him they could find an ally and they would strengthen him and had built him a spine from cuticle containing proteins and chitin built up in layers and fed with long protein strands into his own flesh and own spine and nerves and his body had accepted it as his own. And now. Now, after the incident with the wolf, the Soulkeepers had repaired his shoulder in a similar fashion, building him a new shoulder blade, for the wolf's fangs had torn muscle and powdered bone and they were part of him now, all a part of him, and he was part of them, and they were happy to accept Jage into their family for they knew there was no evil in his body, mind or soul and he could help them, help them protect the Sacred for its purpose was important to the world, and he, Jage, was important to the world... and one day, he would understand why they gave him the Sacred to protect.*

Jage's eyes opened, with a start. He ran his tongue around the inside of his mouth, coughed, and sat up. He flexed his new shoulder experimentally, and pressed at it with his free hand. It felt as strong as steel.

On a flat rock by his feet sat a platter of rock, with some fruit, and vegetables, and a long, slick, grey slab of meat. Jage reached out, picked up the meat, which slithered against his fingers as if trying to escape. He knew what he had to do. He had to get strong. He had to grow, and feed, and become powerful; only then could he repay the kindness of the Hexels and help them with their age-old war against the Trallisk; help them protect the Sacred. Help them *deliver* it.

Jage ate the meat, rubbing absently at his chest which itched, just over his heart, and at that moment knew he needed a new name. Something to reflect his merging with the spiders; his acceptance not just into their society, but into their very *genetics*.

From this point, he decided, he would be known as Jageraw.

General Graal rode the black stallion to the top of the hill and turned, gaze sweeping the snowy wilderness and desolate, crumbling city of Old Skulkra. "I know you," he said, eyes narrowing. "I remember you. I remember you well, Old One.'

Graal was half vachine, half albino. Accepted by the vachine society and culture because of his age, his prowess in battle, his tactical expertise as a general, and because – although their history no longer recorded it – he was one of the blood of the first vachine to walk the world, under the watchful gaze of the Vampire Warlords, Kuradek, Meshwar and Bhu Vanesh. Graal was ancient. More than a thousand years old. Ancient slave to the Vampire Warlords. And Graal was *pissed*.

He attempted to calm himself, tried to slow the thunder of clockwork in his breast. But he could not. His teeth ground together, and he tasted his own blood-oil.

A Harvester approached, eyes fixed on Graal, drifting through the fresh fall of snow like a ghost.

"You should calm yourself, Brother," said the Harvester.

"I am fucking *sick* of this charade. I want the vachine dead. I want them slaughtered! I know my destiny, by right of conquest, of kindred, of birth! I know my place, Harvester!"

"It will come," soothed the Harvester. "It will all come. You have shown great patience to this point; why do you grow so agitated? What has disturbed your mind, general?"

Graal was silent for long minutes, pale lips compressed, white face shaded by shadows, gloom, and a cascade of falling snow. His stallion stamped, snorting steam, and he turned the beast to stare across Old Skulkra. The ancient towers and palaces were rimed with snow; its cracked tenements, crumbling plazas, disintegrating bridges, all were sprinkled with a sugary ash and if Graal narrowed his eyes enough, he could imagine the city as it was a *thousand* years ago, when it was the centre of the Vampire Warlords' Empire, when it had been a Seat of Power... and of death, misery, and human desecration.

Graal leapt lightly from his mount, and stroked his pale features, lost in thought. The skin of an albino, and yet the eyes of the vachine? How little they *knew*; how little they *understood* his lineage.

"What troubles you?" persisted the Harvester, drifting close, towering over the man. A hand reached out, five long bone needles, and rested gently on Graal's shoulder.

Graal spat. "The cankers had a simple task: to hunt down an old man and his wounded companion. More than *fifty* cankers I sent, and yet they came back empty in tooth and claw. How could they not possibly find one simple old man and his tart?"

"You fear this man?"

Graal glanced at the Harvester then, and turned away. "No. Fear is not the correct word. I *respect* him, and respect the damage he may cause if left to run riot. This man is Kell, and once he troubled the vachine in the Black Pike Mountains. He and his soldiers called themselves Vachine *Hunters* – and yes, I do appreciate the irony, as sweet as any virgin's quim. They caused vachine and albino warriors alike serious trouble during a four year period. Not only did they slaughter our peoples, they disrupted the blood-oil trade and nearly killed in its entirety the smuggling of Karakan Red which, as we both know, many half-vachine rely on as part of Kradek-ka's... shall we say, experimentations."

"You were sent to deal with this thorn?"

"Yes. To pluck it free. Many times Engineer Priests, and even Archbishops, were sent with elite squads amongst the Black Pikes to hunt down and end this... problem. They returned either empty handed, or not at all. It was said these Vachine Hunters were ghosts, demons, unsavoury spirits sent by God to remove our kind from the face of the planet. Not so. They were men, highly skilled men with a talent for death and *bloodbond*," he spat the word, teeth bared like an animal, "weapons baptised in some ancient dark magick of which we had no knowledge, nor understanding. They were sent by King Searlan, a *magicker* King, after he studied an ancient text and grew afraid."

"And the text?"

"The *Book of Angels*," said Graal, darkly.

"A dangerous tome indeed. I hope it was recovered?"

"No. That was part of my reason for persuading the Engineer Council to allow me to take their Army of Iron south; otherwise, I fear they may not have trusted me with so much singular authority." He smiled. "There was, of course, also inherent panic at their impending shortage of refined blood-oil."

"Of course," said the Harvester, with a sardonic smile. "A well crafted situation. However, this... Kell? You never found him during your time In the Black Pike Mountains?"

"My soldiers tracked him, and with his few men Kell fought a retreat into the bowels of Bein Techlienain; there, the battle raged for hours in the narrow tunnels and across high bridges, until my soldiers were sure the last of Kell's men – and the man himself – were cast screaming and begging into the Fires of Karrakesh."

"And yet, it would seem he survived."

"Yes, he survived," said Graal, voice bitter. "I swear this is the same man, although I never saw his face myself under the Black Pikes." His voice dropped an octave. "I think some of my trusted soldiers were not quite honest with me about those long, dark weeks under the Stone."

"Maybe this new and unfortunate series of events is merely... coincidence? Or possibly a foolhardy, arrogant warrior seeking to step like a ganger into another's skin?" The Harvester seemed to be smiling, although this was unlikely through the narrow slit of its mouth. Harvesters were renowned for having a flatline when it came to humour.

"There is no such thing as coincidence," snapped Graal. He gave a bleak smile. "As I will demonstrate."

He called to a young albino warrior, and sent him to find Nesh, the leader of the cankers sent to find Kell and Saark in Old Skulkra – and to bring them *back*. Nesh was as near controllable as one could achieve, with such an inherently uncontrollable and chaotic blend of twisted species.

Nesh arrived, huge, rumbling, mouth stretched wide open, tiny eyes filled with swirling gold as it watched Graal. The canker hunkered down, stinking of oil and hot metal. Inside, its clockwork clicked and stepped, and pistons thudded occasionally. Nesh was an example of a canker in its prime, although to be in its prime state, a canker must have regressed from both the human and clockwork that created it – to such an extent that the beautiful became ugly, the logical became parody. To be in prime canker state was to be days from death.

"Yes?" grunted the beast, its speech clipped and short. Words caused this creature, fully eight feet in height, great pain to utter. But it was a gift the canker treasured, for not all could speak through corrupted clockwork and fangs.

Graal walked down one flank, observing the open wounds, the twisted, blackened clockwork, the bent gears and pistons. He smiled, a tight smile. To Graal, more than any other albino or vachine in existence, these creatures were abomination. But like a good craftsman, he used his tools well – with Watchmaker precision. No matter the extent of his personal abhorrence.

"You followed Kell's scent? And the stench of the wounded popinjay?"

"Yes."

"And yet… you claim you lost them. In the maze of streets and alleyways?"

"Yes, General Graal. There much dark magick in Old Skulkra. Much we not understand. Much left over from… the Other Time."

"You are lying," said Graal.

There followed an uneasy silence, in which the huge, panting canker glared down at General Graal. Its mouth opened wider with tiny brass *clicks*, almost like the winding of a ratchet, and the small hate-filled eyes narrowed, fixed on Graal, fixed on his throat.

"I obey my Masters," said the canker carefully, "for only then do I get the blood-oil I require." The panting increased. Graal noted, almost subliminally, that the canker's claws were sliding free, silent, well-oiled, like razors in grease.

"My brother became a canker," said Graal, brightly, moving away from the huge beast. "For years I tried to stop it happening, tried to halt the inexorable progress of an all-conquering corruption. But I could not do it. I could not stop *Nature*. For days, nights, weeks, we sat there discussing the possibilities, of regression, of introducing fresh clockwork, of forceful medical excision. And yet I knew, I always fucking *knew*," Graal turned, fixing his glittering blue gaze on the huge beast, "when he was lying." Graal smiled, a narrow compression of lips.

"I cannot tell you," snarled the canker. "You would never believe!"

"You will tell me," said Graal, voice soft, "or I will slaughter you where you stand."

"They will *curse* me!" howled the canker, voice suddenly filled with pain, and fear, and shock.

"Who?"

"The Denizens of Ankarok," snarled Nesh, and launched itself with dazzling speed at Graal, claws free, fangs bright and gleaming with gold and brass, savage snarls erupting in a frenzy of sudden violence as claws slashed for Graal's head and the General, apparently frozen to the spot for long moments, moved with a swift, calculated precision, stepping forward and ducking wild claw swings until he was inches from the snarling frenzy of bestial deviant vachine, and his slender sword plunged into the canker, plunged deep and Graal stepped away from slashing, thrashing claws, almost like a dancer twirling away with a stutter of complex steps. Graal dropped to one knee, and waited. Nesh, in a frenzy of pain and hate, suddenly decelerated and its eyes met Graal's as realisation dawned.

"You have killed me," it coughed, and blood poured from its mouth. It slumped to the ground, more blood-oil flowing from its throat, and its body slapped the damp hillside. It grunted, and there came the sounds of seizing clockwork. Finally, the internal mechanical whirrings died... and with a twitch, the canker died with them.

Graal stood, and pulling free a white cloth, cleaned his narrow black blade. The single cut had disabled the canker more efficiently than a full platoon of armed albino soldiers. His technique was precise, and deadly. He turned, and his eyes were narrowed, his face ash.

The Harvester was watching him closely, almost with *interest*. "So, the Denizens of Ankarok aided Kell? I find that... improbable," he said, voice little more than a whisper.

"I also," snapped Graal, sheathing his sword. "Especially considering the Vampire Warlords slaughtered them to extinction nearly a thousand years ago!"

TWO
A Taste of Desolation

It took Kell and Saark hours to work their way through the narrow tunnels set within the tower block's walls. Despite Kell being broad and bulky, and Saark of a more graceful and athletic persuasion, it was Saark who really suffered – from a psychological perspective. At one point, in a tight space, surrounded by gloom and ancient stone dust that made them cough, Kell paused, Skanda in the distance ahead and below him, climbing over a series of ancient lead pipes as Kell watched; he turned, and stared hard at Saark. Saark said nothing, but a sheen of sweat coated his face, and his eyes were haunted.

"The wound troubling you, lad?" Kell was referring to the stab wound Saark suffered at the hands of Myriam – Myriam, cancer-riddled outcast, thief and vagabond, who had poisoned Kell and kidnapped his granddaughter Nienna with the aim of blackmailing him into travelling north and showing her a route through the Black Pike Mountains. So far, her scheme was working well. And so far, her brass-needle injected poison was failing to worry Kell, for he had more immediate problems; but he knew this situation would soon change. When the poison started to *bite*.

"Aye," said Saark, pausing and wiping sweat from his face with the back of his hand. He left grey streaks across his handsome, indeed, beautiful, features – or they would have been, if he hadn't recently suffered a beating. Still, even with a swollen face he had classical good looks, and once his long, curled, dark hair was washed, and groomed and oiled, and he slipped into some fine silk vests and velvet trews, he would be a new man. Saark touched his side tenderly; Kell's makeshift stitches and tight bandage fashioned from a shirt from a dead albino warrior was as good a battlefield dressing as Saark was going to get. "It's eating me like acid.'

"You should be glad she didn't stab you in the belly," grunted Kell, and looked off, behind Saark, to steep passages *inside the wall* through which they travelled. "Then you'd *really* be suffering, squealing like a spear-stuck pig long into the night."

Saark gave a sour grin. "Thanks for that advice. Helpful."

"Don't mention it."

"That was sarcasm."

"I know."

Saark stared at Kell. "Has anybody ever told you, you're an incorrigible old fart? In fact, worse than a fart, for a fart's stench soon wavers and dissipates; you do not dissipate. Kell, you are the cancerous wart on a whore's diseased quim lips."

Kell shrugged. "Ha, I get abused all the time – only not with your royal-court eloquence. But then," he grinned, showing teeth stained with age, "I reckon we walk in different social circles, lad."

"Yes," agreed Saark. "Mine is one of rich honey wine, clean and succulent women, fine soft silks, the choicest cuts of meat, and gems so sparkling they make your eyes burn."

Kell considered this. He looked around at the dust, the grime, the slime, and the stink of ancient, rotten piping. "I don't see any of that here," he said, voice level. He reached forward, and patted Saark on the shoulder. "Don't worry. We'll be out soon."

"I'm not worried," said Saark, through gritted teeth.

Kell closed his mouth on his next comment; Saark was a proud man, beaten down often in the last few days. What he didn't need was Kell pointing out his obvious claustrophobia. As Kell knew, all men had a secret fear. His? He chuckled to himself. His was the very axe which protected and yet cursed him. Ilanna. His bloodbond.

They moved on, and realised they had lost Skanda in the gloom. They reached a collage of twisted piping, ancient, slime-covered, and after climbing the obstacle, their shoulders barely able to squeeze through the narrow horizontal aperture, they came to a ladder of iron. Kell paused, boots scuffing the edge of what appeared a vast drop. The aperture, between two walls, was barely wide enough for them to descend; add into the equation a wobbling, unsecured ladder, and the descent promised to be particularly treacherous.

"Shall I go first?" said Kell, staring into Saark's open fear.

"Yes. I wouldn't like your pig-lard arse dropping on my head from above. That sort of thing can genuinely ruin a man's day."

"Let's hope I don't get stuck, then." Kell eased himself over the dusty stone, the descent lit by cracks and occasional gaps in the walls; outside, he could see it was growing dark. Kell wondered if the cankers were still waiting. Damn them, he thought. Damn then to Drennach!

The ladder felt sturdy enough under his gnarled hands, and strong fingers grasped narrow rungs as he began to descend. Above, Saark followed, his breathing shallow and fast, his boots kicking dirt over Kell.

"Sorry!" he said.

"Just don't bloody jump," muttered Kell.

They climbed downwards, the ladder shaking and making occasional cracking sounds. After a while, Kell felt a pattering of something dark and wet on his head, and scowling, he looked up to where Saark was fumbling in the mote-filled gloom.

"I hope that's not piss, lad."

"It's blood! The wound has opened. So much for your damn battlefield stitching."

"You're welcome to do it yourself."

"I think next time I will. I can do without a scar that looks like some medical experiment gone wrong. What would the ladies say? I have a perfect torso, fit only for kings, and you would massacre me with your inept needlework."

"Hold a pad to the wound," said Kell, more kindly. "And let's hope you've not infected me with the plague of the popinjay! That's all I need, irrational lust after every young woman that dances by."

They climbed, down and down, for many stories; before they reached the base, Skanda called them from a narrow ledge, which led off between the ancient, crumbling joists of another building. Like rats, they scuttled between the linings of deserted buildings; like cockroaches, they inhabited the spaces between spaces where once life thrived.

For another hour, as darkness fell fast outside, they scrambled through apertures, crawled through dusty tunnels, squeezed through thick pipes containing an ancient residue of oily film, coating their hands with slick gunk, until finally, and thankfully, they emerged from a wide lead pipe which dropped into a swamp. Skanda squatted on the edge of the pipe, watching Kell and Saark drop into the waist-deep slurry, cracking the ice. Then, with the agility of a monkey, Skanda leapt onto Saark's back and clung to the athletic warrior who frowned, and complained, but recognised that to drop Skanda would be to drown the boy. Hardly a fair exchange for saving their lives.

They waded through icy slurry, which stunk of old oil and dead-animal decomposition, despite the cold. They crawled up a muddy bank in darkness and lay on the snow, panting, before Kell hauled himself to his feet and drew his fearsome axe, Ilanna, peering around into the gloom, head tilted, listening.

"Any bad guys, old horse?"

"Don't mock. If a canker bites your arse, it'll be me you come to running to."

"A fair point."

Saark struggled to his feet and stood, hand pressed against his ribs, his slender rapier drawn. He looked down at his fine boots, his once rich trews and silk shirt. He cursed, cursed the destruction of such fine and dandy clothing. "You know something, Kell? Since I met you, I haven't been able to maintain any fine couture whatsoever. It's like you are cursed to dress like the poorest of peasants, and those who accompany you are similarly afflicted by your fashion!"

Kell sighed. "Stop yapping, and let's get away from the city. Believe me, sartorial elegance shouldn't be at the forefront of your mind; getting eaten, now that's what should be bothering you."

They moved away from the crumbling walls of Old Skulkra, away east in a scattering of Blue Spruce woodlands. Finding an old, fallen wall, probably once part of a farm enclosure, Saark built a fire using the remaining stones as shelter, whilst Kell disappeared into the woodland.

"Just like a hero to *fuck off* when there's work to be done," muttered Saark, sourly, as he struggled with damp tinder. Behind him, Skanda scavenged amongst tree roots, puffing and panting, fingers scrabbling at the snow. The noise intruded on Saark's thoughts – fine thoughts, of dancing with leggy blondes at fine regal functions, of eating caviar from wide silver platters, of suckling honeyed wine from a puckering quim, lips gleaming, focus more intent than during any act of war – and eventually, Saark whirled about, eyes narrowed, hand clutching his side, and snapped, "What are you doing down there, lad? You are disrupting my heavenly fantasy!"

Skanda held up three onions and a potato. He smiled. "We need to eat, yes? I am an expert at finding food in frozen woodland." The boy's dark eyes glittered. "That is, unless you wish to starve?"

"And what are you going to cook it in?" sneered Saark. "Your bloody knickers?"

Skanda lifted a small ceramic pot. "This," he said, simply.

"Where did you get that?"

"There's a ruined farmhouse, thirty paces yonder."

Saark scowled further. "Then by Dake's Balls, what am I doing starting a fire here? There's no shelter! A farmhouse will give us more shelter! By all the gods, am I surrounded by idiots?"

He explored the ruins, and they *were* ruins: ancient, moss-strewn, the original stones rounded and smoothed by centuries of rain and snow. There was no roof, only stubby walls, but at least a fireplace which shielded Saark's fire from the wind. By the time Kell returned he had a merry blaze going, and he and Skanda had pulled an old log before the flames. Saark sat, boots off, warming his sodden toes. Skanda was peeling vegetables and chopping winter herbs on a slab of stone.

Wary, Kell stepped through a sagging doorway and frowned. "What is this place?"

"It's a brothel," snapped Saark. "What does it look like? Sit ye down, Skanda's making a broth. He found some wholesome vegetables in the woods, although what I'd give for some venison rump and thick meat gravy I couldn't say." He licked his lips, eyes dreamy.

"These should help," said Kell, depositing a hare and two rabbits on the slab of stone.

Saark stared. "How, in the name of the Chaos Halls, did you manage to catch *those* with a bloody axe?"

Kell winked. "It's all in the wrist, boy." He looked to Skanda. "Do you know how to gut and skin?"

"Does a bear shit in the woods?" snapped the young lad, and Kell smiled, moving to Saark.

"He's a cheeky bugger," said Saark.

"He has spirit," said Kell. "I like that. And we owe him our lives."

"But?"

Kell looked at him. "What do you mean?"

"I've known you too long, old horse. There's always a but."

Kell's face hardened. "He's a compromise," said the old warrior, stretching out his legs and resting Ilanna by his side, butterfly blades to the ground, haft within easy reach should he need it; and need *her* killing expertise.

"Meaning?"

"Meaning I have to *prioritise*."

Saark stared at the old man. For a long moment he analysed the grey beard and the dark hair shot through with grey. Kell's face was lined and weather-beaten, appearing older, more worn, than his sixty-two years.

Saark pulled on his boots. He stood. He stared down at Kell. "Explain prioritise?"

"I must rescue Nienna."

"What's that got to do with this boy?" said Saark.

Kell's eyes hardened. He stood, looming over Saark with a sudden, threatening presence. "I will find Nienna. I will kill Myriam – and whoever stands with her. That is it. That is what my life has become. I care nothing for anybody, or anything, else. If you can't stand that," Kell's face curled into a snarl, "well, I understand *your* misunderstanding, dandy. I suggest you go back to whoring and drinking, just like you know best; that is, if you can find a place that'll let you rut and drink. After all, it looks to me like the albinos have slaughtered most of the good people of Falanor."

"Hey!" Saark thumped Kell in the chest, making the big man take a step back. "Just hang on a minute there, Kell. I stood for Nienna, and I stood for you; don't be twisting this situation around, don't be trying to say I'm no good for anything. If it wasn't for me, Nienna would be dead. Horseshit Kell, *you'd* be dead. I have my vices, yes," his face twisted a little, as if he was pained to recall them, "but I know where *my* priorities lie. And if we abandon this boy, he will die."

"Not so."

"You a prophet now, *Legend*?"

Kell's eyes narrowed. "You have been sent to torture me, Saark, I swear. I should have killed you back in Jajor Falls."

"Why didn't you?" It was such an innocent question, it caught Kell off guard. Saark persisted, clutching his side where blood wept through the makeshift packing of torn shirt. "You're the Big

Man here, you're the warrior, the hero, the bloody legend of song and dance; you're the man with no conscience, the man of the fucking moment and to the Bone Halls with everybody else! Why am I still here, hey? Why am I still walking by your side? Or have you got a sneaky back-handed death lined up for me, also?"

Kell grabbed Saark's shirt, lifting him from the ground and drawing him in close, until their faces were only inches apart.

"Don't push me."

"Or what'll you do, big man? Stab me in my sleep?"

"Damn you Saark! You twist my mind! You twist my words! Everything with you is fencing, a tactical, verbal puzzle to be negotiated. And I am sick of it!"

"Listen." Saark smoothed down his shirt. "I am with you, Kell. I am not your enemy. I will come with you; we will rescue Nienna, of that I am sure. But don't let panic, don't let blind urgency cloud your vision. This boy here; he is innocent. In fact more; without him, we'd be dead."

"Maybe."

"What?" scoffed Saark. "You think you could take on fifty cankers? You dream, old horse. But what I would say to you is this; I am going for a walk, in the snow, to check our perimeter. I want you to talk to the boy. Find a peace with him – here," he tapped his own skull, "in your head. Because you have a problem, Kell, a serious problem they did not choose to address in your *Saga*."

Saark moved away from the fire, and with drawn rapier, stepped through the leaning doorway and out into the cold, bleak woods. Kell sat down for a while, the only sounds the crackling of the fire and the slithering of Skanda's knife. Eventually, as his temper settled, and recognising some worth in Saark's words, he stood and turned and crossed to Skanda, who was just slicing the final strips of meat and adding them to the broth.

"It will be a fine stew," said the boy.

"It smells good already." Kell's hand was tight on the haft of Ilanna. The axe blades gleamed cold. He was standing before the boy, just to one side, and Skanda was busy, intent on his task. An easy target. An easy death.

No, he thought.

Then: why not?

After all, he had been poisoned, infected by the vile escaped prisoner, Myriam, with the aim of blackmailing him to help her save her own worthless skin. Kell's mission was simple, uncomplicated – ride north, fast, and locate Nienna. His granddaughter had also been poisoned with the same toxin; without Kell's haste, she would die, probably sooner than he for she was young and weak. Despite Kell's age, he was as strong as an ox, he knew. But the problem here lay with Skanda. Kell knew, deep down, that Saark wouldn't leave the boy with so many albino soldiers and cankers scouring the woods looking for them. But the boy would slow Kell down. In doing so, Nienna might die... so, to his mind, it was an easy problem to fix.

Kell scratched his beard. He realised Ilanna was still tight in his fist. Her blades gleamed, catching the light of the fire.

Another problem, was that if he left the boy behind, then how long before Graal tortured information from his spindly limbs? Saark had blabbed enough of the story to Skanda to make the boy a threat. Which meant only one course of action.

Kell took a step closer. Still, Skanda did not look up. His hands moved swiftly, preparing more of the fresh rabbit meat. The smell made Kell's nose twitch, but his mind was working fast, one step ahead of something so simple as animal hunger.

"You seek to rescue your granddaughter?" said Skanda, looking up suddenly. Kell nodded, and Skanda lowered his face again. The knife sliced and chopped.

"Yes. She will die without me. She has been poisoned."

"Saark said she was being held at the Cailleach Pass. That's the road to the Black Pike Mountains, isn't it?"

Kell smiled grimly. Damn you, Saark, he thought.

"Yes," he said, voice barely above a whisper. The fire crackled. Firelight gleamed in Kell's dark eyes. He no longer appeared like a hero from legend; now, in this ruined cottage in the midst of the night, clutching his possessed axe and eerily silent for such a big man, Kell was infinitely more intimidating.

"I used to have a grandfather. A lot like you," said Skanda, innocently, oblivious to the threat which lay within inches, within heartbeats, of his delicate and fragile existence. "He died though, a long time ago. I thought he was as strong as ten men, but age wore him down in the end until his mind snapped, and he could no longer speak. He used to sit by the fire, rocking, dribbling, and this was the man who took on a hundred of the enemy at Tellakon Gate. A tragedy."

"A tragedy," agreed Kell, voice low, and shifted his stance a little to the left, to give him better clearance for the strike. Kell licked his lips. He would kill the boy. Decapitate him. It would be clean. It would be quick. And much more humane than leaving the child to be slaughtered by the cankers... eaten alive, in fact.

Kell gripped his axe tight. His eyes went hard. He lifted Ilanna into the air. Firelight gleamed from her butterfly blades. Kell relaxed, and readied himself for the strike...

Saark moved around the perimeter of their camp like a spirit, halting occasionally to listen. The fall of snow acted as a natural muffler, but was dangerous for it hid fragile twigs and obstacles that might give away Saark's position. Still, he edged around a wide perimeter, eyes and ears alert, slender rapier in one chilled hand, and thinking hard on the problem of Falanor.

General Graal had invaded. There had been no demands. Just slaughter.

Why? What did he want?

Saark mulled over the problem as he scouted, crouching occasionally. At one point he saw an owl, high in a tree, its huge yellow orbs surveying a world which appeared, Saark was sure, as bright as daylight to the savage, nocturnal hunting bird.

Saark's mind drifted to Kell. He turned, to where he knew the ruined cottage lay. He considered Kell's motives, and thought of Nienna, but when he thought of her it made him think of Kat, and that was too painful a memory.

Only days earlier, in their pursuit to warn King Leanoric of the impending invasion of albino soldiers led by General Graal, Kell and his companions – Saark, Nienna and Nienna's best friend, Katrina, with her short, wild red hair and topaz eyes, athletic and feisty despite her youth – were riding out a snowstorm in a deserted barracks when three dangerous brigands entered. Myriam, tall, wiry, strong, short black hair and rough, gaunt features, her eyes a little sunken, her flesh a little stretched from the cancer that was eating her from the inside out. Along with her, two companions: Styx, an inexorably ugly Blacklipper smuggler with only one eye and black lips, and Jex, small and permanently angry, with a tattooed face and the physique of a pugilist.

Myriam had injected Kell and Nienna with poison, and Styx

had murdered Katrina using a clockwork-powered *Widowmaker* mini-crossbow. They kidnapped Nienna during the Army of Iron's attack on King Leanoric's forces.

Kat. Murdered. Dead.

Even now, Saark brushed away a tear, and felt guilt and shame well within him. He had loved Katrina, which was ridiculous, even Saark had to admit. He was not just a dandy and popinjay, he was, even at his own admittance, one of the world's best seducers of women. He knew how they worked, how their minds operated, which dials to turn, which switches to flick, how to speak and lick and kiss and caress, and his beauty had brought him scores of lovers, many a cuckold, and so to fall in love with a seventeen year-old university student was simply *bizarre*. Ridiculous in the extreme. He told himself over and over that was not what happened; that it had been a simple tactic on his part to persuade Katrina to give away that most sought after prize, her virginity… but even Saark did not believe his own lie.

And Saark had had the chance to kill her murderer.

And failed.

Bitterly now, Saark smiled. The wounds were still fresh. The hate was still bright. He would have his day with Styx, Saark knew; one way or another, in this world or in the next. He would cut the fucker in two, and drink his blood, and toast Kat's shade towards the Hall of Heroes.

Saark stopped. Orientated himself. He had been drifting. Dreaming. He winced, clutching the pad at his side. It was still warm, and blood still leaked. Maybe he was weak from blood loss? And the recent beatings?

Saark scowled. And thought of Kell. And a sudden dark premonition swept through him.

No. Saark shook his head. Not even Kell would kill a child. Not in cold blood. Surely?

Saark's eyes narrowed.

Could he?

Flitting embers from snatches of story pierced Saark's mind. Snippets of late drinking songs, when the candles were trimmed low and coals glowed dark in the tavern's hearth. The bard would lower his voice, fingers flickering gently over lyre strings as he recounted the Days of Blood, and the atrocities that occurred therein…

All speculation, of course. Nobody knew what *really* happened all those years ago; no soldier had ever spoken of it. Those that still lived, of course, for most survivors had taken their own lives.

Kell, however... he had *been* there. He had told Saark, although Saark was sure Kell didn't recall uttering the words. However, Saark still remembered the look in Kell's eyes.

"I was a bad man, Saark. An evil man. I blamed the whiskey, for so long I blamed the whiskey, but one day I came to realise that it simply masked that which I was. I try, Saark. I try so hard to be a good man. I try so hard to do the right thing. But it doesn't always work. Deep down inside, at a basic level, I'm simply not a good person." And then, later, as Saark was sure Kell was falling into a pit of insanity... *"Look at the state of me, Saark. Just like the old days. The Days of Blood."*

The Days of Blood. The day when an entire *army* went berserk. Insane, it was said. They killed men, women, children, torched houses, slaughtered cattle, torched people in their beds and... much worse. Or so it was said. So the dark songs recounted. And Saark knew Kell didn't have the necessary streak of evil to murder a child he thought might hold him back; and in so doing, be responsible for the death of his granddaughter, the only creature he loved on earth.

"Horseshit," he muttered.

Saark limped back towards the ruined cottage, cursing his stupidity and chewing at his lip.

Saark burst through the listing doorway, eyes drawn immediately to the crackling fire which danced bright after the gloom of the snowy woodland. There was no sign of Kell. Nor Skanda.

"Son of a bastard's mule!" snapped Saark, and heard a grunt. He peered into the gloomy interior, and the darkness rearranged itself into shapes. Skanda was sat, almost hidden, stirring his ceramic pot of broth.

"Are you well?" said Skanda, almost sleepily.

"Yes, yes!" Saark strode forward, and sat on the log. He kicked off his boots and stretched out his feet, warming his toes. "Where's Kell? Don't tell me. The grumpy old weasel has gone for a shit in the woods."

Skanda giggled, and appeared for once his age. "I think you might be right."

Saark peered close. "Seriously. Are you all right, boy? For a

minute, back there, I had the craziest notion that Kell might...
well, that he might..."

Skanda looked suddenly wise beyond eternity. "Let us say,"
whispered the boy, staring into the fire, "that Kell made the
right choice."

There came a crack, and Kell grinned at Saark from the doorway. "Thought you'd got lost out there, lad. Hugging the trees,
were you? Digging in the dirt for more dirt? Or just having bad
dreams about noble and heroic old Kell, the man of the Legend."
Kell grinned, and although the destroyed cottage had little light,
ambient or otherwise, Saark could have sworn Kell displayed *no*
humour.

"We're safe, for now," said Saark. "No sounds of cankers, no
soldiers, no pursuit."

Kell moved close. "Well don't get too comfy, lad. We eat, then
we move."

"We'll freeze!"

"Freeze or die here," said Kell. "Because I'm telling you, it's only
a matter of time before that bastard Graal sends someone..." his
smile widened, "or some *thing*, after us."

"And the boy?"

Kell could read the pain in Saark's eyes. He sighed, and ran a
hand through his thick, grey-streaked hair. "The boy can come
with us. But I'm warning you, if he gets in the way, or either of
you slow me down, then I'll cut you *both* loose."

"You think you can travel faster than I?" stammered Saark.
"Man, I'm damn near *thirty* years your junior!"

Kell leered close. "I know I can, lad. Now get some warm food
inside you. We've got a long, hard journey ahead."

They moved through the woodland and as dawn broke, wintry
tendrils streaking through heavy cloud cover, so the distant walls
of Old Skulkra could still be seen.

Saark called a halt, and gestured to Kell. Kell moved close, axe
in fist, eyes brooding. "What is it?"

Saark pointed. Distantly, the Blood Refineries squatted on the
plain like obscene bone dice tossed by the gods. "I have it in my
mind to do some research," said Saark, voice soft, eyes bright. "And
maybe some damage! Those machines are here for no good."

"I know what they are," said Kell.

"You do? How is that… possible?"

Kell smiled grimly. "I have seen them in action. In another time. Another place. Let's just say, Saark, that to go chasing them now to satisfy your curiosity would end badly for all of us."

"We need to know what we're fighting!"

"So, lad, now we have gone to war?" Kell smiled, but there was no mockery in his tone. If anything, he valued Saark's spirit; especially after they had been through so much.

"They brought war and chaos to Falanor. I would like to return the favour with the blade of my sword."

"A task for another day."

"You would save Nienna over Falanor?"

"I would save her over the world," rumbled Kell. Seeing the look of incredulity in Saark's face, Kell shrugged and said, "Let me quantify it thus – Graal and his soldiers are searching for us, all of us. And those Blood Refineries are their *life-blood*. They will be guarded more heavily than any sparkling gems, than any royal blood. To go there, Saark, is folly. And what would you do? Gather information? For whom? Which army will use your military intelligence? No, Saark, we must travel north. When I have Nienna, when I hold her safe in my arms, then we will turn our gaze on Graal and these white-skinned bastards."

Saark considered this. "That could, taken the wrong way, look simply like you're putting your own needs first."

"Maybe I am, lad, maybe I am. But without me, you'll never conquer these bastards. I am your lynch pin. And I have been poisoned, and even as we stand debating what to do, the toxic venom pulses through my veins. Or had you forgotten this? Without me, you will fail."

"Your arrogance astounds me."

"It is the truth."

Saark sighed, and turned his back on the giant, distant machines. "You say you have seen these Refineries working. I assume they do not bode well for the people of Falanor?"

"The battle was horrific, yes? Leanoric's slaughter devastating?"

"Yes."

"The battle was just a prologue for what is to come. Trust me, Saark, when I say we need to use cunning, use our brains; charging back into that enemy camp is the last thing we should do."

"You will not?"

"I will not. But I admire your bravado, lad. Come. We will head north. This is a battle for another day."

Saark hung his head, and they moved back into heavy woodland, tracking along in parallel with the Great North Road.

They walked all day, and Kell muttered about pains in his knees. The landscape was beautiful, with hidden hollows filled with virgin snow, woodland branches, stark and bare, pointing white-peppered fingers at the bleak, blue-grey sky. Heavy swathes of conifer forest clutched the contours of the land like a lover. Streams lay frozen like snakes of diamond. The air was crisp, cold and fresh.

Kell marched ahead often, eyes scanning the landscape for signs of enemy activity. At every hilltop he would drop and approach on his belly, so as not to silhouette himself to scouts. His keen eyes tracked the lay of the land, the contours of forest and river, of hillside and mossy nooks, of boulder fields and silent farmhouses.

At one point before midday Kell spent a full half hour watching a farmhouse; no smoke curled from the chimney, and there was no sign of life. They approached warily, driven by hunger and cold, to find the farm hastily abandoned. As they walked across a cobbled yard chickens clucked in a nearby coop. Kell gestured.

"Kill them, and bag them up. Fresh meat will do us the world of good."

Saark stared at Kell's back. "What?"

Kell stopped, and turned. "Kill the chickens. I will find us furs, woollen cloaks, dried beef. Go on, lad."

"You kill the chickens," snapped Saark.

"Is there a problem here?"

"Only peasants kill chickens! I am used to *my* fresh meat served on silver platters, garnished with butter, herbs and new potatoes, a little salt, not too much pepper, and brought to me by a plump serving wench with breasts bigger than the bloody bird she's serving!

Kell stared hard at Saark; the swelling in his beaten face had subsided, but he was still bruised, his lips cut, his skin scratched, and he looked a thousand leagues from the well-dressed dandy Kell had met in the tannery back in Jalder. "Well," said Kell, considering his position, "here, and now Saark, you're a peasant. You look like a peasant, and you stink like a peasant. So kill the damn chickens."

"I will not kill the chickens. I am no serf!"

341

'You will kill the chickens or go hungry," snapped Kell, and stormed off into the farmhouse, kicking open the door and leading the way with the gleaming blades of his axe.

Saark stood for a moment, staring at the empty doorway and muttering curses. A hand touched him lightly on the arm, and Skanda grinned up at him. "It's all right, Pretty One, I'll kill them. Despite my appearance, I have a talent for it."

"Are you sure?" muttered Saark, eyes dark, lips pouting.

"Leave it to me." Skanda carried a rough bronze dagger, which he placed carefully between his teeth. He moved towards the coop and the clucking hens within.

"I'll just… find some firewood. Or something." Saark waved to Skanda, then turned and started rooting around. "What we really need are horses," he said, and crossed to the stables, knowing there would be no beasts there – in times of flight, who would leave a horse? – but willing to search all the same. As he approached, the stables were dark, and silent. Rubbing his chin, he threw open the doors to reveal a total lack of thoroughbred stallion. "Hmm," he muttered, cursing his luck. Would it have hurt, for just this once, to give them a bit of good fortune? For a change? Instead of the gods throwing soldiers and deranged creatures into the battle at every damn pissing turn?

Saark turned, leant his back against the stable door, and heard a strangled *cluck*. He winced. He had been truthful, in that his food *was* normally served on a silver platter by a wench whose breasts would suffocate three men, never mind one; but the reality of the matter, and something that shamed him, was that his life of high society had ill-prepared him for chicken slaughter. He had no idea how one slaughtered a chicken; nor any inclination to find out.

Another deranged *cluck* emerged from the coop, and Saark winced again, almost in sympathy. A sympathy overwhelmed only by his ravenous hunger. Then, suddenly, behind him something went *clack* in the gloom of the dingy stable interior. He whirled about, slim rapier drawn, eyes narrowed.

"Is there somebody there?" he snapped. "Show yourself! Don't make me come in there after you!"

Nothing. No reply. No movement. No sound.

Saark glanced back to the farmhouse, but there was no sign of Kell, and anyway, Saark resented being made to look a fool over something as ridiculous as the murder of a chicken. He pushed into the stable and lowered his head, as if this movement might somehow aid his night vision. He walked along the stalls, nose wrinkled at the stench of old dung and damp straw. The place recked as bad as a rancid corpse. "Come out, now, before I lose my temper!" he said, voice raised, and as he neared the end stall he slowed his pace. Whoever it was, they had to be in there.

Saark leapt the last few feet, rapier outstretched, and blinked. There, huddled in the stall, was a donkey.

Saark and the donkey stared at one another for a while, and Saark finally relaxed. The donkey gave a husky bray, and tilted its head, observing the tall, lithe swordsman.

"Damn it, they left you! You poor little thing." Saark opened the door, and finding a lead on the wall, spent several minutes attaching a halter and then leading the donkey out through the stables. Kell was just appearing from the farmhouse with a collection of items wrapped in a blanket as Saark emerged into wintry sunlight.

They both stopped, staring at one another.

"You found a donkey. Well done," said Kell.

"The miserable whoresons left her! What a horrible thing to do; they could have at least set her free. Well, she can come with us, carry our provisions. I'm sure I saw a basket somewhere."

"Well," said Kell, thoughtfully, dumping the blanket on the snow-peppered ground. "I've certainly no objections to taking a donkey with us. It's a long journey, and many a donkey has surely proved its worth during my lifetime."

"Good," said Saark, rubbing the donkey's muzzle. "I think this beast has had enough mistreatment for one year."

"Yes. And I reckon there's good eating on a donkey," said Kell.

There came a long pause. "So, you'd eat the donkey?" Saark said.

"Saark, if I was starving lad, I'd eat your very arse cheeks. Now get this stuff in the basket. Did you kill those chickens?"

Skanda emerged at that moment with five birds tied together by the throat. He handed them to Kell, who took the dead chickens and glanced sideways at Saark.

"What?" snapped the swordsman.

"For shame, Saark. Getting the boy to do a man's job. *Your* job, in fact. You!"

"He offered," said Saark, miserably, and returned to the stables to find the basket.

• • • •

They moved fast for the rest of the day, only stopping early evening to have a cold meal of dried beef and hard oatcakes. Saark led the donkey, which he'd named *Mary* – to a rising of Kell's eyebrows, and an unreadable expression. Saark shrugged off the implied criticism, and walked slightly ahead of the group. But on one thing they all agreed. Mary did indeed lighten their load, and the farmhouse had been a store of many provisions, from bread, cheese, a side of ham, dried beef, oats, sugar and salt, and even a little chocolate. Kell found a bottle of unlabelled whiskey, which he stowed deep in the basket. He thought it best not to let Saark know, for the last time Kell drank an excess of whiskey it had ended in a savage brawl, with Saark taking a beating under Kell's mighty fists. But, obviously, Kell had no intentions of drinking any whiskey now. He was off the whiskey. It was for medicinal purposes only, he convinced himself.

The sky stretched out, streaked with grey and black. What blue remained was thin, like a bleak watercolour portrait, and just as night began to fall they breached a hill and Kell pointed to a long, low, abandoned building made of black bricks. It had several squat chimneys, and by its overgrown look, gates hanging off hinges, missing bricks and smashed windows, had been empty for a considerable amount of time.

"You knew this was here?" said Saark.

"Aye," nodded Kell. "Camped here a few times. It's an old armoury; rumoured, or so I've heard it told, to have made the finest weapons, helmets and breastplates in Falanor!"

"Safe?"

"As safe as anywhere else during the invasion of a wicked enemy army. I'll scout ahead, you wait here with, ahh, Mary."

Saark watched Kell descend a steep bank of tangled branches smothered in snow. The huge warrior stopped at the bottom, scanning, searching for footprints. Then, wary and with Ilanna drawn, he disappeared from view. He returned a few minutes later and waved them down, and both Saark and Skanda were more than happy to leave the biting chill of the wind behind. Despite new woollen jackets and leather-lined cloaks from the farmhouse, the cold still crept easily through to the depths of their bones. Falanor in winter was not the best place to travel, nor camp.

They slid down the snowy hill, the donkey's hooves digging in deep, and Saark tied Mary up outside the deserted armoury and ducked through the doorway, closely followed by Skanda.

Kell stood, hands on hips, looking around. They were in a huge, long, low-ceilinged workshop; benches lined the walls, set out in L-shapes at regular intervals, perhaps fifty in all stretching off into the gloom. Also ranged around the black, fire-damaged walls were curious iron ovens, and other machines with handles and tubes and strange gears, all black iron, many now rusted into solid blocks.

"Been empty a while," said Saark, whispering, but not realising why he whispered.

"Aye," nodded Kell. "Come on, it's too cold in this room, but there's lots of side rooms. I think this place has been used by travellers for nearly two decades now. Hopefully, somebody has laid a fire."

Saark and Skanda followed Kell through the huge chamber, and their eyes wandered to abandoned benches where ancient tools rested on work surfaces. "It's like they left in a hurry," said Saark, eyes following contours of rusted tools. There were hammers and tongs, files and pincers, and other tools in curious shapes Saark had never before seen; but then, he was a swordsman, not an armourer.

Kell approached one room to the side; the door closed, and he suddenly stopped. He turned and stared at Saark, features hidden in the gloom; then he seemed to win some internal debate, and stepped forward, pushing open the door–

The black longsword slashed for his throat and Kell swayed back with incredible speed, axe slamming up, the spike at its tip carving a long groove of channelled flesh up the albino soldier's face. His chin and nose disappeared like molten wax in a spray of milk white blood, and he screamed, and Kell brought back his gleaming axe, eyes narrowed, and yelled, "It's a trap! They saw us coming! Be ready!" He stepped forward with a mighty swing, halving the soldier's head, and then turning his back on the small room.

"They?" said Saark, drawing his slender rapier, and gaped with open flapping mouth as a flood of albino warriors raced through the gloomy old armoury; there were no war cries, no shouts, no screams of battle; only an eerie silence and thudding of boots.

A soldier fell on Saark and he parried the blow with a clash of steel, batting the ineffectual sword strike aside and drawing his blade across the man's throat. Flesh opened, parted, without blood – like slicing the throat of a corpse, thought Saark sourly – but all other images were slammed from him at the sheer number of soldiers in the armoury. Kell had been right, it was a set-up, a trap; they'd been waiting. Saark parried another blow, slammed his blade back in a shower of sparks, and exchanged several strikes before piercing his blade through the soldier's eye. Beside him, Kell's axe swung, but was hampered by the close confines fighting. He glimpsed the great blades behead an albino in a flail of long hair and gristle, and Saark *shifted* as the great Ilanna hummed past his own face.

'Kell!' screamed Saark, his face thunder, and he skipped to the side to give the old man more killing space. He spun low under a warrior's blade, and shoved his own sword up, brutally, into the soldier's groin. The albino screamed and fell, slipping on his own unspooling entrails, and Saark spun to shout at Skanda to run – but the boy had vanished. Good, breathed Saark as he prepared himself. The armoury was full of the enemy, so many he couldn't count them; what had it been? A platoon? Twenty men? Or… Saark paled, even in the gloom. If a company waited, there'd be damn near a hundred soldiers. And even Kell could not battle such odds.

There were seven down, now, and outside the sun dipped below the horizon. Darkness flooded the room. Swords gleamed. Boots stamped. The only light was a surreal glow, the sun's dying rays reflected off smashed glass; more soldiers ran at Kell and Saark, and the men defended themselves with skill, sword and axe rising and falling, deflecting blades and cutting into flesh with savage, sodden *thumps*. More albino warriors fell, and Kell slapped Saark's shoulder and pointed. They backed away across the chamber, only to hear boots thudding outside a short corridor. They were surrounded! Saark tasted fear. At the end of the day Saark was a swordsman, and an incredibly skilled one – once, he had been the King's Sword Champion, and although Saark had fought in battles before, he much preferred the consummate test of skill during one-on-one combat. In war, he hated the randomness, the chaos, the unpredictability; the threat of an axe in the back of the head when you least expected it. No, for Saark the honour and prestige was in single combat – where the victor took the spoils, wine, gold, women. But here, now… this was fast turning into a charnel house. It was out of control.

The soldiers hung back, wary. Saark could just make out their ghost-white faces in the gloom. He reckoned on about thirty, but that didn't include those coming round behind.

Thirty! If Kell and Saark had been caught on open ground, they would have been slaughtered. Surrounded and butchered like dogs. But the albino soldiers, perhaps knowing the inherent skill of their quarries, had sought subterfuge and covert attack; this had backfired, for close quarters combat meant Saark and Kell could fight a tight battle and not easily be surrounded.

"They're coming in," snapped Kell through gritted teeth. His face and beard were covered once more in blood and gore, only this time white, and glistening in what little ambient light remained. Ilanna filled his terrible hands, the edges of the butterfly blades glimmering. "You cover this side, I'll–" but his words were left unfinished, as a *blast* of blackness, of energy, a series of pulses in concentric circles like the spreading ripples in a lake after heavy impact cannoned through the confines of the armoury, and Kell and Saark were picked up amidst a surging charge of debris, old hammers, bits of battered armour, tools and dirt and even an anvil, and they seemed to hang for a moment before being accelerated in a swirling chaos across the room to hit the wall. Saark felt like his head was turned inside out, his teeth rattled in his skull, strings of bowels ripped out through his arse-hole. Kell groaned, and staggered to his feet with blood pouring from his nose. He lifted Ilanna, teeth grinding as the wall of albinos advanced… and at their core there was a tiny, ragged albino woman, with straggly white hair and bright crimson eyes and a face that was ancient, and lined, and haggard, and Kell knew upon what he looked for this *this* was an albino *shamathe*, a dreaded white magicker, and Kell shook his head and knew he had to kill her fast and put her down *in an instant* for her magick was awesome, potent, a product of earth and fire and blood and raw wild dark energy–

Ilanna slammed up, blades gleaming, but the second energy impact picked Kell up and pulped him against the wall, where the entire brickwork buckled and collapsed outwards in a shower of rubble and dust and broken beams. The armoury croaked and sagged, walls groaning, and Kell was half-buried under a pile of bricks as the air around him and an unconscious Saark rippled and surged and then was seemingly *sucked* back into normality like a rubber band returning to its original shape.

The albino shamathe cackled, and capered forward like a jester, but a tall soldier stepped to the fore, placed a hand on her cavorting shoulder and calmed the witch. "Well done, Lilliath," he spoke, words gentle, and drew a long black blade. "But... I will finish this." Lilliath nodded, hair wild and wavering.

Jekkron, tall, elegant, a warrior born, loomed over Kell who was groaning, eyelids fluttering. The old soldier had lost his axe amidst bricks and snapped timber joists. He opened his dust-smarting eyes and snarled through bloodied teeth but the albino smiled, and gave a single nod of understanding; his black sword lifted high, then hacked down at Kell's throat.

THREE
Clockwork Engine

"So, he has betrayed us?"

Silence echoed around the Vachine High Engineer Council. The two Watchmakers present squirmed uneasily, for this entire concept was anathema to everything in which they believed, and aspired.

"That's impossible."

"Why impossible? A canker, by definition, should be impossible. We are the Higher Race, the Blessed; we are at the pinnacle of flesh and technological evolution. What then is a canker? A mockery of our genetics, a mockery of our humanity, a mockery of our vachine status. The vachine should be perfect; the cankers remind us we are not. How, then, can it be construed that Graal's betrayal is an impossibility?"

Another voice. Old. Revered. Serious. "He has served us for a thousand years. You... *young* vachine do not understand what General Graal has done for us. Without him, and without the work of Kradek-ka, we would never have achieved such an exalted state; we would never have reached our current evolutionary curve, plane, and High Altar. Graal accelerated our species. Without him our race would be dead."

Silence met this statement. Great minds contemplated the implications of their discussion.

A voice spoke. It was young, nervous, a chattering of sparrows next to the wisdom of the owl. "The clockwork is all wrong," said the voice.

"Meaning?"

"The algorithms... they tell of the Axeman."

"What is this *Axeman*?"

"The Black Axeman of Drennach."

Again, another pause. Around the table, some of the elder vachine lit pipes and puffed on smoke laced with the heady narcotic, blood-oil. A silence descended. Several elder vachine exchanged glances.

"The clockwork engines are never specific, but they speak of a terrible killer, an axeman named Kell – but is he friend or foe? The machines will not say. They just bring up his name again, and again, and again."

"We must assume he is the enemy. Every other human to set foot in Silva Valley has had nothing but evil and destruction in their corrupt and festering hearts."

"Is that not to be expected?"

"Meaning?"

"We *feed* on them; they are like cattle to us."

"Still, we must assume this *Black Axeman* is evil, a scourge to our kind. But then, we are straying from the real problem here; that of General Graal, and what he is doing with our Army of Iron."

Silence greeted this.

"Has the report come back, yet? From Princess Jaranis?"

"There has been no communication; nothing."

This was considered. Digested. And then one of the Watchmakers stood; in the structure of the vachine religion, only the Patriarch ruled over the Watchmakers, and the Watchmakers were few enough now to make their rank a dying breed – only five of them left. General Graal was Watchmaker; this was the element of their new information which made the High Council so nervous. Nobody wished to sound like a Heretic; nobody wished their clockwork poisoned, their flesh to be torn and twisted forcibly into *canker*.

She was called Sa, small of stature, but with flashing, dangerous eyes. To cross Sa was to be exterminated. "We have little evidence," she said, voice smooth, eyes fixing on every member of the Engineer Council in turn. She walked around the outside of the huge oval steel table, and stopped at the head where once, in good health, the Patriarch would have sat; today, as on many days, he was confined to his bed. It was rumoured he coughed up blood-oil, and his days were numbered. "We cannot simply condemn

General Graal in his absence; he should be able to defend himself against the *diabolical accusations* that have taken place over this table. What is happening here?" Her eyes glowed. "We used to be *united*. Now, we are crumbling. We will adjourn, and no more will be spoken on this matter until Graal returns in the spring after Snowmelt. Is this agreed?"

There came a murmur of agreement, and the Engineer Council disbanded, the hundred or so members flooding out into the warren of the Engineer's Palace, and beyond, to Silva Valley. Finally, only Sa and Tagor-tel, another esteemed vachine Watchmaker, were left. Their eyes met, like old lovers on a secret tryst.

"I don't think it will be enough," said Tagor-tel. "I do not trust the old General. And... isn't that why Jaranis was despatched? To keep an eye on proceedings?"

"The weather is against her."

"Convenient. For Graal."

Sa puckered her lips, brooding. "I, also, have noticed *changes* in Graal. However, I do not see how one man could be a threat to the High Engineer Episcopate. To the Vachine Civilisation! Even *with* our obedient Army of Iron under his direct control. What would he do? Turn them against us?" She laughed, a sound of spinning flywheels.

Tagor-tel shrugged. "I doubt he would have the *persuasion*. The alshina have served for too long." He thought for a moment. "We need to discover what happened to Jaranis. She had the Warrior Engineers, did she not? Walgrishnacht? He is one of our ultimate soldiers. If anybody will return word, he will."

"We will see. But let us assume, for a moment – away from concepts of heresy – that Princess Jaranis has failed. That she and her entourage are *dead*. What then?"

"We can ask..." Tagor-tel paused, and checked the chamber, making sure they were alone. His voice dropped. "Fiddion."

"You think he will cooperate?"

"He has, shall we say, *passed* us sensitive information before. Graal seems to have some bond with the Harvesters; and the Harvesters play by their own rules. It is worth a try. For whatever reason, Fiddion despises his own kind."

"Do it. Contact Fiddion. Let us see if the Harvesters know what Graal plots."

• • • •

Sunlight glimmered between towering storm clouds, rays of weak yellow that cast long, eerie shadows over the forests surrounding Old Skulkra. Graal strode through the camp, trailed by three Harvesters, one hand on his sword hilt, his pale-skinned face unreadable. Albino soldiers moved from his path, and he stopped only once, head turning left, as the snarls from the canker cages set his teeth on edge. Damn them, he thought. Damn their perverse twisted flesh! They reminded him, painfully, of his brother. Dead, now. Murdered, so he later discovered, by the bastard Kell and his bloodbond axe. "I'll see you burn, motherfucker," he muttered as he continued through the camp and reached the edge of the tents where albino soldiers still had campfires burning.

Several soldiers looked up at his approach, glances subservient, as if waiting for instruction. Graal did not acknowledge their existence. Instead, his eyes were fixed on the three huge black towers which sat on the plain: angular, cubic, squat, their surfaces matt black, their intentions not immediately fathomable.

"Are we ready?" said Graal.

"We are ready," hissed one of the Harvesters, sibilantly.

"Is he here?"

"He is here, General Graal."

"Good. It is about time."

Graal strode out across the plain, and the closer he moved to the Blood Refineries, the larger they seemed: mammoth cubic structures, the black surface of unmarked walls flat, and dull, like scorched iron. Wisps of snow snapped in the air as Graal strode across frozen earth, and as he came near his nose wrinkled. He blinked. The corpses, four thousand in total, stripped of armour and boots, had been laid out in rows before the three Blood Refineries. Graal glanced down, but no flicker of emotion showed across his pale face. He had more important matters on which to worry.

The Refineries towered, and he walked in their shadow. There was a man, tall and lean and bearded, reclining against the first Refinery. Graal reached him and stopped. This was Viga, Kradekka's personal Engineer Assistant, come to oversee the Blood Refineries and their absorption. He had travelled all the way from the Black Pike Mountains to help.

"Well met, Graal," said the man, eyes glittering, and Graal could just distinguish tiny vachine fangs, like polished brass, peeking over his bottom lip.

"I thought you would never come," said Graal, fighting hard to keep his annoyance in check. He was not used to being treated so… casually. "Was the journey difficult?"

"More difficult than you could comprehend," said Viga, rubbing at his beard. "Although I hear you suffered some disturbance yourself; something to do with an old, bearded soldier? A resident of Jalder, or so I was informed."

Graal forced a smile. "A nothing," he said. The Harvesters were watching him, waiting for his command; as if waving away an insect, he gave instruction, and the Harvesters started to lift the half-frozen corpses and feed them into long, thin slots at the base of the Refineries. It took very little effort: the instant a body touched the slot, it was sucked inside. A deep thrumming seemed to well up beneath the ground, and Graal fancied he could sense, if not necessarily *hear*, the huge but subtle clockwork engines within the Blood Refineries; mashing up bodies, extracting blood, and refining it into blood-oil: the food of the vachine world.

The bearded man turned, and watched for a while. Then he tutted. Graal stared into his eyes, and the man lowered his head.

"There is a problem?"

"Kradek-ka's daughter."

"She was always a problem."

"Do not be *flippant* with me, Graal; you know her existence is the reason you stand here now, you know the experimentation Kradek-ka performed on her was the central reason why we can *do this*; without her, without Anukis and her," he laughed, "her *jewel*, there would be no quest for Kuradek, Meshwar and Bhu Vanesh."

"You are of course, correct," said Graal, and straightened his back. Beside them, the Harvesters continued to pick up corpses and feed them into the Refineries. Deep inside, now, the meshing of gears could be heard; and huge pendulous blades working.

Graal glanced up, at the towering wall of the Refinery, and then back to Viga. He reached out to place a comforting hand on his arm, but the man recoiled.

"No. You must not touch me. I am impure!"

"We are all impure," said Graal, head tilting a little; he could see, now, that the man before him was a man ready to crack, a vachine teetering along a blade-edge of insanity.

"We should never have treated her like that. It was wrong of us to push her; to humiliate her!"

"It is too late for regret," said Graal, voice steady.

"Not so! She has escaped, gone looking for her father! Nobody should have undergone such humiliation!"

"Well, she will save us the quest," said Graal, voice hard now. This man's weakness was starting to upset him. He had great respect for Viga, especially as Kradek-ka's most trusted Engineer servant; but to whine thus? To whine was to be weak; and Graal so *hated* the weak. He placed his hand on sword-hilt.

"This whole situation is an abomination," continued Viga.

Graal drew his sword, and shook his head, and stepped close to the man and the blade touched his throat, cold black steel pressing flesh and his fangs ejected, suddenly, with a hiss of fury but Graal leant on the blade and blood bubbled along the razor edge and he felt Viga relax beside him. "It is too late to back out now," said Graal, voice little more than a whisper.

"I know that. It's just… she was an innocent vachine! We ruined her life!"

"She is in the past…" said Graal. "So be silent, and be still, and be calm; the Refineries must work, and we must build the store of energy… of magick! Only with the Refineries at optimum power can we bring about the return of the Vampire Warlords!"

"But you do not have the Soul Gems," whimpered Viga, from behind Graal's blade.

"I am working on it," growled Graal, and sheathed his weapon.

Viga had gone. Graal sat on the ground, cross-legged, and watched as the last of the bodies was fed into the huge machines. He looked around, as flakes of falling snow whipped back and forth in the wind. The distance was hazy, just like Graal's memory.

In silence, the last of the Falanor corpses were fed into metal holes. Then the Harvesters did a strange thing. They moved, each to their own Blood Refinery, and they spread arms and legs wide and shuffled forward towards blank metal walls – so they were stark contrasts illuminated against wide plates of iron. And then they – *merged*, sinking into the metal of the Refineries, becoming for a moment at one with the machines as flesh became metal and iron became flesh, and Graal blinked, licking his lips, nervous for just an instant – not nervous of pain or mutilation or death, even his own death, but nervous in case it *did not work*. Graal blinked, and the Harvesters were gone; absorbed into the machines. Distantly, he could hear a tick, tick, tick, as of huge, pendulous clockwork.

He smiled grimly. They called it Interface. Where the Harvesters used special ancient magick to refine blood, into that chemical agent the vachine craved, and indeed *needed*, to survive.

Blood-oil. The currency of their Age.

Graal sat, grimly, thinking about Kradek-ka. The vachine was a genius, no doubt; he had helped usher in the civilisation and society they now enjoyed. However, he was unpredictable, and a little insane. And his daughter was another problem entirely. Graal's face locked. She was yet just another problem he would have to face.

General Graal sighed, and sat staring at the exhaust pipes on one of the Refineries; slowly, the pipes oozed trickles of pulped flesh to the snowy ground. Graal brooded, waiting for his Harvesters to return.

If only all life was as simple as war, he thought.

When the Vampire Warlords return, there will be more war. He smiled at that, and dreamed of his childhood... over distant millennia.

They called him Graverobber, and he lived amidst the towering circle of stones at Le'annath Moorkelth... The Passing Place. The name, and nature, of the stones had long since been lost to the humans who inhabited the land, with their curious ways and basic weaponry. But the Graverobber knew; he had researched, and learned, and been privy to a knowledge older than man or vachine.

He sat, squatting at the centre of the stone circle, watching the snow falling around the outskirts. He loved the winter, the cold, the snow, the ice, the death.

He looked down at himself, analysing his body in wonder. This is what he always did. This is what made him what he was. Narcissistic was not something in the Graverobber's lexicon, but had it been there he would have agreed; for the Graverobber loved himself, or rather, he loved what he had *become*. What had been made of him, by the Hexel Spiders, over a long, long, long period of time... a journey so long, so arduous, so painful, he no longer remembered the beginning. Now, only now, he knew that he was nearing the end.

Jageraw looked down at himself, at his twisted, corrugated body, his skin a shiny, ceramic black like the chitin of the spider, *the spider I tell you – can you smell the hemolymph? It flows in my veins and in my blood* and he stared down; his limbs thin, painfully thin, so thin you would think they would snap but Jageraw knew they were piledrivers, ten times stronger than human bone and flesh and raw tasty muscle; a hundred times more powerful yes yes. His head, he knew, for he had seen it reflected in puddles of blood, was perfectly round and bald and he had slitted eyes and a face quite feline, like the cats he used to eat, *I like those cats, tasty, all mewling and scrabbling with pathetic claws* against his ceramic armour until he snapped their little necks and ate them whole, fur, whiskers and all.

Warlords!

He almost screamed, for he had made himself jump.

He had dreamed about them. About the Warlords, the Wild Warlords, the Vampire Warlords, the precursor to the vachine that lived in the mountains; their kindred, from baby to ape and beyond, and he laughed, a crackle of feline spider and something else dropped in there like oil in water; the cry of a child.

And now! The sheer concept made Jageraw shiver. For the Warlords were an enemy to be feared, he could sense it, he could feel it, and Jageraw had played out the dream, the events to come, the promise, the *prophecy* yes I did in my mind a thousand times; and despite his strength, despite his awesome killing powers, despite his supernatural abilities of skipping and murder; well, he was afraid.

"The King is dead, the King is dead, the King is dead," he crooned to himself, voice a lullaby, voice music to his own ears, on a different level of aural capability, if not to the pleasure of anybody else. He knew it would happen, for he had seen it would happen, and the mighty had fallen, the great had toppled, and King Leanoric the Battle King was dead and his army erased and fed into the machine, the nasty black machine to make the drug for vachine.

The Graverobber rocked, chitin covered in a fine layer of snow. He heard a laboured breathing, panting, something under the hunt; interesting, he thought, because usually – in these odd scenarios – he got to feed on both hunter *and* hunted. A double feast. Lots of food for Jageraw. Lots of food including (he winked at himself and I like it, I do like it) those slick warm organs. How he did like a bit of kidney to wash down the old claret; how he did lust after a morsel of shredded lung. Tasty as a pumpkin.

The breathing was louder now, but it was hard for the Graverobber to see through thick tumbling snow; it swirled this way, it swirled that way, it swirled every damn way, but it certainly got *in the way*. Jageraw hunkered down, muscles bunching, and decided to kill the *hunted* first. Then turn on the attackers and rip off their heads, no matter how many there were. Three or thirty, it made little difference to the Graverobber; when he was in the mood for killing and feeding, then he would take his time and savour and hunt, until all of them were dead. They left a stink trail worse than any cesspit odour; it was never hard to follow.

The *thing* burst through the circle of stones and stopped, stunned, when it saw the Graverobber. Jageraw half leapt, but checked himself and twisted in mid air, landing lightly, on all fours, like a cat. Jageraw stared suspiciously at what could only be described as a *thing* in his very own circle of stones. Surely, Le'annath Moorkelth had never been witness to such a creature? But then, Jageraw had never seen a canker, and certainly nothing as twisted with clockwork and golden wire as *this* specimen.

"Help me!" growled the bulky, deviant, clockwork creature. It struggled to form the words, for its mouth was wrenched back, jaws five times wider than any normal mortal man's. Thick golden wires were wound around and *in* its flesh. Every single breathing moment looked like an agony of pain and suffering.

The Graverobber's head tilted, and he moved lithely forward, pacing, like a cat. He stopped by the edge of the stones; there was a myth that he could not, or would not, pass beyond. But it was simply a myth; Jageraw could do what the hell he liked, especially when searching for food and a sliver of kidney which tasted so fine and slick on its way down his throat, yum yum.

The soldiers were toiling up the hill under snow; but there were many. Quickly, Jageraw counted. At least a hundred. He turned, eyes narrowing at the deformed creature in his circle *his damnfire circle of stones! his home!* and he had two choices; kill the creature, or hide it. If the soldiers saw him, and they looked well armed and trained and not liable to put up the weak comedy fight of the average villager with screams and skirts and pitchfork; if they saw Jageraw, they might decide he was on the military cleansing agenda.

The Graverobber turned, slowly, and eyed the canker. Damn. That would take some killing, he realised.

So, instead, he leapt, cannoning into the shocked warped creature and in a *flash* of connection and integration and blood-oil *magick* they stepped sideways through time; skipped, simply, a few seconds *forward*. Making Jageraw and the hunted canker, effectively invisible.

The world had been, or at least *seemed*, young and wild and violent, to General Graal. Wild Warlords ruled the land with gauntlets of spiked steel and fangs of brass, and nobody, *nobody* questioned their authority. Theirs was an authority of fang and claw, steel and fire; of impalement and decapitation, where the only rule was that there were no rules: and humans were truly the despicable cattle of legend.

Graal dreamed. And in his dream, he *lived*...

Graal rode the six legged stallion through tall crimson grass towards the marshes, where blue flamingos squawked and flapped heavily into the night sky, bright by the light of the moon, recognising his inherent threat upon approach. Flamingos had far better, more primal, instincts than men. He cursed, wishing he had his power lance; he would have speared a bird for supper. He grinned at that, blue eyes narrowing, fangs ejecting, and turned his mount and rode for the nearest village. This was a new area, new settlements, and they did not know him; at the gates he leapt from his mount, head high, eighteen years of life stark on his cruel, narrow face. When they saw him, his eyes, his fangs, his talons, the five men on the gate shouted and started to heave closed the heavy timber portal but Graal strode forward, slamming a hand through the thick timbers with crunches of destruction. The men screamed, shouting for help, two grabbing long spears of black ebony and steel. Graal stepped in, batted aside a spear, pulled the man towards him and snapped his neck like tinder. He lifted the man, mouth cracking open, and plunged his fangs into the flesh, rooting for the jugular. Blood fountained, coated his pale skin, soaking his white hair, and he laughed as he drank for the blood was nectar and the high took him in gossamer wings and flew him through velvet heavens—

Pain slammed him, and he stared down at the spear protruding from his chest. Near the heart. Too damn near the heart! Graal dropped the ragdoll corpse, cursing himself, his youth, his naivety, his greed, his addiction to blood and the high which brought recklessness to feeding. He had forgotten the second man with the spear. Such a simple omission; to assume he had fled in fear and panic.

Graal grabbed the spear, embedded in his own flesh and bubbling with black blood through his fine white silk shirt; he swung it, knocking the panic-stricken guard from his feet, then snapped the haft and strode forward, towering over the man. "You want to impale me, little creature? Like this?" Graal plunged the broken spear down, into the man's eye, and he screamed and gurgled and kicked for a while, blood a fountain, gore bubbling. Graal stood, and pulled free the broken splinter of wood, a stake he realised, from his breast. An inch. An inch away!

Graal brayed at the moon, a howl long and mournful, and when he lowered his head it was to see the line of villagers approaching. There were thirty of them, dressed like peasants, stinking of woodsmoke and shit and piss, their faces bubbled with toxic disease, their hair lank, eyes lifeless, and could they not see his sheen, could they not read the supremacy in his very fucking skin tone?

They carried weapons, and coolly Graal slicked back his hair, full of fresh blood and its heady scent, and surveyed the array of swords, daggers, sharpened stakes, and even a few pitchforks (oh, the fools!). One woman carried a bundle in outstretched, shaking hands and Graal nearly vomited with laughter. Garlic. For the love of the Bone Halls, garlic? How pure and most beautifully ridiculous! Did she not realise? Did they not realise? Graal adored garlic. Most vampires did. It helped take away the breath of the dead...

Graal pushed back his shoulders, stepped away from the two corpses, and grinned. This seemed to shock the villagers; maybe they were expecting him to flee. Instead Graal moved fast, fast into them, a fist through a chest there plucking free a beating heart, ducking a sword strike by a clumsy village idiot with no teeth, his index finger driving into a woman's eye and beyond, into the brain, taking a longsword from another man and cutting his legs free in a single stroke and then Graal was into his stride, and into the slaughter, and the sword sang and slew, cutting heads from shoulders, hands from arms, arms from torsos, and Graal took particular delight in slicing a pregnant woman in two from the crown of her head, straight through fat chest and pumping spasming heart and belly and child, right down to her groin. A twin murder with a single sweep. Beautiful! Economical! Damn, in fact it was sheer Art.

Within a few heartbeats of human duration, Graal had killed all the villagers. He heard a cough, from beyond the gates, and kneeling, Graal

pulled free a heart with a wrenching tear of clinging tendons and strands
of muscle, then strode to the gates, where he surveyed the five stocky vam-
pires, all mounted, all staring down at him.

"Yes?" said Graal, head high, arrogance shining in his eyes despite his
youth. He bit the heart like an apple, and savoured the texture, savoured
the warm slick muscle in his mouth and throat, and then squeezed the
warm organ like a fruit, draining the remaining blood off into his mouth.
"You caught me during a moment of indulgence. May I be of service?"

"Mount up. There's work to be done."

"Slaughter?" Graal's eyes twinkled.

"Is there any other kind?"

Graal sat, watching the Refineries, the dripping pipes, listening to
the churn of clockwork machinery. All gone, he thought. Long
dead, and gone. Just like his mother, the queen, and his father,
the king. Killed. Murdered! *Slaughtered* like human cattle. Graal's
lips drew back, making his face incredibly ugly, a baring of the
vampire within him, trapped within his now weak flesh, the flesh
of the combination, the pathetic shell of the vachine.

We will be free again, he nodded.

We will be free.

He stood, and stretched his back, and rolled his neck, and gazed
around. Behind him, the war camp was running smoothly; the albino soldiers ran like – he laughed, a little – like clockwork. They
cooked and cleaned, oiled weapons and armour, sharpened blades,
tended to prisoners and the cankers; they needed very little organ-
isation from Graal, for they were like insects, workers in the hive,
busy with their own little jobs and all part of the Great Wheel.

Graal turned back to the Refineries and waited, patiently, until
in the blink of an eye the Harvesters oozed from metal walls,
pulling free as if from a thick liquid. They moved before Graal, a
triumvirate of consummate evil. Graal smiled. Evil was something
he could work with.

"It is complete?"

"As you wish. The blood-oil is refined. Do you not feel the rise
in energy? The surge of usable power?"

"No. It will come to me later, in the dark hours."

The Harvesters reared up, long fingers of bone stretching out,
and to an onlooker if would have appeared – for just an instant –
as if the Harvesters were about to attack Graal, slice his head from

his shoulders, peel the skin from his vachine bones. But they did not. They prostrated before him in a low bow, faces pressing the earth in an almost unprecedented show, and one they would certainly never have replicated before any other vachine. The Harvesters accepted Graal as Master. He smiled, controlling his urges of madness and almost panic-fuelled hysterics, for these creatures were so awesomely powerful that what Graal was actually witnessing was an acknowledgement of what he was about to achieve; what was to come, not what had passed.

The Vampire Warlords.

The Harvesters stood. One said, "What of the Soul Gems?"

"Kradek-ka is searching for the one remaining Gem; the other two are… safe, for now. But he knows where to look. We had… help."

"Will he hold strong?"

"Yes, despite his madness."

"And yet, there is still a thorn to be plucked?"

Graal nodded. "Kell. The Black Axeman of Drennach. I know this."

"What will you do?"

"I have sent the Soul Stealers," he said. "Kell is a dead man."

FOUR

Echoes of a Distant Age

A blur slammed past Kell, whose eyes were fastened on the dark blade descending for his unprotected throat, and Kell knew he would die there, half buried by rubble, head pounding from the force of *shamathe* magic and he had never felt anything like it, so *odd*, but the blur came from the edges of his vision and connected with Jekkron, the tall albino warrior, and with a blink Kell realised it was *Skanda* the skinny little boy, and Skanda's arms and legs were wide and wrapped around Jekkron who took a step back, his face frowning in annoyance at this interruption to murder. Jekkron raised a hand, as if to slap down the annoying boy who clung to him. And then he started to scream, and he started to scream high, and loud, like a woman peeled, like an animal skewered... Skanda hadn't just wrapped around Jekkron, he was *burrowing* into the man, his head snapping left and right and chewing and tearing flesh, and his hands and feet had claws and they tore into the albino soldier, who staggered now, dropping his sword, both fists beating down at Skanda who eased *inside* Jekkron by just a few inches, and with a terrible force of magick, ripped Jekkron's skin and muscle from his chest, belly and thighs. Skanda landed, carrying the skin and muscle like a thick white cloak, and Jekkron hit the ground unconscious, seconds from death. His blood flushed out as if from an overturned cauldron.

In the sudden confusion, only Lilliath saw what happened, the rest of the soldiers simply witnessed their leader going crazy and slapping at himself; Lilliath capered to one side, over a pile of rubble, to see a donkey staring at her. Lilliath stopped, crazy hair wavering, and Mary the donkey turned slowly around, and with a vicious bray, planted both hooves in the shamathe's face, sending her tumbling back over the pile of collapsed bricks.

As Jekkron, conscious again and gasping like a fish, struggled to rise with his lack of albino flesh, so Kell grunted and hauled himself to his feet. Skanda stood before him, staring at the gathered soldiers with a face less than human, his black teeth glinting with Jekkron's white blood, and hands lifted up and held like comedy claws. Except the joke was no longer funny.

Skanda fell on the dying soldier, and ripped out his throat with his teeth, and used claws to slice down Jekkron's ribs and pull free internal organs, which he held up for the soldiers to see. Then Skanda bounded forward, and in a sudden wave of fear the albino soldiers scattered, as Skanda screeched and screamed after them, and suddenly Kell and Saark were left alone.

Kell limped to Saark, who was just regaining consciousness. Blood leaked from his ears, making his long, dark curls glossy. Both men stood, and leaned on one another weakly, and Saark gazed down at the terribly savaged, torn-apart body of Jekkron. His eyes fastened on glinting pools of milk blood, nestling in hollows and peppered with drifting brick dust.

"Did you do that to him?" coughed Saark.

"It was the boy."

"Skanda? No! No way could a small child…"

"He is *not* a small child," said Kell, and with a grunt heaved himself upright and gazed across to the unconscious body of the shamathe. Her face was black and purple. "Your mule has a fine aim."

"Mary did that? Great! And by the way, she's a donkey, not a mule."

"Same difference," muttered Kell. "Come on, we need horses. We need to put leagues between us and them."

"What about Skanda?"

"I have a feeling," said Kell, voice hard, unforgiving, "that the boy can look after himself."

Kell lifted Ilanna, and gazed down at Lilliath. He hefted the axe high, and suddenly Saark was there, hands held up. "Whoa, Big Man, what are you doing?"

Kell scowled. "She tried to kill us, Saark. You surely don't want her following? Doing *that* to us *in our sleep*?"

"You can't kill her, Kell. She's an old woman. She's uncon- scious! For the love of the gods!"

"She's a white magicker, and she deserves to die."

Saark planted himself between Kell and the unconscious shamathe. "No. I won't let you! It is immoral. If you kill her, Kell, then you are as bad as the enemy; can't you see?"

Kell gave a great and weary sigh. "Very well," he said, eyes nar- rowed, face pale from dust. "But if she comes near us again, *you* can sort the bitch out. Let's find some horses."

They moved around the exterior of the deserted armoury, Saark leading Mary by her halter, and indeed found horses tethered. Dis- tant screams echoed through the forest. Whatever Skanda was doing to the albino soldiers, he was keeping them occupied – and their minds far away from their mounts.

There were six beasts tethered here, all seventeen-hand geld- ings, and Kell and Saark raided saddlebags for provisions and coin, then picked the most powerful looking horses. Saark tied Mary's lead to his mount's tail, and the men mounted the beasts under moonlight and cantered up a nearby slope, and away, into wood- land, into the drifting, falling snow.

They did not speak.

They were simply glad to be alive.

They rode for an hour. Several times Saark suggested pausing, and waiting for Skanda. Kell simply gave Saark a sour, evil look, and Saark closed his mouth, aware he would not get far with Kell when the old warrior was in such a stubborn temper.

Finally, they made a cold camp, wary of lighting a fire lest it attract more unwanted military attention. Saark, in particular, was in a bad way. Whilst Kell was seemingly strong as an ox, Saark had suffered several beatings, and a loss of blood from the knife wound at the hands of Myriam; whilst better than he had been, stronger and a little more clear-headed, the constant bat- tering was taking its toll on the man. He had deep, dark rings around his eyes, and his face was drawn and gaunt with exhaus- tion and pain.

"This is wrong," said Saark, as they stretched out an army tar- paulin between two trees to give them a little shelter. To their backs was a wall of rock from several huge, cubic boulders which must have tumbled from the nearby hills hundreds of years before, and this left only a single entrance from which the wind and snow could intrude.

"Which bit is wrong? Pull it, Saark, don't bloody tickle it."

"I'm pulling it, man, I'm pulling! I simply have a reduced mobility due to the wound in my side; or maybe you hadn't bloody noticed me getting stabbed?"

"I'll notice you getting stabbed in a minute, if you don't help erect this damn shelter," growled Kell. "My hands are turning blue with the cold! So go on, what's wrong, man?"

"Running away, leaving Skanda to face the soldiers, demons, and whatever else fills this magick-haunted forest."

Kell tightened a strap, and sat on a rock, rummaging in a saddlebag. Nearby, Mary brayed, and Kell scowled at the donkey. "Listen, Saark. You didn't see what I saw – the boy, he ripped that soldier's skin and muscle from his body like a rug from a floor. Peeled it off, complete! Then bit out the soldier's throat and cut out his organs. Don't start moaning to me about leaving a little boy in the woods; Skanda is no boy like I have ever seen."

"What is he then? A camel?"

Kell frowned at Saark, and motioned for the tall swordsman to sit. In a low voice, a tired voice, Kell said, "I told you what I saw. If you don't believe me, then to Dake's Balls with you! You get out there in the snow and look for the little bastard. Me, I'd rather put my axe through his skull. He gives me the creeps."

"You are incorrigible!"

"Me?" snapped Kell, fury rising. "I reckon we brought something bad out of Old Skulkra; invited it out into the world with us. I fear we may have done the world a disservice. You understand?"

"He saved us," sulked Saark, ducking into the makeshift shelter and resting his back against cold, damp rock. He shivered, despite his fur and leather cloak. "You are an ungrateful old goat, Kell. You know that?"

"Saved us?" Kell laughed, and his eyes were bleak. "Sometimes, my friend, I think it is better to be dead."

They shared out some dried beef and a few oatcakes, and ate in silence, listening to a distant, mournful wind, and the muffled silence brought about by heavy, snow-laden woodland. Occasionally, there was a *crump* as gathered snow fell from high branches. At one point, Kell winced, and took several deep breaths.

"You are injured?" Saark looked suddenly concerned.

"It is nothing."

"Don't be ridiculous! You are like a bull, you only complain when something hurts you *bad*. What is it?"

"Pain. Inside. Inside my very veins."

Saark nodded, his eyes serious. "You think it's the poison?"

"Yes," said Kell, through gritted teeth. "And I know it's going to get worse. My biggest fear is finding Myriam, and the antidote, and not having the strength to break her fucking neck!"

"Do you think Nienna is suffering?"

"If she is, there will be murder," said Kell, darkly, fury glittering in his eyes. "Now get some sleep, Saark. You look weaker than a suckling doe. You sure you don't want some more food?"

"After seeing the result of that albino's corpse ripped asunder? No, my constitution is delicate at the best of times. After that spectacle, I have lost appetite enough to last me a decade."

Kell grunted, and shrugged. "Food is food," he said, as if that explained everything.

Saark slept. More snow fell in the small hours. Kell sat on the rock, back stiff, all weariness evaporating with the pain brought by poison oozing through his veins and internal organs. It felt as if his body, knowing it was shortly to die, wanted him to experience every sensation, every second of life, every nuance of *pain* before forcing him to lie down and exhale his last clattering breath.

The dawn broke wearily, like a tired, pastel watercolour on canvas. Clouds bunched in the sky like fists, and the wind had increased, howling and moaning through woods and between nearby rocks which seemed to litter this part of the world. On the wind, they could smell fire. It was not a comforting stench. It was the aroma of *war*.

Kell, chin on his fist, eyes alert, Ilanna by his side, jumped a little when Saark touched his shoulder.

"Have you been awake all night, Old Horse?"

"Aye, lad. I couldn't sleep. Too much on my mind."

"We *will* find Nienna," said Saark.

"I don't doubt that. It's finding her alive that concerns me."

"Shall I cook us breakfast?"

"Make a small fire," said Kell, softly. "Hot tea is what I need if these aged bones are to survive much more rough life in the wilderness."

"Ha, it's a fine ale I crave!" laughed Saark, pulling out his tinderbox.

"I find whiskey a much more palatable experience," muttered Kell, darkly.

They drank a little hot tea with sugar, and ate more dried beef. Kell's pain had receded, much to the big man's relief, and Saark was also looking much better after a good sleep and some food and hot tea. They huddled around the small fire, then stamped it out and packed away their makeshift camp. They were just packing saddlebags when Kell hissed, dropping to a crouch and lifting Ilanna before him. Her blades glittered, and in that crouch Saark saw a flicker of insanity made flesh.

Skanda walked from the trees, smiling with his black teeth. He stopped, and tilted his head. On his hand rode the tiny scorpion with twin tails. It seemed agitated, moving quickly about the boy's hand and never halting. Its tails flickered, fast, like ebony lightning.

"I found you," he said. He tilted his head. Kell rose out of his crouch, cursed, and continued to pack the saddlebags, turning his back on the boy with deliberate ignorance.

"Are you hurt?" said Saark, rushing over.

"No," smiled Skanda, "but I led those soldiers on a merry chase. I was not surprised to find you gone when I returned to the old armoury." His eyes shone. "I think I upset Kell, did I not? The great Legend himself."

Kell turned, and smiled easily, although his eyes were hooded. "No lad, you didn't upset me. But I didn't worry about leaving you behind, before you get any noble ideas about friendship and loyalty."

"Have I offended you? If so, I apologise."

Kell placed his hands on his hips. "In fact, boy, you have. You have a rare talent, don't you? The ability to kill."

Skanda stared at Kell for a long time. Eventually, he said, "It is a talent bestowed on the Ankarok. I can kill, yes. I can kill with ease. My small size and odd looks do nothing to highlight the bubbling ancient rage within."

Kell stared into the boy's eyes.

A darkness fell on his soul, like ash from the funeral pyres of a thousand children.

It is not human, he told himself.

It is consummately evil.

I should kill it. I should kill it *now*...

His hands grasped the haft of Ilanna, his bloodbond axe, and he took a step forward but a shrill note pierced the inside of his skull, and he realised Ilanna was screaming at him, warning him, and the note fell and her words came, and her voice was cool, a drifting metallic sigh, the voice of bees in the hive, the song of ants in the nest...

Wait, she said. *You must not.*

Why not? he growled.

Because he is of Ankarok. The Ancient Race. They were here before the vachine, and before the vampires before them; they invented blood-oil, and mastered the magick, and they know too much.

Kell snorted. He felt like a pawn in another man's game. I am being manipulated, he thought. But is my sweet blood-drenched Ilanna telling the truth? Or is she lying through her blackened back teeth because she *wants* something of her own...

This was Ilanna, the bloodbond axe, and she was in control, or so she liked to think. Blessed in blood-oil, and instrumental, or so Kell believed, in the Days of Blood, she offered him a tenuous link with madness, a risk which Kell readily accepted because... well, because *without* Ilanna he would be a dead man. And if Kell was a dead man, then his granddaughter Nienna was a dead girl.

He should die.

Why? Because you say so?

Kell breathed in the perfume of the axe. The aroma of death. The corpse–breath of Ilanna. It was heady, like the finest narcotic, like a honey-plumped dram of whiskey; and Kell felt himself float for a moment, lost in her, lost in Ilanna... *I am Ilanna, she sang, music in his heart, drug in his veins, I am the honey in your soul, the butter on your bread, the sugar in your apple. I make you whole, Kell. I bring out the best in you, I bring out the warrior in you. And yes I ask you to kill but can you not see the irony? Can you not see what I desire? I am asking you not to kill; I am asking you to spare the boy. He is special. Very special. You will see, and one day you will thank me for these words of wisdom. Skanda is Ankarok, he is older than worlds, look into his insect eyes and see the truth, Kell, understand the importance of what I am saying for we will never have another opportunity like this... he will help you find Nienna... help you save those you love.*

You bitch.

I am stating the truth. And you know it. So grow up, and wise up, and let's get moving and get this thing done; Lilliath is leading the albino soldiers through the woods. They are coming, Kell, you must make haste...

368

Kell opened his eyes. He realised both Saark and Skanda were staring at him; staring at him hard.

"Are you well?" asked Saark, voice soft.

"Aye, I'm fine."

"We can stay a while longer, if you need rest," said Saark, suddenly remembering his own sleep with a sense of guilt. He had allowed Kell to sit up all night; it had been selfish in the extreme.

"No. The soldiers are coming. We should move."

Skanda's eyes went bright. "You want me to go back into the woods? Find them? Kill them?"

"No." Kell shook his head, eyeing the scorpion perched on the boy's hand. Seeing the look, and misreading its meaning, Skanda hid the tiny insect within folds of rough clothing, and Kell made a mental note to check his boots in the morn. "We're heading north. At speed. We're going to find Nienna. We're going to rescue her... or die in the process!"

Myriam crouched beside the still pool, its circumference edged with plates of ice, their layers infinite, their borders a billion shards of splintered and angular crystal. Beautiful, she thought, breathing softly, pacing herself, and then her gaze flickered up, above the ice, to her own reflection and her teeth clacked shut and the muscles along her jaw stood out in ridges as she clenched her teeth tight. But here, she thought, here, the beauty dies.

She had short black hair, where once she had worn it long. Once, it had been a luscious pelt that made men fall over themselves to stroke and touch. Now, she cropped it short for fear the rough texture and dull hue would scream at people exactly what she was: dying.

Myriam was dying, and she still found it difficult to admit, to say out loud, but at least now she had in some way acknowledged it to herself. For a year she had harboured denial, even as she watched her own flesh melt from her bones, and she'd continually conned herself, thinking that if she ate better, exercised more, found the right medicines, then this illness, this fever would *pass* and she would be well again. However, for the past three years now she had grown steadily weaker, flesh falling from her bones as pain built and wracked her ever slimming frame. She had often joked how the rich fat bulging bitches in Kallagria would pay a fortune to have what she had; now, Myriam joked no more. It was as if humour had been wrenched from her with a barbed spear, leaving a gaping trail of damaged flesh in its wake.

Myriam had travelled Falanor, attempting to find a cure for her sickness. She eventually tracked down the best physicians in Vor, and spent a small fortune in gold, stolen gold, admittedly, on their advice, their medications, their odd treatments. None had worked. What she had gained from her vast expenditure had been *knowledge*.

She had two tumours, growing inside her, each the size of a fist. They were like parasites, but whereas some parasites were symbiotic – would keep the host alive so that they, also, could live, these tumours were ignorant, killing the host which supported them. Her one small triumph would be they would also die. Yes. But only when Myriam died.

Myriam stared into her reflection, the stretched skin, the gaunt flesh, drawn back over her skull and making her shudder even to look at herself. Once, men and women had flocked to her. Now, they couldn't stand to be in the same room, as if they feared catching some terrible plague.

I am a creature of pity, she realised sadly. Then anger shot through her. Well, I don't want their fucking pity! I just want my fucking life back! I have only existed on this stinking ball of pain for twenty-nine winters. Twenty-nine! Is that any age to die? Are the gods laughing at me, mocking me with their sick sense of humour? How fair is that, that others, evil men and women, or useless, stupid, brainless men and women, how is it they get to live – and I do not? Who made that choice for me? Which rancid insane deity thought it would be fun?

Tears coursed her gaunt cheeks, and Myriam bit back the need to scream her anguish and pain and frustration through the frozen trees. No. She breathed deep. And she did what she always did. She thought about this day. And she thought about the next day. And she knew she had to take one day at a time, step after step after step until… until she reached Silva Valley. There, she knew, they had the technology to cure her. Using clockwork, and blood-oil, and dark vampire magick.

However, persuading them? That would be a different matter.

Fear flashed through her, then, and she licked dry lips. Her mouth tasted bad. Tasted like cancer. She grimaced, and her belly cramped in pain and she brought herself back to the present with a jolt; they had not eaten for two days. And the sparse woodland in the low foothills leading to the great feet of the Black Pike Mountains contained little game. She would have to work hard if she wanted supper.

Myriam was a skilled hunter. Before her affliction, she had won the Golden Bow three times in a row at the Vor Summer Festival. Now, the cancer ate her, and had sapped her strength, made her aim less true. But she was still a devastating archer, nonetheless.

Myriam crept through the woods, her boots treading softly on hard soil and patches of snow. She picked every footfall with care and stopped often, looking around with slow, fluid movements, her ears twitching, listening, her mind falling in tune with the winter trees.

There!

She saw the doe, a young one, rooting for food. Were there any parents close by? The last thing Myriam needed was a battle with an enraged stag; if nothing else, it made the meat damn tough.

She saw nothing, and eased herself to her knees, allowing her breathing to normalise, to regulate, as she notched the arrow to the bowstring and with a slow slow *slow* measured ease, drew back the string, taking the tension with her ever-so-slightly trembling muscles.

The arrow flashed through the woodland, striking the doe from behind, between the shoulder blades, and punching down into lungs and heart. It was a clean kill, instant, and the doe dropped. Myriam felt a burst of joy, of pride at her skill; then she stood, and the smile fell from her face like melting ice under sunshine.

Death. She shivered. *Death.*

Myriam crossed the forest floor and drew a long knife; expertly she sliced the best cuts of meat and placed them in a sack, blood oozing between her fingers. Then she stood, looked around, eyes narrowing. Something felt wrong, but she couldn't place her finger on it; however, Myriam trusted her senses, they were fine honed and reliable. If the element which felt *out of key* wasn't here, it must be back at camp. Her jaw tightened.

Myriam moved like a ghost through the trees. The world was silent, filled with snow and ice, and occasionally snow clumped from trees with a tumbling rhythm.

She approached the makeshift camp, trees thinning where huge fists of rock punched upwards at the sky, dominating her vision. Myriam felt her throat dry for a moment, for the Black Pike Mountains were a panorama indeed, a line of domineering peaks that lined her sight from the edge of the world to the edge of the world. Each peak she could see reared black and unforgiving into the sky, many damn near ten thousand feet. And beyond, she knew, they got much bigger, much more terrifying, and much more savage.

Myriam stopped, head tilting. The camp was quiet. Too quiet. Her eyes scanned right, where they could see the narrow trail which led from the Great North Road to the gawping maw of the Cailleach Pass; it was along this, she knew, Kell would finally come, head hung low, poison eating him, begging her for the antidote, for her to relieve his pain, for her to slit his throat and end his torment. Only Kell would not; he would be thinking of Nienna, and her suffering, and how he could save her instead.

A cold wind blew, and Myriam shivered. Snow fell from the trees behind her, making her jump, and she realised she had dropped the sack of meat and had notched an arrow to her bow without even realising it. *Kell*, the wind seemed to whisper. *Kell. He will gut you like a fish. He will cut out your liver. He will drink your blood, bitch!*

Scowling, Myriam grabbed the sack and stalked into their small camp, where the men, Styx and Jex, had built an arched screen of timber and evergreen fronds, for protection against the wind. Within this semi-circle they'd dragged logs for seats, and built a fire in a square of rocks. The fire burned low. Again, Myriam's eyes narrowed. To let the fire go out was foolish indeed; here, in this place, it meant the difference between life and death.

"Styx?" she said, voice little more than a murmur. Then louder. "Styx? Jex? Where are you?"

The camp was deserted. Myriam's eyes looked to where Nienna, their young prisoner, had been seated; there were deep marks in the snow created by her boots. A struggle?

"Damn it."

Myriam left the sack at camp, and followed tracks through the woods, kneeling once to examine a confusion of marks. She cursed; they had been using the camp for nearly a week now, and there were too many contradicting signs. Something rattled nearby. Myriam's head came up. She broke into a run, arrow notched, and skidded to a halt before a series of huge trees swathed in ivy, creating an ivy wall on two sides like a corridor; against this backdrop Nienna struggled, and even as Myriam watched Styx, squat, black-lipped Styx, with pockmarked skin and his left eye, uncovered, nothing more than a red, inflamed socket – she watched him push the blade to Nienna's throat and snarl something incomprehensible on a stream of foul spittle down her ear.

"Styx!" shouted Myriam, moving swiftly forward. She stopped, looked left at Jex, who simply shrugged. The small tattooed tribesman was not in charge of Styx; Styx was a free agent. He could do what he liked. Or so Jex's simple philosophy ran.

"She bit me!" snarled Styx. "This bitch has been nothing but trouble! Now I'm going to teach her a lesson." His free hand dropped down Nienna's side, to her hips, where he started to tug at her skirt. Nienna struggled wildly, and the knife bit her throat allowing a trickle of blood to run free.

"No, Styx," said Myriam. "This is not the way."

His head came up, black lips curling back over the blackened stumps of his drug-rotted teeth. His dark eye glittered like a jewel. "She's trouble, Mirry, I'm telling you! What I have in store for her will break her spirit; you'll see, it'll bring her back to the real world. Either that, or one of us will wake up with a knife in the heart."

"Put the girl down," said Myriam, voice deadly calm.

"And what if I don't?"

Myriam lifted her bow and sighted down the arrow. It was aimed at Styx's one remaining good eye, and Styx knew she was a good enough shot to pull it off, despite the illness which troubled her aim.

"What are you doing?"

"Exerting my authority."

"You're being a fool, Myriam. We've been through some shit together, girl, and now you'd turn on me? I don't bloody understand! This little bitch needs taming; you've watched me rape a hundred women before, young, old, fit, fat, diseased, what's the fucking problem with you now?" He gave a nasty grin, teeth like a fire-ravaged forest of stumps. "It's not like you haven't tasted a bit of screaming young pussy yourself. You always said the bigger the fight, the better the bite."

Myriam stared at him, and she knew she was willing to see him die. Because if he harmed Nienna and Kell went *berserk* then she would never make it to Silva Valley, where the vachine technology could make her whole again, make her well again; turn her into a *woman* again. And also, only if she admitted it to herself, she was a little frightened of Kell. If they abused Nienna he would never stop till they were dead; as it was, they walked a fine line between angering the old warrior, and turning him into a permanent merciless enemy, one that would hunt them to the ends of the earth.

"If you hurt the girl, Kell won't help us reach Silva. If we don't reach Silva, then you won't get your Blacklipper contacts; remember? The ones that will make you *rich*. The ones that will lead you to the three kings of the Blacklippers and all that precious gold beyond."

That stopped Styx. His eyes narrowed. In a voice like mist in a tombyard, he said, "What do *you* know of the three Kings?"

"I know enough," said Myriam, her arrow still aimed for Styx's face. Nienna had stilled in his arms, but the blade rested against her throat, a very real threat. A bead of sweat broke out on Myriam's brow, and her elbow gave a tiny tremble.

Styx saw this. He smiled.

With a *whoosh*, Myriam released the shaft which slammed through the air, piercing the lobe of Styx's ear and rattling off through the trees. He yelped, hand coming up to his lobe, and in doing so released Nienna. She ran to Myriam, cowering behind the tall woman's legs, and when Styx looked up she had another arrow notched, ready, steel point aimed at his face. There was a snarl on Styx's face; but worse, there was hatred in his eye, deep and glittering, and although Myriam had seen that look before a thousand times, she had never seen it directed at *her*. It chilled her. Styx was a very dangerous man; and not an enemy she wished to invoke. However. If Nienna was *damaged* in anyway, then it compromised her situation with Kell, finding the vachine, and living to see the next winter. For she knew, as certain as water flowed downhill, that these were her last few months on earth.

"I think you just made a big mistake," growled Styx. He held up his hands, his knife glinting a little with traces of Nienna's blood. "But don't worry. Don't panic, little Myriam; I am no danger to you. I value the Blacklipper contacts and their great wealth *more* than I value killing you in your sleep." He glanced at Nienna. "Or tasting her foul juice."

Styx lowered his hands, and walked past Myriam and the cowering form of Nienna; he disappeared into the woodland, and Myriam released a long breath. She glanced at Jex.

"Not such a good idea," said Jex, eyes fixed on Myriam.

"You think I don't know that? You think I'm a village idiot?"

"No," said the tribesman, carefully. "But I *do* think you should have let him have his fun with the girl; it would have kept him happy, not harmed her too much, and as he says – it would have tamed her spirit just a little." He shrugged. "Now you have to watch your back. From both fucking directions."

"You can watch it as well," smiled Myriam.

Jex did not return the smile. "Some things in life, we do alone," he said, and moved off through the trees.

Myriam finally lowered her bow, and placed the arrow in her sheath. Nienna moved around to face Myriam, and her hands were shaking. She looked up, and at first Myriam wouldn't meet her gaze.

Then their eyes locked, and Myriam studied the tall girl before her. She was pretty, with a rounded and slightly plump face. Her hair was a luscious brown down to her shoulders, and her eyes bright green, dazzling with youth and vitality. For a long moment Myriam hated her, despised her, was jealous to an insane degree of her youth, and beauty, and strength, and health, whilst *she* was slowly being eaten from the inside out, turning into a husk of degenerative cells. Hate flooded Myriam, fuelled by envy, and she wanted to smash Nienna's face open with a rock; split her head and watch the brains come spilling out. But Myriam breathed deeply, controlled herself, and fought the evil in her veins, in her soul. She forced a smile to her face.

"Thank you," said Nienna.

"Don't be too grateful," grunted Myriam. "You're still my prisoner… until the mighty Kell arrives, and shows us a way through the mountains."

"Still – Styx would have…" she shuddered.

Myriam smiled. "Don't think about it. He's a bad man, aye, but at least it's nothing personal. He hates all women. Come to think of it, he hates all men." Myriam turned, and started back through the trees with Nienna close behind. Nienna was still shivering.

"Why do you travel with such hateful creatures?" said Nienna, her voice low, almost conspiratorial. "It must darken your soul to see such evil at every turn. To witness such horror, and do nothing to halt it."

Myriam stopped, suddenly, and Nienna almost crashed into her. "I saved you, didn't I, little Nienna?" Her tone was mocking, her eyes flashing angry. "Darken my soul? Child, you know nothing of me, or my life, of my horrors and pain and suffering. Don't think because of one little moment, one tiny lapse in my self-control that I'm suddenly a mother figure. You're here for a reason, and that's to draw Kell. That's why I helped you. I care nothing for your suffering. In fact, I wish I'd let Styx rape you – he was right. It would have taught you to shut your bastard mouth."

She stalked off ahead, leaving a confused and now terrified Nienna behind. Nienna trotted after her, tears on her cheeks, and filled with a complete and devastating misery.

Kell managed an hour's sleep. In it, he dreamed. He dreamed of Ilanna, his axe; he dreamed of murder; he dreamed of the Days of Blood. *He stood, muscles bulging, tensed as if pumped on drugs and violence, and his whole body quivered, and his mind flitted and could not settle on a single thought, like some butterfly caught in a raging storm. Blood smeared his face and arms and he glanced down, and Kell was naked, naked and proud and bulging with sexual arousal. His entire body was smeared with blood, and blue and green whorls of paint which were intricately complex and he frowned for he did not remember being painted, or tattooed, but then they did not matter for they were an irrelevancy... Kell leapt down from the stone wall and stood in the street, Ilanna in his hands, a snarl on his face, and refugees were streaming past him, sobbing, faces blackened with soot as behind the city burned, huge towers of fire screaming up into the skies. Kell watched the men and women and children stream past him, and Ilanna said something in his mind with a soothing caress and she sang, and Kell twitched and a head rolled, and blood fountained and Kell moved and allowed the twitching body to spray lifeblood over the butterfly blades of the great axe...*

"Ugh!" Kell sat up, shivering, and pain washed through him like honey through a sieve; slowly, an ooze, spreading gently through limbs and veins and muscles and organs and into... into his *bones*.

It's the poison, he told himself.

It's getting worse.

He pulled his cloak tightly about him. The wind howled. Kell licked his lips. What he'd give for a drink. Gods, he'd kill for a drink. And then he smiled, face black in the moonlight, eyes glittering like some dark devil's, and he remembered the unlabelled bottle of whiskey deep in the basket on Mary's back.

It was a matter of moments to get the bottle and retire back to the phantom warmth of his cloak; the wind stirred eerily through the trees. Kell pulled out the cork with his teeth and an odour of sour, cheap, nasty whiskey filled him. He did not care. He breathed in the scent like drugsmoke; he revelled in its base oil consistency, in its hints at raw energy and amateur production. This was a whiskey made by unskilled peasants. This was a whiskey in which Kell could identify, not like the rich honeyed slop the aristocracy of Saark's social circle enjoyed. This was fire water, and Kell drank it.

He took several gulps, and it burned his throat.

He took several more, and a haze filled his mind.

The pain of the poison left him.

And Kell slept, whiskey bottle cradled like a small, adopted child.

The moon was high in a cold, crystal sky. Nienna sat, wrapped in blankets, listening to the soft snoring of Myriam by her side. The woman turned in her sleep, stretching out long legs. For a moment – a fleeting moment – Nienna considered running. She had tried twice before; the second time, Myriam had caught her and explained, using the back of her hand, what she would do the next time Nienna ran. Now, Nienna slept with her ankles bound so tight her feet would be blue by morning. And anyway, she had seen Myriam operate her bow. She was a lethal, very deadly young woman... who could kill over great distance. It made Nienna shiver in horror and anticipation.

Nienna drifted in and out of sleep, as she had done since her *kidnapping*. Such a simple word, and yet it embodied day after day of a living hell. Riding in front of Styx, and then Jex, they had shared her burden, swapping her often so as not to tire the horses with extra weight; they had ridden north, fast, as if Myriam feared Kell would take up immediate chase. Nienna knew Saark wasn't going to take chase; she had watched him beaten and then stabbed with a long, sharp dagger. Even now, Nienna was sure

Saark must be dead and she shuddered, on the edges of sleep, once again picturing the beating, hearing every crunch, every slap of impact in her nightmares. Even now, she could see the blade slide so easily into his soft flesh, and thought no, it cannot be, cannot be happening, cannot be true, but blood poured from Saark and it was true and Myriam had come to them and they had ridden away into the snow, without a backward glance...

Nienna thought back. Back to Kat. Katrina. Her friend. Now dead. Now a corpse, rotting in the cold bunkhouse where she'd been nailed to the wall by Styx's *Widowmaker*. Nienna thought about that weapon. Thought about it a lot. With a weapon like that, she could really even the odds – no matter that she was a thin, physically weak, and hardly able to lift a longsword. With a *Widowmaker* she could punch a hole through Styx's face and run for the woods...

No. She would have to kill all three if she expected to escape.

But Kell! Kell would come and rescue her! Surely?

Maybe Kell was dead, spoke a dark side of her soul. He went into battle with King Leanoric – against the albino army. Maybe now he was just another corpse on the battlefield, crows eating his eyes, rats gnawing his intestines. She shivered, and gritted her teeth. No! Kell was alive. She knew it. Knew it deep in her heart.

And if Kell was alive, then he would come for her.

Nienna drifted off into sleep; coldness ate the edges of her flesh where skin poked from behind the blankets. She snuggled down as far as she could go, and her eyes suddenly clicked open. What was it? What had woken her? She was instantly wide awake – totally awake – and adrenaline surged through her system.

Nienna sat up. Her eyes searched the darkness. She turned to her right, and looked down at Myriam; the lithe woman snored softly, face lost in a haze of tranquillity that softened her features, made her more feminine. Nienna realised that when Myriam was awake her face was a constant scowl, as if she hated the world and every waking moment upon it.

Nienna turned to her left, and nearly leapt from her skin at the face mere inches from her. She felt the edge of the *Widowmaker* crossbow prod her under the blankets, and she nodded quickly as if to say, "I understand". Styx moved his mouth to her ear and whispered, "Scream, and I'll blow a hole through you, then I'll slaughter Myriam in her sleep and make my own way to Silva Valley."

"I won't scream," panted Nienna, fear a bright hot poker in her brain.

Styx pulled free the blankets, and lifted Nienna up by her elbow. Her eyes fell, and locked on that wood, brass and clock-work weapon. She was sure she could hear a tiny *tick tick tick* from within the stock. As if it was somehow powered by clockwork.

"What do you want?" she whispered.

Styx ignored the question, and eased her away from Myriam. Nienna gazed back at the sleeping woman, confused; it had been Myriam who, on both of Nienna's escape attempts, had heard the flight. Myriam slept light, like a dozing feline. Now, however, she continued to snore.

"Don't worry about her. I drugged her soup. She'll not be troubling nobody tonight."

Nienna felt icy fingers claw her heart. Realisation sank from her brain to her feet. Styx meant to rape her. Tonight. Now. And there was nothing she could do about it; not a thing on earth.

Styx marched Nienna through the woods, and he was panting hard, and he stunk of sweat and… something else. Liquor? Gin, like they used to sell in the Gin Palaces of Jalder?

Nienna was numb, not from the cold, but from fear. She allowed herself to be manhandled through the woods, stumbling. She did not complain. She could not complain. Fear had become her Master. Fear had stolen her tongue, and seemingly, her recent will to fight.

Finding a spot, Styx threw her to the ground. She landed heavy, a tree root slamming her spine and making her cry out. Even this was not enough to snap her from her cold embrace. She watched, with a mixture of horror and revulsion as Styx struggled from his leggings, one hand still holding the Widowmaker pointed loosely at her prostrate form.

Then, with the lower half of his body naked, he grinned at her and she hated him, there and then; she wanted him dead like she had wanted no other person dead in the world, ever. This man had killed her best friend. And now, this man sought to remove her chastity by force.

"If you touch me, I will kill you," she said. She wanted her words to come out strong and proud, like a sneer of contempt for this petty hateful specimen. But her words dribbled out, a mewling from a kitten, the slurred and feeble trickle of the wanton inebriate.

Kell will come, she thought with tears in her eyes. *Kell will rescue me!*

But he didn't come. Here, and now, Nienna was on her own.

Styx dropped his Widowmaker to the frozen woodland carpet, and pulled out a knife. The blade gleamed. He smiled, showing stubby black teeth. "I think it's time we got to know each other a bit better, pretty one," he said.

FIVE
Dark Vision

In the hills above Old Skulkra a small squad hunkered behind rocks. One, the tallest of the men, a soldier with broad shoulders and narrow hips, held a long tube filled with a series of finely shaped lenses to his eye. The delicate mechanism glittered when it caught the dying rays of the winter sun.

"Can you see him?" asked Beja.

"Yes. He returns," said Cardinal Walgrishnacht. His voice was even, devoid of emotion, but his dark vachine eyes shone. He watched, apparently impassive, as the scout approached. The man bowed low, as befitted somebody as exalted and dangerous as Walgrishnacht.

"You saw what happened?" snapped the Warrior Engineer.

"Yes," said the scout, eyes lowered to the snow. "General Graal called out his daughters, the Soul Stealers. Our Princess was..." he swallowed, then lifted his head and met Walgrishnacht's powerful clockwork gaze. "She was beheaded," he said.

Walgrishnacht stood, stunned, and when he looked around there were tears in his eyes, tears staining his pale cheeks. Never, in twenty years of combat and murder, had Walgrishnacht cried.

Beja watched the Cardinal of the Vachine Warrior Engineers, that specially chosen and infinitely deadly elite squad who had followed – secretly, in reserve – in order to protect Princess Jaranis should events turn sour. A violent blizzard had separated the two groups, and stubbornly the proud Princess pushed on regardless, no doubt eager to observe General Graal's progress and report back to the High Engineers instead of making textbook camp until the storm broke.

Now, she was dead. And Walgrishnacht could not quite believe the turn of events. General Graal was, and had been, a servant of the vachine religious culture for nearly three centuries. With Kradek-ka, he had helped usher in a new age of advanced clockwork technology, which elevated their race from savagery to high art. Graal was a founding member of Engineer Council Lore, and a harsh advocate and defender of the Oak Testament. Graal had been instrumental in the taming of pale-skinned creatures, the *al-shina*, from beneath the Black Pike Mountains, and of training these soldiers in warfare and tactics; thus, he was the strategy behind many successful invasions and harvesting north past the Heart of the Mountains in Untamed Lands. After the recent breakdown of several Blood Refineries, it had been Graal who spearheaded Council and carried the vote to invade south. In High Engineer Philosophy, Politics, Ethics, History and Honour, Graal was unquestionable, and untouchable. He was Core to the Vachine Society. Integral. Like a Heart Cog.

Walgrishnacht chewed his lip, and wiped tears from his face with a long, brass talon.

"What shall we do?" said Beja, voice soft. He fidgeted. His body echoed uncertainty.

Walgrishnacht stood and stretched with a tiny *tick tick* echoing from his clockwork internals. He stared off across distant snow-fields, to the camped army of albino warriors; and he knew, in his heart, in his soul, that in an unprecedented move they were betrayed. But what was Graal's plan? What were his goals? Whatever they were, they did not involve saving the vachine race from blood-oil extinction...

Walgrishnacht shook his head. Confusion spun like a snow-storm. The whole situation was... inconceivable! Impossible! Unwarranted! And yet there had been murder, and worse, *betrayal*.

Walgrishnacht turned on Beja. "We must take the platoon back to Silva Valley. We must explain that General Graal has betrayed the vachine, and everything our world stands for."

"We may not survive the mountains," warned Beja, not through fear but tactical understanding. He was aware they may never deliver the message, and thus *warning*, to the Engineer Council.

Walgrishnacht nodded. "We will give our lives to cross," he said. "The High Engineers must reconvene the War Council and assemble the Ferals – for if Graal plans an invasion after the snows have passed, and Silva Valley is unprepared…" He left the sentence unfinished. They both understood; without warning, Graal with his highly trained, disciplined, and *experienced* Army of Iron would roll through Silva Valley like a tidal wave. In an ironic twist, it was the General who commanded the army, not the Council. But then – the General was incorruptible, was he not? Walgrishnacht's face fell into a maelstrom of hatred. "Instruct the men. We move in ten minutes."

"As you wish, Cardinal."

The Warrior Engineers readied their packs and weapons, a sombre mood descending on the platoon. Then, as they headed back north through deep snow, away from Old Skulkra and the sour betrayal that had occurred, so in the distance a howl rent the air, a long, high-pitched note that seemed to linger in the deep forests and dark places of the night.

Beja looked to Walgrishnacht. "Wolves?" he said.

The Cardinal showed no emotion. "Maybe," he said. "Move out."

Anukis, of Silva Valley, had been born to Kradek-ka, one of the founding fathers of modern vachine society. Kradek-ka, like his father before him, had risen through Engineer ranks until he attained the exalted position of Watchmaker. He had achieved this level by ingenuity, cunning, and a technical skill which far outweighed most who lived in Silva Valley. Kradek-ka's *skill* had been with clockwork; not just the machining of parts, or the intricate assembly of clockwork components, but with the *design* of new clockwork machines – machines which, more importantly, could integrate with the vampire society, keeping the dying race alive. This engineering also formed the basis of their religion, *accelerating* them in an evolutionary arc which left them… superior.

However. With his daughter, Anukis, Kradek-ka made changes. For a start, unlike normal vachine, Anukis could not drink the refined narcotic blood-oil, which every vachine relied on to sustain their clockwork mechanisms and, it was said, lubricate their clockwork souls. No. Anukis was different. Anukis was special. Anukis could not take the blood-oil like normal vachine. She could not mate with the magick. She could not feed as a normal vachine would feed... and, technically, this made her unholy, her very existence sacrilege to the High Engineer Episcopate.

Still. Here, and now, Anukis had other problems to worry about.

She was tall, and beautiful, and in possession of long, flowing, golden curls which shone and sparkled in the sunlight. Her fangs were brass, and as she had recently found, her clockwork was built to a more *advanced* design than any in the vachine society had before witnessed. Kradek-ka had made her a Goddess – and in making her a Goddess, had at the same time cursed her, and condemned her under Vachine Law.

On a mission to find her father, Kradek-ka, whom the Silva Valley needed to repair their malfunctioning Blood Refineries, Anukis had soon found herself in position of victim, of slave, at the hands of Vashell, one of the youngest ever Engineer Priests to achieve such a rank; and a vachine who had sworn to love her until the end of time, marry her, and sire a hierarchy of proud and vicious vachine warriors. That was, until the day he discovered her impurity, her living sacrilege. After vicious humiliation, they thus set upon a mission to discover her father's whereabouts within the dangerous and daunting Black Pike Mountain range. After a series of violent events which saw Anukis discover her true nature – that she was no longer vachine, but something *more pure*, something infinitely more primal... a word which taunted her with its haunting echo of millennia – *vampire*, she was *vampire* – Anukis had been separated from Vashell, and the kidnapped Falanor Queen, Alloria, and found herself on an Engineer's Barge deep within hidden tunnels under the Black Pike Mountains, drawn inexorably towards the fabled Vrekken in the hope it was an esoteric pathway which led to her missing father, whom she believed trapped in the near-mythical world of Nonterrazake.

The Vrekken.

The Vrekken roared. It surged. And it *pulled*... nearly half a league across, and filling a cavern of such incredible scale it veered off around Anukis to impossible heights, distant sheer walls glinting with dark rock and lit by wrist–thick skeins of mineral deposits.

The Vrekken howled, like a primal giant in pain. It was a huge circular portal, a juggernaut of churning spirals leading down in massive, sweeping circles towards a savage cone depth... a whirlpool, thought Anukis, eyes taking in the scene in an instant, head tossing back golden curls as her lips came back, brass vampire fangs snarling in horror, her clockwork ticking inside with increased rhythm as gears stepped and cogs spun, twisted, clicked, and Anukis grasped the edges of the Engineer's Barge. There was nothing she could do. The powerful current had her, pulled the boat towards the Vrekken, towards its vast circular sweep and tears ran down Anukis's face for here, *here* she had discovered her true identity and suddenly realised what her father wanted of her – to help revert the vachine to the pure, to the *vampires* of old, and away from the twisted merging with deviant clockwork technology, away from a reliance on the *machine*.

Anukis breathed out in a hiss.

And sped towards the huge underwater whirlpool...

The Engineer's Barge was tugged, then flung into the Vrekken and caught like a toy. It powered in circles, nose in the air leaving a wide wake through churning waters and Anu spun down, and down, and round and down and she realised the mighty whirlpool consisted of *layers* and she passed down, through layer after layer of this oceanic macrocosm, of whirling dark energy, of raw power and violent fusion and screaming howling thrashing detonation and mighty primordial *compression*, and she thought...

There is no fabled Nonterrazake. It does not exist.

Just death. Death in this place...

Anukis screamed... and waited to be crushed, eyes closed, hunched down on the brass barge with its thumping clockwork engine, her heart thundering in her ears like the ticking of the strangest, deviant clock. Spray burst over the barge, drenching her, and she could taste salt and bitterness and the whole world was a confusion. Round and round she spun. Down down through dark layers. She felt the pressure, and heard squeals as the Engineer's Barge started to buckle, to compress and crunch and fold in upon itself and Anukis hunkered down further, a ball of foetal fear, and then there came a crash and wrenching of iron and something slammed her face and darkness rushed in like a surge of sea water into a drowning ship – and Anukis remembered no more.

A dark lake lapped a dark shore. It was raining, fat droplets pattering across the lake. Anukis fluttered open butterfly eyelids that felt stretched to the point of breaking, and wondered if she were dead.

But then pain slammed her like an iron oar, and she realised she couldn't be dead; the world hurt too much, and in her experience, this sort of pain only came from being *alive*. With a tiny hiss, her vachine fangs ejected, and then retracted. This, too, told her the world was real. Only *Man* could have invented the vachine.

She pushed herself up on her elbows, and listened. Nothing, but the lapping of water and the fall of rain. She frowned. Wasn't she *inside* the mountain? Then, slowly, as if dissolving from a dream, a gentle rhythmical *hush hush hush* came to her ears, and she looked up, and her mouth dropped open. Above her, the Vrekken spun, massive and violent and dark, a whirlpool in the sky, black and blue and gold and laced with traces of occasional purple. Rain fell from the mighty whirlpool, and Anukis climbed to her knees, and then to her feet, her body aching, every joint complaining, her eyes still fixed – locked – to the truly stunning and magnificent sight above. For long minutes everything was forgotten, but slowly Anukis came round, her clouded mind clearing, and she was brought back to the present. She glanced right, to where something lay crumpled by the dark lake's shore. She began to walk, soft boots silent on slippery wet rock, and with a start she recognised the crumpled thing; it was the Engineer's Barge, crushed into a loose tangle of metal as if folded and squeezed in a giant's mighty fist. With a quick movement, Anukis looked down at herself, as if fearing, for a few seconds at least, that she had been crushed also. But she hadn't; and except for a dull throbbing in her bones, as if her internal frame had somehow taken a battering but left her flesh intact, she felt fine. More than fine. She felt... invigorated!

Glad to be alive.

She stopped and gazed around, and wondered if this was Nonterrazake, the fabled mythical underworld and, more importantly, the secret home of the *Harvesters*. She moved to the wall, which followed in parallel with the lake's shore, and began to walk, footsteps quick, urgent now, for she was certainly trapped down here, in this underground place, and of one thing Anukis was certain beyond all doubt: there was no way she could head back up through the Vrekken. It was a one-way journey.

She stopped, by a small tunnel. She would have to crawl. She got down on hands and knees and peered in. She could see light, a distant eerie glow, and began to crawl through the rock. Gradually, the mountain beneath her hands, and indeed above and around her, began to fade, a graduated change from black through grey, and finally to the colour of ivory. Of bone, bleached and old. Beneath her hands the rock was no longer black, but a rough-textured white. Her nostrils twitched, for she could smell fresh, cool air. She emerged into a larger tunnel, and saw immediately she was in a mass of inter-connected tunnels which led off, seemingly randomly. Anukis swallowed. She imagined wandering down here in a labyrinth, forever, or at least until she starved and died.

She picked a tunnel at random, and walked across rough bone floor, hand trailing against bone-smooth walls, her mind working. She looked up; the ceiling was high, vast, and it was from above cool air flowed. It caressed her skin, soothing, like a sigh from a lover.

Anukis quelled a savage laugh. That sort of life was over for her. It had been since Vashell's... *abuse*.

Vashell. She remembered his love. His words of kindness. Then his hatred, and actions of violence. Beating her. Making love to her. Fucking her. She smiled. There was a difference; a big difference. And then their quest, their journey, their *fight*. Right up to the point where she ripped off his face, and left him scarred and bleeding beyond all recognition because of her powers of newly awakened vachine dominance.

Where are you now, *lover*? she thought. And she could not keep the bitterness from her mind.

She walked. It could have been hours, or even days, for down in this bone-white place, this place of caverns and caves and tunnels, time seemed to have no meaning. And although this strange underground labyrinth of Nonterrazake was empty, and silent, Anukis could not help but feel she was being watched.

Several times she would turn, fast, a superspeed vachine flick of body and head dropping to attack crouch, fangs out and claws extended for battle. But every time she was met with a vision of simple, gleaming bone.

I am not alone, she told herself, feeling paranoid.

I am not alone...

They watched her. Hundreds of them. They glided silently through the labyrinth, but here, in this place, they were partly invisible; for these were the Halls of Bone, the place which had spawned them, the place from which they had been granted life.

They were the Harvesters. And this was their *World*.

The Harvesters watched Anukis, curious, for a very select few made it through the Vrekken alive and they wondered what elements of blood-oil magick she carried in her soul to make it so. But then, she was a daughter of Kradek-ka, and this answered much; and made the drifting Harvesters *smile* beneath their ornate robes of white and gold thread.

Shall we kill her? came the pulse through bone. It was communal, hive-mind, shared by all. It was a question asked not to other Harvesters, but to the sentient world of bone around them. They thought the same question at the same time, as if they were clones, and the answer which whispered back came from the very bone-roots of the mountain under which they ruled: Skaringa Dak. The Great Mountain.

No. Let her find her father. Let them speak.
She has much to learn.
Much to understand.

The Harvesters allowed her to drift by. There were thousands now, drawn from their blending with the bone walls and columns by curiosity, and the sweet smell of her blood... and the sweeter smell of her soul. They drifted like ghosts, long tapered fingers extended as if tantalised by her organic fluid presence. But she never saw them. For in this place, they were genetic chameleons.

Unwittingly, Anukis was guided like a pig into a trap. And eventually she found herself at a small cave, a circular opening, a wide pale interior decorated with rugs and a desk. Shelves lined the bone walls, and every single one held a tiny clock, all ticking, all transparent, so that a million cogs thrashed as one, and a million gears made tiny stepping, clicking motions. Anukis blinked, for this sight was unreal; as unreal as anything she had expected.

"Anu?"

"Daddy!"

Kradek-ka rose from the padded chair of white leather and Anukis leapt, tumbled into his arms, and his face was in her golden curls and she fell into his scent, of tobacco and clockwork oil and hot metal. He still smelled the same. His arms were tight about her, soothing away her troubles. She cried, a little girl again, her tears flowing to his leather apron, and the old Watchmaker finally moved her gently backwards and smiled, a kindly smile on the face of a wrinkled, ancient vachine.

"What are you doing here? This is a dangerous place!"

"I have come for you. To rescue you!"

"Rescue? No, no, no. Did you not read my letter?"

"What letter?" Anukis's brow furrowed, and Kradek-ka made a tutting, annoyed sound. "I left a letter for you. With Vashell. When I realised I had to come away."

"Vashell has been... evil, to me."

Kradek-ka frowned, then, and his face was no longer the face of a kindly old vachine; now, he appeared menacing, and suddenly, an infinitely dangerous foe.

"That explains much," he said, softly, and moved to a nearby bench. Idly, he lifted a tiny clockwork device and began to fiddle with the delicate mechanism. As his hands moved, so the clockwork machine began to alter and change, sections flipping out and then over themselves, rearranging like an intricate puzzle, over and over and over again in an apparently infinite cycle. Eventually, Kradek-ka placed the item down.

"What is happening, Daddy? I am confused. Why are you here? What are you doing here? The Blood Refineries are breaking, the vachine of Silva Valley – your people – are beginning to starve!"

"You must brace yourself for what I am about to tell you," said Kradek-ka, and his eyes now looked old, older than worlds, and Anukis felt a shudder run through her body. In a strange way, Kradek-ka no longer resembled her father, even though his features had not changed; suddenly, he seemed alien, an altogether different creature.

"This does not sound good," said Anukis quietly, allowing herself to be led to a low couch. She sat, and Kradek-ka sat in his chair, and their hands remained together.

"The Blood Refineries are failing because..." he looked away for a moment, eyes seemingly filled with tears; tears of blood-oil, at least. "They are failing because I engineered it so."

"What? You seek to kill the vachine?"

"*No!* That is, not directly. I had to instigate certain events. I had to make sure General Graal, or whoever else, took the Army of Iron south. Invaded Falanor. It is for a greater purpose." His voice dropped to a low rumble. "A higher purpose."

"I do not understand."

"And nor should you." He smiled. Anukis did not like the smile.

"What are you doing, daddy? You left us! Shabis is dead!"

"I know this," said Kradek-ka, face serious, eyes gleaming. "But it had to be so."

"I killed her," said Anukis, hanging her head with guilt.

"This, also, I know."

"And you do not hate me?"

"You are pure, Anu," he was suddenly smiling. "Shabis chose her own path; and it was the wrong path. You came to me, you sought me out. I hoped it would be so. For together, we can find the remaining Soul Gems, and we can…" He stopped, suddenly, and his teeth clamped shut.

"This is too strange," said Anukis. "It is like a surreal, drug-induced dream. Have I imbibed blood-oil? Am I really hallucinating, back at my apartment in Silva Valley? Will Vashell bring a surgeon to bleed out the poisons? Tell me this is so."

"I have much to tell you, Anukis. I have much to tell. But soon, you will understand. And soon, I hope, you will choose to help me. You will help… us all."

Kradek-ka motioned, and Anukis turned, and gasped at the Harvesters standing silently in the doorway. She could see perhaps twenty, but also saw their pale bony figures spreading off into the surreal hazy gloom of the bone place.

Anukis's fangs and claws ejected, but Kradek-ka squeezed her hand. "No. They are friends."

"They have been hunting me!"

"But now you are here. Now you are safe. They do not understand the bigger game. I do."

Anukis was staring, hard, eyes narrowed, mind a maelstrom Everything was wrong. Nothing fit like it should. The world felt… *seized*, like old clockwork. Like a rusted puzzlebox.

Suddenly, Kradek-ka stood, drawing Anukis up with him. His eyes gleamed. "Don't you understand, Anu? I made you special! I made you special for a reason! The day is coming, when the vachine will regress! We will return to a time of ancient power, of ancient mastery!" His face contorted into a snarl. "Now we are second-hand, kept alive, kept whole by clockwork machines." He spat across the desk, where thousands of tiny intricate machines lay. "It was not always thus."

"You saved the vachine," said Anu, voice small.

"I cursed them!" he said. And his eyes glittered. "And now I will uncurse them."

"What do you mean?"

"We will bring back the Vampire Warlords, Anu," he said. "And then you will see what a species can achieve!"

Alloria, Queen of Falanor, wife to the Warrior King Leanoric, Guardian of all Falanor States, knew instantly the moment her husband died. It felt as if she had been stabbed through the heart.

She had been walking a path through high mountain passes, not long after she left Anukis who in turn set off in the Engineer's Barge, in search of her father. Queen Alloria, alone now, and carrying a satchel with few provisions and extra clothing which Anukis had given her from the Barge's stores, was navigating a particularly treacherous path of sharp frozen rocks, a sheer cliff to her right, a vast drop of maybe five thousand feet to her left, down sharp, scree-covered slopes which ended in a tumbled platter of massive cubic rocks. Her hands, once delicate and manicured, the nails perfectly filed and painted with tiny scenes, skin soft from rich creams and unguents, were now hard and scabbed and ingrained with dirt. They reached out, touching the rock wall for security lest her vertigo tip her over the edge of the slope, and laugh at her fall as she kicked and screamed her way to becoming a bloody pulped carcass at the bottom.

Alloria breathed deep. She calmed her mind.

Then the pain came, slashing through her heart like a razor, and she gasped, and heard his cry across the miles, across the skies, across the mountains, across the void; and Alloria knew as sure as the sun would rise that Leanoric, her true love, the man she had betrayed and who had, against all probability, *forgiven her*; she knew he was dead.

Alloria gasped, and fell to her knees. Overhead, an eagle swooped, then dropped and disappeared into the vastness of the canyon. Alloria clutched her chest, and the pain was intense and she could hear Leanoric's scream which suddenly cut off – in an instant – as he was slain.

"Oh, my, no," was all she managed to whisper, and knelt there on the rocky trail, rocking gently backwards and forwards as desolation filled her like ink in a jug; right to the brim.

She knelt there. For long hours. And cried. She cried for his death. She cried for her boys. And she cried for her betrayal of Falanor, her foolish *foolish* betrayal, which sat with her, sat bad with her, like a demon smothering her soul.

It was only as darkness fell, and she heard the distant cries of wolves that she was prodded into action. She climbed wearily to her feet, drained beyond any semblance of humanity. It had all been too much; the invasion, the rape, the abuse, the kidnapping. And now that her husband was dead, and she knew in her heart he was truly gone, there seemed little left to live for. *But what about your children?* asked a tiny part of her conscience, and she smiled there on the mountain ledge, as clouds swirled heavy above her and light flakes of snow began to snap in the wind. Of course, she thought. Her children. Sweet Oliver, and handsome Alexander; oh how she missed them. She picked her way along the trail in the fast-falling gloom. But then, who was to say they had not also been slain? They had been with Leanoric as he checked his armies in those last fateful days of Falanor's rule. Surely they were still with him, in the fast-falling panic following the swift invasion by Graal's Army of Iron? The albinos had marched on Jalder, then headed south with speed, taking every city and town and village they came upon. They allowed few to escape; and those who did escape were hunted down by the terrible beasts known as *cankers*.

Alloria shuddered again. She looked up. Above her, light fell swiftly from the sky. Velvet caressed her vision. She cursed herself, cursed herself for her self-pity, and cursed herself for knowing too much. Graal. Graal. She touched her hand to her breast, remembering the gems.

Whilst she knelt, weeping, the mountain night and the savagery of nature had crept in on her. Now the Black Pikes would seek to test her mettle, her agility, her stamina and her courage.

Alloria stumbled over a rocky ledge, and nearly pitched into the chasm far below. Panting, and with hands raw from scraping rock, she moved on, telling herself constantly that Oliver and Alexander were still alive; that Leanoric would have had the foresight to hide them somewhere safe. But deep down in her heart, in her soul, she did not believe it... even if she could not feel their deaths as acutely as that of her king, her husband, her lover, and ultimately, her soul mate.

She stopped, suddenly. She turned to face the vast drop. She could no longer see it, for night in the mountains was darkness as she had never before experienced; a total immersion of vision, and senses, and soul. But she knew the drop was there; she could feel the gaping presence, the mammoth opening of space and cold, snapping air. Snow landed in her hair. She ignored it. She stepped up onto the lip.

I should die, she realised.

There is nothing left to live for.

General Graal has won.

"Wait there, little lady," came a soft whisper.

Alloria jumped, startled by the gentle voice. However, she recognised the tone, and yet the words seemed alien to her at the same time. She shook spastically, with fear, with adrenaline, with apprehension at her impending suicide.

"I cannot see you!" she hissed.

"But I can see you," came the voice, at once gentle and powerful and harsh and merciless. Strong hands took hold of her, and eased her back from the slash of precipice. Before her, waves of ice crashed down onto invisible rocks of awesome destruction.

"Vashell? Is that you?"

"Yes," came the rich, powerful voice of the vachine. "It is I."

"Have you followed me?"

"Let us say we travel the same path," came his words, at once soothing and deeply terrifying. Alloria had witnessed his cruelty first hand; and his violence. She was afraid.

"How can you see in the dark?" she murmured, heart beating a rampage in her chest. She realised, then, that she needed her blue karissia; just to help her sleep. Always to help her sleep.

"I have special vision," said Vashell. "I have clockwork eyes. Now, come, the snow is growing heavy; in an hour we will be trapped on this narrow path. I know of a cave a distance ahead where we can take shelter. By the gods, woman, you are freezing! Have you no cloak?"

Alloria struggled to free her cloak from the satchel she carried, and Vashell helped. Once encapsulated within fur and leather, she felt better; a little better. But the death of Leanoric still bit her, like wolf fangs through her heart.

"This way. Hold my hand. I will lead."

Alloria stumbled along the trail, with Vashell leading the way. She did not trust the man – she smiled, and corrected herself. The *vachine*. But then, she had little choice, and in all actuality, no longer cared. If he was going to rape her, slit her, toss her ragdoll body down the mountain, then so be it. Surely, she deserved no less? Alloria had lost the fight and fire in her heart.

They struggled on against worsening weather. The wind howled like a stabbed banshee. The snow pummelled them with padded fists. At one point Alloria fell, with a grunt and a small cry, and she felt herself reeling and sliding towards a violent chasm – but Vashell was there, strong hands pulling her back, and he held her, and she shivered and knew it was not from the cold; she was impervious, now, to ice. It was for the loss. The deep, drowning, terrible loss of her dead husband, her dead children. She knew she would never be sane again.

"Here. We are here."

Alloria could see nothing but white and gloom, but felt a sudden lessening of the wind and horizontally lashing snow. Vashell led her far back into the cave and it was curiously warm. He sat her on a stone, and using a bundle of small sticks, lit a tiny fire in a circle of blackened rocks. This place had been used by many travellers, it would seem.

Firelight filled the cave, and although little heat was produced, the illusion was enough for Alloria, for now. She moved closer, stretching out fingers to the meagre flames, and then her head snapped up as she remembered the vicious fight between Vashell and Anukis (so long ago, *drifting through ancient dreams*)… a fight which had ended with Vashell losing his *face*.

Even in the darkness, in the flickering firelight, his face was nothing less than a terrible mess; strings of flesh covered cords of tendon and visible bone; some scar tissue showed where the vachine's accelerated healing was trying frantically to compensate for such a savage wounding. But it hadn't done enough.

Vashell lowered his face; his eyes were full of pain, and shame. With head lowered, he said, "Once, my Queen, you found me beautiful." She said nothing. He looked up, glittering eyes meeting hers. "But not any more, I think."

"Beauty is more than the skin on your bones, Vashell. It is here, in your heart, in your soul, and mirrored by the things you do. And no, sadly, from what I have seen of you, and the horror of which I heard you speak, I am not prepared to think of you as a beautiful soul."

"I have done... questionable things," said Vashell, head lowered once again. His hand held a dagger. It glinted, blade black in the firelight. Suddenly, Alloria's eyes fixed on that blade, and she swallowed, tasting a thrill of raw metal fear.

She realised, with a dawning like a virgin sun, that she was antagonising a tormented man. He shuffled back a little, and breathed deeply. Here was a vachine warrior not to be trifled with. According to Alloria, he had slain children – impure, Blacklipper children – in their beds. He had no qualms about killing women. He was a predator; the ultimate predator. And he killed not to survive; but because he had an intrinsic enjoyment of the concept, and indeed, the act.

Outside, in the darkness, distant through the snow, a wolf howled.

Alloria shivered, and stared at the cave opening. She was no match for a wolf. When she had decided to head off through the mountains after her release by Anukis, she had never considered such things as wolves, or bears, or even now, as she thought about it, wild men, brigands, outlaws on the mountain trails. She shuddered. Maybe death was still the answer? But on her own terms. By her own hand. Not ripped apart by the wild.

Vashell stood and moved to the cave entrance. Then he turned to her. His destroyed face was creased in... in what? She could not tell whether it was humour, or hatred. Vashell had lost the ability to display facial expressions. Indeed, Vashell had lost the ability to show his face.

"The wolves are coming," he said.

"How do you know?"

"I can hear them. A winter pack. White wolves. They are the worst."

"Why the worst?" Her voice seemed, to her own ears at least, incredibly small.

"Because they are the most hungry," he said, with a twisted smile that showed teeth through the holes in his cheeks.

Alloria looked away.

"They are following your scent. They must have been tracking you for hours. There's precious little meat on these bare hills."

"Then I will die," said Alloria, lifting her head, eyes blazing.

"We all die," said Vashell, turning back to the cave entrance.

Outside, there came a fast padding, and a snarl. Slowly, Vashell backed towards Alloria; his athletic frame partially blocked the cave entrance, and she suddenly realised that Vashell had no sword, only the knife which she had seen him with earlier, a blade stolen from the Engineer's Barge during his escape several days ago.

Then she saw the wolf. It was large-framed but scrawny, lean and athletic and hungry-looking; its fur was a mix of shaggy white streaked with grey and black, its eyes a wide-slitted yellow, its fangs old and yellow and curved like daggers. It was far bigger than any wolf Alloria had ever seen in Falanor, and its claws rasped on the cave's floor. It stopped, head tilted, surveying the two people. Vashell, poised, did not move. He seemed frozen to the spot – either in fear, or gauging his enemy.

Then more wolves arrived, and they were snarling and hissing, drool spooling from ancient fangs as they moved as a pack into the cave which, with its too-wide opening, allowed them in three abreast. There were five, now; then eight. Then twelve. Their fur bristled with snow melt, and each wolf had a narrowed, hungry look. A haunted look. They were willing to die in order to feed.

Alloria heard herself utter a small whimper. Vashell did not turn, but she saw his muscles tense.

The lead wolf snarled, a sudden, aggressive sound, and leapt at Vashell in a blur...

SIX
Stealers' Moon

Jageraw travelled with care, avoiding men, avoiding albino soldiers, avoiding cankers and avoiding anybody he thought might be a threat – which meant anything *alive*. The pain in his chest was worse now, and often made him gasp and he would mutter to himself, "Not pretty, not pretty," and rub at his armoured chitin as if by rubbing the area he could ease away the pain.

The canker Jageraw had saved back at Le'annath Moorkelth was gone, fled through the forest. He was an odd one that canker, yes, thought Jageraw, bitter for a moment that none wished to share his company. Did he stink? Was that it? Stink of fish? All Jageraw got out of the twisted clockwork creature was its name: Elias. Then it was gone, floundering and stamping through the forest, easy meat for soldier's crossbows yes yes. He regretted now not eating the Elias. It was a pain, spitting out the cogs, but cankers could taste quite prime.

As he moved, so he thought of the Hexels.

They had saved him.

They had honoured him.

Now, Jageraw knew his task.

Muttering, he stumbled on through forests and snow, stopping occasionally to hunt down some unsuspecting traveller or refugee, but even the slick feeling of raw kidneys or liver on his tongue, or even – the *joy!* – a succulent lung, did nothing to ease the pain in his chest. And the further north he travelled, the more the pain burned.

• • • •

It was late afternoon, sky darkening, as Kell rode his steed up a steep hill, reins in one hand, the other on the haft of his saddle-sheathed axe. He drew rein atop the summit, and Saark came up beside him, silent, considering. Mary the donkey brayed, the noise loud and echoing, and Kell threw back a bitter scowl.

"Don't even think it," said Saark.

"What?"

"She's invaluable. And Skanda is enjoying riding her. You wouldn't take such a simple pleasure from the boy?"

Kell stared hard into Saark's eyes, and what he saw there he did not understand. Kell knew that he was good at reading men, but Saark was a true conundrum. Complex, unpredictable, Kell knew deep in his heart he would make better progress if he left Saark behind. And that was the answer, he realised. Singularity.

Pain lashed through his veins, and Kell gritted his teeth, swooning in the saddle. The world blurred and reeled, and he grasped the saddle pommel with both hands, face pale, eyes squeezed shut, and focused on simply breathing as the world in its entirety swirled down in wide lazy blood circles. He heard Saark's voice, but it was a garbled, stretched out series of meaningless sounds. And in the middle of it all there was a taste, and the taste was whiskey, and he knew that if only he could have another drink then everything would be all right again, and the pain would go away again, and no matter that it made him violent because he was in a violent world on a violent mission and the whiskey would *help him* achieve his goal; waves of pain pulsed through him, and then a moment of darkness, and then he was breathing, gasping at the cold air like a drowning man coming to the surface of a lake.

The world slapped Kell in the face, and he was gasping, and Saark was asking him if he was well. Kell took several deep, exaggerated breaths, and looked right to Saark. He gave a nod. "It's the poison, lad," he managed, voice hoarse. "When she bites, she bites real hard."

"We need to rest," said Saark. "Somewhere warm, some hot food, a good sleep. We've been through a lot." He winced, clutching his wounded side instinctively. "And we stink like a ten day corpse."

"Speak for yourself," barked Kell.

"Kell?" It was Skanda. His eyes glittered. Again, now they had stopped, the scorpion sat on his hand and seemed to be watching proceedings. Kell eyed the insect uneasily, and made a mental note to tread the bastard underboot at the first opportunity.

"What is it, lad?"

"There is a village, yonder. Creggan. I have travelled there before. It is getting late, we should move."

"Where?" Both Kell and Saark squinted, looking off over gloom-laden, snowy hills which dropped in vast steps from their position, like folds in a giant's goose-down quilt.

Skanda pointed. "Come. I will show you." He reached out, and the lead between Saark's horse and Mary fell away. Skanda cantered the donkey forward, and the usually stubborn beast (on several occasions, Saark had had to practically wrestle the donkey into ambulation) obeyed Skanda without hesitation, nor braying complaint.

Saark shrugged, and Kell scowled. Skanda set off in a seemingly random direction from the high ground near the Great North Road. Saark followed, his gelding stamping and snorting steam. Kell waited for a few moments, pulled free the unmarked whiskey bottle, and drained the last few drops. He licked his lips, and despite hating himself for it, hoped to the High Gods that there was a tavern.

The village was small, a central square with hall and tavern and a few shops. All seemed closed and empty and dead on this cold winter evening, another apparent victim of the Army of Iron. Kell and Saark had Skanda wait by the outskirts as they rode in, weapons drawn, eyes wary as they searched for albino soldiers. Nobody walked the streets. Most of the houses seemed deserted.

"Has the Army of Iron been through, do you think?"

Kell shrugged, and pointed to the tavern where thin wisps of smoke eased from a ragged, uneven chimney. "I don't think so. No bodies in the road, for a start. But let us find out." He dismounted at the tavern, and thumped open the door. Inside was warm, a fire crackling in the hearth. A long bar supported three men, all stocky and dour, who jumped as the door opened, their eyes casting nervous to the intruders, hands on sword hilts. A tall, thin barman gave a nod to Kell, and Kell entered.

"Do you have rooms?"

"How many?"

"Two."

"Yes. It'll be five coppers a night. Will you be wanting warm water? 'Cos that's another copper."

"Warm water is a prerequisite to cleanliness and holiness, my man," said Saark, entering the tavern and smiling, leaning forward over ale-stained timbers.

The barman stared at the ragged, bruised, tattered dandy, without comprehension.

"He said 'yes'," grunted Kell, and dropped coins on the bar. Then to Saark, "Go and get the boy, and stable our horses."

When Saark had left, Kell eyed the barman. "You have a cosy little town, here, barman."

"And we would keep it that way. An army passed through, killing everyone in surrounding towns," his eyes were bleak, his mind full of nightmares, "of this we know. We would ask you to keep your knowledge of Creggan to yourselves. We have nowhere to run, you understand?"

Kell nodded, and ordered a whiskey, which he downed in one. Then, when Saark returned after stabling the horses and Mary, Kell pushed past him on his way to the door.

"Hey, where are you going?"

"Out."

"Out where?"

"Just out," grinned Kell, but it was a grin without humour.

"Old horse, I have a question. Why did you only purchase two rooms? A little odd, I thought."

Kell's grin widened. "You love that damn creepy Ankarok boy so much. Well. You can bunk with him. Maybe he'll stop you behaving like an idiot!"

It was later. Much later. Darkness had fallen, and with it a fresh storm of snow. Kell had returned, brushing flakes from the shoulders of his heavy bearskin jerkin, and now sat eating a meal at a corner table in the tavern. It was a pie filled mostly with potatoes, a little ham, and thick gravy. Kell also had a full loaf of black bread, which he sliced thickly, smothering each slice with butter. Skanda sat, facing Kell, eyes fixed on the old warrior, watching the man eat. On three occasions Kell had offered the boy food, but the thin-limbed urchin waved it away.

"You need something warm inside you, lad," said Kell, relaxing with a full belly, eyes kind now he was out of the cold, the wind, the snow, and immediate threat of battle. He was getting old, he realised. Damn it, he *was* old! And, thinking of their pursuit after

Nienna, he realised just how ancient and worn he really felt. To the core.

"I am not hungry," said Skanda.

"You must eat something."

"If you could ask for a little warm milk?"

Kell nodded, and called over a serving girl. She returned shortly with a cup of warm milk, and a tankard of ale for Kell. Both Kell and Skanda sat, drinking their drinks and watching the tavern gradually fill. The village of Creggan was not as deserted as it first seemed.

"Where's Saark got to?" said Kell, after a while. He was watching a group of men in the corner, and noting their ease of movement, and how they hardly touched their drinks. They seemed like military men to Kell, but one had a taint to the lips, as if he might be a blossoming Blacklipper. Blacklippers were men, and women, who had found a taste for the illegal and hard to come by *blood-oil*, so revered and necessary to the vachine. Most Blacklippers had little idea the narcotic juice they purchased was refined from human blood. Nor did they realise it was destined for a market so… esoteric: that of the vachine civilisation deep within the folds of the Black Pike Mountains. Most Blacklippers simply lived for the moment, and took their pleasure – including blood-oil – when and where they found it; the one downside, of course, being that the more a person used blood-oil, the more their lips, and eventually, fatally, their very *veins* stood out black from their skin. When a Blacklipper's veins stood out like a battlefield map in ink, one could count their remaining weeks on one hand.

Skanda sipped his milk. "He went out."

"Where to?" Kell frowned. "He said he was having a bath."

"He said he had things he needed to buy."

"Hmm," said Kell, and placed his chin on his fist. By his boot, no more than a hand-span away, Ilanna leant against the edge of the rough-sawn table. And under his left arm lay sheathed his Svian knife; usually, his last resort weapon on the few occasions he was parted from his first love. Ilanna.

The tavern was crowded now, but curiously subdued. They all know, then, thought Kell. They understand that Falanor has been invaded and they have missed the network of searching soldiers through sheer luck. No obvious roads led to Creggan. They had been overlooked. By the villagers' demeanour, they understood what would happen if a second pass came upon this little haven.

Kell's practised eye picked out that every man wore a sword, or long knife. Even the women who came in wearing thick woollen dresses and cotton shirts were armed. This was a town living in fear. It was palpable, like ash on their skin, like plague in their eyes.

Skanda finished his milk, and stood.

"Where are *you* going, lad?"

"I'm tired. I am going to sleep."

Kell nodded, and watched the thin boy weave his way through the crowded tavern. Smoke washed over him, and a serving girl approached. She asked if he wanted a drink. Kell looked down at his ale. He looked up at her. And he considered.

"Bring me a whiskey," he said at last, voice hoarse.

Saark sat in hot water, the wound in his side stinging like the fires of the Chaos Halls, his limbs bruised like a pit-fighter's, but still happy as heat flowed through his damaged flesh and aching bones. He settled back with a sigh. The stench of blood, and sweat, and dirt, of battle, of cankers, of sleeping in the forest, of albino brains and albino gore, all were scrubbed from his now pink and raw skin. And even better, he had asked around, and purchased some rich bath herbs, and perfume, none of it as fine as the scents used in the Royal Court in Vor, but a damn sight more refined than stinking of horse-sweat and death.

Saark sighed again. The water lapped the edges of the bath rimed with excised scum. He stared happily at the new clothes – clothes he knew, in his deepest of hearts, were a wasteful extravagance, and certainly not geared for travelling across the country – but still of necessity to one such as Saark. He was addicted to buying clothes and perfume as some men were addicted to whiskey, or gambling on dog fights. Because, he knew, with fine clothes and perfume matched to his natural beauty, the whole heady mix led to one thing, and one thing only: amorous meetings with pretty young ladies.

Saark closed his eyes, picturing the many women he had conquered. And yet Katrina's face kept returning, invading his imagination, pointing a finger of accusation. I am dead, she seemed to be saying. You told me you loved me. Now I rot under the soil and you *did not stop it happening*!

Mood soured by ghosts, Saark climbed from the bath and towelled himself dry. He stood, shivering a little and staring at himself in a full length brass mirror. The wound was healing in his side; it still leaked blood occasionally, but it *was* getting better. The stitches were holding fine. The swelling in his face had gone down, so he no longer looked like a horse had danced on his features, and many of his bruises had faded to yellow, and many, incredibly, had gone.

I heal fast, he thought with a smile. But not mentally, he realised, with a grimace.

He dressed, in a bright orange silk shirt with ruffles of lace around wrists and throat, and bright blue woollen leggings. He'd also bought a new *snow leopard* cloak, long down to his ankles, fine doe-leather and lined with snow leopard fur, or so he'd been told; although he doubted it. Still, it added a nice splash of white to set off the orange of his shirt. And would undoubtedly be warm on the road.

Saark draped a cord over his neck, settling a bright green pendant at his throat, and then buckled his rapier at his side. He drew the weapon, a blur flickering silver in the mirror, a stunning display of skill and accuracy; then he winced, slowly, and held his side. "Ouch," he muttered. "Not there yet, lover. Not there yet."

Leaving his old clothes in a pile for the tavern's serving girls to burn, Saark returned to his room and opened the door. Skanda was seated, on one of the narrow sparse beds, but his face was wide as if celebrating a rapturous applause, and something long, and brass, lay loose along his arm. Saark stepped inside and closed the door. He laid his cloak on a chair and moved to Skanda.

"What are you doing, boy?" he asked, voice low, words not unkind.

Skanda did not respond. His eyes were open, but there was no comprehension there. Saark's eyes travelled down to the brass object. It was old, very old and worn by its look, and quite ornate. Saark had seen similar objects in the houses of doctors when he'd had swordfight wounds stitched. It was a needle, a brass needle, used to inject fluids into the human body. This was affixed to Skanda's arm; or more precisely, his vein.

"Skanda," breathed Saark and moved as if to remove the needle. There came a rapid clicking sound, and his eyes moved fast and he leapt back. The scorpion was there, twin tails raised in threat, pincers flexing as it watched Saark with its many tiny black eyes.

Saark released a hiss of breath. "Damn disgusting little thing," he snapped, and drew his sword, eyes narrowing. "I'm going to cut you in two!" But then he understood the situation with a stab of insight. The scorpion was protecting its master.

How can that be? thought Saark. It's an insect! A poisonous little arachnid with no compassion or empathy for *anything*. Why would it protect the boy?

Slowly, Saark sheathed his sword and held out his hands. "I was simply going to remove the needle and put the boy to bed. You know? Make him more comfortable?"

The scorpion surveyed him for a few moments, then lowered its stings and scuttled back within Skanda's loose clothing. Warily, Saark pulled free the needle with a tiny squirt of blood, and put it to one side. Then he lifted Skanda onto the bed and laid him out, covering him with a thin blanket. "There you go," he muttered, and thought back to his own childhood, his father hanging by the throat, his mother screaming, and the long, long, long weeks of being utterly and totally alone.

Saark's eyes shone with tears. "I'll look after you, lad. You see if I don't," he said.

Saark reckoned he created quite a stir when he walked into the smoky, crowded tavern. The crowd certainly parted to allow him passage, and he ignored the many stares as he crossed to Kell and seated himself opposite the axeman, back to the crowd.

"What," said Kell, "in the name of horse-shit, are you wearing?"

"I call it *Orange Blossom in Winter*. I think it's quite alluring. I think the ladies are noticing me." He smiled a broad, happy smile.

"Mate, every bastard is noticing you, from the lowliest mongrel backstabbing thief to the dirtiest, sleaziest whore in the village. What the hell were you thinking, Saark?"

"I was thinking it's been awhile since I had some female company."

"I thought you were over that?"

"Kell, my friend, you do not understand men, nor women. This is not something I want; this is something I *need*. I cannot control myself, no more than you control your... your swinging axe."

"Saark, we are staying one night. What possessed you to dress like a peacock?"

"It is my way."

"And you stink! Gods, it's like you've been showered with every tart's knicker-drawer lavender bottle in the country! You'll have the bastard albino soldiers on us in an instant if you step into the wilds of Falanor stinking like that."

"You are so uncouth."

"I thought you'd overcome all this crap? I thought we were on a mission?"

"What?" Saark looked incredulous. "*What?* Overcome? You confuse, old horse. Indeed, there is nothing here for which to overcome, because this is a question of breeding, this is a question of sophistication, and this is an embodiment of culture – something intrinsic, not just learned. And, because I have been forced to endure your company and travel in extraneous hardship, just because I have been forced to sleep in shit, and eat shit, and listen to shit, does not mean I thus *crave* shit. No. You know I am used to the finer aspects of life, and despite this being a poor backward peasant village," several of the men in the tavern scowled and muttered at these brash, arrogant and loudly delivered words, "filled with dirty, low-born peasants whose only knowledge is how to feed pigs and kill chickens," he laughed, a bright tinkling of crystal windchimes, "that doesn't mean to say I have to denigrate myself to the lower echelons of a rude base society. Understand?"

"You're a horse's dick, Saark."

"I rest my case."

"Meaning?"

"When faced with superior intelligence, culture and argument, you instantly revert to the base gutter which spawned you. I do not blame you for low-born behaviour, Kell, in fact sometimes I am envious; how I wish I wasn't so beautiful, and charming, and irresistible to the ladies." Saark took this moment to have a good look around, and although his eyes lingered on several buxom wenches, the sight of their moribund attire, cracked and broken fingernails and dowdy knife-hacked hair made him turn back to Kell with a scowl and deep sigh. "However. I am cursed thus, and so must make the most of my natural endowments, and indeed, the nature of my beast. And what a beast it is."

"I'd forgotten," said Kell.

"What do you mean, old horse?"

Kell bared his teeth, and drained his tankard. "We've been through some battles, Saark lad, some hard shit, and you've proved yourself to be tougher than I anticipated. You're a good swordsman, with a strong arm and keen eye, and enough mental toughness to face any enemy."

"But?"

"But the minute you touch any form of civilisation, you regress to the pig-headed sugar-mouthed hard-cocked brainless stinking village fucking idiot I've always loathed." Saark opened his mouth, as Kell hefted his axe and stood, stool scraping the straw-covered stone flags. "And if I hear another sugar-coated pile of goat's bollocks from *you*, I'll carve my name on *your* arse." Saark's mouth closed again, and Kell stalked through the crowded tavern and stepped out into the night.

"Really!" said Saark, and grinned, then winced as the stitches in his side pulled tight. He laughed, half in pain, half in joy at this simple touch of civility. He moved round the table, taking Kell's place with his back to the wall, and noticed with surprise that quite a few of the tavern's stocky peasant farmers were throwing him dark, menacing scowls. Saark waved cheerily, and they returned their dark glances and mutters to the bar, and flat ale.

"Now, what shall I do?" murmured Saark, and rubbed his chin. It was slightly pink from shaving, but by the gods it felt good to be rid of the stubble and dirt. He had groomed his moustache carefully, using a little oil supplied by Bess, the tavern master's daughter. The rest he had rubbed into his hands and smoothed through his long, dark curls. Saark knew he cut a tall, dashing, handsome figure. But after the beating by Myriam's men, resulting in a head like a sausage-stuffed pig's stomach, he had been knocked temporarily out of the womanising game. But now... *now* most of the bruises and swelling were gone, and Saark understood the dark, smoky interior would hide any remaining blemishes. Like a cat, he was ready to play. Like a lust-fuelled bull, he was ready to charge! He grinned. Saark was back, baby, Saark was back!

His eyes wandered the room, and he drank his ale and ordered another, which he also downed. Several women looked at him, and smiled. Saark graded them silently, methodically, placing them in a mental hierarchy of whom he would bed first provided no finer lass entered the premises. Such was his confidence, and experience, it never occurred to Saark that a lady might turn him down. That was something which happened to other poor unfortunates.

So intent was Saark on scrutinising the women on display, like prime beef at a cattle market, that as he was finishing the dregs from his fourth tankard of ale two men approached. He didn't register until they were standing directly before him.

"Hello, lads," smiled Saark, placing his tankard down with a *clack*. "What can I do you for?"

"The popinjay asks what he can do for us," laughed the first man. He was big, with a round head, rough-cropped hair, large ears and ruddy cheeks. In his fist, he held a longsword, point lowered. Saark's eyes followed the blade to the ground.

"That's a good question," replied his companion. "A very good question indeed. A damn fine question, if I be honest."

"Listen," said Saark, leaning forward a little as if sharing a conspiracy, "much as I'd like to sit here and trade stunning witticisms with two grand but obsequious fellows, who are both obviously the core intellectual firecrackers of this entire inbred ensemble, I really feel I must rise and circulate in order to integrate with the finer female brethren contained within this squalid den of congenital primates."

"You see," said the first man. "There he goes again. Spouting all that crap. Horseshit, I says it is."

"Aye. And he stinks like horseshit, as well." Then to Saark. "You hear that, boy? You stink like horseshit."

Saark sighed, and there came a little tearing sound. One of the men yelped, and went rigid. Saark's eyes were suddenly dark, and contained less humour, and his face and dandy clothing seemed somehow just that bit less ridiculous. "That little prick you feel against your leg, my friend – and I can *tell* you're a man who enjoys feeling little pricks against his leg – well, it's the point of my rapier. Let me assure you, my weapon is tempered from finest Jevaiden steel, and probably cost more than this entire village; indeed, I spend a good half hour a day keeping it sharp ready for the hour I need to teach some uncouth big-eared boy a lesson. Now, I'd advise you not to move quickly because the point is a single twitch from slitting your femoral artery – that's the main one, which runs through your groin and will empty your pathetic body of blood in less than two minutes." Saark leaned forward. His eyes glittered. "I've killed thirty eight men with that cut. Not a single man didn't writhe and scream like his intestines were filled with molten lead. You hearing me nice and clear, village idiot?"

Both men nodded, and stepped warily back from the dandy. Their faces had turned pale.

Saark stood, and sheathed his rapier, and turned his back on them with a show of contempt. He glanced once again around the room. His face displayed open disappointment at the sport on offer. Saark sighed, and strode to the door. The smoke, and perhaps a little too much ale, were making him dizzy, with the added consequence of polluting his new finery with a stink like a tobacconist's smoking shed. He stepped out into the night, pulling his snow-leopard cloak tight around his shoulders and looked up into the falling snow. He leant his back against the wall and took several deep breaths, head spinning a little. Damn the grog! he thought, hand on sword-hilt.

"Hello," came a voice, a female voice, and Saark found himself staring at a tall, lithe, robed figure. In the darkness the robe seemed to glimmer like velvet, and from the edges of the hood he could see bright blonde hair, a fan of translucence. She was a little taller than Saark, but rather than intimidate, this excited him. She held herself erect with a natural nobility, and her half-shadowed features were finely sculpted, high chiselled cheekbones, flawless skin and dark, half-hidden eyes.

"Well, hello there," smiled Saark, and stroked his chin, and wondered suddenly at the capriciousness of life, the gods, and most importantly, women. "What's a pretty thing like you doing out on a cold, dark, snow-laden night like this? Surely, you must allow me to escort you somewhere warm where you might partake of drying your fine, moonlit-shadowed hair, and maybe partake of some fine Gollothrim brandy distilled from ripe plums and cherries teased from the superlative orchards of the south."

"Oh, you speak so fine and handsome, sir. You are not from these parts?"

"Alas, no, simply riding through. But I think you may entice me to return! You live here, no?"

"My parents are dead. I spend some time with my uncle in Jangir, the rest here with my aunt. She has a small farmstead."

"Wonderful! Is it nearby?"

"A goodly trek, sir. But what of this brandy of which you speak?" She moved closer, and Saark smelt her musk. It infected him, immediately, like a heady liquor injected to his vein, a toxic narcotic injected to his brain. If I die tonight after enjoying this fabulous woman, I would die a happy man, thought Saark, as he moved close to her and her eyes were still hooded and he reached out, stroked away a stray strand of hair and she giggled, and he leant forward, intoxicated by alcohol and her scent and their lips touched, the briefest of intimations, a promise of flesh and excitement to come. The woman turned away, a teasing, calculated movement which was not lost on the dandy. He enjoyed it. It was all part of the game.

Oh, thought Saark, you're good; you're very good.

"My room is this way," said Saark, gesturing to the tavern.

"It would be unseemly for me to trudge through the tavern common-room. Is there a… more discrete entrance?"

"I'm sure we will find one, my sweet," purred Saark, and reaching out he took her arm and they moved through the snow, and he said, "What is your name, my princess?"

"My name is Shanna," she whispered, voice husky with an anticipation of impending violence.

Saark moved to the bed, and lowered the wick on the lantern. He had taken the woman to Kell's room – after all, the boy Skanda was sleeping deeply in their shared quarters, and Saark knew the old goat wouldn't be needing his bed. Well, not for the intimacies of a lady, at any rate. The ambient air was filled with warmth, and positive energy, and the scent of Shanna which seemed to take Saark and spin him up and around in a frenzy of need and recklessness. He breathed deeply, and Shanna moved to the bed, and lowered her hood, and removed her cloak. She wore a short, white dress, and Saark moved to her and placed his hands on her shoulders and she murmured, a little in pleasure, a little in lust, a little in need, and Saark kissed the pale skin of her neck, kissed through her fine blonde hair and she wriggled in his embrace as if he tickled her, pleasured her, and it was all like a dream seen through a distorted piece of glass. Saark stepped away, panting. "You are beautiful and luscious indeed," he said, and kicked off his boots.

Shanna moved to the lantern, and lowered it more. When she looked up at him, her eyes were dark, like pools of liquid ruby. Her face was gaunt, but stunningly beautiful. When she smiled, Saark melted like butter in a pan. He groaned, and moved to her again, and kissed her, and his arms were over her and touching her, and she writhed under his touch in lustful agony and then took his head, suddenly, in a powerful grip and stared deep into his eyes.

"I think I am in heaven," whispered Saark.

"You soon will be," promised Shanna, and there came twin crunches as her fangs ejected and her head dropped for his throat and a fist of insanity punched through Saark's mind – but not enough to inhibit twenty-five years of military training and real-world combat. Saark swayed back, twisting fast, stepped back and away in shock; then he leapt at her, both boots slamming Shanna's chest and using the impact to kick himself backwards, through a somersault to land lightly on his feet by the door, facing her.

Shanna's hands had come up to her chest, head tilted, the smile still on her lips. There was no pain. Now, her visage was one of mock disappointment. "What? You would spurn me so soon, my beautiful and verbally sophisticated lover?"

Saark cast his gaze past Shanna, to where his rapier stood – useless – by the window. He grinned, a nasty sideways grin without humour as his hands levelled before him, and he stared at the vachine and took a step to the left. Shanna followed his direction with intimacy, and eased towards him.

"You would have bitten me," he said, eyes fixed on her long fangs, and then on her eyes, and he cursed himself. Her eyes were crimson, the red of the albino warriors who hunted them. And yet she had fangs, like the vachine creatures from beyond the mountains. "What the hell *are* you?"

"You wouldn't understand, Saark, my sweet," she said, and lunged at him.

Saark swayed to one side, and cracked a right hook against her cheek, spinning away to the other side of the room. Shanna touched her face, lower lip extending a little. She pouted.

"A little excessive, Saark, don't you think?"

Only then did he realise he had not told her his name. Something chilled inside him. Some primordial instinct told him this woman, or vachine, or whatever the hell she was, was very, very dangerous. And she was looking for him. Hunting him.

Shanna leapt again, and blocked three fast punches. She grabbed his throat and groin in one swift movement, and hurled Saark across the room where he hit the wall, hard, and landed in a heap, wheezing, head spinning, and then she was there, kneeling beside him, and she took hold of his long fine oiled curls and snapped back his head in a vicious movement. From the corner of his eye he saw her fangs extend that little bit more. They gleamed, like brass.

"You're going to taste so sweet, my love," she smiled, completely aware of the irony.

"No," he croaked... as her fangs dropped for his throat.

Kell marched through the snow, boots crunching, the glass of the whiskey bottle cold against his skin under heavy jerkin. He stopped at a narrow crossroads, and looked about. The village was quiet, eerie, dusted with mist and falling snow, most houses sporting lights subdued behind heavy curtains. The villagers knew what would happen if soldiers from the Army of Iron discovered their little safe haven, tucked away between low hills; and they guarded their anonymity with jealous fear and an understanding of a savage retribution if discovered. Wise, he thought. Very wise.

Kell looked up and down the twisting lanes, his breath steaming. He took out the whiskey bottle. He took a long drink. Honey eased into his veins. He thought of Nienna, he felt bad, and he knew if he got drunk he was doing nobody any favours, least of all his poor, kidnapped granddaughter. He knew, then, what he really *should* do was hurl the bottle down the street and go and get his horse and ride after her to the Cailleach Fortress. But he did not. He felt his mind crumbling, disintegrating, like a mud wall before a spring flood.

He started off down a narrow street, unsure of where he was going. The whiskey tasted good on his lips, hot in his throat, and he craved more. Much more. He knew, as did all drinkers, that he could use the excuse of the poison in his veins; however, deep in his heart he realised he was only cheating himself. He needed no whiskey to cover that pain. The pain he could live with. He had lived with worse; much worse. The reality was: he needed the whiskey, because *he needed the fucking whiskey*. It was that simple.

Kell stopped. Squinted. "It cannot be," he muttered and moved to the end of the street. He barked a short laugh, and ran his hand through his beard, and then through his shaggy grey-streaked hair. "Well, I'll be damned." And he recognised the beautiful irony. If the poison went too far through his veins, seeped into his organs and heart, then he really would be damned.

It was a distillery, a long, low building built with its back against a wall of rough-hewn rock carved from a steep hillside. The windows were dark, like torn out eye-sockets. Several were smashed. Behind, in what Kell presumed was a courtyard, squatted the old boilerhouse chimney, appearing far from the best of health. Kell assumed the distillery was long out of use. His eyes gleamed. I wonder if they left any casks behind? he mused, and laughed. Of course they didn't. Only a madman would do that.

Kell moved to the door, and forced it open. He placed his half-empty whiskey bottle in the long pocket of his jerkin, and with Ilanna in both hands, stepped inside.

It was gloomy, but a little starlight from shattered clouds filtered through a broken roof, a cold silver light which emphasised shapes without giving any real form or sense of solidity. Kell squinted, and his eyes adjusted, and he smiled. He was in the tun-room, and as he walked forward realised the distillery building *dropped* beneath him allowing for a double-height interior, but nestled in what appeared a single-storey shell. It was housed in an excavation. Kell stopped, boots rasping, and peered down from the walkway on which he stood. Beneath, he could see large, solid lids for the circular wash-backs. His eyes moved, counting. There were six below ground level, and six above, surrounded by an iron frame and timber gantries. Kell tested the handrail, and it crumbled beneath his powerful fingers. He grunted.

"What a waste! Letting a fine building like this rot and die."

He walked between the wash-backs and stopped, warily, beside a rail which overlooked a lower section of the distillery reached by twin sets of iron stairs. His eyes took in the wash chargers and wash-stills, with their odd copper shapes which looked as if they'd half melted, the metal sloping towards the floor like molten candle-wax, only to harden again. They look like garlic bulbs, he thought, and took another drain of whiskey. He grunted at the continued irony. The only bloody whiskey in this entire place was the cheap, nasty blend he carried in his paws.

"Damn it. What I'd give for a single malt."

Outside, the world seemed to flood into darkness. Clouds, passing over the stars and moon. Kell squinted, for despite having incredibly acute vision, he knew age was getting the better of him and his eyesight was not as good as it once was. "I can still pin a wolf to a tree at fifty paces with my axe," he muttered, and stared down at the steps. They looked far too dangerous to descend. But beyond, he knew, was the warehouse. Would it have barrels of whiskey? He doubted it. But if there *was* some nectar stored there, it called to him, taunting, drawing him as if down some invisible umbilical.

No.

"No."

Kell took a deep breath. His fists clenched, and he stared at the bottle in his hands. It was poison, he decided. And it would kill him faster than Myriam's injected toxin.

You used to have strength, he realised.

You used to have willpower.

Once, you could have stopped. Once, you would have cast away the piss. Once, you would have been a man. A man who ruled the bottle, instead of the bottle ruling his world.

Kell hurled the whiskey bottle out over the spirit-stills, and there came a mighty *boom* followed by a clattering, skittering sound. Then silence rushed back in, like the ocean filling a hole.

"Interesting," came a gentle, feminine voice.

Kell did not turn. His senses screamed. The hairs across the back of his neck prickled, and he forced a grin between tight teeth. He reached up, and slowly rubbed his beard. "The fact that I chose to launch the bottle, or the fact that you were sneaking through the dark?"

"Neither," she said. "I was told you were dangerous, and I was simply pondering the best way to kill a fat old man."

Kell turned, Ilanna in both hands now. His eyes narrowed, and he took in the tall, lithe albino woman, her crimson eyes, her brass fangs, the silver sword sheathed at her hip. She moved elegantly, and stopped, one hip pushed forward slightly giving her an arrogant, defiant stance. She had a gaunt face, and cropped white hair. She was pretty. Dake's Balls, thought Kell, she was beautiful – but maybe forty years his junior. He grinned. "I don't die that easy," he rumbled, rolling his shoulders almost imperceptibly to loosen the muscles.

"But I'm sure that you do," she smiled, and drew her sword.

"That's what the other vachines said," he soothed, head dropping a little, eyes now pools of blackness. He was pleased to note the annoyance in her expression; not just at his recognition, and knowledge, but at his tone of voice. His was not a sermon of arrogance; his was the voice of a known truth.

"Do you want to know my name?" she purred stepping forward. Beneath her, the gantry creaked and Kell looked warily to one side.

"Not really," he said. "You fucking vachine all smell the same to me; decayed flesh, hot oil, and mangled clockwork."

She snarled, a bestial sound far from human. Her fangs slid out yet more, with tiny *crunches*. "My name is Tashmaniok. I am going to sup your blood, Kell. I'm going to savour it running down my throat. I am going to taste your most intimate dreams. I am going to drink your soul. I will lead you to the brink of despair, to a razor-edge of desolation, and you will teeter there like a maggot on a hook and then, only then, when you beg for death, when you plead with me for release... only then will I show you *real* pain."

Kell grunted. "Stop talking. Show me." But even as the words left on a hot exhalation of air she leapt, a sudden striking blur, and Kell's axe lifted deflecting the sword blow with only a hair's breadth between life and death. He stepped forward, mighty axe swinging, to deflect a second, then third blow – and as sparks flew, so the axe twisted, reversed, and swept close to Tashmaniok's face causing her to leap back.

Kell grinned at her. "You're quick, pretty one, I'll grant you that. But you talk a whole bucket of clockwork shit. Be careful, lest I spill your ticking gears over the gantry."

Tash said nothing, but lowered her head and attacked, her sword flickering in a stunning series of frenetic bursts, showing dazzling skill and a precision Kell had rarely met in a human. But then, Tashmaniok was far from human. She was vachine.

Kell deflected the blows, struggling, sweat beading on his skin, but the whiskey was numbing his brain, and so much recent fighting had tired his mighty muscles. Blow after blow he halted, sparks showering the old distillery, only for Tash to twist her blade and attack again; slowly, Kell was forced back to the iron steps leading *down*.

Tash paused, head high, eyes gleaming. She twirled her sword, experimentally, as if loosening her wrist after a brisk warm-up session. She showed no fatigue. By comparison, Kell was sweating heavily, and he felt sick. He could taste bad whiskey and old bile. Doubt flared in his breast, but he quelled it savagely. Now was not a time for doubt. He had killed better than Tashmaniok. He had killed far better.

"You're good, girl," he said. "But I reckon you should work on your speed. I've seen one-legged whores move faster than you."

Tash smiled, with genuine humour. She lifted her head a little, and some distant beam of starlight caught her eyes, which sparkled. "Old man. Save your breath for battle. For I've not seen anything special as of yet; and to think, they call you a Vachine Hunter."

She's answered that question, thought Kell sourly. She was sent by General Graal. Their little war party had not escaped so easily. Indeed, Kell realised, now Graal felt it was personal. An intuition told him things had changed; strangely, Kell felt like Graal *wanted* something. But what the hell did he want other than Kell's head on a plate? What could Kell offer the warped general?

Tash stepped forward, fluid, sword singing a figure of eight; Kell slammed his axe horizontal, and Tash did something with her sword, a technique Kell had never before experienced. His axe clattered off down the walkway behind her, and Kell felt something large and dark fall through him, like a rock down a well. He stood, stunned for a moment, and Tash moved fast leaping, both boots slamming his chest. With a grunt Kell staggered back and fell from the steps, rolling violently down the rattling, iron construct to lie, stunned and bleeding, at the foot.

Kell groaned, and pushed himself up, then slumped to his chest once more. He rolled onto his back, tasting blood, and watched Tashmaniok walk lightly down the iron staircase. She strode, stood over him, her body framed by the sculpted shapes of spirit-stills in the gloom. Dust motes floated in the air from Kell's pounding descent, and he coughed, clutching his diaphragm, face contorted in pain.

Tash twirled her sword once more, humour on her lips. But her crimson eyes were hard. Like glittering rubies.

"Graal told me to be careful," she murmured, and lowered herself to one knee, so that she straddled him. Kell could smell her natural perfume. She smelt good.

"Aye?" he growled.

"But I don't understand why. You're nothing but a whisky-drunk old man who's seen better days." She lifted her sword high in both hands, and Kell watched the silver blade without emotion. His eyes were dark, like the soul of a canker.

Tash twitched, and her sword plunged down.

SEVEN
The Cailleach Fortress

Nienna watched Styx advance, wintry moonlight glinting on his dagger. His cock was a narrow worm in the moonlight, and she realised with a start she had aroused him. Or her vulnerability had. She bared her teeth in a snarl. I'll bite it off, she thought, and images of blood descended into her mind and she knew, knew she was not strong enough to take on this man, this escaped prisoner, this *killer* but she would make him suffer, she damn well knew, and she would make him wish he'd never met her.

Styx dropped to his knees on the ground, and Nienna cringed, but she played on her fear and exaggerated her suffering and weakness, for it allowed him to grow confident and close – and then she would strike, like a viper. Styx shuffled closer, knife before him, but she could see him falling into lust and she had seen that look before, on the faces of college boys during their first encounter with a woman. They lost control. They lost intelligence. By the Bone Halls, they lost everything that made them attractive in the first place!

Nienna stayed still, like a frightened mouse.

Styx's scent overpowered her before his physicality; he stunk, of sweat, of sword oil, of excrement, of bad teeth and bad breath and the blood-oil which stained his lips from the inside out, like a parasitical disease.

He was panting. His knife lowered. His eyes half closed as he lusted towards her, lips puckered, and she hit him with a right hook, just like her grandfather had shown her, her weight dropped into it, power from the shoulder, all her strength and weight and might and hatred and fury and fear powered into that single devastating blow which rocked Styx back on his heels – and made him open his eyes, and laugh at her.

Nienna's mouth dropped open.

Styx lifted the blade. "For that, bitch, I'm going to cut you up."

Nienna felt piss trickle down her legs, and she knew she was doomed and dead and worse; a slave to this terrible man.

Something appeared from nowhere, a blur, a wrist-thick length of wood which connected with the side of Styx's head. Blood and saliva showered from his mouth, along with a tooth, and in slow motion Nienna watched him writhe sideways, body a jellied doll, and hit the earth unconscious. He twitched, and lay still.

Myriam loomed from the darkness. She stood over Styx, face contorted in rage. The tree branch descended again, smacking Styx's head so hard the wood disintegrated in her hands, separating into three discrete sections which tumbled to the earth.

Nienna sat, hands clasping frozen roots, unable to speak.

"Come here, child," said Myriam.

Nienna obeyed, scrambling to her feet to stand, staring down at Styx. Blood ran from his ear. His lips were fluttering, and blue. Nienna looked up at Myriam, who placed a protective hand on Nienna's shoulder.

"Have you killed him?"

"I hope so."

"You could stab him?"

Myriam spun Nienna around, and crouched, staring into her eyes. "Child, this is no place to murder an unconscious man. I have done... terrible things. In my past. In my life. Things so awful you could never comprehend. However. You might not believe this, but I still have some pride. Styx did something bad here tonight; but I have given him a warning – a final warning. If he wishes to take it further, then I will kill him. It's that simple. He obeys my rules, or he's food for the maggots."

She stood. Nienna stared up at her, but said nothing. Then Nienna tilted her head. "Are you in pain?"

"What?" snapped Myriam, eyes scanning the dark woodland.

"You look like you're in pain. It's in your face. In your eyes. All the time. I don't understand."

"Yes," hissed Myriam, eyes narrowed. "I am in constant pain. The gods have decided I am their plaything; they have a task for me, and if I do not succeed then I die, I die soon, I die in great agony, I die horribly. Why, little chicken, what's it to you?" She forced a smile, through her rage, to take the sting from her words. But Nienna could still see the low-level bright agony, like a fishing-line through her face, through her brain, and it reached out to Nienna. To her empathy. She could not bear to see somebody suffer.

"Where do you hurt?"

"Walk with me. Back to the camp," said Myriam. As she walked, she sighed. "It hurts everywhere, little one. In my muscles, in my bones; in my head, in my belly, in my groin."

"Should I rub your muscles?"

Vehemence flared in Myriam for a few moments, like exploding lava erupting into the ocean, but mentally she calmed herself. She hated pity. But this was not pity; this was empathy. A different breed entirely.

Myriam sighed. Nobody had touched her in years. "That would be… odd," she said, and tilted her head. "But welcome, I think."

They reached the camp. Jex was sharpening his sword. He glanced up. "Did you find him?"

"Found him and warned him," said Myriam. "Go and see to him, if you like."

"I will. We may need his skill if we meet any of those albino bastards. With just two of us, it would be foolhardy indeed." Myriam nodded, and watched Jex lope off through the woods.

"Dawn is coming," she said, and moved to the fire, throwing on a few more logs. Sparks danced. "Come and sit."

Nienna moved to Myriam, and as the tall woman sat, stretching her legs out, lifting her head with a groan, Nienna moved behind her, and placed hands on shoulders. "My grandfather taught me this," she said. She began to squeeze Myriam's muscles, and felt knots of tension there. Myriam might look cool and relaxed, but she was a tense mess of taut muscle and rigid fear. Nienna closed her eyes, and allowed her hands to follow the flow, to kneed Myriam's neck and shoulders easing away tension. For a while she rubbed, and probed, and stroked, and when she opened her eyes Myriam groaned, a low ululation of almost ecstasy.

"Is it helping?" asked Nienna.

"It is wonderful," said Myriam, and turned, looking back at the girl. "It's been too long since I was touched." Then she laughed, and shook her head, her short black hair laced with sweat. "Forgive me. Ignore me. I am foolish."

Nienna saw the tears in Myriam's eyes, but wisely decided not to comment. Instead, she analysed the harsh, gaunt features, the sunken eyes, the thin white scars, the brutality of ravaged flesh. Here was a woman close to death, realised Nienna. And yet, she was a killer. She had poisoned Nienna, and Kell; did she not deserve to die? And Nienna realised. Myriam simply wanted what everybody in the world wanted. Life. A simple basic necessity, the one thing so many seemed to take for granted, the one primal commodity so many pissed against the wall with their pointlessness, their pettiness, their crime and greed and self-pity. Life. So huge, and yet so undervalued at the same time.

"What are you thinking?" whispered Myriam, her eyes locked on Nienna and there were tears in her eyes. She grinned, a young, girlish grin, and tilted her head and for a moment Nienna saw sunshine, saw youth and vitality and beauty and it all faded, crumbled into a pan of disintegration leaving Myriam's savaged face as an encore.

"I am thinking you were once pretty," said Nienna.

"And I'm thinking she'll soon be dead," snarled Styx, who'd staggered forward, blood soaking his hair, covering his face, to lean against a tree. In one hand he held a Widowmaker. Behind him, Jex stood, sword drawn, eyes unforgiving.

"So you both turn against me?" said Myriam.

"You've taken it too far with the girl," said Jex. "She's just another plaything; just like all the others. And they never bothered you before, woman. They never *got to you* before. You should have let Styx fuck her, have his fun. We would have dealt with Kell when he arrived. You are wrong about this situation, Myriam. You have changed."

"What?" she laughed, easily, fluid, eyes never leaving the Widowmaker. "I have not changed! This is about ownership, or leadership; I've got both of you bastards out of many a tight situation. Without me, you'd still be in jail. Rotting."

"Aye," nodded Styx, "that is correct. But now we're going to kill you. And take the girl. Rape her, and peel her skin from her screaming, twitching limbs. We'll have such fun, such sweet fun; she'll dance a jig a'right. Then kill her, as well, and bury her for the worms to feast. And you know something else, Myriam?"

"Surprise me," said Myriam, voice low.

"I might just fuck you. Aye. Give you one last farewell going over, before the cancer – or my knife – steals that which you think is so precious. You want to live, Myriam my sweet?" He grinned, showing stubs of teeth through black stained lips which glistened with spit. "Do you want to live, bitch?"

"Life is precious," whispered Myriam.

"So is death," snarled Styx, and lurched forward, fresh blood pumping down his bruised face, free hand flexing, the Widow-maker held high and pointed at Myriam's face. His eye was narrowed and filled with death. Behind Myriam, Nienna cowered in abject fear.

There came a *slam*, and the top of Styx's head exploded, his entire upper cranium removed in the blink of an eye by a steel-tipped black bolt. A shower of skull and brains rained down. Blood washed down Styx's face, the expression stunned for a moment, then he slammed down on the frozen soil of the woodland carpet.

Myriam lifted her own Widowmaker from between her legs, where it was concealed by her loose cotton shirt. She pointed it at Jex, and the tattooed man had gone pale despite his ink; he dropped his sword, and lifted both hands, palms outwards, showing submission.

"He was right," said Myriam, her voice a bitter epitaph. "Death is also precious. All death. Why did you do it, Jex? Why did you turn on me? We had something... special, here."

"He offered me more," came the short man's reply. He shrugged, eyes glittering, and smiled. "But now the odds have turned against him. Put down the 'Maker, Mirry. You know you don't want to do this, we've been through way too much." He looked at Styx's exploded head, which glistened crimson in a pool of blood. "Just like I *know* you didn't want to do that."

"Take your shit, and leave," said Myriam.

Jex eyed her for a while, then stooped, lifting his sword and sheathing the weapon. He shrugged again, turned, and drifted through the trees. Myriam released a long, shuddering breath, and sat back down, the Widowmaker loose between trembling fingers.

"He would have killed you," said Nienna, touching Myriam's shoulder.

"I know that! It's just – we go back. Way back. We went through some hellish times together, child. A world you would never understand." She turned and stared at Nienna. "It's not the killing that bothers me. I've killed priests with their baubled knickers round their ankles. No. It's the loss. The betrayal. I don't understand it." She laughed then, and climbed wearily to her feet, rubbing at her eyes. She stared off through the woods, which grew light with the approach of dawn. "It shouldn't have ended like this," she whispered. "We should have been stronger."

"Myriam?" Nienna reached out, touching her arm.

Myriam whirled, her face a mask of snarling animal hatred. The Widowmaker was high, pointing at Nienna's face. "Don't touch me!" she snarled. "If you touch me again, I'll remove your damn face!" With that, she stalked off through the woods leaving a shocked and chalk-white Nienna staring at the slowly cooling corpse of Styx.

Nienna sat for a long time. She watched Styx stiffen. She had never seen death like this before, close up, casual; she had never before been the spiritual prisoner of a corpse.

I should like this, she thought.

I should be filled with joy.

She pictured Katrina's face. Styx had murdered her; cut short the young woman's blossoming life. This was her revenge! This was her moment! A time for Nienna to internalise emotions and find some kind of closure.

It should have been wonderful! thought Nienna.

However, if this is revenge, why does it feel so wrong?

Eventually, she stood and stretched and moved to the packs the group had carried. Nearby, a horse whinnied. Nienna rummaged around until she found some small, hard oatcakes. She sat back on a log and ate, slowly, with small rabbit bites. As she ate, her gaze dropped, lower and lower, past Styx's shocked and destroyed face, past his narcotic-stained lips, to the Widowmaker lying on the frozen ground with his fingers still curled around the stock. Nienna continued to eat. Would it be hard to use? she thought. How hard could it be?

She stood, finishing the food. Myriam's voice cut through Nienna's thoughts of escape.

"Don't be fooled," came her softly spoken words. "It takes weeks of practice. And against somebody like me, with a deadly eye, the steady hand and eye of the hunter, and a killing edge you could never possess?" Myriam stepped forward from the shadow of the trees. "Well girl, you'd die real quick."

"I wasn't thinking…"

"Shh." Myriam held up a single finger. "Sort through Styx's pack. Save anything you think you can use, dump the rest here. We're riding out."

"I thought we were waiting for Kell?" said Nienna, her voice small.

"We will. At the Cailleach Fortress."

"I thought you said it was haunted?"

Myriam grinned, her face skeletal, and gaunt with the cancer. "We'd better make a pact with the ghosts, child; for if Jex comes back, we'll need a fortress to fend him off. He's a warrior of great skill."

"Kell will kill him," said Nienna, hope bright in her eyes.

"Maybe," said Myriam, gathering her bow. "Maybe."

They rode through a winter landscape, down narrow unmarked tracks and threading between wooded hills. Myriam knew the trails and paths like the back of her hand; never once did she falter when they reached a fork or series of scattered trails. Nienna, riding on Styx's horse, contemplated making a break for it often, but the Widowmaker hanging close by Myriam's right hand, and indeed her skill with her yew longbow, made her think twice. Myriam told Nienna the short clockwork-powered crossbow could kill at a hundred paces; Nienna didn't want to find out the hard way.

As night approached, so did the Black Pike Mountains. They were huge, rearing from beyond the summit of a hill as they breached the rise on steaming mounts. Nienna coughed a gasp. She had seen the Black Pikes, but never this close; and when she saw the reality of their massive, stunning, brooding mass, the sheer weight of their squat and terrifying majesty, all thoughts of exploring them with student classmates went the way of campfire smoke.

"They are truly… stunning," said Nienna, almost lost for words.

"They are deadly," said Myriam, drawing rein. Her mount snorted, stamping cold, and she calmed the beast with soothing words in his ear. She gestured, with a broad sweep of her arm. "The Black Pike Mountains, thousands of leagues of impassable treachery. There is no forgiveness there, Nienna. Only hardness, and a willingness to see you die."

"One day, my friend and I were going to explore the passes. We were going to climb to Hawk's Peak. It is said to be beautiful beyond belief. We were going to camp, and paint the beauty of the scene in oils to show our friends back at university."

Myriam snorted a laugh. "Paint? Girl, Hawk's Peak is a place of wolves and bears, of bandits and blood-oil smugglers. There is beauty, I'll grant you, but there is only one guarantee; death for the unwary."

"You have been there?"

"I have travelled much in the Black Pikes."

"So has my grandfather."

"This, I know," said Myriam, eyes glittering. "It is why I need him so. Come on. We need to make camp. I can feel more snow in the air, and if it rolls down from the Pikes we'll wish we had a roof over our heads."

They made camp that night by a tumble of boulders, and Myriam cooked venison over the fire on a spit. Fat sizzled, dripping into the flames, and Nienna watched, entranced.

"Never seen meat cook before?" asked Myriam, sitting with her legs spread wide, her quiver of arrows before her, checking the length and integrity of each shaft, the quality of each tip, the helical fletching of each arrow so they would rotate in flight.

"When I lived with my mother, we never ate meat."

"Why not?"

Nienna shrugged. "She thought it was inhumane."

"How odd," said Myriam, frowning. "Animals are there to be eaten. They have no other use. What the hell did you eat, then, child?"

"Can you stop calling me child? I have seen seventeen winters pass."

Myriam grinned, and her gaunt face looked almost friendly. Almost. "Habit. And compared to me, or rather, compared to the horrors I have witnessed for the past decade, you are indeed a child; shall we say, a child of innocence? However. What did you eat?"

"Bread. Vegetables. Roots. Mushrooms."

"What a veritable platter of delights you must have enjoyed. What about succulent meat compressing between your teeth, juices running down your throat and chin, what about the perfect flavour of roasted venison?" She pulled out her knife, and cut a slice from the roasting spit. She held out the knife to Nienna. "Go on. Enjoy."

Nienna ate the venison, and it was indeed a dream. She had eaten meat, of course; sometimes with Katrina, or occasionally at Kell's when the grizzled old warrior had enough coin. But it was usually dried beef, softened in soup. Nothing as fresh and mouth-watering as this.

"It's good, yes?" grinned Myriam.

"Very good."

"See! You are my prisoner, and yet you have never feasted so well."

Nienna looked down, then up, into Myriam's eyes. "Why did you poison me?" she said, slowly, after a long connection. "Why did you poison my grandfather? I never did get a straight answer. You were too busy tying me to a tree."

The humour left Myriam's face. She cut herself a strip of venison, and chewed the tip as she stared into the flames. "You have heard of the vachine," she said. It was not a question.

"A tale to frighten children," said Nienna, carefully. Once, in Jalder, only a few weeks previous but feeling like a thousand years, she and her friends had laughed about the Old Tales, the Days of Blood, and the Legend of Three – the Vampire Warlords! And, of course, the *vachine*. Ghosts from the mountains. But that had been before the invasion of the Army of Iron; that had been before the albino warriors, and Nienna witnessing the cankers. She shivered, even as she thought of the huge, terrifying beasts. Surely, in a world that contained cankers, an ancient race that drank the blood of humans was not so hard to believe?

"They exist. In a place called Silva Valley. I believe they can make me well again, I believe their vachine clockwork technology can cure the cancers inside me."

"Clockwork technology? So that is how the vachine work?"

"They drink blood-oil. Refined blood. It is blessed with a dark magick. It is what makes the clockwork *work*. Without blood-oil, the vachine break down; they perish."

"And you would become one of these creatures? Just to stay alive?"

"Would you rather *die*?" hissed Myriam, suddenly. "Would you rather crawl under the earth, have the worms eat your eyes? You watched Styx die earlier today. Was there joy in that? Pleasure? Or are the wolves and maggots even now feasting on his corpse?"

"But surely we go somewhere… *better*, after we die."

Myriam gave a savage laugh. "You want to live with the gods? You want to travel the Elysium Halls? It is a dark comedy, Nienna, told to soldiers to make them fight in battle. There are no Halls for the Heroes. There are no rivers of nectar, no fountains of wine, no Eternal Feasts of the Martyrs. It's all a dark, savage sham."

Nienna remained silent. She did not agree with Myriam. Because, if there was nothing after life, then what reason *was there* for life? There had to be something better. Something more noble. Or it would mean people... like her father, and her best friend Katrina... it meant their deaths had been a bitter, final end.

"Why poison us, then?" persisted Nienna, eventually, after she had watched the passion slowly ebb from Myriam's cheek.

Myriam cut another slice of venison, and ate it thoughtfully. "Kell has travelled to Silva Valley. He knows the vachine."

"What? My grandfather?"

"Aye. Your grandfather."

"He would have told me," said Nienna, after a thoughtful pause.

Myriam grinned. "Told you everything, has he?"

"I know he was in the army. And I know he went through the Black Pike Mountains. But – *knows* the vachine? I don't understand?"

"He knows them, because he worked for the king; an elite group, under King Searlan, the mighty Battle King. They hunted down and destroyed vachine. They were assassins, Nienna." Her voice was soft. Her eyes glowed like jewels by the light of the fire, fuelled by passion, and a need to save her own life. "Kell knows the vachine better than any man alive; for to kill something as deadly as vachine, you have to understand it. And Kell understood them all right."

"My grandfather was no assassin," said Nienna, voice firm.

"Well, you can ask him when he arrives. For he has only days. The poison will be biting him now; he will be suffering, a great pain in his veins, in his muscles, in his bones. The worse the pain gets, the more he will strive to save himself."

"Then, why do I feel no such pain?" said Nienna, suddenly, sharply.

Myriam gave a small shrug, staring into the fire.

"It was a *lie*," whispered Nienna, eyes wide, as sudden understanding flooded her. "You told him I had been poisoned to make him come here! That was... evil!"

Myriam shrugged again. "I thought the trophy of his own life might not be enough. However you, my sweet little apple," she reached forward and cupped Nienna's chin, "you are precious enough to be worth saving."

Nienna shook her head, disengaging Myriam's grasp. "You are evil," she repeated, her eyes narrowed.

Myriam stood and stretched, a languorous movement of long limbs. She was every inch the hunter; the killer. "Maybe so. But my priority lies with myself, so don't get too high and mighty, *child*. At the end of the day, you're simply a bartering tool and to me, worth more than my soul."

"It must be savage to live in your world," said Nienna, her face dark thunder.

"Indeed it is." Myriam's face was twisted and sour. "I welcome you to try it, sometime."

They rode for long, silent hours, hooves clopping through hard-packed snow, wrapped in blankets and furs against the cold of a now mercilessly chilling winter. It was late afternoon as they appeared from the edge of scattered deciduous woodland to see the full majesty of the Black Pike Mountains rearing before them. Whereas under the woodland canopy they had been afforded glimpses, nothing had prepared Nienna for the sheer exhilaration of the Pikes.

The books and stories told of at least three thousand peaks, each a jagged tooth in a maw which split the land in two; not a single peak was under two thousand feet in height, whereas many topped seven and eight thousand, where the air was thin and crevasses seemingly endless. There were few paths which led into the Black Pikes, and of those who discovered a route, few returned. It was said all manner of creatures lived in those echoing valleys, in caves and tunnels and on high treacherous ledges; it was also said such creatures were best left to the imagination.

"Big," was all Nienna managed, awe caught in her throat like a plum stone.

"They'll take you in and spit you out," said Myriam, kicking her horse into a canter. "Come on. There's our destination."

The rugged landscape, scattered with a million jagged rocks, sloped down towards an ancient black fortress which spanned the neck of a valley. The walls were black, and seemed to gleam in the weak afternoon light. Weaving around thick grass and irregularly shaped rocks, many larger than a cottage, they progressed across the land until Nienna's eyes took the tiny toy fortress and reassessed its size and scale. The Cailleach Fortress was *mammoth*. And it was subtly ruined, Nienna realised, the closer she came. Her eyes began to pick out fault lines in the very structure of the fortress. In some sections of the towering, defensive walls, great cracks ran from battlements to foundation, and in other areas towers leaned, and the whole structure took on a disjointed air. Closer they moved, until Myriam called a halt and they squatted like tiny insects against a giant world canvas. And Nienna realised quite clearly that the Cailleach Fortress arraigned before them was *twisted*. Nothing was straight. No wall, no tower, no archway, no section of battlement.

"It is said," came Myriam's voice, a soothing whisper, cutting through the eerie silence which Nienna realised with a start had descended, "that the Black Pike Mountains, offended by this in-trusion of man, sent roots under the fortress and twisted this great monument of war into a mockery of Man's achievement."

"Really?"

"Yes. Others claim a dark sorcery resided here, committing evil necrotic deeds, and the magick twisted and broke every stone used in its vast construction. Whatever the truth, there is no doubt the place is haunted. Nobody will live here. Nobody will even *camp* here."

"And we are going in?" Apprehension.

"Yes. I have learnt that if you keep your head down, the ghosts leave you be. They are nothing but sighs in the wind, the whispers of the dead in your ear, and in your nightmares. You must be strong, Nienna, but do not fear; nothing can hurt you in this place."

"You are sure?"

Myriam gave a narrow, nasty smile. "Nothing but me, that is."

Nienna returned the thin smile. "I had not forgotten. I don't think I ever will."

Night was falling fast, huge storm clouds filling the skies in a tumultuous celebration. Thunder rumbled, a deep-throated ex-halation. In the distance, hailstones drummed the earth.

"Come on. At least there is shelter."

Nienna followed Myriam at a fast trot, and thoughts flitted through her mind. Escape! Turn her horse and run. But then, a sensible part of her soul realised: where to? How would she find Kell in this wilderness crawling with cankers and albino soldiers from the Army of Iron? He could be anywhere. Better to let him come to her. Better to let him take the initiative, and be prepared for chaos when he found Myriam. For Nienna knew, with a sour feeling in her belly, with images of death in her brain, it would be better to aid Kell, for she did not have the power nor the skill to finish Myriam alone. With a bitter nod to reality, she realised she had little enough will to kill in the first place. Killing was for soldiers. Killing was for assassins. And Nienna was neither; she celebrated life, and love, and honour. Death was for fools.

They moved on, and within minutes the Black Pike Mountains were swept with a sheet of pounding ice. It flooded the world, obscuring the sky, obscuring the mountains. Nienna bowed her head as hail slammed her like needles. She lifted the edge of her cloak, but still ice stung her face, and no matter how she tried to shield herself the storm always found a way in. It crept around collar and cuffs, around ankles and tiny vents at the edges of her boots that she didn't realise existed. Cold air crept into her clothing and chilled her, and she cursed it. The Black Pike storm seemed to have all the advantages.

"Not long, now," said Myriam, unnecessarily, and Nienna looked up. The fortress loomed closer, slightly askew and slick with ice and snow. The black walls seemed darker. The battlements glossy. The world was dark, except for the Cailleach Fortress – which *gleamed* with a sort of eldritch witch-light of dark energy.

"What kind of stone is that?" said Nienna, slowly, as they grew closer and closer, and the toy fortress reared above them, towered above them at an angle which made the world feel wrong. When everything was out of the vertical, it made a person's brain hurt.

"It's not stone."

"What is it, then?"

Myriam threw Nienna a dark look. *Shut up*, that look said, and Nienna's teeth clamped tight. "I don't know," she whispered, mind distant. "Something alien".

From a distance the Cailleach Fortress had appeared of normal proportions, but now Nienna realised her perceptions, as well as every vertical wall, were askew. It was big. No, bigger than big. It was *massive*, but also out of proportion. The doorways could accommodate a man twice the normal height, and every single archway or window or archer's firing slit was double the size, as if the fortress had been built to accommodate an army of giants.

They slowed as they approached the main gates, which were open, like the sleeping mouth of a waiting predator. Myriam halted, and her horse pawed the frozen earth nervously. A warm wind sighed from the gates in an easy rhythm, like breath.

Myriam glanced back, and gave a tight smile. "Do not be afraid," she said, and led the way into the corridor of darkness.

From the edges of the world shadows rushed in with a tumbling swirling hissing, like a million snakes trapped in the vortex of a storm, and Nienna's hands came up clasping her ears, clasping her skull as her eyes widened and her horse whinnied in fear, head lowering, hooves booming ancient cobbles, and as her pupils dilated to accommodate the gloom she saw the blurred shapes of the dead converge on Myriam... and then turn, blank black faces focussing and fixing and tilting, and then rushing towards her with a gestalt scream, a merged noise of agony from a thousand years past...

EIGHT
Blood Taint

Kell's mind was spinning and he could taste silver – just like during the Days of Blood. Poison pulsed through his veins, through his organs, through his system, pulsed with the steady beat of his heart and the whiskey was negated, and he was sober again, and she was kneeling above him, beautiful, stunning, deadly, with her bright silver sword and bright fangs gleaming that *vampire* gleam in the starlight. This burned Kell. Burned him with shame. The king was there, old, serious, his eyes boring into Kell and the other warriors as they made the bloodpact, and blood pulsed from the wounds in their wrists, mingling in the golden bowl and flowing down channels, seeping down narrow tubes to *infuse* the weapons which seemed to glow with an inner black light. Kell stooped, lifting Ilanna, and with this dark blessing she was *his* and she whispered, *It will never be the same again, and, I will be with you forever, and I will never let you down, Kell, trust me, I will never leave you* and this touched a chord, touched every tingling nerve in his strung out, drug-infused body for *she* had left his bed, left his house, left his life, despite their vows and their promises and there and then Kell wrenched free the wedding ring and tossed it away in the darkness of the cellar beneath the temple in Vor. "I will never be a slave again," he whispered, unaware of the irony of his promise even as he spoke the words, for to become bloodbond with a weapon, to follow the Old Lore and the sap veins in the Oak Testament, a man ensured he was a slave for eternity.

"No," hissed Kell, back in the present, and he was young and strong and immortal once again, and he twisted fast, a blur, a subtle shift and Tashmaniok's sword scored a bright fire line down his cheek and struck the floor with a grinding squeal and Kell reached almost leisurely beneath his arm, drawing out his slightly curved blade, his Svian, and he thrust it up into Tashmaniok's groin and she gasped, and went rigid, and he held her there impaled on his knife and slowly crawled from beneath her straddle, so that his bearded face came level with hers. Her sword slashed at him, but he batted it aside and jerked the Svian knife, and Tash gasped again, for eight inches of steel were deep inside her flesh, deep inside her *womb* and holding her tight to Kell in an embrace. Her fangs gleamed. Kell smiled. "I was born in the Days of Blood," he hissed, and stood, and Tash rose with him for she had no option, and her vachine blood-oil ran down her legs and Kell's free hand grasped her throat and squeezed and her face, beautiful and pale and with eyes wide, crimson wide and fixed on Kell with a mixture of hate and admiration, they narrowed and Kell lifted her above his head, suspended by blade and throat, and her sword clattered to the ground, and her blood pattered like falling rain and with a *scream* Kell hurled the vachine across the chamber and she bounced from the wall, fell and landed like a cat, on all fours, then in a *blur* she was gone into the darkness; through the wall with a *crash* of buckling timber, and away into the night.

Kell staggered, then righted himself, and took several deep rushing breaths. He moved to Ilanna, aware she had saved him again and it felt bitter in the back of his mind; like an old betrayal.

He took up the great axe, and moved to Tashmaniok's spilled blood. She was a strong one, he realised. One of the strongest he had ever faced. And yet there was something else there; something more subtle. An element of the ancient.

"Saark," Kell breathed, suddenly realising his danger, and he rushed to the broken boards where Tash had made her exit, out into the snow. What greeted Kell's vision was a confused tableau, a scene from a tapestry of nightmare. Fire roared through the town. Men charged with swords. People ran, screaming. Everything seemed a sudden chaos. Kell's eyes narrowed. These were no albino warriors, no Army of Iron; these were *Blacklippers*, the amoral – no, the *immoral* criminals who once kept the trade of *Karakan Red* flowing into the vachine empire in Silva Valley. This, Kell knew. But why attack this village? Why now?

Starvation, realised Kell. The Army of Iron had invaded. Power politics had shifted. The Blacklippers could no longer ply the same trade; and they were criminals at heart, the diseased, the outcast, the toxic. Would they sit back and wait for a new harvest? Or would they flood from the Black Pike Mountains in their hundreds and take what they could?

Fire roared. Sparks glimmered in snow-heavy skies. Chaos roamed the streets. Violence stalked, screaming, on legs of iron, and arrows whistled through the gloom, punching villagers from their feet, hands clawing at fletches.

Kell squeezed from the hole, and ignoring Tashmaniok's footprints in the snow leading away, out into the forests, out into the wilderness where, within a short distance the blood droplets from her punctured wounded body *ceased*... instead, Kell moved forward into the chaos of the village, face grim, fire shining in his eyes, and with the Days of Blood reverberating in his soul like... a blood echo.

Saark screamed like a girl as Shanna's fangs descended for his throat, and he kicked and struggled and punched at her face but she held him in an impossible grip, a vice of steel, and a terrible vulnerability flooded Saark and he went suddenly limp, submissive, accepting his fate.

Fangs touched his neck. They were impossibly cold. Like ice.

"No," he whispered.

"Yes," she said, and her breath tickled his flesh.

Subliminally, he heard the door open. Kell! he thought, in a sudden triumph, with a desperate surge of energy which rushed his system like an emetic. His eyes flickered open, and Shanna's fangs sank deep, through skin, through muscle, and Saark screamed and started to struggle once more, a fish on a hook, unwilling to give up and die and a voice, a cool cold *young* voice spoke.

"Put him down," said Skanda, in little more than a whisper.

With a snarl, Shanna hurled Saark across the room and dropped to a crouch, blood on her fangs, on her chin, on her talons, and her eyes were narrowed and she hissed, "You!"

Saark hit the wall, hit the floor in a heap, moaning. His fingers came to his throat, saw his blood, and he whimpered. Outside, there came a *roar*, and a whoosh of flames. Armed men charged down the streets, and the sounds of battle swept through Creggan. Saark was confused, his mind swirling. Something pulsed in his neck like a second heartbeat. He imagined he heard a tiny *tick tock, tick tock*, like the smallest of mechanical engines. He shivered in premonition.

Skanda moved into a half-crouch, and he circled Shanna, the vachine snarling at him, Saark's blood on her teeth. She licked it, delicately, until it was gone.

"You should have died a long time ago," hissed Shanna.

"We are back," said Skanda, the young boy looking out of place, sounding out of place, as the sudden battle raged outside the tavern and people screamed in the street below. Metal clashed on metal. More fire snarled through lantern-oil soaked thatch.

"You will die again," pointed Shanna, her claw bloodied, her face more feral than human, now.

"Whatever you say, Soul Stealer, daughter of *Graal*," smiled Skanda with full understanding. And he *clapped*, and with the clap came a sound like thunder, and from beneath the floorboards flooded a surge of insects, of beetles and lice, of worms and maggots and weevils, and they spread across the floorboards as the window was suddenly *battered* by flies and wasps, by crawling things and flying things and spiders and hornets and the room was suddenly *alive* as cockroaches swept the floor and walls like a tide erupting from the dark places of the filthy town, and this surge of insects swept around Skanda's feet, swirling like a fluid, a fluid of carapace shells and wings and claws and legs and fangs and Skanda pointed at Shanna whose face was drawn in horror, in revulsion, and the tide of insects flowed to her and up her legs and she turned and screamed and leapt for the window, crashing through glass which splintered and drove into her flesh in long jagged shards, and the insects stung her and bit her and she fell, landing heavily, glass daggers driving deep into her body so that blood gurgled at her mouth and she groaned, and yet still she stood, and ran, dodging through the battling influx of Blacklippers who fought a cruel battle with villagers in the streets.

Skanda moved to the broken window, and tasted her blood, wiping a smear down his tongue. Then, as the sudden calling of insects began to dissipate, crawling into walls and back under floors and squeezing above rafters, heading back for the shadows and the damp places, places of rotting food and rotting flesh, so Skanda moved to Saark and helped the man to his feet. Skanda touched his fingers to Saark's throat, where twin puncture marks *glowed* like molten metal.

Their eyes met.

"You have a long life ahead of you," said Skanda, voice sour.

"I understand," said Saark.

"I do not think that you do."

"I am still human," said Saark, fear in his eyes, in his voice, as if by voicing the fact he could somehow make it real. He touched his neck again, self-consciously.

Skanda nodded, features dark and hooded. "For a little while, at least," he said.

"What will happen to me?"

"It will take time. It was not finished. You will see."

"You are age-old enemies? The Ankarok, and the vachine?"

"Yes. But we are coming back, Saark. We have been called. And there is nothing they can do."

"You can help us!" hissed Saark, suddenly. "Help us drive the albinos back, beyond the Pikes!"

"We have something more radical in mind," said Skanda, and then the small boy whirled about, and was gone, and Saark was confused but through his confusion he knew one thing was certain: this was a parting of the ways, as if Saark and Kell had brought him far enough, and now Skanda was strong enough to travel and *fight* alone, and Saark was reeling, and vomiting, kneeling there amidst broken shards of glass and the crushed shells of a hundred insects, vomiting onto the floor of the room.

Finally, he gained his feet, and found his rapier, and sheathed it on the third attempt. He staggered to the jagged window. Outside, chaos rampaged through the streets. The Blacklippers, the vagabonds from the Black Pike Mountains, were on a raid. Fire savaged the town. Saark smiled a very bitter smile; the villagers had done everything to evade the searching eyes of the Army of Iron – and in so doing, had left themselves open for a closer, just as evil, threat.

As Saark watched, he saw a great figure striding down the street. He had a full beard and wore a bearskin jerkin which made him look even larger than his natural size, which was huge enough to begin. Saark saw two Blacklippers charge Kell, swords out, glittering, and Saark wanted to shout "Watch out!" but the words stuck in his throat like vomit and Kell turned at the last moment and his eyes were dark death and his axe swept up, cutting one man from groin to sternum in a spray of entrails and half-digested slurry, and bone shards glimmered white in the glow of the burning houses, then the axe twisted and cut sideways and a Blacklipper's head rolled, black dead lips tasting frozen mud. But then Saark fell to his knees, neck pulsing, blood pulsing, his veins burning from the inside out, and on a blanket of glass and crushed insects, he passed into a realm of blissful unconsciousness.

Saark coughed, and floated in honey, and the world was perfect and *he* was perfect. He sat up. His vision swam. And then the world seemed – so clear. He stood, crunching glass, and pain jabbed him in the neck and he remembered the bite but even as he remembered it, so it started to fade, as if the memory was a drift of smoke. He had heard stories of the savage marshes to the east of Falanor, where tiny blood-sucking creatures swam the waters. They attached themselves to a man, or to a stricken donkey or cow, and injected a local anaesthetic before beginning a long, hard feast, gorging on the creature's blood. The man, or animal, unaware of anything amiss, was bled dry by the blood-suckers; if three or four attached, then weakness, porphyria, vertigo and death would occur. What struck Saark now *now* was that he felt as if a blood-sucking little bastard had attached to him; but he did not realise it. And even as the thought entered his mind, so it became clouded, and vanished, and he could see Kell outside and he checked his rapier and ran to the stairs and out through the deserted tavern.

"Where's Skanda?" snarled Kell, upon seeing Saark.

"I'm very well, thank you," snapped Saark, eyes flashing with anger.

"Where's the boy?"

"He's gone," said Saark, suddenly weary. He rubbed the bridge of his nose. Around him, fire roared and Kell grimaced at three Blacklippers, who saw his gore-stained axe and thought better of attack. "I was – ambushed, by a vachine. Skanda helped me, cast some weird ancient magick shit, and all these insects came from nowhere. I got a feeling he no longer needed us. He left."

Kell nodded. "We need our horses."

"And the donkey," said Saark.

Kell gave him a sour, twisted look. "And the donkey," he said.

In the shadows of a church tower, Jageraw watched it all. As snow fell, he'd seen the fat old warrior with the terrifying axe which spoke to him, which *knew him*, and he watched the slick dandy and the two death-cold Soul Stealers... oh how he knew them, knew them from Graal, Graal the bad man the wicked man!

Jageraw rubbed his chest, rubbed the burning there, and it was getting more urgent and it would never stop until he reached his destination. But that was a long way a terrible way, no pretty there, no pretty at all!

For hours he watched the Blacklipper raiders finishing up, and only when the cold dawn arrived and the town was deserted except for corpses did Jageraw climb steadily from the old church tower. He crept through the streets with his bag, pulling free a heart here, a kidney there, a spleen here, and some tasty precious lungs there.

Then, with his sack full of organs, full to the brim with squelching delights, he slung it over his shoulder and headed for the forests and trails no longer used by man.

It was hours later, and it was dark, and cold. Kell and Saark had rode hard for what seemed an eternity, until the blazing cottages and the vachine killers and the *danger* seemed, at least for now, far behind. It was Kell who finally pulled rein, and they sat on a low wooded hilltop, the distant fires obscured by snowfall and the haze of a welcome distance. Finally, Saark said, "How are you, Kell, old boy?" There was no mockery in his voice. Only concern.

"I have felt better. Much better."

"Back at that town, one came after you? A vachine, I mean?"

"Yes."

"Me also. She... scraped out my emotions like offal from a sack, and left them glistening on the road like so many spilled entrails. I feel unclean, Kell. I feel like she polluted my soul."

Kell turned to Saark. "They were sent by Graal, and the bastard wants us dead. Or he wants... something. Something else, although I cannot figure what." He lowered his head, and for long moments looked like nothing but a weary old man. He rubbed at his eyes, his cheeks, his beard. He sighed, and in so sighing gave in to decades of weariness, to decades of a hard life, and a harder fight.

"Are you injured?" said Saark, at last.

"Only my ego, lad. She was fast, by all the gods." He grinned then. "But if I am to be slain, then let it be by one so beautiful! She was stunning beyond belief!"

"Mine also. She hooked me like a fish. I fear I am becoming predictable." He sighed, and touched unconsciously at the collar of his cloak, beneath which lay the indelible fang-marks. He could feel them, burning. "Once, even such a beauty would have made me snarl and pucker, and flirt and push away; make her work for the privilege, you understand? Now, I fear, I am a slave to my trade."

"And what trade's that, boy?"

Saark smiled, and rubbed again at his neck. "The trade of dishonesty," he said.

They made a rough camp before nightfall, deep in the woods, and Kell risked a fire. With little food between them they ate sparsely, but took comfort in the flames.

Kell fell into a brooding silence, and winced occasionally. Saark realised it was the poison in his veins, in his organs, in his bones, and he made no comment; instead, he fell into his own weird and deviated brooding.

As Kell fell asleep, watching the fire, so Saark took a little time to move away from the camp seeking solitude. His side was still incredibly sore where Myriam had stabbed him, a bitter event which still filled his mind with dark fury and images of an almost *sexual revenge*. His fingers traced across the dried blood mask which caked his skin. He winced, and pulled up his shirt. His fingers traced the contours of the wound and he jumped, eyes growing wide, then narrowing. The wound had healed. Completely. There was not even the ridge of a fresh scar.

Saark fumbled in the darkness for a while, trying to see the wound, but he could not. And fear touched him, then. Shanna had bitten him. His fingers came up to his neck, and he realised these two wounds, also, had gone. What had she done top him? What strange vachine magick had she poured into his veins?

Saark returned to the camp, and wrapped himself in a fur-lined cloak, and watched the fire and tried to sleep, but he was infused with a strange bubbling energy and sleep would not come. So, instead he watched Kell snoring by the fire, and wondered what powered the man: blood and gristle, like the rest of humanity? He smiled grimly. Or maybe Kell, too, was an esoteric meshing of flesh and clockwork?

Kell dreamed of Nienna. She was seated beneath the arch of the Cailleach Fortress. Strange rocks littered the ground. The Black Pike Mountains grumbled in the background, like an angry father.

"I am sorry," said Kell, walking towards her, both hands out-stretched, but she opened her eyes and they were blood red, and she opened her mouth and it was a vachine abomination, and her fangs crunched free and she hissed the bestial hiss of the vampire... and leapt for him, and he batted her aside, watched her roll in the dirt and dust, cracking her head against a rock. Blood flowed, but instantly healed, blood rolling backwards up her flesh as skin and bone melded, hot wax running together. "What are you?" he screamed at his granddaughter, *What the hell are you?* and she leapt again, long claws stretching to tear free his throat...

Kell sat up. He spat. He noticed Saark watching him and scowled. "What you looking at?"

"A grumpy old stoat?"

"Fuck off."

"You did ask."

"You didn't need to answer."

"What are you thinking about?"

"Rescuing Nienna."

"What about the poison in your veins?"

"DAMN THE POISON IN MY VEINS!" Kell screamed, face almost purple with rage, and then he realised he was standing, axe in hands, glowering down at Saark who had leant back, hands out, face open in shock.

"Calm down," said Saark, eventually, as Kell subsided.

"I am... sorry," said the big man.

"You need to learn to lighten up a little."

"You can always fu... Yes, yes, I see." Kell made a growling noise. "I am sorry. I will attempt to be more amenable. I will talk with you, Saark, and I will be a gentleman." He gave a rough cough, and pain shivered through his features.

"You are dying," said Saark, gently.

"Yes. It grows unbearable. Excuse my rage."

"We need to find this Myriam bitch."

"Yes," sighed Kell, weary with the world.

"I am looking forward to some payback," said Saark, with a narrow smile.

They rode for hours. The clouds dissipated, and the sun, although weak, was warm and pleasing on their skin. On this morning, heading north, the world seemed a much happier, warmer place.

"Talk to me," said Saark, after a while, hunched over his saddle, face lost in distant dreams.

"About what?" grunted Kell.

"Anything."

"I'm not in the mood for talking."

"I need you to take my mind off... something."

Kell stared at Saark, hard. But said nothing.

"I'll begin then," coughed Saark, and thought for a moment. "Don't you think," he paused, contemplating a myriad montage of memories in his laconical mind, "that's there's nothing sweeter in this world than a ripe, eager quim?"

Kell considered this. "Meaning?" he growled.

"It means what it says."

"Meaning?"

"Come on Kell, talk to me, confide in me, I'm bloody *bored*, mate, and you need some cheering up. I nearly died back there at the fangs of *Shanna* or whatever the shit she was called, and I want some fun. I want some philosophising. I want some banter, my man – it's what I thrive on! I want some *life*!"

Kell stared at him. He cleared his throat. "After all we've been through, after all the things we've seen, after all the battles we've endured; how can you be *bored*?"

Saark spread his arms wide, and grinned. His humour had returned. Pain no longer seemed to trouble him. He was bright as a button; brighter, in fact. So bright he *shone*. "Hey," he said, "you know me. I am a hedonist. Drink. Women. Gambling. Fighting. Thievery. Debauchery. It's a dull day when the Bone Underworld shuts its gates."

Kell coughed again, and looked away to distant mountains. Then he returned his stare to Saark. "Do you not think," he said, slowly, one great hand holding the reins of his horse, the other nestled almost unconsciously on the saddle-stashed Ilanna, "do you not think I, also, enjoy such things?"

Saark considered this. "Pah! You are Kell the Hero. Kell the *Legend*. You're idea of a good time is rescuing fair damsels in distress, hunting down vagabonds and returning stolen monies to the authorities, hell, you probably even clean your teeth before you go to bed."

"You met my granddaughter, yes?"

"Of course, a fine fillet of female flesh, she was." He coughed, and rubbed the bridge of his nose. "If you don't mind me saying so."

"I do, as a matter of fact," said Kell, voice hard. But he let it pass. "Obviously, I have a granddaughter. So then, where did she come from?"

"Your daughter would be the logical conclusion," said Saark, smugly.

"Yes. My daughter. Proof of my prowess, surely?"

"Ha. I am sure I have many daughters! One is not proof of prowess, simply a proof of simple, common luck."

"Meaning?" Kell's voice was cold.

"All I'm saying is that ale has a lot to answer for."

"And your *meaning*?"

"Well," said Saark, losing a little of his comfort zone, "I know many an ugly bastard who's sired a child. The Royal Court wine is strong, and when drank in plentiful consumption can lead, shall we say, to amorous connections best left to the annals of dreams." He considered this, as if through experience, his mouth twisting a little. "Or maybe nightmare."

Kell coughed, eyes glittering with a dangerous shine. "You trying to say something, lad?"

"Only that alcohol has sired many children. One daughter, and hence granddaughter, is no display of excellence in the art of amorous seduction."

"I'm not talking about seduction. I'm talking about love... no, no I'm not." Kell frowned, rubbing his beard. "I always was rough around talk of such things. What I mean to say is, I obviously had a wife."

"Yes?" Saark smiled politely. There were many responses he could have made, but wisely chose to utter none.

"Well," struggled on Kell, "I had a wife, and I was married, and we had a child. A girl. A little angel. I loved her with all my heart, and I was a brute I know, but it was the first time in my life I realised I would kill for somebody, and I would also *die* for somebody. That was a new one on me. That was something unique."

"I have heard it is a magical experience," said Saark, a little stiffly. "Although I have never experienced it *first-hand*, myself. *Despite* being a father many times over."

Kell grinned, and it looked wrong on his face, Saark observed. Where was the scowl? The hatred? The fury?

"Well lad, you missed out on a rare experience, for all your talk of hedonism. For nothing beats a high like childbirth – and I should know," his voice dropped to a dark realm, "I've taken every bastard drug in Falanor."

They rode in silence for a while, whilst Saark digested this information. *Well*, he thought, *there's more life in the old donkey than I realised!* "Go on," he said, finally. "What happened to your wife?"

"How did you know I was treading that particular territory?"

"I have spent an eternity in courts, with nobility, and royalty, and peasants who thought they were nobility. One thing they always want to speak about is their wives. Too fat, too thin, small tits, tits like a pig's bladder, carping, harping, moaning, whining, legs always open, legs always shut. It's all water off a greased duck's back." Saark smiled. "So, what's *your* story?"

"I was illustrating a point," growled Kell with a nasty look.

"Am I supposed to understand the point? Or does that bit come later?"

"Just listen," growled Kell. "The point is, I am no longer with my wife. She is not dead. We separated. It was the best option."

"What did you do?" asked Saark, voice a little more understanding now.

"I was a bad man," said Kell, words so soft they were almost lost in the sigh of the wind. "I was the toughest, meanest fucker you ever did meet. I maimed, I hurt, I tortured, I killed. I was infamous. My name was feared throughout Falanor. And I... I *revelled* in it, in the notoriety. Many a time we would stop at an inn, and I would leave my wife in the room and come down to the drinking bar, and drink whiskey, drink far too much whiskey, and as the night progressed so I would lie on the bar, bare-chested, laughing off challenges as a host of women rubbed ale into my hairy chest, or drank fine wine and passed it by mouth to my mouth, and then, when I was ready, I would pick out the biggest, meanest, hardest village bastard and take him outside and humiliate him. I'd never kill him, no, I was not a complete animal – although nearly, lad, nearly. But I'd always leave him with something to remember me by. Once, I punched a man so hard, when he came round he snorted two teeth out of his nose. Another time, I indented my knuckles on a man's skull; damn lucky I didn't kill him. He was unconscious for five weeks."

"And you waited by him for his recovery? Surely that was, at least, a fine and noble gesture! You showed that you had some modicum of honour. You cared enough to find out the result."

"Nonsense!" thundered Kell, filled with rage for a moment. "I met him, ten years later, when I was drunk. He showed me my knuckle imprints on his skull. Said he'd been a pit fighter for nigh twenty years, and never known a man punch as hard as I had."

"Well, your infamy was well placed, then," said Saark, coldly.

"You're missing the point, lad. The point is, I was a bastard to my wife. No. The point *is*, I was a hedonist, much like you; I disrespected my wife, I wallowed in violence, and ale, and whiskey, and the women threw themselves at me in those days, when I was the hardest fucker in the tavern and willing to take on any man in the village or town or city – and beat them all! The women were mine, they were at my disposal, they were there to be used and I used them. And my wife left me. And my daughter hated me. And I am lucky to have even a simple contact with Nienna. I am lucky to have my granddaughter."

Kell fell into a brooding hunch, and his eyes were hooded, his face dark.

"And the outcome of your sermon *is*?" said Saark brightly.

"Appreciate what you've got," snarled Kell, bitterness at the forefront of his mind. "I was like you, Saark, although you have only a limited intelligence to realise it; I was a mad man, a bad man, and I took no prisoners. Ale, whiskey, drugs, women, I took it all with both hands. But it did me no good. Ultimately, it left me hollow and brittle and broken."

"You look far from broken to me," said Saark, voice soft.

"You only see the shell," snapped Kell. "You don't see the empty cancerous holes inside. Now, be as you will, boy, do what you will with no respect for others; but I swear, one day, when you're old, and your time is spent, and you are riddled with arthritis and have no children to weep your passing, and no grandchildren to sit on your bouncing knee and ask with bright wide eyes, aye," he laughed, "they'll ask for stories of your travels with *Kell the Legend*; well, Saark, my lad, if you have been nothing but a dishonourable fellow – one day, one day you'll realise that your bloody time ran out. And you'll die, sad, and unloved, and alone. Even more alone than me." Kell smiled then, and kicked his horse forward, breaking free of the snow-laden forest and looking out and on to the looming Black Pike Mountains.

Saark scowled. Kell had touched a nerve, and his thoughts swirled like a winter storm. "You miserable, *miserable* old bastard," he muttered, and cantered after the old warrior, hands tight on the high pommel of his gelding's saddle.

Saark called a halt, and they sat under snow-heavy conifers, staring across a bleak landscape. Distantly, the Black Pike Mountains mocked them. They were getting close. As Kell grew weak, so they were getting close. And he knew Nienna was out there, just as he knew thousands of enemies were out there. Kell raged inside, and wanted to tear out his beard and his hair. It was a bad situation; a bitter situation! The world had become a savage place. But then, wasn't that what his victims thought as his great axe, his great *demon-possessed axe*, clove them from crown to crotch? You are an old man, and yet you walk with demons. You are an old man, and you converse with evil. You stalked the streets of Kalipher during the Days of Blood...

"Do you hate all vachine," said Saark, suddenly, looking back to Kell.

Kell grunted. "Eh?"

"No. Really. Do you hate them?"

"I hate what they stand for."

"Which is?"

Kell considered this. "They are not of this world by choice. They merge with machines, and in doing so, drink the refined blood narcotic of those they have slain. I reckon that's an unhealthy place to be, don't you, lad?"

"What happens when a vachine bites you?" said Saark, voice soft, but Kell, preoccupied with his own pain from the poison in his bones, and thoughts of finding Nienna, missed any subtleties or nuances which may have emerged from Saark's voice or facial expression.

"Well lad, it starts to turn you," said Kell.

"What does that mean? Turn you?"

Kell shrugged. "They give you blood-oil, and take your fresh blood. It's, not a poison exactly, but more a chemical that works in harmony with the clockwork machines inside any clockwork vampire. Without the clockwork..."

"Yes?"

"You suffer. Suffer long and hard. Until you beg for the clock-work to be inside you."

"Great. And how do you get this damn clockwork?" scowled Saark.

"You either visit Silva Valley, or a skilled Vachine Engineer. It's a religion, apparently." Kell barked a laugh, and slapped Saark on the back. "Why lad, not been bit, have you?" He roared suddenly, at his own incredible witticism, his own great humour.

"Of course not," said Saark, face straight. "Because then I'd be a vachine, and you'd want to cut off my head."

"Nonsense," boomed Kell, his mood seemingly lightened. He leaned in close. "I like you. You're my friend. For you, maybe I'd cut out only one lung."

Kell cantered ahead.

Saark frowned, a heavy dark frown like the thunder of worlds. "Wonderful," he muttered. "A vachine *killer* with a sense of humour."

Snow fell heavy, drifting in great veils across the world. Wrapped heavy in furs, they rode through day and partly through night, before finding a shallow place amongst rocks to camp. They built a fire, abandoning their subterfuge for the simple act of wanting to stay alive. Mary and the horses huddled together for warmth, and Saark sat now, face illuminated by flames, watching Kell sleep. Saark did not feel tired. He could feel his blood pulsing through his veins. Eventually the snow stopped, and the sky brightened, and looking upwards the moon seemed so incredibly bright. Saark smiled, and welcomed the cold.

He drifted for a long time, analysing his life and wondering, again, why sleep would not come. Was it the blood-oil working through his veins? Creeping through his organs? He smiled as intuition nagged him. Of course it was. He was changing, just as Kell had predicted in his summary of what happened after a vachine bit. And that meant? He had to imbibe clockwork of some sort? Saark frowned. That sounded like a bucket of horseshit. Surely Kell was wrong.

Then the pain arrived, a distant, nagging pain which grew brighter and sharper and keener with every passing heartbeat. And then twin stings shot through his mouth and Saark might have cried out, he wasn't sure, but he fell to the snowy ground and smelled crushed ice and the trees and the woodland and a rabbit shivering in a burrow and the stench of Kell, his sweat, bits of food in his bushed beard, stale whiskey on his jerkin. Saark looked up, from the snow, shivering, looked up at the moon. Again, the pain stabbed through his jaws and his teeth seemed to rattle in his skull. The pain was incredible, like nothing he'd ever felt, far surpassing the stabbing at the hands of Myriam; far outweighing the feeling of any blade which had ever pierced his flesh. He wanted to scream, but the pain swamped him, and it was a strange pain, a honey pain, thick and sweet and sickly and almost welcoming... almost.

Saark heard the sounds, then, as if from a great distance. Crunches of tearing flesh and snapping bone rattled through him, and with horror he rocked back onto his arse and touched his face, touched his teeth where long incisors had pushed through his upper jaw. He touched the fangs, felt their incredible, razor sharpness; he sliced his thumb, watched blood roll down his frozen moonlit-pale flesh, and his eyes went wide. His nostrils twitched. The smell of blood awoke something animal within him; no, not something animal, something deeper, something more feral, base, primitive, something which he could not explain.

"What is happening to me?" he said, his words thick and slurred, his head spinning. Then his head slammed right. His eyes narrowed. He fixed on Kell. Not only could he smell the detritus of human stench; now, he could smell Kell's blood.

Saark moved onto his hands and knees, and crouched, and stopped, his eyes focused on Kell, the smell of Kell's blood in his nostrils. He could smell every droplet. Every ounce. It pulsed sluggishly through Kell's veins and to Saark, here, now, the world receded, changed, and the only thing in the entirety of existence was this group of rocks, this campfire, this snow-filled moment with Kell, asleep, head back, snoring, throat exposed. Saark could see the pulse in Kell's neck. It went beyond enticement, through lust and need and into another realm which meant more than life and death. Saark wanted blood. Saark *needed* blood. If he did not drink Kell's blood he would surely die; he would surely explode into a billion fragments of pain only to be reformed again and torn apart again over and over for ever and ever and ever unto eternity.

Slowly, Saark crawled across the snow.

Under waxen moonlight, Kell slept on.

NINE
The Harvest

The wolves crept into the cave, and Alloria stood frozen with fear, her eyes locked to the lead wolf, huge, black, yellow, baleful. "Stand back," came Vashell's voice, and Alloria turned, slowly, as if fearful the moment she presented her back it would be leapt upon, huge jaws fastening over her head and ripping it easily from her shoulders.

Slowly, Alloria retreated. The fire was warm by her back. Her mouth was dry, eyes wide, breath coming in short bursts. Her hand dropped to her lower belly, an unconscious act of protection, an act of the maternal – although her boys, if they lived – which she doubted – were many, many miles away. In a different world.

Vashell eased past her, his terribly scarred face demonic, his eyes narrowed, his clockwork ticking, gears stepping. Alloria jumped, noticing he carried a short stabbing sword in powerful grip. He had taken it from her pack. He was hunched, powerful shoulders ready for battle... which did not come. Vashell *growled*, a low animal sound, bestial and yet mixed curiously with the sounds of subtle clockwork, as if this were a gift bestowed by engineers rather than Nature. The wolves tilted heads, and under his advance they began to back away, still rumbling threateningly, but heads lower now, submissive, as if bowing down before their master.

Vashell stepped out into the storm. The blizzard whipped him. Through veils of snapping snow and ice, the mountains reared, eternal, powerful, immortal.

The wolves continued to back away, until another was set forward. It was massive, bigger by a head than even the biggest wolf. Its fur was jet black, its eyes green and intelligent. It was the prodigal, a natural born leader of the pack, a beast in its prime. Vashell stood and stared at the wolf, which carried something in its jaws. The others had made a decision, and retreated, allowing this huge creature the ultimate choice of attack or retreat.

Vashell stopped, and stared, eyes narrowed, throat still making the strange clockwork growling. And he stared without emotion at the object, the trophy, carried between the jaws of the wolf. Alloria followed Vashell out into the blizzard, arm coming up to shield her eyes, and she gasped. For between its jaws, the magnificent and powerful wolf carried the head of a Harvester.

Alloria placed her arm on Vashell's steel bicep. "Don't attack," she said, urgently. "Maybe it is a friend? Any enemy of the Harvesters is surely an ally of mine..."

But before Vashell could make any informed decision the wolf stood, a fluid blur, then stretched languorously. Its every movement held contempt for Vashell. With every nuance, every glint of those bright green intelligent eyes, the wolf seemed to say: *I know you, you are vachine, I do not fear you, I do not fear the Harvesters, I will rend you and slay you until you are no more.*

The severed head, hanging by a thick flap of skin and spinal column, was blank and white and smeared with dirt. The tiny black eyes were lifeless – but then, Alloria thought, they always looked like that. The narrow nasal slits no longer hissed with their customary fast intake of breath.

Slowly, the wolf dropped the Harvester's head to the snow. It licked its lips, again embodying contempt, then accelerated into an attack so fast it was a blur of black...

Vashell stumbled back, sword slamming up but the wolf's jaws rattled left and right, clashing bone with steel and almost disarming Vashell. He rolled, battle instinct returning, dropping one shoulder and shifting, hitting the ground, coming up fast in a crouch with sword ready, head down, eyes narrowed. The wolf's huge pads hit the snow, and it shook itself like a rain-drenched dog. It chuckled, a huge rolling rumble, turned to face Vashell, then attacked again with a savage scream, a bestial show of prowess. Vashell launched himself forward, sword held two-handed, intending to power the weapon into the wolf's lungs and beyond, into the pumping heart.

But the wolf twisted, one huge paw lashing lazily across Vashell's face and sending him tumbling, skidding over snow towards the treacherous precipice. Below, rocks waited, ten thousand pointed daggers which mocked him.

The wolf paced around in a tight circle, and to one side sat the rest of the pack, a few yelping, all pelts covered in a fine sprinkling of snow, whilst on the other side stood Alloria. Her face was shocked, for without Vashell to protect her she would be dead in an instant.

The wolf moved forward, slowly, head lowering, green eyes fixed on its intended victim. "No!" gasped Alloria, hand to her mouth, and she realised in horror how in this savage wilderness, in the Black Pike Mountains which she had so casually underestimated, she now relied on one who, a few days earlier, would have quite happily slaughtered her. How mad was the world? How ironic? A sick sense of humour, for sure.

Vashell grasped at his sword, fingers clasping steel, and the wolf bunched for the final leap, a snarl erupting from its muzzle as its whole frame tensed and muscles writhed like snakes under fur and it leapt, and Vashell's sword came up but was knocked aside, away, down, spinning onto the rocks far far below and Vashell rammed arms and legs between himself and the beast, and its fangs snapped in his face, fetid rotting breath rolling down his throat and he screamed, the vachine screamed as clockwork gears went *click* and a surge of blood-oil strength powered through veins and with awesome effort he heaved, and twisted, and rolled from the ledge of the high mountain pass. The wolf was dragged into the gap by its own weight, and claws slashed wounds down Vashell's throat, jaws snapping, as it was suddenly whipped away, spinning, into oblivion. Vashell's hands snapped out, grasped rocks, but his body slid over the edge and his fingers grappled and his healing fingers cast for purchase. If he'd had his vachine claws, he would have been safe. Instead, he slid for several feet on near-vertical icy rock, his movements panicked, until his boot wedged in a narrow V, nothing more than a crevice for hardy mountain flowers. He caught his descent. He glanced down. The huge wolf spun away, silent, eyes fixed on him with that bright green gaze. And then it was gone in swathes of mist, smashes of blizzard, and Vashell struggled for a minute and wearily heaved himself back onto the frozen trail where he lay, panting.

Alloria was there, cradling his head, but Vashell pushed himself to his feet and turned to face the rest of the pack. He clenched his fists and snarled at Alloria to get back in the cave, his words almost unrecognisable as human, his head lowered for the final battle which he knew he could not win...

The wolves sat, watching him, then turned as one and disappeared into the storm.

Alloria helped Vashell into the cave, and he slumped, breathing harsh, blood running from the claw gouges in his throat. "Let me help you," she said, and tearing a strip of cloth from her clothing, went as if to bind the wound. Vashell caught her by the wrist, and shook his head.

"I do not need your help."

"You are bleeding."

"I've bled before. I'll bleed again. Listen, you want to make yourself useful, go and get the Harvester's head. They left it. Like I won a prize." He smiled weakly, face a horror mask of scars and weeping wounds.

"I cannot."

"You will not?"

"I *cannot* touch that thing. It's abhorrent!"

Vashell jacked himself to his elbows, then sighed and left the cave. He returned holding the dead head by the spinal tail, and he threw it next to the fire.

"What were you thinking? Cremation?"

"Not yet," said Vashell, and started warming his hands. They were battered, scratched from the fight with the black wolf, and from saving himself the terrible fall. "Look in my pack. There's some dried cat, and my hunting knife."

"Cat?"

"I caught a small snow panther. Or rather, it attacked me in a frenzy of hunger. Without a sword, it was difficult; but my dagger eventually made a good job of it, although I would rather have used vachine fang and claw." He dropped into a silence of brooding, and Alloria felt it wise to remain quiet.

She moved, and rummaged through his pack, pulling out strips of dried meat and the knife. As she turned, she saw Vashell had taken the Harvester's head and stood it on a rock. The spinal column had curled around the bloodless stump like a snake around a staff. Alloria shivered.

"It almost looks alive," she said.

"I am," came a faint, drifting, almost unheard voice from the Harvester's mouth. "Fetch me some water."

Alloria stood, frozen, but Vashell carried a small bottle to the creature's lips and poured. The Harvester spluttered, and wetted its mouth, and Alloria watched in absolute disgust as the water leaked from the creature's severed neck stump.

"But it's dead!" she cried, finally, moving to Vashell as if for protection; but he knelt before the head, and Alloria found herself doing the same thing, her eyes locked on those tiny black orbs, almost fascinated now as a tongue licked necrotic lips.

"Thank the gods you came," hissed the Harvester. "I thought I would spend an eternity in that beast's stinking maw."

"How can you still live?" said Alloria, stunned into gawping stupidity.

"Hold your tongue woman. He has limited strength." Vashell's brow was narrowed, but he did not show the surprise he ought to. Which meant he had seen this kind of thing before.

"They are immortal?" whispered Alloria.

"Not immortal," said Vashell. "Have you ever seen a cockroach?"

"Yes, once they infested the palace stores; we lost much food, and it took the servants an age to sort the problem. What of them?"

"If you take a knife, and cut off a cockroach's head, it takes the tough little bastard a week to die. And the only reason it dies? Because it can no longer eat and sustain its body as a complete entity. Harvesters are the same. Decapitation can sometimes be the end; but not always."

"That's unbelievable."

"Believe what you like, woman. But I have seen this before, once, when I was a child. Hunting snow lions with other vachine royalty; I was along for the ride, with my father. We had a Harvester with us, a tracker named Graslek. The lion surprised us in a circle of rocks, and as we fought a hasty retreat it bit off Graslek's head. My father carried the severed head back to the other Harvesters, who returned it to their world. I do not know what happened then, all I know is that the head talked the entire journey back. Gave me nightmares for months. My mother had to calm me with a strong blood-oil infusion."

"What happened to the snow lion?"

"Regrettably, it survived. Loped off into the peaks with half of a Harvester's body for a prize. Ruined the hunting trip."

Vashell sat down, cross-legged before the head. A tongue wetted lips, and at its request Vashell poured a little more water onto its eager, questing tongue. Five times more he did this, and gradually the Harvester's eyes grew bright, its features more relaxed.

"What is your name, Harvester?"

"Fiddion."

"How long ago were you…"

"Killed?" The Harvester chuckled, a low and nasty sound. "I have become arrogant, it would seem. I was performing a religious rite. I was secure in my own observation skills; I did not see, nor sense, that wolf approach. But then, maybe the Nonterrazake have removed some of my skills. In their eyes, I would deserve such a humiliating punishment."

"You have been cast out?" said Vashell, eyes wide in shock. It was the greatest show of emotion Alloria had ever witnessed from the vachine, but hard to read on his scarred features.

"Yes. And although it shames me, their treatment of me burns with hate. I would avenge myself on those who did this; I would bury their whole world under fire and ash!"

"What did you do?" asked Alloria, in awe, and Fiddion's small black eyes turned on her.

"You dare ask that of me, child? Begone! Away! I am not here to lay my soul bare before *humans*. That would be base and pathetic. But what I would seek…" he paused, small eyes blinking in a long, slow movement more to do with thought than anything else. "Yes. I would seek to give you information."

"Why?" snapped Vashell, feeling uneasy. Everything in his vachine world spoke of honour and loyalty to the Engineer Religion, to the Episcopate and Watchmakers; and they in turn, the vachine as a whole, trusted the Harvesters implicitly. They had fought wars together. They had died together. Whatever information Fiddion wished to share, it was born from bitterness, resentment and a need for revenge. And for Vashell, this sat worse than any ten year cancer.

"I would give you information," said the Harvester, "you can make an informed choice. Would you save your race, Vashell? Would you nurture the vachine into a new millennium?"

"We can do that without your help," said Vashell, quietly, but his eyes flickered with nervousness, almost like the orbs of a hunted creature. He knew he wasn't going to like what he was about to hear; he knew, instinctively, it would change his life forever.

Fiddion laughed. Quite a feat for a severed head. His spinal column seemed to relax and contract with delicate slithering sounds, like snake scales gliding over rock.

"Listen, *vachine*," he said, and his black eyes glowed like the outer reaches of space. "Your whole race, your whole religion, your whole world is threatened. By the Harvesters. By Kradek-ka. By General Graal and his stinking Army of Iron. They work together, can't you see?"

"To do what?" snorted Vashell.

"To bring about the return of the three Vampire Warlords. They are like Dark Gods, and once they walked these lands with a malice and depravity you could never comprehend. The world shivered when they awoke; and it breathed again when they died."

"They are legend," said Vashell, head tilted, one side of his scarred face illuminated by the flickering fire. Wood crackled, and woodsmoke twitched his nostrils. Outside, the wind howled mournfully and Vashell felt a great emptiness, a bleakness, in his soul. "Even if they did return, they would do us no harm. We are of the same blood. We are allies!" But even as he spoke the words, he could see the twisted logic of his own argument. They were not of the same blood. That was the whole point. The vachine were a hybrid clockwork deviation.

"No," said Fiddion, almost sadly, although Vashell was sure sadness was an emotion denied the Harvesters. "You are vachine. You are a dilution, my friend, of the feral wild Vampire Warlords; the vampires of old. Your clockwork is anathema to everything they believed in. Your race would be an abomination to everything they stood for; alien to their very essence."

Vashell shook his head. "We are mighty," he said. "We would fight them! We would destroy them!"

"No, because you will already be dead."

"What?" mocked Vashell. "The entire vachine civilisation? Don't be ridiculous."

"And do not be so arrogant," snapped Fiddion. "That is your curse!"

"And how would this miracle occur?"

Fiddion went silent for a while, face impassive, but then he licked at narrow lips showing his pointed teeth. "I do not know," he said, finally. "It was not introduced to our One Mind. All I know is that it involves Graal, and his army, his recent invasion of Falanor and the rivers of blood-oil now being gathered for the great magick required to resurrect the Vampire Warlords."

"You are forgetting one thing. Graal invaded Falanor on *our* instruction; on the command of the Engineers, and the Watchmakers."

"Yes. But why?"

Vashell frowned. "Because we run dry of blood-oil."

"But *why*, Vashel? Use your intellect, use your mind, don't allow the stagnant mental decadence of a thousand years pollute your ability to reason."

"The crops began to fail. The Refineries needed fresh blood. Some of them began to break down; to become inefficient. Do you think Kradek-ka had a part to play in all of this?"

"I think we can guarantee that," said Fiddion gently.

"What must I do?" But it came to him, a strike of lighting in the thunderstorm of his raging mind. Clarity sparkled like sunlight on a raging sea. "I must find Kradek-ka. I must track Anukis. She has gone to her father; but she does not understand his betrayal of the vachine." Understanding pulsed through him in waves. Kradek-ka had made Anukis, his daughter, in a different mould; when he introduced clockwork to her, it had been different, advanced, like nothing before ever seen by the vachine. She was awesome. And now Vashell knew why. She was an instrument, somehow, a tool to be used in bringing back the Vampire Warlords.

"Kradek-ka has a larger part to play in this than you could ever believe," said Fiddion, and Vashell nodded, and he knew Fiddion, the bitter, desecrated Harvester, was right.

Vashell turned. He stared at Alloria. He blinked. "You understand all this, woman?"

"I understand thousands will die," she said, voice small and yet run through with a fine-lode of iron. Alloria took a deep breath. After all. She was Queen of Falanor. "Our fates are entwined, are they not?" she said. "The people of Falanor. And the vachine. It is not a simple case of invasion. The puzzle is far more intricate than that."

Fiddion's eyes adjusted, and focused on Alloria. She felt her breath catch in her throat; felt her heartbeat stutter and stop. "You are correct," he said, eyes boring into her like the granite and diamond drill-bits used for mining under the Black Pike Mountains.

"The Vampire Warlords will kill you all," Fiddion said, voice little more than a whisper. Then his tiny black eyes closed, and he slept.

Winter in the Black Pike Mountains was a savage, relentless mistress. The nights were long, hard, cold, the frequent storms a show of temper like nothing seen across the Four Continents. For Alloria, shivering in the corner of the cave, peering occasionally at the motionless, decapitated head of the Harvester, and fearing a return of the feral mountain wolves, it seemed to take a month just for the cold dawn to arrive.

With light came an abatement of the storm, and the mournful howling reduced to nothing more than occasional, scattered shrieks. Snow flurries decorated the cave mouth, random snaps of hail and gusts of ice-chilled wind.

Alloria sat, nearer the fire now, arms wrapped around her legs, hugging herself in a need for heat. Terrible icy draughts entered the cave, and she could feel her teeth chattering, jarring her skull. She had never experienced such savage weather in the warm southlands of Falanor. She looked over to where Vashell slept, and envied him his peace. His scarred face seemed strangely calm, his breathing regular.

What have I got myself into? thought Alloria, and gave a deep, bitter sigh. How violently her world had changed in a few short weeks. From her rape and abduction at the whim of General Graal in an effort to subdue King Leanoric, through to a nightmare journey through Falanor, and secret subterranean tunnels under the mountains, to her final accidental rescue by the vachine Anukis, Alloria's life had become a journey of insanity and confusion. Abused, both physically, sexually and mentally, she knew she teetered on the edge of breaking. And yet... and yet her country, Falanor, needed her. King Leanoric used to say: I am the Land, and the Land is me. Now, Falanor had no King and Alloria was – as far as she could ascertain – the only living member of royalty. Sourly, this led to her boys and she sank deeper into depression.

What did life matter now if her babes were dead?

Why did anything matter?

And she thought back, further. Images of betrayal flittered through her skull. She could picture a gem. A small, dark gem. With a sour taste in her mouth, she refused the memories, and pushed them away, feeling pain at simple understanding. Betrayal, echoed the halls of her memory. *Betrayal.*

Smoothly, Vashell rolled to his feet. He glanced at Alloria. "Somebody is coming."

"Who?"

Vashell ignored her and drew his knife, staring at the cave entrance. A few moments later, like a ghost from the snow, came a figure. He was tall, athletic and broad-shouldered. He moved warily into the cave with short-sword drawn, then stopped, staring at Vashell.

"Llaran!" exclaimed Vashell, and took a step forward, then paused, and lowered his face. When he glanced up, his eyes were bright with tears. Llaran lowered his sword, and his face softened.

"Vash? Is that you?"

"Llaran, little brother, it's been a hard fight."

Llaran moved closer. Icicles clung to his hair and heavy furs. His boots were crusted with ice. He stopped, staring at Vashell, his handsome face shocked, his mouth open. Llaran flexed his golden claws, and his vachine fangs ejected.

"They took your face, brother." His voice hardened a little, but then in a flurry of movement he lowered his sword and stepped in close and held Vashell. Vashell felt tears on the scars of his cheeks. The salt stung his tattered flesh.

"Aye, they took my face. But not my honour! Not my dignity! I am still more violent than you could believe possible! I am still vachine at heart, at soul!"

"I don't doubt that," laughed Llaran, releasing his older brother and moving towards the fire with an easy, relaxed, rolling gait. He stopped beside the head of the Harvester, looking down in open wonder, then with a sudden movement he slashed his sword across the Harvester's face, toppling the head into the fire. The Harvester's eyes snapped open and it began to scream, a terrible high pitched sound as flames curled around skin and licked into eyes and scorched flesh. A stench filled the cave. Vashell surged forward, but Llaran's sword came up – a swift movement. Suddenly, his eyes seemed hard and the smile had gone from his face. Noisily, and still screaming, Fiddion's head burned.

"What have you done?" shouted Vashell.

There came a clatter of noise from the mouth of the cave, and three vachine stood there, swords drawn, the bulk of their armour and furs blocking out the cold snow-light.

"We've been hunting this traitor for weeks," said Llaran, lips a narrow line of bloodless ice. "Now, as you can see, his fate is sealed. But you, dear sweet brother, you are a bonus I did not expect!"

Llaran turned to the three vachine warriors, who slid out claws and fangs in readiness for battle. Llaran stepped back towards the wall of the cave, and in a voice full of malice as he stared at his older brother, said, "Kill him. And kill the woman, too."

General Graal rode his steed to the top of the hill, hooves crunching snow and dead leaves, and scattered woodland detritus. He dismounted and calmed the beast, feeding it a handful of oats from his saddlebag. The night sky was a patchwork of black and grey clouds, and moonlight shimmered in shafts illuminating a vast city landscape below. Graal's eyes narrowed, as he watched ten thousand albino soldiers – the Army of Iron – moving into position with the precision of...

Graal smiled.

Why, with the precision of clockwork.

Silently the ranks of albino infantry assembled. To the rear, hidden by woodland, Graal knew the cankers had been released from their cages. However, hopefully they wouldn't be needed for the sleeping, unwary populace of Vor – Falanor's Capital City. The main problem with cankers was they were *too* vicious, too bloodthirsty, too brutal; they savaged a corpse without refinement allowing precious blood to pump free during frenzy and savagery. No. The trick was an ice-death using ice-smoke. Freeze the bodies of human cattle, encase them in ice – so that the Harvesters could reap the Harvest at their leisure.

Graal turned, eyes narrowing, checking the distant shapes on the Great North Road. The huge black outlines of the Refineries loomed, rumbling gently as they were dragged by teams of horses. This time, everything would come together neatly with no surprises. This time, the mission – cause and effect – would slot neatly into place. There would be no... *wastage*.

Graal returned his eyes to the waiting Army of Iron. Moonlight glinted on dull black armour, on unsheathed swords, on matt helmets. Special soldiers had been sent ahead to hunt down and silence any sentries, any woodsman, any stragglers who might alert the population of Vor to their impending slaughter – to their impending *harvest*. Graal smiled a narrow smile. After all, he didn't want to waste precious time hunting down the terrified. Not when ice-smoke could make a neat kill in the first place.

Below, Harvesters were assembling, drifting eerily, like wood-spirits, through the ranks of motionless soldiers. Graal's chest swelled with pride at his men, his albino ghosts. Graal's blue eyes sparkled, and his head tilted, and he acknowledged the *irony* of the phrase. *Albino* was not *quite* correct.

At the head of the infantry now, the Harvesters stopped. Their chanting was low, a monotone, little more than sighs on a winter wind. Their hands, with long bone fingers, lifted towards the sky and Graal felt a *pulse* of magick thump through the ground, passing beneath his boots and on down, down the steep hillside, through gullies and streams and rocks, through narrow channels of peat bog and patches of sparse woodland until it met the Harvesters and from their feet, from the soil, rose the ice-smoke. It billowed, thick wreaths and coils, like ice-snakes under the precise control of their masters. The ice-smoke grew, rising, obscuring the Harvesters and the infantry and Graal felt a stab of pleasure as he knew, *knew* this mission would be successful, and with its success came the total subjugation of Falanor. After that, only one thing remained.

The mammoth clouds of ice-smoke were huge, now, and Graal watched impassively as they rolled out, flowing down hills to en-compass and swallow the first of the buildings on the outskirts of Falanor's capital city; there were no screams, no shouts of alarm, and this, Graal acknowledged, was the beauty of such an attack. It was clean. Silent. Efficient. There was no wastage.

The ice-smoke flooded across cottages, tenements, factories, bridges, rivers, parks, a writhing coiling turbulence of freezing cold with a motionless army of killers waiting behind. This was not a battle, not an invasion; this was simple butchery. And Graal revelled in it.

Finally, there came a scream. But by then, the ice-smoke was moving fast as if accelerating with the downward slope. It spread like a flood, and within a few short minutes the entire city was bathed in white, as if a huge blanket of mist had settled gently in the early morning darkness. Only this time, the mist was deadly.

Graal turned to his horse, and from an oiled leather sheath removed a slender, black battle-horn. It was said it was made from the thigh-bone of a god, but Graal smiled grimly at this nonsense. The horn was made from something much, much worse.

He placed the horn to his lips, and blew a long, single ululation which echoed mournfully across the sea of ice-smoke. With unity and proud synchronisation, the Army of Iron moved forward into the sleeping city streets.

And the slaughter began.

The weak winter sun had risen in a raped sky. Purple bruised clouds lay scattered, the welt-marks of the abuser. The ice-smoke had nearly dissipated, but still long coils, like dying ice-snakes, writhed in the streets. Graal rode his mount, hooves clattering cobbles, and he surveyed his handiwork. Corpses lay in piles to either side of every alley where he looked. Men, women, children, all white and blue and purple, frozen in sleep, frozen in the act of running, their bodies motionless. Some, he knew, were still alive, the ice-smoke purposefully not killing them, just seeking to retain every precious drop of blood. However, death was usually a realistic consequence. Except for those of incredibly strong disposition.

Graal rode his horse down the main thoroughfare, a wide cobbled street lined with baskets of winter flowers and where once King Leanoric, and his queen, Alloria, had ridden carriages in procession, the streets lined with cheering people, happy people, good people, unaware of the fate shortly to befall their land, their country, their species.

Graal halted before the Rose Palace, and it was a wonderful site to behold. Huge iron gates were skilfully melded into a battle scene, and protected long lawns, now piled with corpses, Graal noted, those of servants and retainers, and the King's Royal Guard, their red jackets frosted with ice. The building itself was staggeringly beautiful. Commissioned seven hundred years previously, it was built from white stone, marble and obsidian, and the mortar was mixed with silver which glinted, even now, in this weak winter sunshine. Graal cantered across a frozen lawn, hooves crunching grass, and he dismounted by the wide, flowing marble steps. A Harvester, Tetrakall, was waiting for him.

"You did well," said Graal, removing his gauntlets.

"Lambs to the slaughter," replied Tetrakall with a shrug of his elongated, bony shoulders.

"Still. Your magick is something which impresses. And I am not an easy man to impress."

"You should see the magick of my homeland," said Tetrakall, taking a bobbing step forward, his head lowering a little, his blank eyes staring into Graal's. "We weave dreams, we weave magick, we harvest souls and use them for... things I cannot vocalise, things you would never understand."

"One day, I will visit," said Graal, voice low, and he meant it. The Harvesters thrilled him in a way he found hard to express. They did not scare him – well, maybe a little – but the only thing he truly understood was that they were from an ancient time, a time before the Vampire Warlords. And this in itself was something of which to be wary. Still. They had a pact; a symbiotic agreement. The vachine got the blood for their refineries. And the Harvesters... well, they took something else.

Graal moved past Tetrakall, and Dagon Trelltongue was waiting for him. The man, once trusted advisor to King Leanoric, a man who had betrayed the people of Falanor for his own life, betrayed his king and queen, gave a deep bow and fear was etched deeply into his face as if by carefully applied drops of acid. He had aged since Graal had last seen him. He had aged considerably. Grey streaked his hair, fear squatted in his eyes like black toads, and his mouth was a trembling line of persistent terror.

"You have conquered," said Dagon, his bow lowering further, the tone of his voice unreadable. He had seen what cankers could do first hand; he did not want to be their next victim.

"Yes. And you, also, did well Trelltongue. You have–" Graal smiled. "Why, my man, you have slaughtered your own people. How does that feel, pray tell?" Graal moved close. Could smell Dagon's terror. He reached out, and stroked the man's hair, his long finger tracing a line down Dagon's jaw. "You are responsible for the ease of my success, you are responsible for perfectly traced plans, responsible for the fall of Falanor. I wonder, little man, if you sleep soundly in your bed at night?"

Dagon looked up, then, a sharp movement. "Alcohol helps," he said, smoothly. And there was a spark in his eyes, but Graal held his gaze and the flame died to be replaced by cold dread. A knowledge that every waking day he would have to live with the guilt of betraying a nation.

"Come with me!" snapped Graal, and led Dagon across the Welcome Hall with its gold and silver mosaics depicting the Trials of Gerannorkin, through several long chambers still resplendent with huge oak tables filled with baskets of winter flowers from the South Woods, then right, down more corridors to a huge library. Graal was sure of his path. To Dagon, it appeared Graal had been there before. Many times.

In the ancient library, wood gleamed and stunk of rich wax and polish. The smell of well-tended books invaded Dagon's nostrils, and a stab of recognition and nostalgia pierced his mind; he had sat here with King Leanoric on many occasions, as they shared coffee and brandy and discussed affairs of state. Now, the place seemed cold and dead, as cold and dead as the king. And whilst it could not be said Dagon Trelltongue was directly responsible for the invasion of Falanor – it would have happened with or without his input, his revealing of tactics and military positions, and his betrayal, his information, had certainly made the life of General Graal and the Army of Iron easier.

Dagon noticed a bag in the General's hand, and they moved to the centre of the library. Towering bookcases reared around them, and Graal gestured to a series of low leather reading couches. Dagon sat, on the edge of a couch, as if he might flee at any moment. Graal smiled at this.

From the bag he took a small mirror and placed this flat on a table. Then he seated himself, and stared down at the silver glass. Softly, he whispered three words of power, and the glass misted black, then swirled with sparkles of gold and amber. Then a face materialised and Graal smiled. It was his daughter. One of the Soul Stealers.

"Tashmaniok."

"Father."

"Did you find them?"

"We found them."

"Did you kill them?"

"No, father."

Graal disguised his annoyance well, with only a tightening of muscles in his jaw betraying the fact he did not appreciate such news. "What happened?"

"Kell, the old warrior, turned out more resourceful than we anticipated. He was bloodbond. But more. There was something else about him, father; something we do not understand."

"He is mortal, like the rest of them," spat Graal, suddenly losing his cool. "You must destroy him!"

"Is this pride speaking, father?" She smiled a cold smile, and Graal knew, then, he had raised her well.

"Not pride." He was cool. "Necessity. What of the other? Saark? Did he have that which we seek?"

"We could not ascertain."

"You were fought off?"

"Saark had help."

"From whom?"

"A little boy summoned insects from the wood, the floors, the air. His name was Skanda. I have read about him, in your *Book of Legends*, and in your *Granite Throne Lore*."

Graal frowned. "Impossible. Skanda is dead! The whole Ankarok race are dead! The Warlords saw to that, millennia past!"

Tashmaniok turned from the mirror, then returned to gaze at her father with unnerving, crimson eyes. Her gaze was cold; unforgiving. "Still," she said, smoothly, unperturbed. "Skanda was able to toss Shanna aside as if she were a simple village girl. And he carried a scorpion."

"Did it... have two tails? Two stings?"

"It did," said Tash. "Now do you believe us?"

"I believe there is dark magick at play," scowled General Graal. "Where are you?"

"Heading north," said Tashmaniok. "We picked up their trail leading away from the burning town. It's a long story. However, Skanda no longer travels with the two men. There is little between here and the Black Pike Mountains; we can only assume they head for the Cailleach Fortress."

"I will send some help. Something special," said Graal.

"Yes. We underestimated these men. It will not happen again. No more mistakes. We will peel the skin from their bones."

"Do it. And Tash?"

"Yes, father?"

Graal blinked, slow and lazy, like a reptile. "I love you, girls. Don't ever forget that."

"We never forget it, father."

The mirror returned to a shimmer of silver and Graal stood, stretching his spine. He moved to a narrow window in the library wall, more of an archer's slit than a true window, which had been filled with lead-lined glass. He looked down from the Rose Palace, over the vision below.

The first of the Refineries was being hauled up the main cobbled street, its darkness, and angularity, seeming to block out pink pastel light from a winter sun. Graal turned to Dagon, deep in thought.

"You know it is said this man, Kell, is blessed by the gods," said Dagon, slowly, looking sideways at Graal.

"That is not so," said Graal. "He is mortal, like the rest of you... with your *feeble* human shells."

"No," said Dagon, and his voice held a splinter of triumph. "He is Kell. He is the Legend. He carries the mighty Ilanna. He may not be a part of *your* culture, but he is certainly a part of ours."

"You know something else?" Graal strode in fury to the cowering man, and hoisted him into the air by the throat. Dagon's legs kicked and he choked, and slowly Graal released the iron in his grip.

"No, I swear!"

"Speak, or I'll rip out your windpipe and eat it before your fucking eyes!"

"All I know is what Leanoric told me! He said Kell was a Vachine Hunter, way back, years ago for the old Battle King. He roamed the Black Pike Mountains, slaying rogue vachine who troubled our borders. We did not know, back then, that these were outcast, the impure, the damaged, the unholy. We did not know there was a *civilisation!* We did not realise vachine were a discrete species, an entire race! If we had known, we would have sent our armies!"

Graal dropped Dagon to the polished, wooden floor. He moved back to the window.

"Kell is a special man. He has special knowledge."

"He knows how to kill vachine," said Dagon, rubbing his throat.

"Soon he will learn to die," said Graal without emotion, as he watched soldiers loading Blood Refineries with the first of the frozen corpses from the ravaged city of Vor.

TEN
Echoes of a Childhood Dream

As Saark crawled towards Kell, towards his pulsing blood-stench, the hunger deep in his veins and soul, so a new devastating pain lashed through him in waves. Saark hit the ground, hard, and lay there panting, face pressing the snow, and feeling as though he was being beaten with helves. He looked up, strained to see if Kell had noticed, and then wrenched at his own face as the fangs – having made their presence known to him – retreated back into his skull. Saark screamed a silent scream of pure agony, then rolled onto his back and allowed the cold night to claim him.

At dawn, Saark awoke to Kell's whistling. He was covered by a thick blanket, and warm soup bubbled over a fire. With aching limbs, Saark stood and tested himself. Numbly, he realised there was no longer any pain. Whatever had poisoned him, blood-oil Kell called it; well, it had gone. And he still had his head, which he shook in disbelief; and *that* meant nothing had given him away to Kell.

Approaching the fire, he slumped down and Kell smiled. "If you sleep out in the snow like that, lad, you'll catch your death."

"It was the fight. In Creggan. It took a lot out of me."

"Aye," said Kell. "Well, let's eat fast then saddle up. We have a long day through enemy-infested country ahead of us. And I dare say, those two bitches from the Bone Fields will be somewhere behind, sniffing on our stinking trail."

"Do you... do you feel all right?" said Saark, softly, not quite meeting Kell's gaze.

"I feel as powerful as ten men," growled Kell. "Come on. I want to find Nienna."

The canker stood in the shadow of the ancient oak woodland on the summit of Hangman's Hill, a natural chameleon on the outskirts of the desecrated, crumbling monastery. Snow fell, drifting in light diagonal flurries and adding a fuzzy edge to reality. The canker was huge, the size of a lion, but there the similarity ended. Muscles writhed like the coils of a massive serpent beneath waxen white skin, the smooth surface broken occasionally by tufts of grey and white fur, and by open, weeping wounds where tiny cogs and wheels of twisted clockwork broke free, ticking, spinning, minute gears stepping up and down, tiny levers adjusting and *clicking* neatly into place. Only here, in this canker, in this *abnormal* vachine, the movements were not so neat – because every aspect of the canker's clockwork was a deviation, an aberration of flesh and engineering and religion; the canker was outcast. Impure. Unholy.

As evening spread swiftly towards night, the sky streaked with purple bruises and jagged saw-blades of cloud, so the canker watched two men progress, like distant avatars, making their way gradually across the snowy plain. The small entourage zig-zagged between stands of lightning-blasted conifers and ancient, pointed stones, one stocky man leading two horses, the second, more slender and effete, master of a laden donkey. The canker shifted its bulk, aware it was invisible to the men, blending as it did with the ancient tumble of fallen stones and thick woodland of thousand year oaks, and doubly hidden by the haze of wind-whipped snow. It turned, superior clockwork eyes observing the trees, their gnarled trunks and branches full of protrusions, whorls and nubs of elderly bark. A product of ancient vegetative inter-breeding, a meshing of woodland technologies – of nature, and soul, and spirit. Like me, thought the canker, and smiled as far as such a bestial, twisted, corrupted *creation* could smile; for its mouth was five times the size of a human mouth, the jaw jacked wide open, lips pulled high and wrenched upwards over the skull with eyes displaced to the side of its head. Huge fangs, twisted and bent in awkward directions, glistened with saliva and… blood-oil.

Blood-oil. And blood-oil magick. The basis for an entire vachine civilisation; the nectar of the machine vampires.

The canker smiled again, a bitter smile as it remembered its long past, as it remembered the pretty *man*, and this time the thoughts behind the grimace were as equally twisted. For the canker was deviant, unholy, cast out by the Engineer Episcopate, and however conversely, employed by the very vachine Engineers who had condemned it. The canker could hunt. And it could kill. And in some small way attempt to find a token retribution, some faith, some hope for that entwining symbiotic battle of flesh and clockwork which had twisted the canker since shortly after its meeting with... Graal. When *clockwork* had been introduced to fresh human flesh.

Graal. Now, there was a man to hate.

The canker was obedient. It had been bribed with a future promise of returned and retuned flesh, of fresh new mortality, of assimilation into a purebreed human where it could return to a life of normality; without the eternal internal pain of battling machinery.

I can do it, thought the monster. I can *find out*.

And if not? Well, the instruction had been complicit.

I must kill, it thought.

For it is the only way to be sane.

The canker watched the two men dwindling into twilight, drifting ghosts, and even from this great distance it could smell the oil on their weapons, the sweat in their clothes, the unrefined *blood* in their veins. Hunger pulsed in the canker's brain, amidst a turmoil of gears and cogs and painful memories, *so painful*; brainmesh, it was called. And it hurt worse than acid.

In eerie silence the canker stood, stretched powerful muscles, and padded down the hill between elderly gnarled oaks.

"I thought you said there was a fortified town out this way?" grumbled Kell, stopping and leaning on his axe with a weary sigh. Snow swirled around his boots, and the huge tangled bearskin across his broad shoulders sat crusted with rimes of ice, shining silver. The two geldings halted behind him, and one pawed the frozen earth with a heavy, iron-shod hoof. "It'll be night soon; I could dearly do with some hot food and three hours in a soft bed, away from this bastard snow."

"Ah, Kell old horse, you are so narrow-minded in your basic warrior's vision!" Saark grinned at the old soldier. As the day had advanced, he had begun to feel better and better, more fit and healthy than he had for years. It was a miracle, he realised, with a dark, grim, bitter humour. "A plate of simple peasant vegetables? Surely that cannot be your only lust? What of the warm inviting thighs of some generously proportioned innkeeper's daughter? What of her eager lips? Her fast-rising bosom? Her peasant's need to please?"

Kell hawked and spat, and focused on the dandy. "Saark mate, you misunderstand me. Exhaustion is the first thing on my mind; followed by an ale, and then a need to get to Nienna before something *bad* happens. And look at you! I cannot believe you bought such ridiculous clothes back in Creggan. You should have been born a woman, mate. Too much pompous lace and courtside extravagance. It's enough to make an honest woodsman puke."

"But Kell, Kell, dear Kell – born a woman, you say?" Saark smiled, his perfectly symmetrical teeth displaying a boyish humour that had broken many a woman's heart. "Is that because you find me secretly attractive? Through all our battles, all our triumphs, the mighty Kell, grizzled old warrior, hero of *Kell's Legend*, superior in strength and violence to all his many enemies… *secretly*, all along, he was a boy-fancier and lusted after a slice of Saark's pork pie!"

"You go too far!" stormed Kell, and lurched forward, mighty axe Ilanna held in one hefty fist, face crimson with embarrassment and sudden rage. "Don't be smearing me with your own backward deviant wants. You might enjoy a roll with a man; I do not. The only use I have for a man," he hoisted his axe purposefully, "is to detach his head from his fucking *shoulders*."

Saark took a step back, hand on sword-hilt. His smile was still there, but mistrust shone in his eyes. He knew Kell to be a good friend, and a mighty foe; honourable, powerful, but ultimately compromised by a bad streak of temper made worse by even the smallest drop of whiskey. "Kell, old boy," his words were more clipped now, for the stress of the journey – and the hunt for Nienna – was wearing hard on both men. "Calm down. I was only jesting. Soon, we will find a tavern. Hopefully, one without vachine bitches and Blacklipper raiders. And then, *then* you can satiate your own personal lust."

"What's that supposed to mean, lad?"

"I'm sure they'll have a drop or ten of Falanor's *Finest Malt*."

Kell made a growling sound, more animal than human, and took another step closer. Saark, to his credit, stood his ground. He may have looked like a rampant peacock loose and horny in the midst of a silk market, but he had been King Leanoric's Sword

Champion. Many times, he had been underestimated – usually at the expense of somebody's life.

"You in the mood for a fight, lad?" snapped Kell.

Saark held up one hand, shaking his head, eyes lowered to the snowy ground. "No, no, you misunderstand." He gazed up then, reading Kell's pain. Nienna had been gone far too long, and their quest to find her seemed as hopeless now as it had when the land of Falanor was overrun by the albino Army of Iron.

Ultimately, Kell's missing granddaughter was a thorn in this great lion's paw; but one nobody could easily extract. Only Kell could do that. And the chances were, the search and rescue would be carried high on the back of mutilation, murder and annihilation. Kell was not a forgiving man.

"My friend, you are worse than any irate vachine. Calm down! I was just trying to lighten the mood, old horse."

"I'll lighten your bowels," growled Kell.

"You really are a cantankerous and stinking donkey."

"And you are a feathered popinjay, too damn fond of your own song. Shut your mouth, Saark—I can't say it any plainer—before I carve you a second smile."

Saark nodded, and they understood one another, and they moved on through the now heavily falling snow.

"There's the town," said Saark. "It's called Kettleskull Creek. Fortified with high walls. Brilliant. We might get an uninterrupted sleep! And it looks like the Army of Iron did not pass this way; probably too eager to get to Jalder, and the ripe harvest found there."

"Kettleskull Creek? What an odd name."

"It's fine, Kell. They know me."

"By the way you say 'know me', do you mean there are fifteen bastard children?"

Saark tilted his head. "You know, Kell, for you that's pretty good. No. I have only four bastard children I know of, although I'm sure there are many more in the provinces." He gave a wry smile, eyes distant, as if reliving a catalogue of pretty women. "I did a lot of travelling in the name of the king. So many beautiful ladies. So little time."

But Kell wasn't listening. He had turned, was looking down their back trail. In the distance huge brooding hills blackened the sky through the twilight snow. Kell searched from left to right, both hands clasped on Ilanna. "Let's get to the town," he said.

"A problem?"

"We're being followed."

"You sure?"

Kell turned, and the look in his eyes chilled Saark to the marrow. "Your skill is wooing unsuspecting ladies, lad. Mine is killing those creatures who need to be dead. Trust me. We are being followed. We need to move now… unless you relish a fight in the dark? In the ice?"

"Understood," muttered Saark, and led the way towards the high walls of the stocky timber barricade.

Saark had spoken the truth, the villagers knew him, and they lifted the bars on the twenty foot high gates and allowed the two men entry. As Saark turned, smiling, he faced a porcupine of steady, unsheathed swords.

"What's the matter, lads? Did I say something to offend?"

"Gambling debts," muttered one man with strange, black tattoos on his teeth. He was tall and rangy, with dark looks and bushy brows that met at the centre of his forehead. "Let's just say that last time you was here Saark… well mate, you made a swift exit."

Saark gave an easy laugh, resting back on one hip, his hand held out, lace cuff puffed towards the ranger. "My man, you have read my very honourable intention. I have indeed decided to return in order to pay off my substantial gambling debts." Saark moved to his saddlebag, fished out several coins, and tossed them over with an air of arrogance. The tall man grunted, catching the coins, fumbling for a moment, then examining the gold carefully. Slowly, the swords were sheathed one by one. Saark gave a chuckle. "Peasant gold," he said, head high, eyes twinkling as they challenged the group of men. Several went again for their weapons, but the tall man stopped them, and waved Saark on.

"Go on, about your business. But don't be causing any trouble. There's enough in Kettleskull who have cause to challenge you, King's Man."

"No longer King's Man, I think you'll find."

"As you wish."

They strode down the frozen road, and Kell muttered, "'Peasant's Gold'?"

Saark gave a thin smile. "It does one no harm to be occasionally reminded of one's place."

"Surely you meant 'Stolen Gold'?"

"That as well," smiled Saark, sardonically.

The main inn, *The Spit-Roasted Pig*, squatted beside a huge, warehouse-type building, dark and foreboding, set back from the road and piled high with snow. Kell stared up at the structure, then dismissed it. He followed Saark towards the inn.

"Remember," rumbled Kell, grabbing Saark's shoulder and pulling him rudely back. "Keep a low profile in here. We restock, refuel, then we're off again to find Nienna. No funny business. No women. No drinking. You understand? "

"Of course!" scowled Saark, and held apart his hands, face a platter of innocence. "As if I would do anything else!"

Kell stared at the half-full bottle of whiskey as Myriam's poison began to eat him again. The bottle squatted on the bar, filled with an amber delight, a sugary nectar which was sweet, oh so sweet, and it called to him like a woman, called to him with honeyed words of promise. Taste me. Drink me. Absorb me into your blood, and we can be one, we can be whole. I will take away the poison, Kell. I will take away your pain.

Around Kell the noise of the inn blurred, and fell into a tumbling swirling spiral of downward descent. Only him, and the whiskey, existed and he could taste it, taste *her* on his tongue and she was delight, summer flowers, fresh honey, a virgin's smile, and how could Kell possibly say no to such an innocent invitation? How could he refuse?

Slowly, he reached out and grabbed the bottle. It was aged twenty years in oak vats. It had cost a pretty penny of gold, but the gold in his saddlebags was stolen from the albino army, the invading Army of Iron; and Kell cared nothing for their loss.

"I'm going to my room," said Kell, tongue thick, mind swirling, focus dead.

"There's a good lad," said Saark, eyes glittering with a different distraction, and watched the old warrior depart.

Saark loved many things in life. In fact, there were so many pleasures that in his humble opinion made life worth living, he doubted he could list them all. A child's laughter. Sunlight. The clink of gold on gold. The soft kiss of a woman's lips. The velvet skin on the curve of a hip. The slick handful of an eager quim. Liquor. Bawdy company. Bad jokes. Gambling...

Saark coughed, innocent and unaware, eyes on a buxom wench across the tavern who'd caught his eye. She had long red hair and a cheeky smile. Then the heavy blow knocked him from his feet. He hit the ground, confusion his mistress, and he swam through treacle and felt himself being dragged. Another two blows sent him spinning into darkness. When he came round, groggy and stunned, a cold wind caressed his skin, but it felt good, good against the swellings on his face, tortured flesh battered and bruised after a pounding of helves. What happened? he thought, dazed. Just what the fuck happened?

"Not so cocky now, are you, King's *bitch*?" snarled a face close to his, bad breath and garlic mixing to force a choke from Saark's lips. In the gloom he fought to recognise his assailant, but his mind was spinning, and the world seemed inside out.

"I'd lay off the garlic next time," advised Saark through bleeding lips. "You'll never get intimate with a lady when you stink like a village idiot." There was a growl, and a boot connected with his ribs, several times. Then he was hefted along, dragged through snow, and over rough wood planks. He felt splinters worming into his hands and knees, but it was all he could do to scramble – and be dragged – along.

"Watch your footsteps, lad, wouldn't want you to drown," came a half-recognised voice, and laughter accompanied the voice and with a start Saark realised there were men, many men, and this wasn't a simple dispute over a spilt tankard of ale; it was a lynching party. A sadness sank deep through him, like a sponge through lantern oil. He was in trouble. He was in a barrel of horseshit.

Saark was dumped to the ground, which echoed ominously, and boots clattered around him. Saark waited for more pain, but it didn't come. Curled foetal, he finally opened his eyes and took a deep breath and spat out a sliver of broken tooth. That stung him, that tooth. Anger awoke in him, like an almost extinguished candle wick. This was turning into a *bad* day.

What happened?

He was laughing, joking, there was smoke and whiskey, they were playing at the card table. The villagers from the gate. He was taking their money like honey-cakes from a toddler – winning fair and square, for a change, and not having to resort to the *many* gambling tricks at which he was so good. Then… a blow from behind, from a helve, his face clattering against the table and taking the whole gambling pit with him. Boots finished him off. He didn't see it coming.

But why? In the name of the Holy Mother of Falanor, why?

"He's awake. Sit him up, lads."

Saark was dragged up, forced onto a chair, then tied to it with tight knots. Saark tested his bonds. Yes, he thought. There was no breaking free of those! He gazed around, at so many faces he did not know. Except for one. What was the man's name? Jake? Rake? Drake? Bake? Saark suppressed a giggle. It was the rangy man from the village gates...

"What's this all about, Stake?"

"The name is Rake, dimwit." The circle of men chuckled.

Saark looked about uneasily, and rolled his neck. He could still feel the press of his narrow rapier against his thigh – but had no ability to reach the weapon. Like all villagers, they underestimated the danger of such a narrow blade; what they considered a "girl's weapon". If it wasn't an axe, pike or bastard sword, then it wasn't *really* a weapon. Saark gave a narrow smile. Very much in the mould of Kell. They would find out, if he was given opportunity. Of that, he was sure.

"Surely I don't owe *that much* money," said Saark.

The circle of men closed in, and he could read anger, rage even, and a certain amount of *affront* on their faces, many bearded, several pock-marked, all with narrowed eyes and clenched fists and brandished weapons.

"Look around you," said Rake, unnecessarily thought Saark, although he deemed it prudent not to be pedantic. "Fathers. Brothers. Sons."

"Aye?" Still Saark wore confusion like a cloak.

"Enjoyed many a pretty dalliance during days passing through, haven't you Saark, *King's Man*? When you arrived, word went round fast. Here was Saark, an arrogant rich bastard, unable to keep his childmaker in his cheese-stinking pants."

Saark eyed the circle of men once more. Now he understood their almost pious rage. "Ahh," he said, and realised he was really in trouble. "But surely, gentleman, we are all men of the world? I could perhaps recompense you with a glitter of gold coin? I could make it worth your while..."

"You took my daughter's *virginity*, bastard!" snarled Rake, and punched Saark with a well-placed right hook. The chair toppled and Saark's head bounced from the planks. Beyond swirling stars, he saw a broad, still pool of gleaming black. More confusion invaded him. What *was* this place?

The men righted the chair, and Saark had to listen to the sermon, how rich arrogant bastards shouldn't poke around with their poker where they weren't welcome; how families had been destroyed, children cast out, bastard children born, yawn yawn. Get to the point you dullards, mused Saark, as his gaze fell beyond the men to what looked like a *lake* of black oil. It gleamed in the light of the lanterns, and suddenly Saark felt extremely uneasy. He noticed planks across the oil, resting occasionally on rusted iron pillars, and over which he had been dragged. Then he noticed, as they almost materialised from the gloom, huge, ancient machines, of angular iron, with great clockwork wheels and gears, meshing and interweaving. So. An old factory. From Elder Days. Abandoned. Derelict. With no *understanding*. But here they were, in the bowels of the old factory, the sump, where cooling oil was once stored. But one bright element drove through Saark's thoughts like a spear through chainmail.

Why bring him here?

He grinned, a skeletal grin. He wasn't leaving this place, was he?

They were going to drown him in the oil; and it would swallow him, and leave no mark of his passing.

He stared down into the black pit, motionless now, but as a man moved on the wooden planks so tiny ripples edged out and betrayed the liquid viscosity of centuries-old scum, filled with impurities and filth, and the perfect *hiding* place for *murder*...

With senses fast returning, Saark counted the men. There were twelve. *Twelve?* He didn't remember accosting twelve women, but then the nights were cold and long in Kettleskull, Saark was easily bored and so, apparently, were the local housewives and daughters. Was he really that decadent? Saark stared long and hard into his own soul, and with head hung low in shame, he had to admit that he was.

"What are you going to do?" he asked, finally, watching as Rake tied a knot in a thick length of rope. A noose? Wonderful, thought Saark. Just perfect.

"We are going to purify you," said Rake, face a demon mask in the lantern light, and moved forward, looping the rope over Saark's neck.

"No you're not, lads," came a voice from the darkness. Then Kell stepped forward, his shape, his *bulk* hinted at by the very edges of lantern light. In this gloom it mattered not that he was over sixty years of age; he was large, he was terrifying, and Ilanna held steady in bear's paws was a horrible and menacing sight to behold. "Now put the dandy down, and back away from the chair."

The men froze, helves and a few rusted short-swords held limp and useless. Rake, who held Saark in a tight embrace – a bonding between executioner and victim – stared at Kell without fear. His eyes were bright with unshed tears.

"Go home, old man. We have unfinished business here."

Kell gave a low, dark laugh. "Listen boy. I've been killing men for over forty years, and I've killed every bastard who stood in my way. Now, despite your violence on Saark here, I understand your position, I even agree with you to a large extent..."

"Thanks, Kell!" moaned Saark.

"... but this is not his time to die." Kell's eyebrows darkened to thunder. His voice dropped an octave. "I have no argument with any man here. But anybody lays another finger on the wandering peacock, and I'll cleave the bastard from skull to prick."

Time seemed to freeze. Kell's words hung in the air like drifting snow... and as long as nobody moved, the spell was cast, uncertainty a bright splinter in every man's mind. But then Rake screamed, and hauled on the noose which tightened around Saark's throat, dragging him upright, chair and all, his legs kicking, heels scraping old planks, and Kell took four long strides forward. The terrible axe Ilanna sang through the air and Rake's head detached from his body, and sailed into a dark oil pool. There was a *schlup* as Rake's head went under. His body stood, rigid in shock for several heartbeats as blood pumped from the ragged neck wound. One leg buckled, and slowly Rake's body folded to the floor like a sack of molten offal.

There was a *thunk* as Ilanna rested against the planks, and Kell's gaze caressed the remaining men. "Anybody else?" came his soft words, and they were the words of a lover, whispered and intimate, and every man there lifted hands in supplication and started to back from the chamber.

Kell turned to Saark, reached down, and with a short blade cut the ropes. Saark stood, massaging wrists, then probed tenderly at his nose. "I think they broke it."

"No less than you deserve."

"And I thought you were my knight in shining armour!" scowled Saark, voice dripping sarcasm.

"Never a knight. And no armour," shrugged Kell. He lifted his axe, heavy shoulders tense, and glared around.

"What's the matter, Kell?" Saark rolled his neck, and pressed tenderly at his ribs. "Ouch. And look at that! The bastards tore the silk. Do you know how much silk costs up here? Do you know how *hard* it is to locate and procure a fine tailor? Bloody heathens, bloody peasants... no appreciation of the finer things in life."

"Take out your pretty little sword," said Kell.

"Why?"

"DO IT!"

There came a scream. And a *crunch*. It was a heavy, almost metallic crunch. Like an entire body being ripped in half. This was followed by a thick slopping sound, and ripples spread across the black oil pool towards the men.

"That sounded interesting," said Saark, his recent beating forgotten. He drew his sword, a fluid movement. The way he held the delicate rapier spoke volumes of his skill with the weapon; this was not some toy, despite its lack of substance. Saark's speed and accuracy were a thing to behold.

"Interesting?" snorted Kell, then ducked as a limp body went whirring overhead. It hit a wall of crumbling stone, and slid down like a broken doll, easing into the black ooze. The stunned face, with ragged beard and oval brown eyes, was last to disappear. Kell and Saark watched, faces locked in frowns of confusion; then they spread apart with the natural instinct of the seasoned warrior.

The single lantern, brought by Rake and his men, spluttered noisily. Its stench was acrid and evil, but not as evil as the shadows cast by the stroboscopic wick.

Kell took a step back. More crunches and screams echoed from the darkness, then fell gradually to an ominous silence.

"What is it?" whispered Saark.

"My mother?" ventured Kell.

"Your humour is ill placed," snapped Saark. "Something just silenced eleven men!"

"Well," grinned Kell, "maybe it'll have the awesome ability to silence you! Although I doubt it."

"I am so glad we're both about to die," hissed Saark. "At least I'll die in the knowledge that you were ripped apart too."

"I don't die easy," said Kell, and rolled his shoulders, eyes narrowed, lantern-light turning his aged greying beard into a demonic visage. His eyes were hooded, unseen, but Saark could feel the cloak of solid violence which settled over Kell's frame; it felt like a high charge of electricity during a raging thunderstorm. It was there, unseen, but ready to strike with maximum ferocity.

The creature came from the gloom, moving easily, fluid, despite its bulk, despite its size. It was a canker, but more than just a canker; this was immense, a prodigy of the deviant, and Kell grinned a grin which had nothing to do with humour.

"Shit," he said, voice low, "I think Graal saved this one for us."

"It's been looking for us," said Saark, eyes narrowed, some primeval intuition sparking his mind into action. "Look at its eyes. There's recognition there, I swear by all the gods!"

Kell nodded, hefting his axe, movements smooth and cool and calculated as he stepped forward. The canker was on a narrow bridge now, a thick plank of timber which bowed under its weight. It stopped, eyes fastening on Kell, fangs drooling blood-oil to the wood.

"Looking for me?" said Kell.

Within the canker's flesh, tiny gears and cogs spun and clicked. Its huge shaggy head lowered, and Saark had been right; there was recognition there. It sent a thrill coursing through Kell's veins. Here, he looked into the maw of death. And he was afraid.

"Graal sent me," said the canker, its voice a strange hybrid of human, animal and... *machine*. A clockwork voice. A voice filled with the tick-tock of advanced Watchmaking. Its huge shaggy head, so reminiscent of a lion, and yet so twisted and bestial and deformed, tilted to one side in an almost human movement. That sent a shiver of empathy through Kell. He knew. Knew that once these creatures had been human. And it pleased him not a bit to slay them. "I am a messenger."

"Then deliver your message, and be gone," snapped Kell, brows furrowed, face lost in some internal pain which had nothing to do with age and arthritis, but more to do with the state of Falanor, the invading Army of Iron, and the abuse to *humanity* he was witnessing at the hands of the expanding vachine empire.

"He wants to speak with you. He wants you to return with me."

Kell grinned then. "He's worried, isn't he? The Great Graal, General of the Age – worried about an old warrior with impetigo and a drinking habit. Well, once I said that if we met again I'd carve my name on his arse. That promise still stands."

"He needs your help," said the canker, voice a low-level rumble. "Both of you."

Kell considered this. "Well. I bet that was hard to admit." He rubbed his beard. "And if we say no?"

"You are coming with me. One way or another." The voice was one layer away from threat; but threat it was.

Kell stepped forward, rolling his shoulder and lifting Ilanna from her rest against the floor. *Kill it,* whispered the bloodbond axe in his mind. *Kill it, drink its blood, let me feast. It is nothing to you. It is nothing but a deformation of pure.*

Kell shrugged off Ilanna's internal voice – but could not ignore Saark's. He was close. Close behind Kell. His voice tickled Kell's ear. "We can take it, brother. After all we've been through, you can't let Graal dictate. He's sent this *special messenger* and there's a reason. I'd wager it has something to do with you hunting va-chine in the Black Pikes!"

"And I would second that," said Kell, and launched a blistering attack so fast it was a blur, and left Saark staggering backwards, mouth open in shock and awe as Kell's axe slammed for the canker's head. But the beast moved, also with inhuman speed, with a speed born of clockwork, and it snarled and dropped one shoulder, the axe blade missing its face by inches and shaving tufts of grey fur to lie suspended in the air for long moments. Then reality slammed back and the canker went down on one shoulder, rolling sideways and missing the pool of oil by inches. It launched at Kell, huge forepaws with long curved talons slashing for his throat, but Kell side-stepped, axe batting aside the talons and right fist can-noning into the beast's head. Again he struck, a mighty blow and a fang snapped under his gloved knuckles. The canker's rear legs swiped out, and Kell leapt back and the canker charged him but Ilanna whistled before its face, checking its charge. They circled, warily, amidst the glittering pools of oil. Saark had stepped back, to the edge of one pool, crouching beside the sputtering lantern, rapier in his fist but eyes wide, aware he was no match for a canker in single combat but willing to dive in and help at the soonest opportunity. Suddenly, he darted forward, the razor-edge of his rapier carving a line down one flank. The canker squealed, rearing up, head smashing round as flesh opened like a zip, and coils of muscle spilled out, integrated with tendons and tiny clockwork machines which thrummed and clicked and whirred. A claw lashed out, back-handing Saark across the platform in a flurry of limbs. He rolled fast and lay drooling blood, stunned. Kell attacked, but the canker snarled, ducking a sweep of the axe and slamming both claws into Kell's face, knocking the old warrior back. Kell went down on one knee, and the canker reared up, grinning down through strings of saliva and blood-oil – then turned, head twisting, focusing on Saark who had crawled to his knees, eyes narrowed.

"Don't you recognise me, Saark?"

"Yeah. I reckon you look like my dad."

"Truly? You cannot see my human flesh... the woman I used to be?"

Saark scowled, crawling to his feet, rapier extended amidst soiled lace ruffs. Then, he frowned, and his head moved and eyes locked with Kell. He breathed out, and staggered as if struck from behind. "No," he said, and moved closer to the canker. "It cannot be."

"I was a woman once, Saark." The canker settled down, a clawed and bestial hand moving back to the wound in its flank, and pushing spilled muscle into the cramped cavity. "They chose me... because of my association with you. Because... once we were..."

"No!" screamed Saark, and images flowed like molten honey through a brain twisted with rage and horror and disbelief. For this was Aline, an early love of his life, his childhood sweetheart. They had spent months wandering the pretty woodlands south of Vor, making love in shadowed glades beside burbling brooks, carving their names in the Tower Oak, words entwined in a neatly carved love-heart, whispering promises to one another, sneaking through cold castle corridors on secret love trysts – the stuff of young love, of passionate adventure; the honour of the naive. But it was never meant to be. Aline was cousin to royalty, and her arranged marriage and fate were sealed by a father with huge gambling debts and a need to secure more land and income. Their parting had been swift, bitter, and involved five soldiers holding a sharp dagger to Saark's throat. He still had a narrow white scar there, and his battered fingers came up to touch the place now. Through words choked with emotion, he said, more quietly than he intended, "Aline, it cannot be you."

"They did this to me, Saark. They knew it would hurt you. They knew it would persuade you. I must take you both back to Graal;

only then, will they make me human again. Only then, can I be a woman again."

Saark's gaze shifted, from the abused deviation of his childhood sweetheart, to the fully erect, ominous figure of Kell. Kell's eyes were shadowed, but his head gave a single shake. A clear message. *No.* Saark looked back to the canker, and only in the eyes dragged back sideways over the skull, only in a few twists of golden hair which remained, only in a certain set of wrenched facial bones which, if imagination wrapped them around a normal skull could mentally reconstruct a *face*... did he recognise the woman of his childhood. "No," he said again.

"Help me," pleaded the canker, head lowering, submissive now before Saark who felt his heart melt and his brain lock and his soul *die*.

Saark, gazing down, rapier forgotten, reached out with his delicate, tapered fingers. He touched Aline, touched the pale skin, the tufts of fur, worked in horror over the merging of flesh and clockwork. And then she – it – screamed, high and long and Kell was there, looming over her, Ilanna embedded in the canker's back narrowly missing the spine. Kell placed a boot against the canker, tugging at his axe which had lodged awkwardly under a rib.

"No, Kell, no!" wailed Saark, but Kell wrenched free the butterfly blades which lifted high trailing droplets of blood and a shard of broken rib and several strings of tendon, and the canker whirled low, claws lashing for the axeman in a disembowelling stroke which missed by a hairsbreadth and on the return stroke Aline smashed a fist into Saark's chest and he was powered backwards, almost vertical, his legs finally dropping and he hit the ground, rolled, and splashed into the oil with desperate fingers scrabbling at the platform like claws...

Kell leapt again, axe whirring, and he and the transmogrified woman circled with eyes locked, then struck and clashed in a blur of strikes which left a trail of sparks glittering in the gloom. "Get out!" snarled Kell, glancing back to Saark. "Get out of here, lad, now!"

"Don't kill her," whispered Saark.

"She can never change back, don't you see?" snapped Kell, axe slamming up, claws raking the blades. He staggered back under the immense impact, and jabbed axe points at the canker's eyes. It snarled, head shaking, spittle drenching Kell. "It's a one way process! You cannot *revert*!"

The canker was pushing Kell back, claws lashing out with piledriver force, and Saark could see Kell weakening fast. Within moments, he would be dead; dead, or drowning in oil. With an inhuman effort, Saark's fingers raked the harsh boards and his legs kicked against thick, viscous oil. He rolled onto the deck, panting, and levered himself to his feet where he swayed. He grabbed at his rapier, but sheathed the weapon. Kell saw the movement, and his face went grim, went dark, his eyes becoming something more – or indeed, something *less* – than human.

"Aline." Saark's voice was a lullaby. A song of nostalgia.

The canker paused mid-snarl, but did not turn. Its eyes were fixed with glittering hatred on Kell, his back to the oil, his axe resting against wooden boards. His chest was heaving, and his jerkin was sliced by claws showing shredded flesh beneath.

"Will you help me?" came the voice of Aline. And Saark could hear her, now, hear her tone and inflections entwined around the audible ejaculations of an alien beast.

"Yes," said Saark, with great sadness. "I will help you." He hooked his boot behind the lantern, and with a swift kick sent the flask of oil sailing across the platform, where it shattered against the canker and flames exploded outwards. Fire roared, engulfing the canker which screamed a high-pitched *feminine* sound and spun around in a tight circle, fighting the fire with claws whirring and slashing at itself as flesh burned and fat bubbled and clockwork squealed. Kell came at a sprint, head down, axe in both hands, and both he and Saark hammered down flexing planks into the darkness in the direction of the ancient factory exit...

The canker lowered to its haunches, burning, then glared through flames at the fleeing men. It roared, and charged after them, its burning flesh illuminating the way. Tufts of glowing fur fell from its burning body, into the oil, which slumbered for a few moments after the canker's passage and then suddenly, erratically, ignited. Fire roared along the surface of the oil pools, overtaking the canker and licking at the heels of Kell and Saark, sweating now, eyes alive with the orange glow of roaring demons, and they ran with every burst of speed and energy they possessed as heat billowed around them and sparks exploded and the *roar* and *surge* of fire was something both men had never before experienced...

"We're going to *die*!" screamed Saark.

ELEVEN
Fortress of Ghosts

Kell ran on, and did not reply to Saark's panic, just heaved his bulk along flexing planks with fire at his boots, a stench of burning chemicals filling his nostrils and smoke blinding him. He choked, gagged, and the fire overtook the two men who ran on blindly, across yet another narrow plank into darkness and smoke and behind them the roar of fire drowned the roar and screeches of the burning canker and suddenly both men slammed into the welcome ice-cold night air, flames belching from the orifice behind as they hit the snow and rolled down a gentle slope to finally slide together, turning slowly on ice, to a stop, Kell's great bearskin jerkin glowing and smouldering.

The two men coughed and choked for a while, entwined like scorched lovers, then untangled themselves from one another. Kell staggered to his feet and hefted his axe, staring up at the factory doorway, brows furrowed, fire-blackened face focussed in concentration as his eyes narrowed and he readied himself in a centuries-old battle-stance.

"Surely not?" whispered Saark, climbing to his feet and spitting black phlegm to the snow. His fine clothes were blackened, scorched tatters. Beneath, his flesh was burn-pink in places. He patted his head, when he suddenly realised his hair was on fire.

Kell did not reply. Just stood, staring at the doorway where an inferno raged. And then something moved, a huge cumbersome ill-defined shape within the shimmering portal, a demon dancing in the fire, an image of molten rock against the stage of a raging inferno, and Saark thought he saw the shape of the canker, of his twisted childhood sweetheart, of Aline, stagger within the opening and then slump down, clockwork machines *glowing* as they finally succumbed to the heat and ran in molten streams. Then the roof of the factory belched and slumped, and with a great groaning roar it collapsed bringing part of the walls down with it, and burning rubble filled the doorway and all was gone and still, except for the bright fire, and the demons.

"How could Graal do that?" whispered Saark, eyes still fixed on the blaze. All around the factory, snow-steam hissed like volcanic geysers.

Kell stared at him.

"To a woman, I mean," said the scorched dandy.

"Graal will do what he has to. To get the job done."

"I want his head on a fucking plate," snarled Saark, suddenly. "I want that man dead."

Kell gave a curt nod, and turned his back on the inferno. "We all want him dead, lad." He sighed, then. And gave a narrow smile which had nothing to do with humour. "But at least he's showed us one thing."

"And what's that?"

Kell's face was a dark mask, his eyes pools of ink. Unreadable. "He thinks we're a threat. He went to a lot of trouble to bring us in. And that means we are a danger not just to Graal, but to the whole damn vachine invasion. And… I think we have something he wants. Ilanna, maybe? I do not know. But we will find out, I promise you that." Kell began to walk, back towards the stables. It was time to leave. It was time to leave Kettleskull Creek *fast*.

Saark stood, stunned, watching Kell's back.

Fire crackled, and sparks spiralled up into a clear and frozen night sky.

Kell turned. Grinned a sour, twisted grin. So much for a warm, soft bed! "Come on, lad. What're you waiting for? We have to make *General Graal* earn his coin. And he'll have to move faster than that to catch us."

In silence, and with sombre heart, Saark followed Kell into the night.

It was a day later, and darkness was spreading fast, a vast jagged purple shroud easing out from the towering blocks of the Black Pike

Mountains, questing knife-blades stealing into the real world like a disease spreading from its host. Kell reined in his horse, and climbed stiffly from the saddle. The pain from the poison was with him again, in his blood, in his bones, and he grinned with skull teeth. At least this fresh agony took away the lesser evils of arthritis and torn muscles from battle. At least it focused him – *focused him* – on impending death.

Nobody lives forever, old man, he thought to himself. And I wouldn't want to! But by the gods, it would be sweet to taste life long enough to see the bastard Graal dead and buried.

Saark's boots hit the frozen ground, and he rubbed his eyes. "I ache like a dog in a fighting pit."

"You look just as rough."

"Thanks, old friend."

"If I was your friend, I'd hang myself."

"You're a regular old charmer, Kell."

"There she is." He pointed, and Saark took in the majestic sweep of the mountains, an endless block of vast peaks, sheer and violent and ragged. Cold wind and snowstorms swept down from the Pikes, as if it was some epicentre for gratuitous weather and intent on inflicting misery across the civilised world.

"They're just so… big!" said Saark, eyes once more sweeping the mammoth portrait before him. It was an oil painting, a violence of blacks and greys, purples and reds. "And beautiful," he added, voice touched with awe. "Totally beautiful."

"You ever been here before?"

"Once, in my younger days. Alas, I believe I was pretty much drunk for the entire trip. And I rode it in a fine brass carriage with two women of, shall we say, dishonourable disposition. One had a poodle dog. What tricks that yapping snapping little canine could conjure!"

Kell snorted, and started over the hillside. Rocks lay strewn everywhere, building in intensity as the ground rose towards the vastness of the sky-blocking Pikes. Saark followed, still talking.

"One of the women, a ripe peach named Guinevere, had a neat trick whereby she would take a long, thin block of cheese, and upon removing her corset…"

"Stop." Kell turned. "There's the fortress."

"Cailleach?" Saark gave a tiny shudder. He glanced around, at the fast-falling gloom. The wind howled in the distance like slaughtered wolves. "Hadn't we better wait till morning?"

"No. We're going in. Now."

"It's turned dark," warned Saark.

"I'm the worst fucking thing in the dark," snapped Kell.

"I'm sure you are, old boy. But my point is, the rumours state this place is, ahh, haunted. And correct me if I'm wrong, but more specifically, haunted at night. Yes?"

Kell chuckled. "I thought you were a modern hedonist? I didn't think you'd believe in ghosts."

"Well, yes, I don't, but when you hear so many fireside tales…"

"Popinjays drunk on watered wine," snapped Kell, and surged forward, allowing his horse to pick a trail through the rocks. Muttering, Saark followed at a reasonable distance, telling himself that if wild beasts or haunted *things* attacked, then at least it would take them time to consume the bulk that was Kell, thus giving *him* time to flee.

As the hill dropped to a flat plain, so the rocks became not just more intense in their regularity, but larger, more ominous. Many were smoothed by centuries of weathering, and bands of precious minerals ran through many a cottage-sized cube.

The hugeness of the subtly twisted fortress came ever closer, and as darkness fell through the sky, so Kell ran his gaze over the dark stones, the cracks, the jigged walls and battlements. Above the battlements, leading back to the keep and the rocky valley beyond, which the fortress seemed in some way to *protect*, stood several slightly leaning, slightly twisted towers. Most had no roof, just great blocks which had shifted and settled, to give the appearance of some puzzle – or at least, a madman's example of architecture.

"It's depraved," said Saark, eventually.

"It's old," said Kell.

Staring at the warrior's broad back, Saark, said, "The two go hand in hand, Kell, old wolf. But what I mean is, look at it, the whole thing, it's – well, it's not straight, for a start. I thought they would have brought in some decent builders. Architects who could draw a straight line. That sort of thing. Not some epileptic draughtsmen who spilled the ink and let idiots loose with a trowel!"

Kell stopped and turned. His eyes were glinting. "*Shut up,*" he said.

"Yes, fine, no need to be rude. You only needed to ask."

There was an old road, made of the same strange dark stone. Many cobbles were missing, and filled with dirt and frozen weeds.

Much was obscured by wide patches of ice. Kell picked his way carefully to the road, and they moved down it, towards the huge maw of a leering archway. The Cailleach Fortress reared above them in the gloom, defined by moonlight and foregrounded by the immense power of the sentinel Black Pikes.

"The archway is a guardian," said Kell, voice little more than a whisper. "Listen. She will speak to us…"

"What?" snorted Saark, voice dripping sarcasm. Yet as he stepped forward, so warm breeze rolled out to greet him and he halted, shocked, hackles rising on the back of his neck. "What's going on?" he growled. "What kind of horse-shit is this?"

"Be quiet, boy," hissed Kell, glancing at Saark, dark eyes glinting like jewels. "If you value your bloody life. Follow me, say nothing, do nothing, do not draw your weapon, don't even shit in your kerchief unless I give you permission. I've been here before; and there are rules."

"Rules?" whispered Saark, and despite himself, despite his new found… strength, from impure blood, he moved closer to Kell. "I don't like this place, Kell. It has a stench of evil, in its very rocks, in its very bones."

"Aye, lad." They moved beneath the huge gateway. Beyond, darkness wavered like the oesophagus of some huge, breathing creature. "So follow me, be a good lad, and we both may get through this alive."

"You really think so?" whispered Saark, and the final dregs of light were cast from the sky.

"No," said Kell, "I'm just trying to make you feel better." And with that, he disappeared into the void.

Saark walked, his eyes narrowed, his mouth shut, his fist wound tight about his mount's reins and his arse puckered in terror. Behind, he heard Mary the donkey braying and he wanted to turn, to shout "Shut up you stupid donkey!" but he did not; he had neither the nerve nor the energy. Fear coursed through him like raw fire. It filled his mind with ash.

They walked, boots echoing on cobbles. Shapes seemed to drift around them, ghosts in silk, sighs caressing cold skin, and Saark realised he had new, heightened senses. He could feel more, sense more, smell more. He could smell his own stench of fear, that was for sure.

Something brushed his cheek, like a kiss, and he fancied he heard a giggle of coquettish laughter. Something tightened in his chest. It had not occurred to him the ghosts – or whatever depraved spirits, or dark magick these creatures were – it had never *occurred* to him they would be *women*. He felt a caress down his thigh, and another kiss on his cheek. His resolve hardened. The whole thing felt wrong, and then he caught sight of a figure ahead and she walking towards the two men. She was tall, eight feet tall, and very slender and narrow, both of hips and limbs. Her skin was dark, and shined as if oiled. She wore a black silk robe which rustled, and the hood was thrown back to reveal an almost elongated face, high and thin with pointed features and narrow, feline eyes. Saark looked into those eyes and realised the pupils were horizontal slits. They looked wrong. Saark swallowed. The tall woman stopped, and only then did Saark realise she was both insubstantial, like a drifting haze in the darkness; and that she carried a black sword strapped at her hip. Ha, thought Saark. A ghost sword? And yet he knew, in his heart, it would cut just like the finest steel.

"Who passes in my realm?" came her voice, and it was note-perfect and absolutely beautiful.

"I am Kell. Once, I served your people."

"Kell. I remember. You slew the vachine. That was good."

Kell bowed his head, as if offering obeisance to royalty. He stayed like that for what – to Saark, at least – seemed an exaggerated length of time. Then he stood, and back straight, stared into the ghost's eyes.

"May we pass, lady?"

She lifted a ghostly arm, and pointed at Saark. He shivered, and felt suddenly light-headed as if… *as if his brains were rushing out of his ears and a million memories flowed like wine like water and he was dancing and laughing and drinking and fucking and he was watched from a million years away by eyes older than worlds and he felt himself judged and he felt himself wrenched through a mental grinder and then–*

Saark was kneeling on the cobbles, panting, and his head pounded worse than any three-flagon hangover. Slowly, Saark climbed to his feet, and ignoring Kell and the ghost, unhooked a water-skin from his saddle and took a long, cool draught.

"That hurt," he said, eventually.

"There is a taint on this one," said the ghost, pointing to Saark but talking to Kell.

"Aye. I know. But he's with me."

"It runs bone deep," said the ghost, and Saark froze as he realised what she meant. His infection. His bad blood. His newly acquired and gradually transforming *nature*. What had Kell said? He'd killed *vachine* for these creatures? So they were enemies, and she knew Saark for what he was – or at least, what he would become.

"He's still with me," said Kell, staring at the apparition and, with his traditional stubborn streak, refusing to back down. Eventually, the tall, dark lady gave a single nod, and glided away, disseminating as she moved into spirals of black light which eventually whirled, and were gone.

"What a bitch," breathed Saark, releasing a pent-up breath.

"Halt your yapping, puppy, lest I cut off your head!" snapped Kell, and strode forward, leading his horse.

Saark clamped his teeth tight shut, and followed Kell. Behind him, Mary brayed, and Saark scowled. To his ears, it was an abrasive, mocking, equine jibe, and if there was one thing Saark hated, it was being laughed at by a donkey.

They emerged into the courtyard before the twisted, disjointed, deformed keep. Behind them, the tunnel was dark as the void, sour as a corpse. Saark breathed cool ice air, and thanked the gods he was alive – and not just alive, but with his *affliction* still his own.

Kell was panting, and they looked up at the sky in wonder. Hours had passed, and strange coloured starlight rimed the frozen mountains and peaks.

"Grandad!" screamed Nienna, and sprinted across ice-slick cobbles from the doorway of a small, stone building. She leapt at him, wrapping herself around the old warrior and he hugged her, buried his face in her hair and inhaled her scent and welcomed her warmth, and her love, for without Nienna, Kell was a bad man, a weak man, a lesser man; a dilution. With her, he was whole again. Filled with honour, and love, and an understanding of what made life and the world so good.

Kell dropped Nienna to the cobbles, and she half turned as Myriam appeared at the doorway. Myriam gave Kell a curt nod, eyes bright, head high, proud and wary and strong despite the cancer eating through her. She gave a smile, but it was an enigmatic smile and Kell could not read her intent. She looked past Kell, to Saark, and he saw her eyes glow a little.

"How are you feeling, dandy man?"

"Better now your knife is no longer in my guts. But be warned, Myriam, your time on this planet is finite. You made an enemy of me for life; one day, I will slit your throat."

"But not now?" She moved forward, still athletic despite her gauntness. "Why not, Saark? What's stopping you? The poison which eats Kell even as we speak?"

"Enough!" bellowed Kell, and stomped forward, loosening Ilanna and swinging the great axe wide. For a moment only fear shone like bright dark flames in Myriam's eyes, then she shook her head and strode forward to meet him. If nothing else, she had spirit, and courage enough to match her cunning and evil.

Myriam halted before Kell, and looked into the huge warrior's eyes. She was tall, and proud, and she matched Kell for height. "Do you want to live, Kell, or do you want to die?"

"I don't die easy," he growled.

"You never answered the question."

"Where's the antidote?"

"Close by. However, I have another insurance policy I need to show you; otherwise, what's to stop you cutting me in half with that huge axe? Ilanna, she's called, isn't she?" Myriam smiled, then, and Kell did not like the smile. There was knowledge there, but more. There was an intimacy.

"You are playing games," said Kell. He glanced over to Nienna. "Did this woman hurt you, girl?"

"No, grandfather. And much as I hate to say it, she saved my life. Styx wanted to rape me, and kill me. Myriam murdered him. Jex left."

Kell nodded, and leaned in close to Myriam, aware her hand was on her sword hilt but knowing, as he had always known, that he could cut her in two before she cleared weapon from scabbard. "You play a dangerous game," he said, threat inherent in his tone.

"Yes. The game of life and death. And I choose life. And so should you. Don't be a hero, Kell. Don't be a jangling, bell-adorned capering village idiot."

"I say kill her," said Saark, and he moved closer, his slender rapier drawn. There was a quiet, dormant rage bubbling beneath the surface of his foppishness. "If we let her live, she'll stab us in the back. Again. And this place isn't so big; we can find the anti-dote to the poison."

"Stab you in the back?" laughed Myriam. She focused on Saark. "I'd save that pleasure only for you, my sweet." She smiled, easily.

Saark growled. Kell held up a hand. "Enough." He focused on Myriam. "You have bought a truce for now. I will take you through the mountains. But the poison is seeping through my system. If I do not have the cure soon, I will be useless. And the Black Pike Mountains is no place where a warrior should be useless."

"I will give it to you – soon," breathed Myriam, calmer now that imminent threat was gone. But she knew; Kell was like a caged lion, one moment passive, submissive even, the next a raging feral beast. "But first, you must see this." She lifted her hand, then, and turned it so her palm faced upwards. Across her skin danced a tiny flame, and the flame grew until it was an inferno of silver flames all contained on the palm of her hand. The flames twisted and curled, and then formed themselves into a vision. In the tiny, glittering scene Kell stood on a high mountain pass, with Nienna behind him, cowering against frozen rocks. Saark was nowhere to be seen. Huge beasts loped forward, their fur white, their fangs terrible. They were snow lions, there were three of them, and they were mighty, their fur bright white, three males with bushy manes and yellow eyes. Kell roared and charged the snow lions, and claws smashed aside his axe. In the scene, the third lion circled Kell, leaping nimbly up the rocks and then drop-ping down before Nienna. She screamed, her scream tiny and a million miles away. The lion grinned, and lunged for her, but Myr-iam rushed past, her sword sticking into the lion and making it rear, blood gushing from a savage throat-wound and spraying bright crimson against snow and fur. The lion stumbled back, and went over the cliffs – and in the tiny vision, Myriam took Nienna in her arms and cuddled the terrified girl.

Slowly, the image faded, and Myriam closed her hand.

"You are a magicker!" gasped Saark, taking several steps back. "A witch!"

"Nothing so dramatic," snapped Myriam, scowling. "But I have certain prophetic skills. I may not be able to use magick for pain and destruction, as some can and do; but I see things. This was my vision. And yours, too."

"Clever," said Kell, face dark.

"If you kill me, then the lion kills Nienna." Myriam tilted her head. "You see how the puzzle pieces are coming together? To make a whole?"

"The game is not finished. Not yet."

"Still. We are a partnership."

"Is that why you killed Styx? Because you worked out another way to persuade me?"

"Yes. The power of the Black Pike Mountains brings out the magicker in me; but you are correct. I knew none of this when I poisoned you, and as we drew close to the Pikes then the dreams began, the visions, the pains in my heart."

"I will take you where you want to go," said Kell.

"To Silva Valley? Through the Secret Trails? The Worm Caves?"

"Yes."

"You swear?"

"If you save Nienna's life, as in that vision, then I swear. Now get me that damn antidote! I feel as if you have my balls in the palm of your hand, and I don't bloody like it!"

"Maybe one day I will," soothed Myriam, and turned, and disappeared back into the small stone room at the foot of the keep. She emerged with a tiny vial, and tossed it to Kell. He shook it. There was a small amount of clear liquid within.

He unstoppered the vial, and stared at Myriam. Then knocked it back in one.

"It will take a day or so, but will cleanse the poison from your system. This, I swear."

"And what of Nienna?" growled Kell, voice dark.

"I was never poisoned, grandfather!" smiled Nienna. "That was a lie. A lie to bring you here."

Kell stared for a long time at Myriam. She hid it well, but she was terrified. Eventually, Kell blinked, and relaxed his hand from the terrible haft of Ilanna.

"Now, we can kill her," smiled Saark, and glanced to Kell for support. "Yes, Big Man? Is that what you have in mind?" He was too eager. Too eager for death.

"No," said Kell. "You saw the magick."

"Pah!" snapped Saark. "She conjured that from thin air; it is an empty ruse, a courtside conman's trick, a slick cock up your arse, my friend. Do you not see?"

"It may or may not be real." Kell had a stubborn look on his face. His voice was low. "And maybe I have my own business now, in Silva Valley."

"Your own business? Like what?"

"That would be my business."

"You are worse than any mule," frowned Saark, and sheathed his rapier in disappointment. "Listen. Can we at least rest before we set off on some foolhardy mission through the most treacherous mountains the world has ever known? I stink. I stink worse than the donkey. In fact, I stink worse than you, Kell!"

Kell stared at Saark, and realised the man was saving face. He urgently wanted Myriam dead, and it was still there in his eyes, a burning coal. But for now, Kell could rely on Saark not to unbalance the equilibrium. But long term? Whether Kell believed in the vision or not, whether Kell chose to kill Myriam or not, Saark would one day have his way. And that sat bad in the back of Kell's mind, like an old bone buried by a dead dog.

"We have time," said Myriam, and stepped aside, pointing back into the small room – which in turn led to a small complex of apartments, empty and cold now, but which once must have housed a gatemaster and his family. "We can build a fire. Heat water. It is better than camping in the snow and ice."

Nienna led the way inside, followed by Kell, who struggled to squeeze Ilanna's huge butterfly blades through the opening.

Saark looked at Myriam. She smiled, and tilted her head.

"I have one question."

"Which is?"

"Where was I in the vision?"

"But you don't believe in it, dandy."

"That doesn't matter. Where was I?"

Myriam shrugged, and moved into the building.

"Playing damn games with my head," Saark muttered, and followed with a certain amount of apprehension.

The main guard room was small, but Myriam had built a fire in the hearth filling the limited space with heat. The group slept on under their travelling blankets, but the stone plinths in the chamber used as beds were hard and unforgiving, uncomfortable and deeply cold. Outside, the wind howled from the high passes of the Black Pike Mountains, rasping and ululating through guttural corridors and wide, slightly skewed battlements. Even in the guard room, every line was just a little bit out of square. It made for many complaints, as each bed seemed to be trying to roll its occupant to the floor, or twist them into an unsubtle heap.

Kell slept a deep sleep without dreams, his rage at last satiated in his quest for Nienna. For this simple pleasure, he was thankful. It was also a sleep of recovery, as the antidote to Myriam's poison went to work on the toxins in his blood, in his muscles, in his organs, eating away at the chemicals that would make Kell a dead man. But at the back of it all was the secure knowledge that Nienna was unharmed, and that he was by her side, his axe in one hand, his bulk and ferocity and skill a barrier to any who might now threaten her.

Nienna slept uneasily. The Cailleach Fortress was not just unwelcoming, but deeply unnerving. As she lay, thinking about her dead friend Katrina and all the good times they'd been through, and contemplating the young woman's death for the thousandth time, so she would hear gentle whispers like draughts from the higher reaches of the chamber, or hisses and bangs, like popping stones in the fire. Nienna thought of her mother, a long way distant, lost and lonely – possibly even dead. Had she fallen when the Army of Iron invaded Falanor? Was she dead and buried, food for worms? Or had she found an escape? After all, she was a very resilient woman. She was the daughter of Kell.

Saark, on the other hand, tossed and turned, his teeth hurting him, his blood hurting him. His heart raced through his ears, pounded at him with hammers as his body fluctuated from a heart rate of one beat per minute, leaving him gasping for oxygen, then shooting up to two or even three hundred beats, racing through his chest like a steam-powered clockwork engine and making him claw his blankets in panic, the world a swirl of weird colours and surreal smells and sounds as his senses adjusted, and he felt himself dropping into the world of the altered human...

Eventually the feelings passed, and Saark was just falling into an exhausted sleep after three nights of wakefulness when he sensed somebody close to him. A hand touched his chest, lightly, and Saark's eyes flared open in panic. It was Myriam. He remembered the last time she had been this close; the stab of the knife, the wound in his guts, eating soil. Saark grabbed her wrist, a savage hard movement, but Myriam did not complain. She was there, beside him, her breathing slow, her eyes glittering.

She leaned close, so that her words tickled his ear, and Saark was a split second from drawing his punch-dagger and feeding it to her eyeball. "I would speak with you," she said, words gentle.

"Last time you wanted to speak with me, you stabbed me in the belly."

"That was different." She seemed to be fighting something, and her face twisted. "I am... different."

"Really? That is a surprise."

"Damn you, Saark! Come outside."

She stood, and he let go of her wrist, leaving enraged marks where his surprisingly powerful grip had scoured her flesh. He watched her leave, a cold wind and curls of snow entering the warm guard room on her departure. Cursing, Saark rolled from his hard bed and pulled on trews, boots and cloak. He stepped outside, closing the door quietly behind him, and was hit in the face by a snap of wind-driven snow. He gasped. The cold reached into every gap in his clothing and bit him like a piranha. He cursed. Then cursed again. He saw Myriam further ahead, sheltering under a huge towering buttress of stone. Saark put his hand on the hilt of his rapier, and walked towards her, grimly. If there was any foul play, he would gut her like a fish.

The sky was dark, but a glowing edge to the horizon signified the beginnings of dawn. Snow and wind whipped and shrieked. Saark gazed up at the massive keep, huge and black, slick with ice and slightly jigged from the vertical.

Walking towards Myriam, one hand holding the neck of his cloak together, he snapped, "What the shit do you want, woman? It isn't normal to be out in this."

"You'd better get used to it. We have a long way to go."

"What do you *want*?"

Myriam met his gaze, then. "I wanted to say I am sorry. About before, in Falanor, when I..."

"When you stabbed me in the guts? You bitch."

"Yes. I was. I was fuelled by hatred, by need, by a lust for life. It has made me irrational. Unpredictable. And I confess, a little... insane." She took a deep breath. Looked off, over the skewed fortress battlements. "I would make amends. I would say that I am sorry. That is all."

"Kell is taking you to the Silva Valley. We are here because of you."

Myriam shook her head. "I cannot explain it, but you are here for a greater good. This is what the magick has shown me, taught me, revealed to me."

Saark's eyes were hard. "You'll not con me with your half-penny tricks, bitch. I've seen plenty of part time conjurers in my time; and in my experience, the only thing they crave is silver coin. Amazingly, this impending accrued wealth always coincides with a 'greater good'. Crazy, wouldn't you agree?"

"You can believe what you wish. But Kell believes, and that is for all our benefit."

"Yeah, well, the old goat's a rancid fool."

"I will say it again. I am sorry. You can take it with grace, and acknowledge that I may have changed – that, bizarrely – spending time with Nienna has, shall we say, *altered* my view of the world. She has touched me. She has changed me. And now, because I have changed, the magick runs deeper through my veins. In sacrificing my hate, in stepping away from my rage, I can see more clearly."

"Good for you, girl! What do you want? A big sloppy kiss?"

"Curb your cynicism," she snapped, and he could see tears on her cheeks. Saark chewed his lip, and considered stepping close to her, holding her, hugging her, telling her he forgave the vicious stabbing back in the woods. But his mind shifted. She was a chameleon. She was out for self-preservation. He did not believe she had changed, but still sought personal profit at their little group's expense.

"Ha! I'm going back to bed. Save your sob stories for Kell. He's a sucker for a dying woman."

"But you, Saark? What do you care about?"

Saark gave a dark smile under the glowing edges of a rising winter sun. "Why, I'm a soft touch when it comes to myself."

"So we are the same, then?"

Saark stared at Myriam, stared at her hard as the truth of her words bit him. He opened his mouth to speak, then closed it again. She was correct. They were *exactly* the same. Saark used people for his own ends. He always had, and he always would. He was vain, narcissistic, and totally enveloped with furthering his own pleasure – and life. Shit, he realised. Shit. In Myriam's position, would he have acted the same? Would he have stabbed somebody, poisoned another, in order to force them to help? And he knew, deep down in the glowing embers of his ruptured heart, that he probably would.

With shame touching him, he turned and went back to his cold bed. And the pounding of the rampant vachine blood-oil in his veins echoed right down to his soul.

Soon after dawn they followed a narrow alleyway through the fortress, winding between towering dark walls which exuded not just cold and gloom and abandonment, but an inherent *dread* which seemed to be a part of this long-deserted fortress. People had not only died here, it felt as if their souls had been sucked into the very stones, distorting them, tearing them free.

Kell led the way, walking his skittish horse with Nienna in the saddle. He didn't want to let her out of his sight. Nobody would take his granddaughter from him again; not without stepping over his dead body first. Next came Myriam, dressed in warm winter garb, her face seeming more shrunken on this freezing morn, her eyes ringed with purple and black, her breathing rasping and shallow. And behind came Saark, a wary eye on Myriam, listening to her ragged cancerous breathing and wondering how long she really had left. She wanted to reach Silva Valley, but according to Kell it was a hard, brutal journey and Saark could not quite puzzle out why he was still agreeing to do it. Surely, he could turn around now? He had Nienna. He had the antidote. And even if he believed Myriam's magick, her supposed prophecy, if he headed away from the Black Pikes then surely he would never see a pride of snow lions. How, then, could he lose Nienna to attack? It was strange. Saark decided to question Kell in private when the opportunity arose.

Within the hour they were free of the Cailleach Fortress, and in a narrow valley which ran beyond, through a narrow pass with massive, sheer towering walls. It was terribly gloomy in the pass, and huge rocks littered the floor, in places rising in piles which the group had to scramble up and over, slipping and sliding on wet rocks and ice. The horses struggled on gamely, and with pride Saark watched Mary – more agile than them all, despite carrying a heavy load on her back. The donkey did not complain, but willingly climbed each hill of loose rock to stand, staring down at the cursing humans with an almost equine arrogance.

After a while, Kell called a halt. "It's no good taking the horses any further, unless we intend to eat them."

Everybody stared at him. "You can't *eat* a good horse," snapped Saark. "What a waste of a fine creature!"

Kell grunted. "It's meat, like anything else. But the path will grow ever more treacherous; best now to let them free. They will soon start to slow us down. If we release them here, there's a chance we may find them on our return."

"Our return," said Myriam, softly, eyes distant. She smiled a skeletal smile. "Maybe some of us won't return? Instead, we will find paradise."

"In your dreams, Myriam," said Saark unkindly, and slapped his mount's rump, watching the beast slither back down the pathway and canter to a halt. The group emptied saddlebags, and then Kell stared meaningfully at Mary.

"No," said Saark.

"She'll be a pain in the arse."

"Nonsense! Mary is a fine beast, agile as a goat, the stamina of a lion. Where I go, Mary goes."

Kell peered close, and grinned. "Is there something I don't know about you and that mule?"

"Mary is a donkey. And don't be so crass."

"Why not? You've fucked everything else in existence."

"I resent that, axeman."

"Why so? I've never seen one so rampant. You'll be chasing Myriam next!" He roared with laughter, some good humour returned, and slapped Saark on the back. "Come on lad. Walk ahead with me. I wish to talk."

They moved on after releasing the horses, and Saark led Mary, her rope wrapped around one fist. Behind, Nienna walked with Myriam, and Myriam smiled down at the girl. "Is it good? Good to be back with your grandfather?"

"Yes. I have missed him terribly. I knew he would come for me."

"I... I wanted to apologise, girl. For the way I treated you. And treated him. I have been selfish beyond reason."

Nienna shrugged. "What I don't understand is why we are still here. Why we are heading through the mountains. I thought he would leave you when you gave him the antidote; in fact, I thought he would cut you in half." She smiled, a weak, cold smile, her eyes glittering.

Myriam sighed. "I have done... bad things, Nienna. I admit that. And I deserve Kell's hatred. And even yours."

"I don't hate you," said Nienna, smiling gently. "I see your pain, understand your agony. I pity you, Myriam, not hate you."

Myriam's eyes went dark. "Well girl, sometimes pity is far worse."

Ahead, Kell had halted. The towering walls were silent, looming, filling the narrow pass with shadows. Water trickled and gushed in various places, and had frozen solid in others, either in fingers of sculpted, corrugated ice, or in vast, hanging sheets. Occasionally, stones rattled down the sheer iron-stained flanks of this interior slice from the mountain range.

"We must move with care," said Kell. "There have been many rockfalls here over the years. Any loud noise could bring down the Pikes on our bloody heads. We all understand?"

"Aye," nodded Saark, rubbing Mary's muzzle.

They set off again, down a rocky slope, boots slithering. Eventually, Saark said, "Kell, I have a question."

"It better not be about sex," growled the huge warrior.

"No no. Not this time. I was simply wondering why we are still here?"

"Think about it."

"About Myriam?"

"No, you dolt. About the two vachine who Graal sent to kill us. I was thinking about them; thinking a lot. Graal has invaded Falanor, wiped the whole damn army of Leanoric under his boots. So then. What next? We stumble through his camp like blind men through a brothel, and by some bloody miracle manage to escape. What *should* Graal do? Continue his expansion in the name of vachine blood-oil gathering? Or spend considerable resources sending killers after us? Why? Why hunt us down? He knew we were heading north. Why waste two of his best killers? Surely he has more important fish to fry."

Saark considered this. "He knew your history, Kell. About being a Vachine Hunter for the old Battle King."

"Exactly. But that should not worry him; what's the worst I could do? Harry a few stray vachine scum in the mountains? Hardly a threat to his war effort, don't you think?"

"What are you getting at?"

"Graal knows I was heading north. He knows I know the Pikes. Maybe – and this is just a thought – maybe he thinks I'm heading for Silva Valley. The homeland of the vachine. But then, surely I would be slaughtered the minute I arrived?"

"So you think Graal wants to stop you finding Silva Valley?"

Kell nodded. "Yes. He thinks I know something I don't. There is some great mystery here, some puzzle we need to unravel. I think Graal is not playing for the vachine; I think he works his own game, I think the conniving bastard is up to his own bowel-stinking tricks. But what? What could he possibly be doing? And *why* would he think I was a threat to his plans?"

"I see your reasoning. And now I see why we're heading north, instead of south back to the relative comfort of Falanor – such as we'd be able to find. If Graal doesn't want you here, this is probably the best place for you to be."

"Exactly!" growled Kell. "Silva Valley, that is where the answers lie. The more we travelled north after Nienna, the more I realised that Myriam's goal is our goal. She wants immortality; I want answers. Our only chance of stopping this damned invasion is to confront its source. We need to know more about these Harvester bastards, we need to know where the albino soldiers come from – but more importantly, we need to find the source of the vachine."

"You cannot take on an entire nation of clockwork killers," said Saark, hand on Kell's shoulder.

"You just do it one head at a time," snapped Kell. "You'd be surprised what a pyramid you can build."

"I think, old horse, that sometimes you are crazy."

Kell nodded sombrely. "I'm just the way the world made me."

More snow fell, a light scattering making rocks treacherous and slippery. After several hours of the narrow pass they emerged into a circular valley with a frozen tarn at its floor. All around reared jagged teeth peaks, and Kell put his hands on his hips, breathing deeply, staring out at the stunning, desolate beauty of the place.

"Kingsman's Tarn," said Kell. He pointed, and the others followed his gaze. "Up that way is Demon's Ridge, the first of our trials. If we can get up there by nightfall, we'll be safe from anything that follows."

"You're being followed?" said Myriam, eyes narrowed, hand straying to her longbow.

"I guarantee it," said Kell. "Graal seems to have a passion to make me dead. Well, as he's going to find out, I don't die easy."

"You keep saying that," snapped Saark.

"Ain't it true, lad?"

"I'm not disputing its truth, just pointing out that it grates on my nerves every time you say it."

Kell laughed, seeing Saark's uneasiness. A cold wind howled down over the tarn, and rushed past them like a phalanx of cold angels. "I understand now! You are so much out of your natural environment, it hurts."

Saark frowned. "What do you mean?"

"The royal court," Kell sneered, "with its golden goblets, bowls of honey fruit, its randy middle-aged courtiers with powdered wigs and silk panties and glossy leather boots – that's your world, Saark. The world of easy sex and animal sex, of whiskey-wine and the best cuts of meat full of thick fat juice and spiced herbs from a different continent! The world of the dandy. The fop. The rich idiot with too much gold and nothing between his ears, nor his legs, I'd wager. That, Saark, my favourite horny, perfumed goat, is the world to which you belong. Your natural setting. But this. This!" He stared around, at the wilds, the rugged ridgelines, the whipping flurries of snow, the ice, the storm-filled skies; a place of natural wonder, and brutality, and death. "This is my place," he finished quietly.

Saark pushed ahead, leading Mary. "That way, you say?"

"Yes. Across the heather. There's a rocky path we can follow further on, an old stream bed leading up to Demon's Ridge. You'll struggle with that damn donkey, though."

"I'm not leaving her behind. Not here," said Saark, patting her fondly.

"Aye. Well, I suppose there's good eating on one."

"What?" Saark's voice was ice.

"Her meat will be a bit stringy, but it'll do when we're starving on the crags."

"She's not for *eating*," scowled Saark. "That would be a crime!"

"Aye. A crime to my belly, is what I'm thinking. But come on. We have a long way to go."

They rose from Kingsman's Tarn in the basin valley, and within an hour the wind was howling across the rock faces and cutting through their clothing. Each pulled on extra woollen shirts and dug out thick cloaks, as high over the ridges snow danced and threatened heavy falls.

"I expect," said Saark, grunting as he jumped down into the old stream bed and turned to guide Mary, "that the snow can easily block our passage. Render our journey impossible. That sort of thing?"

"Aye," said Kell, panting, putting his hands on his hips to gaze up the narrow incline ahead. Although snow was present, it was surprisingly shallow and banked to one side of the old stream bed. Kell picked a path to the left where his boots could still grip the stones, and he led the way up the slope.

Their progress was slow, and before long all four were panting, and struggling to move forward. Despite cold and ice, the small rocks of the old stream bed shifted under boots, making the scramble difficult.

Still, they pushed on.

Out of the wind it was hot work climbing, and they played an annoying game of removing clothing, then suffering the bite of wind and putting it back on. Saark cursed more than the others, and Nienna was silent, her face strong, eyes focused on the task, pushing herself on much to the silent pride of Kell. She is definitely of my blood, he thought. She has the strength of ten lions!

Darkness was gradually falling as they reached the final section of the steep trail, which grew worse for perhaps the final hundred metres of ascent up to Demon's Ridge. The ridgeline had vanished now, and all they could see was rock and ice, boulders and channels in the mountain rock.

Saark stopped, and glanced back at what they had climbed. He grinned over at Nienna. "You're doing well, girl." She nodded, but no smile came to her face. She was exhausted, hands cut, feet sore, the cold seeping into her bones, the wind shrieking in her brain. "I am trying, Saark. Really trying." Her voice was the voice of a child again, and weariness her mistress.

Now, the climbing got harder and they struggled on, clawing at the frozen rocks, dragging themselves up steep inclines and past huge boulders. Mary the donkey was, as Saark predicted, surprisingly agile, but as he peered further and further up the trail, he wondered for how long she'd be able to manage.

They struggled on, sweat pouring down faces, making their hair lank and skin chilled by the wind. Myriam suffered the worst, for with her savage cancer she had grown weak, and grew weaker with every passing day. Her face and eyes were fevered, and she drank water often, hands shaking with fatigue and dehydration. At one point she stumbled, and Saark was there in the blink of an eye, moving with incredible agility and speed, grabbing her arm before she toppled back down the steep road of stones. She smiled in gratitude to him, leaning on him heavily as she fumbled for her water bottle again. Saark scowled, and let go.

"I should have let you go," he snapped.

"You're still sore about that knife wound, aren't you?"

Saark said nothing, but moved ahead. Myriam watched him with bright fevered eyes.

Kell was first to reach the summit and stand on the heady heights of Demon's Ridge. He planted a boot either side of the ridgeline, hands on hips, hair and beard caught by the wild, whining wind, and gazed out over the stacked ridges and endless teeth of the Black Pike Mountains. They filled his vision like nothing else ever could, and Kell caught a breath in his throat, filled with emotion, filled with dread, and filled with a deep certainty, an intuition that this was his last time in the Black Pikes. He knew, as sure as night follows day, that he would die here. The Pikes would claim him. For Kell, this time, there was no going home.

Melancholy hit Kell like a fist. He helped Nienna climb up and stand beside him on the high ridge, gazing out across the staggered realms of hundreds of mountains which stretched off to a distant, dark horizon. Trails of dry snow curled in the air, and each mountain was subtly different, many purple or black or grey, many with snow on flanks and peaks; but they all shared one thing in common. Each was a savage barbed pike, a threat to life and love, and without an ounce of mercy in the billions of tonnes of rock which carved out passes and channels, gulleys and scree slopes. These were the Black Pike Mountains. All they brought to humanity was suffering and death.

Saark arrived next, panting, his dark curls drenched with sweat. Mary the donkey followed him, struggling up the last section, but once on the ridge was sure-footed and seemed unconcerned by the vast drops surrounding them. Saark patted her muzzle and looked to Kell. "You move fast for an old fat man," he said.

"And you climb well for an effete arsehole."

Saark gazed out. "I don't like the look of that. Too many places to die!"

"It's beautiful!" said Nienna, voice filled with awe.

"Yeah," muttered Saark, taking in great lungfuls of air, "as beautiful as a striking cobra. Girl, this place is no place for mortals. The Black Pikes were put here by the gods to keep us away from the Granite Thrones!"

"The Granite Thrones? What're they?"

"Tsch," scowled Kell. "That's a myth."

"In my experience, nine times out of ten myths are based on fact."

Kell shrugged. "Whatever. That does not concern us. What *does* concern us is getting to Silva Valley; it's a long, hard haul my friends."

Myriam climbed the final stretch, and stared at the donkey's arse blocking her path. Saark clicked his tongue, and Mary moved out of Myriam's way, eyes flared, ears laid back along her dark-haired skull.

"This is no place for an ass," said Myriam acidly, stepping up onto the ridge.

"I wish everybody would stop complaining about my donkey," moaned Saark.

"Who said I was talking about the donkey?"

They laughed, and stared out in wonder. The world seemed much larger, a vast sweeping canvas. Nienna turned a full circle, eyes absorbing the magnificent splendour as the wind swooped and howled, crackled and snapped.

Kell laid his hand on Nienna's shoulder. "Is this what you wanted, girl?"

"What do you mean?"

"That day, when the Army of Iron invaded Jalder. You said you were bored. You wanted a taste of adventure. Well, you've been given adventure all right. You've been given adventures enough to last you a lifetime!"

"It's not what I expected," she said, in a small voice, remembering the evil people she had met, the pain she had endured, the friends she had lost. And most of all, she pictured Kat, a victim at the hands of Styx's Widowmaker crossbow. Nienna realised she was glad Styx was dead. He was a bad man, and had deserved everything. "I realise now. I did not understand. It would have been better to stay at home, go to university, raise a family." She took a deep breath, and looked up into Kell's eyes as the wind whipped her dark hair. "But I am here now, and this thing is happening to our world. The Army of Iron will not stop, the vachine will not stop – not unless we stop them, right?"

Kell chuckled. "An old man, a haunted child, a cancer-riddled woman and a foppish dandy. What chance, in the name of the Bone Underworld, have we really got?"

"You sell us short, old man," said Saark, smiling, his eyes twinkling as his gaze moved back down the trail they had traversed. The smile dropped from his face, as if he'd been hit by a helve. Distant, by the tarn, where the pass led from the Cailleach Fortress, something moved. "We have company," snapped Saark, hand on the hilt of his rapier.

The group turned, looked down, and stared.

Distant, two pale-skinned figures emerged. They were tall, lithe, athletic, and moved with a balanced ease across uneven ground. Even from this great remoteness it was clear they were Graal's daughters, the vachines who had attacked Kell and Saark earlier. They were the Soul Stealers. And they still hunted Kell's blood.

"I thought we'd scared them off," said Saark, voice little more than a whisper.

"No chance, lad," said Kell, eyes hooded. "And look. This time they brought friends."

Behind the two women, on long chain leashes, came the cankers. There were three of them, but these were smaller than previous beasts and appeared, almost, like bow-legged horses. Only these seemed to have no skin. Bloody, crimson flesh gleamed, even from this distance. One of the skinless cankers screeched, and the sound echoed through the basin valley like a woman being stabbed, reverberating on high spirals of wind. It was a chilling sound.

"Time for us to move on, I think," said Saark, mouth dry, voice a whisper.

"Let's go," agreed Kell, and they headed down the opposite side of Demon's Ridge as far below, in the valley, the Soul Stealers sniffed the air and started forward in pursuit.

TWELVE
The Black Pike Mountains

General Graal knelt on luxurious rugs, his body naked and oiled, and grasped the black sword in shaking fingers. He had imbibed drugs, the leaf of the Truaga Plant, and allowed his blood to be filtered through KaKa Leaves. And although he was considered an amateur in circles of magick, this simple spell taught by Kradek-ka, this simple mind-to-mind communion using blood-oil as a signal carrier was something at which Graal was becoming peculiarly adept. For he knew he would need this skill when the Vampire Warlords returned...

Kuradek, Meshwar and Bhu Vanesh.

It had been an age since they walked the lands. An age since they sat on the Granite Thrones. But their time was about to return, and Graal could feel their apprehension in the Blood Void; could feel their frustration and eagerness, and ultimately, their desire to return with their toxicity, with their plague.

"Kradek-ka?" he whispered.

"I am here," said Kradek-ka, the telltale *tick tick tick* of his vachine clockwork filling Graal's mind and making it difficult to concentrate over such distance.

"I am finished here. Falanor is a conquered land."

"Yes. You have conquered it, Graal; you have brought a bloody retribution for their past; for the times of Ankarok. Servants they again shall be! And, as a consequence, we have enough blood-oil for the Summoning. But still, we need the third Soul Gem. Without it, we will have no control of the Vampire Warlords.

With all three Soul Gems, we will be Masters." He laughed, a cold cruel laugh.

"Does Anukis know?" said Graal.

"No. She is a simple fool. She believes me, and she trusts me; after all, I am Watchmaker, I am Engineer! She was polluted by her mother as a child, I fear, fed simple morals and indoctrinated in the way of vachine; she wishes to see the vachine society expand and prosper, despite what they did because of her impure nature; despite what Vashell was forced to do – by coercion, and by magick. But she will come round, Graal. She will deliver the Soul Gem voluntarily... And if she does not? Well, I will rip the Gem from her chest with my own teeth. The Engineer Religion must end here. It is time for a new Empire. An Empire based on Blood and Sacrifice and Vampire Plague!"

Graal said nothing for a moment, and thought of his own daughters, Shanna and Tashmaniok. If they had carried a gem of infinite power, of destructive soul magick buried deep within their own flesh, if they had carried a key to controlling the ancient vampire gods – would he sacrifice them? He smiled then. Of course he would. For they were only flesh, and bone, and what Kradek-ka and Graal planned... Well, that was immortality. Power. And total control.

"What of the second?" said Graal, then. "Have the three moons aligned?"

"The moons are aligned," confirmed Kradek-ka. "And even as we speak, Jageraw is in the mountains on his strange deviant course. As the Book of Angels decreed, the Gems had to be implanted in Guardian Souls. When released, only then would they have the true power to control the Vampire Warlords."

"So we have Anukis. We have Jageraw. Our *lady*, our *contact* implanted the third... have you found her, yet? Have you found the Guardian?"

"Yes." Kradek-ka's voice was soft. Clockwork gears stepped and clicked with a vague, background buzz. "I know the Guardian now."

"Did she choose well? Is the Guardian known to me?" said Graal, voice grave.

"Let us just say this answers a puzzle which has haunted us for many a day, General Graal."

The brass chamber in the Engineer's Palace was cold, and eerily quiet at this hour of the night. Sa entered, pulling a high-collared shimmering iron gown tight. Her eyes burned with annoyance. "This had better be good," she snarled, striding across the metal floor, boots ringing. Then she stopped. She stared at Walgrishnacht and the three remaining members of his platoon.

The Cardinal and his vachine warriors were in a sorry state. Their flesh was cut and burned, by weapons and by ice, and their armour and clothing was in tatters showing signs of many a battle. The vachine warriors wore bloodied bandages with pride.

"You came through the mountains?"

"Through the Secret Paths," said Walgrishnacht.

"And you have news," said Sa, briskly.

"Princess Jaranis is dead. General Graal had her murdered. I assume this precludes invasion."

"It is not your duty to *assume*," snapped Sa, eyes narrowed. "You were pursued?"

"By cankers," said Walgrishnacht, voice level. Tagor-tel gave a short hiss, air rushing past his vachine fangs. He gestured to Sa, who nodded. For cankers to attack vachine was unheard of. Unbelievable! Even to utter such a breath was heresy in the Engineer's Palace.

"You can prove this?" said Tagor-tel, voice low and filled with poison.

Beja stepped from the shadows, and he carried a sack. Unceremoniously, he upended the cloth and a huge, deformed canker head rolled out, leaving blood-oil smears on the chamber floor.

Sa took an involuntary step back. She met Walgrishnacht's steel gaze.

"We are not the enemy here," said the Cardinal, and she noted his hand was on his sword-hilt. He had a finger missing.

"Do you realise to whom you speak?" hissed Sa, invoking her Watchmaker status.

"Yes," said Walgrishnacht. "But it looks to me that Graal intends to invade. You must call the War Council. If you do not pull our troops, and our *Ferals* back from Untamed Lands, we will be defenceless. Silva Valley will be defenceless!"

Sa gave a nod. She turned to Tagor-tel. "Any news from Fiddion?"

"No. He has been strangely silent."

"Then call the War Council," said Sa, voice bleak. "Come the spring, it appears we go to war."

• • • •

Kell and his fellow travellers made a hasty descent into a narrow pass which led through the mountains. Tension was eating them, now. On their trail were two cross-breed vachine albino killers. Which meant... what? That the vachine and albino soldiers were breeding? Saark shivered at the thought as he moved lithely across rocky ground, and a cold wind laced with ice caressed him.

"You're going to have to leave the donkey," said Kell, finally, as they stumbled through a narrow inverted V, leading to a rocky ravine.

"No."

"It's not up for debate, Saark. With those bastards on our tail, we need to put down more speed. She's slowing us down." Kell placed his hand gently on Saark's arm. "My friend. If Mary is with us when the cankers come, they will tear her to pieces. You know this."

Saark nodded, and with a tear in his eye he patted the donkey's muzzle, removed the heavy load from her back and took a few essentials from the bags, before slapping her rump with the hilt of his rapier. With a startled "eeyore", Mary cantered back down the trail, then turned and stared at Saark reproachfully with large, baleful eyes.

"Go on. Shoo!" he yelled. Looking back to Kell, he grinned. "I love that beast," he said, and Kell nodded, eyes hooded, hand on the Ilanna's matt black shaft.

"Let's move," said Kell, eyeing the high ridgeline above. Distantly, he fancied he could hear canker snarls, but shook his head. It was the wind in the crags. But they were coming, he knew. The albino women and the cankers. They were coming, all right. He could feel it in his bones. In his very soul.

Kell had been right to abandon Mary. They moved with more speed now, although both Nienna and Saark complained bitterly at the pace; and Saark more-so than the young woman. On Kell's direction, they angled right, up a steep rocky slope filled with flat plates of granite and slate, boots stomping and sliding to send yet more rocks scattering and clattering to the valley below. Kell pushed them hard, and after fifty minutes or so all were streaming with sweat, pain flashing bright patterns through their brains. Saark paused, and gazed down the scree slope.

"I can see Mary!" he said, almost triumphantly. Then stopped dead, as from a narrow chimney in the opposite wall of rock loped the three cankers. They stopped, snarling and drooling, and spread out, circling the donkey, great paws padding and claws drawing sparks from the hard ground, eyes fixed, travelling in lazy pendulous sweeps. Mary eeyored in panic, eyes wide, ears laid back on her terrified skull. Saark found his heart in his mouth, terror running through his veins. "No," he muttered, gripping his rapier as Mary hunkered down in terror, bunching her hind quarters to do the only thing she knew how; to kick. "Not the donkey!" wailed Saark. But, after a few brief circles, the cankers broke away like a squadron of hunting falcons, and padded along the bottom of the valley floor.

"Shh!" said Kell, motioning for the others to lower themselves to the ground, killing their skyline. Then he glanced up. Above them reared a high wall of granite cut through with lodes of glittering quartz, diagonal bands that gleamed and sparkled. He fancied he spied a narrow aperture. A narrow squeeze would be good to slow down the cankers – or at least force them to come through in single file. But they hadn't been spotted yet; if they stood and ran now, it would draw the cankers to them immediately. If they were lucky, the cankers would lose their scents.

"They're heading off down the ravine," whispered Saark.

Kell nodded.

Myriam shifted, and a rock rolled down the slope, bouncing as it reached the bottom to send a hollow clatter reverberating through the rocky wilderness. The cankers stopped, a sudden movement, and all three heads turned to stare up at the hiding adventurers.

"Well done, bitch," hissed Saark.

Kell stared at the cankers. He had never seen anything like them. Their skin was translucent, showing the crimson of thick muscles cut through by clockwork machinery within, all twisted and deformed just that little bit – a characteristic which set them apart from pure vachine. It was a twisted merging of clockwork technology and flesh made real.

Their eyes were blood red, faces elongated almost into horse muzzles but much wider, much larger, showing curved fangs which twisted and bent in seemingly random directions. They moved on all fours like huge lions, but as they turned and bounded up the slope Kell and Saark blinked, realising they had hooves.

"Mother of Mercy," whispered Saark, drawing his rapier.

"Run!" screamed Kell, suddenly, breaking the spell. Nienna and

Myriam sprinted, sliding up the scree, with Saark and Kell close behind. Kell pulled free Ilanna and kissed her butterfly blades. "Don't let me down this time," he muttered.

I am here for you, Kell. Here to kill for you. As you know I always will.

They sprinted up, as best they could. The cankers moved fast, faster than a human, and spiked brass claws emerged from hooves sending showers of sparks scattering down the scree slope. Myriam reached the narrow aperture first, and lifted free her long bow. She notched an arrow and touched a fletch to her cheek in one swift movement. An arrow flashed through the gloom, hitting a canker high in the shoulder. It squealed then, with a high-pitched whinny, twisted and corrupt. The cry of a dying horse.

Nienna ran into the gap in the rocky wall. It was the width of a man, the walls green and slick and slimy. Moss lined the floor in a thick layer, and above, about twelve feet from the ground, several large fallen rocks had formed a wedged, uneven roof.

"Come on!" shouted Nienna, fear etching her face and voice like acid. She pulled free a long knife, and stood, waiting, watching.

Saark reached Myriam's side and turned. He was an agile and quick man, made faster by his bite at the teeth of the albino vachine. He had left Kell behind, labouring, for once his prodigious size and strength working against him. Kell was panting hard, sweat running in rivulets down his face, into his beard, and he powered on, Ilanna in one mighty fist as the first of the cankers came up fast behind him... at the last minute Kell screamed and whirled, Ilanna slamming through flesh and knocking the canker back down the slope, where it rolled and thrashed past its sprinting comrades. Kell came on a few more steps. He was twenty paces from the aperture, but the cankers were too close. Another arrow flashed, close over Kell's shoulder and into a canker's throat – the beast reared, emitting the strange screaming horse-shriek, but dropped to the ground and charged on. Kell's axe slammed in an overhead sweep, connecting as the canker leapt for his throat with long brass claws, and Ilanna bit through muscle and flesh, snapping bones with terrible crunches. The canker twisted, trapping the axe and rolling away, tearing the great butterfly blades from Kell's sweating grip. The third canker leapt, but Myriam's arrow flashed, striking the beast through the eye. Kell shifted left as the beast hit the ground beside him, thrashing, and he leapt on its back, great hands taking hold of its long equine head and wrenching back with all his strength, his muscles writhing, and for a long moment they were locked, immobile, a bizarre double-headed creature from a deformed nightmare – then there came a mighty *crack* as Kell snapped the beast's neck. The canker fell limp, mewling, and Kell ran back to his embedded axe, taking hold of the shaft and wrenching the weapon free. Panting, and covered in huge globules of canker blood, he turned and ran for the crevice.

"Well done, old horse!" beamed Saark, as Kell reached the wall of rock. The old warrior glanced up, lips tight, saying nothing. He turned, and watched the two injured cankers climb to their feet. Even though Ilanna had cut a huge chunk from the beast, breaking bones within, it shifted itself and they could see the huge *open* wound – enough to fell any bull or bear – and watched as *inside* the wound thin golden wires seemed to flow, twisting and entwining around broken bones, pulling them with little cracks back into place, into alignment, then wrapping around and around and around, binding, strengthening, as all the time the ominous *tick tick tick* of slightly offbeat clockwork clicked across the empty rock space.

"Inside," growled Kell, squaring himself up.

"They can fit," said Saark. "The cankers are smaller than others we've met. Kell, the bastards can follow us."

"Not if I have my way!" he hissed, eyes like glowing coals. Myriam and Saark followed Nienna into the narrow gap, and Kell lifted Ilanna above his head as the cankers orientated themselves on the man and dropped their heads, growls emitting on streams of saliva.

Kell swung his axe, striking the rocky wedge above. The wall *boomed*, sparks spat in a shower, and above the rocks trembled. Again Kell struck the wall, and again, his huge muscles straining, Ilanna shrieking and singing in simple joy and the cankers charged, their brass claws raking the rocks and for a final time, Kell slammed his axe into the wall and above there came a rattle, followed by cracks as three huge rocks shifted, and one fell, the second fell atop it, and their combined weight brought a wall of granite tumbling into the gap as Kell leapt back, stumbled back, dust billowing out and slamming him like a wall of ash. Kell coughed, choking for a moment, blinded, dust in his beard and eyes. He dropped his axe, rubbing at his eyes and coughing some more, and Saark patted the old man on the back.

"Well done, old boy."

Kell picked up Ilanna and surveyed the blockage, his eyes following it upwards. He grunted in cynicism. "Let's see how long that holds. Not long enough, I'd wager."

"You're ever the sweet voice of optimism."

"Get to chaos, Saark. And next time, try using that pretty little rapier instead of standing by watching me fight!"

"Hey!" Saark spread his hands. "You seemed to be doing such a fine job! You didn't need my little prick in the middle of your hero battle; after all, you are *Kell the Legend*. They wrote poems about you."

Kell stared beadily at Saark, then pushed him heavily in the chest. "Go on. Follow Nienna and Myriam. Let's get out of this shit hole before a mountain of rocks comes down on our heads."

"Don't push! You'll wrinkle the silk."

Kell shook his head and sighed. "Some things will never change," he rumbled.

They moved as swiftly as they could through the gloom, and more snow began to fall. They found a cave, and Kell allowed Myriam to build a small fire. "They know where we are, anyways," he said. "And I think we all need something warm inside us."

Myriam made a thin soup in a shallow pan she carried in her pack, and as they sat shivering in the small damp cave, warming hands over the meagre flames, Myriam stirred the soup, and fixed Kell with an odd look.

"You know, Kell, when I was younger I was a student at the University of Vor. We had many texts there; it was during that time I found I had a small affinity for magick."

"Illusions, you mean," snorted Saark.

"Even so. There were many texts I studied before... before my affliction."

"And?" Kell had made a mug of coffee, and held it between his great bear paws. It looked a little ridiculous. Out of scale. He drank the bittersweet brew, and sighed, feeling caffeine and sugar fire through his system. That feeling was closely followed by a ravening hunger. How long since they had eaten? How long since they did anything except grab a sleep of exhaustion, or a meal of dried meat as they fled yet more danger? Oh, for a fine steak, a tankard of honey-mead, and new potatoes garnished with herbs and butter. Kell found his mouth watering. Horse-shit, he thought. Things were going to get a lot worse before they got better, that was for sure.

"I think I know these two women who follow, in pursuit. These, as you say, blend of albino and vachine. Of what you speak is a rarity; if the texts are to be belicved."

Kell stared at her. "They had texts on the vachine at Vor University?"

Myriam gave a strange smile. "Yes. They were kept under lock and key, obviously. King Searlan, as his father and grandfather before him, did not want the vachine made common knowledge to the populace. It was bad enough having Blacklippers running blood through the mountains, feeding any impure vachine willing to buy Karakan Red, without further adding to dark legends."

"And that's where you found out about merging human with clockwork?"

Myriam nodded. "Yes. When I contracted my…" her face contorted a little, and her eyes darkened despite the fire, "my *cancer*, when I had exhausted my funds on employing ridiculous and pointless physicians who took my money and made recommendations, none of which worked, then I turned to *knowledge*, I turned to those secret books I knew existed in the Vor Vaults. I knew which Professors held the keys. I persuaded them, one way or another, to give me access."

"You mean you used sex?" blurted Nienna, meeting Myriam's gaze.

"Don't look at me like that, girl. I did not – and do not – want to die."

"None of us want to die," said Nienna. "But we don't always get a choice." She bared her teeth in what might have been a smile; a smile tainted by memories of Kat.

"You say you think you know these women? Explain."

"They fit a description I once read. In an ancient text."

"Hold on," said Saark, holding up his hand. "I've been close to one of these killing bitches. Real close. And I'm telling you she wasn't a day over the age of twenty."

"That isn't the way it works," growled Kell.

Myriam nodded. "They do not age; or not as you and I understand the ageing process. A vachine with regularly updated clockwork – well, they could live for hundreds of years. And these two – Shanna and Tashmaniok they were named – they were famous for many dark deeds. They were known as the Soul

Stealers! And they were there at the Siege of Drennach. They were there during the Days of Blood."

"They were?" said Saark, eyes wide. He glanced at Kell. "Hey. *You* were at the Siege of Drennach! It's in the poem. It's part of the Legend!"

Kell licked his lips, eyes down, and sipped his coffee. He leant forward with a grunt, and stared into the pan. "Is the soup ready?"

Myriam tasted it, then reached into her pocket and added more salt. "Soon. Let the meat soften. I, also, find it hard to chew."

Kell sat back, and as he stared into the fire he said, "The Siege of Drennach was a bad time. Many died there. Nobody cared about Drennach, back then. We felt like we'd been deserted, by the King, by the people of Falanor. We were left out there to hang. There were only three hundred, a quarter what the garrison should have been, especially in a place that big. When the savages came from over the rolling desert dunes, wearing flowing robes and carrying tulwars and spears with golden heads that shimmered in the sun... well, each man on those walls knew he was dead meat. The savages had War Lions on leashes, huge beasts trained to fight in pits and then, at Drennach, trained to attack the defenders on the walls." Kell shook his head, and sighed. "It was a bad time; a time of death." He looked up. "I did bad things, then. I was a cruel man." His face hardened, eyes narrowing. "A very bad man."

"But you never saw these *Soul Stealers*?" asked Saark.

Kell shook his head. "Never heard of them, lad. And when I had my little encounter back at the distillery, I did not know the bitch. She seemed to know me, but I assumed that was because they were hunting us – sent by Graal, no less. If there was anything deeper, anything from back at Drennach, well, she gave me no sign."

"One thing is for sure," said Myriam.

"Oh yeah?" snapped Saark.

"They are deadly."

"I think we should eat, now," said Kell.

"Grandfather?"

His face cracked into a smile. "Yes, little monkey?"

Nienna returned his smile. "You said you were a bad man. Were you... were you *really* bad?"

"Only to the bad men," lied Kell, shivering as he spoke the words, shivering as flickering red images of gore and torture rampaged through his mind; shivering, as he remembered his daughter.

Kell forced the memories away. No. Not now.

Now, he had a different agenda. To keep Nienna alive.

And to end the madness in Falanor.

He could only do that by remaining calm, and thinking things through, and not drinking whiskey and losing his temper. He could only do these things by *not* being Kell the Legend. His Legend came from his evil, dark deeds, from blood-oil and whiskey, and from the Dog Gem soul of Ilanna. From Ilanna.

Kell coughed, and accepted soup from Myriam.

"I should be dead," he said, and sipped the hot, thin broth.

"But you are not."

"I deserve it," said Kell, fixing eyes on Saark.

"That's up for debate," smiled Saark, weakly. "You continually claim to be a bad man; and yet I see you perform good deeds all the time. Good deeds that help people; look at Nienna. You *saved* her, Kell."

"To save myself," he grunted.

Saark laughed, a tinkling sound in that strange cold place. "You are indulging yourself, old man, you have this image of yourself and you will not, *can* not admit that good exists inside you. Well, mate, whatever you say. But you and I both know, even if you had not been poisoned, you would have strode across this world with your axe in hand, slaying any bastard who got between you and your granddaughter."

"There you go," said Kell. "You admit it. I would have slain any who stood before me. That is not honourable. That is not strong. That is weak, Saark; I am a weak man. A strong man would not use his physical strength as do I. A strong man would not... *abuse* his gift."

"The only abuse here," said Saark, "is your lack of table manners. Look! By all the gods, you're spilling soup down your jerkin. You're a scruffy bastard, Kell. It's in your beard and everything! Can you not connect hand to mouth? Can you not retain a simple soup in your orifice?"

"I'll shove my fist in your orifice if you don't stop mewling."

"Ha, and there was I defending your honour and integrity."

"I need no man for that," said Kell.

Myriam had been watching bemusedly as the two men squabbled, then sat, staring at Kell. "Kell."

"Yes, lass?"

"I am confused. And a little worried."

"Spit it out."

"Well, as to why you are still guiding me to Silva Valley – to the vachine. I don't want to wake up – or not wake up – with an axe in the back of my skull. I am tired of looking over my shoulder. Weary of living in fear. And I recognise I have earned this by my actions. To you, and to Nienna. I am deeply sorry."

Kell grinned, looking down into their meagre fire. "You have pushed me a lot, Myriam. Pushed me beyond the boundaries of accepted behaviour." He glanced up. His eyes glittered, then he shifted his gaze sideways to his granddaughter. Nienna was looking up at the cave walls in fascination, as if she'd found a particularly original composition of poetry embedded in damp stone. Kell shook his head. He could not understand her continual enthralment. "The thing is, lass, if you'd pulled that trick on me a few years back, with the poison – well girl, you'd now be dead. The minute the antidote touched my lips I would have split you down the fucking middle like a log." He rested back, soup finished, hands on his knees. He sighed. "However. I am trying. I am trying to be... not good, but *better*. I am trying to be a *tolerable* man, for Nienna, to show her a fine example. Ironically, I am trying to do this in the midst of an invasion. But a man must strive." He ran his hand through his thick, shaggy, unkempt hair. Then scratched at his beard, rubbing away a smudge of soup. "And we have the same goals. The same destination. Silva Valley seems to be the place with answers. I am Kell. And I sorely want some answers."

"I have a trade."

"Another one?" growled Saark. "The only trade you deserve is a blade between the ribs."

"Quiet," snapped Kell, scowling. "She's done bad things. We all agree this. But then, Saark, you are hardly the angel. I have not forgotten what you did with Kat. You are a predator. What did the men say back at the village? At Kettleskull Creek? 'Saark, an arrogant rich bastard, unable to keep his childmaker in his cheese-stinking pants.'"

"Oh. You heard that, did you?"

"I heard it, lad." He glanced at Myriam. "What are you thinking?"

"Information. About the Soul Stealers."

"Go on."

"You promise not to kill me?"

"If I'd wanted to kill you, you'd already be dead."

Myriam nodded, realising that her life hung by a thread, and that thread was called Nienna. She swallowed.

"The Soul Stealers. They are creatures of the Black Pike Mountains. That is what I read."

"Yes?"

"Their father is said to be an ancient servant of the Vampire Warlords. They do his bidding. I read that for hundreds of years the Soul Stealers have been employed in an attempt to bring back the Vampire Warlords – and if they do, these Warlords will use the vachine and the albinos and the Harvesters... all will be subservient, all will turn the world into a dark place of chaos."

Kell considered this. "I have heard this tale before," he said. "About these Warlords, although under a different name; it is a fiction used to frighten little children by the fire. It is a nonsense."

Myriam shrugged. "There is a place, Helltop, a mountain-top hall, a sacred place of the vachine. It overlooks Silva Valley, from thousands and thousands of feet up. It is said to be the home of the Soul Stealers. It is said that they cannot be killed except in that place, for it is a source of their power, the source of their own collective soul. And when they kill, every soul they take flows back to the Granite Thrones which reside there."

"I have heard of the Granite Thrones," said Nienna, suddenly. "It is where the Blood Kings once sat. We did it in Classical History in preparation for Jalder University." She went quiet, then. She was continually reminded of a life she no longer had.

Kell nodded, remembering shoving his Svian deep into the vachine who attacked him. He should have pierced her core, with a blow like that. He should have destroyed her clockwork engine. "You think we'll have big trouble with these Soul Stealers?"

"I guarantee it," whispered Myriam.

With the dawn they set off through an icy valley, and a stone path rose in a series of switch-backs for perhaps two thousand feet. They climbed this narrow pathway in silence, hands cold and tucked into furs and pockets, and with faces tortured by the biting, howling, bitter mountain wind. Kell led the way in grim silence, brooding. When Nienna asked how long they had before the Soul Stealers and the cankers caught up with them, he just smiled grimly and shook his head.

At the rear travelled Saark, and Myriam dropped back, boots kicking loose rocks. She walked along beside him for a while, in silence, as jagged walls reared around them and far above, an eagle soared.

"Have you forgiven me yet?" she said, smiling.

"No. Fuck off."

"Harsh words, Saark."

"Not as harsh as sticking a knife in an unsuspecting man's belly."

"That was a mistake. I admit that now."

"Not easy to forget, nor forgive."

"Still, I am sorry. I apologise. I would never, ever do it again." She met his eyes. "I mean it, sincerely, Saark. It was a mistake." She gave a short laugh, like a bark. "I must admit, the more I have got to know Kell, the more I admire him. He is so strong, powerful, a giant to walk the mountains with."

"Careful girl, I think you're getting a bit wet down there."

Myriam looked at him, her face humoured. "You think so? Because of Kell, or because of you?"

Saark stopped for a moment, staring at her, then continued to walk the steep trails, calf muscles burning, feet throbbing inside his boots, his pack a dead weight across his spine – as if he carried a corpse.

He shook his head. Smiled. "I must admit, girl, I do tend to have that effect on young women." He considered this. "And middle aged women. Hell, even grannies. It's rare I've met a woman alive who doesn't want a bit of the tender Saark loving."

"Do you really think that much of yourself?"

"No. Women think much of me. I am simply along for the ride."

"Have you ever been in love?" Saark's smile fell, and immediately Myriam realised her mistake. "I am sorry," she said.

"No. No, don't be. I shouldn't bottle my guilt and self-loathing inside; it's an unhealthy combination. Yes. I have been in love. Twice. One was taken away from me, for an arranged marriage."

"And the other?"

"The other was married to another," said Saark, voice a croak, eyes filled with tears. He waved away her concern. "Ach, both were a long time ago, although some bastard seems intent on reminding me of past miseries. Have you ever been in love?"

"No," said Myriam, tilting her head to one side. "I admire men, for looks or physique, but if I am totally honest, then no man has ever grabbed my heart. And then, well, I became ill, and it has eaten away at me, robbed me of youth and my looks, even my bodyweight. It is a savage punishment. The gods have a sick sense of humour, don't they? They seem to use most of it on me. No wonder I became so bitter."

Saark was watching her. "I admit," he said, voice soft, "once, you must have been a bonny lass."

"Enough to turn your eye, Sword Champion!" she snapped, "But no more."

"I'm sorry. I did not mean to offend."

"None taken," but her voice had become more brutal, more desolate.

"It must have been difficult. Watching yourself fading away."

"Yes, Saark." Her voice was little more than a whisper, and they came to a narrow set of large boulder-type steps, blocks carved from the mountain trail. Kell had helped Nienna up, and was ahead. Saark leapt lightly up, then turned and as Myriam climbed, she slipped... Saark moved so fast he was a blur, and caught her wrist. He lifted her onto the stone step, her hand in his, one hand on her hip. They stood for a moment, looking at one another, then Saark stepped back and coughed, releasing his hold.

"Watch your step, girl. That's a three thousand foot drop. And I bet you don't bounce much on the way down."

"Thank you."

"Pleasure."

They moved on. "Imagine," said Myriam, "if you suffered a horrible scarring to your face. Or you were trapped in a fire, and ended up with face and hair on fire leaving you brutally burned and ugly. How would you respond?"

Saark shivered. "It is a fate worse than death," he conceded. "I would be an easy victim for a torturer. This is my weakness, I admit. The minute he touched my face, I'd whimper like a girl and spill any and all secrets I carried."

"Vanity is a curse," said Myriam.

"Ahh, but only when you're not as beautiful as I."

"You are a real romantic," said Myriam, voice hard.

"I try," preened Saark, missing the irony – or choosing, at least, to ignore it. "I try, my sweet."

At the top of the climb they came to a plateau coated in hard-packed snow. Their boots crunched and, despite their ascent, a world of further, higher peaks spread around them in a glorious, full panorama. Nienna spun in circles, giggling, and Kell breathed deep. The wind was curiously still on this mountain summit, and Kell pointed with Ilanna, across a high ridgeline peppered with ice.

"Wolfspine," he said, simply.

"Looks dangerous," muttered Saark.

"It is," replied Kell, darkly. "We must take great care." He ruffled Nienna's long, dark hair. "And especially you, little monkey." But Nienna did not reply; her eyes were wide at the sight of the ridge they were to traverse.

Wolfspine. A half-league in length, a narrow, undulating ridge perhaps a foot in width, and with sheer four thousand foot drops to either side. The path itself was an inverted V of stone, black, slippery, frosted with lace patterns of ice.

Kell led the way, across a slightly curved plateau of snow, boots crunching. The air was still, and calm, brittle and cold, and bright light glared painfully from white snow.

Saark caught him up. "We are wonderfully ill-equipped for this," he said.

"You think I don't realise that, lad?"

"Just thought I'd mention it."

"Just try not to fall off, eh?"

"I'll certainly do my best on that account."

They stopped, where the mountain plateau rose and narrowed to the Wolfspine. Distant, through a haze of low cloud, they saw the next peak, the next Black Pike connected by this insane walkway of treacherous, icy rock.

"Is there no other way?" whispered Saark.

"No. The next five peaks are impossible to climb, and this ridge rises and dips, but links each peak together; without it, there would be no way to Silva Valley. The mountains form a protective barrier. In deep winter, this place is impassable – to all but the mad."

"Ha, and I suppose you're going to tell me you've done it?"

"I have," said Kell, voice low. "But I had ropes, and boots with spikes, and proper ice-axes."

"Can we do it now, do you think?"

"We're going to find out, Saark. There's no point going back. And… I want you to go first."

"Me?" squeaked the dandy, his fear palpable. "Why not you? You've all the damn experience. What do I know? I just drink wine and fuck pampered plump beauties. This is out of my bounds, Kell old horse. This is so far out of my world I should be paddling among the stars."

"I must take the rear," said Kell.

"Why?"

"In case those bastard cankers come back."

"Oh. Yes. A fine reason."

Kell stood, staring along the ridgeline. He glanced back at the near-flat plateau. It stretched off, then fell away into a darkness of seemingly endless valleys and tumbling mountain slopes. Beyond, he could see Falanor stretching away, see her hills and distant villages, her frozen rivers and snow-covered forests. Here, he knew – here was the point where Falanor fell behind, vanished, was eaten by the mountains. Here was the point of no return.

He remembered his time before, in the Black Pikes, hunting vachine.

"Damn," he said, and his gaze swept the world. Everything was clear and still and unbearably dazzling. It was like the gods had painted the world in pastel shades. Kell watched Falanor, and felt as if Falanor stared back. Help me, she said. Purify me. Make me proud.

"I'll be back," growled Kell, turned his back on Falanor, and started to climb up to the Wolfspine ridge.

"They're coming."

Nienna's voice was high in panic. Kell turned, glanced back over the undulating ridge. They were picking their way carefully over the narrow ribbon of stone, and clouds had shifted, a mist enclosing the small group, muffling sounds and at least, for a while, hiding the heart-stopping sheer drops to either side.

Kell drew Ilanna, and stood. He heard the snarls. The mist moved in patches, sometimes clearing, sometimes thickening. Then it cleared on their back-trail, and Kell saw the two crimson equine cankers. They moved fast along the ridge, sure-footed, drooling, their eyes fixed on their quarry, on fresh meat, on palpable fear.

There came a *whoosh* by Kell's ear, and an arrow punched into the lead canker, just below its face. It roared, feathered shaft erupting from its flesh, and pawed at the buried arrow for a moment, snapping the shaft. It roared again, and charged, pace increasing.

"Saark," growled Kell. "Go on. Get Nienna to the next peak. There is a resting place on the top of the mountain, a stone shelter. It would be easier to defend than here."

"And what about you?"

"I'll stay awhile, see what happens."

Another shaft hissed from Myriam's bow, and hit the lead canker in the eye. It reared then, screeching an impossibly high screech, and toppled from the mountain, sliding down the terrible slope at first, then connecting with a large rock and soaring out into the void. The mist swallowed the canker, and the monster was gone.

Now, as the mist cleared in patches, from further down behind the cankers strode the Soul Stealers. One lifted her bow, and too late Kell focused and *realised*. An arrow flashed, and Ilanna rose – but too slow. The arrow nicked his cheek, leaving a fine line of blood as it continued its trajectory... behind Kell, and into Myriam's throat. She gurgled, gasping, clawing the shaft and staggering back. She hit the ground, pitched sideways, and before Kell could grab her, slid off the ridgeline and into the vast, swallowing mist of the mountain void.

Nienna screamed.

Kell scowled, and turned back. Another arrow flashed for him, but with a rising rage and casual arrogance Ilanna snapped up and the arrow was deflected, cracking off into the mist.

Kell faced the final, charging canker.

And the Soul Stealers beyond.

"Come on," he growled, lowering his head. "Come and eat my fucking axe."

THIRTEEN
Kindred

Vashell stared at the three vachine warriors, and heard Fiddion's
Harvester head crackling in the fire as flames consumed flesh, and
felt Alloria move away, behind him, giving him combat space.
Vashell breathed deep, and settled into a rhythm of battle. They
were underestimating him, he knew, because he had no face or
claws or fangs, but Vashell was a warrior born. He hefted his knife,
and stepped forward as the first of the vachine attacked...

It moved fast, leaping almost horizontally at Vashell who dropped
his shoulder in a blur, knife ramming up into the vachine's belly
and ripping savagely sideways as he took the vachine's short black
sword in his fist, and twisted allowing the moving body to slam
against the wall with a splatter of blood. With a short hack, he severed the vachine's head and blood-oil flowed free from the neck
stump. Nobody else had moved. Vashell squared himself to the
other two creatures who stared, stunned at what they'd just witnessed. They separated as far as the cave would allow, and as the
wind howled mournfully outside, Vashell caught sight of his
brother from the corner of his eye; Llaran was smiling.

"What's funny?" snarled Vashell. "The fact I'm going to sever
your spine?"

"You cannot stand against us."

"Watch me."

With a battle shriek Vashell attacked, ducking a sword strike and
slash of claws, elbowing the vachine in the face and front-kicking
the second, leaping figure back to the wall. He leapt himself, and

sword blades clashed, and he reversed his sword thrusting it under his own arm and into the chest of the vachine leaping at his back. The creature gurgled, and clockwork whined and clicked, and Vashell withdrew the blade, turned fast and lopped off the second man's head... continuing the fluid move with a roll of hips, drop of one shoulder, his left arm bearing the knife coming up, a clash of steel sending sparks scattering through the cave as the short black sword came high overhead to slam through the third vachine's shoulder, and deep down into lungs. Clockwork machinery, spinning and moving, could be seen through severed, wide-open flesh. Vashell tugged free his blade, and split the vachine's head clean in two showing a cross-section of skull and brain – closely meshed with fine gold wire and tiny, micro-clockwork. The head peeled in two, like fruit-halves, and Vashell heard the sounds and turned fast – but Llaran had gone. Fled, into the snow.

Alloria was standing, hands before her, panting hard. Vashell leapt to the fire, and using the tip of his sword flicked Fiddion's head from the flames. It was a blackened, crisped ball, a globe of stinking fried pork and fat ran from orifices, and steam rose from the cooling, over-cooked meat.

"Hell," hissed Vashell, his vachine blood-fury still raised as his eyes narrowed, and he contemplated following Llaran into the snow. To be betrayed by his own brother! He could not understand it. But then he thought about it, and he could. Vashell was no longer beautiful vachine; and he had lost his fangs and claws, that which made him holy, that which endeared him to Engineers and Watchmakers alike. If they had taken him back to Silva Valley, he would have been executed as impure. Burned, like a common criminal. Quartered, like a captured Blacklipper. Vashell spat into the fire. "Bastards." Now, he could never go home, and that burned worse than any loss of face.

"Listen... to... me..." croaked Fiddion.

Vashell moved to the cooling head, and knelt. He reached out, touched the scorched flesh. He shook his head. "I cannot believe it. You tough little bastard. Can you hear me, Fiddion?"

"Listen carefully. Vashell. The Vampire... the Warlords, they will return. Kradek-ka and Graal, they will make it so. A... summoning. They will..." He coughed, then, and a tiny raw pink tongue darted against scorched, blackened lips. "They will take Anukis. To Skaringa Dak. Helltop. To sit on the Granite Thrones. She has the Soul Gem, you see? You must stop this." He coughed – or at least *choked* – again, ejecting a long thick black stream of gore. "Help Anukis," said the Harvester. "Help the vachine race."

"You don't know what you ask," said Vashell, eyes full of tears which stung his tortured face. "She has taken everything from me; my fangs, my claws, my vachine life. She took my pride and my dignity – stripped me of everything and left me as outcast! Even if I saved Silva Valley, saved the entire vachine civilisation – they would still turn on me and execute. Don't you understand?"

"That is why you must help," said Fiddion, quietly. "Now put me back on the fire. None, none must know my secrets."

Vashell obeyed, placing the Harvester's crisped, smouldering head back into the flames. The fire roared for a moment, bright green flames soaring to scorch the roof of the cave. Then the head burnt fiercely; in minutes it was nothing more than an outline of ash, which crumbled, vanishing into glowing embers.

Alloria was there. She placed a hand on Vashell. He looked at her.

"What will you do?" she said.

He glanced back at the vachine corpses, their blood-oil staining rock and ice. Then he stood, and shook free the queen's grip. He lifted his short black sword and examined the blade. Then he bared his teeth, where once his vampire fangs had sat.

"I will fight," he said, eyes lost in shadow.

It was like a dream. A dream watched through fog. A dream watched through refracted glass. Kradek-ka took hold of Anukis by the throat and he pinned her down, and she screamed and struggled and the Harvesters helped, long bone fingers piercing and cutting her flesh and the brass needle was long, and dripping with globules of amber fluid, of sweet sweet *honey* and Kradek-ka, face twisted in animal hatred, plunged the needle into Anukis's neck and her struggling slowed and ceased and she watched the scene from outside her body, and felt good, and felt warm, and memories faded and everything in the world seemed cosy and kind and simply *right*.

It had taken days of preparation, but Anukis had grown strong, had grown calm, had filled herself with yet more love for her father. He sought to make the vachine strong, to accelerate their civilisation; his was a noble cause. And when he pioneered new technology, she would be accepted back into Silva Valley, no longer blood-oil impure, no longer outcast. She could return to her old life. With Kradek-ka, her father, by her side.

Now, they travelled ancient mountain tunnels. The walls were of purest white, and the Harvesters who travelled with Anukis and Kradek-ka, numbering perhaps thirty strong and making her shiver when they crept up behind, smiling curiously with long bone-fingers extended, carried small white globes which lit the way with a dull, feverish light.

Kradek-ka led, with Anukis usually one step behind. Occasionally he would smile back at her, at his eldest daughter, at his *special* daughter, and her mind swam a little as she tried to remember why she was there. The gold liquor the Harvesters gave her in the morning and evening, it seemed to have dulled her senses and made the world flicker like beautiful candlelight, and yet it confused her at the same time. It was most strange.

"You are a delight to behold," said Kradek-ka, remembering her earlier struggle, her fight, her animosity. But then, all emotions were easy to control with a subtle infusion of drugs. Just like all physical aspects were easy to control with a little introduction of melding clockwork.

They walked, through endless tunnels. Sometimes the walls were smooth and curved, corridors wide and paved as if used by great armies or royalty; other times they became angular, the white tiles gleaming and slightly off centre, awkward to look at as if they were plucking to unravel your mind. Then they would walk across rough hewn stone, sometimes dry as desert sand, other times slick with water or a clear, viscous slime. But two constants remained; the walls were always white, and the tunnel floor always sloped up.

They climbed. For hours, they climbed.

Occasionally they would come across rest rooms, low-ceilinged and scattered with beds. Kradek-ka would allow Anukis to sleep, to regain her strength. Kradek-ka never slept and would stand at the foot of her bed, watching her, staring at her, until she drifted into a world of dreams, of before the horror and bloodshed, when she used to sneak at night through the city streets of the Silva Valley, avoiding Engineers on her way to the Blacklippers for a bottle of Karakan Red.

When she awoke, Kradek-ka was always there, the Harvesters like ghosts in the background, or out in the tunnels, watching, drifting around, their purpose esoteric and unfathomable. Anukis often wondered if Kradek-ka stood watching all night; or if, when she slept, he would move away and entertain himself. However, he was always there when she awoke. Once, she might have found it creepy. Now, however, she found it comforting. Her father, the Watchmaker, was watching over her. He was all-seeing, all-strong; he was the backbone of the Vachine Empire. He had invented the Blood Refineries. He would save the vachine. He would expand the vachine. He was immortal. He would care for Anukis, forever.

They travelled on, and sometimes they would pass huge caverns, high up on narrow stone walkways with golden wires to grasp in order to steady oneself. Below, the white ground appeared soft, and pulsed with an inner white light. Harvesters collected there, and looked up in their thousands. Sometimes they watched these intruders – for that was how Anukis felt – and they would pass beyond the massive cavern confines. Other times, the Harvesters would lift their long, bone fingers and Anukis could not tell whether it was in salute, or in condemnation.

On crossing the fourth or fifth cavern filled with thousands of soundless Harvesters, Anukis turned to her father. "There are so many of them," she said, face ashen, strange pains in her chest, deep down in her clockwork.

"Yes. Nobody from Silva Valley, no Engineer, no Watchmaker, not even the Episcopate have seen these Halls. They are a holy place, and we are lucky indeed to pass through and remain unharmed. Usually, they would descend on us in thousands, and we would be instantly husked."

"Why, then, do they allow us passage?"

"Because we have something important to do," smiled Kradek-ka. "Something that will benefit them immensely."

"What do we have to do?" said Anukis, face a little slack. The drugs were starting to wear off, and the pains in her clockwork were increasing, and so strange, she thought, so odd that she needed the honey liquor more often now. She thought of the past; had she always needed the honey liquor? She did not remember taking it before, when she was a free vachine of Silva Valley… but then, the entirety of her early life was fuzzy and just a little bit twisted, and she let the memories go, let them slide away as more of the honey drug slid down her throat and eased into her veins and she was at peace.

Kradek-ka patted her hand. "Don't worry about it, sweet little Anu. You will see. Everything will be fine in the end. I promise."

Anukis nodded, and then they came to a sleep chamber, and she slept.

Anukis sat in a white place. The trees were blinding, dazzling, their white and silver leaves shimmering. Water tinkled nearby, white water in a white-rock stream. It was filled with natural music. It calmed her.

Looking down, she sat on spongy white heather, her legs curled beneath her. She was naked, except for marks under her skin; dark imprints of clockwork which made her grimace at the mechanical. Anukis slid her vampire fangs in and out, revelling in the slick smooth movement. Yes. Kradek-ka had made her well.

Anukis peered around for a long time, her mind sleepy, the world a strange place, her ideas not connecting, her memories fuzzy and distorting, reverberating like a skewed dream. It may have been a thousand years. It may have been a micro-second. Time seemed to have no time, here.

Anukis heard a sound, and through the white woods strode a woman, tall, naked, stunningly beautiful. Her long hair shone in the diamond light. She smiled when she saw Anukis, who hissed in fear...

It was Shabis! And Shabis was dead.

"I killed you, sister," she said, voice impossibly soft, eyes lowering in shame.

"No. Vashell killed me," Shabis said, and embraced Anukis, kissing her cheeks and lips. "You tried to warn me. I would not listen. I should have listened to you, sister." Tears shone in her eyes. "I was drunk on his love like wine; I was addicted to his lies, like I was to the blood-oil of our corrupt society."

"Father will make it good again."

"Do not listen to him!" The sudden flash of anger in Shabis's eyes shocked Anukis, and she took a step back. Her feet sank into soft moss. She was stunned by the ferocity; the sudden change.

"Why not?" Anukis was gentle.

"Because! He is a liar. He has always done things for his own ends. We have never factored into his equation; I know that now. I can see clearly. I understand Kradek-ka as I understand no other, and he is evil, and he will destroy our vachine civilisation."

"No, he will make it strong again! He loves the vachine, he has nothing but honour towards the Episcopate and Silva Valley." But Anukis felt suddenly hollow, as if she had been scooped empty by a giant claw. Somehow, she recognised the truth in Shabis's words. Somehow, she glimpsed through the encompassing lies.

"You are wrong, Anu," said Shabis. "We were always his tools. His weapons. Only I was the expendable one. He used Vashell, used Vashell to drive you *here*."

"Where is here?"

"You are in the Harvester's Lair. They are a created thing, like a machine, like a clockwork engine. They were created by the Vampire Warlords... created with only one purpose."

"Which is?"

"To harvest blood. Yes, now they help the vachine and help convert the blood to blood-oil; but that is only to keep the dream alive, to keep the workings of the machine alive. Soon, you will see the power of their onslaught. They will turn against the vachine, Anukis. And they will be led by Kradek-ka."

Anukis frowned. "Once, not long ago, I was cast out by my own people. The vachine of Silva Valley humiliated me, and I was destined for death. I set out with Vashell to find our father – he was captured by the Harvesters. I swore I would seek vengeance on the vachine, for never had I felt such pain. Surely, if Kradek-ka seeks to destroy the vachine... no, it is all too confusing. It is all too insane!"

"The vachine are your race," said Shabis, gently. "You cannot destroy a whole race because of what they did to you. Genocide is never the way, no matter how unholy you perceive the enemy, Anukis. Our father intends to kill the vachine. All of them. And that includes you."

"Now you are being ridiculous. Father would never hurt me."

"Not yet. Because he needs you. But the time will come."

The scene started to fade around Anukis, and she swallowed, mouth dry with fear. She was being dragged away from this ethereal plane, away from whatever bright, shining existence Shabis inhabited. And she had no control. No control at all.

"Needs me?" she said, speaking quickly, lethargy leaving her momentarily. "In what way does he need me?"

"Ask him about the Soul Gems," whispered Shabis, even as she faded away and was gone.

• • • •

Anukis awoke. The walls pulsed white. Kradek-ka was watching her. He smiled, but his eyes were dark, his fangs gleaming gold. Kradek-ka was vachine. And yet, now that she thought about it, she had never, ever, ever seen him take blood-oil. And when Anukis was considered *unholy*, he had not just known about Karakan Red and the Blacklippers… he had known Preyshan, the *king*.

"Tell me about the Soul Gems," said Anukis, moistening her lips with her tongue.

There was a flicker in Kradek-ka's face, but then it was gone. He smiled in serenity. "I don't know what you mean."

"The Soul Gems. Why do you need me, father? Where are we going?"

"We are going to celebrate a holy ritual. On behalf of the Harvesters. We are giving thanks that they help the vachine with blood-oil; that we are all holy together."

"Something is wrong. You are their prisoner."

"Yes. A prisoner of sorts. Only until I help them… perform a certain ritual."

You don't need me."

"You are coming," said Kradek-ka, his voice hard and brittle as iron. Then he softened a little. He took a deep breath. He reached out, and helped Anukis rise from the soft, white bed. His hands were gentle. His claws gleamed, sparkling like silver in the diffused light.

"I will stay here. I feel weak. I need to sleep."

"No. Time grows short. You will come now."

Anukis met her father's gaze. "No, father. I will not," she said, voice icy, breaking free of the honey drugs in her veins and mind and wondering just what game was being played here. Anukis was sick to the heartcore of being pushed around, told what to do, used and abused and taken advantage of. She had come through the Vrekken, risked her life for her father, and yet this did not *feel* like her father; he felt like an imposter, a chameleon, something which changed its skin to please and was yet different inside. A different organism.

Kradek-ka, still smiling, slammed out his fist. At the end, his claws were extended and they were impossibly long, huge curved silver and gold blades which pierced Anukis's throat, driving through her windpipe and neck muscles and spine, appearing at the back of her neck in an explosion of blood that decorated the white walls. With the force of the blow Anukis's body danced like a dropped corpse in a noose, and Kradek-ka stood there, holding Anukis in the air, a punctured ragdoll. Anukis gurgled and kicked, not quite believing the strength of Kradek-ka, not quite believing her own weakness, and not quite believing what had just happened.

"My girl," said Kradek-ka, eyes glowing impossibly dark. "You will do exactly what you are told," he said, and retracted his claws.

General Graal moved to the Blood Refinery. The cold night breeze cooled his naked body. Without clothing and armour, he was tautly muscled and very, very lean. Graal's skin was perfectly white, like fine porcelain, and when he turned the moonlight caught his features and gave him a surreal, dead look. As if carved from stone.

"The Sending Magick is ready, general," came the sibilant hiss of a Harvester, bobbing as it walked towards him. Graal nodded, and moved through the snow, feet crunching, to where the huge Blood Refinery squatted, fat and black and bloated, like a burnt corpse in the sun, like the full belly of a corpse-fed battlefield raven. He turned back, looked at the Harvesters, and beyond, down into Falanor's capital city of Vor. Many buildings burned fiercely. The temples. The libraries. Smoke spiralled into the dark winter sky, fireflies of ash dancing like insects. Graal's nostrils twitched, and he could smell distant smoke. He turned back to the Blood Refinery. It reminded him of an overfull insect.

"We are finished here," he said, voice low. "You know what to do."

"Yes," hissed the Harvester.

Graal stepped forward, and pressed his naked body against the Blood Refinery. He started the incantation, and felt the Sending Magick flow through ancient iron and *into* his veins and flesh and bones, and he flowed with the magick and was absorbed by the magick, and it smashed his skull with a sudden bright pounding and he flowed with it, and the destination was clear and he felt every component atom in his being broken down and disseminated then reintegrated into a whole, and Graal laughed for this was what insanity must feel like and he revelled in it, this was what being a god must feel like and he bathed in it, gloried in it, and lost his own mind to it all, and it was Good.

Graal swam. He leapt. He flowed. It took a million years.

He eased like a blood cell through the veins of the universe.

He trickled through time, like a virus through an organism.

Graal no longer existed, for his matter was part of all matter, and the magick *tugged* at him, and *directed* him and only through the bindings of the spell did he retain some semblance of identity and was not spread across an infinite plane.

And then everything was dark. And it was over.

It felt like being born. Pain lashed him with a million stings in every atom of flesh, and Graal would have screamed but the pain was too great. He squeezed from something soft and slick, pus-filled and flexible and yielding. He slapped to the floor, trembling as if suffering a violent seizure, and cold fluid poured out after him and covered him with thick ice ichor. He felt hands on him, or felt *something* on him, and they were hard and pointed and pierced his flesh accidentally. He was manhandled into blankets and he realised, with a moment of panic, that he was blind. Towels rubbed his body, rubbing life back into his flesh, rubbing gooey liquid from his eyes, and gradually a soft diffused light began to wander into his eyes and skull. Only then did Graal cough, and disgorged a huge stream of thick pus which pooled on the floor to lie, quivering, like dark blood.

"You did well," said Vishniriak, and the Harvester patted him gently in a rare moment of connection.

Graal focused on the Harvester, but could not speak. His vocal chords were raw, as if rubbed by a grater.

"I felt like God. I felt like Death," he finally managed.

Vishniriak nodded, in understanding. He had travelled The Sending. He understood exactly what Graal meant. To travel the Lines of the Land by magick was to be a part of the earth, of the mountains and oceans and forests and bedrock. It was to lose identity. Without powerful bindings, a mind would snap. But Graal was strong. Graal was very strong.

Graal stood, and clothing and armour were brought for him. He dressed slowly, feeling old, feeling more old than the Black Pike Mountains. Finally, he strapped well-oiled armour into place, and a short black sword by his side.

He nodded at Vishniriak. "Has Kradek-ka arrived?"

"Yes, general."

"And he has the girl?"

"He has, general."

Graal smiled then, his eyes gleaming. "Kell is coming to us. We must prepare," he said. "The time is ready for the Vampire Warlords to return." And he strode confidently, arrogantly, from the chamber deep within the bowels of Skaringa Dak.

FOURTEEN
Wax Nest

The world was shrouded in mist. Kell stood, poised on the high mountain ridgeline, the world around him a blanket interspersed with vast drops and glimpses of the rearing, Black Pike Peaks.

Ahead, the mist thickened momentarily, obscuring the two Soul Stealers. Only the canker came on, and more vachine longbow shafts whistled from the mist and Ilanna slammed left, then right, cutting arrows from flight... as the canker, close now, and amazingly nimble for its bulk, bounded along the narrow, undulating rock path and leapt at Kell with a savage snarl, an ejection of saliva, and Kell's axe slammed left but the canker ducked, equine head swaying back. Claws hammered at Kell but Ilanna deflected the blow on a fast return sweep, and he took a step back, the mist suddenly parting around him to reveal vast drops from nightmare. He ducked another swipe of curved claws and set his chin in a grim line as he clenched teeth hard, brows furrowed, and felt himself descending dropping plummeting into a blood red rage...

I will help, said Ilanna.

Yes, said Kell.

A flickering staccato of images rampaged through his mind. It was the Days of Blood – again. And he welcomed it. *He stood, muscles bulging, tensed as if pumped on drugs and violence. His brain ached, and random chaos bounced around the cage of his brain. He lifted Ilanna, and she sang, she sang a high beautiful song only this time THIS TIME the world could hear her lullaby and the people running down the street fleeing the insanity of the army they stopped, and turned, and listened to*

*the stunning ethereal voice of Ilanna as the perfect hypnotising notes re-
verberated through fire and smoke and sounds of slaughter, and the
fleeing refugees paused and Kell strode amongst them Ilanna cutting left
and right, and they did not flee, and they did not retaliate, they simply
stood staring at this blood soaked figure at Kell's rage and his fury and
his madness as Ilanna slammed left and right with economical accuracy,
and they had love in their eyes, love for Ilanna's Song, and they welcomed
death and in welcoming death their blood fed the butterfly blades and
when they were all dead, all cut up in pieces on the muddy cobbles, so
Kell fell to his knees amongst the men and women and children, and he
cried, his tears running through a mask of blood and he cast Ilanna away
and screamed "WHAT HAVE I DONE?" and he knew then, that he was
cursed, that he was evil, that ultimately he was trying to be good and just
and honourable; but deep down, he was simply a very bad man.*

Kell blinked.

The canker was on him, fangs an inch from his throat and his
eyes met the mad crimson gaze and he dropped Ilanna between
them, and thrust her up and *out*, blades punching a huge hole up
through the beast's great, cavernous chest, and Kell's legs braced
and his teeth ground, and he stood there, strong, a powerhouse,
with the impaled canker kicking on the end of his axe and with
neck muscles and arm and shoulder and chest muscles bulging, his
face purple with effort, and he lifted the kicking squealing canker
up, high up into the air and stood there, feeling a wonderful power
flooding through him, feeling strength and godliness teasing
through flesh like a divine orgasm. Ilanna began to sing and the
canker kicked, like a lizard on the end of a spear. Kell jerked the
axe, blades cutting deeper into the huge beast, fully twice his size,
great equine head thrashing with teeth gnawing invisible bones,
and Kell thrust forward again, the blades so deep now that thick
gore flowed out, over his head and torso, drenching him in entirety.
With a final thrust Ilanna severed the canker's spine. It went suddenly still on the end of the axe. With a mighty scream, Kell
wrenched Ilanna sideways, half severing the dying canker's body
into two discrete pieces, which flopped with slaps of thick dead
meat. Bloody clockwork components scattered, many tumbling
down the mountain's flanks, clattering, brass and crimson gears still
stepping, wheels spinning, cogs shifting. Kell lifted Ilanna in the air,
one-handed, as the mist parted and the Soul Stealers locked eyes
to him and he grinned, grinned through his mask of canker blood

and Ilanna began to sing. She sang a high beautiful song, which rang out across the mountains and valleys, echoed across snow-fields and frozen tarns. It was long and eerie and mournful, a song about murder, a song about death. And as she sang, so the Soul Stealers paused, and they stood for a long time listening as the dead canker slowly shifted, and slipped from the mountain ridge, vanished into the abyss. Eventually, Kell lowered Ilanna. The Soul Stealers turned, and disappeared into the swirling white vapour.

"Grandfather!" came Nienna's shout. They were far across the ridgeline now, Saark guiding the young woman. Kell turned, moved away from the canker's blood pools and stopped. Gazing down where Myriam had fallen, he tried to differentiate her corpse from the distant slopes and jagged rocks. He could not.

"Damn it," he snarled, then loped across the ridge at great speed, showing no fear of heights, showing no worry at the vast slopes veering off to either side. For Kell, vertigo was something that happened to other people.

Saark and Nienna moved on, through the eddying haze, and Kell eventually caught them up as they climbed towards the next mountain top. As they breached a rise, a savage steep scramble which did its best to cast all three back down the mountainside, so a wind snapped around them and the mist cleared, and the world of the Black Pike Mountains opened like God peeling the top off the world.

"Stunning," said Nienna, simply.

Kell grunted.

Saark helped the old warrior up the last scree of rocks, and they stood in silence staring at the black granite wilderness, and the sweeping fields of snow. It was quite light where they stood, although the wind bit into them like ice knives.

"You did well," said Saark.

"I reverted," said Kell.

"Meaning?"

"Something happened to me. Something happened to Ilanna. Something bad."

"I don't understand."

"I think only Ilanna understands. I think, sometimes, she plays her own game, Saark. She sang to the Soul Stealers – there was a connection there, what kind of connection I am not sure. But they retreated. They fled."

"You killed the canker. Maybe they were scared of you?"

"No," grunted Kell, rubbing his beard and leaning on the axe. Her blades gleamed black in the harsh winter light. "No, they were frightened of Ilanna. I think."

"Where do we go next?" asked Nienna, hunkering down in her clothing. Her face was drawn, ashen, her eyes red from crying. The death of Myriam had stunned her.

Kell pointed, to where a huge mountain reared high above the others. It was formidable, even at this distance, with twin horns of overhanging rock rearing near the summit and spreading out, so the beast in its entirety resembled the skull of a ram.

"Skaringa Dak," he said. "Otherwise known as Warlord's Peak."

"That's one ugly mountain," said Saark. "And it's big. Too big, Kell. Look at the distance we have to cover! We can't be dragging Nienna all that way."

"We must. But rest assured, we go *through* the mountain, not over the top."

"Kell, that's Silva Valley you're talking about. It's an entire *civilisation*, by all the balls of the gods! You cannot fight the world, old friend."

"One step at a time," said Kell.

Saark sighed, and Nienna moved to him, hugged him. "I can't believe Myriam is gone," she said. Saark nodded, but said nothing. It did not surprise him, and he had to admit, he had wanted her dead. However, now the deed was done, guilt stabbed him like a tiny knife in the belly. She had been a victim of the cancers eating her body, her bones. She had given in to madness to chase an impossible dream. And her only reward now was lying dead and broken, a smashed doll, at the foot of the terrible Black Pikes.

"Yes," he said, finally, and hugged Nienna tight. It was a simple connection, a simple sharing of warmth and humanity. And in this dark place of stone and ice, it felt necessary.

"Come on," said Kell. "We have a long way to go."

"You're mad, old man."

"Maybe," he said, face dark. "Let's get moving, before those bitches forget Ilanna's song and come back."

She swam through darkness, and at last there was no pain. It had happened so suddenly. The arrow in her throat, rolling from the high ledge, then… a long, rattling descent. She hit rocks, and was conscious for a while of great darkness hanging over her like a guillotine blade waiting to drop. Then, she supposed, she died. There was a long period of nothing. And then fire seemed to rage through her veins, potent and raw, the most powerful injection of energy she had ever, ever felt. She felt something cold against her chest, and with a jerk she shuddered in huge lungfuls of cold mountain air. Only then did she feel the pain at her neck, and everything came rushing back and she opened her mouth to scream but a hand clamped over her face, muffling her. She thrashed for a while, arms and legs kicking in chaos, but something immeasurably strong pinned her down, holding her still, and she felt the fire raging through her and it hurt, hurt so bad, hurt worse than anything she'd ever felt and seemed to rage for a million years. Then her eyes flickered open and she stared into a gaunt, pale, beautiful face. The face of the Soul Stealer. She tried to struggle in sudden panic, but Shanna held her tight and smiled a hollow smile and showed her fangs, which were stained with blood.

"Be still, child," she hissed. "It will not take long."

She looked to the left and Tashmaniok came into Myriam's plane of vision. She carried something and Myriam frowned. Then another punch of pain spun through her and she convulsed, unable to breathe, her heart filled with pure white agony as she slammed into cardiac arrest.

"Now," said Shanna.

Tash knelt, and in her hand was a tiny device, a cross between the innards of a watch and an insect made from gold wire. It scampered from Tash's hands, and moved across Myriam's skin as she stared down at it, pain slapping her in waves, her eyes following the tiny clockwork machine in terror. "This is the latest technology," came Tash's soothing voice, as the clockwork spider paused over Myriam's spasming, fractured heart, lifted a leg, and with a high-pitched screeching drilled a hole through her breastbone.

Myriam screamed, thrashing, and again Shanna clamped the woman's mouth, cutting the sound off with a sharp slap. The tiny clockwork machine cut downwards, opening a dark hole in Myriam's chest, and then climbed in. It reached back, and did something – as if closing a zip. Then it crawled into Myriam's heart and long tendrils of gold wire ejaculated from tiny needles, encircling Myriam's dying, fluttering organ and encapsulating it. Tiny sections of the clockwork machine broke away, and began to travel through Myriam's body. She spasmed, and convulsed, her limbs twitching, her eyes rolling back, froth foaming from her mouth, fingers and toes clenching and then suddenly *erupting* with brass claws, and her teeth broke out with *snaps* as fangs pushed from her own gums. They were made from gold. They gleamed.

Finally, Tash threw Shanna a knife. Shanna slashed her wrist, and allowed a gush of dark blood-oil to spill into Myriam's open mouth. She convulsed again, as if taking poison, her teeth stained crimson, and black, her tongue lolling around like a fat eel. Then, finally, she went still.

Shanna wrapped a cloth around her wrist, binding it tight, then climbed from Myriam's still, lifeless body. She moved to Tash, and placed her hand on the Soul Stealer's shoulder. They waited, motionless, watching Myriam with interest.

"Did it work?" said Shanna, finally.

"If they do not bind, she will soon fall apart," said Tashmaniok without emotion. "Like succulent cooked meat pared from the bone. Like a desecration of all that is human." Then she turned, and stared up the mountain flanks to Wolfspine. Her eyes narrowed, still remembering the pain of Ilanna's song piercing her skull. It had skewered her brain like a spear. Her soul. Even now, she was shivering.

We will find you soon enough, old man, she thought.

We will see how long the magick lasts in your axe!

All pain fled. It happened in an instant. Myriam sighed, and breathed out. She felt, ultimately, at peace. Devoid of the agonies which had wracked her for so long, the cancers which had eaten her and supplied constant pain. She had suffered an eternity, the pains fading to a background agony, a persistent throb which just became normal to everyday existence. Only in sleep did the fire sometimes abate; and there was always a vast disappointment in the morning when Myriam awoke to find she still suffered.

But... Not now.

She felt it, as an emotion, as injected knowledge. The clockwork had moved through her body, combining with blood-oil, combining with the virus of the vampire, and all three had worked in harmony. Cancers were obliterated in a moment. The arrow wound in her throat had bubbled, and slowly healed as she slept. Her pain had gone, all pain had gone, and she floated in a warm secure place not unlike a womb.

Her eyes opened. It was dark. They were in a small, warm cave. Shanna and Tash sat on rocks by the fire, watching her.

Slowly, Myriam sat up. She was wary. These were the enemy.

Then she looked down at her hands, and a thrill of fear and excitement flooded her. Her fingers ended in claws. She blinked. She reached up to her throat, remembering the savage arrow-wound which had, effectively, punched her from the summit of the ridge. The flesh was smooth, uninterrupted by wound or scar.

Then her hands moved to her teeth, and touched gently at the fangs there.

She looked at the Soul Stealers.

"You have made me vachine?" she said, softly.

Shanna nodded.

"You have removed the cancer from my body?"

Tash stood, and crossed to her. She held a shard of mirror, which Myriam took and stared into. She sank into that mirror, then, sank into the silvered glass as if being sucked down into a lake of beautiful mercury.

Myriam stared at her own face. Her flesh had filled out, and although she was pale, she was radiant with health. No longer did gaunt eye-sockets dominate her face with purple rings. Her eyes sparkled like fine-cut gems. When she smiled, her teeth were white and strong, not knuckle-dice wobbling in a corrupt jaw.

Myriam looked down at herself. Her clothing was battered and tattered and torn, as befitted somebody who had slid down the mountainside. But her hips were full, legs powerful, her fingers strong, the flesh filled out and defined by muscle.

"There is one more thing you must do," said Tashmaniok, kneeling beside Myriam.

"Anything," she wept, "anything at all."

"You must swear your soul to us," she said, voice gentle. "You must swear it by the blood-oil that flows in your veins, by the blood-oil that lubricates your clockwork."

"I will swear with all my heart!" cried Myriam, and put her face in the palms of her hands as she thanked the vachine for giving her health, strength, and ultimately, her life.

"Good," said Shanna, also leaning in close. "Now, my little virgin vachine, we have a job for you."

• • • •

They walked through the darkness, down a narrow rock trail.

"This is insane," said Saark, for the tenth time.

"Shut up," growled Kell, for the tenth time.

"We'll break our bloody ankles, man!"

"What, so you'd wait here for those vampire bitches to hunt you down, would you?" snapped Kell. "Stop being such a court jester, and get on with the job, lad."

Saark shrugged, and moved on. In truth, the dark held no problem for him. Not now. Since Shanna bit him, his eyesight, and especially night vision, had increased tenfold. Now, the night was like a green-tinted summer's day. No longer would he have trouble falling over things drunk in the night. Now, there was no night.

However, despite increased strength and vision and stamina and healing, Saark was having other problems. Like the stench of blood. Here, and now, walking the mountain trails in snow and ice and whipping, freezing wind, he could smell Kell's blood more than anything. But Nienna's was also there, a more subtle, more gentle sweet fragrance; like the scent of roses, when compared to nettles. But with great force of will Saark was learning to master this weakness, or what he saw as a flaw in his new-found gift – or maybe curse? – and was able with great strength of mind to suppress the urges to extrude his still-growing vampire fangs and leap on Kell, devouring his throat and heart-blood.

The only problem had come when Kell killed the canker, lifting the beast up on the end of his axe and shaking it over his head, emptying its blood and blood-oil and guts over himself in a carnage orgy of gore. The sheer stench hit Saark like a wall, rolled over him like an explosion of rampant forest fire, and it was all he could do to hide his crazy rolling eyes, his extending claws, and not jump on Nienna's back and tear out her spine. In that moment, he wanted Nienna more than anything on earth, with a feeling of emotion and raw need greater than anything he had ever had to endure. Forget sex; sex was as rancid milk to thick clotted cream. This desire for blood, this urge this lust this mockery was more powerful than the sun and the moon. Brighter than the stars.

Nienna had turned, seen him advancing on her, and smiled weakly, meeting his crazed eyes. It was the smile that did it; broke the spell and caged the savage beast growing inside Saark. Without that *connection* of love and trust, he would have leapt on her and chewed out her soul.

Now, Saark fought himself.

He fought the new urges which drove him, using internal logic to battle the growing needs of a blossoming half-infected vampire. All he needed was clockwork integration to make him whole, and he would be a changed person, he realised. All he needed was a Watchmaker, and he would no longer be Saark. Saark would be dead. A stranger would stand in his shell. He would be corrupt. He would be lost.

"Damn it," muttered Saark, clawing himself, a thrashing of internal turmoil.

"What's it now, dandy?" snapped Kell, turning and scowling. Saark could see him as clearly as in daylight. He could see the pulse of blood at Kell's throat. It made his mouth go dry with longing.

"These damn vachine," snapped Saark irritably. "Don't you just fucking hate them?"

"Every last one," said Kell, turning back to the trail. "They need exterminating like a nest of cockroaches." He moved on, picking his way with care and helping Nienna when she needed help. Behind, Saark's eyes gleamed with malevolence.

They rested two hours before dawn, eating dried salted beef and rubbing warmth back into limbs bitten by cold. Saark had wandered off for toileting, and Kell sat close to Nienna, looking down into her eyes with concern.

"How are you, girl?"

"Frightened," she said.

"We have to do this, you understand?" he said. She nodded. "We have nowhere else to run. The bastards have taken over Falanor; we must fight the invasion at its root."

"What will you do when we arrive?" she asked.

"I will find these Watchmakers, I will find those who control the Army of Iron, the people who rule Graal. First, I will ask. And when they snarl in superior arrogance, then, then I will fight, and I will take their top Watchmakers hostage, force them to withdraw their soldiers from our land."

"Do you really think you can do this?"

Kell nodded. "I'll give it my best damn shot," he said.

"A fine plan," said Saark, approaching from the path to the large ring of rocks where they were seated, "with, I can see, only three major flaws."

"You heard all that?" said Kell.

"Aye, I heard some."

"What did you hear?"

"About finding the Watchmakers, holding them hostage, that sort of thing."

"By God, lad, you've got some incredible hearing."

"No, no," said Saark slowly, "I was on my way back."

"You were all the way over there. Shitting behind that rock. I could smell you. You stink worse than any boy-lover's perfume." Kell shook his head, frowning. "And lad, you move quiet. Did you say you used to be a thief?"

Saark shrugged, and stroked his chin. "Is it time to move?" he said. "I have a feeling those Soul Stealer bitches are close on our trail."

"Yes. Not far now," said Kell.

"Not far from what?"

Kell stood, and stretched, and his mood visibly darkened. "The Worm Caves," he said. "So don't get too comfortable, lad, because we have a lot of sneaking to do. The Worm Caves are no place for mortals. They ooze death."

"You can't be serious," said Saark, eyebrows rising. "You mean the *Valentrio* Caves? Shit. No, Kell. I've heard the tales, about the white worms which inhabit that place. In fact, they were from the same bloody bard who sang about your bloody maudlin *Kell's Legend*. Which just goes to show what a barrel of donkey-shit those songs really are." He grinned, a sour grin. "Maybe there's no danger after all?"

"Funny," said Kell, and threw Saark his pack. "Believe me, there's danger all right. So empty yourself now; this is no place to be needing a shit break. Let's go."

Shivering even more, and far from pacified by their talk, Nienna followed Kell, and Saark brought up the rear. The aroma of their blood twitched his nostrils, more tantalising than ever, now. He scowled, eyes narrowed. Damn this curse, he thought bitterly. Damn it to the Dark Halls! Damn it to the Bone Underworld!

The archway was small, and carved in a blank wall of rock with no other noticeable features. It would have been easy to miss the opening, if you hadn't known it was there.

Saark stood back from the black arch and looked up at finely carved script. His brow furrowed. "I've never seen lettering like that, before," he said, then wrinkled his nose. "Gods, it stinks in there."

"The *leski* worms," said Kell, voice soft.

"Have you even seen one of these worms?"

"Only once. From a distance. They have teeth as long as your forearm – but that's all I saw, I was too busy running in the other direction. They have a poisonous bite, lad, so don't get too close."

"That's comforting. What does the writing say?"

Kell shrugged, and started removing unnecessary kit from his pack. "Empty your pack of junk. You're going to need to travel light. There are some narrow places in there, tight places. Places a man could get easily trapped."

"But I thought you said the worms were big? Fangs as long as a horse's dick, or something?"

"They are, but they compress their bodies to squeeze through narrow apertures. Like a rat, Saark." His eyes twinkled. "You should know all about that kind of vermin, coming from your Royal Court background. And anyway, to answer your question, the script reads, 'Seek Another Path'."

"That's it? That's the warning?"

"That isn't good enough for you? With a stench of death like Dake's arse pumping out?"

"You have such a way with words, my man." Now, with his pack somewhat lighter, Saark drew his rapier and ran a finger along the blade. He re-sheathed the weapon. "Let's get going. Before I change my mind."

"You can always head back. Woo those vampire killers with your charm."

"What, and have them bite me, turn me into one of them? That would be insane!"

"Yes," said Kell, eyes glinting, "we wouldn't want that, lad, would we? Then I'd have to cut your head off!" He gave a low rumble of laughter, and slapped Saark on the back.

As they moved to the entrance, and Kell stooped to enter, Ilanna before him, Nienna touched his arm. "Grandfather?"

"Yes, monkey?"

She smiled at that. "I'm scared," she said.

"Don't be. I'll protect you."

"I know you will. But… I'm still scared."

Kell turned, and righted himself. He lifted Ilanna, looked at her curious matt black butterfly blades – so unlike any other weapon he had seen. She was older than the mountains, so the legend went. And indestructible. He kissed the blades, then bent down, and kissed Nienna on one cheek. "Just stick close to me, little lady. Don't be frightened of the dark. Kell walks beside you."

Nienna nodded, eyes full of tears. Her adventure was not quite what she'd expected. Not when so much blood and death was involved. Not when good women like Katrina had to give their life for nothing; for the honour of thieves and murderers. She sighed. And followed Kell into the gloom.

The Valentrio Caves were dark for perhaps a hundred metres, and then the floor seemed to shine with a very pale, sickly light. The darkness closed in fast, with claustrophobia in one fist, and haunting echoes in the other. Within minutes Saark had closed the distance from his rear guard, and was almost treading on Nienna's heels.

"Kell," he hissed, after perhaps ten minutes where they followed a level, winding passage.

"What?" said the old warrior.

"The light. On the floor. By Dake's Balls, what is it?"

Kell grinned, face a skull in the pale, ethereal glow. "Slime. From the worms. They must secrete it. Or something."

Saark's face fell. He looked ill. "Shit," he said. "I wish I'd never asked."

"Don't worry," soothed Kell, seeing Nienna's face from the corner of his eye. "This tunnel system is vast; it stretches for hundreds of miles under the mountains, vertically as well as horizontally. You can travel here for weeks and never see a worm. The *leski* are primitive, they have no understanding. They just eat and breed."

"Sounds a bit like us sophisticated humans," muttered Saark.

"Come on. Let's get moving. We have a long way to go."

They walked, boots making odd sounds on the sticky, luminescent ground. Saark realised, unconsciously, that he had his rapier drawn. He cursed himself, and sheathed the weapon, frowning. At least his rising fear and claustrophobia were good for one thing; they were taking his mind off the sweet, cloying smell of Nienna's blood, distracting him from the ever-present rhythmic thumping of her heart. He shook his head. What are you becoming, Saark? he asked himself, and didn't like to consider the answer.

They moved for hours, and sometimes the glowing floor would end and they would ease through deepest gloom, guided by mineral veins in the rock and marble walls. Sometimes, the corridors would narrow as Kell predicted, so that both Saark and Kell had great difficulty squeezing through and only Nienna was able to pass with ease. Occasionally, they came to areas where huge boulders had dropped, crushing part of the tunnel and making it near impossible to pass. Several times they had to squeeze beneath a chunk of mountain that, if it shifted, would crush them like an ant beneath a boot. At one point the crushed section was extended, and Saark found himself on his back, scrambling along with limbs scratched and dust falling in his eyes and his panting coming in short, sharp bursts. Panic was an old friend clutching his heart, and he was coughing and choking and pushing up at the immeasurably huge rock above and wondering if he was going to die until Kell's rough hands grasped his scruff, and hauled him the rest of the way under the obstacle.

Saark sat there, choking, covered in grey dust and looking pathetic. He wiped his sweating, dirt-streaked face, and glanced up at Kell. "Thanks, old boy."

Kell gave a single nod, and stood, stretching his back. "It's going to get more enclosed ahead."

"Just what I need," said Saark.

"I'm just warning you."

"Well, don't! I'd rather have a sour, nasty, bad surprise."

Again, they picked up the trail of glowing passageways, this time rising steeply until the tunnel emerged onto a small platform overlooking a cavern. As they approached, they could see the slime-glow increase in intensity, and this warned the group; they moved slow, hunkering down as they broached the rise. The small platform was just wide enough for the three of them; and what they saw left them crouched in stunned silence.

Below, in what appeared to be a naturally carved cavern, a massive affair strewn with stalactites and stalagmites, there were pods; corrugated, white, each pod about the size of a horse and divided into six or seven bubbled segments. They lay, motionless, not glowing but pale white, almost luminescent. And there were hundreds of them. Thousands. Littering the cavern, many of them packed in tight, crammed together.

"What," said Saark, with a completely straight face, his voice low and carefully neutral, "are those?"

"I don't know," said Kell.

"But you said you've been here before!"

"Yes, but I've never *seen* those before!"

"Are they, you know, something to do with the worms? Maybe they hatch, or something? Like eggs?"

"Possibly," said Kell, giving a small shiver. If they hatched, the group would be immediately overrun.

"Look," said Nienna, pointing. Kell lowered her finger.

"I can see it, girl."

They were *pulsating*. As if they were breathing.

"What now?" whispered Saark.

"I reckon we could go down there and cut one open," said Kell. "Then we'd know exactly what was inside. Exactly what we're dealing with."

"*What?*" snapped Saark. "Are you out of your mind, you crazy old fool? You might set them all off, then we'd be fucked for sure. And here's another thought – if they are eggs, then what in the name of the Grey Blood Wolf laid them?"

Kell nodded. "I suggest we circumvent."

"I would second that," agreed Saark.

They moved to the right, still watching the thousands of pulsating, segmented cocoons, or eggs, or whatever the organic objects were. They looked dangerous, and that was enough for the party.

Taking a right-hand tunnel, Kell led the way once more, wary now, Ilanna in his great fists. He was more alert, eyes straining to see ahead, ears listening for sounds of any approaching enemy. He wouldn't let Saark or Nienna speak now, and they travelled in morbid silence, ears pricked, nerves suspended on a razor wire.

The tunnel wound on, ever upwards, crossing many more in a complex maze. Kell chose openings with a sure knowledge, and Saark made a mental note not to get lost down here. The Valentrio Caves were a maze like nothing he had ever witnessed.

Eventually, the low-ceilinged corridor ended in a small chamber. It glowed. There were eight of the slowly pulsating, slowly *breathing* pods blocking their path.

Kell halted, and held up his fist. Saark and Nienna froze, peering past him. The chamber, floor lined with sand, was small. The pods filled it entirely, leaving nothing but narrow passages between each throbbing slick body of luminescent white. Nienna shivered.

"I don't want to sound like a pussy," whispered Saark, "but is there another way around these... these *blobs*?"

"It'll be all right," said Kell. "I'll lead. Nienna, stay close behind. Saark, bring up the rear."

"Why do I always have to go at the back?" he whined. "What if one of the quivering little bastards wakes up and jumps on me?"

"Well," smiled Kell, "it won't be the first time you've taken it from behind."

"You are a jester, Kell. You truly should be capering like an idiot in the King's Court."

"Can't do that," growled Kell. "The king is dead."

They moved into the narrow spaces between the segmented bodies. Each cocoon was tall, as tall as a man, and most at least as long as a horse, high in the centre and then tapering down in staggered segments towards the tips, which seemed to glow, changing suddenly from pale white fish-flesh to jet black, and then back.

Saark shivered. Kell moved with his jaw tight. Nienna desperately wanted to hold somebody's hand, for she could feel the fear in the air, smell the metallic scent of these pulsing cocoons. Kell brushed against one, and for a moment the pulsating ceased. In response, Kell, Saark and Nienna froze, staring in horror at the huge bulbous thing.

"You woke it!" mouthed Saark, urgently, face screwed into horror.

Kell gripped Ilanna tighter, but after a few moments the regular rhythm of the creature resumed. The group seemed to breathe again. They crept past, six, seven, eight of the cocoons, and then Kell stepped out into the opposite tunnel and breathed deeply, shoulders relaxing. Nienna stepped out behind him, and Saark turned to stare back at the corrugated pods. "Well thank the bloody gods for that!" he grinned, as his rapier swung with him, tip at knee level, and the point of his decorative scabbard cut a neat horizontal line across the nearest pod's fleshy surface. There came a hiss, a bulge, then a thick tumbling spill of white splashing out like snakes in milk. A scream rent the air, so high-pitched the group slammed hands over ears and grimaced, then ran down the tunnel as the scream followed, perfectly in rhythm with the pulsing of the *thing's* body.

"You horse dick!" raged Kell. "What did you do that for?"

"I didn't do it on purpose, did I? Can I help it if their skin is as flimsy as a farm maiden's silk panties? I barely touched the damn thing!"

"Come on," said Nienna, pale from the screaming, and she led them on a fast pace up a steep corridor. Suddenly Kell lurched forward, grabbing Nienna and bundling all three into a side-tunnel. They stood, in the gloom, and watched the albino soldiers pounding past. Kell counted them. There were fifty of the very same black-clad albino warriors who'd invaded Falanor.

"So, this is where they hide," whispered Kell, face grim.

"I am assuming," said Saark, in a quiet, affable voice, "that this place wasn't crawling with *either* egg-pods, nor albino soldiers, the last time you came through?"

"It was twenty years ago," snapped Kell. "I've slept since then."

"And got drunk many times," responded Saark, voice cool, eyes shaded in the gloom. "You've brought us into a hornet's nest, old friend. How many albino soldiers are here?"

"Let's find out," said Kell.

They moved back up the tunnel, which rose yet again on a steep incline that burned calves and sent shivers through straining thighs. They travelled for an hour, and three times more they came across squads of albino warriors wearing black armour and carrying narrow black longswords. And several times they passed along the lips of vast caverns, each full of pulsating segments, glowing, quivering cocoons. The third time they did so, Saark called for a stop. Down below, they saw several albino soldiers moving through the chamber, and one stopped, resting a hand on a quivering flesh segment.

"They're changing colour," said Saark.

"Eh, lad?" said Kell.

"The pods. They're no longer translucent. Now they are a deep white. Like snow. Look."

Kell peered. He shrugged. "So what?"

"And their pulsing is slower," said Nienna.

"So what?"

"You're an irascible old goat," snapped Saark. "The point is, each chamber seems to be some kind of birthing pit. That's my opinion. And these things are looked after by the albinos."

"Why would they do that?"

"Maybe they like to hatch worms," said Saark. "Maybe they are building a worm army!"

"That isn't even funny," said Nienna, eyes wide.

"Who said I was joking?"

"Shut up," said Kell. "Look. Something is happening."

They watched. A hundred soldiers marched into the cavern, and arranged themselves around a circle of five pods. A tall albino warrior stepped forward, and drawing a short silver dagger, he cautiously inserted it into the nearest pod and, with intricate care, cut a long curve downwards. Flesh bulged, and was followed by a flood of white which sluiced across the stone floor. There followed a tumble of cords, like thin white tree roots, and then there was a shape nestled amongst the mess, amidst the thick strands and gooey white fluid. It slopped, spread-eagled to the floor, and several of the soldiers stepped forward and...

"Holy Mother," said Saark, mouth open.

"So this is where the bastards emerge," growled Kell.

"What are they?" whispered Nienna, stunned by what she saw.

The soldiers wrapped the newly born, nearly-adult albino soldier, naked, flesh white and pure, scalp bald and glistening with milk, limbs shaking and unable to stand without support, in a blanket. The man was like a newborn foal, weak and quivering. The surrounding soldiers led the blanket-trussed newborn down a corridor in almost reverent silence.

"They're hatching," said Saark, without humour. "The human maggots are hatching."

"They're not fucking human," snarled Kell.

"Well," continued Saark, in the same cool, level voice, detached and not quite believing as he tried to comprehend the magnitude of what he was witnessing, "what actually *are* they, then?"

"They're the enemy," said Kell, "here for us to kill."

"An interesting viewpoint," came the smooth, neutral voice of the albino warrior. He stood, and behind him were thirty soldiers. All had bows bent, arrows aimed at the three peering intruders. "They are, in fact, our alshina larvae. As you so quite rightly put it, young man, we are not human. This is where we are hatched – eggs laid, implanted, and hatched by our queen." He drew a short black sword, and used it to point. "Ironic, that you refer to us as the *albino*. That would be *your* arrogance speaking. To think we are simply humans without pigmentation. Man, we are a different *species*."

He turned, then, and surveyed the bent bows of his warriors. Several smiled.

"What do you want?" growled Kell, and slowly stood. He flexed his shoulders, and his face was thunder. Saark stood next, and he placed a warning hand on Kell's shoulder.

"Look," said Saark. "They have Widowmakers."

The dandy was right; some of the warriors carried the same weapon that Myriam and her little band had used back in Falanor; the same weapon which had taken Katrina's life.

"If you know what these Widowmakers *are*," said the leader, smoothly, with no hint of fear or panic, "then you obviously know what they can *do*. I suggest you drop your weapons. My soldiers have been primed to kill the girl first."

"Why, you bastards," frowned Kell, stepping forward. The Widowmakers lifted in response to his antagonism. They were surrounded, heavily outnumbered, and even the mighty Kell could not fight with thirty arrows in his chest.

"We have to do it," urged Saark, and was the first one to lay down his rapier. Nienna, wide-eyed, fearful, threw down her own sword and reluctantly Kell knelt and placed Ilanna reverently on the rocky ground.

"Take care of her, lads. I'll be wanting her back real soon. And if there's a single mark on her, I'll be cracking some skulls."

"Fine words," smiled the leader, but then the smile fell like plague rain. "Restrain them."

They had hands tied tightly before them, Kell grumbling and growling all the time, facing out into the great hatching chamber where yet more newborns were eased from their larvae pods and into the cool air of the chamber; into the real world. Like insects, thought Kell with a shudder. They are hatched like insects.

He was spun round by surprisingly strong hands, and a huge white-skinned soldier smiled at him, crimson eyes fixed on his, hand on the hilt of his short black sword. "You'll be cracking skulls will you, Fat Man?" he hissed.

Kell's head snapped forward, delivering a terrific head-butt that dropped the albino warrior in a second, and had him crawling around in circles, blinded.

"There's the first one," growled Kell. "Any more fools want to try me out for size?"

The leader pressed a razor dagger to Nienna's throat. He still retained his air of calm, of clarity, as he stared down at his disabled soldier who – even as he watched, died on the floor. His skull was indeed cracked. Broken, like a raw egg.

"Anything else, Kell, anything at all, and I'll cut her up. A piece at a time."

"You've made your point, lad," said Kell, showing no surprise that the leader knew his name. "Just as I have made mine. So tell me – what happens next in this vile and acid-stinking albino piss-hole? You got any more surprises for us?"

"Just one," said the leader, words soft as he caressed Nienna's trembling throat with his blade. "Somebody wants to meet you."

"And who would that be? My mother?"

"No," said the leader. His crimson eyes twinkled. "His name is Graal. He's been expecting you."

FIFTEEN
Soul Gems

Skaringa Dak was a huge, evil mountain, even by the usual standards of the Black Pikes which in themselves had a reputation for being huge, evil, merciless and downright impenetrable. Skaringa Dak towered over surrounding peaks, and to one side, between hooked crags and violent obstacles, if one was to stand *just right* between jagged teeth, a person might, when the mists and snowstorms cleared, see the distant, widening spread of Silva Valley, home of the vachine, home of the engineered vampire race.

Near the summit, surrounded by glossy knives of rock sat ragged slopes containing millions of glossy, polished marble daggers, impossible to traverse on foot and a natural – or maybe not so natural – barrier to the flat circle of Helltop, five hundred metres beneath the mountain's true summit.

Helltop.

A place of mystery and magick for ten thousand years, surrounded by walls and fissures, crevices and crags, hooks and knives, and accessed only by a narrow, sloping tunnel which led deep inside the bowels of Skaringa Dak, and welcomed the foolish to explore.

Helltop.

A five hundred-metre circle of flat rock, polished marble, inlaid with natural lodes of silver and gold so that it twinkled under snowmelt. The surrounding peaks lay deep in snow, but not so the circle of Helltop. Helltop was immune to snow. Some said it was a volcanic fissure from deep within the mountain that channelled heat

550

from unfathomable places; others said it was acts of evil magick which had taken place there over the centuries, ranging back past even the Vampire Warlords of Blood Legend – and which lingered, invisible, like esoteric radiation.

Set in the centre of Helltop and criss-crossed with thick bands of gold and silver in the glossy floor, sat the three Granite Thrones. They were ancient, and hewn by primitive hand-tools centuries before. They were jagged, and rough, and basic. And they were *old* beyond the comprehension of modern civilisation. Before the three Thrones there was a small, circular pool of liquid, like a glass platter of black water. This natural chute fed down, *down* through a thousand vertical tunnels, natural fissures and chutes and stone tubes cutting through the rock to the very roots of the mountain. These were the arteries of the mountain. These were its *life*.

Graal stood beside the Granite Thrones dressed in a white robe. Wild mountain winds whipped his fine white hair, and his unusual blue eyes surveyed this, the scene he had awaited for nearly a thousand years.

A mournful howling echoed through the mountains. Graal smiled. He could feel the *pull* of so much blood-oil and its associated magick of the soul. Now, all they needed were the Soul Gems and the Sacrifice to finalise and bind the spell. To bring back the Vampire Warlords. To *control* the Vampire Warlords.

Graal looked left. Kradek-ka, Watchmaker of the Vachine, gave him a single nod. He checked on Anukis, his daughter, who stood, swaying, blood-oil on her lips, her eyes rolled back, the honeyed drugs in her veins flowing thick now with a necessity of oblivion.

Graal opened his arms, and he opened his mind, and he *felt* the mountain beneath him *within* him and he felt its great veins of silver and gold, and they were one for a moment, he, Graal, and Skaringa Dak, and he knew this was the mountain of the Vampire Warlords: Kuradek the Unholy, Meshwar the Violent, and Bhu Vanesh, the Eater in the Dark. *Can you hear me, children?* he whispered, flowing through the mountain's vast caverns and tunnels, flitting like a ghost through the hatching chambers of his Army of Iron.

We hear you, sang the Soul Stealers.

Have you brought them to me? he whispered.

We have brought them to you, sang the Soul Stealers.

Then we have the final Soul Gem, he said. His eyes flickered open and he stared at Kradek-ka. "We have all three," he intoned, voice like a lead slab, the flesh of his face quivering as if in prelude to a fit.

"Then we must prepare," said Kradek-ka, and placed his hand gently over Anukis's chest where her heart, a heart entwined with the clockwork augmentations of the vachine, beat with the ticking of a finely engineered timepiece.

Under her skin, something glowed in response to his touch, in response to Skaringa Dak, in response to Graal and Helltop and the Granite Thrones. Beneath Anukis's skin, beating with the pulse of the clockwork machinery which kept it alive, glowed the implanted Soul Gem.

Snow whipped Vashell as he crouched, hidden in a narrow V of rock, and stared with open mouth down at the plateau of Helltop. "I cannot believe it," he hissed, and glanced back down to Alloria. She was weak with cold and fatigue, even wrapped in furs from the wolves Vashell had skinned to keep her warm. "Fiddion was right. They seek to bring back the Vampire Warlords!"

Alloria tried to creep under an overhang of rock, out of the wind and the blizzard. She was dying, Vashell knew, and guilt tore at him. But this was different. This was the vachine. This was Silva Valley. Now, in this place, he realised what evil magick they were about to perform... and more importantly, what sacrifice they needed to make it work.

Blood-oil was not enough.

Graal needed the souls of the clockwork vampires.

Thousands of clockwork vampires.

But *how* could he do it? None of the Old Texts spoke of the Ritual of Bringing, or the Summoning. And pages had been savagely cut from the Oak Testament, so it was said, by the First High Episcopate Engineer in order to stop evil filling the world. The pages had been burned. It was the only way.

So how did Graal *know*?

You bastard, thought Vashell. You would sacrifice our people.

You would sacrifice the entire vachine civilisation! And for what?

To rule beneath the Vampire Warlords? But understanding eased into Vashell's mind, then; a deep and intuitive understanding. No. Graal was too arrogant. Too power hungry. He would seek to rule the Vampire Warlords. To control them. Not to *become* one of them, but to be their Master.

"You are insane," Vashell whispered. And he knew what he had to do. He had to stop them. When the Soul Gems were presented to the Granite Thrones, he had to stop them – to kill the carriers. Or at the very least, to kill the Soul Stealers. For only with the Soul Stealers could the Soul Gems be extracted and used for the Summoning. So it was written in the Oak Testament.

Vashell watched, as *something* tied tight with golden wire was dragged onto the platform. It had black, corrugated skin and was making feeble mewling noises. It was big, and powerful, but – impossibly – subdued.

Vashell felt sorrow. And he felt pride. He felt guilt. And he felt an incredible compression of the mind. He had always loved the vachine. He had been a prince of the Vachine Empire, and yes, since his impurity at the hands of Anukis he was outcast and could never return to the place he loved; the place which folded neatly around his heart and soul like a fist. But he could do something. He must do something. He was the only one who *could*.

He stared, through tears, at the mewling creature. And blinked as he recognised, there beside the gleaming chitinous monster, Anukis. Sweet Anukis! And the puzzle pieces fell into place. Anukis carried a Soul Gem. That was why Kradek-ka made her so special, so *advanced*, and used his technically brilliant vachine engineering to keep her alive; to create a *prime*. That was why he allowed vachine society to turn against her, so that when this time came, when the need to sacrifice so many of Silva Valley came, then Anukis –

Vashell went cold.

Anukis would be ready, he thought.

Ready to kill. Ready to murder.

Ready to sacrifice...

Vashell realised with a sick feeling in the pit of his stomach that the whole thing had been a game, a clever strategy, instigated and plotted by General Graal and Kradek-ka in order to bring back the Vampire Warlords. They had planned, and plotted, and hijacked the Blood Refineries, necessitating orders from the vachine to invade Falanor in search of new fresh blood-oil... when in reality what they did was gather raw materials to allow the rebirth of the Vampire Warlords.

Thousands of humans. Thousands of vachine.

All dead, and about to die, just so the Three could walk again! He would stop them. He would halt their plans.

Vashell reached for his bow, and with freezing fingers notched a deadly arrow to the string. He turned and peered back over the ridge. Who to kill? Who was the most effective target? If he only had *one shot*? Kradek-ka? Anukis? Sweet Anukis... tears stung his eyes, and he brushed them away. Or Graal. If Graal was dead, surely they could not continue?

Vashell heard the tiniest of sounds, like metal claws on rock, and he turned, and went terribly cold.

Two women stood, almost nonchalant in their easy posture. Their fangs gleamed, and their claws gleamed, and one had long white hair tied back into tails, and one had short hair spiked by the blizzard. They carried swords. They were smiling.

"What on earth," said one, tilting her head so as to accentuate the beautiful curve of her face, "are you doing up there?"

Vashell moved fast, bow smashing round, shaft releasing like a striking cobra.

There was a snarl, a slam, and a tearing of flesh.

Alloria whimpered, and backed away through the snow.

The Soul Stealers ignored her as they briefly fed.

Now, weaponless and bound, a squad of ten from the Army of Iron marched Kell, Saark and Nienna without relent through the underground tunnels of Skaringa Dak. Their commander, tall and arrogant, was an albino named Spilada, and he led the way – in fact, seemed the only one in the group to *know* the way. They marched all day, sweat pouring down faces, muscles burning and screaming during internal tunnel ascents, many of which were scrambles, extremely dangerous scrambles when hands were tied tightly before them. At one point Nienna slipped, stumbled, and began to slide down a long slope of scree towards a gaping black chasm. One of the soldiers grabbed her by the scruff, hauling her whimpering body away from a sheer, vast, underworld crevasse.

Kell turned to Spilada. He smiled, a warm and amiable smile, only the fury raging in his eyes telling a different primal story. "Anything happens to the girl, and I'll eat your fucking eyes out," growled the old man.

"And receive ten swords in your back," came Spilada's terse response.

"Yes," grinned Kell. "But *you'll* have no face, and eyeballs dancing on your open cheekbones."

"Shut up. And walk."

"Whatever you say," growled Kell, and with a nod and courage-building smile to Nienna, started up the scree slope.

At the top they stopped for a short rest on a ledge of black rock. Below, the scree slope led off to a massive drop which fell away into echoing blackness. The air was strange, at some times freezing cold making the group shiver, at others bearing wafts of raging hot air which brought them out in streams of sweat. Kell and Saark were kept seated apart, but Nienna was allowed to sit near Saark.

"How you doing, girl?" grinned Saark after he had regained his breath.

"That was incredibly hard," she said.

"Yes, we're not mountain climbers, right?"

"No." There came an awkward pause. Around them, the white-skinned soldiers sorted out their kit, all the while keeping a close eye on the prisoners. Kell sat to the left, legs dangling off a small drop, face calm but eyes murderous. They could sense his violence from a league away. "What's going to happen, Saark? I'm frightened."

"I don't know, Little One," he soothed. "What I do know is that it was a mistake coming here. Kell thinks he can take on the world; yet now, here, he's just a broken, captured old man."

"He's still Kell," said Nienna, voice soft, pride and belief shining in her eyes. "He is The Legend. He slew Dake the Axeman. He was the Hero of Jangir Field. He turned the tide at the Battle of Black Beach, carrying Dake's head back to the King. He was at the Battle of Valantrium Moor. He's a hero, Saark. He cannot be beaten!"

"He is still a man," said Saark, gently, thinking of the other side of Kell, the dark side of Kell, the murder in his eyes, the murder in his axe, and ultimately, his part in the Days of Blood. Unreported massacres. Cannibalism. Torture. The rape of the dead...

"He's more than just a man," said Nienna, hope in her breast. "He is Kell."

Saark nodded, not willing to remove her spark, her hope, but staring around at the ten warriors with a sense of painful reality. He smiled, still thinking of these soldiers as albino. But they were not. They were... Saark shivered. Shrugged. He had no idea what they were. Part insect? They were shells, he realised. Something else, something *old*, living inside a human shell.

Kell stood, and stretched, back still to the soldiers. He turned, and two looked up from honing swords, watching him closely. He smiled in a friendly fashion, and moved over to them. "I need a piss," he said.

"Over there," gestured a soldier, with a nod.

"And how do I get my cock out? You've tied me tighter than a fishmonger's purse strings."

"You'll not be untied, old man."

"Better come and hold it for me, then."

"No. I have a better idea." The soldier smiled, a wax, fake smile. "Just piss in your pants. You old warriors all stink of piss anyways; it's said you make incontinence pads out of leaves in the forest, but I don't believe it myself. I think you just line your britches with old shit. It all adds to the rancid stench of the legend."

Kell shrugged, easily. "No problem. If that's what you want." A pool of piss leaked out from one boot, forming a puddle of glistening yellow and Kell stepped closer to the men, trailing a stream of piss and both soldiers, with backs to the scree slope now, dropped their gazes in disgust.

"Not here, you dirty old fool!" snapped one soldier, and glanced up –

Into Kell's boot. It was a massive blow, catching the soldier under the chin and lifting him high into the air, and backwards. He tumbled down the scree slope in a clatter of rocks. The second man rose fast, started drawing his sword, but Kell stamped on his hand and he let go of the blade; twisting, Kell stamped down a second time, boot catching the pommel and striking it downwards. The sword blade punched through scabbard, a diagonal strike down through the buckling man's left calf muscle, right through flesh and into his right foot, pinning his legs together. He toppled, screaming, clawing at the bloodied blade.

At the edge of the scree slope there came a short scream as the sliding soldier was ejected into the abyss. He took a clatter of stones with him. Then silence followed his long descent into oblivion.

The rest of the soldiers leapt into action, drawing swords and Kell turned on them, eyes glowing, teeth bared. "Come on, you heaps of walking horseshit! Let's see what you're made of! Let's see if the maggots fight as well as they breed!"

"No," came a soft voice. Spilada held Nienna, one hand clamped around her throat choking her, the other with a short skinning knife, blade gleaming. Even as Kell watched, face thunder, Spilada let go of her throat, grabbed her hand, lifted it before the group and with a swift, tight cut, snipped off the little finger of her right hand. Nienna screamed, there was a spurt of blood and she went down on her knees weeping, cradling the mutilated limb, rocking. Her finger lay on the ground, like a tiny white worm.

Spilada stepped forward, and as Kell surged at him he lifted a finger and placed the skinning dagger against Nienna's throat. He smiled a cold smile. Kell stopped. He lowered his face. The flat of a sword smashed the back of his skull, and he went down on one knee. Boots waded in, and they kicked him, eight soldiers kicked him, but he did not go down. He simply took the beating, blood on his teeth, eyes never leaving Spilada even under the heaviest of blows.

Saark leapt to Nienna, cradling her, tearing off a section of his shirt and binding her cut finger as best he could. He glared up at Spilada. "What are you doing? She's just a child!" he snarled.

Spilada shrugged. "Next time, I'll cut off her hands. You men, you listen, you *will* cooperate. This is no game we play." He turned back to Kell, who had stood now the beating ended. The soldiers backed away from him warily, as if they surrounded a wild caged bear. In the background, the man whose legs were pinned together by his own sword whimpered. Spilada made a strange tight gesture, a flicker of fingers, a signal, and another albino slit the wounded man's throat in a rush of white blood. He gurgled for a while, twitched, and was still.

"I will kill you," said Kell.

Spilada shrugged. "You will cooperate. Do I have your cooperation? Or shall I fetch my bag of razor-knives?"

"I will do as you ask," said Kell, gently. He lowered his head. He did not look at Nienna.

"Hush girl," said Saark, and the soldiers now bound Kell's feet – a loose binding, an effective hobbling which allowed him to walk, clumsily, like a prisoner. Saark hugged Nienna. She was crying in pain and shock.

"He cut off my finger!" she wept, staring at the bloodied section of shirt tied tight around her stump. "He cut it off! What kind of men are these? We should never have come here!"

"They're men who'll do much worse if we don't cooperate," said Saark, nostrils twitching at the stench of blood which filled up his nose and mouth and mind with a whirling red vortex of sudden lust. "Come on." Saark helped Nienna to her feet. She swayed, with pain and shock.

"Can she walk?" snapped Spilada. "If not, we'll toss her into the canyon."

"I can walk, you bastard," Nienna snarled, suddenly venomous. There was pure hate in her eyes. Spilada smiled at the vision.

"We have a little Hellcat here, I see."

"A Hellcat who'll cut your throat."

Spilada's smile dropped from his face like a stone down a well. "Enough talk. Walk or die."

Nienna nodded, and Saark helped her to stumble to her grandfather. Kell looked at her then, sorrow in his eyes, tears on his cheeks and in his beard.

"I'm sorry," he said.

"It's not your fault!" wept Nienna, and tried to hug him, clumsily due to her bound wrists.

"I caused you injury. I will never forgive myself."

"You were trying to get us free," she said.

Kell scowled. "I should never have brought you here, child. This is a place of death." His voice dropped, turning to a growl. "Or very soon, it will be." His eyes strayed to Ilanna. She had been placed in a sack with other weapons, and one soldier carried it over his shoulder. But Kell could see her outline. And he could hear her voice.

In time, she said. *It will come.*

I promise you that, Legend.

Kell nodded, and the group moved into another narrow tunnel which led, as ever, upwards.

After many more hours, during which they were allowed only short rests – mainly for the sake of Nienna, who had dropped into a subdued, bitter silence – they emerged from another steeply-climbing tunnel onto a platform in a vast subterranean cavern. Now, the soldiers carried lit torches, for the glow of worm slime had faded behind them. Fire sputtered and whipped in wild underground breezes, howling from unseen high places, crags and hollows, high tunnels and caves. The platform led out over a narrow stone bridge, wide enough to let three men walk abreast but with no guard rails. It arched slightly over a vast abyss, and disappeared into darkness which the torchlight could not penetrate.

"There's somebody on the bridge," said Saark.

"You've better eyesight than me, lad," said Kell.

"You first," grunted one soldier, and prodded Kell. Kell climbed a few short rough-hewn steps, and out onto the windy, underground bridge. It was damp, and looked slippery. Wary, Kell stepped forward, but the bridge was solid under his boots. He walked with care, followed by Saark and Nienna, and then the soldiers from the Army of Iron spreading out behind with Spilada at their core.

"By all the gods, it's Myriam!" said Saark, voice rising a little in surprise.

"Does she have her bow?" snapped Kell.

"Yes! She must be here to help." His voice dropped. "But... something is wrong," he said, head tilting to one side. "How could she have survived that fall?"

"Probably got stuck on a ledge," muttered Kell. "Don't think about that now... what we need to think about is *escape*."

"If we fail, we die," said Saark, looking into Kell's eyes.

"Then we die," said Kell softly. "I have a knife in my boot. When we get close to Myriam, follow my lead."

"Stop the talk!" snapped Spilada from the rear. He drew his sword. "Unless you want ten inches of steel in your spine!"

Kell and Saark were quiet, moving forward across the slick stone bridge. The wind snapped at them with hungry jaws. The abyss loomed. Myriam was smiling as they came close.

Kell gasped, for her hair was thick and lush, her gaunt face no longer gaunt, but finely chiselled and defined by beauty; her figure, her limbs, her hips, all were powerful and athletic, and her flesh was healthy, even in this cold subterranean hollow, not the waxen pallor of the near-dead. Now, she was beautiful again. Myriam was no longer a slave to cancer and the fear of death. Myriam was a woman in her prime.

"Kell..." warned Saark.

And Kell knew, knew the risks, knew Myriam might not be *with them* but the opportunity was too good and the location too neat not to use for his own ends, his own plan, and battle rage swamped him and he could not be a prisoner, could not be bound like an animal heading for predicted slaughter and yes they might all die, but better to die fighting! He stumbled, tripped on the bindings which locked his legs together in a prisoner's hobble, and went down on one knee. The tiny knife in his boot cut up, through leg bindings and wrist bindings with one swift harsh movement and as Kell arose in a blur of action Saark had turned to him, and Kell slashed his bonds, in the same movement his arm snapping back and launching the blade which embedded to the hilt in Spilada's eye. The soldier screamed, grappling at his face and Kell leapt down the bridge, fist slamming one man to break his cheekbone and send him rolling, to topple from the span. Another drew his sword but as it left the scabbard Kell was in close, head-butting the man and taking the weapon neatly. A back-handed swipe cut his head from his shoulders, the short blade rammed through another's man's chest to the hilt, and Kell tossed the soldier's blade to Saark who leapt to Kell's aid. They cut their way through three men in as many seconds, leaving the kneeling figure of Spilada behind them on the bridge. The clash of steel on steel echoed through the vast cavern. Nienna, shocked by the sudden violence, the acceleration of battle, blinked, then stared at the kneeling figure of Spilada. He held the hilt of the small knife, gently, as if readying himself to pull it from his eye-socket. With a growl, Nienna leapt forward and slammed the heel of her hand against the hilt of the blade, driving it deep, through Spilada's socket and into the brain within. Spilada slumped back, legs kicking, and Nienna dropped to her knees and was sick on the bridge.

Saark battled the remaining soldiers, and Kell dropped to one knee, opening the sack in the hands of the dead soldier. Slowly, reverently, he drew out Ilanna. She squirmed in his hands, her haft almost like *skin* to the touch, and Kell stood and his eyes were fire and his mouth was a grim line. "Saark, step back," he said.

Saark stopped, and backed away. Kell strode forward, rolling his shoulders.

The enemies stared at him, and their eyes moved to the axe. So, thought Kell, they know her. "Come on," he said, voice little more than a whisper of mountain breeze.

The remaining soldiers turned and fled, dropping their swords, sprinting along the bridge and disappearing into the black.

The wind howled, increasing in fury. Kell turned back to Saark, and Nienna, and the figure of Myriam who had not moved during the battle. However, she had not drawn an arrow to aid them. Kell scowled, and strode forward, with Saark joining him.

He stopped short of Myriam. He placed Ilanna against the stone of the bridge with a dull iron clank.

"You're looking well, lass," he said, calm, meeting her gaze which now shone with good health and bright vitality. Myriam laughed, the tinkling of a summer brook over marble pebbles.

"You can see what happened," she said, and as she spoke they could spy her tiny vachine fangs. Her nose twitched. Nienna came to stand behind Kell and Saark, peeping at Myriam, face confused.

Myriam made eye contact. "Nienna." She smiled, face radiant. "It feels wonderful, Nienna... truly, I am whole again, truly, I am at the peak of my physical prowess!"

"Step aside," sighed Kell. "I can see you're not here to help, and I have not the will to fight you."

"What?" mocked Myriam, suddenly. "The great Vachine Hunter, not willing to fight the terrible, evil vachine which stands before him? I thought you were Kell? I thought you were a Legend?"

"What do you want?" said Saark, voice soft.

"Ahh, the suckling vachine speaks!"

"*What?*" snapped Saark, face pale, etched with worry.

Myriam looked past Saark, to Kell, meeting his iron gaze. "He didn't tell you? The dandy didn't share his great secret? Back in the town, he was *bitten*, Kell. I can smell it! He's half-turned, but without the clockwork it's a slow and painful process." She dropped her gaze back to Saark. "Had any strange pains, boy? In your fingers? In your teeth? In your heart?"

"Shut up," growled Saark.

"Or what?" grinned Myriam. "You'll rip out my throat with your fangs? Go on Saark, show your friends your teeth. You can't hide it now, can you? Only the dark down here has been concealing your shame. But there's nothing to be ashamed of, Saark! Nothing, it's wonderful, it's a rebirth! Don't you feel your senses singing? Can't you hear the beat of the Mountain's Heart?"

"What do you want?" said Kell, voice level, refusing to look at Saark. Saark took a step away from Kell. Fear etched his features like moonlight.

"I am to escort you," said Myriam, returning her gaze to Kell. "I was to take you from the soldiers, but you had to have your little sport. Still. I said you would come quietly." She winked, and her tongue licked her vachine fangs. Somewhere, almost unheard, there came the *click* of changing gears. "For old time's sake."

"Stand aside, Myriam," said Kell, lowering his head and the rage of battle welled in him again and he was finding it harder to control, and he could hear the screams of the dying and the mutilated, the burned and the raped during the Days of Blood. And their blood ran in his mouth and down his throat, and he was eating their raw meat with the others, with the damned, with the possessed. That wasn't me, said Kell. But he knew different. And a hundred souls screamed from his past and pointed at him with cold dead fingers.

"No," said Myriam, still making no move for her weapon.

"So be it," said Kell, and hefted Ilanna – as a *whoosh* hissed through the air, and something unseen slammed past at incredible speed and Kell was knocked to the ground with stunning force. Kell was up, a blur of movement, blood on his mouth and eyes narrowed. He whirled on Nienna and Saark. "Get back!" he screamed. "Back along the bridge! They're here!"

"This is a place of blood-oil magick," said Myriam, gently, and drew her own short sword. It was silver, and it glowed, just a hint, but enough to show it was no ordinary weapon of base metal. "And the Soul Stealers are strong here, Kell, so strong... stronger than you could ever comprehend."

Nienna and Saark were running, and Kell turned back to Myriam. His intention was obvious. Never leave an enemy behind; especially not one with a bow. Ilanna came up, black butterfly blades dull by comparison to Myriam's silver sword, but infinitely more threatening. He launched at Myriam, but she danced back, silver sword parrying the blow. Again, something whistled past Kell, so fast he did not see, and something fine and hard wrapped around his face. With Ilanna in one hand, he clawed at the substance, pulling at it but it wriggled, and he saw it was a fine gauge golden wire. More whistles and moans of wind surrounded him, and suddenly there was a flurry of activity as the Soul Stealers passed, their flight one of magick, and the gold wire wrapped around Kell's face and head and neck, and the wire was around his arms, pinning them against him and strapping Ilanna to him, and he fought and struggled, but they drew tight and he screamed as they cut through clothing, cut into his flesh, then they were squirming, moving, writhing as if they had a surreal intelligence, a form of metal life, and Kell's legs were tightened and he hit the bridge, watched the wire as it seemed to *expand* and grow and wind around him, and around him, until he could not move, could barely breathe, locked to his axe like a dark lover.

Kell watched, witnessed Saark and Nienna hit the bridge further along. There came light slaps as the Soul Stealers landed on the stone, vachine fangs bared, eyes crimson and burning. They moved close to Kell, and Tashmaniok knelt, and stroked his face and beard interwoven by gold wire, and she smiled, then turned back to Myriam who had sheathed her sword.

"Bring him," she said, and in raw agony Kell passed into darkness.

SIXTEEN
Warlords

Vor, capital city of Falanor, sat in silence, desolate, a ghost town. Fine snow whipped along the dead streets. Darkness bled into corners like leaking ink. Occasionally, lightning cracked the sky like a bad egg.

On a hill overlooking the city squatted the Blood Refineries. They were dark, brooding, terrible in their monstrous design and purpose. The wind hummed around the huge vachine-built edifices, as if conveying a lament for the slaughtered, the drained, and the desecrated.

Above this gentle storm of snow, there came a crackle of high electricity. Not lightning, but a web of incandescent fingers which trailed across the sky in bursts, illuminating the clouds, melting the snow, filling the sky with a lightshow of wonder and bestial primitive ferocity. The only audience were encamped soldiers from the Army of Iron left behind to guard the Blood Refineries, and they emerged from tents and shielded eyes, gazing up in wonder, heads tilting, mouths forming lines of compression... and of understanding.

"So it begins," said one, his words a whisper in the storm.

More crackles leapt across the sky, this time blood red and turning the night into an electric storm of crimson. The Refineries started to hum, to vibrate like caged animals in shackles desperate to break free. The horizontal bursts of electricity filled the sky, no longer bursts but sheets of sparks and webs and fire, which finally *discharged* with tornadoes of bright burning light against the Blood

Refineries... and the world was filled with noise and concussion and raw energy as General Graal, hands raised in the Black Pike Mountains, on Helltop, on the Vampire Warlords' Seat of Power, so he drew this source of blood-oil magick and allowed it a channel *home*.

They had assembled on Helltop, and Graal walked along the line of Granite Thrones, his back to them, showing contempt for their weakness, but also hiding his joy at their capture. Kell was dumped to the slick smooth ground, and he grunted as he hit the floor and glared up at Graal with undisguised loathing. Nienna was weeping, the wires which bound her cutting into flesh and drawing blood, and Saark said nothing, his mouth a bloodless slit. Graal turned.

"Stand them up."

Unceremoniously, the Soul Stealers dragged Kell, Nienna and Saark to their feet, and they shivered as the cold mountain wind kissed them, and gazed around at the silent dark gathering. There were soldiers from the Army of Iron, a silent honour guard for their General and Watchmaker, Kradek-ka. Of the three Granite Thrones, two were occupied. The first, by a young woman with long, golden curls and the fangs of the vachine. Her face was slack, drugged, her eyes rolled back in a skull which showed the marks of a beating. Her throat still sported a huge puncture wound, half-healed by advanced vachinery, and softly through the silence, the tick-tick-tick of her clockwork could be heard. On the second throne was a strange, crumpled, black-skinned creature, his skin more like insect chitin than real flesh. He was tied, as were Kell and Saark, with tight golden wire and although they could read no expression in his face, his eyes held a deep and ancient rage... and yet also understanding, and submission, and cooperation. For Jageraw, this was the culmination of his purpose and his existence. This was his destiny, and they needed no bonds.

Kell hawked, and spat on the ground. Distantly, thunder rumbled through the mountains, the Black Pikes displaying unease and raw, limitless power. He scowled at Graal, and looked slowly around, at the soldiers, at Kradek-ka who displayed a facial expression of intense focus, and then to the Soul Stealers and Myriam, their vachine subordinate, who had helped capture them and truss them like goats ready for sacrifice.

"At last. Kell. You have arrived. We have been waiting for you."

Kell growled something incomprehensible, and spat again. "I made a grave mistake the last time we met, Graal. I should have carved you out a skull-bucket and pissed in it. However. The error is mine, but one I'll not make again."

Graal gave a low, level laugh, but his eyes held no humour. He looked up at the torn sky. Then back to Kell. "Can you not feel the *shift* in power, Kell? Old man, can you not feel the vibrations in the air, and smell the sickly-sweet blood-stench of a hundred thousand victims? They are coming back, tonight, and all we lacked was the final Soul Gem. My beautiful daughters, here," he moved around Tashmaniok, his hand sliding around her hips as he walked, and she tilted her head to smile at Kell, a dazzling show of beauty, "they did well to find it and deliver it to evil."

"What horseshit is this?" snarled Kell. "We have no Soul Gem!"

"But you do," said Graal, voice lover-soft, moving close to Kell, "and it is buried inside," he touched his own chest, "integrated with the heart, and it will be such a shame to cut it free because, sadly, a side effect of removing the Soul Gem is... death."

He turned and moved back to the Granite Thrones. He reached out, and touched the huge solid artefacts, face serene, for he knew everything was ready, everything aligned, in place, and nothing – not even Kell – could stop them. Nothing on earth could stop the Vampire Warlords.

Graal raised his arms to the sky, and the sky crackled with horizontal sheets of crimson electricity. The Soul Stealers moved to him, stood slightly back, pale faces bathed in a glow of blood-oil magick. The wind shrieked through Helltop like a million banshees. The snowstorm whipped and snapped, and the sky, still full of awesome primal power, an awe-inspiring *Summoning*, turned red and black as it filled with blood-oil streaks of energy. The snow itself turned red, into frozen blood snowflakes, and crimson flakes fell around Helltop like tears from the slain, which is what they surely were.

"They are coming," said Graal, and looked to Kradek-ka. "Are you ready?"

"I am ready," said Kradek-ka, face impassive.

Kell struggled against the wires which held him, then glanced across at Saark. "Lad? Can you hear me?"

Saark looked at Kell, weariness and defeat shining in his eyes like emerald tears. He gave a single nod.

"Can you help me get free?"

"I doubt it," whispered Saark. "And even if I did, you would slay me."

"What are you talking about?" hissed Kell, face a contortion of effort and fury. Around them, the bloody snow thickened, and more discharges rent the sky. The wind howled like death, moaned like a widow, screeched like a castrated priest.

"I was bitten. I am changing. I will become like her." He gestured to Myriam with a nod of his head. His voice was as bleak as a midwinter sacrifice. Then he looked at Kell, full in the eyes, face contorted in fear. "You are the Vampire Hunter," he said, voice almost sardonic. "I will never sleep soundly again." His eyes dropped to the floor, his dark curls whipped by the savage wind.

"Listen, lad," growled Kell, trying to control his temper, "the only one I'm going to kill around here is that annoying fucker Graal. So get your claws out, or your vampire fangs or whatever, and get me free of this fucking wire! You hear?"

"I cannot," said Saark. He was filled to the brim with melancholy. He had resigned himself to death. He sighed, like a tumbling fall of worlds.

"You will not!" snapped Kell, and watched uneasily from the corner of his eye as Kradek-ka drew a long, curved, matt black blade. "Help us get free, you dandy bastard! Look. I promise I'll not kill you. There. I've said it. You can't let them do this..."

Saark shook his head, tears running down his cheeks. "Truly, Kell, it is out of my control."

Kell stopped his struggling. The gold wire bit his flesh like razors. He was pinned to Ilanna, the greatest of slayers, and the irony was he could not get a hand free to wield the mighty weapon. *If only I could get one arm free,* he thought. *I would welcome the orgy of violence! I would bathe in blood again. Just like the Old Days.*

Suddenly, the energy and horizontal sheets of lightning and fire died, along with the wind and the snow. The sky was a terrible, flat black, as if they gazed up into a slab portal of nothing, a huge and endless void. Silence settled like ash. The world became an incredibly still place.

"What's your next trick?" shouted Kell. "You going to pull a rabbit out of a horse's arse?"

Graal stared at Kell, as if seeing him for the first time. Then he gazed down, down at a small pool of black which nestled at floor level before the Thrones. The Arteries of Skaringa Dak. The life-blood of the mountain itself. Kell blinked, seeing the pool for the first time; it was black, black as ink, black as moonlit blood, black as the Eternity Void.

Graal spoke, and when he spoke it was as if he communed with the mountain, with Skaringa Dak Herself. "Mighty Vrekken, hear my call, rise up for me, rise up and do my bidding!" and his hands crackled with blood-oil magick and Graal knelt, and plunged his hands down into the pool and his eyes were closed and blood ran from his eyes and ears, staining his pale white skin red, and his body vibrated and twitched as if in violent epileptic spasm, and then Graal kicked backwards, sprawling to the ground at the foot of the three Granite Thrones, but quickly stood, coughing up blood and spitting it to the rock. He grinned over at Kell, teeth stained, then towards the motionless figure of Kradek-ka.

"We need the Soul Gems," he whispered.

Kradek-ka approached Anukis, and her eyes seemed suddenly normal and sane as she gazed into the face of her father, the father who had nurtured her from womb to womanhood and whom she had trusted with all her heart. "No," she said, golden curls trembling, vachine fangs baring as the dagger plunged into her chest, tearing through white cotton and cutting deep through to her heart... Anukis screamed, and started to thrash madly despite her golden bonds, splashing blood upon the Thrones, and Kradek-ka grasped her throat, steadying her, and cut a deep circular hole in her chest, the tip of the knife slicing through skin and breast-bone to prise free the Soul Gem which had lain dormant inside her, a parasite, beating with her heart since birth.

Kradek-ka took the Soul Gem, and turned to Graal, and behind him his daughter writhed on the Granite Throne in the throes of death, blood bubbling up her throat and down her chin like a crimson mask. But Kradek-ka ignored his kindred, and lifted the Soul Gem for Graal to see. It was small, the size of a thumbnail, and a perfect cylinder of matt black which gleamed under a coating of Anukis's blood-oil.

"And the next," said Graal, blue eyes shining. His words, although softly spoken, carried across the surreal, impossibly quiet plateau of Helltop.

Kell's head snapped left, to Saark, then down, to Nienna, who was watching with a kind of morbid fascination as Kradek-ka approached the corrugated black creature that was Jageraw. *They think one of us carries a Soul Gem!* screamed his mind, suddenly. But which one? And something pierced his mind like a splinter, and he smiled a sour smile as he realised what made him special, what made him such a terrible, evil killer. There was something alien inside his flesh. Something which had corrupted him. Something in his heart, put there during the Days of Blood.

In silent shame Kell replayed his past, the horrific deeds he had committed, and surety settled in his mind like honey in a pot. The Soul Gem was inside him. It had polluted him. Turned him bad, like an alien cancer. And now they were going to cut it free. And then he was going to die... but at least die a pure man, at least die a *good* man. Now, he truly understood.

Kell struggled against the wires, and Nienna looked up at him and she smiled, and it was a terribly sad smile that filled him with an empty, rolling void. He could not stand for this! He would not stand for this. But the more he struggled, the more the golden wires bit his flesh until he was slick and slippery with his own blood and his own lacerated skin. "Bastards," he was growling, "bastards!" he screamed, his voice booming across Helltop and the Black Pike Mountains but it did not matter, it made no difference as Kradek-ka's blade sawed through Jageraw's chitinous armour and the creature made no sound, made no struggle, even as the blade bit flesh and cut through to his heart, prising out the Soul Gem on its tip to lie, nestling in Kradek-ka's palm like an excised insect.

"The Hexels hid you well," said Kradek-ka, and his eyes were locked to Jageraw's and he smiled, head tilting. "The Soulkeepers gave you the weapons to live, little boy. They turned you into something... something *else*. So you could protect this Soul Gem, the First Soul Gem, until the time of the Summoning. We owe you a great debt."

Jageraw nodded, and closed his eyes, and died in silence.

Something seemed to sweep across Helltop. It was an *emotion*, a *pulse* of energy. "They can feel us," said Graal, licking bloodied lips. "The Vampire Warlords acknowledge us."

"One more," said Kradek-ka, and turned towards Kell, and Saark, and Nienna.

"One more," nodded Graal, and walked slowly forward, the Soul Stealers close behind, their footsteps matching his, their white hair glowing in the odd light from an unseen moon.

"You were the hardest to hunt down," said Graal, his smile crooked, his words hoarse.

"Let me fight you!" raged Kell, struggling with all his might, blood slick across his entire body and soaking his clothing as the golden wires bit. "I'll not die like this, you fucking whoreson! Not on the end of a butcher's knife! Let me fight, I say!"

Graal tilted his head, and turned, and stared strangely at Kell. Then he laughed, a chuckle so base and evil it sent Kell into a paroxysm of fury. But his words stopped Kell dead.

"Not you," said Graal, and reached out, and stroked Kell's bearded cheek. "You do not have the Soul Gem, old man. Whatever gave you that idea?"

And it was like a hammer blow, for if Kell did not carry a parasitic evil within him, something which had polluted his humanity, made him carry out evil acts like no other... then the fact was, he was simply a bad man. But this mammoth shock was followed by a realisation.

"Gods, no!" he hissed, as Graal moved to Nienna and Kell's mouth dropped open and how could it have happened, how could the girl carry something like that inside? Without anybody knowing? Without showing any adverse signs? And now Graal was going to carve her up like a pig on a block, and she would die in this desolate lonely terrible place so that *They* might live... and Kell could not stop it.

Graal looked down at Nienna. "Be still, little one. This will soon be over," and he smiled and reached out and touched her skin and tears were coursing down her face, and Kell was frothing at the mouth in rage and frustration and he was the greatest warrior of Falanor, the greatest *Legend* of the age and he could do nothing to save his beautiful, innocent granddaughter...

Graal moved on, past Nienna, and took hold of Saark who jumped, as if waking suddenly from a dream. Graal dragged the tightly wired dandy across the platform and Kell hissed, mouth dry, eyes blinking fast.

"Kell, hey, what's going on?" yelled Saark, starting at last to try and struggle, shocked from his reverie and maudlin coma by the very real events about to unfold. "What are you doing?" he shouted into Graal's face. "Get off me you fucker!"

Graal paused, then sat Saark on the Granite Throne, stepping back as if to admire a fine sculpture. "Didn't you realise?" said

Graal, voice little more than a whisper but carrying clear across the silent, reverent platform. "I thought she would have told you?"

"Who? What the hell are you talking about?"

From the cave entrance came Alloria, only now her skin glowed and her eyes dazzled and her fingers ended in brass claws. Tiny fangs protruded over the Queen's lower lip and she walked slowly, languorously to Saark, to the King's Sword Champion, to her ex-lover, and she moved beside the Throne and looked down at him with a mixture of pity, and love, and understanding.

"I'm sorry it was you," she whispered.

"What have you done?" said Saark, voice dropping low, dangerously low. "Oh Alloria, you have betrayed everything, what have you done?" And it fell into place, puzzle pieces tumbling into position, and that was why Graal went for her after the initial invasion of Falanor – not just as a bartering tool against the King, but because... she was *his*.

"It took a while for her to love me," said Graal, crossing to Alloria and kissing her, and she responded, one hand coming up to rest against Graal's cheek. "But once infected with blood-oil, once a slave to the clockwork, once she became *vachine* she grew to know her place, she grew to understand the world with open eyes. She was a great tool in leading Vashell here, and in finding the traitor, Fiddion. But then, I digress." He motioned to Alloria, who moved to stand alongside Myriam – both women changed by the blood-oil bites, the infection of the Soul Stealers. Both watched, fascinated, as Kradek-ka approached Saark with his small black knife.

Saark glanced over, at the other thrones. Anukis was dead, slumped to one side. Jageraw was a motionless mass of bloodied insect-armour woven with dark human flesh. And now... now it was his turn!

"No!" he yelled, and started to struggle. "Kell, Kell do something! But Kell could do nothing, and their eyes met and Kradek-ka reached forward and with his iron vachine grip, pinned Saark back against the Granite Throne. Saark could not move. He was motionless, not just in Kradek-ka's hold, but in horror, and terror, and his eyes were on the tip of the curved blade which moved slowly, inexorably toward him; and he thought back, thought of Alloria and what they had together, the love they had together and it had all been fake, all been an act and she had been charged with *implanting* the Soul Gem into a host for safe-keeping, and he had been that host, their love a mask to hide her real intentions, and Alloria had been a spy for Graal and a traitor to her husband and the people of Falanor and hate ran deep through Saark's veins, then, as he understood; maybe she had not been willing at first, but what had fuelled her? What in the name of the Seven Witches had fuelled the Queen of Falanor to betray everything she loved? As the knife cut deep, and Saark gasped, and ice forced into his flesh and cut into bone with a grating, grinding sound Saark's eyes met with Alloria's and she smiled at him and there was no sorrow there and she was completely *vachine*, she was no longer human and rage and hate flowed strong in Saark but he could not move and pain flashed up and swamped his mind and the knife cut deep and carved a circle the size of a fist from his flesh, and he gasped, unable to breathe as he was mutilated, and he did not struggle and did not scream and the pain and ice were everything, all consuming, swamping his vision and he gasped, again, and saw as if through a veil of blood the Soul Gem excised from his own savaged body and he coughed, and blood splattered from Saark's mouth, and he felt everything and the world fall away and down into a blood red pool of darkness.

Kradek-ka turned, in silence, as Saark slumped to one side behind him, blood running down the Granite Throne and onto Helltop. "No!" screamed Kell, struggling pointlessly, and Nienna was weeping and Kradek-ka handed the three Soul Gems to General Graal, who took them, took the three small matt black cylindrical jewels – the source of so much agony and pain and blood and death and power.

"Now, we call the Vrekken," he said.

Skaringa Dak was huge and brooding and ominous, once volcanic with a million natural arteries and channels and tunnels and veins, now dormant but home to the swirling underground whirlpool, the Vrekken; it overlooked Silva Valley to the North, dominating the skyline of the vachine civilisation and controlling the flow of the Silva River from deep inside the Deshi caves and beyond, where the Silva River flowed deeper into the heart of the Black Pike Mountains.

Now, as General Graal's blood sacrifice and blood-oil magick Summoning sent ripples of energy through the natural arteries of Skaringa Dak, so the Vrekken, that mighty underground whirlpool, roared a noise so loud it made the mountain tremble and there came a distant *boom boom boom* as water pressure increased a million-fold and with the power of the ocean, the power of the mountains, the fury of the *land*, the Vrekken reared from its deep bottomless pit and water heaved through tunnels millennia deserted, black and cold and shimmering like blood. It pounded through corridors and caverns, smashing up through a hundred breeding nests of Graal's white-haired soldiers, up up up through thick arteries as the mountain trembled and the world trembled and billions of gallons were forced under enormous pressure into the Silva River, out through the gaping maws of the Deshi Caves, out with such incredible pressure and a wall of water reared like the rising head of a striking cobra and slammed at once down Silva Valley crushing houses and temples, warehouses and palaces, and thousands of vachine were slammed with such force they were crushed, compressed down into a mash of flesh and corrupted clockwork components. Thousands ran, streaming down pavements and jewelled roadways, but the wall of water pounded along and they were gone in an instant. The Engineer's Palace was torn in two, one half picked up like a toy and dashed along the expanse of Silva Valley, bounced from mountain wall to mountain wall as tens of thousands of screams rent the air and the mighty force of the Vrekken crushed the occupants of Silva Valley... and the vachine civilisation therein.

The roaring seemed to last a thousand years. It echoed deafening through the Black Pike Mountains, like mocking laughter. And... as soon at it had come, the might of the Vrekken was gone, leaving Silva Valley flooded, a churning platter of dark black waters. Where once the valley had sat, now was a surging, seething lake.

Slowly, the violence faded and the new lake settled, calming, to be still.

Silva Valley was no more.

And the dead screamed unto eternity.

On Helltop, they stood in silence. The roaring of the Vrekken, the flooding of Silva Valley, the extinguishing of the vachine civilisation had taken perhaps five minutes. Kell, eyes narrowed, stared hard at Graal. "What have you done?" he said.

"It was a necessary sacrifice," said Graal.

"You exterminated their colony like insects."

Graal's eyes gleamed. "And soon, you will see why!" He gestured to the Soul Stealers, and Shanna and Tashmaniok moved to Anukis, and tossed her corpse aside. Then they did this to Jageraw, leaving smears of dark blood on the Granite Thrones. Finally, they grabbed Saark, who was wheezing, eyes closed, the huge fist-sized hole in his chest showing shattered breast-bone and the open cage of smashed ribs. Within, his heart beat with a slow, irregular rhythm – like a fist opening, and closing, and opening, and closing. They tossed him to one side, where he rolled over and Nienna ran to him, and nobody stopped her.

"Saark!" she said, face wet with tears. But she could not hold him, for she was bound too tight.

"All is well, Little One," he grunted, and forced himself into a sitting position. He looked down at his open chest in horror, and when he smiled blood glistened on his teeth.

"Saark, don't die," she wept.

"I don't think I have much choice in the matter," he managed, voice hoarse. Then he winked at Nienna, and coughed, eyes closing in pain. "Did I ever mention you're a stunning young lady? A real catch."

"You'll never change," laughed Nienna through tears.

"I wish…" he winced again, the agony plain on his face, "I wish I had just a few more years. So… so many women, still left, to please." His head slumped forward, and breath rattled from his lungs.

Kell gazed out over the distant, flooded Silva Valley, and turned back to Graal. Graal and Kradek-ka stood before the Granite Thrones. The pool before the Granite Thrones – down through which Graal summoned the Vrekken – was an empty hole, deep and bottomless, all water sucked free when the Vrekken threw its hydraulic fury at Silva Valley.

Graal and Kradek-ka stood, either side of the hole. They faced the Granite Thrones. They seemed to be waiting. Kell glanced left, to Myriam and Alloria; both were entranced by the sight, by the Summoning, and the air crackled with dark energy. The Vampire Warlords were coming. It was written in the sky. Written in the stone. Kuradek the Unholy. Meshwar the Violent. Bhu Vanesh, the Eater in the Dark. The world would descend into chaos. And the Vampire Warlords would build a *new* Empire.

Kell looked right. The Soul Stealers were entranced, their bright crimson eyes fixed on the Thrones. This was the moment. This was the time. If Kell could break free now, he could... what? A cold realisation dawned. The Summoning magick had been cast. The spell was done. All the deaths, the blood-oil, the sacrifice... the Soul Gems had done their work, summoned the Vrekken, destroyed the vachine, killed enough vachine souls to bring back the Vampire Warlords from the Chaos Fields – from the Blood Void.

What could Kell possibly do? Even if he murdered Graal and Kradek-ka, it would make no difference. The Summoning was *happening*. It was an unstoppable Force of Nature. Of Chaos. Of *Magick*.

I can help you, said Ilanna.

No, you cannot, said Kell.

He is coming, be ready, said Ilanna. Kell scowled. His gaze swept the platform. He could see the stars again, but a blackness like smoke rolled out against the night sky, blocking out the stars in three hazy patterns. Kell blinked. Was he imagining this haze-filled sky? He lowered his eyes, and shook his head, and all the fight had gone out of him. They were here, Saark was dead, he and Nienna had failed. They had thought they were so powerful, so clever, bringing the fight to the enemy – when in fact, all they did was deliver Saark and the Soul Gem to Graal.

And he came, from the edge of the scene, from between the rocks where before there was no passage, and he stepped from smoke and he was barefoot and danced on the glossy slick surface of Helltop. He was six years old, with thin limbs and pale skin, he was ragged and tattered, wore torn clothes and had black, shiny teeth. His eyes, also, were black, and they shone with an ancient wisdom, with the decadent wisdom of the Ankarok. Skanda danced, twirling and weaving, a slow dance to unheard music, perhaps the music of the stars and the magick and the Summoning itself, and Kell watched the little boy with his mouth open, and a sour needle split his brain and Kell scowled, for Skanda was part of this evil too and if Kell could get his axe free he would make them all pay, for the blood and the death. Kell watched Skanda dance, and the Soul Stealers turned and fixed eyes on the little boy, and they drew their silver swords and leapt at him with sudden violent snarls and the world seemed to *tilt* and come rushing back into place and Kell watched in awe as Skanda danced between the impossibly whirling sword blades, and he leapt and twirled and danced, and the blades hissed and sang around him, a glittering web of death and Skanda lifted his eyes and they met with Kell's, there was a *connection* and Skanda smiled and he lifted his hands and from his hands flowed... insects. They came in a flood, crawling and skittering, flying and buzzing and stinging, they poured from Skanda's hands and now his mouth opened and they flooded from his throat and rushed past the startled Soul Stealers who dropped to their knees in defensive crouches as Graal suddenly turned, realised what was happening and his face turned from bliss to fear, his eyes darkening, his mouth opening to scream but the insects flooded out, over the plateau and over Kell who panicked, squirming in his bonds as worms and maggots and cockroaches and wasps flowed over him, smothering him with their insect noise and acid and...

Kell blinked. The gold wires fell away, eaten by insects.

Kell looked down, at Ilanna grasped in his mighty, lacerated, blood-drenched hands. Slowly, he looked up, and saw the Soul Stealers, and Graal, staring at him. Skanda danced on, a mournful dance, insects still pouring from his mouth and his little boy's feet slapped pitifully on the slick ground. Graal pointed at Kell. "Kill him!" he screamed, with a sudden insane fury and the Soul Stealers stood, then leapt at Kell who brought Ilanna up in a savage sweep and stream of sparks, batting aside both swords and knocking the two female killers back.

Kell took a step forward. He lowered his head. "I am Kell. And I am mightily pissed off."

The Soul Stealers leapt again, and Kell moved with awesome speed, a blur, an age of pent-up rage and frustration unleashed in a few swift heartbeats. Swords struck Ilanna, were cast aside and she sang as she cut for Tashmaniok's neck but the Soul Stealer back-flipped away, too fast, and her fangs came out and her claws grew long and they could hear the *tick tick* of stepping gears and clockwork wheels. She leapt at Kell, snarling, and was caught on the flat blades of Ilanna but twisted, one boot between the axe and herself, and pushed herself away into a roll as Ilanna sang a finger's breadth from her throat. Shanna attacked, sword slashing, claws trying to gouge Kell's eyes. He stumbled back, and she came on, snarling and spitting and Kell was forced further back until the rock wall halted him and he fought a short, furious battle, axe and blurring sword flickering to a discordant song-clash of steel. Kell ducked a sword strike, jabbed with his axe but Shanna shifted, avoiding the blow. Tashmaniok came in on Kell's right, and sweating now, slowing, the old warrior back-handed an axe strike at her face which she easily avoided.

"You're getting slow, old man," taunted Tash.

"You're going to die, old man," laughed Shanna.

"Then we'll eat your granddaughter," said Tashmaniok, all humour gone. She was neither sweating, nor panting; she showed no signs of exertion. Kell, on the other hand, was a sack of shit. He was covered in his own blood, in lacerations from the tight cutting wires, and his sweat was stinging his many wounds and fuelling his fury. But the vachine killers were right; he was old, and he was tired, and he was tiring. Fury and rage could only last so long. Kell had only minutes... *seconds*... to live. They knew it. And he knew it.

"Catch," said Skanda, from between the two Soul Stealers, and he threw the twin-tailed scorpion and Kell tried to dodge but the scorpion landed lightly on his chest, just under his throat, and before he could do anything both tails flexed and struck like the twin heads of a striking snake. The scorpion stung Kell, who yelled in surprise as the Soul Stealers turned on Skanda for a moment, distracted, swords a blur as they frantically attempted to kill this boy of the Ankarok, but he danced, tantalisingly, forlornly, between their blades. Then there came a sharp *crack*, and Skanda smiled an ancient blood-oil magick smile and watched as *time* cracked and Kell stepped in two, and looked at himself, looked at his twin, his clone, his double, one a few steps out of time meaning he was not one, but two. The Kells stared at each other, stunned into silence, and the Soul Stealers stood still with mouths hung agape. The two Kells turned, like a mirror image, and with roars that shook the air launched themselves at the Soul Stealers, twin Ilanna axes singing a curious humming chorus of axe-blade death. Swords and axes shrieked, and now that each Kell fought only one enemy his confidence and speed and agility returned, and with savage necessity the original Kell forced Shanna back against a wall, his axe strikes accelerating as she grew more and more frantic, and she called out for help, "Tash!" a shriek of the condemned as Ilanna batted aside her sword blade for one last time and with a mighty roar, a bestial battle-scream Kell lifted the butterfly blades of his bloodbond axe and they came down in a savage vertical strike that cut Shanna from skull to quim, and slopped her bowels and clockwork components to the Helltop plateau. "No!" wailed Tash, distracted by her twin's destruction, and Kell's axe cut through her neck, sending her head rolling along the stone ground, slapping slowly to a halt by Graal's boots.

Skanda smiled, and clapped, and the twin-tailed scorpion ran onto his hand and up his arm. He clapped again, and there was a second *crack*. The air felt greasy, full of smoke, and the second Kell disappeared as time jigged into synchronisation, into a linear snap of reality.

"Don't ever do that again!" snarled Kell, turning in rage, his head pounding as if struck by a mallet, but Skanda had gone. He ran to Nienna, and Graal was shouting orders to the soldiers surrounding the Granite Thrones. Even now, dark smoke was coalescing on all three Thrones, and Kell shook Nienna, dragging her away from Saark's body. "We must go," he growled, eyes wild.

"Bring Saark."

"I reckon he's dead!"

"Bring him!" she shrieked.

Kell grabbed the limp body of Saark, grunting as he slung him over his shoulder for the dandy was heavier than he looked, then dragging Nienna behind, he sprinted for the only exit available – the empty pool, the hole, sitting stagnant before the three Granite Thrones. Graal had drawn his sword, and as Kell charged so he turned and his face was death, his eyes twinkling sapphires, and the sword came up and Kell screamed and hurtled towards him, axe coming up and smashing Graal's sword aside as Ilanna cut a long streak down Graal's left cheek, peeling his face open like a fruit, and Kell's last glimpse before they were swallowed by the hole was that of three tall, smoke-filled figures seated on the Granite Thrones. Their eyes were blood red, and they were watching him. Kell, Nienna and Saark fell into the chute, into the vertical tunnel below, and in the blink of an eye vanished from Helltop.

They fell.

Fell, towards the distant, booming Vrekken.

On a high peak above the flooded Silva Valley sat four Vachine Warrior Engineers and two Watchmakers. Walgrishnacht's eyes were bleak, his face drawn and haggard as he surveyed the destruction of Silva Valley below. Their escape had been a miracle. Many had died following.

"Nobody could have predicted this," said Sa, voice gentle.

Tagor-tel placed his arm around her shoulders, and they sat for a while, thinking of the thousands who had died, smashed and drowned below them in the echoing caverns of the Vrekken.

"We must call what remains of the vachine armies," said Walgrishnacht, standing, and he turned and stared at the distant peak of Skaringa Dak. Above it, blackness swirled like evil personified. "We must summon the Ferals."

"It is too late!" wailed Sa. "Can you not feel it? Can you not feel *them*?"

"I do not understand," frowned the Cardinal.

"Graal has summoned the three Vampire Warlords," said Sa, tears running down her cheeks. "With or without our armies, this means the end of our civilisation."

Walgrishnacht drew his sword, which gleamed black in the moonlight. "Only when I am dead, and my proud blood-oil stains the battlefield, will I believe this is so," he said, and gestured to the few remaining members of his massacred platoon. "Let's move out," he said, brass fangs gleaming.

The wind crooned across the peak of Skaringa Dak. Graal, pushing his peeled cheek back into place with a squelch, turned and faced the Vampire Warlords. They were huge, and dark, their skin swirling smoke, their eyes raging blood, and they stood – in unity, as one – and first Kradek-ka knelt, and then, slowly, General Graal knelt and a chill terror flooded him like nothing he had ever felt. For the Vampire Warlords were terrible, and they were death, and they had changed and brought something *else* back with them from the Chaos Fields, from the Blood Void, from the Halls of Bone. All around the platform soldiers knelt to show terrified obeisance, and Myriam and Alloria knelt also, the wave of total fear washing over them and making piss run down their legs.

"General Graal," said Bhu Vanesh, the Eater in the Dark, and blood eyes tilted in a smoke face to survey his subordinate, to survey his slave, and Graal nodded, unable to speak, the terror like thick flowing ash in his mouth and his brain and he was a child again – how had he thought they could control these ancient, bestial, primitive Warlords?

Kuradek stood on the Granite Throne, and peered off across the desolation of Silva Valley. He smiled, face swirling gently, every feature a blur, every breath a rattle of chaos. "Silva Valley is destroyed."

"Yes," managed Graal, forcing words between clenched teeth.

"You have done well, slaves."

"Yes," forced Graal.

Meshwar the Violent stepped away from the Granite Throne, and for a moment Graal thought he might disappear; like this whole Summoning was a bad nightmare, and the magick which had brought the Warlords back might restrict them to the Thrones. But it did not.

"Gather your soldiers," said Meshwar, surveying the warriors from the Army of Iron, heads bowed, fear and chaos worms in their rotten, spinning brains. Meshwar's gaze was bleak. His voice was an intonation from a different realm. From a world of chaos. "Gather them all. Now is time. Now we go to war."

"Against whom?" trembled Graal.

Blood eyes glowed. "Against *everyone*," he said.

III

VAMPIRE WARLORDS

PROLOGUE
Portal

The wind howled like a spear-stuck pig. Black snow peppered the mountains. Ice blew like ash confetti at a corpse wedding. The Black Pike Mountains seemed to *sigh*, languorously, as the sky turned black, the stars spluttered out, and the world ceased its endless turn on a corrupted axis. And then the Chaos Halls *flickered* into existence like an extinguished candle in reverse.

A sour wind blew, a death-kiss from beyond the world of men and gods and liars, and smoke swirled like acid through the sky, black and grey, infused with ancient symbols and curling snakes and stinging insects. The smoke drifted down, almost casually, to Helltop at the summit of the great mountain Skaringa Dak. The Granite Thrones, empty for a thousand years, were filled again with substance. With flesh.

The three Vampire Warlords, as old as the world, as twisted as chaos, formed against the Granite Thrones where they were summoned. *Almost*. Their figures were tall, bodies narrow shanks, limbs long and spindly and disjointed, elbows and knees working the wrong way. Their faces were blank plates on a tombstone, eyes an evil dark slash of red like fresh-spilled arterial gore, and yet their worst feature, their most unsettling feature, was in their complete physical entirety. For in appearing, they did not settle. Did not solidify. Their nakedness, if that was what it was for the Vampire Warlords wore no clothing, was a diffusion of blacks and greys, a million tiny greasy smoke coils constantly twisting and writhing like an orgy of corpse lovers entwined, cancerous entrails like black snakes, unwound spools of necrotic bowel, and their flesh relentlessly moved, shifted, coalesced, squirmed as if seeking to strip itself free of a steel endoskeleton forged from pure hate. Their skin coagulated into strange symbols, ancient artefacts, snakes and spiders and cockroaches and all manner of stinging biting slashing chaos welcomed into this, The Whole. They were not mortal. They were not gods. They were something in-between, and oozed a lazy power, terrible and delinquent, and none could look upon that writhing flesh and wish to be a part of this abomination. Their skin and muscle and tendon and bones were a distillation of entrapped demons, an absorption of evil souls, an essence of corrupt matter which formed a paved avenue all the way back to the shimmering decadence of the vanishing Chaos Halls.

The Vampire Warlords turned their heads, as one, and stared down at the two men... the two *vachine*, who had summoned them, released them, cast them into ice and freedom.

And the Vampire Warlords laughed, voices high-pitched and surreal, the laughter of the insane but *more*, the laughter of insanity linked to a binary intelligence, a two-state recognition of good and bad, order and chaos, pandemonium and... lawlessness.

"You," said Kuradek, and this was Kuradek the Unholy, and his skin squirmed with dark religious symbols, with flowing doctrine oozing like pus, with a bare essence of hatred for anything which preached the word of God upon this decadent and putrefying world. In the history books, the text claimed Kuradek had burned churches, raped entire nunneries, sent monasteries insane so that monk slew monk with bone knives fashioned from the flesh-stripped limbs of their slaughtered companions. Kuradek's arm lifted, now, so incredibly long and finished in fingers like talons, like blood-spattered razors. General Graal, mouth hung open in shock and disbelief, hand pressed against his face where Kell's axe had opened his cheek like a ripe plum, nodded eagerly as if frightened to offend. Fearful not just of death, but of an eternity of writhing and oblivion in a tank of acrid oil.

"Yes, Warlord?" Barely more than a whisper. Graal bent his head, and stared in relief at the frozen mountain plateau beneath his boots. Anything was better than looking into those eyes. Anything was better than observing that succulent flesh.

"Come here, slave."

"Yes, Warlord."

General Graal straightened his back, a new anger forcing him ramrod stiff and his eyes narrowed and he stepped up onto the low plinth where the Granite Thrones squatted like black poisonous toads. Kuradek was standing, and the other Warlords, Meshwar the Violent and Bhu Vanesh, the Eater in the Dark, were seated, gore eyes glittering with an ancient, malign intelligence.

"You sought to control us, just as the Keepers controlled us," said Kuradek.

Silence flooded the plateau, and all present lowered heads, averted eyes, as a wind of desolation blew across the space, chilling souls. Graal, teeth gritted, did well to maintain that gaze. Now he was close, he could make out finer details. The skin, the flesh of coiling smoke, of writhing symbols, of constantly changing twisted imagery, was glossy – as if wet. As if *oiled*. And now he could see the Vampire Warlords' vampire *fangs*. Short, and black, like necrotic bone. Not shimmering in gold and silver like the vanity of the vachine. Graal ground his teeth. Oh how they must have laughed at the narcissism of the vachine sub-species. How they must now be revelling in such petty beauties the vachine had heaped upon themselves.

"No, I..."

Graal stopped. Kuradek was staring at him. Foolish. He could *read Graal's mind*. Kuradek made a lazy gesture, and for a moment his entire being seemed to glow, the smoke swirling faster within the confines of its trapped cell, Kuradek's living flesh. General Graal, commander of the Army of Iron, was punched in an acceleration of flailing limbs across the granite plateau. He screamed, a short sharp noise, then was silent as he hit the ground and rolled fast, limbs flailing, to slap to a halt in a puddle of melted snow. He did not move. Kuradek turned to Kradek-ka, who half-turned, as if to run. He was picked up, tossed away like a broken spine, limbs thrashing as he connected with a rearing wall of savage rock. He tumbled to the ground, face a bloody, smashed mask, and was still.

Now, the other Warlords stood. They moved easily, fluid, with a sense of great physical power held in reserve. All three gazed up as the Chaos Halls gradually faded and the stars blinked back into existence, one by one. Now, the wind dropped. Total silence covered the Black Pike Mountains like a veil of ash.

"We are here," growled Meshwar, and as he spoke tiny trickles of smoke oozed around his vampire fangs, like the souls of the slain attempting escape.

"Yes," said Bhu Vanesh. Also known as the Eater in the Dark, Bhu Vanesh was a terrible and terrifying hunter. Whereas Meshwar simply revelled in open raw violence, in pain for the sake of pain, in punishment without crime, in murder over forgiveness, Bhu Vanesh was more complex, esoteric, subtle and devastating. Before his imprisonment, Bhu Vanesh had prided himself on being the greatest vampire hunter; he would and could hunt anything, up to and including other Vampire Warlords. Before their chains in the Chaos Halls, Bhu Vanesh had sought out the greatest natural hunters in the world and let them free in forests and mountain landscapes, using himself as bait, himself as hunter. When the hunt was done, with his captured victims staked out, he would gradually strip out their spines disc by disc, popping free of torn muscle and skin and tendons, and he would sit by the camp fire as his hunted victims screamed, or sobbed, or simply watched with stunned eyes as Bhu Vanesh savoured his trophy, licked the gristle from the spine in his fist, sucking free the cerebrospinal fluid with great slurps of pleasure. Bhu Vanesh was the most feral of the three Vampire Warlords. He was the most deadly. An unappointed leader...

Bhu Vanesh was the *Prime*.

Meshwar pointed to an albino soldier. "You. Soldier. Get Graal." The man gave a curt nod, and crossed to the General, helping him wearily, painfully, to his feet. Graal leant on the albino soldier, panting, blood and snot and drool pooling from his smashed mouth, his battered face. His pale vachine skin was marked as if beaten by a hammer.

Kuradek strolled across the clearing, and a cool wind blew in as the world was restored to normality, as blood-oil magick eased from the mountains like a back-door thief slinking into the night. Kuradek climbed up a rocky wall, his thin limbs and talons scarring the rock. Pebbles rattled down in the wake of his climb. Then he stood, on a narrow pinnacle of iced slate, and gazed out over Silva Valley, once home to the vachine civilisation, now flooded, thousands of vachine drowned to seal the magick that would return the Vampire Warlords to the mortal realm.

Shortly, his brothers joined him, and the three tall, spindly creatures, their shapes a mockery of human physiology, their flesh constantly shifting in chameleonic phases of smoke and symbols, stood tall and proud and surveyed the world like newborns.

"The vachine are dead," said Kuradek.

"Mostly," observed Meshwar.

"Those that live need to be hunted," said Bhu Vanesh, a smoke tongue like a rattlesnake's tail licking over black fangs. He anticipated the hunt in all things. It was what gave his existence simple meaning.

"Not yet," said Kuradek. "We are new again to this world. We are weak from escape and birth. We need strength. We need to build the vampire clans. Like ancient times, my friends. Like the bad old days."

"Suggestions?" Meshwar turned to Kuradek, narrow red eyes glowing with malevolence.

"I remember this country," said Kuradek, looking back over hundreds of years, his mind dizzy with the passage of time, coalescing with images of so many people and places and murders. "This is the homeland of the Ankarok."

Bhu Vanesh made a low, hissing sound.

"They were imprisoned," said Meshwar. "Just as we."

"Yes. We must watch. Be careful. But until then, I feel a stench in the air. It is an unclear stench. It is the stench of people, of men and women and children, *meat*, unhealthy and unclean, with no pride or power or natural dignity. We must separate, my brothers, we must head out into the world and," he licked his black fangs, eyes glinting by the light of the innocent moon, "we must *repopulate*."

"So we go to war?" said Meshwar, and his voice held excitement, anticipation and… something else. It took little for Meshwar to become aroused.

"Yes. War. Against all those deviants, lacking in vampire purity!"

ONE
Underwurlde

Events were a blur for Saark, the rich dandy, the flamboyant womaniser, for all that interested him in life was fine wine and raucous sex, silver platters of finely carved pig-meat, juicy eyeballs soaked in thin apple sauce from the figarall fish caught in iron traps under the Salarl Ocean. He was obsessed with pleasure, with joy, his own unstoppable and unquenchable *lust*; Saark was a hedonist, a narcissist, a nihilist, and unashamed of his open succulent fire. And yet now, now it was a blur. His life was a blur, and everything in it filled with a dreamlike quality, a haze of misunderstanding, of confusion – and more importantly, of–

Pain.

The knife cut into his chest and he may have screamed, his kicking limbs lurching in epileptic spasms. The knife was burning hot then ice cold, burning, burning as the tip skewered his skin, and his muscle, and sawed rhythmically and with razor-eagerness through his breast-bone leaving him gasping, teeth clacking repeatedly, fingers flexing as he begged *begged* to make it stop make it stop, but the face over him was hard and brutal, the face of the vachine Watchmaker, Kradek-ka and Saark's blood flushed down his chest, his belly, and he felt something removed from him.

Saark lay there, gasping, flopped like a fish on the Granite Throne and black snow fell and a cold wind whistled, disturbing his long black curls. The wind smelled good, smelled of ice and freedom beyond the mountains, beyond this imprisonment of the blade which had sundered his pale weak brittle flesh. The mountains. The Black Pike Mountains. Skaringa Dak. Helltop.

These names were distant, now, tails of smoke, and his blood pounded in his veins and he was different. Saark had been infected by the bite of the Soul Stealer, her venom pumping round his veins and infusing him with the *toxin* of the vachine, the vampires, a second-rate disease for a second-rate hero... Saark laughed. Blood bubbled around his lips from punctured lungs. He felt like he was dying. And he knew: surely he was.

Saark could ascertain noises, shouting, the clash of weapons, but they were all gone and lost to him. Consciousness fled like a startled kitten, and when he awoke the cool granite of Helltop was pressing his face like a lover. He heard more shouts, and sobbing, and one eye could see the dark sky filled with a *portal* into the Chaos Halls, the Blood Void, the Bone Graveyard, and a fist of fear punched through Saark as he listened to the steady *thump thump* of his heart, open to the world, and slowly his hand crawled across the ground. His fingers crawled across his own slick flesh, slick and cold, drenched in iced blood, and he found a hole gaping over his heart, and his fingers could feel the trembling of his *heart* within because he was open to the world, carved up like a pig on a slab, and that was so sweet, so ironic, so frightening.

A hand soothed his brow. Beyond, he could feel a terrible presence, of death and hatred and omniscient rage. The Vampire Warlords had arrived. And Saark, even in his disorientated state, knew desolation.

"It will be all right," soothed a voice in his ear, and he recognised Nienna and he smiled, and her hands were stroking his face. He could see fear in her eyes, though, and knew then he would die. What could she see? How could she save him?

Saark tried to speak, but could not.

Saark tried to move, but could not.

Distantly, through a mesh of fractured thoughts, words came to him, all tangled, interlaced, like the stranded threads of cotton his mother used to repair his trews. *We must go. We must! We cannot! He's dead. Bring Saark. Bring Saark. He's dead.* They echoed backwards and forwards, reverberating as if they were a drunk's uneven song in the bottom of a sediment-layered tankard. *Bring Saark! Bring him!* A woman's shriek. Oh how he longed for a woman's shriek, but that was a different world, a different age.

Movement. Ice. Cold. Wind. And then–

Plummeting. A feeling of weightlessness. And Saark remembered no more.

On the icy plateau of Helltop, with the Vampire Warlords solid and real behind him, newborn demons and dark gods and *vampires* from the Chaos Halls, Kell, with Saark over one shoulder and dragging Nienna behind him, his mighty axe *Ilanna* in one huge fist and rage and fear pumping through his breast like molten hate, Kell leapt for the hole in the mountain's summit, leapt for the vertical tunnel so recently brimming with waters which spilled out, were *forced out* under awesome pressure to flood Silva Valley and drown the vachine living within...

Kell's logic was simple. Leap down the vertical tunnel. *Escape!* It had water, down there, somewhere, spoke his desperate mind; and that would cushion their fall. If not? Well, a grim side of Kell's soul decided, if *not* then sudden impact, sudden death, it would be better than living as slaves to the vampires.

Kell blinked. General Graal was in his way.

Nothing stood in Kell's way.

In reflex, Ilanna flashed up, smashing Graal's sword aside as if wielded by a tottering toddler, and in the same movement singing blades sliced Graal's left cheek apart as if paring tender braised beef from bone. Graal stumbled back with a shriek, and Kell and Saark and Nienna tumbled into the hole, into the ancient tunnel worn through rock by a million years of probing melt-water. In that instant, Kell glimpsed three figures on the Granite Thrones. They were fashioned from black smoke. Their eyes were blood red. And they were watching him.

Gravity caught Kell in its fist and pulled him downwards, separating him from his companions. All thoughts and fear were smashed aside like a blow from a helve. Acceleration became his mistress, fear glued his teeth shut, and Kell fell into a headlong dive that seemed to last forever...

The tunnel was long. White. Images flashed and blurred before Kell's eyes. He tumbled occasionally, hitting the sides of the vast tunnel wall but they were smooth, worn by floods and ice and a raging torrent. His hair and beard streamed behind him. Tears eased from old eyes. He dragged Ilanna, his axe, his sweetheart, to his chest and lowered his chin and waited for a terrible impact...

It never came. Gently, the tunnel curved and Kell was sliding, then free again and falling, diving, and he heard a distant scream but could do nothing. He glanced back, and saw only darkness. Again, he was cradled by a curve in the tunnel, and friction slowed him, burning the flesh of his hands and he yelped, in surprise, in shock at sudden raw agony but it told him one thing, one certainty: it hurt like a bastard, and that meant he was alive. This was no dream. Kell narrowed his eyes and gritted his teeth and fell through Skaringa Dak – dived, through the heart of the mountain.

Tunnels flashed past. Some lit with mineral deposits. Some were huge, caverns dissecting the tunnel through which Kell fell and he thought, *where is all the water?* And he realised, *a flood, a flood of magick, drowning Silva Valley, drowning the vachine civilisation…* and then he hit another curve, which slowed him, and he was sent tumbling through air and darkness and plunged into water so cold he gasped, ice-needles driving through his eyeballs and brain and numbing him. He was deep under, and he clung to Ilanna. *I will not let you go, I will not lose you, my love.* With a sudden spurt of anger Kell punched upwards, powerful legs kicking, and he broke the surface with a splutter and desperate intake of air. He went under again, but fought upwards and as he gasped and breathed, he saw the nearby glow and kicked out for it, his strokes urgent, cold battering through his old bones.

It was a beach, of sorts. Kell kicked and struggled, then flopped uselessly onto his back, great chest heaving. Kell had never been one for swimming, and he hated the water with a vengeance.

Pain and fear ran rampant through his blood, and Kell pushed himself to an upright position and cleared his nostrils with snorts, head spinning. He heard something then, a crying, a thrashing in the underground lake. *Nienna!*

Dropping his axe, Kell surged back towards the freezing lake. "Nienna!" he boomed, and his voice reverberated back a hundred times more powerful, a cackling of demons.

"Grandfather!" shrieked the young woman, "I've got Saark, help, he's dragging me under!"

Kell kicked off his boots, muttering darkly, and with the surreal and ghostly glow behind, leapt back in to the freezing waters, powering over to Nienna and taking the dead-weight of Saark's body from struggling hands. Kell struck back for the shore, Nienna following, and they lay there on the black sand panting, exhausted, shivering with core-biting cold, and Kell rolled Saark to one side and growled and said, "You should have let him sink. What sense, Nienna, in rescuing a corpse?"

"He's not dead," panted Nienna.

"I watched them carve out his heart!" snapped Kell, weary now, and crawled and stood, and rubbed his hands together. "Of course he's dead! Now we need a fire, girl, or we'll also die in but a few short hours."

"But..."

"Nienna! Stand up! Get moving. Keep moving."

She stood, and they looked around. The shore of the vast underground lake seemed to stretch off for eternity. The cavern was vast, endless, and the glow came from eerie stalactites and stalagmites which sat cloaked in some kind of fungus. Kell moved to one, and peeled back a little. He sniffed it. He touched it to his tongue. "I hope it burns. Because," he gazed around, long grey hair plastered to his shivering scalp, "if it doesn't, we're going to die down here."

The beach was littered with stones and rocks, of a million different descriptions, all washed up over millennia. Kell set Nienna to gathering the glowing fungi, and he found several rocks, striking them together until he found a combination that gave a spark. Back from the water, near a cluster of flowstone and stalagmites, Nienna piled the scraped fungus and Kell knelt, feeling foolish, shivering violently. He struck sparks in the fungus, and on the fourth attempt it glowed, and flames flickered. An odd-smelling smoke rose and heat blossomed from glowing flame-petals. Kell glanced up. "Get more," he said.

"Bring Saark to the fire," said Nienna.

Kell ground his teeth in annoyance, but gave a nod. He moved back down to the lapping shore. He bent, and lifted the dandy, and retrieved his axe. He carried both back to this odd subterranean campsite and threw down the axe. He laid Saark out. Saark's eyes opened.

"Thanks, old man," he said, voice a hoarse whisper. "Thought you were going to leave me out there to die."

"Saark! Gods, man! You tough little cockroach!" Kell moved Saark closer to the flames, and stared in awe at the savage chest wound. He could see Saark's heart beating within, pulsating with very, very slow thumps. Kell shivered. Saark was a hair's-breadth from death.

Nienna returned, and they piled more fungus on the fire. Flames roared and within minutes steam was rising from their sodden clothes. Saark's eyes had closed, and Kell gestured to Nienna. They stepped away from the fire.

"There is nothing I can do for him," he said, sadness buried in his eyes, in his voice. "I wish there was, Nienna, truly I do. It is a miracle he has lasted this long. He must have lost a lot of blood."

"Can you not stitch him? I've seen you sew wounds before!"

"No, Little One. It is too wide. It's straight through the bone. We must... sit with him. But when it is time to move on, well..." Kell gripped his axe tight, trying to convey understanding through gesture.

Nienna understood clearly, and she punched Kell on the arm. "No!" she hissed. "You're not going to kill him! I won't let you."

"We cannot take him with us, girl. Look around you! I doubt very much we will survive. How foolish, to try and drag a guaranteed corpse."

"He may be a guaranteed corpse to you," said Nienna, eyes cold, voice in the tombworld, "but he's a fine friend to me, and I will not leave him. You go if you wish, *grandfather*. But I will find a way to get Saark back to the sunshine."

Kell sighed, and watched Nienna return to Saark. He ground his teeth, and rubbed at his temples, and moved back to the fire as the chill of the underground cavern bit him with tiny fangs. *She has the stubbornness of her mother in her,* he thought bitterly, but that only led to further painful memories, of ancient days, and Sara, and Kell closed that door with a violent shove.

Saark moaned, and his eyes fluttered open. "Where am I?" he murmured.

"You should be dead," growled Kell.

"Nice to see you, too, you old bastard."

"I'm simply being honest," prickled the aged axeman.

Saark coughed, and Kell rubbed at his beard. "I reckon we'll need to be moving soon. Don't want those Vampire Warlords ramming claws up my arse."

"How long have we been stranded?"

"A day, maybe."

"If they wanted us, they would have found us," said Saark, voice a croak, eyes watering. "Is there anything to eat?"

"No."

"Anything to drink?"

"Just brackish, oily water. At least the lake will sustain us."

Saark laughed, then grimaced in pain. "You bring me to the finest places, Kell."

"Yeah, well, we ain't married yet, are we?"

"At least you acknowledge there might still be time. Ha!"

"Not whilst I'm breathing, lad."

"Where's Nienna?"

"Gathering more fungus. It burns well, but with a strange smell."

"I recognise that smell, Kell. It's drugsmoke. You're keeping us all high. Well done, that man. I thought my pain had receded; it's because I've been inhaling a natural narcotic for the last few hours. Don't you feel the buzz?"

Kell bared his teeth, face eerie by the light of the fire and the glowing, fungus-covered stalagmites. "Yes. But what you're feeling – that may be the smoke, I agree, or it could just be the vachine blood which now runs through your veins in a torrent."

There was an awkward silence.

"Listen," said Saark, finally, eyes shifting uneasily.

Kell placed his hand on Saark's, and patted him. "Don't you worry, lad. I know you think I'm an insane vachine killer... well, I *am* an insane vachine killer, but you're one of us. You're a friend. I promise to you, here and now, on my honour, on my blood, on my axe, that I *will not* kill you – vachine, or no vachine. That settle you?"

Saark coughed. Blood rimed his lips. "Thank you. But you do not know what you promise. You do not know how it feels."

"Explain it to me."

"Wait. Somebody's coming."

"How can..."

Saark grinned. "*Vachine* senses. They are good, Kell. Very good."

Kell rose, Ilanna in his great fists, and scanned the black shoreline with narrowed eyes. If it was the Vampire Warlords, immortal deities or no, Kell would give them a taste of his axe they'd never damn well forget!

And if it was General Graal come sniffing around after blood and violence? Kell smiled, a nasty smile on such a wise, old, ravaged face. Well, Graal had it coming from a long way off.

A figure picked its way carefully along the shoreline, gradually materialising into a woman. She was tall, limbs wiry and strong, but whereas once she had sported short, cropped black hair, now it was long, gently curled, and luscious like the pelt of a panther. Whereas once her features were gaunt, ravaged by cancer, sunken eyes and narrow bloodless lips, her flesh stretched like ancient, oil-stained parchment, now her skin was smooth and pale like marble, her face proud with high cheekbones and glittering dark eyes. She was a striking figure. A beautiful woman. She had the tiny, pointed teeth of the vachine. The gentle, slow *tick tick tick* of the machine vampire. A clockwork vampire.

"Myriam!" snarled Kell, and readied himself for battle.

Myriam approached, warily, both hands held wide to show open palms, no weapons. Her eyes met Kell's, and she knew there was death waiting there; but then her eyes met Saark's, and a smile touched her lips.

"He is still alive," she said, voice no longer the croak of the dying.

"No thanks to you, vachine bitch. Arm yourself, Myriam, because by all the gods I'll cut you from head to quim, whether armed or no."

"I have not come to fight," she said, stopping, boots crunching on the stones of the dark beach. "If I'd wanted you dead, I could have picked you off from five hundred paces with my bow. And you know that's true, old man."

Kell grinned. "Yeah. Well. I don't die easy." He moved forward, lowering his head, face full of rage and thunder, Ilanna lifting a little and seeming to *glow* black in anticipation of battle. Myriam had betrayed them, allowed Kell and Saark and Nienna to be caught by the Soul Stealers, *aided* in their capture by the Soul Stealers and delivered to General Graal trussed up like festival turkeys for summary execution. She was the enemy, through and through. She was a vachine contortion. A puppet. She must die.

"No!" screeched Nienna, dropping her armfuls of fungus and racing across the beach to stand before Kell. She held her arms wide. "No, Kell, no! Don't do this."

"Get out of my way, child, or you'll feel the back of my hand."

"Hard brave words from the Black Axeman of Drennach!" she sneered. "Such heroic spit to threaten a little girl."

Kell focused on Nienna for the first time. "She will betray us.

She is the enemy. She must die. Have you forgotten so easily what happened on the bridge? I have not."

"Hear her out, grandfather." Nienna's voice softened. *"Please?* She has her bow. I've seen how incredible she is with that weapon – devastating! She could have easily killed us from afar – all of us."

"Girl, you are fast becoming a thorn in my side!" Kell snapped, but lowered his axe, aware he was putty in her fingers, and knowing deep in his soul he would regret allowing Myriam to live.

"Yes, but surely I'm a thorn on a rose?" she said sweetly, and turned to Myriam. There were tears in Nienna's eyes. "Myriam? You have come to help?"

"Yes, child," said Myriam, and smiled, and there was love in her eyes. "Kell released me. From imprisonment. From thrall. From slavery."

"Explain," growled Kell.

"When you killed the Soul Stealers, Kell. They infected me with their blood-oil, their disease, and used clockwork to change me into a full vachine. I was theirs to command, not just through words or gratitude, but by – it is *hard* to explain. They took a part of my soul, and I took theirs. We were joined. I could not refuse them; Shanna and Tashmaniok were a drug for me. I was their marionette. But when you killed them, I was dazed for a while, and then their essence faded back to the Chaos Halls and I was set free. And then I saw the Vampire Warlords, I listened to their words, and I was filled with an absolute terror. I ran, Kell. I was frightened. I slipped away from Helltop and came looking for you. Believe it or not, you people are the only family I have."

Kell grunted, and slumped down beside Saark, who was panting heavily. "Well, you've found us in a sorry mess. I hope those bastard vampires don't come after us, for we are in no real state to defend."

Myriam moved forward, keeping a wary eye on Kell and his axe. "May I examine Saark's wound?"

"Go ahead. The lad will be dead by tomorrow." He fixed a beady eye on Myriam. "And you had a great part to play in that, girl."

Myriam knelt, and peeled back the torn linen pad which Kell had placed over the wound. "It has begun to heal," said Myriam.

"Nonsense," snapped Kell. "And even if the flesh healed, I've seen wounds like that before on the battlefield; he'll surely be riddled with infection. Gangrene will set in turning his flesh into a stinking putty. He will die, horribly, there is no doubt. And in a great amount of pain."

"Kell, shut up!" breathed Saark, scowling. His eyes fixed on Myriam's. "What's happening to me?"

"It is the vachine blood-oil in your veins. You have changed, Saark. You already know this. You now possess accelerated healing powers, and no infection will touch your tainted blood." She glanced at Kell. "The old man is wrong. There will be no gangrene for you; no maggot-filled infections. Your flesh is clean, because no bacteria can face the vampire parasite."

"Why so?" asked Kell, intrigued.

Myriam gave a small smile. "His flesh is cursed. No infection will touch him. Nienna! Bring me some of the fungus; the more yellow, the better."

Nienna carried some to the hunter and knelt by her side, watching carefully. "Can you help save him?" she said, voice soft, eyes wide. Nienna was in a permanent state of shock; she had seen too much death. Her childhood had been stripped away like bark from a tree, leaving her scarred and naked.

"Watch." Myriam tore the fungus into pieces, and taking a flat rock, began to crumble it between her brass vachine claws. "Mulgeth weed, it also grows in the Stone Lion Woods – in the cold, dark, damp places. It has many precious properties for those who live in the wilds."

"It burns well," said Kell, "although I wouldn't smoke it in a pipe, that's for sure."

"Some physicians use it," said Myriam. She opened her pack, now at her side, and removed a tin cup. "Nienna, run down and gather water from the lake," she said, handing the cup. She turned back to Kell. "Mulgeth weed removes pain, aids in healing, and yes, we can even eat it. But if one was to use it for too long, it would destroy a person's brain from the inside out; it delivers a slack jaw and permanent yellow drool. Soon, any such over-indulging individual would be down the Shit Pits at the docks shovelling fish-heads for a living."

Kell leaned close to Saark. "Hear that, lad? No downsides for you, then."

"Kiss my rosy arse, Kell," he coughed, wincing in agony.

Nienna returned, and dripping water into the crushed Mulgeth weed, Myriam kneaded it into a thick paste. Then, she leant forward and packed the hole in Saark's chest with gentle fingers. He groaned, a low sound of agony, and once Myriam had filled the hole she covered the wound with a bandage taken from her pack. She took another pouch, and from this a small, brown glass vial. She unstoppered it, and dripped a single drop of clear liquid into Saark's open mouth. Within seconds, he was snoring.

Myriam turned to Kell. "Now we must discuss Falanor. We must stop these Vampire Warlords."

Kell snorted. "We are trapped under the mountains, lass. What would you have me do? Topple the damn peaks on their heads?" Then his eyes turned dark. "And your words are fine and brave, coming from one who fled the enemy. Fled from them, yes, or maybe, instead, you are still in league with Graal and his bastards?"

"No," said Myriam. "The Vampire Warlords, they are terrible indeed. Dark creatures from the Chaos Halls. They were banished there once before, but Graal and Kradek-ka brought them back using blood-oil magick to open a portal! But I know their plans, Kell. I heard enough, before I was able to slip out down the passages into Skaringa Dak. I heard enough to bring the information to you!"

"Go on," said Kell, listening, brow furrowed. "But that part of your story where the mighty Kell saves Falanor and rides home on the arse-flanks of a pig carrying the severed heads of three Vampire Warlords in a tattered old onion sack, and sucking on the honeyed teat of a rescued virgin, well it needs to be excised right at the start."

"Grandfather, listen to her," said Nienna, sitting cross-legged on a stone. "What have you got to lose?"

"All our lives?" suggested Kell, but muttered something unheard and scratched his beard. At least the oily lake had sluiced him clear of blood, gore and vachine brains, vachine clockwork. He was feeling barely human, for a change. "Go on girl, let's hear it. Then I'll focus on getting my granddaughter clear of this unholy shit-hole, and back to some semblance of sanity."

"Not in Falanor, you won't," said Myriam, voice soft. She glanced down at Saark, face now relaxed in peace, then back to the old, grizzled warrior. "There are three of them. Kuradek the Unholy, with a passionate hatred for all human religions. His favourite pastime was slaughtering monks and ladies of the cloth; or even worse, changing them into vampires and letting them loose on their colleagues. He burned churches and temples to the ground, then would eat their ashes, laughing that his shit would be baptised in holy fire. Now, he intends to return to the northern city of Jalder. He will control the northern half of Falanor, and build up his army of albinos and... and *vampires*."

"They killed everybody in Jalder," said Kell, voice cold and hard. "I was there. I saw it."

"No, Kell. They killed *many* in Jalder. But men are more resilient than you give them credit. They hid. In cellars and attics and warehouses. In the sewer systems, in the shit cauldrons of the tanneries. Kell, many survived, trust me. Kuradek knows this, and he will hunt them down, turn them into his vampire slaves. Into parasitical puppets he can control."

Kell took a deep breath. He thought of his few friends in Jalder, old men, old warriors from back at Crake's Wall, Jangir Field, the Siege of Drennach, and the Battle of Valantrium Moor. If any could have survived the ice-smoke, then surely these were the men?

"I don't know," said Kell, slowly. "It was a miracle I survived the invasion. If it had not been for Ilanna..."

"This is what Graal told Kuradek. This is what I heard."

Kell nodded. "And what of the other two bastards? They going to set up a nursery and wean baby vampires with bottles of blood?"

"No, Kell. Meshwar the Violent will head south, rule Falanor's capital, the city of Vor. There, Graal believes even more rebels survived the ice-smoke invasion. There are thousands of tunnels beneath the city, a huge and sprawling complex. When Graal's invasion began, many fled into the tunnel and sewer network. Many hid. And Vor is vast, as you well know. It is Meshwar's job to hunt down these people, weed them out, turn them into his vampire horde."

"And the third?"

"Bhu Vanesh. The Eater in the Dark. He is a hunter, from the old days," said Myriam, and she rubbed at her eyes, weary now despite her vachine blood. Terror edged her words, and Kell noticed a slight tremor to her hand. If she was faking her fear, then she was a very good actress. But then, Kell had met many a good actress in his years of battle across Falanor. He'd killed a few, as well; on stage, and off.

"And what is his wonderful plan?"

"He will seek to take control of the Port of Gollothrim."

"Ship building?" said Kell darkly, brow furrowed. "He would seek to expand their dirty little empire west? He wants transport for his army, doesn't he, Myriam?"

"Yes. His albino slaves and vampires will take the existing navy, and also build him an extended fleet of ships. With this new, mammoth navy they will head west across the Salarl Ocean – expand their Vampire Dominion across the world!"

"What of Graal?"

"He will go with Bhu Vanesh. Oversee the ship-building. One could say he has been... demoted. Graal thought he could control the Vampire Warlords. But they are all-powerful. They have other plans."

"Graal always was an arrogant bastard. And I didn't get to carve my name on his arse with my axe. Not yet, anyways. Still, l at least carved him a new cheek flap."

"Graal was less than complimentary about that," said Myriam, flashing a dark smile. Her eyes met Kell's. "You understand what all this means, axeman? You *do* understand?"

Kell sighed. It was a sigh from deep down in a dark place weary of carrying the weight of the world. "I'm a retired soldier," he said. "I'm a simple man, a man of bread and cheese, of coarse wine and nostalgic memories of battle. It was never meant to be this way. I was supposed to live out my final years in Jalder, see this young lady through university, maybe travel the Black Pikes one last time before dotage crushed my rotten teeth in his fist, and watched my mind dribble out my ears."

"We have to stop them," said Nienna, who had been listening, quietly, head to one side. Her eyes flashed dark.

"We cannot," said Kell.

"You can!" snapped Nienna. "If anybody can halt this madness, Kell the Legend can!" Hope was bright in her eyes. Her hands and lips trembled. Her focus was complete.

Kell shook his head. "I'm an old man, Nienna," he said gently. "My back hurts in the cold. My knees hurt on stairs. My shoulder is an agony every time I lift the damned axe. And, and this will amuse you, Myriam, for it is your damn fault... the *poison* is still in my bloodstream. The poison *you* put there. Lingering, like a maggot under a rock."

"I gave you the antidote," said Myriam, her lips narrowing.

"Which does not always work?" Kell raised his eyebrows. Myriam remained silent, chewing her lip. "I thought not. With your eagerness to become a vachine, you killed me, woman, as sure as putting a dagger through my heart. Your antidote bought me time. But the evil liquor is still there: in my veins, in my organs, in my bones. I can feel it. Eating me, slow and hot, like an apothecary's acid."

"I am so, so sorry about that," said Myriam, but knew her words meant nothing. She had been dying, from a cancer riddling her every bone. To coerce Kell into helping her, she poisoned him with a rare toxin from a breed of *Trickla* flowers found far out west beyond the Salarl Ocean. Her antidote, however, had not been enough; or maybe the poison had been rampant in Kell's system for too long. What did he have now? Weeks? Months? A year? By saving herself, Myriam had effectively condemned Falanor's greatest hope. Falanor's last true hero. Myriam felt this irony slide through her like honey through a sponge, and she smiled a dry smile, a bitter smile. By her actions, Myriam may have condemned the world.

"I do not believe it," said Nienna finally, placing hands on hips. Her eyes were narrowed, brows dark with thunder. "Are you sure, grandfather? Sure about all this? I watched you fight those Soul Stealers. You killed them! Like they were children!"

Kell laughed sharply. "Oh, how the young do so romanticise. They almost had me, girl; if it had not been for Skanda's help, I would be slaughtered horse-meat on a butcher's worn wooden slab." His gaze transferred to Myriam. "You came here for help. To help yourself, yes, through fear of your new masters; but to help Falanor was an after-thought. I am sorry, Myriam. Battle weighs heavy on my old body, and my twisted mind. There is nothing I can do. For once, Falanor must help Herself."

Myriam bowed her head. Tears lay like silk on her cheeks. "So be it, Kell," she whispered.

They travelled for hours down narrow tunnels barely wide enough to accommodate Nienna. Eventually, when exhaustion crept upon Myriam, the hardy and seemingly tireless vachine, and Nienna was like the walking dead, they called a stop in a small alcove. It was cold, and damp, but then so were all the tunnels under Skaringa Dak.

Nienna lay, wrapped in a thin blanket, her finger stump throbbing. After an albino soldier amputated her finger in retaliation for Kell's defiance after they had been taken prisoner, events had moved so fast, so frantic, she had barely a moment to consider her new severance. But now. Now, despite her exhaustion, sleep would not come. Her eyes moved through the darkness lit by strange mineral lodes, and came to rest first on Kell, snoring, lost in the realms of distant dreams and memories and battles; then on to Myriam, breath hissing past her small, pointed fangs. Vampire fangs. *Vachine* fangs. Nienna rubbed at her finger, and winced as pain flared up her hand, up her arm. Kell had expertly stitched the wound, the *amputation,* slicing a flap of skin and pulling it over the neatly cut bone. He had tears in his eyes. Tears of sorrow, but also of guilt. He blamed himself. He felt completely responsible. And Nienna supposed he was, to a large extent; but then, if he was to blame for the loss of Nienna's little finger, he was also to blame for saving her life time after time after time. She could forgive him one small mistake, if mistake it was. She grimaced. In war, they all had to make sacrifices. And at least she was still alive.

Nienna rubbed her finger. It had been the most painful moment of her life, and the act of butchery, the look on the albino soldier's face – well, it was something she would never forget. Just like Kat's murder was something she would never forget. The vachine, the cankers, the soldiers, the battles – her grandfather striding with axe in hand, with *Ilanna* in hand, and turning from an affectionate old soldier, a retired old soldier, white-haired, funny, loving, ruffling her hair, cooking vegetable soup, polishing her boots with spit and polish and hard elbow grease, chastising her for neglecting her studies, nagging at her to smarten up her clothes, eat better food, be nice to her mother even when her mother shouted at her, neglected her, allowed her to starve. Nienna laughed bitterly. Oh yes. Her mother. A good strong woman, everybody said. A religious woman. Pious. When she died, she had earned a place in the Bright Halls. But Nienna remembered a different aspect to her character. Nienna's mother, Kell's daughter – Sara, the daughter who had disowned Kell and swore never to speak to him again. Well, to Nienna she was a cold woman. A hard woman. A woman of iron principles. A woman who made Nienna's flesh creep, made her hackles rise, a woman who'd made her life a misery with constant religious studies, muttered prayers and the eternal, submissive worshipping of the bloody gods!

Damn the gods, thought Nienna.

Let them burn in the furnaces of the Blood Void!

Let them rot in the Chaos Halls!

Yes. Kell might be a hard man, a drinker of whiskey, a pugilist, he might be a butcher and all the other things people called him – and what she had seen. But he had a core of goodness, Nienna knew. He had a kind heart. A kinder soul. And to her, no matter how others tried to deviate matters, he was still a hero. He was Kell. Kell, the Legend.

Sleep finally came.

And with it came a dream, a dark dream, a dream in which Bhu Vanesh hunted her, panting and giggling through a dark, deserted city, through empty streets and temples and cathedrals, running over slick greasy cobbles. And as he caught her, his fangs gleamed and he reached for her succulent throat...

As Nienna tossed and turned in her sleep, so Myriam's eyes flickered open. She uncurled, like a snake unfurling from the base of an apple tree. Myriam stood, and stretched, revelling in the feel of new muscles, new bones, and the death of the cancer within. How could cancer survive in a being which was itself a predator? A cancer on civilisation? How could cancer cells eat her own, when her new vachine cells were far more aggressive and vicious and violent than anything *Nature* could possibly conjure? Where Nature had failed, man had stepped forward. Myriam's eyes narrowed. In her opinion, the vachine were the pinnacle of evolution. It could get no better than this.

Gently, she reached down. Beneath Kell's arm was sheathed his Svian, his reserve blade for when Ilanna was lost. It was also, according to ancient, esoteric legends (although Kell would never admit it as such), a ritual suicide blade. For when times got bad. Real bad.

Myriam withdrew the Svian. The pattern of Kell's snoring altered, then he snorted and relaxed again, and she toyed with the blade for a few moments, running her finger up and down the razor edge. A bead of blood appeared on her pale white finger. She licked it clear, tongue stained berry-red for just an instant. Then it was gone, the blood-oil was gone, and she gave a little shiver.

Inside Myriam, something went *click*. She felt the rhythm of springs and counter-weights. She felt the spin of gears. She felt the stepping of advanced clockwork mechanisms, entwined with her flesh, her bones, her organs. And Myriam revelled in her *advanced evolution*.

Could she let anything get in the way of her vachine existence?

Could she let *Kell* get in the way?

Of course not.

And something pulsed deep in her mind. In her heart. In her *clockwork*.

She felt the need growing. Growing strong. And Myriam did so need to feed. It burned her, like a brand. Like birth. Like death. Like existence. *Existence*.

Myriam lifted the Svian blade. It glinted in the reflected luminescence of the mineral-layered walls.

Her eyes shifted to Kell.

And her smile was a cruel, bloodless slit...

TWO
Warlords

General Graal was sucked through the blood-magick lines, and it felt like dying, and felt like being born, and eventually he was lying on a cold tile floor in a kitchen, staring up at the smoke-stained, wood-beamed ceiling in the High Fortress at Port of Gollothrim. The *High Fortress*. He smiled a sickly smile. It was also known locally as *Warlord's Tower*.

The world was a blur for Graal. First, he could smell woodsmoke. Then he could smell the sea, a distant tang of salt, the taste of fresh sea breeze. Stunned, for the blood-oil magick *sending* was like being punched into the earth by the fist of a giant, Graal gradually fought for his senses to return. He heard distraught sobbing. He breathed, breathed deep, and inside him clockwork went *tick, tick, tick*.

Graal moved his head to the left. Kradek-ka lay unconscious, blood leaking from his eyes. His flesh was pale and waxen, and at first Graal thought he was dead – until he heard a tiny stepping of gears, witnessed the gentle rising of Kradek-ka's chest. Then Graal looked right, and jumped at the savagery of the sight...

Bhu Vanesh was there, seven feet tall, narrow, smoke-filled, long arms and legs crooked. One hand held a limp figure, a plump woman bent over backwards, blood dripping freely from where her throat had been entirely ripped out. Her eyes, dead glass eyes, were staring straight at Graal. He shivered. Bhu Vanesh turned a little, as if sensing Graal's return to consciousness. Blood-slit eyes regarded him, but Bhu Vanesh did not break from his task: the task of feeding. His second hand held another woman, this time slim, petite almost, and wearing the white apron of a kitchen attendant. She had long blonde hair, very fine, like silk, which spilled back from her tight entrapment revealing her throat, pale and punctured and quivering.

As Bhu Vanesh sucked vigorously on the plump woman, his eyes watched Graal. Graal stared back. Then Graal's gaze shifted to the slim blonde woman's eyes, and they were frightened, face contorted in pain. Her hands were clenching and unclenching, and for a moment Graal felt sympathy which was instantly dashed against the jagged towering shoreline of his cruelty.

Graal stood, and watched, and knew with a malicious joy that Bhu Vanesh was weak. Weak from the Chaos Halls. Weak from travelling the lines of blood-oil magick; the Lines of the Land.

Eventually, the plump woman closed her eyes. She shuddered. She died. Bhu Vanesh withdrew his fangs with squelches, and dropping the plump kitchen woman with a newly slashed throat, he lay the blonde on the kitchen tiles, and slit his own wrist with a talon. The black and grey smoke coiled back, and a thick syrup oozed free. He allowed this to drop into the slim blonde's mouth, and then knelt back on haunches and watched. Graal said nothing. There was nothing to say.

The blonde started to writhe and contort, her body spasming, trembling, muscles growing taut then slack, taut then slack. Black oil seemed to bubble at her mouth, then flowed out of her eyes and ears and quim, staining her white uniform and pooling under her body.

Graal looked left, out through a narrow window. He was uncomfortable watching the vampire change. It reminded him too much of his youth, and some very bad times. Bad times which had been excised from his memories – until now.

Graal observed the dawn, a wintry grey-blue sky. Distantly, he could make out the sea, and a phalanx of seagulls crying as they swept past his vision. Gollothrim. The Port of Gollothrim. The Fortress. Was it still occupied? Graal shivered. They'd soon find out...

Returning his gaze, he saw the transformation was complete. The blonde woman stood, and seemed uneasy in her shell. Her eyes were now black – jet black, and unnaturally glossy as if filled with a cankerous honey. This, this was the sign of a Vampire Warlord's servant. Graal remembered, now, his thoughts flowing back through a long history, a longer deviation.

"You." Graal was snapped back to the living, the present, and realised Bhu Vanesh was pointing at him. Graal stared for a moment, then glanced at the woman. She was smiling, showing her own vampire fangs. Dead, but alive. The undead. Not like the sophisticated clockwork vachine at all...

"Yes?" snapped Graal, anger flooding him. Anger, and bitterness, and regret. What had he done? He glanced down at the waxen figure of Kradek-ka. What had *they* done?

"Take Lorna to the Division General's quarters. He is here. I can smell his fear. Lorna will begin my recruitment. She is the First."

"Yes."

"And Graal?" Bhu Vanesh's voice was a low, low rumble. Those red eyes cut through Graal's nerve like an assassin's garrotte.

"Yes, Warlord?"

"Forget your manners again, and I will cut off your head and suck out your brains."

Graal paled. He bowed his head a fraction. "Yes, Warlord."

A winter sea breeze caressed the stone corridors of Port Gollothrim's High Fortress as Graal led Lorna, this newly baptised and transformed vampire, towards the central control point of this south-western Falanor city. Prior to the Vampire Warlords' resurrection, Graal's Army of Iron had not made it this far; which meant, in theory, the population of the city was sound. Those, that is, who had not fled after Vor was sundered.

Graal paused, and stared from a high window. Below, the city appeared deserted. And then he saw them, a group of rough-looking men down by the seafront. Huge walls lined the front, presumably to halt high tides or violent storms. Graal's eyes strayed, and he saw a woman, further down. She carried a babe in her arms, and walked quickly, nervously, looking often over her shoulder. She reached a small line of cottages and ducked quickly into a doorway. So. Port Gollothrim was still home to... Graal smiled. Fresh meat. Templates. Vampire templates. But where were the soldiers? Called away to fight his Army of Iron, in Vor? Possibly.

Graal rubbed his chin. His torn cheek was stinging, but even now he could feel accelerated vachine flesh knitting together. He would be healed by the next morning.

He felt Lorna's eyes on him. He turned. "What are you looking at?"

"A nervous man."

Graal stared, hard, then smiled a cold thin-lipped smile. "So, Lorna, bitch, Bhu Vanesh's First, born straight into our world of horror by simply being in the wrong place at the wrong time. You think you are so powerful? Let us see you perform. Perform, like a dancing monkey jerking on the puppeteer's strings."

Lorna's head tilted, and she observed Graal, and he felt the clockwork of his heart accelerate a little. Then she turned, and Graal led her no more. She moved fast, bare feet padding the cold stone flags, white kitchen apron stained with blood and the black gore from Bhu Vanesh's veins. Her neck showed the twin bites of the vampire. Her skin glowed in an ironic mockery of life.

Now, Graal followed. Lorna needed no guidance.

She accelerated, and Graal had to jog to keep up. Down long corridors, up steps, until they burst into the Division General's chambers and surprised the five men there. Division General Dekull stood beside a large polished oak table, with four other men; all wore military uniforms of black and silver bearing the Falanor crest. The table was filled with maps, and several glasses of half-drained wine.

Dekull, a large man with bull-neck and over-red complexion, thinning brown hair and large hands, stared for a moment in abject confusion. "Who the hell are you?" he growled, red-face forming into the frown of a man who did not take interruptions lightly. Then Lorna squealed in sudden bloodlust, real *blood* lust, and a burst of energy fired her and leapt at him, fastening arms and legs around him, teeth lusting for his jugular. He staggered back, knocking the table over. Wine spilled across maps. He tried to grapple with the newborn vampire, but there came a sudden *crack* as she snapped his arm like tinder, and Division General Dekull screamed, high-pitched and animal, and this slammed the other men into action. They drew swords and charged as Graal watched impassively from the doorway.

Four swords slashed at Lorna in quick succession, as her knees came up, bare feet on Dekull's chest and she kicked up and backwards, through a somersault, landing behind one soldier. Swords clanged together in discord. Lorna's fist punched into one man, and *through* him, bursting free of his chest in a splatter of blood. She stood, holding his jiggling body upright, then let him fall as the three remaining men leapt back, faces uncertain, eyes narrowed. Lorna took a long lick of slick blood from her elbow to her still-clenched fist. Her black eyes gleamed.

"Come on," she growled, voice feral and husky.

One man screamed and charged, and she deflected his sword blow on her left arm where the razor-edge peeled her skin back like flesh from soft-braised pork. Her right hand dropped, grabbed his crotch, and ripped back hard detaching chainmail trews, penis and testes in one mangled lump. The other two men edged towards the door, then one, Command Sergeant Wood, turned and kicked his way savagely through the leaded window. He climbed out onto a high ledge and disappeared from view. The final man dropped his sword with a clatter. Division General Dekull was kneeling, blood pooled around him, nursing his broken arm. Bone protruded from flesh, a savage break, a sharp stick pointing at the roof.

Lorna strode to the surrendered soldier, and knelt before him. She seemed almost tender. The man, a young commissioned officer named Shurin, trembled as urine leaked down his legs and pooled around his feet. It stank bad.

"I didn't mean it," Shurin whispered, eyes imploring. "I beg forgiveness."

"There is no forgiveness," said Lorna, and he was on his knees before her and she took his face in her hands, a palm against each cheek and she was smiling and Shurin's piss gurgled as it swilled around them, and she pulled his face towards her, as if they were parted lovers returned for a final kiss; then she lowered her fangs, and they sank into his flesh, and he screamed and began to kick, to struggle savagely in the nature of any trapped beast and the piss-stink of the coward. Lorna sucked Shurin, and drank him hard, and left his deflated corpse like a limp doll on the flagstones.

Lorna stood. She licked blood from her lips. She radiated power.

Graal was examining his fingernails, his air one of debonair cool, his eyes detached from the bloody scene before him. He knew the situation; understood it inherently. Until Lorna killed, and fed, she was not true vampire. Now, with this fresh intake of blood, she was almost there. Almost. Now, in the same way the vachine used clockwork to finalise their victims' transformation to vachine, Lorna had to make her own slave; her own *ghoul*. It was the Law of the Vampire. One of the Old Laws. For the vampires were a race of the enslaved...

Lorna was advancing on the barely conscious figure of Division General Dekull. His broken arm cast odd shadows against the wall. Outside, the winter sun was a copper pan pushed into the sky.

"You missed one."

"What?" Lorna's head snapped round.

Graal looked up. Gestured to the window. "You missed one. Sloppy."

"I saw no help from *you*," she snarled, blood still slick on her fangs and causing her frail blonde hair to clump in rat tails around her face.

"This is not my freakshow," smiled Graal, coolly, and turned his back, departing the chamber to look for Kradek-ka. Behind him, he heard Lorna's soothing words. First, he heard the *crack* as Lorna put Dekull's arm back in line. His scream shook the rafters. Then she fed, and fed him her blood, and in so doing spread the black blood of Bhu Vanesh, from killer to victim. She spread the disease. Spread the curse.

It was night.

Graal sat in his large, almost regal sleeping chambers, nursing a glass of port at a smooth-waxed redwood table. Across from him sat Kradek-ka, face still battered from his collision with a jagged mountain wall. He looked far from his usual composed, serene self.

Outside, a large pale moon hung in the sky like a pancreas cut free by a drunk surgeon. Yellow light filtered into the sleeping chamber, and tumbled lazily across Graal and Kradek-ka's sombre features.

"So it is done," said Kradek-ka, and took a drink from his glass. Graal nodded, and rubbed his eyes. Bhu Vanesh's vampiric plague had swept through the High Fortress in less than a day. Now, he had a hundred and fifty vampire slaves, a jagged hierarchy ruled over by Lorna and Division General Dekull. Dekull had shown himself to be a formidable taker to the cause; and of course, once he was under Bhu Vanesh's control, the Vampire Warlord instantly had access to Dekull's emotions, his thoughts and, more importantly, memories. The instant Bhu Vanesh's blood was in Dekull's veins, they shared a hive mind. Bhu Vanesh knew the layout of the High Fortress, the Port of Gollothrim, the details of Falanor army units, and everything else of military interest. He had absorbed the Division General's mind. This was one of his *talents*.

And now, night had come.

Bhu Vanesh lifted the portcullis, and with the baleful yellow moon glaring down like a disapproving eye of the gods, had pointed out into the city. Before him, arranged on a cobbled court-yard, were a hundred and fifty vampires. They were soldiers, stablehands, cooks and cleaners. Each wore twin marks at their throat. Each had gloss black eyes. Each could smell fresh blood. Out there, in the city, in the world…

"Expand my slaves," said Bhu Vanesh, stalking back from the portcullis, head bobbing a little, legs working with curious joints and making him even less than human. Not that it took much imagination. In the gloom, the flowing smoke of his flesh was even more pronounced.

Silently, the flood of newborn vampires headed into the night, spreading out, disseminating, each on a personal mission of feed-ing and violent coercion.

"It's done," agreed Graal. Bitterness was in his mind, on his tongue, in his soul. He licked his own vampire fangs. The feeling from Bhu Vanesh was tangible. He hated not just humans, but the albinos *and* the vachine. His arrogance was total. To Bhu Vanesh, everything that walked or crawled was inferior. A slave. There to be used, toyed with, and ultimately consumed as food.

"We must take him. Take them all! Send them back to the Chaos Halls!" Kradek-ka had the light of madness in his dark va-chine eyes. He was a Watchmaker! A Royal Engineer of Silva Valley! He was not used to being a slave…

"Sh!" snapped Graal. He glanced around the chamber. He gave a narrow smile. "I think our elite brethren are the kind to employ many, many ears. Let us just say I understand your frustration, and I agree with your train of thought. What we must do is strike when he is at his weakest."

"With each new slave, he grows stronger. With each drop of fresh blood, he grows more ferocious! You know the legends as well as I, Graal. What I want to know is why the magick failed us? Why, by all the gods, did we lose control?"

Graal shook his head. "It was a cheap dice-trick. A card con, like the sailors pull down on the docks. Who wrote the ancient texts? The servants of the Warlords. They wove betrayal into the narrative, after all, who would summon them back without be-lieving in their own mastery? What incentive in being a slave? A puppet? We were cheated, Kradek-ka. And our arrogance, and greed, allowed us to be cheated. Without our efforts, without our lust for power, the vachine would have remained in Silva Valley.

We were kings of a small pond; now we are fucking slaves, just like the rest of them."

"*'Thus how thee mightye are crushed lyke shelles againste thyr throynes,'*" misquoted Kradek-ka, and poured himself another glass from the crystal decanter. The port glimmered, like blood, in his glass. Somewhere, out in the city, a human gave a terrible scream. Several cracking sounds followed. Then a deep silence flooded back in.

Graal and Kradek-ka's eyes met.

"How do we solve this, and still remain dominant?" said Kradek-ka.

"Our first step is to kill Bhu Vanesh."

Kradek-ka nodded, and nursed his drink, and listened to the vicious hunting far out in the darkness.

Command Sergeant Wood sat on the roof of the High Fortress, the Warlord's Tower, and brooded. His short sword sat across his knees, and he squatted, huddled beneath his thick army shirt, shivering uncontrollably. Not just from the cold, the wind, the ice, but from everything he had witnessed. And more. The things he could see unfolding in the city beneath him. Horrible things. Nightmare things.

King Leanoric was dead. That was news he handled well. Even the invasion, the Army of Iron – unbeatable, invincible! – as a soldier, this was information which he could grit his teeth and try to plan for. Blood-oil magick. Ice smoke. Cankers. All these things Command Sergeant Wood had witnessed, and fought, and after Leanoric was smashed at the Battle of Old Skulkra, Command Sergeant Wood – with several platoons of elite men – had headed south to warn his superiors. But their way south had been blocked by hundreds of cankers, snarling, roaming free. It took Wood and his men three days to circle the beasts, and they had two encounters which lost Wood six men. It had been a grim time. But still, a time Wood could fight with fist and sword and mace. But now? Now this… *abomination*.

Command Sergeant Wood observed the city below. The Port of Gollothrim. The city of his childhood. A city he loved with all his heart, all his soul. As a boy he had run riot through the narrow cobbled streets, stealing from market traders, organising other orphans and vagabonds into a tight unit that preyed on rich merchants and dealers in silks, spices and diamonds. He was caught at the age of sixteen after robbing a spice magnate, who died from a heart attack during the robbery, and Wood was sentenced to hang. But he'd been rescued from the gallows by a kindly old Captain, Captain Brook, and afterwards joined Brook's Company as a helper, sharpening swords, oiling armour, cooking for the men. Now, here, Command Sergeant Wood had risen as far through the non-commissioned ranks as a soldier could go. He was tough as an old boot left for months in the desert sun, harder than the thick steel nails which held together the Falanor Royal Fleet. But Wood had a soft spot for his men, and even more so, his *city*. The Port of Gollothrim. *His fucking city!* Which was under attack from within...

Command Sergeant Wood had fought cankers and vachine, so he was not averse to surprises. The speed with which the High Fortress was taken was hard for Wood to comprehend, and to *accept*. But even more so, was the changing of people into these... *creatures*.

Wood spat on the high roof, and his eyes tracked a vampire through the distant streets below. There came a tinkling, the smash of glass, and the vampire entered through the window. Wood heard screams. He shook in rage, his fists clenched, eyes narrowed. Then, silence flooded up to him through the icy darkness.

"You were a hard one to find," said Lorna, and Wood uncurled smoothly from his crouch on the edge of the High Fortress roof. His eyes moved beyond her, but she was alone.

Despite his size, his barrel chest, his large hands powerful enough to crush the spine of any man he'd fought, Wood leapt nimbly down to the flat roof, slick with damp and ice, and slashed his sword several times through the air.

"You come here for me to teach you a lesson, girl?"

She laughed at that. A pretty, tinkling sound. She ran a hand through her fine blonde hair, and her claws lengthened, her fangs gleaming under the baleful yellow moon.

"I think it's the other way round, Command Sergeant *Wood*."

"So you know my name."

"You will make an extremely useful addition to our ranks. After I play with you. After I *suck you*." She grinned at him, eyes mischievous, and he reddened. Wood was not a man comfortable with sex. Never had been, never would be.

He smiled grimly. *Join your ranks? I'd rather die first. Rather cut my own throat with a rusty fucking razor. Rather string myself up by the balls! But... Hopefully, it wouldn't come to that.*

She attacked, fast, in the blink of an eye – and came up short, almost impaling herself on the point of Wood's sword. She backflipped way, then moved sideways, and Wood tracked her.

"You move fast for a fat man," she said.

"Come closer, girl. I'll show you a little bit more."

She snarled, and her gloss black eyes narrowed. Then she charged, in a series of bounds, and leapt ducking under Wood's slashing sword, but he slammed a left hook that pounded her head, knocking her sideways into a straight right that spread her nose across her face. Wood's boot smashed her head, and even as she hit the stone he stamped on her chest, then her face. She lay stunned, and Wood moved swiftly, picking her lithe, seemingly frail body up and lifting it high above his head. He leapt onto the battlements edging the roof of the High Fortress, and gazed down to the distant cobbles of the courtyard.

"Bhu Vanesh will kill you for this!" Lorna mumbled through broken teeth. Her shattered, swollen cheeks changed the shape of her face. Wood gave a short nod.

"He should come find me himself, then," snapped the old soldier, in the same military bark that had sent hundreds of men scuttling across many a desolate parade ground. His powerful shoulders bunched and he launched Lorna into the air. He watched her fall with interest, and when she hit the cobbles it was with a sickening crack. Wood fetched his sword, then returned to the edge of the roof. Glancing down, he watched Lorna start to move, her broken, snapped shape starting to writhe, beginning to squirm. Somebody ran to her, and she gradually climbed disjointedly to her feet and glared up at him.

"Hell's balls!" Wood snapped, and ran for the far end of the roof. Here, he knew, there was a tunnel he could use to escape. But what to do? Where to go? How could he fight such creatures? How could they *die?*

And it came, in a flash of brilliance. Of inspiration.

He would travel the city, and gather to him those who still lived. The criminals, the smiths, the soldiers, the market traders. And they would arm themselves.

And they would fight this scourge.

With a new objective, a *military objective*, Command Sergeant Wood loped off into the darkness.

Jalder was Falanor's major northern city and once a trading post connecting east, south and west military supply routes, known as the Northern T. Sitting just south of the formidable Black Pike Mountains, and separated by the Iron Forest, Jalder had been the first city hit when the vachine invaded south from the mountains and their stronghold, Silva Valley, and using their albino ranks, the Army of Iron.

Since that invasion, where General Graal had used a mixture of blood-oil magick and cunning, first to take out the northern scouts and guards, then to infiltrate Jalder's Northern Garrison and slay the entire regiment based there with not a single loss of life to his own army – *since* those days, months earlier, since the flooding of magick summoned *ice-smoke* which chilled and killed, and allowed soldiers to run riot capturing and murdering the vast majority of Jalder citizens – well, for those that remained, life had been unbearably hard.

It could have been expected that all would die, such was the hardship in Jalder. The ice-smoke froze people in their beds, froze traders selling wares at market stalls, murdered children playing in the street. And those not killed had been rounded up by the Army of Iron, and even worse, many were eaten when a unit of rogue cankers broke free and rampaged through the streets, ripping out throats and snapping off heads.

The Army of Iron had moved south, leaving behind a token garrison of three hundred albino warriors and five ethereal, ghostly Harvesters in order to patrol the deserted city of Jalder, mopping up stragglers and warning Graal of any military activity behind his advancing lines.

Twelve weeks had passed.

And incredibly, some people had survived.

They lived in sewers, and attics, in the tanneries and deserted fish-stores, they scuttled like cockroaches beneath the floorboards of once-rich, proud dwellings, they hid in the towers of Jalder University, in the dungeons of Jalder's Marble Palace, in the Dazoon Clocktower and the old guild spice-houses. They scrabbled for food like vermin, dressed in rags, their weapons rusted. But they survived. They *existed*. And slowly, warily, they began to fight back.

The resistance was led by a small, narrow-faced man known simply as Ferret. He was slim, wiry, but incredibly strong for his size after a life of hardship as a thief, a pit-fighter, and later in His Majesty's Prisons, including a stint in the terribly harsh *Black Pike Mines*. What Ferret lacked in brawn he made up for with speed and accuracy, dirty-fighting and the ability to use his mind. In those first days when the ice-smoke rolled through Jalder, he had been safe in the dungeons – until two albino soldiers went through the cells systematically killing all prisoners. When they came to Ferret, he'd been curled in a ball in the corner of his cell, crying, begging for his life, covered in snot and sores. The two soldiers opened the cell, and one studied his nails whilst the second moved in for the kill – gurgling as Ferret leapt forward, out-stretched fingers punching through and *into* the soldier's throat. He took the dying warrior's sword, hefted it thoughtfully, and split the second albino's skull straight down the middle with a single blow. Turning back to the first man, with finger-holes through his oesophagus pouring white blood, Ferret took hold of his hair and hacked free his head.

Three months ago.

Three months!

How things had changed. How life in Jalder had changed for those poor unfortunates still left. The Harvesters roamed the streets, directing the patrols. Many of the humans remaining were soon killed… killed and *harvested*. The old, frail, weak, scared. The children had proved resilient; good at hiding, and learning quickly to kill in packs with youthful ferocity, and without remorse.

And gradually, they had all come to Ferret. This small man, this skinny man, with his lank brown hair and pockmarked features like the arse of a pig. He was one of the downtrodden, one of the underdogs. But hell, Ferret had come good. Ferret had shown that it was all about *the mind*. All about planning, and thinking, and instruction. Not simply violence, but the *planning* of violence.

Ferret gathered those stray and directionless men and women and children to him; he organised them into groups, the children into food foraging parties, the woman into units who practised with swords and bows during the day, and mended armour and fashioned arrows by night. They discovered underground tunnels near the river, and set nets to catch fish thus providing fresh food and protein. They used the old furnace chambers of the tanneries to cook their food, so that smoke and fumes would be carried up high brick chimneys and away on distant winds. They slept, huddled together under old furs and blankets the children found in rich merchants' houses, and always with weapons to hand. Once, a unit of five albino soldiers found a sleeping pit – the battle had been fierce, but short, with twenty people slaughtered including one of Ferret's trusted "Generals", as he liked to call those he promoted and put in charge.

In those first days, the resistance had numbered maybe five hundred: the strays in the sewers, those hiding in attics and cellars, shivering in the cold dark places. Now, they were no more than two hundred. Slowly, systematically, they had been rooted out and killed. It depressed Ferret more than he could ever admit, and now, as he sat in his little control centre deep within an old tannery building, cold, silent, the huge cauldrons empty, the fires gone out, he waited with three of his Generals for his best weapon, his most trusted ally, his most vicious soldier – a twelve year-old girl they called Rose. Beautiful on the outside, but sharp with thorns beneath.

Rose was a slim, quiet thing. But she had proved herself time and again as the most capable *soldier* in Ferret's resistance. She was superb at gathering intelligence: where albino soldiers would patrol, if there would be Harvesters, what was happening in the outside world. She had her own routes through the city, and Ferret did not ask. Her results were what counted, and Ferret did not need to know the details.

All he knew about Rose was that her parents had been killed when she was young, maybe four or five years, and she had survived in the city from that early age on her wits and intelligence and intuition. She was a born killer, despite her angelic appearance. She was dangerous beyond compare.

Her tiny bare feet pattered down the corridor, and Rose glided into view; warily, for she was always wary; but with an easy and confident manner. She was a girl in tune with this odd underground environment.

"Hello, Rose."

"Ferret," she said, her dark eyes glancing to the Generals, then around the room. "Nice hideout."

"You have information?"

"Of course. You have payment?"

"Yes." Ferret smiled, his narrow face breaking into genuine humour. *Never trust anybody who did something for free*, he thought. With Rose, he had to buy her information. Usually with precious stones, which he had children through the city scouring rich merchants' deserted houses to find so he could keep this particular human gem in active service.

Ferret tossed her a small velvet bag of rubies. "Here you go."

Rose snatched the bag from the air, and looked around suspiciously. She frowned, then seemed to relax. Ferret tuned in to her senses; he had never seen her frown. Was there something wrong? Had she seen, or sensed, something he had not?

Ferret felt his alertness kick up a few degrees. He loosened his sword and knife at his belt, but kept the smile on his face for Rose. He glanced to the three Generals; all huge men and proven warriors, despite their soiled garb. It was hard to keep clean fighting from the sewers. They stunk like three-week-dead dogs. All except Rose, that is. She was perfectly clean, her simple black clothes fresh as virgin snowfall, her shoulder-length black hair neatly brushed. Nothing about her indicated a covert lifestyle of information gathering, and the secret murder of albino soldiers.

Rose tipped the rubies onto her small, white hand. They looked wrong, somehow, sitting there in the girl's palm. Then, in one swift movement she ate them, swallowing with a grimace, and glancing up to Ferret. She allowed the velvet bag to drop to the stone floor.

"The albinos know where you are," said Rose.

Ferret felt a thrill of fear course through him, tugging his senses like drugsmoke, pounding through his head, flowing like molten lead through his veins.

"What? This place? They know about *this place*?"

"Yes," said Rose, and glanced around. As if nervous. Ferret had never seen her do that before; never seen her portray anything but the utmost calm, secure in her knowledge that she was unobserved, had not been followed. Now. Now she was different. She was out of character. Ferret grimaced, as he realised the emotion she carried like raw guilt. Rose was *scared*. "They are coming for you," she added, almost as an afterthought.

"Tonight?"

"No. Now. *Now!*"

Even as the words brushed past her lips on a warm exhalation of air, so there came a scream of bricks and torn steel, and a shower of rubble cascaded into the underground chamber. Bricks clattered in the control centre, dust billowed, and Ferret and his generals had drawn weapons, were standing ready, as one *of the vampires* leapt snarling from the dust, so fast it was a blur, hitting one general in the chest and bearing him to the ground with talons slashing open his throat. The large man convulsed, started to thrash, choking on his own blood, on geysers of blood as he flopped around, arms and legs kicking, but pinioned to the ground as if the vampire was a heavy weight.

Ferret licked dust-rimed lips. The vampire was tall, thin, with white skin and a near-bald head. Long ears swept back, and it turned a narrow, elongated face towards him, eyes red, fangs poking over its lips and with a start, with a *jump* that nearly kicked his balls through his belly, Ferret realised this was Old Terrag, once a butcher down on the markets by the Selenau River, an expert with a cleaver by all accounts, and now an integral part of the resistance in Jalder. Old Terrag was one of Ferret's most trusted men. Now, he had changed...

The vampire snarled, lowering its head as the cut-open general slowly ceased his thrashing, blood dropping from fountain to bubbling brook, and with a blink the huge war hammer hit the vampire in the face, sending it catapulting in a flurry of limbs across the room. Ferret glanced at Blaker, and gave a nod. The huge general had kept his wits about him and crept through the billowing dust. Even when Ferret had not. *Shit. That won't happen again. Well, over my dead body. Especially over my dead body!*

Ferret glanced back to Rose, but the young girl had gone. "Damn," he snarled, as the vampire hit him in the back and his face smacked the stone floor, hard. Stars flashed through his skull, and he was blinded. He could hear scuffling, hissing, snarling, and Ferret jacked himself up and began to crawl. There came a *crack*, like wood breaking, and a terrible scream. This was finished off with a gurgle. Ferret searched around for his sword, and as his vision cleared his fingers curled around the short, sturdy blade. He found a wall, and realised most of the lanterns had gone out. Smashed. Only one weak flame burned, and Ferret scrambled around until his back was to the wall, and he crouched there, sword touching the ground, looking, listening. *Use your brain, damn you! Think!*

Three generals. Two definitely dead. And a hammer blow to the face for the attacking bastard. A blow which should have cracked the vampire's skull in two like a fruit on a chopping block, had simply stalled it for seconds. *What have they done to you, Old Terrag? What did they make you?* But Ferret knew. He'd read the stories. He'd heard the old tales, warped and twisted fantasies passed down through generations. Old Terrag was a *vampire*. And much, much stronger than the albino soldiers who patrolled the streets of Jalder making Ferret's life miserable.

There came a roar, and Dandig attacked with his axe. Ferret squinted, saw something squirm through the dust and still spilling rubble from the hole in the roof. The two figures clashed, one a huge bear of a man, his neck as wide as Ferret's thigh, his biceps not much thinner, a black-hearted bastard of a killer who only obeyed Ferret because he didn't know where the gold was kept – or in fact, that there was no gold at all. The axe swept for Old Terrag, who swayed back, changing direction, leaping, bouncing from the wall and launching at Dandig from above. Clawed hands took hold of Dandig's head, as the axe on its return sweep made a *humming* noise lashing under Old Terrag's elongated, stretched out body. And whilst still airborne, the vampire twisted Dandig's head, and Ferret waited for the *snap* of breaking neck but it was worse, much worse as the vampire kept on twisting and tendons crackled and popped and the head *came clean off*. Blood fountained. Dandig's confused body collapsed like a sack of sloppy shit.

Ferret tried to lick his lips, but could not. Fear had drained him of spit.

Old Terrag straightened, *damn, he'd always been a tall bastard*, and stared for a while at the pumping body on the floor. The head had rolled off into the shadows, and Ferret knew the man would have been completely pissed off. Dandig wasn't a man used to losing.

Ferret fought down the urge to splutter a histrionic giggle.

Old Terrag turned that blood gaze on Ferret and his balls retracted to pips. "Your turn, Ferret," hissed the vampire and Ferret was frozen, a statue, a carving from ice, and the vampire launched at him and he wanted to scream and curl up in a ball, to crawl away to some dark recess and lie there until he decomposed. *There there, Fador, soothed his mother and tucked him under the thick sheep-wool blanket but the dark was all around, those tales from Uncle Grimmer still vivid and bright in his child's colourful imagination, the clockwork vampires and clockwork werebeasts creeping through the dark with talons longer than a man's forearm... prowling... ready to strike...*

He blinked, and Old Terrag was on him, flying at him, arms out-stretched and he jerked up his sword in sheer panic, no timing, no skill, just a flurry of scrabbling and movement and the blade flashed and Old Terrag impaled himself on the blade. Ferret heard steel bite through flesh, through bone, through muscle, sliding through Old Terrag's chest, through his heart, to exit on shards of spine.

They squatted there, together, like lovers, and Old Terrag's out-stretched clawed fingers took hold of Ferret's face and their eyes met. Ferret licked his lips. The vampire was shivering on the sword, impaled, and Ferret could see the tip of his blade on the other side of the vampire's body. Old Terrag trembled, and hatred etched the drawn back skin of his face, *its face*. Ferret thought he was dead, then. It still had the strength to twist off his head. Like it did with Dandig. Shit.

Then Old Terrag closed his eyes, and smiled, and died.

Ferret waited for a minute, waited to see what would happen. Then he scrambled from underneath the body and put his boot on the vampire's chest, withdrawing the short sword. Its heart. He had pierced its heart!

He leant against the wall for a few moments, breathing heavily, then wiped sweat mixed with brick-dust from his brow, leaving a muddy red smear on his sleeve.

"You can cut off their heads, as well," came the gentle voice of Rose, as she emerged from the dust.

Ferret coughed, and snorted snot to the ground. "You've seen them killed?"

"A few," she said. "The eastern quarter of the city is all but over-run. All your rebels." She smiled, sadly. "All of them... *changed*."

"How are they changed? With magick?"

"With a bite. To the neck. Then they seem to die, and they come back to life and are quick, and strong, and hard to kill. As you saw." She glanced at the three twisted corpses of Ferret's Generals; three hardy men, grim men, men who had slaughtered albino sol-diers for fun. But one vampire had killed all three. And would have killed Ferret, if not for a twist of fate. Of luck.

"Shit. We have gone to the Bone Graveyard!"

"No. We are in Jalder. You must tell your people. They will lis-ten to you. You must tell them how to fight. How to kill..." She glanced at the corpse of Old Terrag. Already, it had gone black, crinkled as if cooked, and the stench was unbearable. "How to kill these creatures."

"I will," said Ferret. "Come with me, Rose."

"No."

"It's death out there!"

"I know." She smiled. "But I have things I must do."

His name was Vishniriak. He was a Harvester. He was a leader amongst the Harvesters. He came from under the Black Pike Mountains and was tall, wearing thin white robes embroidered with gold religious symbols and threads. His face was flat and oval, his head hairless, his nose tiny slits which hissed when he breathed. And eyes... small black eyes without emotion, but glittering with a feral intelligence.

He stood on the battlements overlooking the city of Jalder, and the wind howled, and his robes flapped and whipped, snapping viciously. He turned to his left, and stared at Kuradek the Vampire Warlord with tiny black eyes.

Hate flowed through him.

Vishniriak, and the Harvesters, hated the Vampire Warlords. But he knew they were tools. And a good workman uses the best of tools.

To the Harvesters, the Vampire Warlords were the best of tools.

"Send them," said Kuradek, his flesh swirling, flowing, and Vishniriak knew that one day there would be a reckoning, and one day they would fight; but now. Now they were allies. With a single goal.

Vishniriak looked down into the courtyard, the same place where months earlier a flood of albino soldiers, the Army of Iron, had marched down into the city of Jalder under cover of ice-smoke and slaughtered most of the population, corpses ready for the *Harvest*.

Now, there were nearly a hundred vampires, pickings from the hardiest men and women and children who had stood against the albino soldiers still active in the city. But not now. Not now.

It had been fascinating for Vishniriak to watch, and no matter how much he hated the vampires in principle the domino effect of their transformation had been stunning and swift. Kuradek had found three humans, infecting them, making them his primaries, his ghouls, then sent them out to find and infect others. Like a plague they swept through the eastern quarter of Jalder. Until none were left.

It had taken two nights.

Now, they would ease out into the city like a brass medical needle penetrating a succulent vein.

And they would hunt. They would convert. They would feed.

Until no humans remained.

THREE
Zone

"I hope you're not going to use that?" Nienna's voice was gentle. And very, very close.

Myriam started, and turned, her movement reflected in the Svian blade. "Child. You move quiet for a... mortal." She smiled. The irony was not lost on Nienna. Myriam glanced down at Kell, snoring gently, face relaxed in sleep, just another old man. Another retired soldier. How easy it was to be deceived, for Myriam knew he was the greatest killer on the continent. She moved to replace the knife in Kell's under-arm sheath, and with a *slap* her wrist was enclosed in Kell's mighty fist. Despite her accelerated vachine strength, the power of the clockwork, Kell's grip was like a steel shackle and she could not move. He opened one eye.

"Finished your game?" he growled.

"No game," said Myriam.

"I wondered if you'd try."

"Maybe I'm not that foolish," she said, and winced as the grip tightened, forcing her to drop the blade – which Kell took from her, neatly, and sheathed it with a whisper of oiled steel on leather.

"Maybe you are," he said, sitting up and releasing her. She rubbed her pale flesh, glancing at the angry-red welts where his fingers had crushed her.

"You're still strong, for an old man."

"Better believe it," he grunted, and stood. He kicked Saark, who opened an eye to observe Kell like a lizard from a hot rock.

"Come on, dandy," he growled. "We're moving out."

"You could have just told me."

"I find a boot up the arse infinitely more persuasive."

"I was having such sweet dreams, of a buxom young tavern wench I once entertained. She could do amazing things with fresh cream and cracked eggs. You should have seen the foam!"

Kell stared at him. "So then, even your new vachine blood has done nothing to kill your wayward libido?"

"If anything, Kell, it has made me more rampant!" Saark stood, and smiled, and stretched himself, muscles aching from an uncomfortable, cramping sleep. But at least he could stand. At least he could stretch. "Now, my old and bedraggled friend, I can do it all night." He touched his chest, tenderly, remembering the savage wound and his near-death experience. He cast it from his mind. It no longer mattered; he was not dead. He was alive. And he was going to drink deep from the cup of hedonistic fulfilment.

"Yes." Kell coughed. "Well. Be careful where you stick it. You've gotten in enough bloody trouble already."

"Like I always prophesied," announced Saark, brightly, "you are the miserable, moaning voice of doom! You should learn to lighten up, Kell. Look at me, heroically skipping along the jaws of death and you don't hear me whining like a little girl with a broke skipping rope. But you, Kell, Kell the mighty Legend, after all we've been through and lived and endured, still you're bleating like a lamb on a cliff ledge without its mama. It's like adventuring with my fucking grandma. What next? A stick? Incontinence trews? Senility? Oh, but you're already holding hands with *that* old goat." He winked.

Kell snorted, and scowled, but did not reply. Saark was right, but Kell could not help but have dark thoughts. It was simply the way he was built. With age came great wisdom. It also came with a great amount of moaning. Kell snorted again, and cursed the day he'd met the dandy.

Nienna moved to Saark, and touched his breast lightly. "How do you feel? How's the wound now?"

"Healing," said Saark, and pressed his own hand to the chest-wound. "Myriam's drugs helped me sleep." His eyes moved to the now-beautiful vachine, with her long dark curls and flashing, dangerous eyes. She stepped out into the tunnel, surveying the route ahead. Her hips were wide, legs powerful, waist narrow, breasts full beneath a tight leather jerkin. Saark licked his lips. "I had very sweet dreams," he said, finger lifting to touch his tongue, and then dropping to touch his chest unconsciously.

Nienna saw the look and gesture, and said nothing, but frowned, and turned away. Back to Kell. "Do you trust Myriam?" Her voice was quiet, and she watched Saark move down the tunnel towards the newly changed vachine. She felt a sudden bitterness then, for they had a connection now; a bonding. They were both newly changed, both a *different* breed to the human. Myriam and Saark were vachine. Whereas she, Nienna, was human. Human, and young, and weak. Too young for Saark. Her eyes narrowed again. For a fleeting moment she wished Shanna and Tashmaniok, the Soul Stealers, had bitten *her*, changed *her* into vachine. Shared their blood-oil. Shared their clockwork. Infected her with their disease. *Then* Saark would have shared with her. He would have looked at her in a different light. Nienna's eyes gleamed.

Kell rubbed his neck, and rolled his shoulders, then his hips, groaning as he worked at the stiffness which came after sleep. "I trust her as much as I've always trusted the conniving bitch. Which is to say, not at all. But what option do we have? She says she can guide us from this place. If she lies, well then, I'll cut her head from her vachine shoulders and we'll make our own way out."

"That would be... interesting," said Nienna.

"So you want her dead, now?"

"Not dead. Just out of the picture." Nienna crossed to Saark, and touched his arm. He turned to her, lightly, a laugh on his handsome face. The gaunt look of the near-dead was fading. His accelerated vachine healing was kicking in fast. He no longer looked like a walking corpse; health and strength had returned. He took Nienna's hand, but was still talking to Myriam.

Kell watched all this, and growled a low growl as realisation struck him. There was something there, between Nienna and Saark. Or at least, there was something there from Nienna. Previously, Kell had always focused on the dandy and his machinations towards Kat, Nienna's older friend, for that had been the obvious flirtation. It had taken his eye from the more subtle approaches of his granddaughter.

"Horse shit," said Kell, and spat on the tunnel floor. "Come on!" His voice was loud and brash. "Let's get moving. You sure it's this way, Myriam, my sweet little angel?"

Myriam gave him a strange look. Her lips curled into half-smile, half-grimace. There was a question in her eyes but Kell stared back, a hard look, a dark look. The same look Dake the Axeman got shortly before his head was cut from his mighty, heroic shoulders.

Myriam shrugged. "Yes. Two days, by my reckoning. Although I'm not sure what we'll do when we get there, the river is too fast to swim, although there are some albino storerooms nearby. Let's hope they're not full of soldiers, hey?"

"Makes no odds to me," grunted Kell. "One way or another, we'll be passing through." He lifted Ilanna, and his meaning was obvious. Myriam did not miss the inherent threat.

"Let's move, then," she said.

When they stopped for the night, it was warmer, and Myriam found some shards of crate for a fire. "It'll be smelt for miles around," muttered Kell unhelpfully, but did not stop her lighting it. They all needed heat. More. They needed the light and morale-boost of a good fire. There was something about the tunnels which invaded a person, chewed its way down into a person's internals… and sucked out their life and guts and soul. The tunnels, indeed, Skaringa Dak itself, was a huge tomb. Being inside the mountain was like being buried alive. Being inside the mountain was like being *dead and buried*.

Nienna found herself a quiet corner, and using a thin blanket given to her by Myriam, tried as best she could to make herself comfortable. Saark approached and knelt beside her, offering her a cup of water. "Myriam found it, down yonder. A pool which doesn't taste of sulphur and shit. It's fresh. Try it!"

"Such small pleasures in life," said Nienna, "that we are reduced to this. Thankful and rejoicing for a simple taste of fresh water."

"Yes, hardly beats the honeyed wine and whorehouses of Vor!" grinned Saark, then looked immediately contrite. He glanced at Kell. "Sorry," he said. "I was forgetting your youth. And my big mouth."

Nienna touched his arm. "I'm not as young as you think," she said.

Saark's eyes glittered. They were dark and entrancing, and Nienna gazed into their rich depths. "Too young, my sweetness, I think," he said with an easy, disarming, friendly smile. And under his breath, "Far too *dangerous*."

"I'm only a few months younger than Katrina," pointed out Nienna. "And her youth wasn't a problem for you."

"Yes. And look how that ended!" snapped Saark, the smile falling from his face. He sighed, and rubbed at tired eyes. "Sorry. Again. I'll not forget what that bastard Styx did. Such a waste. Such a sorrow."

"Yes." Saark pulled gently away from Nienna, and she lay under her blanket, looking at him. His hair was long and black and curled. Even without oils and perfume, he was a picture of masculine beauty. Well balanced. Perfectly formed. Yes, he *had* been through the wars, but recent travel, exercise and constant battle had simply enhanced his athleticism, making him even more of a naturally powerful warrior than when they'd first met. That, and the vachine enhancements... His skin now glowed. His eyes glittered like jewels. He was like... a *god*.

"I'm cold," said Nienna.

Saark gave a long, lazy pause, eyes locked to hers. "That's a shame. That's what it's like, down here in this wasteland." He glanced to Kell again, then back to Nienna meaningfully. "I, too, miss warm and cosy beds, and the easy living. Maybe one day, I'll be able to warm you. But not tonight, my precious." And then he was gone, and Nienna could smell his natural perfume, and she bit her lips and rubbed her eyes and stared at her grandfather. Saark's fear of the old man was palpable. Nienna scrunched herself under her blanket, and tried to think pleasant thoughts. Instead, she dreamed of Bhu Vanesh, hunting her, hunting her through dark citadels... and nobody could hear her screams. Nobody could ever hear her screams...

For three days they journeyed through narrow, winding, underground tunnels. Sometimes they had to climb across savage vertical drops, and on several occasions they came to guard outposts: small wooden buildings, usually empty of everything except wooden cots without bedding. At least this meant they had firewood, and Kell broke up the cots and they burned them at night, as much for the comfort of living flames as for any real heat they produced.

On the fourth day, Kell stopped and tilted his head. Then looked to Saark. "You hear it?"

"Yes. You have exquisite hearing for a human," smiled Saark.

"Helps me to kill," grunted Kell, and carried on.

"What can you hear?" asked Nienna.

"Water. A river."

They continued for another hour, until the tunnel spat them out on a gentle rocky slope. It was littered with rubble, and a sloping shingle bank led gently into a wide, fast flowing and *very* deep underground torrent. Back by the tunnel entrance there was another guard outpost, which Kell approached warily, Ilanna ready in huge fists, and down along the shingle black moss grew, and black vines twisted and turned amongst the stones like narrow, skeletal fingers.

"I'm amazed anything grows down here," said Nienna, crunching down to the water's edge.

"Don't go too close," said Myriam, and placed her hand on Nienna's shoulder. "To fall in, that would be to die. The cold and ice would chill you in minutes."

Nienna twisted away from Myriam's grip. "I don't need your advice. I'm not stupid."

Myriam looked to Saark, who shrugged.

"It's empty," called Kell from the guard hut, then stepped inside. He emerged after a few minutes. "There are some supplies. A sack of grain and weapons."

"Swords?" said Saark.

"Aye," nodded Kell, and threw Saark a thin military rapier.

Saark caught the weapon, and swished it through the air several times. "Well balanced. Good steel." He lifted eyes and met Kell's gaze. "Maybe our luck is improving?"

"Yeah, well don't get too horny. This place is a dead end." He nodded to the river.

Saark glanced up and down the shingle slope, and saw Kell was right. The only access was via the river. Then he noticed a short jetty, in black wood, half rotten and listing to one side. It had been repaired with old rope, but threatened at any moment to crash into the river.

"I get the impression this place isn't used often," said Saark.

"I think the damn albinos have more things to worry about than us, lad. You remember back on Skaringa Dak? The sky going out like a candle? The appearance of those pretty boys, those Vampire Warlords?"

"I remember," said Saark. He glanced up and down the river, and shivered. Then he looked over to Myriam, then back to the thickly churning waters. He could see lumps of ice. "I know what you're going to suggest."

"You do?" Kell looked impressed.

"We have only one option."

"Which is?"

"The river." Saark's eyes were dark. "If we don't build it right, we'll drown, Kell."

"I know that, lad. But if we stay here, we'll either freeze or meet another group of Graal's arse-kissing gigolos. It's one of those risks we'll have to take."

"I'm not a boat-builder," said Saark, eyes narrowed, voice suddenly wary with suspicion. "What do you want *me* to do?"

"Go and cut that rope free from the old jetty. We'll need it for bindings. And I'll sort out some timber."

"What will I cut it with?"

"There's knives in the hut."

"Are they sharp?"

Kell stared at Saark. "I *don't know*, lad. Go and have a bloody look."

Muttering, Saark moved to the guard shack and peered in. It was dark, and damp, wood mouldering, the sack of grain rotten. Saark curled his lips into a sneer, and crept in as if afraid to touch anything. He found one of the knives, blade rusted, hilt unravelling, and stepped back out to the shingle. "This knife is rusty," he said.

Kell looked up. He sighed. "Just do your best, lad."

Saark moved to the jetty, muttering again about being rich, and honoured, and noble, and how manual labour was a disgrace to his ancestors and so far beneath Saark he should live on a mountaintop. He stopped and peered warily at the treacherous footing. Water gushed around the jetty with gusto, bubbling and churning. Reaching out, Saark touched the wood with a grimace, and it was slick with mould. The whole structure shifted under his touch, shuddering.

"Great," he said, hefting the rusted knife and starting to saw at one piece of rope.

Back at the shack, Kell pried free several planks using the tip of Ilanna's butterfly blade, whilst whispering an apology to the axe. She was a killing weapon. A weapon of death. To use her for simple carpentry was total sacrilege.

Myriam built a small fire, and with Nienna's help cooked thin soup. They used a little of the grain, and watched in amusement as Saark fought with the rope, the rusted knife, and even the whole shaking jetty. Despite his usual visual elegance, his élan and poise and balance, the minute he touched any form of menial task it was as if Saark's thumbs had been severed. He growled and cursed, and finally cut free a length of rope, arms waving for a moment as he fought not to fall into the river. Myriam leapt forward, grabbing the back of his shirt and hauling him back.

"Thanks," he said.

"You dance a jig like a criminal in a noose."

"The only crime here," he said, smoothing his neat moustache, "is having to perform basic peasant labour." He stopped. He was close to Myriam, and her hand had slipped from a handful of shirt to the base of his spine. It was as if she held him. Close. Like a lover. He turned, into her, and breathed in her natural perfume. She was sweet like summer trees. Ripe like strawberries. As dangerous and tempting as any honeyed poison.

Myriam was as tall as him, and their eyes met only inches away, and their lips were close. Myriam licked hers, leaving a wetness that glistened. Saark stepped back, breathing out deeply, and saw that both Nienna and Kell were watching them.

"What's the matter?" he growled. "Never seen an artist wrestle with a rope before?"

"A piss-artist, maybe. Let Myriam do it," said Kell. "That way you won't bloody drown."

"The cheek of it!" But Saark handed Myriam the dagger, and retired to the fire. He watched her move elegantly, and climb out onto the jetty to the far end. It trembled and he felt his heart in his mouth. Swiftly, she made a cut and began uncoiling the old, blackened rope. To the left, Kell was gathering a formidable supply of planks, at the expense of the shack's rear-end wall where the wood was more sound.

Saark looked back to Nienna, and was surprised to find her glaring at him.

"Something the matter, little monkey?"

"I'm not your fucking little monkey," she snarled, and Saark lifted his hands, palms out, and shook his head a little, face confused. Nienna calmed, and gazed into the fire. Then she snapped back to Saark. "You enjoy touching her, did you?"

"You have nothing to worry about," said Saark. "You forget, easily, how this was the woman who stabbed a knife between my ribs. I do not forgive, nor forget. Not as easy as you, it would seem."

"Back then she was dying, she was a husk," snapped Nienna. "Now she is… pretty. Beautiful! Her skin glows. She is strong, and the picture of health. And you are both now…"

"Vachine?" Saark laughed. "I've yet to discover if that is a curse I will soon regret. Yes, it has healed me. Yes, my eyesight is a thousand times better, and I do not tire like once I did. But there is a price, I can feel it; there is always a price."

"Bite me," said Nienna.

"What?"

"Make me like you."

"No." Saark frowned. "This is madness. If Kell heard you speak thus…"

"What would he do? He's a grumpy old man. A fucking *has-been*. Bite me, Saark, then take me with you. When we get out of the mountains, we can flee together!"

"Whoa!" Saark leant back, and saw that Nienna's eyes were gleaming, almost with fever. Gently, he leaned towards her and put his hand on her knee. "What's going on inside your pretty head, Little One?"

"Stop treating me like a damn child!" she hissed. "You know what I want!"

Saark laughed easily. "Yes, I am predictable, am I not? But what you ask will get me killed. You know it, and I know it. If we are together, how long before Kell comes hunting us down? How long before sweet Ilanna cleaves through my skull? Where then your childish love?"

"Childish love? How *dare* you!"

"I dare much, little girl," said Saark, and smiled easily, eyes glowing. "If you simply want a quick session with your legs wide, any soldier in the barracks will accommodate you. I can arrange it, if you like. But if you want prime steak, if you want to *feel* Saark's superior touch and skill and expertise, well, you'll have to wait until you're a little older. I'm not the same as the perfumed absinthe drinkers in Vor who seek out little boys and girls for their fun. That is a practice I helped stamp out."

Nienna, with eyes wide, stood and stalked off, just as Myriam arrived and dumped a large coil of rope beside the fire. She sat, and looked at Saark. "You know I heard most of that?"

"I know."

"Do you think it'll work?"

"I hope so. Much as I'd like to taste her youthful sweetness, I'm sure the price would be too high." He glanced again at Kell. "Far too high."

"There is a price for everything in life," said Myriam, giving him a dazzling smile.

"I'd noticed," muttered Saark.

They ate in a tired and weary silence, the gloom and cold getting to them despite their meagre fire. After three hours of grunting and hard work, stomping around in the shingle, Kell had finally fashioned a raft.

They stood, staring at the vessel, and Saark wore a frown like a deviated ballroom mask from the *Black Plague Tribute*, an illegal and anti-royal piece by one of Falanor's most twisted playwrights.

"So, what's that look mean, then?" said Kell, scowling.

"Nothing! Nothing. I mean, is it supposed to look like that?"

"Like what?"

"Like *that*. I mean, all twisted and uneven. I swear by all that's unholy, Kell, you're no bloody carpenter."

"I know I'm not a carpenter," snapped Kell. His eyes blazed with anger. "That's the whole damn point! This is a life and death situation; we must make do with what we have; work with our limited tools. Which means *none*. This is about *escape*, Saark, not pissing carpentry."

"Still." He pursed his lips. "She hardly looks seaworthy."

"*She* is *not* a bloody galleon," snarled Kell, hands on hips, his fury still rising.

"And *I* can bloody see that!" said Saark. "To be honest, I think I might take my chances with the soldiers and demons. If we try and ride the river on *that thing*, we are sure to die."

Kell stared at him for a moment, then shrugged. "Suit yourself. You coming, Myriam?"

"I'm coming," said Myriam, flashing Saark a weak smile. She grabbed one edge, and with Kell they dragged the makeshift raft down to the water's edge, where the water tugged eagerly.

Saark shuffled after them, and stopped, shifting from one foot to the other. "This is starting to feel like a military training camp," he muttered, as he watched Kell making last minute adjustments, pulling several of the binding ropes tight. The timber creaked in protest under Kell's exerted pressure.

"Meaning?"

"Well, we did all sorts of horse shit like this during training. Carry rocks and logs, build rafts, work as a team to get across the river, make stepping stones, swing from high trees, climb like monkeys up pointless walls of rock, run through the mountains, navigate blizzards, that sort of thing. Hah! What a chamber pot of rotting turds that whole thing turned out to be!"

"So, you've built a raft before?" Kell glanced up as he worked.

"Sort of."

"How can you 'sort of' build a raft? You either do or you don't."

"I directed their actions, like a good captain should."

"You mean you let others do the real graft, whilst you sat on your arse thinking about women?"

"Of course," smirked Saark, failing to grasp even the subtlest strand of sarcasm. "That's the way it should be. Royalty and people of breeding doing the commanding, whilst, ahem, no offence meant, but peasants work their fingers to the bone."

"So I'm a peasant, eh lad?" Kell straightened, and rubbed his hands on his jerkin. The skin of his hands was ingrained with dirt. His fingernails were mostly black from impacts during battle. His huge hands wore the hardy skin of sixty years of toil.

"Of course you are!" said Saark brightly. He grinned, and slapped Kell on the back. "But don't worry, old horse! I won't hold it against you! As you say, I've worked with worse tools."

Kell lifted Nienna onto the bobbing wooden raft, and then held out his hand for Myriam, who stepped lightly aboard. The raft bobbed. It looked far from safe. Kell glanced at Saark's beaming face, then stepped on himself. It took his weight, and he placed a hand on the low, makeshift tiller he'd fashioned from the lid of an old cherrywood chest. The raft began to drift from the shore.

"Hey, what about me?" snapped Saark, suddenly. His eyes went wide.

"Better jump for it, laddie."

"Hey, wait, I thought, I mean…"

"Didn't think you'd want to touch my dirty peasant's paws," grinned Kell. The gap was two feet distant now, and the current started to turn the raft. "Better be quick, when the current gets us you'll never make it."

Saark took a step back, and with an inelegant squawk, leapt for the raft. He hit the edge, and scrabbled for a moment, one leg sinking into the ice-chilled waters to the thigh. Then Myriam grabbed him, and hauled him onto the rough-lashed planks where he lay, gazing up, panting.

"You would have left me," he said.

"Don't be silly," smiled Kell.

"You would. I know you would."

"Well, maybe one day you'll learn your lesson," said Kell.

Saark pushed himself up. "And what lesson's that?"

"You never bite the hand that feeds."

The current caught the raft, and with a rapid acceleration they were slammed along the cavern and disappeared rapidly into a narrow, blackened tunnel. To Saark, it felt as though they were being sucked down into the Chaos Halls themselves...

Cold air hit them. They were plunged into total darkness. The raft moved forward swiftly, rocking occasionally, and Saark found himself sitting very, very still. Fear of water was not something that had ever really occurred to him; he had only ever *really* been on the Royal Barge on Lake Katashinka, and even then he'd always been drunk. Now, however, a cold sobriety had him in its fist and every little rock, or shift, every turn and dip and rise made his stomach flip over, and injected him with a sudden nausea and need to be sick. A white pallor invaded his face, but because of the gloom nobody realised his fear.

They seemed to slow for a while, travelling down narrow tunnels, and then emerged into a huge cavern. Fluorescent lodes glinted in the walls, lighting their way, and ice gleamed on rocks and stalagmites.

They plunged into darkness again.

"Does anybody feel sick?" said Saark in a small voice.

"You big girl," snapped Kell. He was concentrating hard, attempting to *feel* the flow of the river, to anticipate – in the Stygian black – whether they were being pulled toward the rows of harsh, jagged rocks, like gnashing teeth, which lined the way.

"No, no, really, I feel incredibly queasy."

"It'll be your wound," said Myriam, not unkindly. She crossed to Saark, and took his hands. "Here. Let me soothe you."

"Yeah, I bet you will," said Nienna, voice small.

"No, honestly, I feel really..." Saark scrambled to the edge of the raft, and threw up noisily over the side. He vomited for a while, and there was an embarrassed silence, and finally Saark sat up.

"How you feeling?" growled Kell.

"That was your fault."

"*My fault?* How, in the name of Bhu Vanesh's *bollocks*, did you come to that conclusion?"

"It's your boat control, isn't it? You're all over the place, man!" He turned to Nienna and Myriam, little more than ethereal white blobs in the dark. "I'm sorry, ladies, to lose my equilibrium in such a way. I'm sure you must feel queasy as well."

"Not I," said Myriam.

"Nor I," said Nienna, eyes flashing daggers. "Maybe you've been sucking on something you shouldn't?" She flashed a glance to Myriam, but it was lost in the gloom, in the surge and sway of the raft.

"Something's coming," said Kell.

"What do you mean, 'something's coming'? What can possibly 'be coming' out here?" But even as Saark was spouting his vomit-stinking words, they hit a sudden dip and the raft fell several feet, splashing with a slap onto a swirl of churning water; Kell fought with the makeshift tiller, which gave a *crack* and came off in his hands. He stared at Myriam.

"That's not good," she said.

"You idiot!" screamed Saark. "You're supposed to be steering the damn thing! Now you've broken it! You bloody idiot! What the hell are you doing?"

"I'm not doing anything," snapped Kell. "This whole game is out of my damn control. But I'll tell you what I *will* do if you keep blaming me for freaks of nature, you freak of nature, I'll be steering your big fat stupid face into the current of my fucking *fist*."

"No need to be like that," said Saark primly – as they hit another sudden dip, and the raft tipped madly and Saark rolled towards the edge, squawking like an infant. "Wah!" he screamed, and Myriam launched after him, grabbing hold and dragging him back without ceremony.

"Get hold of something!" she hissed, and retracted her claws. Then the pain hit Saark, as he realised her *vachine claws* had saved him by hooking into his thigh muscle.

He screamed again. "You punctured me! You grabbed my bloody *muscle!* Are you addled on *Fisher's Weed?* Devoid of your better judgement? Are you insane? Look, I'm bleeding, I've got blood all over my pants, there's blood everywhere, on my pants, and everything!"

"There'll be more soon," muttered Kell. But they hit another drop, and as water washed over them and they clung to the raft for dear life, so it began to turn and rock, and drop into choppy troughs flecked white with foam. A roaring came to their senses. It was loud, and vicious sounding.

"That sounds like a waterfall," said Saark, carefully.

"So it does, lad," snapped Kell.

"You know that shack back there? You remember how it was never used?"

"I suppose I understand, now," said Kell.

Saark turned his moaning on Myriam. "I thought *you* said you *knew* this path?"

"No. I said I could guide us out."

"What, and dropping us off an underground waterfall is getting us out, is it? Am I truly surrounded by idiots?"

Myriam gripped him. Her vachine fangs flashed. "Listen, Saark, I never said I'd been this way before. Only that I knew of tunnels which led out from the Black Pike Mountains. If you're so damn perfect, you paddle us back up the fucking river!"

"Wait," said Nienna, and her voice was soft. She held up a hand. "Listen."

They listened, and heard the roar of fast-approaching falls.

"I hear my imminent death approaching," whimpered Saark, eventually.

"Can't you hear the cracking?"

"Great! A rock-fall as well! Wonders will never cease!"

"No. It's ice," said Nienna.

"Well," beamed Saark, "that's just fine and dandy. Helps us out of our predicament nicely, and with all manner of– HOLY JANGIR FIELDS LOOK AT THAT BASTARD!" It was a black band of nothing and it was scrolling swiftly towards the adventurers on the raft, rimed with an edge of sparkling white ice and dropping *dropping* into a cold vast nothingness filled with blackness and steam…

FOUR
Wildlands

Kell fell, air rushed past him, and he prayed the hefty raft didn't hit him in the back of the skull. Rocks smashed to his left and right, and clutching Ilanna to his chest he managed to angle his body into a dive. He dreaded the impact with ice-chill water, dreaded that harsh impact slam to face and body and soul. He knew it was enough to kill a man, and he knew armour and weapons could drag a man to his death – he'd seen it before, several times, watched warships settle into the ocean like dying dragons, watched men flail and scream, panic invading them as quickly as any ice waters, only to be sucked under heaving green waves and never return. But Kell would never give up Ilanna. He would never give up the Sister of his Soul. Not even if his life depended on it…

Saark screamed like a woman, flapped like a chicken, and did not care that the world could and would mock him. He hit the water with a gasp, went under deep and surfaced flailing like a man on the end of a swinging noose – only to see something huge and black and terribly ominous tumbling toward him – and he realised in the blink of an eye it was the raft *the fucking raft* and he leapt back and twisted, swimming down, *down*, and something made a deep sonic *thump* above and Saark *knew* the bastard would hit him, push him down, drown him without any emotion and he swam, bitterly, secure in the knowledge that he was cursed and he was a pawn and the whole bloody world was an evil gameboard designed *just* for him. Bubbles scattered around like black petals, and eventually, as pain lacerated his lungs and bright lights danced like flitting fish, he struck for the surface, gasping as he emerged in a burst. He bobbed there for a while, in the gloom, listening to the roar of the waterfall, and then his eyes adjusted and he saw Kell, Myriam and Nienna on the raft, dripping, frowning, and staring at him. He scowled.

"Come on, lad," urged Kell. "What you waiting for?"

"What happened, did you all nail yourselves to the bastard thing?" spat Saark, and struck out through the undulating water.

"No," said Kell, taking Saark's wrist and hauling the man onto the raft, which bobbed violently. "*You* simply spent too much time paddling down there with the fairies. What were you doing, man? We thought you'd drowned!"

"Hah. I was simply counting my money." Saark looked up. They'd fallen a considerable way, and behind them the base of the waterfall churned. Steam rose, and ice crackled on rocks. Saark shivered, and then realised he wasn't dying from the cold. "Wait. Something's wrong," he said.

"It's a geyser," said Myriam. "The water here is heated from thermal springs deep below Skaringa Dak."

Saark scowled. "It smells odd."

"Sulphur," said Kell. "You should be thankful for the bath, mate. You were beginning to stink."

"Amusing, Kell. If you didn't have that big axe I'd put you across my knee and spank you. And we all know how you'd enjoy that!"

Kell stared at him. Hard.

"I take it back," said Saark, and watched Kell deflate. "Was only a little joke. At least we're not dead." He brightened. "So many women! And so few days left on this world!"

Kell handed him a broken plank. Saark stared at it.

"What's this?"

"I meant to say. Don't get too happy. It's time to paddle."

"You want me to paddle?"

"Yes, Saark. Paddle. Before we get sucked back into the waterfall's undertow, and dragged down to a real watery grave."

Swallowing, Saark began to paddle. His efforts did not draw comment, although they probably should have.

They sailed through more darkness, a deep and velvet black that brought back childhood nightmares of vulnerability and despair;

and the tunnels soon turned chill again, making all four shiver and regret leaving the warmth of the underground spring. After more peaks and troughs, the sailing started to become rough.

"We're vibrating," said Saark. "What's that supposed to mean?"

There was ambient light again from mineral deposits, and it outlined Saark in stark silver making him appear as a ghost. He was shivering uncontrollably, thin clothing sticking to him like a second skin.

"It means we're in for a rough ride," said Kell. "Get a good hold onto something. And for your own sake, Saark, do not let go."

In the eerie silver light, the river became more and more choppy. Occasionally, they saw rocks appear like shark fins and glide past. Another roaring came to their ears, a gradual escalation of chattering sound as of a thousand insects, and the raft started to rock wildly. Kell clung on grimly, and Saark, with a start, ejected brass claws and stared at them in horror.

"Welcome to the world of the vachine," said Myriam, with a smile, and dug her own claws into the lashed timber planks. Saark stuck his claws into the wood, and hung on grimly, looking sick, looking miserable.

The raft slammed onwards… and the river suddenly dipped, into a vast slope with twists and turns, and Saark was screaming and Nienna clung to Kell whose face was grim and scowling, and they flowed past rocks, and chunks of ice, and the river suddenly widened and hit wild swirling pools, gulleys and troughs, and they were pulled first one way, then another, water splashing over them, drenching them to the bone with freezing ice needles and Nienna screamed. They were spun around again, almost capsized, then accelerated down a wide tunnel past sharp rocks and Saark felt as if he was falling, falling down an endless tunnel of vertical water streams and he knew he would die there, knew he would die after all the pain and suffering he'd been through and it felt bitter on his tongue, wildfire in his mind and he was scowling and shouting and clinging on for life and then –

Then it was calm.

They flowed out into cold winter light. The river swirled through a forest of towering conifers, hundreds of feet high and suffocated by snow. An icy wind bit their cold wet bodies.

Kell laughed, a deep rolling rumble. "We're out!" he breathed, and hugged Nienna, and gazed around, a man filled with wonder, a man seeing daylight for the very first time. He glanced at Myriam. "Well done, girl. You were right! You did well."

Myriam seemed to glow under the praise, and Saark looked down at his damp clothing, ragged, torn, mud- and blood-stained, and then he looked up at the sun. "Are we... safe, in the sunlight?"

"Hardly sunlight, Saark."

"I thought vachine..."

Myriam shook her head. "No. A fiction. The brightest of sunlight might cause you pain in your transformed state, but that is all." Myriam leant closer. "What you have to worry about, Saark, my sweetness, is the fact that you have blood-oil flushing round your veins, but no real clockwork to control it."

Saark gave a swift nod, and wary glance at Kell. "The Big Man said as much. Said I would need to bind with clockwork, although I do not know how such a thing will be achieved. Or, even if I'd want such a thing." He shuddered, and flexed his brass claws.

"You have no choice," said Myriam. "Without clockwork integration, without the skills of the Engineers, you will die."

"Thanks for that," scowled Saark.

The raft swept downriver, and Kell ripped free a plank from the edge of the ragged platform and used it to guide them to the shore, huge neck and shoulder muscles bulging as he fought the heavy flow.

Saark grinned, breathing deep the fresh cold air. After what felt like an eternity in the tunnels under Skaringa Dak, it was good to be free of them again; good to be free of the Black Pike Mountains. Good to be back in Falanor. Good to be *alive*.

"'Kell stared melancholy into great rolling waves of a Dark Green World, and knew he could blame no other but himself for The long Days of Blood...'" Kell turned sharply, scowling at Saark.

Myriam tilted her head. "The poem?"

"Aye," said Saark, and as the raft grounded on a bank of snow, he leapt from it and stared back, as if it was some great sea beast recently slaughtered. "Thank the Halls I'm on stable land!" He placed hands on hips, and watched Kell step from the raft with Nienna clinging to one arm. She looked frail and weak, and his heart went out to her at that moment.

"We need a fire. Food. Shelter," said Kell, matter-of-factly. His eyes were burning. "Or we will die."

"I like a man who doesn't mince his words," said Saark.

"And I like a man who fucking pulls his weight! Now get out there and find us firewood, and find us a shelter, or I swear Saark, you'll be wearing another wide and gaping smile on your belly before the sun is down."

"Fine, fine, a simple 'please' would have sufficed." Saark turned to hunt for firewood, a dandy in rags, but the look on Kell's face halted him. He frowned, turning back. "Yes, old man? Is there something else? Maybe I should stick a brush up my arse and sweep the floor whilst I'm at it?"

"One more thing. No more poetry. Or I'll cut out your cursed tongue, and be glad I done it."

Saark snorted, and headed into the gloom-shadowed forest, muttering, "All these threats of violence are *so* low born, lacking in nobility, so uncouth and raw. Threats truly are the language of the peasant."

Moving into the forest, they found a natural shelter from the wind, and in a small alcove surrounded by holly trees and ancient, moss-covered rocks, built a fire. Myriam was gone for two hours, and returned with a dead fox brought down by a single arrow from her bow. As she went about skinning and gutting the creature, Saark stripped off his wet shirt and laid it on a rock by the fire to dry. He flexed his fast-repairing body, and Kell looked up from where he was sharpening Ilanna's blades with a small whetstone.

"You're repairing well, lad," he said, eyes fixed on the chest-wound cut from above Saark's heart by Kradek-ka on the plateau of Helltop. "I still find it hard to believe you carried that Soul Gem inside you for so long – and realised nothing."

"I was bewitched. Once. And only once." Saark sighed, and stretched out, like a cat in the sun, and ran his hands up and down his arms and flanks, checking himself. "It'll never happen again, I promise you that! And by all the gods, I've taken a battering since I met you." His eyes sparkled with good humour. His pain had obviously receded, and he was more his old self. "Look at all these new scars! Incredible. One would have thought keeping company with *The Legend* would have brought me nothing but women, fine honey-wine, rich meats and incredible fame. But now? *Now*, I'm stuck in a forest after the, quite frankly, most abominable adventures of my entire life, I'm riddled with bruises and scars, been beaten more times than a whore's had hot fishermen, stabbed, burned, chastised and abused, and to top it all the only company I get is that of a grumpy old bastard who should be crossbow whipped in the face for his taste in clothes, whiskey and women." Saark sighed.

Kell looked up. "Shut up," he said.

"See? Where's the witty banter? The dazzling repartee? I wish to discuss literature, philosophy and women. Instead, I get to grub in the woods for mushrooms and onions, dirty my nails like the lowest working man instead of being ridden like a donkey by a buxom farm lass!"

Kell sighed. And looked to Myriam. "Is the meat ready? The stew's bubbling."

Myriam crossed to him carrying a thin metal plate, and scraped a pile of fox meat into the pan. "I'll dry the rest, roll it in salt. We can take it with us."

"Good girl," said Kell, nodding his approval. Saark scowled, and started to remove his trews. "And what are you doing?" snapped Kell.

Saark, half bent, glanced up. "I'm sick of wearing wet clothes."

"You're not removing your stinking trews here, lad. Get out into the forest."

"But it's cold in the forest."

"I am *not* staring at your hairy arse whilst I cook," said Kell, face like thunder. "I, also, have been through much recently. And it's bad enough seeing your homeland torn asunder and your friends murdered by ice-smoke magick and insect-born albino soldiers, without some tart wishing to dangle his tackle over my fox stew. So get out into the forest, and try not to sit in the pine needles. They sting, you know."

Saark stared hard at Kell. "Kell, you're worse than any old fish wife," he snapped, but pulled his trews up and sauntered away from their makeshift camp, swaying his hips provocatively, just to annoy the old warrior.

An hour later, with the winter sun dying in the sky and pink tendrils creeping over the horizon chased by sombre, snow-filled storm clouds, Kell sat back with hands on his belly, and closed his eyes.

Saark was mending his torn shirt with needle and thread supplied by Myriam's comprehensive pack; a woman used to living in the wilds for weeks at a time, the provisions she carried were lightweight but necessary. Salt, arrows, thread, various herbs, and several spare bowstrings. As she pointed out, her bow was her life. It was her means to a regular food supply, and with fox stew in their bellies, it was hard for anybody to disagree.

Nienna was staring into the fire, lost in thought, holding the binding on her severed finger. Myriam moved and sat beside her. "Do you want me to look at that? It should be ready for a fresh dressing."

Nienna sighed, and nodded. "Yes. Thank you."

As Myriam unwound the bandage from Nienna's hand, examined the stitched flesh above the cut finger, and applied fresh herbs to the wound, Nienna found herself looking away, face stony.

The albino soldier under Skaringa Dak had taken her finger to punish Kell for an escape attempt. Now, she felt she was less than a full woman. No longer beautiful. No longer whole. Nienna looked down, and flexed her hand, wincing as pain shot up the edge of her hand and arm.

"Still hurts, yes?" smiled Myriam.

"Like a bitch," said Nienna.

"And you've met a few of those, right?"

Nienna laughed. "I didn't mean you."

"I did," said Myriam. She sighed. "I've done... questionable things." She stroked her own cheek, then rubbed at her eyes. "I'm tired of doing bad things. I have been given a gift. A second chance. I am strong now, and fit, and although in the eyes of the people of Falanor I am..."

"Outcast?" said Kell, softly.

They looked up. He was reclined, his body a shadowy bulk in the gloom of fast approaching night. Firelight glinted in his beard, in his glittering eyes. He may have looked like a big friendly bear, ensconced as he was in his tatty battered tufted old jerkin, but this was a big friendly bear that could turn nasty and insane in the blink of an eye.

"Yes. An outcast. Alien. The enemy." Myriam smiled at Kell, and shrugged. She turned back to Nienna. "Once this is all done, once this game is played out, I will be hunted to my death in Falanor. By every man with a bow or knife. The vachine are seen as evil. I cannot change that."

"They drink the blood of others," said Kell, voice still soft.

"And you eat the flesh of beasts," said Myriam.

"Not human flesh," said Kell.

"To the east, past Valantrium Moor, past Drennach, past the Tetragim Marshes, there are tribes who eat the flesh of men. They see it as no different to cow, or dog, or pig. It's just meat."

"They, too, are evil."

"Why so?"

"It goes against the teachings of the Church. Human flesh is sacred."

Myriam shrugged. "So you mean to tell me if you were ever put in a position where you were going to die of starvation, and human flesh was on the menu, you absolutely would not eat? Not even to save your own life? To save the lives of your children?"

"I would not," lied Kell, throat dry, remembering the Days of Blood, where he had indeed eaten human flesh, and much more, and much worse. "I would rather die," he said, voice husky, eyes hidden.

"Well that's where we differ, then," snapped Myriam, voice hard. "But you should not judge so readily, Kell. I guided you and Nienna and Saark out from that bastard mountain; I saved your lives. This time."

"Lucky for us," nodded Kell, dark eyes glinting in the firelight. And now he didn't look like such a friendly bear. Now he looked far more dangerous. "But enough talk. What are your plans now, Myriam?"

"I will attempt to kill the Vampire Warlords."

This was met with momentary silence. The wind hissed through the trees, and it sounded like the roll of the ocean against a beach. It was hypnotic. Somewhere, snow clumped from high branches. Conifers creaked and sighed.

"Why?" said Kell, eventually, head tilted to one side. It was such a simple question, Myriam was speechless for a few moments as she composed her thoughts.

"It is the right thing to do," she said, eventually, and looked into the fire, refusing to meet his gaze.

"You will die, then," he said.

"So be it."

Kell growled. "This thing is too big for you," he snapped. Graal's Army of Iron is invincible; you know how they took Jalder, and Vor, and the gods only know which other Falanor cities. And I was there at Old Skulkra when the Army of Iron came from the

Great North Road, came from Vorgeth Forest like ghosts." He spat, and rubbed his beard viciously, as if angry with himself. "Those bastard Harvesters cast their ice-smoke magick. No soldier could stand against them!"

"But you still live," said Myriam, softly.

"I am different," snapped Kell.

"Yes, you have your magick axe," she said, half-mocking.

"There is nothing magick about this axe. And before you say it, no, she is possessed by no demon; let us just say Ilanna has an attribute none of you could ever guess."

"So you will not help?"

"I cannot fight Falanor's battles forever," he said.

"It looks like you've stopped fighting full stop," said Saark.

Kell looked at him, and pointed with a powerful finger. "Don't you bloody start," he said.

"Well," scoffed Saark, "look at you, look at everything we've been through, all the fights and the murder and the bloodshed. And the mighty Kell would turn his back *now*? Just as things got worse? The time he is needed the *most*!"

"That's the point, lad. We made things worse. Don't you see? We're pawns in another man's game. Every step we've taken since meeting up in Jalder in that cursed tannery has seen us step closer and closer to the resurrection of the Vampire Warlords. We made it happen, Saark. We fucking made it happen."

Saark shook his head. "That's so much horse shit Kell, and you know it. If it hadn't happened the way it did, it would have occurred another way. Yes, maybe we were set up to some extent – because Alloria had that Soul Gem implanted near my heart by the dark gods only *know* what deep and ancient magick. But the outcome was always written in stone, written in blood. Now we have to stop it."

"No." Kell ground his teeth.

"Why not?" said Saark. "I don't believe the mighty Kell has given up. Or maybe he's just turned soft, heart turned to butter, muscles to jellied jam, maybe the mighty Kell's dick has finally gone limp and he can no longer fuck young boys. But you still suck, don't you Kell?" Saark stood. Kell's head was down. "Is that all you want from life now, you dirty old bastard? To suck horse dick and bury your head in the ground? Wallow in self pity?" Saark sang, and his voice was a beautiful, haunting lullaby:

"He dreamt of the slaughter at Valantrium Moor,
A thousand dead foes, there could not be a cure
Of low evil ways and bright terrible deeds,
Of men turned bad, he'd harvest the weeds,
His mighty axe hummed, Ilanna by name,
Twin sharp blades of steel, without any shame
For the deeds she did do, the men she did slay,
Every living bright–eyed creature was legitimate prey."

Saark laughed then. His eyes glittered like jewels in the gloom of the snow-enslaved forest. "What a load of old donkey shit. You should complain. You've been misrepresented in *legend…*"

Kell slowly stood, boots crunching old pine needles. His eyes burned with fury. With killing rage. His fingers were curled around Ilanna's steel shaft and he lifted her, almost imperceptibly. "You better be careful what you spout, laddie," he growled, and he was gone from the world of humans, he was teetering along a razor blade looking down into a valley of madness. "Somebody might just cut out your tongue."

"What? For speaking the truth? If you don't help us, Kell, if you leave us to face the Vampire Warlords alone, then we will die. And the problem still remains."

"I SAID NO!" thundered the old warrior.

"ARE YOU MAD YET?" screamed Saark suddenly, stepping forward.

Ilanna swept up, a blur, and stopped a hair's breadth under Saark's chin. The dandy grinned. "You good and mad now, old bear?" he said, voice a little calmer.

"Yeah, I'm fucking mad," snarled Kell.

"Then let's go and kill these Vampire Warlords before they do any more damage!"

Kell stared into Saark's eyes for a long minute. Then he seemed to deflate a little. "I will not put Nienna at risk," he said.

"What, I am the reason for all of this?" snapped Nienna. The stump of her finger had been neatly bound, and she was sat, rubbing it thoughtfully. "You wish to protect me? Well, you'd better come with us then. Because I'm going with Saark."

"No, you are not," growled Kell.

"Yes, I bloody *am*. I am a woman. I have my own mind. You do not control me. Or is that what this is all about? It's not about me.

Now, I'm your surrogate daughter... but you couldn't control your *real* daughter, oh no, and she went wild and now you seek to pass off your impotence and lack of control and lack of *fatherhood* on me. Well, I won't have it, grandfather. I am my own person, and to stop me you'll have to kill me."

Kell sat down by the fire, and stared into the flames, chin on his fist. Firelight glittered in his eyes and Myriam, Saark and Nienna exchanged glances.

Finally, Kell looked up, and stared at each of his companions in turn. Slowly, one by one, he met their gazes, and they stared back, defiant, heads high, proud. "I simply want to save Nienna," he said.

Nienna knelt by his side. "To do that, grandfather, you'll have to help us. This thing is wrong, and you know it. We have to do the right thing. We have to kill this evil. I was there, on Helltop; I saw them brought back from the Chaos Halls, just like you, and the terror nearly ripped me in two. These Warlords have not come to Falanor so they can go sleep in comfy beds and have sweet sugary dreams. They are here for blood and death."

"Just like the vachine," said Kell, sharply.

"Yes," said Saark. "Just like the vachine. But I fear we are in the middle of something far more complex than we could ever understand; we are in the middle of some ancient feud. Unfortunately, we're the bastards being persecuted, used as pawns, and I cannot sit by and watch good people slaughtered."

"It will be a hard fight," said Kell, looking around at their faces.

"Is there any other kind?" grinned Saark.

"We may all die," said Kell.

"As I pointed out, you're ever the happy face of optimism. But we're used to you now, Kell. We can put up with your strange ways."

"You'll have to do what you're told, lad," Kell snapped, pointing with a stubby rough finger. "You hear me?"

Saark spread his hands, face filled with pain and hurt. "Do I ever do anything else?"

"Hmph," said Kell, and rubbed his beard, then his eyes, then the back of his neck. "I will regret this. I know it. But if you want to bring down the Vampire Warlords, if you want to spread their ashes to the wind, all of you," again he fixed Saark, Myriam and finally Nienna, with a little shake of his head, fixed them all with a deadly stare, "all of you must do exactly what I say."

Saark shrugged. "Whatever you say, old horse. You have something in mind, then?"

Kell stared at him. And he gave an evil smile which had nothing to do with humour. "Yes. I have a plan," he said.

They rode for two days, both Kell and Myriam realising that they had emerged northeast of Jalder, quite close to the huge dark woodland known as the Iron Forest. The Iron Forest was a natural northern barrier which separated Jalder from the Black Pike Mountains, and rife with stories of rogue Blacklippers, evil brigands and ghosts. Kell waved this idea aside when Saark brought it up one evening, just before dusk.

"Pah," said Kell, the skinning knife between his teeth as he ripped flesh from a hare brought down by the skill of Myriam's archery. Now, as a vachine, she was even more deadly accurate with the weapon. What the cancer had taken away, vachine technology had improved with clockwork. "There's nothing as dangerous in the Iron Forest as me, lad. So stop quivering like a lost little girl who's pissed in her pants."

"Little girl? Piss? Me?" Saark placed a hand to his chest, and winced a little. The wound from Helltop at the hands of Kradek-ka, now nearly fully healed, still stung him occasionally. "I think you'll find that when brigands avoid you, it's nothing to do with your notoriety, nor your mythical axe. It's to do with the great stench of your unwashed armpits which precedes you."

"Boys, boys," said Myriam, holding up her hand. "Please. Stop. Enough." Nienna giggled. Since the pain in her hand had receded, partially due to the natural healing process, partially due to herbs which Myriam mixed into a creamy broth every night and which eased pain and gave sweet, beautiful dreams filled with vivid colours, she had found herself mellowing incredibly. Imminent danger was far ahead, the travelling not so hectic, and she found she was a far different girl from the slightly plump and naive creature who'd been about to enter the academic world of Jalder University. Now, Nienna's muscles had hardened, toned from weeks of marching and climbing, even fighting; her hands were calloused from chopping wood and gathering branches, and there was a toughness about her eyes. This was a girl who had witnessed death, observed horrors beyond the ken of most Falanor nobility. The experiences had strengthened her. Built her in character and resolve. Turned her from girl, to woman.

Kell snorted. "You're a dandy peacock bastard."

"You're a stinking old goat with a prolapse." Saark laughed, his laughter the decadent peal of raucous enjoyment found at any hedonistic Palace Feast.

Myriam shook her head again, somewhat in despair. "Saark! Stop! Listen, we passed some wild mushrooms back down the trail. Please please please, stop arguing, go back there and collect them for me. It would add a great deal to the meal."

Saark sighed. "Well, that depends on my reward." He winked.

Myriam tilted her head. Her eyes shone, but before she could answer Kell butted in, voice harsh. "You'll get the back of my hand if you don't, lad," he growled.

"Ahh, but I know you love me truly," smiled Saark, making Kell's scowl deepen further. Grabbing his sheathed rapier, he trotted off down the fast darkening path. "How far?" he shouted back.

"Ten minutes' walk," replied Myriam.

Saark nodded, and was gone. A ghost, vanished into the angular, bent trunks of the Iron Forest.

"Will he be all right?" said Nienna, face a mask of worry.

"The glib fool can look after himself," snorted Kell, returning to skinning the hare.

Saark trotted along, quite happy, vachine eyesight vivid in the darkness. He pondered the gift of the bite from Shanna, one of the Soul Stealers sent, not to kill him, as he had at first thought, but to bring him to Skaringa Dak for the resurrection – or *summoning* – of the Vampire Warlords. What had Myriam said? He'd been injected with blood-oil, which partially turned him into a vampire. Gave him many of the benefits, but without clockwork to make him truly vachine, then he would die. Saark snorted. He felt far from dead. In fact, he felt more alive than ever! Stronger, faster, tougher, with a higher tolerance to pain and an amazing rate of healing. Saark wondered what sort of match he would be for somebody like… Kell.

He grinned. No. Kell would still kick him down into the Bone Graveyard. After all, Kell was something *special*.

Saark stopped. He'd wandered a little off the trail, and rotated himself, eyes narrowing. There it was. In his meandering thoughts, he'd started through the twisted trunks of the Iron Forest.

"Damn."

The Iron Forest sprawled for perhaps ten or fifteen leagues, a haunted barrier between Jalder and the Black Pikes. This reputedly haunted stretch of woods was made up from ancient towering conifers, spruce and red pine, birch and blue sarl, and huge sprawls dominated by even more ancient oaks, perhaps five or six hundred years old, crooked and black as if their ancient trunks had been burned in savage forest fires. But the trees still managed to live on, in twisted blackened husks.

This woodland was the reason Jalder's walls had never spread far north. And it had also been one reason the Army of Iron, led by General Graal, had managed to covertly approach the city's northern defences without detection.

Saark shivered, suddenly looking around. It was a damned creepy place.

Even though the winter sky was still filled with witch-light, the forest was black. Long shadows and branch-filtered gloom did little to brighten the path. Saark shivered again, picking his way to the trail from which he had so foolishly strayed. He hated forests. And he especially hated forests at night. Saark was a creature of Palace Courts, of feasts and banquets, of jesters and music, laughing and dancing, long silk clothes and powdered wigs, thick white make-up, rouged lips, pungent perfume and slick eager quims. Saark's world was one of money and liquor, and endless long nights of drunken debauchery. Woods were for woodsmen. Forests were for peasants. The whole of the outdoors, in fact, the more Saark considered it, were a peasant's playground. How could one enjoy life grubbing for potatoes? Chopping wood? Slaughtering chickens? He shivered. Surely, that was a life worse than death? But here he was, ironically, stinking like a pauper and probably looking as bad as any vagrant who wandered the back-street gutters of Vor. Saark didn't dare look in a reflective pool; he was afraid of what he might see. Afraid of how far he'd fallen.

Reaching the path, Saark stopped. To his left, he heard a *crack*. He froze.

Horse shit, he thought. There's something there!

An animal? Or a man? He gave a little involuntary shiver, which tickled up and down his spine. He drew his rapier, and the steel shone cold in what trickles of light leaked through the forest canopy.

Saark breathed, a stream of chilled smoke.

Or... was it something worse?

A soldier. An *albino* soldier. Or maybe even a vachine. *Maybe even a canker.*

"Double horse shit," he muttered, his own unexpected utterance startling him. To his right, a clump of snow fell from slumped branches. It crunched through the woods in a subdued way, echoes bouncing back and forth from ancient gnarled trunks.

Saark swished his blade. Well, whatever it was, it'd better stay away from *him!* He'd gut it like a fish! Carve it like a duckling!

Saark looked left, and right. He decided wild mushrooms weren't such a culinary necessity after all, and what he really needed to do *right at this moment in time* was hurry back to the security and *light* of the campfire.

Above, snow started to fall.

Darkness finally drew a veil across the sky.

"You old bastard," he muttered, and began to pick his way back down the trail. Something moved, in the undergrowth to his right. It was something large, ponderous, and as Saark stopped, so the *thing* stopped.

It has to be a canker, thought Saark. His imagination flitted back, to those towering, powerful, snarling evil creatures, huge huge wounds in their flanks showing the twisted corrupted clockwork of their deviant manufacture. Kell had killed a fair few, the mighty Ilanna ripping through towering flesh and muscle and gears and cogs. But Saark? With his pretty little rapier? Against such a creature he was less than effective.

Saark began to creep. In the darkness, something stomped and changed direction, heading for the path. With a start of horror Saark realised it would cut him off. He broke into a panicked run, but ahead something huge loomed out of the darkness, stepping menacingly onto the trail, and its bulk was terrifying, its eyes demonic orbs in the gloom, a swathe of black fur running across its shadowed equine flanks, and Saark screamed, turning, slipping suddenly on iced roots and hitting the ground hard with his elbow, then his skull. Dazed for a moment, he realised he'd dropped his rapier and his right hand scrabbled blindly for the weapon as the great beast moved up the path towards him, looming over him like a terrible huge smoky demon, and Saark opened his mouth to scream as terrifying huge fangs descended for his throat...

"Eeyore," said the demon, and a long hairy muzzle dropped and nuzzled against Saark's chin, leaving a long slimy path of hot saliva across his stubble and well-groomed moustache. Donkey breath washed over him. The donkey stepped back, and there came an unmistakable and unterrifying *clop* of donkey hooves.

"I… I just don't bloody believe it!"

Saark sat back on his arse, found his rapier, and with shaking fingers levered himself up from the icy trail. He stood, and stared at the donkey in the gloom.

"Eeyore," brayed the donkey.

Saark squinted. Then he rubbed his chin. Then he squinted again. He moved alongside the affable beast, and looked at the basket on its back. He rubbed his chin again. "And now I just don't *bloody* believe it! Mary! It's you, Mary! You came back over the mountains! It's me, Saark, your faithful owner, oh I'm *so* pleased to see you, *so* pleased you got away from those cankers and Soul Stealers, you must have come back through the Cailleach Fortress, then headed south down through the Iron Forest, following the trails until, by sheer coincidence, we were reunited! Joy!"

Saark stopped. He realised he was standing in the woods, talking to a donkey.

He rubbed her snout, and Mary nuzzled him. "Still. It's damn good to see you again, old friend." He grinned, and taking her loose dangling rope, led her on the trail back towards the adventurers' makeshift camp.

Stew was bubbling over the fire when Saark stepped triumphantly from the tunnel of trees. "Look, everyone!" he cried. "I found Mary in the woods! My faithful old donkey! She's come back to me from over the mountains! What a coincidence! It's a miracle!"

He beamed around, and Kell, glancing up, continued to sharpen Ilanna. "Good. Get her killed and gutted and skinned; we can put some donkey hooves in the stew."

"Ha ha," said Saark, smile wooden.

Kell stopped his honing and stared. "I'm serious. We're at risk of starving out here. As I've always maintained in the past, there's good eating on a donkey."

Mary brayed, nostrils flaring.

"You jest, surely?" said Saark.

"Leave him be," said Myriam, moving to examine the animal. It was indeed Mary, donkey, beast of burden, and Saark's honourable equine friend. She nuzzled Myriam's hand in a friendly fashion. "Are there any supplies still left in the basket?"

Saark rummaged around, and triumphantly produced dried beef, salt, sugar, coffee, arrows and blankets. "See, Kell, no need to kill my special friend. She has brought us much needed supplies! What a brave donkey. Yes you are, a brave donkey." He rubbed her snout.

Kell grunted.

Nienna moved close, and stroked Mary's muzzle. "I can't believe she found her way back. All that way!"

"Ahh, well," Saark stroked his neat moustache, "a clever creature, is your average donkey. You may think they're stubborn, and a bit docile, but I guarantee they have more brains than the majority of idiots you find in any smalltown tavern." He gave a meaningful glance to Kell, who was studiously ignoring both Saark and the donkey.

"Still. An incredible journey for a donkey," said Nienna. "Admirable. And that she managed to find you in the woods? What a stroke of luck!"

"She could smell his awful perfume," muttered Kell.

"You be quiet, old man," snapped Saark, bottom lip quivering a little, "just because you don't have a donkey of your own."

Kell stood, and stretched his back. He stared at Saark, a broad smile on his rough, bearded features. "Well lad," he grinned, and rubbed at his beard, and ran a hand through his shaggy, grey-streaked hair, and knuckled at weary eyes, then winked, "at least you'll have something to keep you warm under your blankets tonight, eh?"

And with that, he sauntered into the woods for a piss.

FIVE
Regular as Clockwork

Dawn was bright and crisp and cold. Snow clung to bare, angular branches, and in the magenta glow of a new morning the trees did indeed appear to be cast from iron. Most were huge, gaunt, stark against a brittle sky. Saark yawned, stretching, and opened his eyes to see Nienna sat by the fire, to which she'd added fuel and stoked it into life.

Saark rolled from under his blanket and shivered. "By the gods, it's cold out here."

"Did you sleep well, Saark?" Nienna didn't look up, but continued to prod the fire. Her voice was soft, lilting, like a delivery of fine soothing birdsong. Saark swallowed, and breathed deep.

"Yes, my sweet," he said.

She looked up then, and their eyes met, and Kell's snore interrupted the moment like a burst of crossbow quarrels. Saark glanced over to the old warrior, who had turned over in his slumber, boots poking from beneath his blanket. It was as if he was mocking Saark, even in sleep. *I am watching you, boy*, the sleeping warrior seemed to say. *Touch my granddaughter and I'll carve you a second arsehole.*

Saark crossed and sat opposite Nienna. He watched her for a while, her delicate movements, and with a start he realised... On their long journey, she had changed – from child, to adult. From girl, to woman. She was harder, leaner, fitter. Her eyes were creased, and her face, on the one hand weary from endless travelling and the threat of being hunted, was also *radiant* with a new, inner strength. This was a woman who had stared into the Abyss, and come back from the brink.

"How are you feeling?" asked Saark.

Nienna tilted her head, giving a half shrug. "Tired. What I'd give for a hot bath."

"Me too." Saark coughed. "I mean, on my own, not, not with… you." He stumbled to a halt. Flames crackled. Wood spat. In the Iron Forest, snow fell from branches. Mary's hooves crunched snow.

"Am I so hard to look at?" said Nienna, suddenly, tears in her eyes. "Am I so ugly?"

"No! No, of course not." Saark moved around the fire, and placed his arm around her shoulders. He gave her a gentle squeeze. "You are beautiful," he said.

She looked up into his face. Tears stained her pink cheeks. "You mean that?"

"Of course!" said Saark. "It's just, well, Kell, and that axe, and, well…"

"You always say that," snapped Nienna, and rubbed viciously at her tears, heaving Saark's arm from her shoulders. "I think, for you Saark, it is a convenient excuse."

"That's not true," said Saark, and placed his arm back over Nienna's shoulder. "Come here, Little One. And before you bite off my head with that savage snapping tongue, it's a term of affection, not condescension." Saark hugged Nienna for a while, and rocked her, and she placed her head against his chest – so recently violated, now repaired with advanced vachine healing.

Nienna could hear Saark's heartbeat. It was strong. Like him. And she could smell his natural scent, and it made her head spin and her mouth dry. She could see stars. She could look into heaven and taste the ambrosia of a distant, fleeting promise.

Kell coughed. "Sleep well, did you?"

Saark eased his arm from Nienna's shoulders. "Don't be getting any wrong ideas, old man."

Kell leered at him from the dawn gloom. "*I wasn't,*" he said, almost cryptically, and disappeared into the woodland for a piss. Saark glanced at Nienna, as if to say, *See? My guardian devil,* but she was looking at him strangely and he didn't like that look. He knew exactly what that look meant. It was a look a thousand women had given him over the years, and Saark knew about such things, because he was a beautiful man. But worse. He was a beautiful man without morals.

He shivered, in anticipation, as a ghost walked over his soul...

They ate a swift breakfast of dried beef, and set off through the Iron Woods, Saark leading Mary by a short length of frayed rope. The walking was hard; sometimes there were narrow trails to follow, but more often than not these petered out and they had to travel cross-country, Kell leading the way and cursing as he fought the clawed fingers of the trees and tramped heavy boots through snow and tangled dead undergrowth.

After a few hours of walking and cursing, they stopped for a break. Or in the case of Saark, for a moan.

"My feet are frozen! We should build a fire."

"We haven't got the time," said Kell, face sour.

"Yes, but if my toes freeze solid I won't be able to walk. Even worse, I saw one man once, used to work over near Moonlake when we had those real bad falls a few years back. He was stranded, out on the Iopian Plains, out there for days he was. His toes went black and fell off!"

"They fell off?" said Nienna, aghast.

"I've seen this also. In the army," said Kell, removing his own boots and rubbing his toes. "The trick," he gave Saark a full teeth-grin, "is to keep moving. Keep the hot blood flowing. When you languish on your arse like a drunken dandy, that's when you get into trouble."

Saark ignored the insult, and gazed around. "But it is pretty," he announced. "Reminds me of a poem..."

"Don't start," snapped Kell. "I fucking despise poets."

"But look, old man! Look at the beauty! Look at the majesty of Nature!"

"The majesty of Nature?" spluttered Kell, and his face turned dark. "Where we're headed, boy, there's little majesty and lots of death."

Saark considered this, as Mary nuzzled his hand. "And where is that?" he said, finally, when Kell ignored the hint to continue.

"Balaglass Lake," said Kell.

"You're insane," said Myriam. "We can't travel there; it's poisoned land!"

"Whoa," said Saark, holding up a hand. "Poisoned? As in, gets into our bodies and chokes us, kind of poison?"

"Balaglass Lake is frozen," said Myriam. "But not with ice, with toxins. Even in high summer it remains solid, but as unwary travellers wander across its seemingly solid surface, then a pool will suddenly open up and eat them. I saw it, once. Near the edge. Man fell in, up to his knees; over the next few days, the... water, or whatever it is, ate the flesh from his bones. We strapped him down, used tourniquets, a leather strap between his teeth. He screamed for three nights until we could bear it no more and put him out of his misery." Myriam faltered, and was silent.

"A happy tale," snapped Saark. "Thank you so much for lifting my mood!"

"We need to cross it," said Kell. "It's the quickest way."

"Where to?" said Saark, face a frown.

"To the Black Pike Mines," said Kell.

They stood by the shores of Balaglass Lake, but there was nothing to see except a perfectly flat platter of snow. A wind sighed from the edge of the Iron Forest, ruffling Kell's beard as his dark eyes swept the flat plateau.

"You see?" pointed Myriam, behind her. They looked at the animal tracks. "Nothing heads out onto the frozen lake; it's as if the animals *know* it's evil and will suck them down."

"What freezes it, if not the ice?" said Saark, rubbing his chin.

Myriam shrugged. "Who knows? It has always been thus. Styx said his father, and his father's father, had both always known it as such a place. And that only the foolhardy attempted to cross."

"How big is it?" said Saark, peering out across the desolate flat plain.

"Big enough," laughed Kell, and stepped out onto the frozen surface. "See. Solid as a rock."

Saark stared at him. "It's when you say things like that the ground normally opens up and swallows you! You should not tempt the Fates, Kell. Their sense of humour is more corrupt than a canker's brain."

"Ah, bollocks," said Kell. "Come on ladies, we have a mission. You want to save Falanor? Well it won't happen if you all stand there picking your noses."

"I do so under protest," said Myriam, and warily tested the surface with her boot. "Seeing a man scream with only bone sticks as legs taught me never to chance my luck here." Even so, she stepped onto the frozen lake and stood beside Kell. Then Nienna stepped out, and lifted her head proudly, turning to meet Saark's gaze.

Saark stepped from one boot to the other. "You sure there's no way round?" he whined.

"Get out here!" thundered Kell, and turning, stalked off across the plate of ice.

Warily, Saark followed, leading Mary who shied away, trying to pull back. "Shh!" soothed Saark, and slowly, gently, coaxed the donkey out onto the frozen surface.

Myriam, who was twenty paces ahead, turned. "See. Animals can sense it. Sense the death."

"Will you fucking shut up!" shouted Saark, irate now as he fought with the donkey. "Shh, girl, come on, girl, it won't hurt you, girl, please come on, trust me, it won't hurt."

"Is that how you coax all the ladies?" grinned Myriam.

Saark considered this, and frowned. "That's just a damn and dirty misrepresentation," he said. Then smiled. "Although I have to admit, it works sometimes."

Kell and Nienna were ahead, Kell striding through the powdered snow without a backward glance, the mighty Ilanna in one fist, his other clenched tight. Nienna trotted by his side, and glancing back, she saw Saark and Myriam following.

"Does this lake really swallow people, grandfather?" she asked, staring down at her boots. She had come to trust the ground, and the thought of walking on thin ice filled her with a consummate fear.

"Old wives' tales," said Kell, without looking at her. His gaze was focused on the distant line of trees, a swathe of iron-black trunks no bigger than his thumbnails. Half a league, he reckoned. That was a long way to walk on treacherous, thin ice.

Behind, Saark and Myriam were making small-talk.

"Tell me more about the clockwork," said Saark, the rope from a disobedient donkey cutting into his hand and making him wince.

"What do you need to know?"

"You think I will die? Without it, I mean?"

"That is what Tashmaniok and Shanna advised. They may have been lying, though." She peered at Saark. "Why? How do you feel?"

"Wonderful! Powerful, strong, at the peak of my prowess! All pain is gone, my wounds have healed except for the odd twinge;

"I'm thinking maybe this clockwork vampire thing isn't so bad after all. I am faster, stronger, my eyesight more acute; my stamina rarely leaves me, and I have greater resistance to heat and cold."

"And yet you still moan about your cold toes," observed Myriam.

"That's because the moaning bastard will whine about anything!" shouted back Kell.

"By the gods, he has good hearing for a human," frowned Saark.

"Better watch him, then, when you're sat under the blankets cuddling Nienna."

Saark stared long and hard at Myriam. "I was simply offering warmth and friendship," he said.

"Yes," snorted Myriam. "I've seen that sort of friendship a lot during my short, bitter lifetime!"

Saark's eyes went wide. "Me? Really? You think I'd..." He considered this. "Actually, yes, of course you're right. I would. But you're missing the point. With that huge ugly axe hanging like a pendulum over the back of my skull, well, somehow I seem to lose that all-important *urge*." He grinned, but watched Myriam's face descend into pain. "Are you well?"

"Yes! No. It's just, well, I don't want to talk about it."

Saark replayed the conversation in his mind. Something had upset Myriam. What had it been? With his big flapping lips, he'd managed to put his damn soldier's boot in the horse shit again. Saark frowned, then stopped walking, placing his hands on his hips. Mary clacked to a halt behind him, and Myriam turned, a question in her eyes.

Saark moved to her, and he was close, and he could smell her scent, a natural wood-smoke, a musky heady aroma mixed with sweat and Myriam's natural perfume. It made him a little dizzy. It made his mouth dry.

"Yes?" she said.

"Nothing," he smiled, and leant in close, lips almost touching hers, and he paused, and felt her inch towards him, her body shifting, in acceptance, in readiness, in subtle longing; and this was his permission to continue and he brushed her lips with his, a delicate gesture as if touching the petals of a rose and he felt her *sigh*. He eased closer, pressed his body against hers, and they kissed, and she was warm and firm under his gently supporting hands, her body taut, muscular, stronger than any woman he'd held before. He heard her groan, and her kiss became more passionate and Saark understood now, *understood* with the clarity of blood on snow. She had been eaten by the parasite cancer, and retreated like a snail into its shell. Myriam had repressed her lust, her longing, her desires, and it had been a long time since she'd had a real man; a long time since she'd had *any* man. Saark grinned to himself. *I'll show her what a real man is all about*, and he kissed her with passion, with delicacy, with an understanding of exactly what women want, how to bring them out, how to allow them to enjoy themselves – and more importantly, enjoy themselves with *him*.

She pulled back. "You're a dirty scoundrel," she laughed.

"Kiss me again."

She kissed him again, with an urgency now that was suddenly interrupted as Mary shoved her muzzle into Saark's cheek and flapped her lips with a "hrrpphhhhh" of splattered donkey saliva. Saark made a croaking sound, taking a step back, and Myriam laughed a laugh which was a tinkling of gentle chimes.

"I think she's jealous," smirked Myriam.

"I think you're right," agreed Saark. "Go on! Shoo! Bloody donkey! Bugger off!"

Myriam touched Saark's cheek. "I'll be waiting for you. Tonight."

Saark gave a single nod. "I know, my sweetness."

The Iron Forest shifted slowly back into view, but Kell had stopped up ahead. The travellers had become strung out, Kell in the lead, followed by a sullen Nienna walking alone, then Saark and Myriam trotting across the flat lake side by side, their faces awash with laughter and good humour. After a few minutes they caught up to Kell, whose dark eyes were surveying the black, seemingly impenetrable mass of the Iron Forest. It was dark, daunting, huge angular trunks and branches like broken claws. A dull silence seemed to ooze from the forest like an invisible smoke. No birds sang. No sounds came to the group, except for...

"Was that a cracking sound?" said Saark, going suddenly very still.

"Shh," said Kell.

They listened. Beneath, somewhere seemingly *deep* beneath, there came another series of tiny, gentle cracks. The noises were unmistakable, and this time in a quick-fire succession like a volley of crossbow bolts from battlements under siege.

"Should we run?" said Saark.

"A very bad idea," said Kell, softly. "We need to walk. Quickly. And I think we should spread out. Distribute the weight."

"I knew this was a bad idea," said Myriam, ice in her voice.

"Hold your tongue, woman! It's saved us three days' travel, and every day matters with those bastard vampires out there; or had you forgotten our purpose, so busy were you sticking your tongue into the dandy's foul mouth?"

"Let's just move," said Saark, holding his hands out.

They spread out, to a retort of more *crackles* from under the frozen surface of Balaglass Lake. This time, the sounds were nearer the surface; not deep down, like before.

"I'm frightened," said Nienna.

Kell said nothing.

They moved towards the iron-black trees, spreading apart, listening to the cracking sounds. Some were quiet, distant, deep below the surface; but some were loud, rising in volume suddenly until they made Kell's ears hurt. He increased his pace.

Saark was jogging, with Kell to his left, Myriam and Nienna to his right. Mary's hooves clumped the ice behind him, and he stopped, suddenly. He felt the ice beneath his boots *shudder*. Could the impact of Mary's hooves be making it worse? After all, there was some pressure there. Saark turned and stared at the donkey. Mary eyed him warily, and brayed, stamping her hooves as if to ward off cold.

"Whoa!" said Saark. "Don't do that, girl!"

"Eeyore," brayed Mary, as if sensing something beneath the surface of the snow, something like a predator closing in on them fast. Saark glanced up. Kell had made the bank, closely followed by Nienna. The bank was a muddy, root-entwined step, maybe waist height. Kell reached down, and hauled Nienna up to safety.

Saark started to run, then stopped as a crack opened in the surface before him. "Ahh!" he said, more an exhalation of horror than a word, and he took a step back. An evil, sulphurous aroma rose from the crack which zig-zagged before him. It shuddered, the whole toxic frozen lake seemed to shudder, and the crack grew yet wider. Saark ran right, where the crack petered out, and around it with Mary in tow still stamping those heavy hooves.

Saark looked up, saw Myriam had reached the bank and Kell hauled her up a lower, ramped section. Her boots scrabbled and slid in the frozen mud. There! Mary would get up that! *How did I get so damned far behind? What happened there? Are the gods mocking me again?*

He ran for it. Kell grew closer, beard rimed with ice, face screwed into a mask of concern.

"Come *on*, Saark!" hissed Myriam.

More cracks rang out, like ballistae from siege engines; Saark pumped his arms, and Mary trotted obediently after him – and suddenly stopped, hauling back on the rope, rear haunches dropping, a strangled bray renting the air. Saark was jerked back, nearly pulled off his feet, and he whirled, scowling. "Stupid Mary!" he snapped. "Come on! Come on, damn donkey, or I'll leave you out here to sink!"

Mary shook her head, braying, and a shower of spit hit Saark like a wet fish. Saark moved behind the donkey, and slapped her rump as hard as he could. Mary coughed, shook her head again, and launched ahead with hooves flying over the ice. Saark ran after her, saw her scramble up the slope, just as the ice opened up before him and his boots sank in up to the knees. He screamed, flailing forwards, stumbling, fingers brushing the bank. And Kell was there, leaning forward, and their hands touched and eyes met. "Oh no!" whispered Saark.

Kell turned, fumbled with Ilanna. "Grab the axe, lad," he shouted, leaning out. But another crack rent the air, and Saark went under, and was gone beneath the surface of the frozen lake.

"No!" screamed Myriam, but Kell grabbed her jerkin.

"Whoa lass, you can't go in there!"

Chunks of ice bobbed, and Mary brayed forlornly. Snow began to fall from a bleak pastel sky, and they stood there on the bank, watching the chunks of ice, listening to more cracking sounds and praying for Saark. Kell grimaced. What had Myriam said? That the man's legs had eaten away after the toxins of the lake came into contact with his flesh? *But maybe Saark will be lucky*, thought Kell. *Maybe he'll drown.*

Myriam strained again, and Kell picked her bodily up, and moved her away from the edge of Balaglass Lake, her legs kicking, eyes furious. "Put me *down!*" she hissed.

Kell dropped her on the frozen forest floor.

"I'm sorry, lass." Kell shook his head sadly. "He's gone. He's dead."

There came a surge from the lake, and Saark appeared gasping and spluttering, kicking and struggling. "I'm not fucking gone!" he screamed. "Help me out! Now! This shit! It tastes like shit!"

Kell sprinted back to the slope, and lying full length reached out with Ilanna. Saark grabbed the blades, careful not to sever his own fingers, and Kell hauled him onto the sloped bank where he rolled, coughing and choking. Saark was covered in what appeared a thick, oily, black green sludge, and he coughed up some huge chunks which sat, quivering on the frozen mud.

"Fucking horrible! It was fucking disgusting!" He struggled, fighting with his wet clothes until he stood, naked and shivering on the icy bank. He looked at everyone. "What? *What?* Come on, get me some fresh clothes, will you? Out of Mary's basket."

Myriam found fresh clothes, and Kell grabbed handfuls of snow, scrubbing Saark's violently shivering body free of the lake's sludge. When he came to Saark's groin, he handed him a snowball. "Here you go, lad. A man's cock is his own business."

"Myriam," said Kell. "Build a fire. I'll find some water, we need to get the lad cleaned off. And Nienna, can you get some firewood? Good girl." He turned back to Saark, struggling into thick woollens, his fingers almost blue. "What the hell were you doing, lad, putting that damn donkey before yourself?"

"I couldn't leave her!" snapped Saark.

"Well, I hope she was worth it," said Kell with a scowl.

"She is. She is."

"We'll see if you still think that when your flesh is peeling off your bones."

"I'd forgotten that," shivered Saark miserably, and stared forlornly at his boots. They were leaking black dye onto the snow. "The whoresons! Those boots cost a pretty penny."

"I think you've got bigger problems than that," snapped Kell.

Soon they had a reasonably large fire burning, despite Kell muttering about visibility and smoke and announcing their location to every damn soldier, brigand, Blacklipper and cut-throat for a two league circle. Kell found a frozen pool, and cracking it with his axe, bid Saark undress once more and jump into the ice-chilled water.

"But why?" he whined, kicking off his trews.

"Get that shit off your skin. And out of your hair. Don't want to go bald, do you?"

Saark looked at Kell in absolute horror, and undressed with acceleration. However, it took a prod from Ilanna to get a squawking, flapping, *very* unhappy Saark into the frozen pool and he went under, and spluttered up, and scowled and cursed, swore and chattered. He scrubbed at his hair, muttering obscenities to Kell, to Mary and to the world in general. Then Kell hauled him out, wrapped him in a blanket and supported the shivering man to the fire, laying his clothes next to him.

"It's like having a baby again," muttered Kell.

"Well, if you hadn't dragged us across that bloody lake in the first place, I wouldn't be sat here with balls the size of acorns."

"So, nothing's changed, eh lad?" grinned Kell.

Saark was shivering too much to reply.

Myriam and Nienna got a large pan of broth cooking, and Kell disappeared into the Iron Forest searching for bad people to dismember. He returned after an hour, shaking his head, to find Saark slurping his third bowl of soup and in much better humour.

"See?" beamed Saark. "Nothing wrong with me! Nothing at all! I think all these stories about toxic lakes that eat men whole are nothing but horse-shit ghost stories spewed by cranky old woodsmen around their inbred fires." He gave a meaningful glance at Myriam, and then sat back, opening his blanket a little to allow more warmth in.

"By all the gods lad, put it away!" boomed Kell. "We don't want to be looking at that whilst we eat our soup!"

"What's the matter, never seen such an example of prime steak before?"

"I've never seen such a little tiddler!" roared Kell, good humour suddenly returned. "You make the sausages at the butchers seem quite majestic! Now put your clothes on, we've wasted enough time messing around here. We should get moving."

"I have barely recovered from my near death incident," whined Saark, pulling his blankets tighter with a scowl. "The least you could do is have some compassion!"

"I'll have some compassion when you're dead. Get your trews on, I found soldiers out in the forest. *Lots* of soldiers. Enough soldiers to, for example, give us a real bad day."

Myriam stamped out the fire, and they were ready to move in a few minutes, Saark complaining about his wet boots and how he was chilled to the bone.

Snow started to fall heavy, and clung to the angular branches of trees like a white parasite. They trudged through the silent forest, leaving a narrow trail and cutting randomly between the trees in case the soldiers had seen their fire, and came to investigate.

The sky was streaked with ice.

And through this frozen forest world, they moved.

They came upon a deserted farmhouse, a leaning, ramshackle affair with no obvious trails leading to it, or from it. It must have been deserted for years, and the woodland had slowly reclaimed the land, the road and the stables. It still maintained a roof, and that was something, for the snow was coming down thick. Kell was thankful for this; as he pointed out, it would cover their tracks.

Kell allowed them a fire, for without fire, he said, they may die; and to hell with the soldiers.

"If they do come," he grunted, "I'll teach them something new about cold. The cold of an early grave."

With a fire burning in the old kitchen fireplace, and the sky dark outside, the enclosing forest blocked out ambient light and gradually piled high with the fresh fall.

Myriam disappeared into the woods, returning with wild mushrooms and berries from which she made a stew, and Saark busied himself in the stables making sure Mary the donkey had a thick blanket over her back, and was not subjected to too many draughts.

Saark patted her muzzle. "I'd have you in the house with us, but you know what Kell's like. Grumpy old bastard. Soon as eat you as look at you."

"Talking to your donkey again?" said Myriam, almost in his ear, and he jumped.

"By the Chaos Halls, you move quiet, Myriam."

"Just one of my many talents."

She moved in front of him, and draped her hands over his shoulders. She leant forward and they kissed, and despite the cold and the snow, despite the darkness and the distant nagging fear of their mission, of the vampires, of the state of Falanor, here and now they were enclosed in a shield of warmth and desire.

"You coming to my bed tonight?" she whispered, husky, pulling away but not letting go. She was in control now, she was the dominant one, her confidence returned tenfold, her eyes bright and eager. Saark enjoyed this. Enjoyed the reversal. It was stimulating.

"Yes," said Saark, seeing no need at coyness. His hands moved down her back, onto her buttocks, and he pulled her to him so their hips touched. He was hard against her, and he grinned because he knew that she knew; and she knew he knew she knew. They kissed again. "I'm going to treat you so fine, Myriam," he said.

"I know," she smiled.

"Where's that firewood?" came Kell's coarse shout.

"Coming, Legend," grinned Myriam, and filled her arms with chunks from beside the leaning, rickety stables. "And then we'll have some poetry! We'll have some hero-song!"

"Not from me you won't," growled Kell, and slammed the door.

The fire had burned low. They had arranged blankets before the flames, Nienna close beside Kell – *presumably so the old goat can keep an eye on me and her*, mused Saark. But as embers glittered, so too did Myriam's eyes and she rose, taking her blankets with her, and moved to the nearest bedroom. Saark followed, and stepping into the small room, he closed the door.

Myriam moved and opened the shutters. The snow had stopped, and eerie moonlight filtered in at an angle, highlighting her face, her high cheekbones, her smooth, pale skin. Her hair caught the moonlight, and shone like liquid silver shot through with strands of ebony. Slowly, she trailed to the bed and laid out her blankets. In silence, Saark did the same, and then they stood there for a while, staring at one another, like virgins on a first date, simply watching, not rushing, as if not quite sure what to do. Saark moved first, fired by lust and kneeling on the bed, and Myriam came from the opposite side to meet him. He touched her shoulders, and ran his hands down her arms, then leant in close and kissed her neck, and breathed in that musky scent. She groaned, a low, low animal sound from the pit of her stomach, and in that groan Saark sensed years of frustration, of longing, of need, and he caught sight of his own fingers in the moonlight and was shocked to see them shaking. *What's this? Saark, the greatest of lovers, the most incredible seducer in the whole of Falanor, shaking like a child at his first sniff of an eager quim?* He smiled, and enjoyed the sensation, and his hands took Myriam's head and his fingers ran through her hair. It was luscious, a pelt, and he kissed her and their tongues mated, and as they kissed they undressed one another, one item of clothing at a time, their hands that little bit too eager, a little bit too quick with excitement and the promise of what was to come. Saark touched Myriam's naked shoulder, as her hand slipped between his legs and took hold of his throbbing, eager cock. "A better performance than this morning," she purred, and bit his ear. He gave a little jump and grinned, face outlined by moonlight.

"You'd better believe it," he said, and his tongue left a slick trail down her jaw, then down her throat, and he took her left breast in his mouth, pulling slowly at the nipple between his teeth and holding it there as he felt himself *pulsing* in her hands and his own hand dropped between her legs. She was warm there, and wet, so wet, and Saark breathed in her scent and tickled her, slowly, teasing her with two fingers and her back arched and she reclined back on the bed, and Saark lowered his mouth to her cunt, and he played with her and she moaned, and his tongue teased and he nibbled and inside that dark sweet hole he could feel it, *feel* the *rhythm* of ticking clockwork and Myriam was groaning, writhing, and she could take no more and she pulled at him, her fingers eager and grasping, her nails leaving long red grooves down Saark's ribs and hips and he straddled her. Saark looked down. Myriam's face was bathed in moonlight, but more, she was lost, lost in an ecstasy and lost in the moment. She was so beautiful it that writhing, spellbound zone, and it was timeless, and endless, and she took his cock with both hands, pulling him urgently, guiding him into her and he fell, fell down a huge well of honey and spiralling scents, fell into a world of crazy colours which absorbed him, cushioned him, exploded him, and they fucked on the blankets in the moonlight, and it was slow, and beautiful, and sensuous, and Myriam clawed his back and Saark bit her neck, drawing a little blood with his vachine fangs but this made Myriam more wild, and she bucked, writhed, with him entrapped, unable to let go. It was magick, but a magick deeper than anything cast by the so-called magickers in their long silver robes back in Vor. This was a magick of Nature, a magick of the beast, and it was completely natural, a need, a lust, and they came together in a vortex of pleasure and fell down a long black well to the infinite realms of contented sleep.

It was morning. Early morning. A cool wind drifted in through shutters. Somewhere, a bird gave a splutter of song and Saark opened his eyes, looking up into Myriam's face. She rested her head on one hand, raised on her elbow, and she was staring down at him. She smiled, and he saw her vampire fangs, complete with traces of blood. His blood. But he did not mind. In fact, it excited him rather a lot and she noticed this with a purr of appreciation. "Again," she said, a growl, a simple command, and Saark gave a nod, and within seconds they were fucking only *this time* this time it was different and Myriam was more wild, far more feral and something had changed something had *gone* and they kissed and he thrust into her, thrust deep into her so hard he thought he would tear himself apart and they worked together, in perfect rhythm, and sweat was dripping from her face into his and as he rose frantically to an uncontrolled and uncontrollable orgasm so the clockwork went *click* and the brass wires and gold wires threaded from inside Myriam, and the clockwork seemed to *know* Saark was blood-oil infected, and they were needed, and the machines came through Myriam, through her womb and into Saark and he felt a scream well as he came, and in the moment of greatest pleasure, his moment of greatest *vulnerability* so the clockwork burned through him, entered him, and he writhed around and would have yelled and screamed but Myriam's hand clamped over his mouth and her incredibly strong body pinned him, rigid, locked down to the bed as the clockwork inside her *split* and *multiplied* and her eyes glistened and she understood.

Myriam stood, and watched Saark writhing on the bed, his eyes rolled back and white, froth at his lips.

Kell burst in, Ilanna in his great fist, eyes roving. "What's happened? Shit, Saark? Saark?" and he rushed to the bed and Myriam stood back. Saark thrashed, in agony, his body rolling and bucking and a smile was on her lips. Slowly, she dressed.

Kell turned on her. "What did you do to him?"

"I saved his life," she said.

"He doesn't look very well to me!"

"Listen. He was bit. By Shanna. You know how it works, Kell; I know you do. If he didn't get the clockwork, eventually the blood-oil would poison him; like the Blacklippers, but worse, for with them it's not in their bloodstream, only in their flesh. Here, he would have been dead within a week, no matter how strong he said he felt."

"Clockwork? But, how? How did you... " Kell's voice trailed off.

"Use your imagination, old man," said Myriam, and pushed past him, but he grabbed her upper arm. She struggled for a moment, but even despite her *vachine* strength, Kell was stronger. His grip was an iron shackle, his thunderous face doom.

"If you have hurt him..."

"Yes, I know, you'll plant that huge fucking axe in my skull. But just remember your complete lack of trust in a couple of hours when he comes round, and feels better than ever. Just you wait, Kell! I look forward to your apology. I look forward to that stupid pig look on your stupid flat face!" She shook off his hand and stalked from the farmhouse, looking for somewhere to wash. Her anger was tangible. Like blood mist.

"I don't understand," said Nienna, as Kell pulled blankets over Saark's naked body. "She said she gave him... clockwork? So that means now he's a full vachine? How did she do it?"

"I'll explain later," muttered Kell, and checked Saark's pulse. He had settled down, was still, although his eyes were still rolled back in his skull. His breathing was regular. Kell placed his hand on Saark's chest. Within, he could feel a heartbeat, but also a steady *ticking*; like a clock.

"Is he well?"

"Shit," muttered Kell and left the room.

Nienna moved to the edge of the bed, and sat beside Saark. She stared down at his face, and her hand moved, tracing down his beautiful features and coming to rest on his naked chest. She gave a shiver. And then she realised, both he and Myriam had been in here together. Naked. Now everything clicked into place. Now everything fit together.

Nienna's face changed, and the vision that swam across her young, pretty features turned her ugly for just a moment.

Composing herself, and biting her lip, and pushing away images of violence, Nienna stood and left the bedroom.

Myriam sat by a bubbling stream. Ice froze the edges, but it flowed down the centre, pure and fresh and ice-cold. Small blue flowers grew along one bank, where the snow had been held at bay by a line of dark green pine. Her gaze followed the trees up, up to distant heights; she reckoned them to be a couple of hundred years old. Magnificent. Kings of the forest.

She sighed, and dipped her hand in the stream, thinking back to the night, and their love-making, and the absolute total pleasure. Then her eyes grew bright, and she thought now of the clockwork, and Saark's acceptance of the clockwork – for she knew, if it did not work his death would have been instant. He would have died inside her. But that had not happened, and Saark was, now, for the very first time, true vachine.

"'A creature of blood-oil and clockwork,'" she quoted. "'A child of the Oak Testament.'" She had spent precious little time with Shanna, and Tashmaniok, the Soul Stealers who had turned *her* into vachine – and so robbed the parasitic cancer which riddled her of another dark victory. But during that short time, she had learned from them.

And the rest – well, Myriam smiled. The rest was *instinct*.

A hand touched her shoulder. She had not heard him approach, and she turned, and smiled up at him, and winter sunlight highlighted her hair and her smile.

"Myriam," said Saark, and crouched down. Now, his skin was more radiant. Now, he was at the peak of physical strength; of fitness; of *clockwork* enhanced life.

"You feel well?"

"Incredible," he said. And inside Saark, something went *tick tick tick*. His eyes glowed. He reached down and kissed Myriam, and they stayed there for a while, kissing, holding hands, listening to the burbling of the stream.

"We should leave soon," said Myriam. "In case more soldiers come."

"Of course. Kell will be shitting buckets."

"Did I do the right thing?"

"You did the right thing," said Saark, and he could feel it, he knew, inside himself, that without the clockwork he would have died; and it would not have been a good death. What Myriam had done was save him. She had given him a part of her own clockwork engine. Her own machine had divided, and grown, and become a part of Saark, golden wires and brass gears worming into him, meshing with his flesh, building him into full vachine. Real vachine.

"I love you," said Myriam.

"And I love you," said Saark, amazed at himself how easy the words came; although, in all fairness, he'd spoken the words a thousand times to a thousand different ladies. This time, did he mean it? Saark filed that away for later analysis.

"Now, you will never die," said Myriam. "And we will live together, be strong together, forever."

Saark frowned, but Myriam was looking across the stream. She did not catch his face.

"Just think," she continued, eyes distant, "we are so strong, we are like royalty, Saark! We could have anything we wanted! Gold, jewels, land, titles, we could *take* anything our hearts desired!"

"Wait," said Saark, his voice soft. But Myriam continued, pushing on, unheeding of the tone of Saark's voice...

"If we conquered the Vampire Warlords, just think what we could do with their power, Saark?" She turned and looked up at him, and misread the confusion in his face. "We could use Kell, get to the Warlords, slaughter them. We could absorb their power, or use their legions – for that is what they will be doing, right now, as we sit here by this stream. They are creating vampires, creating armies! But we are superior, Saark, we are *vachine* and we could rule the world together!"

"Wait," snapped Saark, pushing back from Myriam and standing. She followed him up, and now it was her face that held confusion. "What the hell are you talking about? Taking anything we want? Ruling the Vampire Warlords? What kind of horse shit is this?"

"We are all-powerful *vachine*, can't you see? Together, we can do anything!" said Myriam, and he caught a glimpse of her brass fangs. They had slid out a little. And he knew; that was a sign – of attack.

"I think you get ahead of yourself, Myriam."

"You said you loved me."

"And I do. But I didn't realise that meant ruling the whole fucking world with you." There was heavy sarcasm in his voice, and Myriam's face flushed with anger.

"Don't turn against me now!" she hissed.

Saark held up his hands. "Whoa! Hold on. We had some great sex last night, and I like you, Myriam, really I do, but I didn't realise I was signing a contract! I didn't think we were becoming partners in the destruction of Falanor!"

"What's that supposed to mean? We'd save Falanor!"

"What, and rule in the place of the King?"

"The King is dead!" snapped Myriam.

"Yes, and we are not able to take his place. What's got into you, girl? What the hell is this madness?"

"It's not madness," she hissed, eyes flashing dangerous, "it's *ambition*. All my life I have been looked down upon, spat at, sneered at, misjudged, pitied, and then the cancer sought to end it all with a mocking final dark salute. But the vachine saved me. And with that salvation, I realised I'd been given a gift. And so have you. And we can use that gift to ascend in power. And to rule."

"I don't want to rule," said Saark, voice quiet.

"I thought we were in this together," said Myriam.

"You mean you thought I was a tactical manoeuvre?" snapped Saark, his own anger rising. "Is that what happened last night, Myriam? Was I just a fuck to get the clockwork inside me, so you claim the credit and use me to do your bidding? I've seen women like you, at court, thinking all men are weak-minded and easily controlled with their cocks. You think you can control us, and get absolutely anything you want. And yes, many times we are; we are weak, and gullible, and we think with our dicks and not our brains. But I tell you something now, Myriam, and you listen to me, and heed my words. I am not weak-minded. And greater than *you* have tried to turn me against Falanor; but I love my country more than I love life, and I will give my last breath to *save* this place, not condemn it; and certainly not to place some second-rate vachine *Queen* on the fucking throne!"

Myriam snarled, and leapt at Saark with claws out, slashing for his throat. He side-stepped, back-handed her across the face and knocked her to the frozen soil.

Myriam wiped her mouth, looked at blood-oil on the back of her hand, and snarled up at Saark.

"You'll regret that," she hissed.

"Show me," he said.

She leapt, and Saark punched her but she bore him to the ground, where he hit hard, grunted, and they both rolled down the bank and into the stream, crushing the swathe of little blue flowers. Myriam's claws slashed for Saark's face, and he caught her hands but one razor tip cut a neat line from his temple to his jaw. "I'm going to slice you open, a flap at a time!" she raged, struggling.

"How quickly love turns to hate," mocked Saark, and kicked her between the legs. She grunted, and Saark's elbow slammed her face, but failed to dislodge her; instead, her hand shot out and thumped Saark's face under the water.

Myriam shifted her body forward, and put her full weight on Saark's face. He struggled, kicking, bubbles erupting in a stream through the ice-cold waters. Myriam smiled, applying as much pressure as she could muster, and she watched him squirm as if through frosted glass, face distorted by the water, and by his struggles, and by his furious anger. He spluttered, and bubbled, and Myriam wondered how long it would take to drown a *vachine*...

"Up you get, lass." The voice was Kell's, and it was colder than an ice-filled tomb. Myriam leapt backwards, twisting into a somersault to land nimbly on the opposite bank of the stream. She glared at Kell, and her eyes dropped perceptibly to the matt black Ilanna nestling in huge bear paws. Kell smiled, and gave a narrow-lipped grimace. "Why don't you come over here," he said. "I have a gift for you."

"Fuck you!" snarled Myriam, and for a second her eyes moved from Nienna, standing pale and shocked, hands clasped before her, eyes wide, to Saark, glaring up at her from the stream and coughing up lungfuls of water. Then back to Kell.

He could see the fear in her eyes. A fear of the axe.

Then she was gone, sprinting through the Iron Forest, and in the blink of an eye she'd vanished through the trees.

Kell jumped down into the stream and Saark took his proffered hand, wrist to wrist in the warrior's grip, and was hauled to his feet. He brushed water off his jerkin.

"If I'd been quicker, I would have said I already had," said Saark, with a painful grimace.

"What? Fucked her?" Kell fixed him with a beady eye. "Lad, it's you who got a good fucking, that's for sure." Kell scratched his beard. "What, in the name of the Seven Gods and the Blood Void, was that all about?"

"A power trip, I think," said Saark, and stumbled up the slippery bank where Nienna reached out and helped him up. He smiled into her face, but she did not return the expression.

"Thank you, Little One."

Nienna scowled, turned, and disappeared through the forest.

Saark lifted his hands in the air. "What? *What?* Why are women so bloody complex? And what did I do to deserve *all of this?*"

Kell whacked him on the shoulder as he came past, and gave a bitter laugh. "You know *exactly* what you did, lad. And there's a hundred pregnant wives across the whole of bloody Falanor to bear witness to that one! However, we have more serious matters at hand."

"More serious than getting drowned?" mumbled Saark.

"Better come pack your stuff," Kell said, and his voice was serious. "There's soldiers out in the woods. Lots of soldiers. I reckon they're looking for something."

"Like us?"

"Yeah, lad. Like us."

SIX
Vampire Plague

Command Sergeant Wood sat on the rooftop, hidden by a chimney, and watched the vampires drifting through the mist-tinged streets below. There were eight of them, a mixture of men and women, and one young girl who reminded him so much of his own dead daughter it brought tears to his eyes. She had long, golden curls, but only the pale face and blood eyes brought Wood crashing back to the present and the world and *reality*. She was a child no longer. No, she was a killer!

Watch. Think. Learn. *Act!*

In the army thirty damn years. Never seen nothing like this. Give me a man with a sword any day! Give me a stinking Blacklipper with a rusted axe, give me a raw recruit with anger in his eyes, spit in his mouth and a dagger in his fist 'cos he thinks I'm a bastard on the parade ground! But this? This... abomination?

Wood considered himself a religious man. He had always thought of the gods as higher beings in control of his life, and always done his utmost never to piss them off, well, as best he could. Wood tried his utmost to be a fair and honourable man, sometimes in battle he slashed his sword across the back of an enemy's neck, maybe stabbed a few through the back of the kidneys as well, but in the scheme of things he didn't lie, cheat, rape or murder. And this was despite being dealt a rough hand in the game of life. For the grey plague to take his wife had been painful beyond bearing; hanging on to her withered hand, weeping, not caring if he died by her side and went down the long grey path to the black waters of the Chaos Halls. No. He'd been ready for that. Sort of. Could bear it. Just. But for his nine-year-old daughter to follow two weeks later... it had been too much to bear. Three days after Sazah's death, Wood tried to take his own life. Tried to hang himself from the polished oak banister of a house now devoid of life and warmth, and love and laughter... and stinking that plague stink, with two corpses filling the beds.

Wood took a length of old rope, and with hands frighteningly steady, formed it into a noose. He tied it with a blood-knot he'd learned when fishing with his brother as a boy; a good, strong knot, not likely to fail. Then he dragged a heavy chair from the bedroom, his daughter's corpse nagging at the edge of his vision, and tied the remaining end to the banister. He stood on the chair, then climbed up onto the banister, one hand against the wall to steady himself. He looked down, to the polished terracotta tiles, and it looked a long way down, looked a long way down into the welcoming well of his own death.

No fear. He smiled. *No fear.*

He would join Tahlan, and Sazah, and they would be together and that would be the end of it. Wood smiled, nodding to himself. He felt himself shift on the chair, and he passed the noose over his neck. The rope had been coarse on his skin, chafing him a little, irritating him – he was a man of small irritations, as his army recruits knew all too well. But this time he did his best to ignore it. After all, he was about to make that final leap...

Then, the door to his house opened, and a wizened old man stepped across the threshold. He was stooped, wearing brown robes and carrying a gnarled, polished walking stick. The old man's name was Pettrus. Once, just like Wood, he'd been a Command Sergeant and the two had met at an old soldier's drinking evening, down at the *Soldiers' Arms*, a dockside tavern of ill repute. The night had been a long one, and when Wood stepped outside for a piss, shuffling down a narrow alley to avoid prying eyes, he'd spotted Pettrus standing by the dockside, staring down into the black, cold, lapping waters, the churned scum and detritus of a busy city port.

"Pettrus? What are you doing, man?"

"I want to die."

"Don't be insane! You're a Command Sergeant in the King's Army! You've got everything a man could want!"

Pettrus turned then, and it was the haunted look in his eyes, the pain, that made Wood realise he was about to jump. There was anguish in the lines of the man's face; pure anguish. He was in mental turmoil. A psychological hell.

"I have nothing!" he snarled, and went to jump... but Wood was there, powerful fist around the older man's bicep, straining to pull him back. They fought for a few moments, struggled and scuffled, and fell back onto the dockside in a slightly drunken heap. They started laughing, and Wood stood, hauling Pettrus up after him.

"I'll buy you an ale. You can tell me all about it."

Pettrus nodded, and they went into the *Soldier's Arms*, through the smoke and crowds to a quiet corner. Wood brought two jugs of frothing ale, brown, bitter and intoxicating.

"Why the hell did you want to do that?" said Wood, slamming his jug down, a creamy moustache atop his real one.

"My wife."

"What's wrong with your wife?"

"Nothing. That's the problem. She's perfect. She's beautiful, well proportioned, long silky black curls, a perfect physical female specimen."

"However?"

"She'll open her legs to any man willing. I caught her, last night, with a young soldier from my own platoon. You hear that? My own *fucking* platoon. I beat him, of course."

"Of course."

"He ran around that bedchamber, trews round his ankles, squawking like a chicken with each punch until I knocked him down the stairs. That shut the bastard up. Then I turned on Darina..."

"You didn't..."

"No, no." Pettrus waved his hand. "We argued. She told me about them. About her lovers. Every week, a different man. Every night I was on sentry duty, she'd come down here, to the taverns, drink her fill and find somebody for comfort. She said she didn't want to be lonely, but we both know that's horse shit."

"Yes."

They drank in silence for a while, then Pettrus looked up, intense, and grabbed Wood's arm. "Thank you. Thank you for saving me."

"Ahh shit, Pettrus. Don't be ridiculous. I did nothing."

"No. No. You saved my life. I owe you."

And from that day they had become good friends, talking often, and helping Pettrus overcome his destroyed marriage. Until the plague hit. Until Tahlan and Sazah died, weight dropping away, skin turning grey, huge sores forming under armpits and in groins, gums peeling back from teeth and forcing them to protrude like on a five-week corpse...

Wood stood on the banister, noose round his neck, looking down into the shocked eyes of Pettrus. The man was older now, retired from the army, powerful but stooped a little. Too much sentry duty, he used to joke. Too much manual work.

"Get down here," he growled.

"Leave me be!" said Wood, tears streaming down his face.

"I'll not let you!" snapped Pettrus. "I thought you were stronger than that!"

"Stronger than what?" screamed Wood, swaying dangerously on the banister which creaked in protest at his weight. "Stronger than a man who watched his family crumble and die, holding their trembling hands whilst they begged for life? Begged me to help them? Spewed blood and black bile and black tears? Stronger than a man cursed by the very Black Axeman of fucking Drennach to the pits of fucking Chaos? Only he's not dead, he's alive and having to live through the same shit day after day after day? Tell me, Pettrus, in all your fucking unholy wisdom, what should I do?"

"Don't jump, is what you should do. Taking your own life is not the answer, my friend."

Wood stared down into those dark brown eyes. He saw a great sadness there, but it was not enough. Not enough to stop him... he went as if to step forward, but Pettrus held out a hand.

"The reason you are not to die, my friend, is because Tahlan would not want it so. She would want you to go on. To live. To be happy. And if you think about it, if you died, would you wish your wife and daughter to follow you to the Oil Lands? No. You know this in your heart, Wood. Trust me. Listen to me."

As he'd been speaking, Pettrus moved slowly up the creaking stairs, each board tuned so that intruders would alert Wood in the night; now, the noise got on his nerves, and he watched Pettrus reach him, and help him down from the banister, and he was covered in tears and snot, and sobbing, but as Pettrus' hand touched his, so the warmth of human contact felt good; it felt so very good.

They drank a bottle of rum, and talked about old times, talked about good times.

"Remember them, my friend."

And the next night, another bottle. And the next. And the next. Until Wood had a warm glow of memories, and of long companionship, and that nasty bite of wanting to die had gradually dissolved.

"Remember them always."

Now, Wood sat on the rooftop, eyes narrowed, watching the vampires. Over the past three nights he'd been making his way slowly, warily, across the Port of Gollothrim and towards the house of Pettrus. Hopefully, the old man would have locked himself in the attic and kept his temper in check. Wood needed to reach him. Needed to plan. Needed the bastard alive, for Pettrus was one of the best tacticians he'd ever met. But the going was slow for Wood, not just because of the rooftop scampers across ice-slippery slate, but because in *hours* he had watched the vampire filth spread, like an evil plague, a virus, oozing through the city like oil smoke. However, unlike the stories, the fireside myths whispered to frighten children in the dark, these creatures moved through the gloomy daylight; even more-so when thick fog rolled in off the Salarl Ocean, obscuring the winter sun. They weren't afraid of the light. And *that* worried Wood right down to his bones.

Now, down by the docks, Wood could hear a riot of activity. Carpenters were sawing and hammering, carving and sculpting, labourers carting huge planks of wood, and ship builders in their hundreds were at work. Wood stood a little, holding onto the chimney, aware that if he slipped and a piece of slate went tumbling to the ground the bastards would be over him like a swarm of insects. He shaded his eyes, trying to see the docks; he could catch glimpses, of bodies hard at work. And of course, their noises echoed through the light mist which had seemed, ridiculously, to have lingered for the past three days now. Or at least, since Bhu Vanesh and his vampire demons had invaded the Port of Gollothrim.

Think. Think. What to do?

Reach Pettrus. But then what?

He shook his head. After all, why were they building *ships* of all things? Wood moved off across the icy rooftop, lowering himself over a stone lintel and down to another. He eased tenderly across ridge tiles, hunched over and trying not to pose a large target, and below in the streets he caught peripheral glances of the creatures, the *vampires*, call them what you will, drifting like ghosts, almost regal in their lazy decadent dawdling.

After another few hours of subterfuge, of careful travel, Wood crouched by a stone gargoyle, glancing past ugly twisted features wearing a stubble of moss and haircream of seagull shit. There. He could see Pettrus' house, a narrow terraced stone building on a steep, cobbled road leading down to the southern docks. The door was open. Wood grimaced. *That was bad.* Even as he watched, he saw two vampires move to the doorway and pause, looking around. There came a subtle *crack* from inside, and the creatures moved in; vanished from sight.

"Bollocks." Wood leapt down to a lower roof, then scrambled to a pipe, swinging his legs over and dangling precariously for a moment, cold fingers clawing, nails dragging on stone, boots kicking uselessly until they found purchase. Wood half climbed, half slid down the iron water-channel pipework, and landed in a heap on the cobbles. He stood, drew his army-issue iron short sword, and approached the door...

Inside, darkness beckoned like a bad nightmare. Wood glanced behind him, licked his lips, and thought better of calling out for Pettrus. It would bring a city full of blood-sucking vermin to the door, that was for sure! But then, he did not need to call out – he heard Pettrus' voice, as grumpy and scratchy as ever.

"Get out, you filthy bastards!" he was snarling, and Wood heard the rasp of steel.

He ran, into the lower quarters where he'd spent many a happy evening drinking brandy and sherry and port, and recounting endless old war stories, tales of campaigns in Anvaresh and Drennach, Torragon and Ionia. Then Pettrus would break out the black bread and cheese, and they'd wash it down with more fine brandy and watch the sun come up over misty rooftops, hearing the call of gulls and distant cacophony of ships unloading their foreign wares at the docks.

Wood ran for the stairs. There came a thud, and a gurgle, and Wood stopped in his tracks. At the foot of the stairs was a dead vampire, chest awash with a flood of crimson, face a rictus mask, fangs gleaming, eyes blood-red and wide and dead. Through the heart. It had been stabbed straight through the heart.

Wood stepped gingerly over the corpse, and eased up the stairs. He heard Pettrus again.

"Come on, you blood-puking bastards! Let's see what you've got!"

"You will not be underestimated again," came a soft, feminine voice, followed by a crunch of wood, and a growl, and the sound of smashing glass.

Wood ran, reaching the landing and spinning into the modest bedroom. Pettrus' sword was on the floor, stained with blood, and he had been flung across the room, hitting the wall, one arm smashing through the window. Blood trickled over his wrist, and his face was slapped, stunned, dazed. Before him, back to Wood, stood a slim girl, no more than eighteen, with long blonde hair and hands focused into claws. She was hissing, a low oozing sound, and hunched ready to spring. To the right, there was another creature, crumpled in a foetal position, hands clasped to chest, panting fast like a heart-attack victim. Pettrus had not been taken easily. But even now, the slim girl was readying to pounce.

Wood leapt forward, shouting "Hah!" as his sword thrust out, but the girl moved fast, *too fast*, spinning as the blade struck, aiming for her heart but missing, and it scored a line under her arm, parting her flowered dress and opening a huge wound but she did not scream, did not moan or cry out in pain but simply took the blow, flesh parting like razored fish-flesh and no blood came out, just flapping bulging muscle revealing yellow ribs within. Wood's blade came back, and she leapt at him, and in reflex his sword shot up and she knocked it away, fist slamming out to thump his chest, the impact a crushing blow that threw him back against the wall, his head ramming back, stars fluttering and she leapt again, pursuing him, and Wood's head twitched sideways where the vampire's fist skimmed his cheek, punching a hole clean through the stone wall. Dust rose, Wood choked, the girl struggled for a moment with fist trapped and Wood side-stepped, glared at her in temper, pain pounding through his chest with hammer blows and realisation in his dark eyes that if her punch had connected, she would have crushed his head like a ripe fruit. His blade lifted, and he struck her a savage blow across the skull, which split her open revealing skull and brain within, a cross-section down halfway to her nose. She did not die. Wood stared with his mouth hung open at the large V of wound, the open skull, the struggling creature who should be dead as a corpse, but was still mouthing obscenities, flapping and fighting, and her fist came out of the wall grey with powdered stone and her fingers were twisted and mangled, snapped and bent in order to retrieve her fist and she turned on Wood, face a horrific open V, eyes split wide apart but still staring at him with recognition, understanding, *hatred*, and Pettrus against the far wall croaked, "Cut off its head!" and Wood's blade lifted wide, and slashed at the girl, and there was a thud as her decapitated split head hit the thick carpet. The headless corpse stood for a moment, and Wood watched it, wondering if the bastard thing would still attack him. What would he do then? Cut off the arms and legs? And what if each body part came after him? He felt an insane giggle welling in his chest and he forced it down with a grunt. *Focus! You've seen worse than this!* But when? When, *really?*

The corpse collapsed, and lay still. Wood gave a sigh, and glanced right to the fast-panting vampire. Its eyes were watching him, and blood was pooling under it.

"I winged it," said Pettrus, pushing himself to his feet and brushing broken glass from his dressing-gown sleeve. "Go on. Kill it, lad."

Wood moved to the thing, wary, sword gripped in a heavily sweating palm. He could feel droplets in his moustache, and on his shining pate. Damn his thinning hair! How would he woo the young ladies now?

His sword slammed down, separating the creature from its head, which rolled a short way and stared up at him, tongue protruding and purple like a great bloated worm.

Pettrus moved to Wood, and slapped him on the back. "Thanks, boy. I had it under control, but you arrived just in time, all right." He coughed, and grinned, and bent to retrieve his own sword.

"Why are you wandering around in your dressing gown?"

"I was asleep, wasn't I?"

"What, *here?* Didn't you have the bloody sense to hide, man?"

"Of course I hid, you buffoon!" chortled Pettrus, and rubbed at his sliced wrist. "I was in the attic! What did you think I'd be doing, painting my arse blue and parading it up and down the docks? I just needed a piss, is all."

"Why not piss in a bucket?" snapped Wood, as usual becoming irate at the old man's obstinacy.

"I'm not doing that, boy. It'd stink."

"You risked certain death because of a piss stench?"

"Not certain death. You turned up. Eh?" He slapped the younger Command Sergeant again, and grinned a mouthful of bad teeth.

"Stop calling me 'boy'. I'm fifty years old!"

"Still a boy to me," said Pettrus, then his mood turned a little sour, and he surveyed the corpses. "We need to do something about this outrage. We need to sort this shit out."

"I agree. They've taken over the whole damn city, and worse than that, it's spreading quicker than the Red Plague!"

"Yes." Pettrus rubbed his side-whiskers. "We need to get rid of them, because unless we do, all the good restaurants will remain closed. And how will I get my steak and port then, eh?"

Wood stared at the old man. There was a twinkle in his eye.

"You always liked a challenge, didn't you?"

"When the Gold Loop Tribes of Salakarr mounted a charge on elephants with spikes attached to their legs, and tigers straining on golden leashes, and with arrows which flamed and spears which had mechanisms to cut a man in two, well, me and the lads did not flinch! We stood our ground, shields high, spears and swords ready, jaws tight and with good hard Falanor steel, good old Falanor backbone, and a bit of Falanor spunk, we turned back those screaming hordes. We did that."

"And your point?"

Pettrus stood straight, as if to attention on a parade square. He held his sword, and ignored the blood, and with proud whiskers quivering, said, "I'm not going to let some dirty blood-sucking youngsters ruin *my city*. We need to get to the Black Barracks. That's where all the old soldiers know to go in times of crisis. The Black Barracks! And when we've got a few of the old boys together, well, Command Sergeant Wood..."

"Yes?"

"We'll give these damn vampires a bloody nose to remember," he grinned.

Graal sat in the high stone tower, head in his hands, mind pounding. It was the worst headache he'd ever had, a flowing river of thumping tribal drums that seemed linked to his clockwork, to his inner gears and cogs, a rhythm in tune with the *tick-tock* of his twisted clockwork heart.

Reaching out, Graal took a glass of brandy and drank deep. He had started to drink more and more, usually just before he was required to see Bhu Vanesh and give the Vampire Warlord an update on progress. Certainly, he drank *after* every meeting. Because, and he knew this to be true, General Graal was now little more than a slave. He had worked so hard to summon the Warlords, with the mistaken belief he would be in control... when in reality they were so powerful as to be beyond physical retribution.

Graal had tried to kill Bhu Vanesh. Just the once.

On the second night, he had crept to the darkened bedchambers where Bhu Vanesh slumbered. The room was filled with blacks, and purples, and crimson colours, candles burned stinking of human fat and corpses littered the floor at the bottom of the bed – evidence of Bhu Vanesh's supper.

Normally, Lorna and Division General Dekull would be standing in attendance; but Graal had witnessed them leave the chamber, and decided it was time to strike.

He drew his thin black sword, and with blue eyes glinting in his pale, white face, Graal stepped daintily over husked corpses, their flesh shrunken and shrivelled over grotesque twisted skeletons thinking all the time how this reminded him of the *Harvesters*, and the way they drained the blood for the Refineries... his mind snapped to the present. Bhu Vanesh reclined on black satin sheets, stained with pools of dark, dried blood. He slept, breathing rhythmical, body still coiling and twisting, each limb fashioned from dark smoke, red eyes closed in dreams of... what did a Vampire Warlord dream of? World domination? World slaughter? An end to fear of imprisonment? Graal had grinned, then, a slightly manic grin. Remove the head, and the body dies. Such was the vampire mantra.

He crept with all the agility and silence he knew he possessed. His sword lifted, so gentle a butterfly could have landed on its razor edge and not been disturbed by its fluid movement. Then, it slashed down, angle and force perfect for removing a head, and Graal watched in lazy-time slow-motion as if through a shimmering wall of treacle and the air felt suddenly *muzzy* with a discharge of magick and Graal realised too late the charms which surrounded this ancient creature. His blade struck Bhu Vanesh and simply stayed there, a hair's-breadth from severing his neck, and slowly Bhu Vanesh rose from the bed in one rigid arc of movement and his red eyes opened and he stared down at General Graal as his sword thumped to the satin sheets.

"You had one chance," said Bhu Vanesh, his voice a portal to the Chaos Halls, smoke oozing from the terrible orifice as he spoke. "That is now gone. Betray me again, and I will suck your bones. Go now."

Graal turned, shaking, and walked past Lorna and Dekull who stood either side of the door, fangs gleaming, red eyes watching him with hunger. He returned to his tower with a panicked *tick tick tick* in his ears as he acknowledged he was vachine, and he was weak, and he was a slave, and he did not know what to do.

There came a knock at the door. Graal drank the brandy and placed the solid glass down with a *clack*.

"Enter."

The man was small, stocky, with thick black hair, shaggy eyebrows, frightened eyes. Once, Graal would have relished the terror in this little man, but not now, not today, not in this life; because Graal was subject to the same rules and the same slavery. He was shackled by fear. Strangled by power. Bhu Vanesh was Warlord. Graal was a worm.

"What is it?" snapped the General.

"I... I've been sent here, because of the ideas I had, I'm a designer, an engineer. I... I..."

"If you stutter again, I'll rip out your throat and eat your spine. Now. Continue."

Graal focused on the man, watched him swallow, could smell the ooze of piss in his pants, could hear the rumbling of his churning guts, smell the acid of his fear-filled reflux. That made Graal smile. To add a razor edge to any conversation always filled Graal with an almost sexual delight. To put the pressure of *death* on a simple exchange of words made Graal feel strong again, powerful, in control. Ha! But he knew it was a false feeling, the imitation of an imitation. So... the feeling of elation dropped like an avalanche from his soul.

"You are building new ships?"

"No, I have a thousand carpenters and riggers carving piss-pots. Of course we are building ships."

"I have a new design."

"I have hundreds of designs. They work well. We have corvettes, frigates, galleons and merchant hulks. We have everything we need, armed with the biggest damn crossbows I've ever seen and capable of punching a hole the size of my whole body through the side of an enemy vessel. What could you possibly offer me?" sneered Graal, and poured himself another large glass of brandy. Below, the shipwrights, caulkers and carpenters worked on, their noise adding to Graal's pounding head and rising temper. Who was this little man? Why did he plague Graal so? And what fucking idiot had sent him up? Graal would kill this fucker, then make sure whoever was responsible got to clean out the sewers for the next year.

"I can build you a metal ship," said the man.

"Ridiculous! It would sink."

The man watched Graal carefully, then shook his head. "No. I have designs, and I have made models. A metal ship will not burn, and is armoured by natural design; it will be smaller and more manoeuvrable than any war galleon you care to pitch against it."

Graal considered this. "What is your name?"

"Erallier, sir. Just think, if I can do this for you, if I and my family are looked after, and not turned into..." He shuddered. Then composed himself. "You will please your," he considered his words carefully, "your *master*, yes? You will have an incredible warship the like of which has never been seen."

Graal nodded. "Yes. You have a month to deliver plans and begin work. See Grannash below, he will issue you with coin and a... *mark*."

"A mark?"

"A ward. To protect you, like those out there," Graal waved a hand in the general direction of the thousands of workmen on the docks. "We can't be having all our workers *changed*, can we? How then would the ships be built? Now. Go. Please me, and I will personally guarantee your family's safety."

"Yes, General. Thank you, General."

Erallier departed, and Graal considered the proposal. A metal ship. The greatest warship ever! Enough to beat the Vampire Warlords? Graal shrugged, and stood, and stretched his back, and stared out at the Port of Gollothrim. Beyond the docks, the navy of Falanor was being gradually recalled. Now, four hundred vessels lay at anchor along the docks and for as far as the eye could see; and to the south in the city's shipyards, another two hundred skeleton vessels were in building progress. Graal had been given a year. One year to build up the navy. And then the Vampire Warlords would seek to... expand. They would travel. And they would conquer. They would take their plague to every corner of the modern world. They would build a new empire!

Graal smiled. And sighed. And pondered. And waited for news. And plotted against Bhu Vanesh. *One day, you fucker, I'm going to eat your heart and take your place. One day. One day!*

To the north of Falanor, where the Selenau River flowed through the Iron Forest and entered the vast realms of the Black Pike Mountains, there was a wall of rock, a half-league wide, jagged and black, sheer and vast. Impassable, and yet beyond there was a road, a black road, a wide road, built over a hundred years by the White Warriors, the soldiers of the vachine, the soldiers of the Harvesters, a secret road from whence the Army of Iron arrived at Falanor's northern borders and thence to the city of Jalder, and beyond.

This mammoth wall of towering rock was a barrier, a shield of sorts, between the world of men and the world of albino soldiers. Between men and Harvesters. Men and vachine.

Snow fell from a bruised sky. The wind howled mournfully from the edge of the Iron Forest, and whipped up in little dancing eddies, creating complex patterns in the snow before scattering and merging once more with undulating fields of white.

Everything was still, and calm – a perfect watercolour of serenity.

Then the black wall shimmered, each chimney and vertical ridge hung with rivers of ice sparkling for a moment as if hoarding a million trapped diamonds... And then the wall was not a wall, but a veil, like a shimmering black curtain. And beyond, a black road stretched away, edged with ice and snow, a blasted road, a desolate road. And as the mountain rock shimmered like insubstantial lace, so there came the stamp of marching boots, and the rattle of armour, and beyond the wall as if seen through mist came ranks of soldiers, their flesh pale and white, their armour matt black, carrying spears and wearing swords and maces at belts. They wore high-peaked battle helmets, and their shields bore silver insignia. The sign of the White Warriors. The sign of the Leski Worms, from whence they were once hatched.

The front battalion approached the wall, then stopped with a stamp of boots. Slowly, they walked forward, and *eased* through solid rock, out onto the snowy drifts. Rank after rank came, until the battalion was free of a rocky, blood-oil magick imprisonment, and they moved out across the snow in a square unit formation – to be followed immediately by a second battalion, another square group of four hundred soldiers, marching out into the cold crispness of Falanor from the black road beyond the Black Pike Mountains. More battalions came, until they made a brigade, and the brigade doubled into a division of four thousand eight hundred soldiers, and eventually, through churned snow and mud, the battalions finally formed into an albino army. The Army of Silver, the silver on their shields glinting with reflections from a low-slung winter sun.

The Army of Silver, led by General Zagreel, moved west from this secretive rock entrance, and they were trailed by a hundred Harvesters, bone-fingered hands still weaving the magick of *opening* and long white robes drifting through snow, tall thin bodies ignoring the bite of the Falanor wind.

Silence flowed for a while, followed by the stamp of more boots, and this time the approaching battalion held matt black shields decorated with insignia in brass, and they flowed from the mountain wall like a river of darkness, their pale faces impassive, their spears erect, swords gleaming black under winter sunlight, ignoring the whipping snow as more and more units and regiments filed out to stand before the mountain wall and then, with the tiniest of sighs, the mountain wall lost its sheen and became solid once more, leaving two full albino armies standing in the snow between the Black Pikes and the Iron Forest.

General Exkavar turned his eyes to the forest, the dark iron trunks twisted and threatening, and a cruel smile crept across his narrow, white lips. Blood eyes surveyed the snow, and he removed his helmet and ran a hand through thick, snow-white hair. He glanced back at his perfectly ordered Army of Brass, and then over the snow fields to the equally professional Army of Silver.

He turned to the bugler. "Sound the march," he said, and his eyes were distant, as if reliving a dream. "We head south."

SEVEN
Black Pike Mines

Kell, Saark and Nienna moved as fast as they could down narrow trails which weaved like criss-crossing spider-webs through the Iron Forest. West they headed, constantly west, and eventually, on one dull morning with light snowflakes peppering the air, they broke free of the trees and looked out over a rugged, folded country, full of hills and rocks, stunted trees and deep hollows. Everything was white, and still, and calm. This was wild country filling in the gaps between Corleth Moor and the Cailleach Pass to the west of Jalder. They were past Jalder now, past the Great North Road; the Iron Forest had done its job, but as Myriam pointed out before her fight with Saark, and her sudden departure, the once outlaw-occupied forest had been curiously devoid of criminal activity. Dead, or just sleeping? Or fled to safer climates?

They stared out over the undulating folds of these raw wild lands. "Looks like rough travelling," said Saark, chewing on a piece of dried beef.

"We're going to need supplies," said Kell, ignoring Saark.

"I *said*, it looks like rough travelling," snapped Saark.

"I heard what you said, lad. But you're stating the obvious. We've had rough travelling ever since we left Jalder, through the tannery and down the Selenau River. What did you expect? A cushioned silk carriage waiting for you?"

"You're a grumpy old bastard, Kell, you know that?"

"Yeah. You keep mentioning it."

Saark bent down, rubbing at his legs. Ever since falling into the polluted lake in the Iron Forest, his skin had flared red, all over his body, stinging him with knives of fire. But Kell had come up with a theory why his flesh had not fallen from his bones, as certain rumours would have it. As a vachine, Saark had accelerated healing. Now, his flesh was being eaten by toxins, but healing just as fast as it was being destroyed.

"So I'll be like this, in a scratching agony, forever?" Saark had snapped, face twisted in annoyance.

"I thought you'd be used to a bit of scratching by now," Kell had smirked.

Now, it was irritating Saark again and he rubbed his legs, and chewed his beef.

"Won't they have food at these Black Pike Mines?"

"Maybe. We're not sure what we'll find, though. Maybe it'll be deserted? Maybe it was ransacked by the Army of Iron on their way through. It could be a burnt shell, smouldering timbers and blackened rocks."

"I assume that would end your wonderful and secret plan," muttered Saark, still scratching.

"It certainly would." Kell took a deep breath, staring up at the sky, then out across the wilderness. "By the gods, there are a thousand places out there for an ambush."

"Hark, the happy voice of pessimism," said Saark.

"Will you stop that damn scratching? It's like standing next to a fucking flea-bitten dog!"

"Hey, listen, I feel like I've got a plague of ants living under my skin. I can't stop bloody scratching. It's not like I have a choice."

"Well, if you'd not been so stupid and put the donkey first, you wouldn't have gone through the damn surface."

"There you go, blaming Mary again. Listen Kell, it's not Mary's fault and I resent the constant implication that she's holding up your weird and unspeakable mission that is so clever you have to keep it a secret!"

Kell leaned close. "The reason I keep it to myself, you horse cock, is so when, shall we say, certain priapic fools started sticking their child-maker into hot, sweaty and untrustworthy orifices, there's no possible chance of a blurted word at the wrong moment. You get me?"

"So..." he frowned, "you think I'd spout our plans during sex? Like some loose-brained dolt?"

"Of course you would, lad. You're a man! You think with your hot plums, not with your brain."

"Oh, and I suppose the great Kell—"

"There's a farmhouse."

The two men ceased their squabbling and followed Nienna's line of vision. Through swirls of snow, half-hidden by a hollow of rocks and heavily folded landscape, there was indeed a farmhouse.

"Any smoke?" squinted Kell.

"None I can see." Nienna clicked her tongue, and led Mary ahead. Ten paces away she stopped, and turned back. "Are you coming? Or shall I go searching for food alone?"

Kell and Saark followed at a distance.

"Stroppy girl, that one," said Saark.

"Yeah. Well. She's sad Myriam has gone, you know? They'd become friends. Been through a lot. Shame you had to start sticking your pork sausage where it didn't belong."

"If you're going to keep on at me, Kell, I'm going to walk with the fucking donkey."

"You do that, lad. No talk is better than your talk."

"I'll watch her arse," muttered Saark, marching away from Kell. "It's a damn sight prettier than your battered face."

The farmhouse was deserted, and had been left in a hurry – presumably when the Army of Iron had marched through this way, months earlier. The travellers hunted through various rooms, scavenging what they could. Fresh clothing, blankets and furs, boots for Saark, salt, sugar, coffee, some raw vegetables preserved by the winter, and some chunks of dried beef and goat from a small curing shed with a slanted, black-slate roof. They found hard loaves of bread, which would soften in soup, onions, and also a large round of cheese sealed in wax which was placed reverently in Mary's basket. It had been a long time since they'd eaten cheese. That would be a tasty reward on the hard, unforgiving trail.

Saark wanted to stay in the farmhouse to rest, but Kell shook his head, forcing them to push on. It was with great regret they left the sanctuary of the building, heading back out into the snow, into the folded wild lands. Soon it fell far behind, and only snow, and heather, and rocks were there to offer comfort.

• • • •

Kell pushed hard, and they travelled long into the night before collapsing into an exhausted sleep. He woke them at dawn, and they pushed on again, grumbling and cold, feet aching, joints aching, growing a little warm with travel but at least now with bellies full of meat and cheese instead of straggled weeds and unwholesome mushrooms from the forest.

The landscape here was warmer to travel, for the shape of the land, the folds and dips, cut down on many a crosswind. Once, Saark had been separated from a unit on military manoeuvres with King Leanoric, and had to walk ten leagues across Valantrium Moor. The wind-chill alone nearly killed him, and it took a week of hot baths, hot liquor and hot women to restore his good humour.

Now, however, there was no promise of hot baths, liquor or women; only a cold prison mine and the prospect of meeting prison guards. Would there be nubile young women included in that gathering? Would there be succulent wobbling flesh? Eager thighs? Clawed and painted nails? Saark doubted it.

For a week they travelled like this, Kell always ahead, his stamina a true thing to behold, especially for one so old. Saark and Nienna had taken to walking together, and for the first few days Nienna sulked with Saark, her lower lip out, face turned away, jealous no doubt of his frantic coupling with Myriam. But Saark worked on her relentlessly, with nothing else to do except talk to the donkey; and gradually, his charm began to break through her iron and ice resolve. On the third day after leaving the Iron Forest, there came a smile, quickly followed by a scowl. After four days, a chuckle. After five, a real bursting laugh of good humour. And by the sixth day she had started to talk again. Internally, he punched the air with joy; looking back through his long life of talking to, and fucking, women, he now realised Nienna had become the hardest challenge. Ironic, that only days earlier she'd been falling over herself to please him. To help him. To couple with him.

"This feels like a never-ending journey," said Nienna.

They had stopped at the top of a low rise, which fell away suddenly in a steep cliff. Kell had gone on ahead to find a safe path down. It gave them a good – if limited – view of the near distance. Anything further was blocked by occasional swathes of mist, or flurries of snow.

"Hard on the feet," said Saark, removing his boots. He scratched his legs, then rubbed at his toes.

"That's quite a stench," said Nienna, smiling to take the sting from her words.

"I think it would win me certain awards, back at the King's Royal Court," grinned Saark, and pulled a face as he rubbed between his toes. "By the Chaos Halls, the old gimlet pushes a fast pace."

"He is a great man," beamed Nienna.

"Yes, with a bad temper and a tongue fiercer than a dominatrix's whip," scowled Saark.

"You do goad him," said Nienna.

"Only to keep the old goat on his cheesy toes. Look at it this way, without me to take his mind off more serious matters, he'd be going crazy with grief! My talk of wine and wenches gives him a simple anchor-point for his short-term anger episodes."

Nienna considered this. "You have, er, enjoyed a lot of wine, then?" she said, carefully.

"And wenches, that's what you really mean, eh?" smiled Saark, easily, and pulled on his boot. He removed the other. "By all the gods, this one is worse! How can a man's feet smell so bad? I do believe I should cut them off and burn them on the fire!"

"I agree."

"Ask me, then."

"Ask you what?"

"Whatever's troubling you, little lady. There's always something troubling you, young... no, no, I take that back. You're no longer young, are you? So I'll begin again. There's always something troubling you, *Nienna.*" He smiled kindly.

"Do you love Myriam?" she blurted out, then bit her tongue, aware she'd probably gone too far.

The smile froze on Saark's face like a rictus of ice-smoke magick. It was a question he hadn't anticipated, and Saark looked down at the frozen rocks, rubbing his chin thoughtfully. His mind swirled. Did he love Myriam? Despite the fights, and the betrayals, did he? Did he *really?* Despite her trying to kill him? To drown him like a flapping chicken?

And bizarrely, Saark realised that he did. But he recognised this was not the time to say such a thing, and especially not to Nienna, here, in this place. What harm her ignorance? What harm protecting her from herself?

"No," he said, finally. Then added, "I have a lot of affection for the girl, after all, ever since she stabbed me in the guts we've been through a lot together." Then a flash of inspiration bit him. "What you think you saw, you did not. We coupled, but it was nothing to do with love, or even lust – it was everything to do with the clockwork. Everything to do with the vachine."

Nienna frowned. "How does that work?"

"I was bitten by a Soul Stealer; her blood-oil infected me. But the vachine are different from the vampires of old, and the blood-oil they carry instead of vampire's blood is like a drug, a living cancer, and without the clockwork machines to control it, it will finally kill you. What me and Myriam did was to save my life. Nothing more."

Nienna looked into his eyes. And she heard it. The *tick tick tick* of the machine vampire. Saark tilted his head, and then gave a short nod. "Yes. It feels... odd. Almost like I carry a weight in my chest. But that is all. Otherwise, I think and breathe and fight and love, just like before."

"Love me," said Nienna.

"I can't do that," said Saark, stiffly. "Kell would cut off my balls, and you damn well know it!"

"You have to live your own life. Don't be scared of my grandfather. I am a grown woman now, you said so yourself." She had moved closer, a lot closer, and despite Saark's accelerated vachine skills he only now realised. He swallowed. He could smell the musk of her skin and something took hold of his mind in its fist and squeezed, gently, and he felt himself losing control. It was always the same. With women. With wine. The temptation would present itself and Saark could never, ever, say no. It was as if his brain was mis-wired, and didn't work like a normal person's brain. He had not the capacity to deprive himself of *any* earthly pleasure. Saark was a slave to hedonism, and had very little real control in his conscious decision making. It was a curse he carried deep.

Nienna was close. He stared at her lips, slick and wet. Her tongue darted out, a nervous gesture, and then Saark was falling into a well of uncontrollable insanity and every trick and nuance and skill fell neatly into place, click click click, like a brass karinga puzzle being worked by an expert's flashing fingers. And she tasted good, tasted sweet, and he was inside her and they kissed, sat there on the rocks, and kissed.

Saark pulled away.

"Oh!" said Nienna, and smiled.

"Oh *no*," said Saark, and grinned. "But shit, Kell will rip off my balls! He'll rip off my head!"

"Rubbish! It was only a kiss." And she giggled, but he could see it in her eyes, she wanted more, she wanted much more, she wanted it all. Saark swallowed, as a hand thumped his shoulder.

"Not far now, lad."

"Kell." Saark's voice was a croak, and he did well to speak at all.

"Did you sneak up on us, grandfather?" said Nienna, turning her head and fixing him with a beady stare.

"Heh, just checking Saark here was being an honourable gentleman. Anyway, come on, there's a cottage up ahead. It's been lived in recently, but it's empty now; probably owned by a crofter. We can have a good rest, I think we've earned it, and approach the Black Pike Mine prison fresh tomorrow, eh?"

Saark stood, and took Mary's rope.

And as Kell led the way, he threw Nienna a look which she missed; she was gazing, distantly, a dreamy look on her face. *Shit. Shit shit and double horse and donkey shit!*

Less than an hour saw them inside the small and cosy cottage. It was little more than a living room and a side-larder, mostly empty except for a few flagons, old mouldy bread and three small sacks of grain. Saark made a nosebag for Mary, filling it with grain and placing a blanket over her back under a rickety lean-to on the south side of the cottage, where there was the least wind.

Nienna prepared a thick broth, and Kell chopped firewood. He got a good blaze burning, and they sat, warm for the first time in what felt like years, bellies full of hot broth and mugs of coffee in dirt-ingrained hands.

"I'd forgotten what it felt like to be a part of civilisation," said Saark, quietly, and sipped his sweet coffee, relishing the heat and the mixture of bitterness and sweetness all mixed in together. A contrast of pleasures.

Kell snorted a laugh.

"What's so funny?"

"Not long ago, lad, this would have been far from your idea of civilisation. Where's all your raw fish on silver platters now? Where are your buxom serving wenches with rouged lips and powdered wigs? I tell you, a curse on nobility."

"Spoken like a true working man," smiled Saark.

Kell stood, and stretched, and Saark eyed the old warrior thoughtfully. He was much leaner than when Saark first met him back in Jalder, hiding in a tannery from a hunting Harvester. The miles, the fights, the climbing of mountains, it had done much to return Kell to a lean, rugged, muscular figure, despite his advancing years. Then Saark's eyes slid sideways to Nienna; here, also there had been a vast change in physical appearance. Whereas she had been slightly plump, and soft, her face carrying the puppy-fat of childhood, now she was slimmer, stronger, more muscular; she carried herself erect and proud, like a fighter. The fat had gone, and there were creases in her face, hard edges around her eyes. A young woman who had seen too much hardship. Still, she was coping, mentally, as well as physically. Saark wasn't sure how long many young women from King Leanoric's court, with their white make-up and long, crafted fingernails, would have lasted in the mountains, or being hunted by Soul Stealers and cankers and rough soldiers from the Army of Iron. No. Not long, he'd wager.

Nienna saw the look, and gave him a dazzling smile. Saark licked his lips. He could still taste her there. It was most pleasant. His ruse about Myriam had worked. Nienna believed him.

Kell moved into the small storeroom, and came out with a pewter flagon. He sniffed it warily, and his face lit up. "It's whiskey," he said, in all innocence.

"Oh no," said Saark. "You know you shouldn't drink that. You *know* what it does to you!"

"Just a small one," said Kell, and smiled easily, and pulled up a chair with a scrape. "Saark, after all the shit scrapes we've been through, lad, after nearly dying on Skaringa Dak and falling through that mountain, the least I can do is have a drink."

"It makes you bad," said Saark.

"No. *Too much* makes me bad. But I know when to stop. I always know when to stop. It's just sometimes I choose not to." He lifted the flagon, and took a hefty drink, then lowered it and smacked his lips with the back of his hand, rubbing at his beard. "By all the gods, that's a rough drop, but it warms a man's belly after a trek through snow, so it does."

"Here." Saark took the flagon, and took a hefty drink himself. He nearly choked as the raw moonshine burned his throat, but Kell had been right, and it warmed him right through.

"It's good, right lad?"

"It's like drinking donkey piss, Kell."

"You should know, mate. You and that Mary lass have got way too close." He laughed, and winked, and offered the flagon but Nienna waved it away. He took another hefty swig, and this time held it there for a while. As he lowered it, Nienna looked concerned.

"No more, grandfather. Saark was right. It turns you bad."

"Ach, I'm a big man, I can take the whole flagon and it wouldn't touch the hole in my stomach!"

"Or indeed, the ego in your skull," said Saark.

"Ha!" He took another big drink, and passed it to Saark, who put the flagon carefully to one side.

"No more, Kell."

"You big girl!"

Saark smiled. "Maybe, but I having a feeling that where we are going tomorrow, the last thing you need is a drink; or even worse, a damn hangover!"

Kell shrugged, easily, and sat down. For a while they sat in amiable silence, watching the fire, then Kell stood again. "I'll go and chop some more wood. You know me. I like to keep active."

Saark nodded, and Kell stepped outside. The world seemed brighter, more whiter than white. He grinned to himself, and licked at the droplets in his beard. They tasted just grand. Snow was falling heavy now, obscuring the sky, obscuring the world. A fluffy silence filled every space. This cottage clearing felt small, safe and secure.

Kell strolled around to the small woodshed, and glancing back to make sure he went unobserved, pulled a hidden flagon from under a pile of logs. He unstoppered the flagon, took a deep breath, and followed it with a long, gulping drink.

"No good will come of this," he muttered, but by then – as it always was – it was far too late...

Night fell. The fire burned low. Kell snored heavily on one side of the room, and Saark lay with his back to the fire, eyes closed, unable to sleep. Inside of him he felt something *shift* and it made him feel nauseous, like he was going to puke. Tick, tick, tick went his steady clockwork-enhanced heart. By all the gods, he thought, it feels *too strange*.

Saark heard Nienna shift, and kneel up beside the fire. Saark turned himself, and looked at her long hair glowing. She moved to him, and lay beside him, and he threw a glance to Kell but the man had drank more whiskey later that evening, and was now sleeping like a baby – albeit a very drunk one.

"We shouldn't," he said, as Nienna kissed him; but not like before, this time it was urgent, and this time she pressed herself into him, eagerly, filled with lust, filled with desire.

"We should." She had waited a long time to get hold of Saark. She wasn't going to let him go now.

They kissed, and she straddled him, and their passion grew and Saark felt himself in that place again, that uncontrollable place and, as he always did, he gave in to it, surrendered unconditionally and kissed Nienna, kissed her hard, with passion, his hands running up and down her flanks, caressing her breasts and she writhed atop him, moaning, and Saark was hard and pressing against her and something intruded on his thoughts and there was a *click* as he realised his error. Something was wrong. Shit. Kell was no longer snoring...

"Up you get, girl."

Kell lifted Nienna bodily from Saark, and placed her to one side. His eyes were glowing embers in the gloom of the cottage, his fists were clenched, his beard glinted with droplets of whiskey, and the firelight gave him the air of a demon.

Maybe he is, thought Saark.

"You too. Up you get."

"We've been here before," laughed Saark.

"No we haven't. This time I'm going to break your fucking spine, I reckon."

Saark looked up into those merciless eyes, and swallowed hard. Kell was not a man to back down.

"I implore you, Kell, there are greater things at stake here than Nienna's honour! Think of Falanor! Think of the Vampire Warlords! And let's be honest, look, the girl is fully clothed, all I did was maul her a bit. Squeeze her tits. Get her hot and ready. No harm is done, really, Kell, I beseech you!"

Kell loomed close. "The harm, fucker, is that you never stop. Ever. And unless I teach you a lesson, you'll come back time and time again. And I can't have that. Now get up, or I'll kick you into a pulp like the fucking dog you are."

Kell's boot swung, and Saark rolled fast, avoiding the blow. He leapt up, wearing only his trews, and lifted his fists slowly, as did the pugilists he'd watched in the Shit Pits.

"I've got to warn you, Kell. I'm vachine now. Stronger. Faster. Harder." His own eyes glowed by the light of the fire.

"Show me," said Kell.

"Stop it!" screamed Nienna, both hands at the sides of her head. "Stop it, both of you!"

They ignored her.

Kell charged, roaring like a bear and throwing a fast combination of five punches. Saark dodged, left, right, ducked, then leapt back and his back slammed the wall of the cottage. But Kell followed him, a right straight thundering a hair's breadth from Saark's chin and implanting a dent in the plaster of the wall. Saark skipped away, and Kell followed again, a whirr of punches coming faster than any drunk should be able; Saark ducked, shifted his weight, then slammed a right hook to Kell's jaw that rocked the big warrior.

Kell halted, and stared hard at Saark.

"Have you come to your senses?" snapped Saark.

"Ha, no, well done boy," he rubbed his jaw, "a fine punch. Let's see some more." He launched at Saark, arms grappling around Saark's own and pinning them to his sides. Together, they crashed through the cottage door reducing it to tinder, and landed in the snow with "oofs" of exploded air. Saark wriggled, the dead weight of Kell atop him, and a stunning blow caught the side of his head, blinding him for a moment, then another cracked his nose and that made Saark good and angry and he felt his fangs ease free and talons slide from fingers and with a scream he heaved Kell aside and leapt up, talons slashing for Kell's throat, but Kell took a step back, swaying, and lifted his fists. "Yes lad! Come on! Show me what this pretty dandy's made of!"

They circled in the snow, Nienna hanging at the doorway, panting. Both men were wary now, eyes shining. Snow fell thick around them, and the whole scene was surreal to Nienna, muffled, silent, as if she was seeing it in a dream, or from the bottom of a frozen lake...

"*Stop*," she begged, wearily.

Again, they ignored her. Saark attacked, aiming punches for Kell who swayed, the punches missing him. Kell's boot lashed out, catching Saark in the stomach, but Saark turned the blow into a backward leap, and he flipped, somersaulting to land on his feet, fists raised.

"A pretty trick, boy-lover. You left a piss-trail of perfume droplets in your wake."

"Funny, because despite the perfume I can smell your stale whiskey and bad sweat from here."

Kell growled, and charged, and Saark leapt over him, flipping again to land in the snow.

"Damn you, stand still and be battered!"

"No, Kell, I don't want to fight you! Don't you understand? There are enough fucking enemies out there to last us a thousand lifetimes! And you want to play here in the snow like little kids?"

"Little kids, is it?" growled Kell, and charged again. Saark leapt high, but Kell was ready, jumping himself with a grunt and catching Saark's legs. He swung Saark like a slab of beef, and the dandy hit the snow hard, head slapping trampled ice, all air smashed from him. Kell put one knee on Saark's chest, and one great hand around his throat. With his free fist, he punched Saark with a crunch, and glared down with lips working soundlessly, anger his mistress.

Nienna ran inside the cottage, and curled her hands around Ilanna. The weapon was cool to the touch, and perfectly smooth, like ice. Nienna lifted the axe, the huge axe, with ease. It was surprisingly light.

I have missed you, came the words in her head, and Nienna jumped. She nearly let go of the weapon, but for Saark wriggling around under Kell and returning punches to the great man's head.

Saark grabbed Kell's balls and squeezed hard. Kell howled, rolling to one side, and Saark scrambled free across the snow, but Kell lunged, catching the vachine's ankle and dragging him back –

Claws hissed through the air.

Nienna blinked. *Am I dreaming?* she thought, mind in a swirl of severed lust, fear and now, wonder.

No. I am Ilanna. I am Kell's axe. Do you remember, back in the Stone Lion Woods? I saved your life, but at the time thought you were too young to shock with my... thoughts. Now, I see, you are a much harder woman. I congratulate you.

If only everybody thought so, dreamed Nienna. She took a step towards the door. Kell and Saark were exchanging punches once more. Saark's newly accelerated vachine status was proving a match even for Kell, and both wore bruised and battered faces like horror masks.

I've missed you, said Ilanna, voice soft and sweet.

What does that mean?

We worked together. In the past. It was a good union. One day soon, we will speak again.

Confused, Nienna stepped out into the snow. "Stop!" she screamed, and held the huge battleaxe above her head. Ilanna gleamed dull, matt black, an awesome sight to behold. "Stop this foolishness! I demand it!"

Kell and Saark paused. Blood dribbled from the edge of Saark's mouth, and one of his brass vachine fangs had snapped. Kell had a blackened eye and blood coming from his nose. He looked superbly pissed off.

Kell gave a sudden laugh, a bark, and lowered his fists. "Whatever you say, granddaughter. I think I gave this popinjay a pasting."

"You think so, old man?" scowled Saark. "I've had grandmothers give me harder blow jobs."

Kell lifted his fists again.

"STOP!" screamed Nienna. "What is wrong with you? Saark, you idiot, stop provoking him! And Kell, what's your problem? One sniff of whiskey and you turn into an uncontrollable beast."

That stopped Kell in his tracks, and he rubbed his beard, and lowered his head, a little in shame, a little in guilt. "Yes," he mumbled, and then looked up again. "Give me the axe."

"Why?"

"Because she is mine."

Nienna chewed her lip. She nearly spoke. Nearly said it – that Ilanna had *talked to her*. But part of her thought it was nothing more than a hallucination brought on by stress, or lack of sleep; part of her thought that maybe she was a little crazy.

Nienna stepped forward, and Kell took the huge weapon. He stared at it thoughtfully, then over at Saark. Saark slowly lowered his fists, paling. Kell wasn't called a *vachine hunter* for nothing.

"Now wait a minute, Big Man," he said.

"Ach, calm yourself, dickhead. If I wanted you dead, you'd be dead." He gestured with Ilanna, pointing towards Saark's chest with the blade tips. His voice lowered to a bestial rumble. "But I promise you this, lad. If you lay another finger on Nienna, I'll cut your dirty vachine head from your fucking vachine neck. Understand?"

"I understand."

"And this time, it's a fucking promise, lad."

"Acknowledged."

Kell lowered the weapon, strode to Saark, and threw his arm around the man's shoulders. "But by all the gods, you've got bloody handier with those clockwork fists, so you have! I haven't had a black eye in thirty years!"

"Wonderful," said Saark, mouth dry.

"This calls for a drink! Nienna, bring out the flagons."

"Over my dead body," said Nienna, scowling.

Kell shrugged. "Was only a suggestion, was all. Let's have some soup, then – and talk about happier times gone by!"

"I remember my father hanging himself," said Saark, voice cold, testing his broken brass fang with his thumb and wincing.

"You always know how to put a pisser on it, don't you lad?" He slapped him, hard. "Come on. I'll tell you about when I lost my first bout of single combat."

"You lost in single combat?" said Saark, raising his eyebrows.

"No lad, of course I didn't. I'm just trying to cheer you up."

"It's big," said Saark, lying on his belly and staring down into the valley. "No. I'll rephrase that. It's a *monster*."

The Black Pike Mines.

Originally built by King Searlan to house the worst and most violent criminals in Falanor, it also became a repository for the Blacklipper smugglers – who, by definition, had probably caused murder in order to get their casks of Karakan Red.

There was a gap in the mountains, and the Black Pike Mines had been built into the gap, the front wall merging seamlessly with near-vertical walls of jagged mountain rock. However, to simply call it a mine or a prison was misleading; this was a *fortress*. The staggered front walls were a sort of keep, and the prison stepped back into the V of an inaccessible, impregnable mountain valley. There was no back door, and only sheer smooth black granite walls for those who wanted to get in – or out. It would take an army to enter the prison mine, and that was the idea. When King Searlan built a prison, he intended his criminals to stay put.

Behind the defendable battlement walls were rows of cells carved into the mountain itself, fitted with black iron bars. Further back, where Saark and Nienna could not spy, Kell informed them, was the Hole. The Hole, or the mine itself, was the place where so many thousands of criminals had been worked to death in the name of rehabilitation.

"It looks like a prison," said Saark.

"It is."

"I know. I'm just saying."

"Searlan wanted his bastards to stay put. That's what they called themselves, back in the bad old days. Searlan's Bastards."

"I expect you put a few good men away there as well, did you?"

"No."

"No?"

"No good men. Only scum."

"How many?"

"What does it matter?" Kell's eyes gleamed. More snow was falling, and the gloom made him look eerie; a giant amongst men, bear-like, with his looming, threatening mass, his bearskin, his huge paws. It was easy to forget he was over sixty years old.

"I'm just contemplating, right, what happens if we get inside that place and a few of the old prisoners recognise you? You understand? Old fuckers carrying some twenty year pent-up grudge. After all, I've known you but a few sparse months, and I already want you dead."

"Thanks very much."

"I'm just being honest."

"Listen, Saark. I must have put over a hundred men in there. And if they cross me again, they'll have a short sharp conversation with Ilanna. You understand?"

"You can't *kill* a hundred men, Kell. Be reasonable."

"Fucking watch me," he growled. "Come on. Get your shit. I know the Governor, a man called Myrtax. He's a good man, a fair man. As long as he kept those gates shut, even the Army of Iron would have struggled to breach the defences; and I doubt very much this pipe in the arsehole of Hell was high on Graal's invasion agenda."

They moved down a narrow track which led to a wide open, bleak killing field. As they moved across barren rock and snow, Kell pointed to four high towers.

"Each tower can take fifty archers. That's two hundred arrow men raining down sudden death. And out here," he opened his arms wide, "there's nowhere to hide."

"You fill me with a happy confidence," said Saark, voice dry.

"I try, lad. I try."

They moved warily across the killing ground, heads lifted, eyes watching the towers for signs of archers, or indeed, any military activity. But they were bare. Silent. The whole place reeked of desertion.

They drew closer. A cold wind blew, whipping snow viciously and slapping it into exposed faces. Nienna gasped frequently, her breath snapped away, an ice shock sending shivers down her spine.

Eventually, they were in shouting distance and Kell halted, Ilanna *thunking* to the snow, Kell stroking his beard as he surveyed the formidable wall and massive gates before him.

"IS ANYBODY THERE?" he rumbled, deep voice rolling out across the bleak prison fortress. Echoes sang back at him from the walls, from the vertical mountain flanks, from the slick, ice-rimed rocks. The wind howled, an eerie, high-pitched ululation.

Silence followed. A long, haunting silence.

"There's nobody here, Kell."

"I don't understand. Why would Myrtax give up his castle? He was a brave man. Loyal to the King."

"The King is dead," said Saark, weary now, sighing.

"Hmm."

There came a *crack*, and a head appeared over the icy crenellations. "By all the gods, Kell, is that you?"

"Governor Myrtax?"

"It's been a long time. Wait there, I'll come down and open the gate."

"Where are the prisoners?" frowned Kell, hand on his axe.

"Gone, Kell. All gone. Wait there. I'll be but a few moments; I have warm stew, a fire, and hot blankets inside. You must have travelled far."

Kell nodded, and rubbed once more at his frosted beard.

"Wonderful!" beamed Saark. "A little bit of civilisation, at last! I'd wager he has some fine ale in there as well, and all we need to make the evening complete is a couple of buxom happy daughters, and…"

"Saark!" snapped Nienna.

"What?"

"Saark!" Her frown deepened.

"I am simply pointing out that a buxom wench could be considered a luxury in these parts." He shrugged. "You know how it is, with me and buxom wenches."

"I certainly do," said Nienna, her voice more icy than the frozen battlements.

Governor Myrtax opened the huge, thick door, which in turn was set in the fifty foot high gates which guarded the prison wall; he stood, a beaming smile on his face, a well-built man who had run to fat. His hair was shaved close to the scalp, and peppered with grey. He wore a full beard, a mix of black and ash, and his eyes were dark, intelligent, and friendly.

Myrtax opened his arms. "Kell! It's been too long! No happy prisoners for me this time?"

"No," snapped Kell, and stepped forward, hugging the man. "Sorry. Not this time. But give a few months and I'll have ten thousand heads on spikes for you!"

"Are things that bad, to the south?"

"King Searlan is dead."

"No!" Myrtax drew in a sharp breath, and his face went serious. "That is grave news indeed." He glanced around, up and down the snowy field where the wind blasted gusts of loose snow in rhythmical, vertical curtains. "Better come inside. We've had Blacklippers sniffing around, the dirty, oil-taking bastards."

Kell nodded, and ushered Nienna and Saark before him. They moved into a long, dark killing tunnel, high roofed and with balconies for archers and stone-throwers used in times of siege. They walked a short way along, and Saark glanced up nervously.

"Don't worry lad. We can trust Myrtax."

Myrtax had stopped next to the second portal. Beyond, they could see black cobbles and streaks of ice. Myrtax turned, lifted his hands, and his eyes fixed on Kell and his eyes were haunted, filled with guilt, and with grief. "I'm sorry, Kell."

There came a rattle of activity and above the three travellers, on the high killing balconies, rose fifty men, convicts, murderers, dressed in rag-tag furs and armour and each sporting a powerful crossbow.

"Truly. I am sorry."

A tear ran down Myrtax's cheek. "They have my wife. They have my little ones. What could I do, man? What could I do?"

"Throw down your weapons," came a gruff bark.

"There's only fifty of you," snorted Kell, dark eyes moving across the ranks of men. But Saark's hand touched his shoulder, and he knew what the dandy meant. Nienna. There was always Nienna. Like a splinter in his side, removing his strength, castrating his fury. "Damn."

Saark tossed down his rapier, and Nienna threw down her short sword and knives.

Reluctantly, Kell rested his great, black axe against the wall. His shoulders sagged. They had him.

Three men pushed into the tunnel, and shoved Myrtax aside where he stumbled against the wall, going down on one knee. They arranged themselves before the travellers, and each wore a snarl as ugly as his features.

"I am Dandall," said the first, a tall, narrow-faced man in his fifties with slanted green eyes. He had scars on his cheeks, and long, bony fingers.

"I am Grey Tail," said the smaller of the three. He was a head shorter than Dandall, slim and wiry, his face round and almost trustworthy, if it wasn't for the black lips of imbibed blood-oil which tainted him with its curse. Kell saw the man's hands were shaking, probably withdrawal from his drug of choice. The veins stood out on the backs of his hands, on his throat, black, as if etched in ink through his pale white skin, a relief roadmap pointing straight towards Hell and damnation to come – for that was where he would soon travel. When a Blacklipper became so marked, he had only limited time on the face of the world. He carried a small black crossbow, which quivered even as his fingers quivered.

"And I am Jagor Mad, because I'm *mad*," rumbled the third, a huge bear of a man, a good head taller than Kell and rippling with muscle like an overstuffed canvas sack. His head was misshapen, and riddled with scars and dents. His nose was twisted, and stubble grew unevenly around wide scar tissue tracts. His fists were clenched, and he carried no weapon like the other two, who both wore short swords. His eyes were gleaming, and his gaze never left Kell.

"I remember you, Jagor Mad," said Kell, almost amiably, although his eyes gleamed in the gloom. "I put one of those big dents in your dumb head, if I remember it rightly. I reckon it should have knocked some sense into you, but I can see I'm fucking wrong."

Growling, Jagor Mad stepped forward, but Dandall's bony fingers spread out, his arm blocking the huge man's path.

"Let me kill him, Dandall, let me rip out his windpipe with my teeth!"

"Not yet," said Dandall, voice soft. He focused on Kell. "You put us all here, my large and wearisome friend. But now," and he laughed, a nasal whining like spent vachine gears, "*now* we three are the Governors of the Black Pike Mines. Behind these doors, we have three thousand *new* soldiers, our new model army! Once, they were convicts, and Blacklippers and *scum*, the freaks and the murderers, the outcast from pretty little Falanor, but now they're under *our* command and we rule these damn mountains, this mine and this fucking fortress!"

Dandall motioned, and Grey Tail stepped forward. The crossbow lifted, suddenly *hissed* and took Kell in the shoulder, punching the large man backwards. He stumbled, but righted himself. He grasped the bolt protruding from his flesh, and blood pumped out through his fingers. His eyes glowed. "Just like a coward," he growled, voice dripping liquid hate, as Jagor Mad stepped forward and with a devastating right hook knocked Kell to the ground. Jagor put one knee on Kell's chest, and grabbed the bolt. He applied weight, and Kell groaned like a dying wolf. Saark leapt forward, but a rattle of bolts from the balcony above clattered around him on the cobbles, and Saark did a crazy dance, hands over his head, trying his best not to get pierced.

"We got you now, Kell old boy," Jagor Mad spat, furious scarred face looming down at Kell as if from a toxin-induced nightmare. "And you know what?"

Kell was swimming, not because of the pain or the bolt – he'd been shot before. But because of the drugs coating the bolt's tip, which even now entered his system forcing him down into a realm of drifting unconsciousness. And as he swam deeper and deeper down down *down*, losing control, losing connection, down into the inky void of bitter lost dreams and terminal disappointments, so Jagor Mad's last words rattled in his thumping, crashing skull...

"Get the girl. We'll torture her first."

EIGHT
Prison Steel

When Kell came round, he was lying in a dark cave, bright winter sunlight spilling in unwelcome and unholy, and thumping his already pounding head with big new fists. For a few moments he thought he'd been on the whiskey again, down that hole, locked in that dungeon, and a terrible dread stole over him and he rifled frantically through the pages of his fractured memory. But then, like the break of a new dawn, images slowly filtered back through the upper reaches of consciousness. Black Pike Mines. Dandall, Grey Tail and Jagor Mad. Crossbow bolt. Right hook... Kell clutched for the bolt, but it had been removed, his shoulder bound with a torn section of shirt which he recognised as Saark's fine lace frippery. *Great,* he thought. *Just what I need. Saved from death by a dandy idiot.*

"Don't worry. There's no badness in there. And if there was, I'll be damned if I was sucking on your foul necrotic flesh."

Kell groaned, clutching his head, and sat up like a bear emerging from hibernation. His dark shirt was torn and bloodstained. The world swam. Then, he thought of Nienna.

He rose, like a colossus, and strode *at* Saark. "Where's my granddaughter?" he roared.

"It's fine, Kell, don't panic," Saark held up his hands, "that Jagor Mad was just putting his fist up your arse. Giving you something big and hard to worry about. I can see her from here, she's tied up in one of the cells across the way. Over there." He pointed. Kell squinted.

Kell took a few moments to analyse his surroundings. To his right loomed the great wall of the Black Pike Mine fortress, containing hefty stone barricades replete with steps and towers on which soldiers could defend against any opposing force. The valley floor ran pretty straight, pretty flat, and was lined to either side by hundreds, no... *thousands* of cells, all carved into the natural rocky walls and fitted with sturdy iron bars. Kell and Saark had been locked in one of these. Nienna, in another.

"Why didn't they separate us two?" he grunted.

"They didn't want you dying; gave me a needle and thread, had me patch you up good."

"Why the hell would they do that? There's three hundred men out there must surely want my blood."

"I thought you said a hundred?" Saark shook his head. "Anyway, they, er, they said something about *sport*, and *entertainment*, words of that calibre, and then something about a trial. They don't want you dead. Not *yet*. Not before you suffered as, I assume, they feel they have suffered under your rough justice." Saark's eyes were gleaming, and he grinned at Kell without humour. "They want to play, Kell," he said.

Kell digested this information. He finally caught sight of Nienna across the valley floor, and gave her a wave, but she seemed lost in a half-sleep, staring at the roof of her cave cell. Kell's tongue probed his dry mouth, and he cursed these people, and cursed the drugs they'd used to incapacitate him. By the Bone Halls, he thought, they'd better finish him off next time or he'd crack a few skulls!

Kell's gaze swept left and right. He could see, perhaps, three hundred men. They were roughshod, most quite stocky from years working in the Black Pike Mines. These were Falanor's worst, most grim and nasty criminals. The murderers, rapists, smugglers, child-killers. Kell stared at them with uncontrolled disgust, and an even bigger disgust at what he must do. He sighed. It was the only choice he had.

"So, come on then," said Saark. He was looking sideways at Kell, eyes narrowed. "What's the big plan now, eh? You managed to get us caught pretty bad, with your so-called *ooh Governor Myrtax is totally trustworthy and we can go in and get something to eat* old horse shit. *And* they've gone and captured Mary. I tell you something, if they cook my donkey, there'll be hell to pay."

"Stop whining."

"Give me some answers then, damn you!"

"Listen to the demands of Saark, the wonderful, masterful, all-powerful vachine shagging vachine coward. I didn't see you doing much to help when they peppered me with fucking crossbow bolts!"

"It was one bolt, Kell. Hark at the power of a man's exaggeration!"

"You're a fine one to speak. If anybody believed your tales, you'd have impregnated half of Falanor by now!"

"Maybe I have! They do say I have a certain way with the women."

"Yeah, and I bet you carry enough pox to drop a battalion. Now shut your mouth, Saark, and tell me what they did with my axe."

Saark frowned, then rubbed his bruised face. He, too, had taken a beating at the hands of Jagor Mad. As the huge oaf declared, he was indeed, at least partially, *mad*. But then, Saark was getting used to taking a beating in the fiery orbit of Kell's legend. After all, that's what friends were for, no?

"They dumped it in one of the cells, I think. Along with Nienna and the rest of our weapons. It's got to be said, Kell, sometimes I wonder who you love the most: Nienna, or that damn axe?"

"The axe'll never let me down," growled Kell, face locked in a terrible anger. "Now listen to me, Saark. This is the plan."

"Wonderful!"

"Take the grin off your powdered mug before I damn well knock it clear. Things are about to get serious, and you need to know what to do."

"Go on, then. Stun me with the geometry of your tactician's mind."

"I'm going to win over the criminals here, and we'll form them into a fighting unit, into an army, and march on the Vampire Warlords! We will take the battle to the enemy. We will attack, first Jalder, then Gollothrim, then Vor. We will kill the Vampire Warlords. We will stop the vampire plague."

There was a long silence. Outside, somewhere high in the mountains, an avalanche boomed. Crashing echoes reverberated from on high, a deafening and terrifying sound which gradually faded into drifting echoes, like a scattering of loose snow.

"Kell, even for you that's madder than a mad dog's dinner."

"Meaning?"

"Well, where do I begin? For a start, all the bastards here hate you and want your blood and spleen. The Vampire Warlords are, er, indestructible. How can you train an army out of scum? What sorry fool will do the training? And even more importantly, even if, and this is a big *if*, you persuaded three thousand hardened criminals to join your cause, what would stop them being criminals the minute we set foot back in the real world? They'd be straight back to killing and raping, I'd wager."

"Yeah. But we have the upper hand."

"Which is?"

"They have no idea what's happening, out there, in Falanor. They saw the Army of Iron passing through, they rebelled against Governor Myrtax and took over the fortress. They have no idea about Jalder being overrun, or Vor or the gods only know how many other damn cities. They know nothing of King Leanoric dying in battle, or of the cankers or the destruction of Silva Valley."

Saark snorted. "And they don't *fucking care*, Kell! Don't you understand? We're dealing with criminal scum here, the freaks of the country, the bastards who are bastards to their own mother's bastards. They don't deserve to live, and they won't fucking help you, I'm fucking telling you, I am."

"Ha, that's so much horse shit," snapped Kell. "You, with your southern queer dandy ways, you have no fucking idea what these men are like." Kell moved close, his voice dropping a little. "You don't get how life works, do you, Saark? You've had silver platters and boiled eggs all your life. You've had your face in so many rich bouncing tits, licking the arse-crumbs from oh so many perfume-stinking nobles' cracks, that you have no *connection* with reality. Most of these men, they're not bad men, not evil men, there are shades of grey, Saark, and we all make mistakes. It's nice to see you're so fucking perfect! In a different world, you would have lost your head a long time ago!"

Saark snorted again. "What the hell am I hearing? You put hundreds of these bastards in here! Listen to the last of the great hypocrites! You hunted them down, Kell, you killed a lot, and you dragged many back to Vor for trial. And now you want them to fight for you? Now you want them to *die* for you? I've met some mad skunks in my time, heard some crazy bloody plans, but this takes the ridiculous plum straight from the mouth of the insane rich. They'll never follow you, Kell, *Legend* or no. They'd rather shit on your grave."

"You'll see," rumbled Kell.

"And what you going to do? Kill the new governors?" Saark laughed.

"That's the idea."

"What with? Your left thumb?"

"If I have to. Now stop your prattling, I'm trying to think and you're carping on like a fishwife on a fish stall selling buckets of fish to rank stinking fishermen."

"What? *What?* Is that an example of how you're going to win over the crowd? Ha ha, Kell, you've got some serious lessons to learn in life. You're about to throw yourself to the wolves."

"We'll see," said Kell, eyes glowing. "We'll just see."

As the day progressed, Kell and Saark watched a hundred or so men sawing wood and putting together some kind of framed structure. Kell brooded in silence, wincing occasionally at his damaged shoulder, and sat with his knees pulled up under his chin, arms wrapped around his legs, wondering how to get out of this mess. Nobody came to their cell, and they were given no food or water. Occasionally, they saw one of the new Black Pike Governors wandering around the frantic building work, and as a hefty softwood frame took shape, Saark put his head on one side.

"Looks like a stage," he said, at last. "Why are they building a stage? Are they going to treat us to a performance of *Dog's Treason*, or maybe a sequence of sonnet recitals based around the life of that great lover, *Cassiandra*? I know! I've got it! They're going to perform *The Saga of Kell's Legend* just for *your* bloody benefit!"

"It's a gallows, idiot. That's why the centre has extra vertical struts. There's going to be a hole through which somebody drops."

"Somebody?"

"I take a lot of killing," said Kell, voice low, eyes narrowed. "Look, there's Jagor Mad. He really is a big, dumb fool. I thought he would have learnt his lesson last time I brought him in. Evidently not."

"What did he do?"

"Aah," Kell shook his head, then lowered his face to stare at the rocky floor of the cave. He kicked his boot against one of the pitted iron bars. "Jagor came from a city called Gilrak, to the west of Vor. All those who wanted to live in Vor, but couldn't afford to live in the capital, well they lived in Gilrak, and what a sorry heap of shit it was. Like a scum overflow. A sewer outlet. Now, the thing about Gilrak was that it was a new city, with the old one, Old Gilrak, lying a half-league southwest. But what few people knew was that the two were connected by old tunnels. So Jagor and a few of his friends came up with a wonderful money-making scheme. They'd kidnap children, take them through the tunnels – so that when a search went out there was no chance of finding the bastards – take them through the tunnels to the deserted city of Old Gilrak, fast horses, down to the coast where bad men from across the sea were waiting on Crake's Beach with boats."

"So he took children and sold them?"

"Yes. Sold them to bad men, for a lot of gold, men who would use them for, shall we say, unspeakable acts. Things a child should never have to go through." Kell's eyes were gleaming.

"Not a happy end for a child?" ventured Saark.

"No. King Leanoric had three genius spies, who eventually uncovered what was going on. Then they passed the information over to me, and the King charged me with stopping the trade. He gave me limitless funds, and the pick of his men. Well. I work fast, and alone, but Jagor had forty men working his trade so I picked out five of Leanoric's best killers. Not swordsmen, mind, not *soldiers*, but *killers*. Men I'd seen in battle, men with real stomach for the job."

"And the job was?"

"Extermination," said Kell, glancing up at Saark. "I've seen the way the justice courts worked in Vor." He spat. "I've watched good men hang, and I watched bad men walk free. I wasn't about to let this little fish escape the pond."

"So what happened?"

"First, we found one of Jagor's scouts. We tortured him, broke his fingers and toes, cut off his balls, held him screaming in a cellar before cutting his throat. The vermin. Well, he told us where the next targets were; where the next children were. And Jagor's kidnappers were getting greedy; they were going to take ten children that night, all under the age of ten. One of my killers took the place of Jagor's scout, and we waited, let them sneak in and take the girl from her little town house in the poor part of the city, then we followed those fuckers back to their camp in the woods, and the place they'd dug down and smashed through into the old tunnel network leading to Old Gilrak."

"What happened next?"

Kell shrugged. "We came on them in the night. Fucking slaughtered them, six of us there were with rage in our eyes and blood on our swords and axes. We massacred them, men and women alike, no mercy. Five escaped into the tunnels, including Jagor Mad. I'd gone in for the kill, we fought and I hit him so hard I put a dent in his skull, broke three bones in my hand but it was worth it. But then somebody jumped on my back, I rammed back my head, ended up with half his teeth stuck in my scalp, but it gave Jagor time to flee. Down through the tunnels."

"You don't make friends easy, do you Kell?"

"Shut up. Well, my men took the kids back to Gilrak and I went down the tunnels after these rats. I followed them all night, caught up with two who were injured, killed them easy enough, then another two tried to spring a trap on me in the dark. Well, Kell doesn't die easy, and I gave them a few things to think about – delivered courtesy of the butterfly blades of Ilanna. Then I chased Jagor Mad all damn night, but the bastard got away. He might look like a big brute, but he ran faster than any frightened schoolgirl, I can tell you."

"How did he end up here?"

"Some of Leanoric's soldiers caught him a week later, north in Fawkrin, heading there with all his ill-gotten gains. I reckon he was going to set himself up as a bandit in Vorgeth Forest, live like a woodland lord. Anyway, because the soldiers had him, he was delivered to the Chief Lord Justice in Vor. Meant he got a trial. Hah! I had to stand there, and them bastards with their fancy words and stupid wigs, they tried to make it sound like I was some bloodthirsty killer, or something..."

"And of course, they'd be right."

"And I pointed out I wasn't the one selling children to dirty bastards from across the sea, and that's when we went into the woods, it was six of us and forty of them. Still."

Kell rubbed his chin. "They had to put him in prison. Too many families weeping and wailing in the courts. Would have looked bad on the Chief Lord Justice. Not even *he* could have stomached a mass public retribution for his bad comedy court system." Kell chuckled. "I'll never forget, all those judges giving me their dirty looks from under powdered wigs. Gods! Enough to make a man puke, it was."

"So... Jagor Mad came here?"

"Yeah. Scowling at me all the way through the courtroom, mouth uttering threats. He was the lucky one; the others got a taste of my axe. And they fucking deserved it."

Saark looked out from behind bars. He tested them, tugging gently, as he had a hundred times that day. "And now they'll give you *your own* trial, to satisfy Jagor Mad's sense of revenge."

"Looks that way."

"What about the others? Dandall and Grey Tail? You put them both here?"

"Aye, lad."

"And what did they do?"

"Dandall killed people. Lots of people. Used to wait down on Port of Gollothrim docks for drunks, men, women, didn't matter to him. He used to use a long stiletto dagger, get them down a back alley and push it through their necks. I reckon he thought he was doing somebody a favour, although it was probably himself. He was lucky there were seargents with me when I brought him in. He'd just done a drunk prostitute, killed her then cut out her eyes. If I'd been on my own, well, he would have got Ilanna in the back of the head."

Saark considered this. "Is there anybody you *don't* try to kill?"

"Yeah. People who mind their own business."

"So Jagor Mad kidnapped children for the sex trade, Dandall was an out and out murderer, what lovely crime did Grey Tail commit? Don't tell me, he was arrested for stealing sugar?"

"No. He used to eat people. Before he was a Blacklipper. Must have picked up that dirty stinking vachine habit – no offence – when he came to this wonderful shit-hole. Grey Tail lived in Vor, our illustrious capital city, quite a rich man by all accounts. Worked as a physician, tending the wounded arses of those too rich to get off them. It took the authorities years to realise that occasionally his rich clients would vanish. He had a big house on a very well-to-do street in Merchant's Quarter. Four storeys it was, very nice stone, big cellar below street level. Used to take the odd client, one who wouldn't be missed too much, take them down there, strap 'em to a chair and then, well then he'd begin."

"There he is now," said Saark, and they stared out at the small, wiry man with the round face. He was directing a group of carpenters, who were hammering planks in place as a makeshift floor. If you looked past the evidence of him being a Blacklipper, he was a modest-looking man who could have quite easily, in the eye of the imagination, been a respectable surgeon. "What *exactly* did he do to his patients?"

"Used to cut them up, piece by piece, and cook them in a little pan. Used to eat their flesh first, he'd gag 'em, slice off a chunk, fry it, eat it. Keep them alive for a few weeks whilst he feasted on their flesh. It was the neighbours who complained; I reckon they got sick of the stench of frying human fat."

"We live in a decadent world," said Saark.

"Aye. Sometimes, laddie, it makes me wonder if the vachine have the right idea."

"Hey, I can always bite you?" He grinned. "You'd become *one* of *us*."

Kell stared at him. "The day you bite me, Saark, is the day I rip off your skull."

"As I said, is there anybody you've met who you didn't try and kill?"

"No. I don't have it in me."

"That's what I thought you'd say. Oh, look Kell, up go the gallows. Hurrah!" Ten men laboured to erect a huge post, which was then strapped into position and secured with cross-struts. The sound of hammering echoed across the flat ground. Kell's face was grim.

"No need to be so happy about it."

"Hey, I'm pretty sure it's designed for me as well, mate. You're not the only one with the honour of being an enemy of the new Black Pike Mine Governors."

"Yeah. Well. We should rest. Going to need all our strength, later, aren't we."

"You really think you can convince them?"

"I hope so," said Kell. "All our lives depend on it."

"Wake up, you fucking bastards." It was Jagor Mad, growling through the evening gloom and between the bars. Snow was falling. Both Kell and Saark awoke, weary, groggy, as if they had been drugged. "Come on, quick, before I call a man with a crossbow."

Kell stood, and stretched languorously, ignoring the pain in his shoulder. "Yeah. Well, lad, that would be your way now, wouldn't it? Shoot us through the bars, in the fucking back, just like the coward piece of sliced horse dick you really are. But look, out there. All your pussy lickers are waiting, watching you. And you know you have to play the game, or some bastard will stick you in your sleep. Not that you don't get that every night, eh Saark?" Kell nudged Saark, who gave a nervous laugh, eyes fixed on the pure hate and rage that filled the trembling Jagor Mad standing before them.

"You will eat those words, Axeman," spat Jagor.

"Show me!"

"Your time will come, soon enough! On the end of a fucking rope!"

"Like that'll stop me," snarled Kell, moving close. Suddenly, he grabbed Jagor through the bars and dragged the huge bear close. Jagor Mad struggled, but despite his prodigious strength Kell was his match. Jagor's face slammed the bars, and Kell pushed his nose against his enemey's as his hands flapped and slapped, and grappled for his sword. When Kell spoke, his words were a low growl, so only he, Jagor and Saark could hear. "I could kill you, Big Man, right here, right now, bite off your fucking nose, put out your fucking eyes and you'd be screaming and then you'd be dead, and you fucking know it, you worthless worm." He pushed Jagor roughly back, just as sword cleared scabbard. The blade rang against the bars, and Jagor was in an uncontrollable rage.

"Wise?" enquired Saark, backing away as Jagor Mad fumbled with the locks.

"Is anything in this world?" snapped Kell. "Or would you rather dance on the end of a rope?"

"Calm," said Dandall, and a hand appeared on Jagor Mad's shoulder, and there were muttered words and the huge Governor strode away, face scarlet. Dandall opened the locks, and behind him were ten crossbow men, all grinning.

"Give up the tricks now, Kell. You're going on trial for your crimes. Either that, or ten bolts in your belly. You decide."

"I'll come quiet," said Kell, "although it isn't my way."

"Oh yes. The Legend." Dandall gave a slick sneer. "Well, it won't get you far in these parts. Not with these men. They like a good hanging, y'see? They like a bit of entertainment to pass away the long, cold winter evenings."

Kell and Saark stepped from their cage. Wind caught them, chilled them, thrilled them. It ruffled Kell's hair and beard, and he flexed his powerful fingers and looked around, like a wild beast in its first few seconds of release. Then he looked down, to where three thousand convicts crowded at the front of the now finished stage and gallows. Kell gave a grim smile. Everybody knew this was a farce, a stage-show; there would be no real trial, just a performance and then some killing. Kell took a deep breath. So be it, he thought.

Kell and Saark were guided down the rocky path, and Kell glanced left. He could see Nienna, clutching the bars of her own cell and watching, face small, white, filled with fear. Kell tried to give her an encouraging smile, but a spear butt jabbed him in the back of the head and he stumbled. Kell stopped, and turned. The man stared at him.

"Do that again, and I'll make you eat it, point first," growled Kell.

The man swallowed, and took a step back.

Dandall laughed. "Don't let the old fool scare you. He knows he can't outrun or outfight crossbow bolts; and at the end of the day, we have his granddaughter. Nienna. And the fun we could have with that pretty sweet slab of meat." Dandall licked his lips. "After all, Kell knows how skilled I am with a variety of blades. And if we were to give Nienna over to Grey Tail there, well," he chuckled, and sniffed the air as if sniffing the aroma of a fine cooking stew, "mmmm, I'm sure there's bits that would taste sweeter than she looks!"

Kell made a guttural growling sound, but said no more. He marched forward, down the path to be swallowed between the jeering, shouting crowd of men. Many punched and kicked out as he passed, but Kell ignored the blows, and marched with head held high, reaching the stage and pausing just for a second to stare up the steps, at the huge thick beam supporting the gallows and a gently swinging noose. Kell gave a sickly, wry smile. He'd sent enough men to be hanged under the supervision of King Leanoric. How ironic, it had come to this!

Kell mounted the steps, and Saark was jabbed up after him. Their boots were hollow, echoing on the planks as they were pushed forward and made to kneel. To one side, ten thick, hand-carved chairs had been set in a semi-circle, and now another seven men approached and mounted a second set of steps, taking their places in the chairs with as much regal air as they could muster. They were old, most of them, and wearing rich clothes and thick gold jewellery. Their eyes were bleak and cold – except for one man, on the end, Governor Myrtax, who was trembling, and kept his head low, eyes studiously ignoring Kell. It was clear he was being coerced, but Kell felt a twinge of disappointment that the man had no backbone. Kell sneered at him, and gazed out on the crowd.

Thousands of faces. Filled with hate. Shouting, and sneering, crying and bellowing. Fists were punching the air. Their hate rolled out and encompassed Kell and he absorbed it, and he used it. He revelled in it. He used it to *focus*. It reminded him of fighting in the *pit*.

Now, Grey Tail and Jagor Mad approached, and took their seats, leaving one final chair free for Dandall who stood, and raised his hands, and gradually the cacophonous roaring cheering noise subsided.

"Men and women of Black Pike Mines!" he cried, and another roar went up and Kell's fists clenched. He glanced over at Saark, who was visibly pale, and trembling. Saark licked his lips and gave Kell a worried smile. Vachine or no, Saark would die in this place. No extra strength or speed could aid him against such numbers. A crowd like this, they were a killing crowd, a lynching mob. They wanted blood, and wouldn't be happy until they had it – even if that meant each other's.

"Hang 'em!" shouted a man near the front, a man with a thick beard and small dark eyes.

"Yeah, we want to see them dance!" cried another.

Kell squared himself to the crowd, and allowed himself to smile. "Why don't you come up here and do it yourself, fucker?" he snarled. "Or have you lost your balls in that face full of beard?"

A roar of laughter rippled through the crowd and Kell grinned. "You are all fools," he said, and the laughter stopped in an instant. "You sit here in the place that imprisoned you, frightened to move, frightened to leave, frightened to fucking *fart*, and you have no idea what's turning in the real world outside!"

"Shut up!" snapped Dandall. "You are here for trial. A trial to determine your death, so I advise you to be silent when I tell you."

"A trial?" roared Kell, and saw Jagor Mad surge from his seat, face red, fists clenched but Grey Tail held him back. "What petty nonsense. And to be honest, Dandall, I don't give a shit about your trial. I reckon you'll all be dead, soon enough."

"What do you mean?" rumbled the bearded man from the front of the audience.

"STOP!" roared Jagor Mad. "This is OUR day, the day when Kell the Legend, *defender of the rich, arse-kisser to nobility, fucker of Queens, the day when he DIES!*"

Kell laughed. His voice was low, but carried to every man in the audience. "If you want me dead so bad, Jagor Mad, why not come do it yourself? Here. Right now."

"I will!" thundered the huge man. "Who do you think will be dropping you on the end of that noose?"

Kell spat out laughter once more. "Just what I thought of you, Jagor. A coward and a lick-spittle, spineless, chicken, hiding behind the decisions of others, hiding behind a hangman's horse shit when out there in Jalder and Vor and Gollothrim the Vampire Warlords have returned, they're killing all your people, your friends, and families, infecting them with vampire poison, turning them into vampire slaves!"

A murmur ran through the audience, and Jagor strode forward and hit Kell with a mighty right hook. Kell did not go down, but instead stared hard at Jagor, blood at the corner of his mouth. "Go on!" he bellowed, "show them what you can do to a man with his hands tied! What a hero! What a warrior! A man to be feared – by chickens!"

Again, laughter ran through the crowd and Jagor went red with embarrassment and anger. "You want to fight me, old man? You want to fight, here and now, and the loser hangs? Then so fucking be it."

Silence reigned. The falling snow hissed gently in a diagonal sleet.

"That would be unfair," said Kell, voice rumbling out slow and measured, a performance as good as any Saark had ever seen. Kell turned to face the crowd. He acknowledged that *they* held the power in this comedy trial; they would demand what they wanted, and would get it through strength in numbers. Kell stared at three thousand faces, hard men, criminals, men who'd survived the mines for many years, the hard manual labour making them stronger, more brutal in a struggle for simple survival. Kell smiled. He glanced at Jagor Mad. "You, on your own, ha, you would be far too easy. I would fight you, Dandall and Grey Tail! All at once. And if I win, I get to speak to the crowd. I tell them of the Vampire Warlords, and the carnage sweeping the real world."

"They don't want to hear your bedtime stories, you old fuck," snarled Jagor Mad. "They want to see blood!"

"Let's show them," said Kell, and lifted his bound hands. "Untie me!"

"No!" snapped Dandall, striding forward with Grey Tail close at his heel. The three Governors of the Black Pike Mines scowled at Kell. Swiftly, he had changed the dynamic of the trial. The three men almost felt as though *they* were back before the noose. "Kell will hang. That will be an end to it."

"You scared of him, Dandall?" said the bearded man near the front.

"Of course I'm not scared of him!"

"Let him fight you, then. You telling me the three of you can't take one old man?" The crowd started to laugh, and the three Governors exchanged glances. Somehow, the tide had turned. There was hatred for Kell, yes, but it didn't outweigh a lust to watch a good fight. Entertainment, Saark had called it. And he'd been right.

At that moment, Saark started to make soft clucking chicken noises. More laughter burst out, and Jagor Mad pulled free a curved knife and pointed at Saark. "I'll deal with you later, dandy," then slashed the knife through Kell's ropes.

Kell moved back, boots pacing the stage as he rolled his shoulders, loosening muscles, wincing a little at the crossbow wound but grinding his teeth and knowing he must show no pain.

Kell reached the other side of the stage, and turned, and lifted his fists in a stance taken by Shit Pit fighters; a roar went up from the crowd and Dandall placed a hand on Jagor Mad's arm. The three Governors looked at one another, gave a nod, and spread out, eyes narrowed, wary. They knew who Kell was, knew him far too well, far too painfully, and despite appearances they knew what he could do. Kell was a killer, pure and simple. But they were experienced. They'd done this sort of thing before.

"Come on lads, let's see what you've got."

Jagor Mad rushed Kell, fists high, purple face filled with hate and rage and spittle flying from lips which thrashed, teeth grinding, and he swung a powerful right hook but Kell swayed back, Jagor's knuckles flashing past his nose, and he slammed his boot into Jagor's groin. As Jagor grunted, and stumbled forward, Kell powered a punch down onto the bridge of the large man's nose and there was a terrible crunch. Jagor hit the planks face first and Kell stepped over him, watching as Dandall and Grey Tail spread even wider apart. They rushed him at once, a concerted attack, and Kell ducked a punch from Dandall, dropping to one knee and ramming his fist into the Governor's stomach, folding him over with an explosion of sour air. In the same movement, his arm powered back and he turned, where Grey Tail had leapt into a kick. Both boots hit Kell in the face, and he grabbed the wiry man's legs and they both went backwards across the doubled-over figure of Dandall, crashing to the boards. Grey Tail slithered around, getting atop Kell and delivering four powerful punches straight to Kell's face before Kell grabbed the man's cock and balls in a single handful, jerking tight, and Grey Tail let out a high-pitched wail as Kell crushed him in one mighty fist, rising to one knee, then to his boots, with Grey Tail dancing and squealing on his tiptoes, "Let go, let go, let go." Kell let go, and slammed a head-butt to his face, dropping the small man and turning into... a punch, which glanced from his cheekbone, and another, which glanced from his temple. Jagor Mad loomed over him, eyes mad with rage, and Kell dodged a third blow and kicked out, boot crunching against Jagor's kneecap and knocking the big man back. Kell stood, and lifted his fists. "It's like fighting three little girls," he spat though saliva and blood. Laughter rippled.

Dandall leapt at him, but Kell side-stepped, ramming an elbow into the man's face as he swept past, lifting him almost horizontally before Dandall thumped to the boards. Then with a roar, Kell charged at Jagor and delivered six punches, which Jagor managed to block, stepping back and back and back until he reached the edge of the stage, stumbled, his questing boot found nothing but air and he fell, face slapping the edge of the stage before he tumbled back into the crowd, who let out a loud jeer. Kell whirled, into a plank wielded by Grey Tail. The wood slapped his face and Kell went down, coughing, stunned, as Grey Tail set about kicking the large axeman. Kell warded off the blows, rubbed blood out of his eyes, then lunged at Grey Tail, grabbing him by balls and throat, hoisting him into the air and launching him into the crowd, who parted, allowing Grey Tail to land heavily. There was savage *crunch*, and his leg twisted beneath him at a crazy angle. Bone poked through cloth. Blood pooled out. Grey Tail screamed for a few seconds, then passed into a no-doubt welcome realm of unconsciousness.

Dandall stood, stunned, as Jagor Mad grunted and heaved himself back onto the stage. His face was battered, a diagonal line of blood crossing from one eye to his jaw, and his eyes held murder.

"Fuck this horse shit," he said, and drew a small knife. Kell's eyes narrowed.

"You upping the stakes, boy?"

"Fuck the stakes, I'm going to gut you like a rancid fish."

"But what about your crowd? They want to see a fight."

"They want to see a killing."

"Never upset your audience, Jagor."

"Fuck the audience."

The large Governor advanced, and Dandall backed away, face pale, recognising a fight now entering a different league; something of which he wanted no part. Jagor lunged at Kell, who backed away, then again, and they circled warily.

"Not so tough without your axe, eh Kell?"

Jagor ran at Kell, who batted the knife to one side and slammed a fist into Jagor's head, then skipped away as the knife slashed for his belly. Now, Kell's back was to the thick wood column and its dangling noose. He could feel the gaping hole of the drop behind him, and glanced back. Seeing his chance, Jagor ran at him and Kell stepped aside, slammed three straight punches into Jagor's face, slapped the knife from the man's hand then took hold of his tattered, bloodstained shirt.

"Is this what you wanted?" growled Kell, and shoved Jagor to the noose, grabbing the rope and lowering it over Jagor's head. Stunned, and coming round an instant too late, Jagor's fists grappled at Kell's bearskin and his boots scrabbled at the edge of the drop.

"What are you doing?" he shrieked.

"You said they came here for a hanging!"

"Not me, for you, Kell, for you!" Jagor's voice was filled with terrible fear, and his knuckles were white where he clung to Kell's bearskin. "No, no, get the rope off!"

"You try to kill me, you up the stakes to *death*, then don't fucking complain when I return the favour!"

"No, Kell, I beseech you, don't do this! I don't want to die!"

"None of us want to die, son," said Kell, and slammed a heavy slow punch between Jagor Mad's eyes. His fingers released Kell's jerkin and he stepped back, and there was a *snap* as the rope went tight and Jagor dangled there, kicking, face purple, hands clawing at the rope but because he was such a hefty, large man, battered and bruised and tired from the fight, he could not take his weight. He kicked for a while, and a cheer went up from the army of convicts ranged about the stage.

Kell glanced over at Dandall, who was white with fear. Kell stooped, picking up Jagor's knife, and his eyes were glittering and Dandall held up his hands. "No, not me, spare me Kell, please."

"Get down on your knees and beg."

Dandall got down on his knees, and touching his trembling forehead to the planks, he begged.

"And these are your leaders?" roared Kell, facing the crowd as behind him Jagor Mad's head and shoulders could be seen, struggling, and below the stage his legs kicked and danced and he refused to let go of that most precious thing. *Life*.

"You would fight for these worms? You would kill, for these fucking maggots?"

"NO!" roared the men before Kell, and he grinned at them, and turned, and sawed through the rope. Jagor Mad fell through the hole and hit the ground with a thump. He lay still, wheezing, and Kell peered down at him, where he squirmed in the mud and snow-slush.

Kell lifted his arms wide, and addressed the convicts. "The Army of Iron came from the north, from beyond the Black Pike Mountains. They slaughtered thousands of people in Jalder, men, women, children, I saw this with my own eyes. King Leanoric's army was beaten, their bodies fed into huge machines, Blood Refineries, to feed the vampire monsters to the north. But then it got worse, gentlemen. The vachine summoned the ancient Vampire Warlords – and they are terrible indeed. They rampage through our land, through Falanor, and none can stand against them. They take your friends and families, your kinsmen and countrymen, they bite them, they convert them to vampires and the world out there will *never* be the same again unless you stand beside me and fight!"

"Why should we trust you?" shouted one man.

"Because I am Kell the Legend!" he boomed, "and when I fight the world trembles! I do not do this for money, or lust, or any petty base desire. I do this because it has to be done! It is the right thing to do! I know many of you here hate me, but that's good, lads, *hate* is a good thing – I'm not asking you to kiss my fucking arse," a few laughed at that, "I'm asking you to help me put the world back together. These vampire whoresons have broken it, and they need a damn good thrashing."

"You put many of us here! We're criminals to you, scum, why the fuck would you care?"

"No, you're wrong, you're men who made mistakes, and yeah a lot of you did bad things, but now's your chance to do the right thing. Falanor needs you. She needs your strength. She needs your trust. She needs your steel. Will you fight with me?"

A terrible silence washed across the gathered men. Behind him, Kell heard Saark's sharp intake of breath. Their future, their lives and deaths, and the lives and deaths of thousands of people, the future of Falanor, all hung here, and now, as if a delicate thread of silk lay threatened by the brute bulk horror of an axe-blade.

Kell folded his arms, as if in challenge to the three thousand men ranged before him.

"Well lads," came a voice from the front. It was the hefty bearded man who'd spoken earlier. "I don't know about youse lot, but I ain't having no vampires shitting blood and shit in *my* bloody country!" He drew a short sword, and waved the dull blade above his head. "I'm with you, Kell, even though it's your damn fault I'm here! I'll fight beside you, man. We'll send these fuckers home and down into the shit!"

"Good man!" boomed Kell. "What do they call you?"

"They call me Grak the Bastard."

"And are you?" roared Kell.

The large bearded man grinned. "You'd better believe it, you old goat!"

"Glad to have you with me, Grak. Now then, lads, are you going to let Grak head out there into Falanor alone? Or are you going to show some brotherly bonding, are you going to fight for your homeland, fight for the future of your children? After all, it's damn fucking unsporting to let me and Grak kill all those vampire bastards on our own! It'd be a shame to have all the hero songs to ourselves!"

"I'll come!" bellowed a short, powerful man with biceps as thick as Kell's.

"Me too! We'll show the vampire scum what the scum of Falanor can do!"

"Yeah, we'll do better than any King's damn army!"

Kell watched the men talking animatedly for a moment, and Saark appeared beside him. Using Jagor's knife, Kell sawed through

Saark's bonds and the dandy grinned at him. "I don't believe what I just saw."

"Men are always looking for something to fight for," grimaced Kell.

"But you're the same!"

Kell stared at him "Of course I am." It was no criticism, just an observation. "Listen – go and get Ilanna. I'm missing my axe terribly."

Saark stared at the big man, with his battered face and bloodied knuckles. "And Nienna? I should release Nienna?"

"That goes without saying," smiled Kell, easily, and turned as Grak the Bastard climbed the steps and moved forward.

"You're smaller than you look, up close," said Grak.

Kell grinned. "Well met, Bastard." They clasped hands, wrist to wrist.

"Only my mother calls me that."

"I have a job for you, Grak, and I think you're the man for the job."

Grak pushed back his broad shoulders, and clenched his fists. "You name it, Kell. I'm yours to command."

"I'll be the General of this here little army. You can be one of my Command Sergeants."

Grak raised his eyebrows. "Promotion is quick in your new army, I see. I'll surely stick around now. Who knows where I'll be in a week? In a year, I'll surely be a god with a big fat arse!" He roared with laughter, slapping his thigh, and many men joined in.

"I want you to round up Grey Tail, Jagor and Dandall. Get them tied up and brought to me."

"You going to kill them?"

"No. They're just blinded by hatred; and to be honest, Grak, I need every good fighting man I can get. These Vampire Warlords – they're like nothing I've ever seen in this world."

"I'll get on it, Kell."

"And Grak?"

"Yes, General?"

"What did you do out in the real world? So that I dragged your arse to this chaotic shit-hole?"

Grak the Bastard grinned at Kell with a mouthful of broken teeth from too many bar brawls. "I killed my last General," he said, turned his back, and strode across the planks of the hangman's platform.

● ● ● ●

Kell stood on the battlements as night closed in. Snow fell on the plains beyond, and a harsh wind blew across the wilds. Kell shivered, and considered the enormity of what he was doing. Kell knew he was no general, but he was going to lead an army of convicts across Falanor and engage the vampires and the Army of Iron in bloody battle. And the Army of Iron *alone* had slaughtered King Leanoric's finest Eagle Divisions, more than ten thousand men. And here, Kell had a mere three.

"It's an impossible task," he muttered, but he knew, deep down in his heart, deep down in his soul, it was something he had to do. Something nobody else would, or could.

Kell sighed, and Ilanna sang out in a vertical slice as a shadow moved behind him.

"Hell, man, I nearly cut off your bloody head!"

"Sorry, Kell, sorry!" It was Myrtax, wearing a fresh robe and rubbing his hands together, eyes averted from Kell's cold steel gaze. "Listen. Kell. I came to apologise."

"Ach, forget it, man."

"No, no, what I did was cowardly."

"Horse shit. You were protecting your family. I would have done the same."

"Very noble of you to say so, Kell, but I know that isn't the case. You would have stood, and fought, and overcome your enemies. I stand before you a broken, humbled man."

"Yes. Well." Kell was uncomfortable. "We can't all be a..." he smiled sardonically, "a *Legend*."

Myrtax moved to the battlements and stared off into the distance. Snow landed lightly on his hair, making him look older than his advancing years. Then he glanced at Kell.

"We're getting old."

"Speak for yourself."

"What you up to, Kell? You want to fight off all the vampire hordes?"

"Aye. It's the only way I know."

"I was speaking with Nienna."

"Yes?" Kell looked sharply at Myrtax. "And?"

"She said you're tired. That you didn't want to come here. Didn't want to do this. You said Falanor would look after Herself."

"Aye, I said that. And it's true." He sighed. "You're right. We *are* getting old. This is a young man's war."

"You're wrong, Kell. This is a time when the world needs heroes. Heroes who are not afraid of the dark. Heroes who will," he smiled, looking back off into the snow-heavy distance, "walk into a fortress prison of three thousand enemies, and turn them to good deeds."

"They can only do what's in their hearts."

"They will fight for you, Kell. I can feel it. In the air. In the snow. They are excited; horrified, frightened, but excited. You have inspired them."

"Maybe. But they won't be inspired when the vampires rip out a few hundred throats and crows eat eyeballs on the blood-drenched battlefields."

Myrtax squinted into the snow. "Somebody comes."

Kell shaded his eyes, and through the haze of snowfall they watched a cart slowly advancing, being pulled by two horses. More men walked beside the cart, which had a heavy tarpaulin thrown over the back.

"Let's go and see what they want. The hour is late, and men don't wander to prisons in the dead of night for naught."

Kell and Myrtax descended the steps, and were soon joined by Saark and Grak the Bastard. They marched to the gates and stepped out, the huge walls looming behind them and seeming to cast a deep, oppressive silence over the world.

"They look cut up," said Saark, voice grim. "Like they've been in the wars."

As they neared, they slowed, and each of the six men carried swords, unsheathed.

"If you've come for a fight, lads, better be on your way," said Kell, hefting Ilanna and taking a step forward.

"We don't want trouble," said one man.

"We've come for help," said another.

"What's your story, lad?" said Governor Myrtax, not unkindly.

"We're from Jalder. The city was overrun weeks back, but near fifty of us escaped through the sewers. Women and children as well. No soldiers were sent after us, and after a few days' travelling, running, we camped up in an old farmhouse."

"I think we should invite them in, hear their story over an ale and broth," said Myrtax.

"Wait," said Saark, holding out his hand. Then he shook his head. "What's under the tarpaulin, gentlemen?"

"It's *them*," snapped one. "Two of the bastards who came hunting us." He looked suddenly frightened, a terrible look on the face of such a big, brutal man.

"Let me guess? They came at you in the night, slaughtered most of you, but you six escaped?"

The man nodded, and Kell strode forward, lifting the edge of the tarpaulin with the corner of his axe. "Did you cut off their heads?"

"No. They're still alive."

"You did well capturing them. They usually fight to the death."

"Well, forty of us died trying. We thought we'd bring them here, to Governor Myrtax. My dad always said he was a good man. He could... put them on trial, or something. I haven't got it in me to kill women, no matter how vile."

Nienna had appeared at the gates, rubbing at tired eyes, yawning. She padded to Saark's side and touched his arm lightly. He smiled down at her, and said, "You not sleep?"

"What, with you all making a racket out here? What's going on?"

"They caught some vampires."

"Oh."

Kell glanced up at Nienna. "Stand way back. These are vicious, especially if they've been tied down for a while. You don't know what they might do."

"Are you sure you know what you're doing, Kell?" Myrtax had gone deathly pale. Saark had drawn his rapier, and Grak held a short stabbing sword in one meaty fist.

Kell shrugged, and threw back the tarpaulin. On the cart lay two beautiful women of middle-years, their hair glowing and glossy, their skin pale white and as richly carved as finest porcelain. They were tied up tight with rope and field-wire, and they moved lethargically as they glanced up, struggling to move. Kell saw the rope which bound them had been nailed to the cart. Their yellow, feral eyes fell on Kell and one hissed, but the other, the more elegant of the two, stared hard at him and rolled to her knees, elegant despite the bindings. She licked her lips and Kell swallowed, mouth suddenly dry, hands clammy on Ilanna. Fear sucked at him, sucked out his courage and almost his sanity.

"No," he whispered.

"You! Bastard!" hissed the vampire.

"What is it?" snapped Saark, running forward and clutching

Kell's huge iron bicep, and he realised too late Nienna was with him, and her run was pulled up short by the clamp of Kell's fist.

The vampire laughed, eyes glittering, snow settling gently on her long dark hair and smooth black dress. She stood, and stared down at them, tugging gently at her bindings, and Nienna fell to her knees in the snow, weeping and staring up.

"What's *going on?*" snarled Saark, feeling the panic of the situation rising.

"Saark, meet Sara," growled Kell, grimly, his eyes never leaving the yellow slits of the tall vampire. "My daughter. Nienna's mother."

NINE
Song of the Ankarok

For a while, Kuradek the Unholy spent his days recovering, basking like a lizard on a rock. The journey from the Chaos Halls had been a long, hard journey, fraught with peril and indeed, filled with violent bursts of fighting simply to survive... even for one as savage as Kuradek.

Kuradek turned several humans into *slaves* and they brought him meat, and fresh blood, the near-dead bodies of children and babes on which he could gorge until full, until bloated. He would lie, in the Blue Palace, on a couch of silk, his skin smoking and squirming with evil religion, and his hatred was palpable, like a haze of ocean fog, and his red eyes surveyed the *turned* and he smiled with crooked smoke fangs.

Slowly, Kuradek fed, and he recovered his strength, and thought long and hard. He brooded. He remembered a time, the time of the *vachine* and he spat out black lumps of smoking phlegm with rage. He reached down and tore off a baby's arm, ignoring the dead blue eyes which stared up from a bloodied pile of infant corpses. He chewed on the fingers for a while, and having gnawed to the bones, moved up to the wrist, sucking at the bone marrow and picking strips of flesh clean with his fangs.

The vachine!

Bastards!

He remembered like yesterday their magick, how they had taken control from the Vampire Warlords by their deceit, them, the slaves he had allowed to live! And even the sacrifice of Silva

Valley did little to cheer Kuradek, even the death of so many va-chine did little to satiate his lust for revenge. For Kuradek knew, *knew* they had expanded north, past the Black Pike Mountains, and there were hundreds of thousands still remaining, still breath-ing air, still breeding human cattle and mixing their blood with foul oil-magick. They were impure, the vachine; they were de-viants of the vampire. They were an outcast race. They were a *clockwork* race, and Kuradek would not have it! His eyes glowed, and his long arms flexed, talons dropping to shriek against stone with an array of sparks. No.

Kuradek would make the vachine pay.

One day.

All of them...

Slowly, Kuradek rose from his bloated slumber and blinked lazily. He stepped up to the high window in the west tower of the Blue Palace, and stared out across the blackness of Jalder. No fires burned, now, and a cold ice wind blew across what appeared a deserted city. And yet... yet he could *smell* those who still lived, could smell the blood in their veins, hear the pumping of their hearts like discordant music, off-key notes, a poisoned orchestra. Kuradek breathed deep, and leapt from the high tower window, landing and cracking the ancient stone flags of the courtyard. A group of the *turned* scattered in shock, then fixed eyes on their master and returned slowly, smiles on pale faces lit by the moon.

Kuradek hissed, and gestured the slaves back, then he moved, running through the darkened streets, moving with awesome speed across snow and ice, talons gripping with surety, smoke-trailing head weaving from side to side as he sniffed, as he *hunted*... he reached a cottage, skidded on ice, kicked the door across the room in an explosion of splinters and stood in the cen-tre of the space. One talon smashed down through floorboards, and the whole room seemed to erupt in violence as screams rent the air and Kuradek leapt down into the hidden cellar where eight people hid, and swords struck at him but seemed to slow through his smoke-filled, symbol-tattooed body then emerge from the other side without harming the Warlord. His talons lashed out, punching holes through men's chests. He grabbed a woman, and his long limbs pulled apart and both her arms came off at the shoulders spewing blood and leaving her screaming, her blood describing fountains across the walls. Kuradek loomed over a four year-old girl with curly brown hair, brown eyes looking up at him in awe and shock and wonderment. He reached down, and with a quick bite, removed her head, swallowing it whole.

Kuradek lifted his smoky muzzle and... howled, howled at the city, at the moon, at the stars, at his tortured past, at his escape from the Chaos Halls, at the bastard vachine and their curse and imprisonment, but most of all, Kuradek howled with enjoyment and hatred and rage and impotent fury and the *joy*, the pure acid *joy* of the hunt.

Throughout Jalder, Kuradek's howls and screams seemed to stimulate the turned vampires into action. They rampaged through the streets, breaking into houses, searching through attics and cellars, finding more hidden humans and either drinking their blood and leaving drained corpses, or as they had been instructed, *turning* them into yet *more* vampires. Into Kuradek's Legion.

For Kuradek knew.

Falanor was full to the brim with human offal. And they would bring the fight to him. They always did. It was their nature. But he would crush them. Unlike a thousand years ago, when the vachine turned on their masters, this time Kuradek and the Vampire Warlords would be ready...

As the hours passed, and day turned to night turned to day, so Falanor fell under the spread of the *vampire*. And unlike the vachine before them, who had sought simple extermination for blood-oil magick, and for sacrifice, the Vampire Warlords sought slaves, sought an army of the impure. For that way, they could expand. That way, they could create Dominion.

In Vor, Meshwar the Violent uncurled like a snake and stood tall, stretching, smoke curling from the corners of his mouth. His blood eyes dropped to survey the slaves before him, and he strode down the once pure regal steps of King Leanoric's beautiful Rose Palace, and stared out through huge iron gates, out over the destruction and desolation of Vor, Falanor's capital city.

Smoke curled along midnight streets, swirling about the feet of many slave vampires bearing the *mark* of Meshwar. He grinned, a smoke grin of tightly reined insanity, and surveyed his handiwork. He was not called *The Violent* for no reason...

In the City Square, a huge pile of corpses burned, their drained, angular figures like wooden stickmen seen through flames. Meshwar's eyes drifted impassively over the thousand or so unfortunates, their clothing, skin and bones turning to ash as fire roared and crackled like feeding demons, illuminating the palace with an orange glow.

What Graal had begun so many weeks earlier with his ice-smoke and blood-oil magick, with his invasion of Vor by the Army of Iron – well, now Meshwar was finishing the task.

The Army of Iron were camped out of the city. All vachine camped alongside them had been taken into the forest and executed. Some vachine had put up a fight, several bands even escaping into the woods; but Meshwar sent squads of vampire killers after them, hunting them down, ripping out throats and clockwork hearts, spilling gears and cogs to the forest undergrowth,

Now, though, now it was all *his*. And the *worm* Graal was the problem of Bhu Vanesh. Slowly, through Meshwar's mind eased a thought web, for he did not think like normal mortals. This multi-threaded strand held ideas of death and destruction for Graal, but also amusement for it would annoy Bhu Vanesh. It would not be long, decided Meshwar, until Graal died a horrible death, despite his misplaced loyalty in their Summoning. To Meshwar, Graal was an imposter. A twisted impure. A melding of that which they sought to stamp out...

Meshwar's eyes surveyed Vor once again, then again, and again, taking in the destruction, the rampage, the *violence*. There, the Five Pillars of Agrioth had been chained and pulled to the ground by teams of horses and cattle. Five thousand years of history destroyed, because it was the history of the Ancient, the history of the *Ankarok*, and they were a pestilence long dead and better ground into the dirt, into dust, even moreso than the vachine.

The Great Library had first been ransacked, the books burned, then the ancient building itself set alight. That had been a particularly pleasing night's work, Meshwar nodded, smoke-filled mouth forming a smile, skin changing and shifting like a chameleon, and the image of the violence flashed across his flesh like moving, animated tattoos on smoke. On Meshwar's skin, the other slaves could see the re-enactment of the Great Destruction, as it would come to be known. Even after fires had died in the

Great Library, leaving the teetering blackened walls smoking and charred, stinking and unstable, so Meshwar had personally led a team of vampires in pulling down the remaining walls until only rubble remained.

"No man should read," emerged Meshwar's guttural voice, as around him his vampires bowed and nodded and wondered when they would be fed. "He does not have the ability to utilise any such knowledge with wisdom and clarity. The only use for a human, is that of a slave."

Now, Meshwar watched the Three Temples of Salamna-shar burn, huge shooting flames of orange and yellow roaring at the night sky illuminating the huge piles of rubble and snow throughout the city on all three sites. Fireflies danced over the once magnificent domes, towers and crystal spires. And Meshwar smiled again. Kuradek the Unholy would have liked this moment. This utter destruction of Falanor religion. The annihilation of man's petty gods and their base vanities. After all, the only religion *now* would be of their own making... worship of the Vampire Warlords.

Meshwar moved to the high iron gates of the Rose Palace. He reached out, touching the ancient, pitted iron, and looked up at the incredible artistry thousands of years old. Then he glanced back to the Rose Palace, in all its glory, and violence flooded his brain but he calmed himself, with small breaths, as a man would calm himself before ejaculation. "No. Not yet." He would destroy the Rose Palace, but it was the single largest symbol of freedom and the Royal spirit of Falanor. It would have to die *last*. But die it would.

Meshwar pointed at a young vampire girl, and she padded over to him. His talons caressed her face, then he lifted her from her feet and clamped fangs over her throat, and bit, and fed, her arms and legs kicking spasmodically as he fast-drained her to a husk. He allowed her skin-filled bones to drop with clacks, and rattle off untidily down the steps.

Meshwar turned, fast, to see the Harvester watching him with a smile on his curious, blank face. Small black eyes were fixed on Meshwar and his own blood-red gaze narrowed.

"You want something, Vishniriak?"

"My clan master would speak with you, Meshwar, great Warlord. It is most urgent."

"I will speak with him when I am good and ready. Not now. Not tonight. I have much work to... attend."

Vishniriak nodded, but the Harvester did not break the connection. Despite looking odd, with his tall angular frame, pale oval face, small black eyes and perfectly white robes embroidered with fine gold wire – despite the filth, and smoke, and fire filling the city of Vor – Vishniriak still carried an air of power, and an air of authority. The Vampire Warlords considered themselves superior to the Harvesters; but the Harvesters did not share the same sentiment.

"It's about the cankers. They have gone."

"I thought they were destroyed? Like all vachine filth?"

"No. There was a leader amongst them. And, against all odds, he has rallied the cankers and they have fled together, north, it is believed."

Meshwar considered this. "I did not think they had it in them; their bestiality is too far removed from any logical thought. Who commands them?"

Vishniriak smiled, head tilting to one side. "He is one of General Graal's impromptu clockwork creations. A second-hand canker impurity with far too many slices of humanity remaining. His name is Elias, once the Sword Champion of King Leanoric. Now, ahh, a *much* altered beast."

"Send a hundred slaves. Hunt them down. Kill them all."

"Yes, Master." Vishniriak bowed his head, an inch away from actually showing respect, turned with a billowing of white robes and disappeared towards the Rose Palace.

Meshwar scowled, face swirling with images of rape and torture and murder in the smoke. Then he relaxed, and decided what violence to inflict on Vor that night.

It was past midnight. General Graal sat at the table, staring into the solitary flame of a candle and thinking of Bhu Vanesh, thinking of Helltop and the Summoning of the Vampire Warlords. So much effort. So much blood-oil magick. So many dead. And all for what?

Graal smiled a crooked smile, and mocked himself. He had harboured such plans! He had thought he, and Kradek-ka, could rule the Vampire Warlords, use them as puppets to build an army and take control of the world! And yet things had turned out different. Things had become... *distorted*. And now, they were as much slaves as those poor lost souls *turned* down on the streets below.

The door opened, and a draught drifted in like plague. Wood slammed with a rattle, and Kradek-ka sat down opposite Graal and glared at the man, at the albino, at the *vachine*.

"I cannot believe it's fucking *come to this!*" he snarled, and bit the top from the bottle with a crunch of breaking glass. "I sacrifice my own *fucking daughter*, I sacrifice the *vachine civilisation* of Silva Valley, and here we are, locked in a tower like two old men waiting to die."

Kradek-ka poured two generous glasses of brandy, taken from the looted and ravaged city below. Even now, at this late hour, they could hear the hammering of ship-builders. Frantic work on the new navy continued. And the ships' skeletons were growing. Slowly, imperceptibly, but they were growing.

"We should kill Bhu Vanesh," said Graal, drinking the brandy. It glistened on his pale lips; glistened against his brass fangs. "We should kill him. It. Now. Tonight." He glanced up, and Kradek-ka was staring at him. "We should send the fucker back to the Chaos Halls."

"We tried. We failed."

"We should try again!"

"We only get one more chance." Kradek-ka smiled weakly. "You know how to do this, and not die in the process?"

"I have an idea."

"Blood-oil magick?"

General Graal nodded, and drank more. "When we opened the gate to the Halls they followed a path between that place and this; every path has a resonance. A bond, if you like. The Vampire Warlords were bound to the Chaos Halls; being here is an unnatural balance. All we need do is give them a *push*, and they'll be dragged back, kicking and screaming. I think. I believe a killing blow will do this."

"Bhu Vanesh is mighty indeed," said Kradek-ka, with fear etched into his face and voice.

"We must attack when he is at his weakest."

"Which is?"

"When he feeds," said Graal, eyes gleaming.

Bhu Vanesh stood and stretched, and stepped down from the dais, staring at the three chained girls. They were shivering in terror, eyes staring at the ground, huddling together like sheep. Bhu

Vanesh smiled at that. For, like sheep, they were about to become *food*. He moved swiftly, grabbing the first girl by the throat and pulling her close, almost as if to kiss. Then his maw stretched wide and the girl screamed, a wavering long high note, and Bhu Vanesh's fangs sank into her throat and started to suck her dry as the other two girls vomited, and squirmed, and moaned and thrashed with horror.

Out of the shadows came Kradek-ka, moving fast, and the spear thrust into the Warlord's back with as much force as the old vachine could muster, born of fear and hatred; the spear rammed through the Vampire Warlord, through his heart and through the girl on which he fed, making her go rigid, puking blood as her limbs twitched spasmodically. Even as the spear thrust struck, so Graal leapt from the high beams of the roof, sword slashing down to open Bhu Vanesh's throat and the Vampire Warlord dropped, pinned to the girl, gurgling and Graal stood, his curved blade dripping blood and looked down with a sneer and spat at Bhu Vanesh, until he realised that the Vampire Warlord wasn't gurgling in his death throes, he was laughing and he slammed upright and rigid in a splinter of time, and fire seared the girl to which he was attached, crisping her instantly to ash. What remained of the spear Bhu Vanesh grasped, and pulled it smoothly through his smoke-riddled body, as the smoke-flesh of his throat ran together and Graal screamed, and attacked in a blistering display of sword skill but Bhu punched him in the chest, caving in his breastbone and ribs with one mighty blow and sending him slamming backwards to roll amongst scattered tables and chairs until he hit the wall, his clockwork pounding, several wheels rolling from the massive open wound. Kradek-ka attacked from behind, and Bhu Vanesh turned, grasped the old vachine's head between both sets of talons, and with a *wrench* twisted his head clean off. Kradek-ka looked surprised. His mouth worked soundlessly, as blood dripped from his severed neck stump. The body spewed blood and tiny brass cogs, then one knee folded, and Kradek-ka's corpse settled to the ground like a deflating balloon.

Bhu Vanesh sighed, and tossed away the head. He pointed at Graal, and grimaced. "I cannot stand traitors," he snapped, and from the shadows eased Lorna, petite and blonde and smiling, and the bulk of Division General Dekull. They lifted Graal with ease. He could not fight. He was slowly dying, with his chest caved in.

"Take him to the Black Tower," snapped Bhu Vanesh, eyes glowing, and he waved his talons to dismiss them and turned his attention back to the two moaning girls who remained. "I am still enjoying breakfast. I will deal with him later."

Graal, his clockwork whining, was dragged from the chamber and out, into the cold stairwell, and up narrow winding steps.

General Graal lay on the floor, panting, pain flooding him like nothing he'd felt in his long, long lifetime. Breathing was hard, with a caved-in chest, and he knew even with accelerated vachine healing powers, this *pulping* at the talons of Bhu Vanesh would take him months from which to recover. *If* he could recover. But then, in a few short hours he would be dead. Bhu Vanesh was toying with him.

So, it was all for naught? How many men, down through the ages of history, have taken great risks only to end up, condemned and dying, in a prison cell? He smiled at that, then winced and vomited blood.

Many. *Many...*

And Graal had *exterminated* most.

Pain rocked through him in waves, and it was so bad, so painful Graal went beyond pain and into comedy. He laughed, laughed because it hurt so damn fucking much. He lifted his head, looked down at the hole in his chest. He could see his own beating heart merged with clockwork. Cogs spun, and gears stepped, but many were twisted and misaligned. The only time Graal had seen that was in the cankers. That thought made him shiver. Sobered him with a slap.

Better death, than to turn canker.

He had seen what becoming a canker did to a man. After all, it had happened to his brother. The brother Kell had killed. Kell! That old bastard. Graal grimaced. *Now there's a fucker who needs his head on a spike! His balls chopped off! His throat opening like a second smile! Far too much testosterone. Far too much of the fucking hero factor, the dirty stinking piece of reprobate horse-shit! Him, and that damn axe... that axe...*

"I'm sorry to intrude," said the little boy, "but it would appear somebody left a door open."

Graal groaned, and his eyes moved to the boy. He was five or six years old, skinny and raggedy looking to the extent he would be taken for a vagrant in any of the fine cities of Falanor. Not that many existed, in the old sense of the word *city*. The boy wore rags, and had no shoes, and he was smiling and his teeth were black, like insect chitin.

"You!" gasped Graal, and struggled to rise, but groaned as pain swamped him and he passed back into a welcome deep honey pool of glorious unconsciousness.

When his eyes fluttered open, Skanda was sitting on the edge of Graal's bed, staring down at him where he lay on the stone flags, still with that disarming smile stuck on his face. "You do look rather ill," said Skanda. "Maybe some medicine is in order?"

"I want nothing from you!" Graal spat, and he would have screamed and attacked, but had not the strength, nor the energy. Instead, he glared with blue albino eyes at the boy.

"I disagree," said Skanda, and he hopped from the bed and Graal cringed, as if expecting some fearful weapon. Instead, Skanda knelt down by Graal and placed his hands on the vachine's belly. Inside him, Graal felt the clockwork slow to a rhythm that was normal, not discordant, not twisted. Pleasure ran through him, tingling every fingertip, and pain fled like rats before a flood.

Graal sighed. Then he blinked, slowly, and allowed himself to breathe.

"Thank... you," he managed, and stared hard at Skanda. "But I haven't forgotten Helltop. I haven't forgotten your part in the deaths of my daughters!"

"Ahh. The delightful Shanna and Tashmaniok. Yes. I am sorry about them. But we need Kell alive. We need the Legend to exist. Or all our plans would be for nothing."

"Our plans?" said Graal.

"The Ankarok," said Skanda, softly, his dark little insect eyes fixed on Graal. "That is why I am here. That is why I need your help."

"There is nothing I can do for you, boy," snapped Graal. "Nothing I can do for the Ankarok! Nothing I can even do for myself..."

"We are alive," hissed Skanda, "and if you help me, Graal, General Graal, Graal the Dispossessed, Graal the Dying, Graal the Fallen, Graal the Slave, Graal the Whipping Boy of the *fucking* Vampire Warlords... then I will help you. *We* will help you."

Graal swallowed, and he looked at the six year-old boy, but it was the eyes, the eyes were old, older than Time it seemed. They were portals, piss-holes straight back to the Chaos Halls.

"What is it you require?" said Graal, voice a little strangled.

"We want our Empire back," said the Ankarok.

"What do you need me to do?"

"We need your blood-oil magick. Ours is trapped. Trapped in the curse that is Old Skulkra. I broke free, broke free and was aided by Kell and Saark. But now, now we are ready to return. General Graal – we will sweep aside these vampires. We will send the Warlords back to the Chaos Halls."

"But we'll have *you* instead," said Graal.

"You will not be a slave," said Skanda. "I guarantee you that. You will rule by my side. You will be a vassal of the Ankarok. You will be a *Prince* of the Ankarok!"

"How do I know I can trust you?"

"Because you have little choice. But also, I could leave you to die. There are others, Graal. But I *like* you." The boy grinned. "I like your tenacity. I like your lack of fear. I like your *will* to get the job done." His smile dissolved. "I like your ability to kill."

"So we would exchange one evil empire for another?"

"Evil is all about perspective," said Skanda. "But these Vampire Warlords thrive on destruction; and what use is that? If you kill all the slaves, who then will *be* the slaves? It is a base stupidity. A flaw in their strategy."

"What do you need me to do?"

"Follow me."

"What about the thousands of vampires in the city below?"

"Trust me," said Skanda, smiling with those gloss black teeth. "They will not be a problem for my power."

"I will come with you," said Graal. "But I have one request."

"Ask."

"When we find Kell, the Legend, I want to be the one who places his head on a spike."

"Agreed."

TEN
Valleys of the Moon

Kell stared at his daughter, and slowly, without taking his eyes off the tall female vampire, he reached down and hoisted Nienna to her feet.

"Mother!" she gasped.

Sara stared at Kell, glanced at Nienna, sneered, and turned back to Kell. "You are looking old, Bastard Father. Soon, soon you will be dead. Sooner, if I have my way."

Kell glanced at Saark. "Go and get chains. And shackles." He stared hard at Sara. "Better make them strong ones."

Saark nodded, and eased through the fortress gates.

"You're looking well," said Kell, staring up at his *vampire* daughter. She rolled her neck, as if easing tension, and smoothed her hands down her black dress. Then she looked at the bonds restraining her hands. They were tight, and blood bubbled around the rope and thin wires, which bit into her flesh.

"I am weak. These fools put a pitchfork in my back. Right through me! The bastards. But soon, when I am strong, I will return the favour!" She turned and hissed at the men, who backed hurriedly away from the cart, lifting their weapons in a parody of defence.

Kell realised, then: Sara had been weakened during a fight in which she killed *forty* men and women. She had been restrained. But soon, *soon* she would snap the wires like cotton thread. She had let them take her; so she could rest. Recuperate. To sleep the sleep of the vampire – like an injured hound licking its wounds, waiting, *waiting...*

Suddenly Kell leapt atop the cart so he was inches from Sara, and Ilanna was between them and she hissed when she saw the axe, and scrambled back as far as the bindings would allow.

"You remember my axe?" said Kell, voice deep, eyes fixed on Sara. The second vampire started to rise, but Kell waved Ilanna at her. At *it*. "Stay down, or I'll cut off your pissing head, I swear! There's no healing a wound like that!" He returned to Sara. "Not even for you, daughter of mine."

"It is a shame it came to this," she said, and licked her lips, showing sharp fangs.

"Indeed," said Kell, gaze locked. "Because now I'm going to have to kill you."

"Please, no," and suddenly she was pleading, voice soft, aggression gone and she dropped to her knees. "I will pray to you, great Kell, Kell the Legend, and I will do your bidding."

Kell gave a mocking laugh. "Like you prayed to your god? And look what he did for you, Sara. He cursed you! He made you like this! The gods? Bah! A curse on all their hairy arses! And all for what? The pain you caused Nienna with your hard ways, your religious learning, your pious necessities. Well, now she is my ward." Kell dropped to his own knees, so they were once again facing each other. His words came out in a low growl. "And you will serve. Or you will die."

"I will serve," said Sara, head low. She glanced at Ilanna.

"Look well on the blades," said Kell, and then climbed down from the cart as Saark approached with shackles. "For vampire or no, they will tear out your soul and devour it. This, you know. This, you have seen."

Saark secured the shackles on ankles and feet, and using a small ratchet tool, cranked them tight until Sara gave a howl and glanced at him, sharply, as if imprinting his face in her mind for future reference.

Kell lifted Nienna to her feet. "Come on, girl. This place is too painful for you."

"What will you do to her?"

"I will not kill her, if that's what you think."

"I... I love her, Kell. She is my mother, no matter all her faults. No matter her poisonous gossip, her force-fed opinions, her casual hate. I *have* to love her. No matter what she's done. That's why she's my mother."

"I know that, love."

"How did she become like this? What happened?"

And as they passed through the gates, into the dark and brooding shadows, Kell whispered, "I don't know, girl. I just don't know."

Kell slept badly. His dreams were dark flashes of black, violet and blood red. In his last dream, he dreamt he awoke and it felt real, felt like it was *happening* and Sara was there, inches from his throat, and she laughed and hissed and her jaws dropped, fangs puncturing his skin and Kell screamed and thrashed but she pinned him down, her strength incredible and unreal as Kell kicked and kicked and kicked, and felt his lifeblood sucked from him, sucked from his gaping throat. Sara would rise above him, dripping blood and grinning in absolute madness – and Kell sat up with a shout, a snap of jaws, and then glared across at Saark lounging in a chair beside his bed.

"What the fuck are you doing here?"

"Good morning to you, Kell."

"What the fuck is that *smell?*"

"It's perfume. *Hint of Venison.*"

"Hint of what, lad?"

"Er, venison." Saark suddenly looked a touch uncertain.

"So, you're telling me you're wearing a perfume that stinks like a charging, honking stag?"

"No, no, it's more a suggestion of an aura of power, over which all women will stumble erotically when they enter the room."

Kell stared at him. "Either that, or they're knocked down by the stench and buggered unconscious by a group of rampant drunk nobility! Ha, Saark, it smells like rancid bowels on a ten-week battlefield. So I hope you don't want a good morning kiss, 'cos I fear I've got kitten breath something chronic!"

"Not at all, my sweetness," he said between clenched teeth. "I just dropped by to check up on you. Brought you some coffee, and here," he lifted a plate from the floor. "Compliments of Myrtax."

Kell uncovered a large tin plate filled with bacon, sausage, four eggs and fried mushrooms. Kell gawped. "By all the gods, that's a breakfast fit for a King!"

"Or certainly a fat bastard, more like. But you eat it all up, Kell, get some strength in you, then we need to talk about what's to be done."

Kell lifted mushrooms on his fork, chewed, looked almost euphoric, then snapped, "What's to be done? Eh? What do you mean, laddie?"

"Well, I refer to the next stage of your thrilling plan. I am curious."

Kell stared at his friend, who had taken the entire previous evening, late though it was, to bathe, sprinkle himself with perfume and a light dusting of make-up from Myrtax's wife's quarters. The Chaos Hounds only knew which wardrobe he'd raided – *now* he wore a pink silk shirt, ruffed with lace at collar and cuffs, and bulbous green silk pantaloons the like of which Kell had never seen. He also wore yellow shoes, polished to a bright vomit shine.

"Listen. I'll have my breakfast," said Kell, uncertainly, still stunned by Saark's garish wardrobe. "You go and gather all the armourers and smithy labourers together. Meet me down the Smith House with them, in about... twenty minutes. That's if they haven't kicked your head in first."

"Meaning?"

"You look like a peacock."

"Yes. Well. 'Tis hardly a fair division of work, I feel," said Saark, pouting. "And I *did* bring you breakfast."

"Eh? Well, I tell you what, next time I'm up to my neck in gore from the killing, I'll make sure *you* get your fair share of the fight as well. Agreed, Saark?"

"Point taken. Twenty minutes, you say?"

"Good man! Go knock 'em out."

And for the first time in what felt like *years*, Kell focused on one thing and one thing only. Gorging himself on a fine fried breakfast. He tried hard to shut out the shouts, laughter and whistles as Saark moved gaily through the old prison grounds, but could not help himself. Kell grinned like a lunatic.

The armourers were a bunch of huge, heavily muscled men – numbering perhaps forty in total, with one single exception. A small, weedy looking man standing almost swallowed by the wall of blackened, bulging flesh. They wore the universal uniform of smithies the world over: colourless leather pants, heavy work boots, and most went bare-chested, a few with leather aprons. The small man was the only one smiling.

"Look at him," nodded Saark, and nudged Kell in the ribs with his elbow. "Stands out like a flower on a bucket of turds."

"I'd keep your voice down if I was you," said Kell. "Smithies are not known for their fine tempers and happy chatter. You liken them to horse-shit, next minute you'll be trampled in it, mate."

"Point taken. Point taken."

"Right, lads," said Kell, standing with huge hands on hips. "You all know what's happening here, so I reckon I'll cut to the shit. We'll be going into battle. All the men here will be fighting men, and they'll need weapons, light armour, and shields."

"Won't we move faster without armour and shields?"

"Ha. Maybe. But we certainly won't live as long against… *them*. Now, I know you have great stores of iron and steel here in the mines. Have you any gold?"

The small man lifted his hand. "I believe there are several bags of coin in Governor Myrtax's underground vault. He kept a certain mint for King Leanoric. We found some large lodes down in the mines, you see. Way deep down, in the dark, where fear of collapse is greatest."

"Good. Good." Kell scratched his chin. "We'll need that to pay the lads. But with regards warfare, this is what I need. Short stabbing swords for close combat. Maybe only," he parted his hands, "this long. I want round shields with rimmed edges, so they can be hooked together, *locked* together to repel a charge. I need long heavy spears, maybe twice as heavy as you'd normally make, and arrows – I want iron shafts with slim heads."

"They'll be heavy for the archers to fire," said a big man, with thunderous brows, shoulders like an ox, and a certain distinct look of eagles about him.

"Yes," nodded Kell, "but they'll also have a lot more *impact*. And believe me, we'll need that for these vampire bastards. They'll take some killing, if they're anything like their dirty, blood-sucking vachine brethren."

"Steady on, Kell," said Saark, sounding a little injured.

"Just telling it how it is."

"The men who came in last night," said the large smith. "They said three vampires wiped out near forty of their friends. They managed to kill one, and after a long struggle they captured the other two. That means these creatures are pretty brutal, if you ask me."

Kell nodded. "They're brutal, I reckon. But they also prey on naivety. If we know what we're fighting, and we know how to kill 'em, and we have some protection – I reckon we can take the fight to them. Another thing we need," he looked around to check he wasn't overheard, "we need steel collars."

"Like a dog collar?"

"Aye. Only these stop the bastards getting their fangs in your throat. You understand?"

"How thick do you want them?"

"About half a thumb-length."

"They'll be uncomfortable. Chafing, like."

"Not as uncomfortable as having your throat torn out and strewn across Valantrium Moor."

"I take your point. Although I'm not sure the men will wear them."

"They will. And those that won't, when they see a friend spewing blood they'll soon change their minds."

"What's the best way to kill these vampires?" asked the small man.

Kell jabbed his thumb towards Saark. "Lads. This is Saark. He's an, er, an *expert* on the vachine, and indeed, that makes him more of an expert on the Vampire Warlords than any of us could ever be. Any more questions about killin' 'em, ask Saark here. I know he looks like an accident in a tart's parlour, but he knows his stuff. I'm off, I need to speak to my daughter."

"*Kell!*" snapped Saark, frowning.

"What is it, lad?"

"You're leaving me here? With *these?*"

"Hey, you chose to dress like a sweat-slippery whore in a disreputable tavern." Kell grinned, and slapped Saark on the back. "Don't worry, lad! If they bugger you rancid, I'll hear the screams and come running to your rescue!"

"Kell!"

"Just remember, some of these blokes have been locked up for *years* without a quim as tasty as yours."

"Kell, my entire sense of humour has gone!"

"Good. Because now is not the time for jokes; now is the time for killing. Tell them what you know, and tell them well. One day soon, our lives will rest on these men."

Saark swallowed, and turned, and looked at the forty hefty labourers with dark eyes under dark brows. A cold wind howled down from the mountains, and from the corner of his eye Saark observed Kell stride away. *What a bastard. A bastard's bastard.*

One of the smiths stepped forward. His two front teeth were missing, and his forearms were as wide as Saark's thighs. "Is that really a pink silk shirt you're wearing, boy?" he rumbled, voice so deep it was like an earthquake beneath the Black Pikes.

Saark drew his rapier. He smiled. "Gentlemen. Allow me to begin your education," he said.

As Kell strode across the rocky earth towards the cells built into the mountainside, Governor Myrtax joined him, jogging a little to keep up with Kell's warrior stride.

"They will work for you?"

"Aye," said Kell. He stopped, and looked across to the smaller man. "I want you to oversee production. I want as many labourers as possible helping make armour and weapons and shields. When we go into battle, each man must have the best, for the fight will be savage indeed."

"Do you think we can win?"

Kell looked Myrtax straight in the eye. "No," he said.

"Then why fight?"

"Why indeed."

"This is insane, Kell! Madness! You say these Vampire Warlords are all-powerful. I saw those vampires the men from Jalder brought in; and they killed forty people! We cannot stand against such odds."

"But it matters that we stand," said Kell, his voice low. "Now tell me, what did you do with Jagor Mad?"

Myrtax pointed. "He's in those cells over there. With the other bastard so-called Governors. Why? Are you going to kill him?" There was a strange gleam in Myrtax's eye that Kell did not like. Kell grimaced.

"No. I need his help."

"His... help?" Myrtax's voice had gone up several octaves. "He'll not help you, Kell, unless it's to throw you in the furnace. He hates you with every ounce of his flesh."

"We'll see. First, I'm going to see my daughter."

"I'll come with you."

Kell stopped again, and turned. "No, Governor. Go to Saark. Help him organise the smiths. Saark is a canny lad, but he's little experience with metallurgy – or indeed, the instruction of people. Especially men. He tends to rile them the wrong way, admittedly by trying to sleep with their wives and virgin daughters, but still. Go. Help me, Myrtax. I cannot do this alone."

The Governor nodded, and hurried off, one hand on his robust and well-fed belly.

Kell continued to walk, glancing up at the skies, a huge pastel canvas of white, ochre and deep slate. Distant, heavy clouds vied for sovereignty. They threatened more snow against the world of Men.

Reaching the cell, Kell saw Sara was alone. The two vampires had been separated through basic mistrust. A wise choice. She watched Kell approach, eyes yellow and narrow, but she did not move from where she lay on the floor, curled like a lizard on a rock in the sun.

Kell sat down an arm's length from the bars, and placed his chin on his fist.

"Sara. What am I going to do with you, eh girl?"

"Knowing you, you'll use that great axe to cut off my head!"

"You are vampire-kind now. Maybe that would be a kindness?"

"My master will find you!" she hissed, suddenly, and leapt at the bars, claws raking out. Kell stayed motionless, and the sharp points of her talons skimmed the end of his nose. For a few moments Sara thrashed and hissed, trying to get to him, to his throat, to his jugular, to spill his blood and drag him like torn offal into her cage where she could gorge and feed... but she could not reach. Kell had judged his distance well. Gradually, she subsided, glancing at him like a sulky child.

"Your master is Kuradek the Unholy?"

"Yes."

"And he has taken Jalder?"

"Go to Hell!"

"You're already there, girl. Help me!"

Kell and Sara stared at one another.

"You know nothing about how I feel," she snapped, eventually, and Kell sat back a little, listening. She eyed him warily. "You were a bad man, Kell. I know your secrets. My mother told me all about you, before she... died." Her eyes narrowed. "And even that event is shrouded by mystery, is it not, great Legend?"

"What happened during the Days of Blood, happened," said Kell, softly. "I am not proud of myself. Not proud of my actions. But I tell you now, there's no need to bring your mother into this. You have reason enough to hate me yourself."

"I can still feel the handprint," she hissed, jabbing a finger at Kell. "Here!" She placed a hand against her face. "It burns me, like a brand, making me a slave to the Great Man, the Great Hero, ha ha! If only the people of Falanor knew the real Kell. The bastard. The wife-beater. The child-beater."

"It was not like that," said Kell, darkly.

"Oh, but it was! You see, it's all about perspective, it's all about purity, and you had neither, you fucking old bastard. You turned on us. All of us. And not just your family, your King and country! Don't you remember? Or has the whiskey rotted your mind as well as your fucking teeth?"

"It was not like that," growled Kell, and his fists clenched. He forced himself to stay calm. "That is in the past. Now, Sara, we must talk about the present."

"What? About how you'll beat my little girl? Nienna never did see past your mask, did she, the little fool. Dragged in by the stories of glory, dragged in by the myth but not the man. I'm surprised you haven't bruised her yet, Kell. Or maybe you have. I'm amazed she's still walking in a straight line. It was my leg you broke though, silly me for forgetting."

"Still the acid tongue, I see," snapped Kell. "Just like your mother! There are bigger things at stake here, now, in this time. Like Falanor! Like the world!"

"Pah! Like you give a damn about anything but your own horse-shit ego and petty desires. Can't you see, Kell, I am part of something *bigger*, now, part of something *powerful!* I am strong, Kell. I could take you, in battle, I could rip your arms from their sockets and piss on your face as you stumbled slipping in the mud." Her eyes were gleaming, cheeks flushed in triumph. "Go on Kell, let me out, let me show you! Or are you still the pathetic, weak, moaning coward you always were?"

"Tell me of Kuradek."

Sara laughed. "What would you like to know? He controls Jalder. We have turned, between us, many thousands into vampires! There is little of the resistance left."

"So they did resist you? That's good. Their spirits still live."

"No! It is foolish! Kuradek is Master, he is incredibly powerful and he knows you, Kell, oh yes he knows you, he remembers you from Helltop and he has sworn to hunt you down, to change you into one of us! Imagine it, Kell, imagine how powerful you would be! Increased strength, speed, and you could never die!"

"You die," snapped Kell. "You die just like everybody else. All we need do is cut off your head, or ram a sword through your necrotic heart."

Sara went quiet.

"You forget," said Kell. "I know your kind."

"You hunted vachine," sneered Sara. "They are weak, spineless, mechanised with their pathetic ticking clockwork! They are an aberration of the pure; they are the weak, the diseased, the freaks." She chuckled. "The vachine are a corruption."

"I hunted vachine," said Kell, and met Sara's gaze. "But I hunted your kind, too. Me. And Ilanna. Do not think I haven't killed true vampires. It was a long time ago, but I remember the taste like it was yesterday."

"Impossible! Vampires were extinct until the Vampire Warlords returned!"

Kell shook his head. "Oh no," he said, eyes glittering. "You are so wrong, with your little mind from little Falanor. You never did travel, did you Sara? Never saw the world and all its mysteries. Well I did. I saw enough to make any sane man crazy. And that's why I know... I know your Master, Kuradek, Kuradek the Unholy – if I kill him, if I remove his head, then I may save all those he has tainted with his evil."

Sara remained silent, staring at him. Eventually, she said, "How could you know that?"

"I do," growled Kell. "Because I have seen things you people could never comprehend. I have walked the dark magick paths to the Chaos Halls. Do you think the Vampire Warlords are the only creatures touched by evil? Sara. I have done... many, sobering things. I believe I am touched by darkness. But I am trying to be good. Trying so hard."

"Well don't! Don't fight it! Come with me, come to Kuradek! He does not want you dead, Kell, he wants you as his General! He knows your power, he knows what you and he could do together! You could overthrow the other Vampire Warlords! You could rule the world! We could be together again... father. We could walk the roads again, father."

Kell had lowered his head. Now his eyes lifted, and there were tears on his bearded cheeks.

"You would take me back?" he said, voice a husky low growl. "After all that I did? To you and your mother?"

"Yes! We could be a family again."

Kell stood, and turned his back to Sara. She stood, in her cage of rock and iron, and stepped forward, grasping the bars. "Come with me, Kell. Come to Kuradek. He waits for you!"

Kell turned back. His knuckles were white around Ilanna. "I'll go to him all right. I'll cut his puking head from his shoulders!"

"No, Kell, no! Wait!" but Kell was striding away, across the rocks, to the cell which held Jagor Mad.

Behind, in her cell, Sara sat cross-legged on the floor. She closed her eyes, and breathed deeply, and the *feeling* of Kuradek filled her, filled every muscle and every atom. She seemed to float, and she breathed deeply, and the world took on a surreal quality, a haze of witch-light, clouds rushing across the skies, dark ghosts walking the rocks beyond her cell like jagged, black cut-outs, holes in the raw core of the Chaos Halls.

"You did well," hissed Kuradek.

"I failed you."

"No. You gave him something to think about."

"He will come for you."

"Yes. And I will be waiting."

"He will try and kill you."

"Yes. But I am all-powerful. He will crumble. Like dust between my claws."

"Are you sure?"

Hundreds of miles away, on his throne in the Blue Palace at Jalder, Kuradek opened his dark crimson eyes and smiled. "Yes, my sweet," he said, smoke oozing from his mouth, skin writhing with corrupt religious symbols that squirmed as if fighting to be free of his dark-smoke skin. "They always do."

Kell's mood could be described as a thunderous rage as he approached Jagor Mad's cell. The three men who had called themselves the new Governors of the Black Pike Mines were sat together, eyes sullen, faces lost to despair. They were awaiting execution. The atmosphere was sombre.

Kell stopped by the bars, and gestured to the two guards who held long spears and wore short stabbing swords over kilts of steel. "Open it."

"But… Governor Myrtax said…"

"Governor Myrtax does what *I tell him, laddie!*" barked Kell, employing a parade ground bellow that once made many a Command Sergeant piss his pants.

"Yes, yes sir," snapped one guard, shaking as he fumbled keys and unlocked a three bar gate, swinging it wide from its slot in the mountain wall.

"Jagor Mad. Step free."

"What do you want?" said the big man, voice husky and low, his face still battered and bruised from their fight. Jagor stepped from his confinement, squinting at the bright daylight, and he stretched his huge frame. His throat was heavily bruised, huge welts showing where the rope had savagely burned him.

"I want your help," said Kell, folding his arms.

"Why would I help you?"

Kell drew Ilanna from his back, glanced at the twin black blades, and hefted her against his chest. "You help me, or I execute you now. Right here. On this fucking spot."

Jagor Mad considered this, and a finger lifted, touching the marks at his throat. "Seems like a fair choice. I'll help you. But don't be asking me to fucking sing and dance."

Kell grinned. "No, I have something far more fun than that planned." He turned to the guard. "Give Jagor your sword."

"What?"

"Are you deaf, lad, or shall I unblock your ears with my axe?"

"No need to be rude," grumbled the guard, and handed Jagor Mad the sword. Jagor took the weapon, face showing a mixture of confusion and suspicion. "What's happening here, Kell?" he murmured.

"Follow me."

"You wish to battle?"

"No, Jagor, you big dumb fool! These vampire bastards threaten the whole of Falanor! I want you alive, because you're a big hard bastard, and I'll not waste a man like you just because you were fighting for your freedom! I respect that. I respect your anger, your fire, and your fucking brutality! You were born to fight, Jagor, not be locked in a cage, not to hang from the gallows. Well, I'm giving you the chance to earn redemption."

"What do you want me to do?"

"There is a place. A hidden place. Where the last of the Blacklipper Kings reside, after their brother was killed by the vachine known as Vashell. Do you know what I'm talking about?"

"I know."

"Can you take me to this place?"

"It is a closely guarded secret amongst the Blacklippers," said Jagor Mad, carefully.

"We are all threatened here," said Kell, eyes glittering. "I need the help of the Blacklippers. I hunted them for decades, aye, and I am their sworn enemy. But now, I am like a brother compared to the nightmare in the dark."

Jagor stared hard into Kell's eyes. He lowered his sword. "I will take you. But they will kill you, old man. With no remorse."

Kell grinned. "I don't die easy," he said.

Kell strode up to Saark, who was sat on a stool eating a plate of sausages from his knees. He glanced up, then leapt up spilling his plate and knocking over his tankard as he saw Jagor Mad looming behind Kell. Saark grappled for his rapier, shouting, "Look out, Kell, he's behind you!"

Kell patted Saark on the arm. "I know, lad, I know. I brought him here."

"What? *What?*" snapped Saark, spitting and dribbling sausage everywhere.

"He's coming with me. To help me."

"Where are we going all of a sudden?" said Saark, lifting and picking his sausages from the snow with a curse and a dirty glance. "I thought you said we had an army to train?"

"Yes. *You* have an army to train. *I* have a problem to solve."

"What problem, what the hell are you talking about? And army? Me train an army? You have to be sky-high out of your fucking donkey skull if you think I'm capable of training a bloody army!"

"You were a soldier, weren't you?" said Kell, and nodded to Grak who appeared, carrying a newly forged steel collar in his powerful hands. Grak stopped, and put his hands on his hips, grinning.

"I was King Leanoric's Sword Champion," said Saark, looking injured, "if that's what you mean?"

"There you go. You were in the army. That's good enough for me. That's all settled then."

"Now wait a minute," said Saark, "I was a commissioned officer, I didn't rough it with the scum in the barracks," he glanced at Grak, and Jagor, and swallowed, "no offence meant, I was in the High Court watching the jesters and eating venison and lobster from silver platters! I was attending the buxom serving wenches and bestowing gifts of fine silver jewellery on nobility! I wasn't eating bloody beans from a pan and scrubbing my boots! I had servants for that sort of thing! Peasants! Like... well, like you..." He stopped.

Grak gave a cough, and slapped Saark on the back, a slap so hard he nearly pitched Saark to the ground. "Don't worry, lad. I'll help you! Grak the Bastard by name, Grak the Bastard by nature. I won't let no fancy big-titted silver-wearing venison-stuffed ladies get in the way of you training the lads. Right?"

"Er, right," said Saark, weakly, and seemed to physically slump.

"After all, if all our lives rest on your scrawny shoulders, I think you're going to need some help. Right?"

"Right."

"I mean, if we're going into battle to face a terrible foe, a foe who is savage and brutal, knows no remorse, is stronger than us, faster than us, more brutal than we could ever imagine – well, we'd be idiots to let a dandy moron train us without any experience or skills, wouldn't we?"

"Er. Yes."

They stared at each other. "Not that I'm saying you're a moron," explained Grak, helpfully, and roared with laughter.

Saark stared at the carrots stuck in Grak's beard, and shook his head. He threw Kell a nasty glance. "So, *Legend*, what wonderful little jaunt are you going to be enjoying whilst I get stuck here with three thousand condemned *convicts*, nary a beautiful woman in sight, and food so bad even Mary would turn up her muzzle in disgust?"

"I'm going to the Valleys of the Moon," said Kell, smiling and nodding.

"What?" said Saark, and placed a hand on one hip in what could only be described as an effeminate stance. "The Valleys of the Moon don't exist! Leanoric hunted for them, for thirty years, after his father had damn well given up!"

"It's said you have to be a mystic to enter," said Kell, cryptically.

"And I suppose you qualify, do you?"

Kell shrugged. "I have three thousand soldiers here. Or I will have, when you complete their training. I need more. It's not enough to take Jalder, or indeed, any of the other cities. The vampires are savage. And the Army of Iron is disciplined, that's for sure. They also rely on magick. We need the magick of the Blacklippers."

"Pah, what are you talking about? Have you been on the whiskey again?"

"It's true," rumbled Jagor, stepping forward. Saark looked again at the sword in his huge hands. It looked like a child's toy. Saark swallowed, for he was within striking distance and Kell seemed extremely laid back. As if he had nothing in the world to worry about.

"Which bit? The fact the Valleys of the Moon don't exist, or the fact that you have to be a village idiot invested with the dribbling liquid brain of a certifiable peasant to even *want* to look for such a mythical artefact?"

"No. It exists," said Jagor. "I have been there."

"And you're a mystic, are you?" scoffed Saark, examining the lace ruff of his sleeve.

"I surely am," rumbled Jagor, eyes flashing dangerously dark. "Watch. I can mystically transfer this short sword into the middle of your head."

"Point taken," prickled Saark, and turned his attention to Kell. "But seriously, Kell, think about it. You know I like to gamble, drink the finest wines, suckle the most succulent foods, dance like a peacock and fuck like a stallion. All the sensible things in life, my man. I've never trained an army in my life! You'd be *insane* to entrust me with such an important directive!"

Kell loosened his axe, and in a sudden movement swung the blade for Saark's head. Saark rolled back, fast, faster than any human had a right to move. His rapier was out, and he'd grabbed up the stool on which he was seated and hoisted it as a makeshift shield. He'd also moved, imperceptibly, so his back was against the wall of the fortress.

Kell grinned. "You see? Defence, stance, back to the wall, and you shifted so that you could attack all three of us, not knowing from whence the next strike would come." Kell sheathed Ilanna. Saark scowled. "It's all intuitive. You'll do just fine, lad. Just teach them about the strength of shield walls, the tactical advantage of a solid fighting square and how to respond in formation to commands. Get them practising. That's what I need. That's what you must do. Lives depend on it, Saark. All our lives."

"Bloody great," mumbled the dandy.

"As I said," roared Grak, "the bastard here will help. I've trained soldiers before. Just see yourself as the commissioned officer, and me as your finely honed tool."

"There's only one finely honed tool around here," mumbled Saark, but forced a smile. "Very well. If train men I must, then train men I must! We will turn back the tide of these evil vampires! Hurrah!" He flourished his rapier. Everybody stared at him.

"But don't think you can sit on your arse and do nothing," said Grak, amiably.

"Er. That's something like what I had in mind. You said yourself, you've trained men before."

"Aye, but I won't put up with slothful bastards. I put my foot down, I do."

"I take it by your story and demeanour, young Grak, that something untoward happened to your last Commanding Officer?"

"Aye. I cut off his hand."

"By accident?"

"Well, it was his accident to be damn disrespectful about the men whilst I was chopping wood."

"I thought you said you killed your General?" interjected Kell.

"Aye, him as well. Why do you think I'm here?"

Saark stared at Kell. "Please?" he mouthed, silently.

Kell turned his back on the dandy, and slapped Jagor Mad on the shoulder, having to stand on tiptoe to do so. "Come on, lad. Our horses are waiting."

"How long will you be?" said Saark, in what bordered on a useless puppy whine.

"A week, I reckon," said Kell, and glanced back. "Don't let me down on this, Saark. You understand?"

"Yes, Kell."

"And Saark?"

"Yeah?"

"Watch out for Sara. She's a wily bitch. I think she communes with Kuradek, so I'd limit what she can see, hear and do. She can spy bloody everything from that cell you put her in."

"Perhaps you'd like me to put a bag over her head?"

"A brilliant idea! Just don't get too close to her claws."

"Yes," said Saark, weakly.

"And Saark?"

"Go on." He sighed. "What now?"

"Don't touch Nienna."

"Like I would dream!"

"I know all about your fucking dreams, lad. If you do it again, the next fight we have, vampire invasion or no, you'll be wearing your feet as souvenirs round your pretty slit throat."

"Any other advice?"

"Keep the men well fed, but work them hard."

Saark put his hands on his hips. "Any *more* fucking advice? Why the *fuck* are you leaving? Maybe you should write me a, y'-know, short manuscript on the art of running a fucking soldier-camp full of scumbag convicts – no offence meant –"

"None taken," smiled Grak menacingly.

"– or maybe you should *just do it yourself!*"

"See you in a week."

Saark scowled as Kell and Jagor moved to the horses, the finest war chargers from Governor Myrtax's stables. Huge beasts of nineteen hands, one was a sable brown gelding, the other charcoal black. Kell mounted the black beast, which reared for a moment and silhouetted Kell against the weak winter sun.

Saark stared in wonder.

Kell calmed the gelding, patting its neck and whispering into its ear, and ducking low over the horse's neck, galloped off through the gates of the Black Pike Mines and out onto the snowy fields beyond, closely followed by the hulking figure of Jagor Mad dressed in bulky furs and standing in his stirrups, giving a final, menacing, backward glance.

"I hope he knows what he's doing," said Saark.

"I hope you do," said Grak, staring at him.

The gates closed on well-oiled hinges, and Saark glared at Grak with open hatred. "I'm going for a bath," he said.

Grak nodded, and watched the peacock strut away, hand on scabbard, a stray sausage stuck to the back of his silk leggings. Grak sighed, and stared up at the sky.

"The gods do like to challenge," he said, and headed for the barracks.

Kell and Jagor rode in silence for a long time. West they travelled, along a low line of foothills before the rearing, dark, ominous Black Pike Mountains. Both horses carried generous packs of provisions, and for a while Kell brooded on his last conversation with Nienna.

"I'll miss you, grandfather."

"And I you, little Nienna."

"I am little no longer," she laughed.

"You will always be a child to me."

He sensed, more than saw, her shift in mood.

"That's the problem, isn't it? You control. I heard what mother said, heard some of the things she accused you of; and I have seen you raise your hand to me on several occasions! You need to learn, grandfather, you need to get in tune with the modern way of thinking! I am a little girl no longer! Understand?"

"When I was a boy," said Kell, "a woman could not... *meet* with a man until she was twenty-five summers! You hear that? Twenty-five years old! And you are seventeen, a suckling child barely weaned from her mother's tit and still lusting after the stink of hot milk."

"How dare you! I can have children! I can drink whiskey! I am a woman, and men find me attractive. Who the hell are *you* to lecture me on keeping myself to myself? I worked it out, Kell. I'm not stupid. You were *twenty* when you sired my mother; and she was eighteen. Barely older than me! And I bet that wasn't the first time your child-maker had a bit of fun with her..."

Kell glared, and lifted Ilanna threateningly. "You need to learn to hold your tongue."

"Or what? You'll cut it out?"

Kell frowned now, as a cold wind full of snow whipped down from the mountains and blasted him with more ferocity than his memories allowed for. Or had he simply been tougher, during his youth? As the years passed, had he simply grown weak? More pampered? Relying more on his *reputation* than any real skill in battle?

Kell was troubled by Nienna, but aware that events were over-taking him fast. He knew Saark would destroy any training he hoped to give his fledgling army. And anyway – an army of bloody convicts? Kell would laugh so hard he would puke, if he could summon the stamina.

And just to make his life more miserable, filled with hardship, filled with pain, the poison injected into him by *Myriam* was starting to make its presence felt once more. It was a tingling in his bones. Especially the joints of his ankles, knees, elbows and wrists. "Damn that vachine bitch," he muttered.

"Are you well, old man? You look fit and ready to topple from the bloody saddle!" Jagor was grinning, but there was menace behind that grin. A low-level hatred.

"I'll last longer than you," grunted Kell, staring sideways at Jagor. "And don't be getting any fancy ideas. I ain't as fucking weak, nor as old, as you think."

Jagor held up both hands, as his horse picked its way through snowy tufts of grass. "Hey, I'm not complaining, Kell. Thing is, I wanted you dead so much – so bad. So bad it burned me like a horse-brand. Tasted like sour acid in my mouth. But when I was hanging by the throat, all I could see were bright lights and hear the voice of my little girl singing in the meadow. I knew I was going to die. I knew I would never see her again. And that hurt, Kell. Hurt more than any fucking noose. But then you cut me down, and saved me. And although that burned me in a different way, I have to concede you spared me. You kept me alive. And one day, if we're not massacred in the Valleys of the Moon, I might get to see that little girl again."

"I didn't know you had a little girl."

"Why would you?"

"I thought it might have come out at the trial."

Jagor Mad laughed. "I told them bastards *nothing*, you hear? *Nothing*. If they'd found out, they would have arrested Eilsha. The Bone Halls only know where my little one would have ended up. At least I spared them the pain of imprisonment."

Kell considered this, turning his head to the left as more snow whipped him, making him smart, and his eyes water. "I am confused, Jagor. You were part of a syndicate that used to kidnap children, and sell them into slavery? Yes? How could you do that, when you have your own little one?"

Jagor's face went hard. "We had to eat," he said, scowling.

"Would you have liked it, if another slaver took your girl?"

"That's different. I would have cut out his liver."

"And so now, you have the right to hang on to yours?"

"I didn't say what I did was right, Kell, and believe me as I lay in my cell night after night, week after week, year after bloody year, I cursed you for catching me, yes, but I cursed myself for my poor decisions in life. Once, I believe I was immoral. Above all those weak and petty emotions. Now, I have changed. At least a little." He gave a grim smile.

"I don't believe men change," said Kell, bitterly.

"So you're the same as during the Days of Blood?" Kell's head snapped up, eyes blazing. "Oh yes, Kell, I have heard of your slaughter. You are legend amongst the Blacklippers – for all the wrong reasons."

Kell sighed, his anger leaving him as fast as it came. "You are right. And by my own logic, I am still a bloodthirsty, murdering savage. Maybe I am. I don't know. You can be the judge of that when we head into battle; for believe me when I say we have many a fight to come."

The night was drawing close, and they made a rough camp in the lee of a huge collection of boulders at the foot of the Black Pikes. Kell stretched a tarpaulin over them as a makeshift roof, which was fortunate as thick snow fell in the night.

Kell lay in the dark, listening to Jagor snoring. Pain nagged him like an estranged ex-wife, and it seemed to take an age for him to fall into sleep. He stared at the stars, twinkling, impossibly cold and distant, and thought about his dreams and aspirations. Then he smiled a bitter smile. What do the stars care for the dreams of men?

He awoke, cold and stiff, to the smell of coffee. He shivered, and looked up to see Jagor crouched by a small fire, boiling water in a pan, staring at him. Kell gritted his teeth. He had allowed himself to fall into a deep and dreamless sleep; not an ideal situation when travelling with a certifiable killer.

"Coffee?" said Jagor, raising his eyebrows.

"Plenty of sugar," said Kell, and sat up, stretching. He was wrapped in a blanket, fully clothed, his boots by his side. Ilanna was by his thigh. She was never far from his grasp.

"You snore like a pig," said Jagor, pouring the brew.

Kell squinted. "Well, I ain't asking you to marry me."

Jagor laughed, and a little of their tension eased. "I like it that you snore, old man. Makes me think of you as human."

"Why, what *did* you think of me?"

"I thought you were a Chaos Hound," said Jagor, face serious, handing Kell the tin mug. "When you followed me down those tunnels to Old Gilrak, well, I knew then I was cursed, knew I was being pursued by something more than human. Hearing you fart in the night – well, old man, that's helping my mind heal."

"That's Saark's damn cooking, that is, the dandy bastard." Kell sipped his coffee. It was too sweet, but he didn't complain; rather too sweet than too bitter. Like life.

"He's a strange one, all right. What's with the pink silk, though? And green pants? And all that stink of a woman's perfume? Eh?"

"I think he thinks he's a noble."

"Is he?"

"Damned if I know," said Kell, and took the proffered oatcake.

"Do you mind if I ask you a question?"

Kell nodded, eating the oatcake and drinking more coffee. After a cold night under canvas, it was bringing him back to life; making him more human. "Go ahead."

"Why do you travel with him? You two seem... so different."

"Don't worry," growled Kell, "I'm not into that sort of thing."

"That's not what I meant," rumbled Jagor, reddening a little. "I mean, him with his long curly hair and fancy little rapier; you with your snoring and your axe. I wouldn't have thought you'd put up with him."

Kell considered this, finishing his coffee. "You're right, in a sense," he said. "Once was a time I couldn't have stood his stink, his talk, his letching after women or the sight of his tart's wardrobe. But we've been through some tough times together, me and Saark. I thought I saw him killed down near Old Skulkra, and I was ready to leave him for dead; but he showed me he was a tough, hardy and stubborn little bastard, despite appearances. I don't know. I like him. Maybe I'm just getting old. Maybe I've just killed one too many men, and like to talk and listen for a change, instead of charging in with the axe. Whatever. Saark's a friend, despite his odd ways. I ain't got many. And I'd kill for him, and I'd die for him."

Jagor nodded, and finished his coffee. "I think we should be moving."

"Aye. A long way to go, and already my arse feels like a fat man's been dancing on it."

"You never were a horseman, were you Kell?"

Kell grinned. "In my opinion, the only thing a horse is good for is eating."

Kell and Jagor Mad rode for another three days in more-or-less companionable silence. Jagor didn't speak about his capture all those years ago, or the recent incident with the noose; and Kell didn't mention the crossbow wound in his shoulder, nor the recent threat of murder. When they did talk, they spoke of old battles and the cities of Falanor, they talked of Kell's *Legend*, the saga poem, and how Kell hated his misrepresentation. As if he was a damned *hero*. Kell knew he was not.

Eventually, as they passed through folded foothills, past huge boulders and a random scattering of spruce and pine, Jagor stopped and looked to the right where the Black Peaks towered. His horse pawed the snow, and Kell's mount made several snorting sounds. The world seemed unnaturally silent. Eerie. Filled with ghosts.

"Easy, boy," said Kell, patting the horse's neck. Then to Jagor, "What is it?"

"We are close."

"To the Valleys of the Moon?"

"Aye."

Kell ran his gaze up and down the solid, looming walls of rock. "I see nothing."

"You have to know how to look. Follow me."

They rode on, and again Jagor reined his mount. He seemed to be counting. Then he pointed. "There."

Kell squinted. Snow was falling, creating a haze, but he made out a finger of smooth, polished granite no bigger than a man. "What is it?"

"A marker. Come on."

Jagor led the way; Kell followed and loosened Ilanna in her saddle-sheath. Then Jagor paused, and Kell saw another marker, and they veered right, between two huge boulders over rough ground; normally, Kell would have avoided the depression – it was a natural and instinctive thing to do whether on horseback or foot. It was too good a place for an ambush.

Jagor led the way between the boulders, and onto a flat path which led up, out of the tiny bowl. "Now look," he said.

Kell stared around, and Ilanna was in his hand as he glanced at Jagor. "I see nothing. Are you playing me for a fool?"

"Not at all, Kell. It's there." Jagor pointed, to the solid wall of jagged black granite.

"You're an idiot! That's impassable."

Jagor shook his head, and said, "Shift to the left. By one stride."

Kell shifted his mount, and as if by magick a narrow channel appeared before his eyes which led *into* the seemingly impassable rock face. Kell shifted his gelding again, and the passage slid neatly out of view, the rocky wall naturally disguising this narrow entrance. Kell stared hard. "By the Bone Halls, that plays tricks on a man's eyes."

"You have to know it's there. One footstep in either direction and the passage vanishes! As you say, like magick!"

"You lead the way."

"You still not trusting me?" Jagor Mad grinned, his brutal face looking odd with such an expression.

"I trust nobody," snapped Kell. "Take me to the Blacklippers. Take me to the Valleys of the Moon."

Saark stood in the snow and the churned mud, and his feet were freezing and he was scowling. The men had been divided into platoons of twenty, as he had watched King Leanoric do on so many occasions. Each platoon was commanded by a lieutenant, and five platoons made up a company ruled over by a captain.

They'd held a contest on the second day, in which crates, barrels and planks of wood had been assembled beside a pretend river. On the other side, behind upturned carts, archers with weak bows and blunt, flat-capped arrows were the enemy. Each platoon had to work together to "cross" the river and take the cart. The platoon which succeeded first would earn wine and gold.

Saark and Grak watched in dismay at first, as men squabbled and fought over planks and crates. But a young, handsome man, Vilias, imprisoned for his spectacular thieving career, gathered together several crates and got three of the platoons crouched behind them for protection from the archers as the other platoons continued to argue, or were shot by archers.

"We need to work together," said Vilias.

"But then the prize is shared between sixty, not twenty!"

"But we still win the prize," grinned the charismatic thief. "One bottle of wine is better than none, right mate?"

Vilias set several men to smashing up crates, and they fashioned several large, crude shields. Then, with five men at a time using the wide wooden shields they worked under protection to build a bridge, crossed the river and stormed into the cart fortress with swords raised and battle screams filling the air.

Afterwards, Saark and Grak called Vilias to them.

"You showed great courage," said Saark, smiling at the man.

Vilias saluted. "Thank you, sir. But it was just common sense."

"Common sense has got you promoted to Command Sergeant, lad. That's extra wine and coin for *all* the platoons under your new command."

"Thank you... sir!"

"You understand that an army is all about working together," said Saark, with his chin on his fist. With his dark curls and flashing eyes, with his charisma and natural beauty, he cut a striking figure now he no longer wore fancy silk shirts and bulging pantaloons. Grak had persuaded him to don something more fitting for the Division General of a new army.

"Yes, sir!"

Vilias returned to his men to share the good news, and Saark sagged, glancing over at Grak who grinned a toothless grin of approval.

"Well inspired!" boomed Grak. "Any army indeed works – and *wins* by all the gods – by the simple act of cooperation. Soldiers watching one another's backs; spearmen protecting shield-men, archers protecting infantry, cavalry protecting archers."

Saark chuckled. "I only *know* because you told me last night after a flagon of ale."

"Still," said Grak. "You *sounded* like you knew what you were talking about! And that's what matters, eh lad?"

"I'm not cut out for this," said Saark, displaying a weak grin. "Only yesterday the smiths came with technical questions about the shields; what the fuck do I know about shields? Succulent quims, yes! Breasts, I could talk all day about the size and texture and quality of many a buxom pair of tits. But shields? *Shields*, I ask you?"

"With things like that," said Grak, "just refer it to me. Say you're too busy to deal with it. Last thing we need," he bit a chunk from a hunk of black bread, "is a shield with the shape and functionality of a woman's flower."

Saark paused. "A what?" he said.

"A flower."

"You mean the slick warm place between her legs?"

"Don't be getting all rude with me," snapped Grak. "I won't take it, y'hear?"

Saark stood, and stretched. Then grinned, eyeing the ranks of men who were now practising with wooden swords as newly appointed Command Sergeants strolled up and down the lines, shouting encouragement and offering advice. Grak had appointed those with soldiering experience, he'd said.

"I suggest we go to the quartermaster," said Saark.

"Why?"

"I suggest we get two flagons of ale and retire to my quarters. You can teach me about warfare, about units and field manoeuvres, and I, well," Saark grinned, and ran a hand through his long dark curls, "darling, I will teach you about *women*."

Kell and Jagor rode into the narrow pass. It was quiet, eerie, and very, very gloomy. Kell eased his mount forward, and the beast whinnied. High above, there came a trickle of stones.

Jagor turned in the saddle, and motioned to Kell to halt. "This place," he said, speaking quietly, "they call the Corridor of Death. It is the only way to reach the Valleys of the Moon, and is always, I repeat *always* conducted in silence."

"Why?"

Jagor glanced up, fearful now. "Let us say the slopes and rocky faces are far from stable. I once witnessed a hundred men crushed by rockfall; it took us three days to dig them out. Most died. Most were trapped, and as we dug, and hauled rocks, and had our horses drag boulders in this narrow shitty confine, all the time we could hear them crying for help from down below under the pile. They cried for help, they screamed for mercy, and eventually they begged for death."

"That is a very sobering tale. I will keep it in mind," said Kell, and glanced upwards. The sheer walls and steeply slanted inclines were bulged and rocky, covered in snow and ice and fiery red winter heathers. Kell licked his lips and shivered. He had no desire to be imprisoned under a thousand tumbling rocks.

They moved on, in silence, whispering soothing words to the horses. Sometimes the trail widened so that three horses could walk side by side; sometimes it narrowed so the men had to dismount, walking ahead of their mounts to allow them to squeeze flanks through narrow rough rock apertures. It did nothing to improve Kell's mood.

Eventually, the passage started to widen and they emerged in a valley devoid of rocks. It was just a huge, long, sweeping channel and Kell instinctively glanced upwards where high above, on narrow ledges, he could spy the openings of small caves.

"I don't like this," said Kell.

"The Watchers live here," said Jagor. "This is where we will be challenged."

"And what do we do?"

"We do nothing," said Jagor, forcing a smile that looked wrong on his face. "If you draw your weapon, they will shoot you down. Let me do the talking. You have been warned."

They cantered horses across the snow, hooves echoing dully, and in the gloom of the valley where high mountain walls – perhaps two thousand feet in height – towered over the two men and cast long dark shadows, so gradually Kell became aware of movement...

Jagor held up a hand and they halted, side by side. Along the ridges scurried small figures, and it was with surprise Kell realised they were children. But as the figures halted their scurrying, and lifted longbows and drew back bowstrings, so Kell realised with sinking horror that these were no normal children. These were Blacklipper children – which meant they had drunk, and continued to drink, the narcotic refined drug, blood-oil, the substance which the vachine needed to survive. But when it was imbibed by a human, it caused a drug *high* like nothing in Falanor, or even beyond the Three Oceans.

Kell watched carefully, making no move towards his weapons, his eyes gradually adjusting to the gloom. There were perhaps fifty children in all, and each was what he knew could be described as a Deep Blood. They had drunk so much of the powerful narcotic, were so entrenched in the liquid's power and dark magick, the essence of the refined blood-oil so necessary to vachine survival – and so condemning of human flesh – that their lips were stained black, and their veins stood out across pale flesh like strands of glossy spider webs on marble skin.

Soon, Kell knew, these children would die.

Soon, they would travel what Kell knew they called the Voyage of the Soul. To an afterlife all Blacklippers believed in. To an afterworld that justified narcotic slavery.

"Throw down your weapons!" shouted one girl, no more than thirteen years old. Her hair was long and black, braided in heavy strips. She was naked to the waist, and her veins stood out like a river-system viewed from mountain crags at night. She carried an adult longbow, a weapon Kell had seen punch an arrow through a hand-thick pine door. The arrow fletch touched her cheek. As far as Kell could tell, her hand did not shake.

Slowly, Jagor and Kell complied.

"Now get off the horses and speak your names, and nothing funny, or you'll have fifty arrows through you!"

"Nice place," muttered Kell.

"Wait till you meet the parents," said Jagor.

"What's that?" cried the girl. "What are you saying? Speak quickly now, or you will die!"

"You are the Watchers," said Jagor, his voice booming out, "and I am Jagor Mad. Your people know me well."

"Yes," said the girl. "Welcome home, Jagor Mad. You may take up your weapon. Who is the man alongside you?"

"His name is Kell."

"Kell, the Legend?" said the girl, her voice painfully neutral.

"Yes," said Jagor, and threw Kell such a strange look the large warrior was moving before he heard the sound of the arrows. Shafts slammed all around him, peppering the snow and thudding home into his horse which reared, suddenly screaming a high-pitched horse scream, and Kell leapt for his axe, leapt for Ilanna as the charcoal gelding staggered back on hind legs, front hooves pawing the air, blood pumping from ten wounds and arrows protruding like the spikes on a spinehog. There was a devastating *thump* as the gelding hit the snow, a huge pool of red spreading fast around the creature and Kell's head slammed up, eyes narrowed, fixed on Jagor as he realised *realised* the bastard had led him into a trap...

"What did you do?" screamed Kell, and leapt forward, Ilanna in his fists and Jagor stepped backwards fast, his own sword coming up with a hiss. Ilanna swung down, and Jagor deflected the powerful blow with a grunt and a squawk.

"Nothing, Kell! Nothing! I did nothing!"

"I'll fucking eat your heart, you whoreson!" he screamed.

"Drop the axe, Kell!" shouted the girl. An arrow slammed between his boots, and Kell stared at that arrow, stared at it hard. A moment earlier, his horse's bulk had protected him. Now, he had no such protection.

Kell glanced up. "What's to stop you peppering me like a fucking deer in the woods?" he snarled.

"I am," came a deep, bass rumble, and from a cave which

blended into the gloom of the rocky wall stepped a man bigger than any Kell had ever seen in his life.

The figure walked forward, dwarfing Kell and even Jagor. His skin was pasty and white, the black web-traces of Deep Blood veins marking him out as an addict of blood-oil; but more, his eyes were black with the oil, his lips, his nostrils, even his fingernails had been polluted by the toxin of his chosen drug. He carried a huge flange mace, matt black and nearly the size of Kell's entire torso. To be struck by such a weapon...

"And you are?" snapped Kell, slowly lowering Ilanna but keeping the beloved axe close to his body; a barrier between himself and the unknown; a last resort between Kell walking the world and walking the infinity of the Chaos Halls.

"My name is Dekkar. I am one of the Kings of the Blacklippers."

Kell bowed his head a fraction, and lowered Ilanna. "I knew Preyshan. I knew him well."

"Yes. But still you must drop the axe and back away," said Dekkar, and flexed his mighty chest. Muscles writhed like dying eels. "I guarantee my children will not kill an unarmed man."

Kell nodded, and Ilanna *thunked* to the snow. He backed away. Dekkar watched, and Jagor Mad moved forward and with an evil grin, placed his short sword – the very short sword Kell had given him – against Kell's throat.

"What's this?" said Kell, softly.

Jagor looked at Dekkar, and his grin widened. "Do you want to tell him? Or shall I?"

Dekkar moved forward, looming over Kell. The huge flange mace lifted, and Kell saw himself reflected as smeared, dulled, featureless colours in its merciless grim finish.

"Jagor is my brother," said Dekkar, his voice laced with irony. "And here, Kell, your name is indeed a Legend – for all present in the Valleys of the Moon are instructed that the Prime Law is that you must die!"

ELEVEN
Blood Temple

Command Sergeant Wood was having a bad morning, it had to be said. He stood in the stone tunnel, Pettrus unconscious on the floor behind him, a cold breeze blowing through with the stink of old sewers, and he watched the two vampires picking their way towards him over the twisted corpses of their brethren.

One was a girl, young, beautiful, with slender limbs and high cheekbones and curly golden hair. But her eyes were narrowed in a look of hatred and bestiality that shouldn't have resided on such a pretty *child's* face. Blood rimed her lips and vampire fangs.

"Shit," muttered Wood. "Shit!"

The second vampire was an old man, crooked and bent and moving in a twisted way, as if something was wrong with his spine. He had a white, bowl haircut, ragged and uneven, that was, perhaps, one of the worst haircuts Wood had ever seen – on mortal *or* vampire. Then recognition hit Wood like a mallet between the eyes.

"Langforf!" he exclaimed, stepping back, his short sword wavering in his grasp. "Langforf, it's me, Wood! Don't you recognise me, man? We fought together in five campaigns!"

Langforf, along with his very bad haircut, growled and leapt at Wood, claws slashing for his throat. Wood stepped back fast, stumbling over Pettrus' unconscious body and hitting the ground hard on his arse with an "oof" that would have been comedic, if it hadn't been for impending death looming over him. Langforf leapt at Wood, landing atop the soldier as if they were old lovers on a secret tryst and eager for sex. Foul breath swept over

Wood, into his mouth and lungs making him choke. It was rotting meat combined with dried, old blood. Wood screamed. Claws scrabbled for him, and he grabbed Langforf's throat, bad haircut bobbing to tickle his own forehead, and they struggled for a few moments with Langforf hissing and spitting foul stuff into Wood's open maw.

"Get it off, get it off!" he shrieked, but of course there was no-body to help him *get it off* and he realised he would have to help himself. He got one hand free, and Langforf's fangs brushed his throat making him squirm. His strength was failing, and for an old bowl-cut, Langforf was surprisingly strong. Wood managed to get a dagger free from his belt and he rammed it between Langforf's ribs. No blood came out, and indeed Langforf continued to struggle with the same strength and determination. Again and again Wood plunged the dagger into Langforf's side, until there was a large squelching hole and something round and slick and evil slid out, nestling in a pool of slime in Wood's lap and making his life just that little bit more uncomfortable.

"Aie!" he screamed, and got the dagger high, between him and Langforf at throat level. Then Wood simply let Langforf descend with his fangs, pushing his own throat onto the dagger and cutting his head nearly clean in half.

Wood scrambled out from under the twitching old revenant, and grabbed his short sword – just as the young girl leapt. Wood hit her, hard, breaking her clavicle and shearing his sword down into her lungs – where it wedged under her ribs and was wrenched from his grasp.

Wood stood there, feeling like an idiot, as the girl took a step back and prodded at the sword as if she'd never seen such a weapon before. She tried to tug it free as Wood looked frantically about for another blade, then skipped back, grabbing Pettrus' sword – too long and fanciful for Wood's normal liking – and leaping forward he slammed the blade through her neck. It jarred, cutting through her spine, and her head came away, lolling grotesquely to one side and held in place by skin and ten-dons. Her red eyes glared at him, accusingly, as she continued to tug at the embedded sword. Wood shuddered, and hacked again, detaching the head. Slowly, a black smoke escaped from her neck as if released from a clockwork pressure valve, and the vampire collapsed.

Wood rubbed his beard with the back of his hand, and crept forward, tugging free his own sword. Then he moved back to Pettrus, who was gradually coming round.

"Got the drop on us, the bastards," he said, surveying the carnage. "But you did well, my friend. Very well."

"I'm getting tired of this," said Wood, grimacing. "I just want my old life back."

Pettrus grabbed him by the shoulders, looked into his eyes. "You know that's never going to happen. Right?"

"I know. I know. I just *wish*. In a sane and normal world, beautiful young women shouldn't try to bite your throat. Or at least, not until they've had a few drinks."

Pettrus chuckled. "Glad to see you've still got that sense of humour," he muttered.

"Yeah, me and most of the city. Come on. We're not far now. And it's still safer travelling down here under the rock than across the rooftops."

"Until you meet bastards in the tunnels."

"Until you meet bastards in the tunnels," agreed Wood.

They moved on, warily now for they had grown lax and complacent in the past few hours, coming upon the previous gathering of vampires with their weapons sheathed and minds tired and blank and definitely switched *off*. It had been a short, hard, savage fight, and Wood and Pettrus both knew they were lucky to be alive. Luck, and combat instinct honed over decades was what saved them. Now, they did not want to run the risk of a second encounter; not when they were so close to the Black Barracks.

It took another hour of careful navigation and creeping through the darkness. Rounding a bend in the rock tunnel, Wood stopped and squinted. He could see a figure at the bottom of the steps leading up to the Black Barracks. To Wood's right, a heavy flow of slow sewage didn't so much move as *coagulate*. Pettrus squinted over Wood's shoulder.

"That's not a vampire."

"Why not?"

"It's Fat Bill."

"Maybe Fat Bill got bit? Maybe Fat Bill is *now* Fat Bill the vampire scourge?"

"Nah," said Pettrus, shaking his head. "He's got his sword drawn. Look. He's guarding the steps."

"*Maybe* he's a vampire guarding the steps from people like us?"

"I don't reckon," said Pettrus. "Vampires don't use swords."

"Of course they do! I've seen hundreds!"

"There's only one way to find out." Raising his voice, Pettrus shouted, "Hey, Fat Bill! Are you a vampire? Do we have to stick a blade through your heart and skull?"

Fat Bill, who must have weighed the same as three sacks of flower, lumbered around in a slow circle and squinted through the darkness. "Any man who tries that better be ready to have their own head crushed," he rumbled, and grinned in the gloom. "By all the gods, is that you, Pettrus? And who's that with you? That skinny gay goat, Wood? It's bloody good to see you both!"

Pettrus and Wood moved along the walkway, and looked up at Fat Bill. He wasn't just fat, he was tall, broad, and both soldiers knew he packed a punch greater than any kicking shire horse. The men shook hands, chuckling, and Fat Bill led them up the stone steps.

"The lads'll be glad to see you."

"Who's here?"

Bill stopped, and turned. He grinned, with most of his teeth missing from brawling. His hair, straggly and white, whispered around his head like cotton. "All of us, Wood. All of us."

They continued, passing a couple more guards whom Wood only vaguely knew; then they emerged into a long, low-ceilinged barracks room.

The Black Barracks squatted on the outskirts of Port of Gollothrim, in what used to be an old warehouse area used for the loading and unloading of cargo; when an industrial accident had destroyed the nearby quays, the area had been pretty much abandoned and left to rot. It was a quiet place, and more importantly for the old men who ran the Black Barracks, a *cheap* place. Whoever said growing old made you generous was a lying bastard. The old soldiers who attended the Black Barracks for weekly drinking sessions and to regale one another with exaggerated tales of valour in their youth, well, they were uniformly tighter than any mother-in-law's hidden purse.

Despite being located in a quiet area of the city, still the barracks had been kitted out as if under siege. All windows had been blacked out and boarded up, and the doors had been reinforced by heavy planks of steel. Lanterns were kept to a lit minimum, and the noise level was a dull mumble as Wood stepped through the door – as opposed to the normal drunken roar that greeted him.

"My God, it's good to see you old boys!" grinned Wood, and for the first time since the vampires had spread through Port of Gollothrim, his heart lifted in joy.

"Wood!" roared a few old soldiers, who stood and smiled in welcome at the two new men. "Glad to see a few bloodsuckers didn't manage to suck you dry!"

Wood strode forward, and slapped a man on the back. "Gods, who've we got here? There's Kelv Blades, never been a better man with a battleaxe or I'm not Command Sergeant Wood! And look! Well met, Nicholas. Who'd have thought The Miser would have left his Gold Vaults, even in times of vampire plague?"

"Got most of it stashed," winked Nicholas the Miser.

"And there's Old Man Connie, Sour Dog, Stickboy Pulp and Bulbo the Dull. Well met! And look, by all the gods, it's Weevil and Bad Socks! I thought you two were dead?"

"It'd take more than a rock on my head to kill me!" rumbled Bad Socks, who climbed ponderously to his feet. He was, as ever, without his boots and his socks did indeed smell bad. He was also nearly seventy years old, one-eyed and his face was so heavily crisscrossed with scars there was little original skin left. He hadn't so much retired from the army, as been forcibly ejected.

Pettrus grinned around as conversation and arguments broke out. "They're all here," he said, meeting Wood's gaze. "What's that? Two hundred of them? *Two hundred!* That's two hundred blades, Wood. Our own little army."

"And not a man here under the age of sixty-five, I believe," said Wood. He was still smiling though. It was good to see so many friendly old faces. Indeed, it was wonderful to realise he wasn't alone and unloved in a hostile world.

"Just think of the experience, though!" said Pettrus.

"Just think of the arthritis!" grinned Wood.

"If any man here hears you say that, you'll get a sword in the guts."

"Yeah, I know. But by the Granite Thrones, it's bloody good to see them all." He raised his voice. "I said, it's bloody grand to see you all! It's good to know I'm not alone!"

"Have you been fighting 'em?" rumbled Fat Bill. "The bloodsuckers, I mean?"

"Fighting and killing them," said Pettrus.

"Good. 'Cos we've got a plan." Fat Bill grinned, but Wood felt his heart sinking. To Wood, the word "plan" was usually synonymous with "trouble", "error" and inevitably, "massacre". "We need some handy men to help carry it out."

"It's nothing to do with robbing the Gollothrim Bank again, is it?" scowled Pettrus. "You know what happened *that time*."

"No," said Fat Bill, and Wood realised everybody was quiet in the Black Barracks, all eyes on Fat Bill, Wood and Pettrus. "This is something infinitely more *juicy*."

Graal was tired. Bone weary. He had never felt so tired before and attributed it to the wounds suffered at the claws of Bhu Vanesh. He reined in his horse at the top of a rocky, barren hill, a stolen black charger from the stables of the old Mayor of Gollothrim, and turned in his saddle. Skanda was close behind, riding side-saddle on a small, grey mare which constantly eyed Graal with nervous eyes, tosses of the head and snorts and stamps.

Skanda pulled alongside Graal, and smiled.

"You are weary?"

"Through to my bones."

"Bhu Vanesh did more than torture your flesh. I think he may have poisoned your soul."

Graal snorted. "My soul was destroyed long centuries ago." He gazed out, across a country scattered with long shadows from a low winter sun. Snow rimed the rocks and trees, frosted the long yellow grass, and clung like diamonds to huge, scattered boulders.

"It will be night soon."

"No time to camp," said Skanda, and dropped from the saddle, stretching his back. "We have too much ground to cover, and tick tock tick tock, the clockwork always moves when you wind it up."

"I'm not sure I agree with your choice of paths." Graal was still gazing into the far distance. His mouth was a narrow, bitter crease, his hands albino pale on the pommel of his saddle.

"The Gantarak Marshes? It is a straight line."

"It's a damn dangerous line. I've heard tales of whole armies lost in the murky, shitty depths. And even now winter insects will be waiting to bite and sting and feed."

"On blood?" Skanda laughed, light gleaming from his gloss black teeth. "How beautifully, deliciously ironic! A blood-sucker feeding from a blood-sucker! I am stunned that you find the concept so hateful. Surely you must empathise with the insect?"

"I despise insects," said Graal, voice a growl. "I find their lack of empathy disturbing."

"What, and you *vachine* are so much better?"

"We look after our own."

"Until you slaughter an entire civilisation to satiate a mammoth greed."

Graal shrugged. "I am what I am. I believe in self-preservation and building on one's triumphs. What other goal to seek other than total domination? Total dominion? *'If one does not strive to reach the pinnacle of vachine development, then one should stay in the ground with all the other worms.'*"

"As spoken by a true vampire prophet. But his logic, and yours, are flawed. For by turning against your own race in your desperate search for an ultimate kingship, you left your flank unprotected."

"Sacrificing the vachine of Silva Valley was a necessary evil! A move on the gameboard of life and conquest, a sacrifice that will lead eventually to ultimate victory!"

"I'm surprised you still feel that way after watching Bhu Vanesh twist Kradek-ka's head from his shoulders."

"There are always casualties in war," growled Graal.

"Indeed there are," said Skanda. "But normally one seeks to wipe out the enemy, not one's own nation."

"It was the only way," said Graal. Then shrugged. "Anyway, plenty more vachine survive to the north who know nothing of my betrayal; I can always go slithering back to them with my tail between my legs." He grinned, an almost boyish grin if it hadn't been for the evil gleam in his cold blue eyes.

"There are more?" Skanda's head snapped up, a little too sharp.

Graal stared at Skanda. "More vachine? Yes. Does that bother you?"

Skanda relaxed, and his words slid out, cool as chilled snake-meat. "Of course not. I know the vachine civilisation wasn't restricted to Silva Valley. How many more?"

"Thousands," said Graal, and grinned. "*Hundreds* of thousands. Far north, north of the Black Pike Mountains which are simply pimples on the arse of the World Beast. North, where the ice rules, where the vachine built their master civilisation, Garrenathon, with the help of Harvesters Pure."

"Indeed," said Skanda, voice still cold, eyes fixed on Graal. "Why, then, do you not reside there? In this *Garrenathon?* Surely you would be received as a great general? Surely you could satisfy your whims of wealth and power and dominion from such a seat?"

Graal shook his head. "Kradek-ka and I, we came here, to Silva. Oversaw the building. So you see? The vachine of Silva Valley were *our* puppets, *our* playthings, right from the start; nurtured, grown, crafted, awaiting the time when we could resurrect the Vampire Warlords. But we underestimated them. Bastards."

"Come. Time to move on," said Skanda, and hopped up onto the mare with incredible agility. His black eyes fixed, once, on Graal, then turned and stared off to the far north. There, he imagined vast, vast cities of ice; a world of huge towers and temples and palaces, filled with a million clockwork vampires, a million *vachine*. "One day, I will find you," he whispered.

"What was that?"

"Nothing. I shall lead the way, Graal. We wouldn't want you falling in the marsh now, would we?"

After the biting and discomfort of two days in the Gantarak Marshes, Graal was relieved to break free onto the Great North Road. Snow fell occasionally, a light peppering that drifted in the wind and frosted the pines which lined the road. They rode north for a while, horses picking their way with ease, but Skanda grew increasingly agitated at this open route commonly used by armies, and now by association, possible *vampire* armies. After all, the Warlords were spreading their new rule, their new *plague*, with acumen. And the Great North Road was the easiest way to move troops up and down the flanks of Falanor...

They cut northeast from the Great North Road just south of Old Valantrium, and travelled east towards Moonlake but with no intention of entering the city – which would either be deserted, or maybe ravaged by vampires, Graal was sure. He had not been privy to all plans set in motion by the Vampire Warlords; but certainly, infesting every city of Falanor was an initial priority.

Graal and Skanda travelled in silence, mostly. Graal thought long and hard on his past actions, on the vachine, their betrayal, the blood-oil legacy, and Kell. Kell. The bastard who had helped his current tumbling downfall... or at least, that was one way Graal saw events. If Kell had not killed the Soul Stealers, then

Graal might, *might just*, have had the strength necessary to overthrow the Vampire Warlords in their initial moment of weakness. Instead, Graal had been slapped aside like a naughty child.

Bastard, he thought. Bastard!

Another two days saw the ancient walls of Old Skulkra edging into view past the rolling snowy heather of Valantrium Moor. Those two days had been a desolation for Graal, two days of plodding across high, exposed moorland, a sharp nasty wind cutting from east to west and carrying ice and snow, no paths to follow in this deserted landscape and a cold sky wider than the world.

Now, as the frozen heather dropped down from the moorland plateau, so Skanda found them a sheltered place and they made camp before nightfall. The sky was the colour of topaz and stars lay strewn like sugar on velvet. Graal built a fire, and for a change Skanda came and sat with him, and both warmed hands over the flames.

"What's the plan when we arrive?" said Graal, eyeing the small boy with distaste. Skanda may look like a child, a young human boy, but Graal knew different; he still remembered his inhuman movements when Shanna and Tashmaniok tried to cut his head from his shoulders. He had danced between their silver swords like a ghost. Like one of the *Ankarok*. The Ancient Race.

"You will see."

"You need my blood, do you not?"

Skanda tilted his head back, and eyes older than the moon surveyed Graal. Skanda smiled, but there was no real humour there, just a mask held in place by necessity and discipline. "Yes. You are observant."

"Well, I didn't think you dragged me all the way out here for my cooking skills."

Skanda shrugged. "Your blood-oil runs thick with the souls of thousands. It is rich with death and slaughter. General Graal, I don't believe I could have found a more worthy and more potent specimen if I tried."

"You will perform magick?"

"I will."

"And what will happen?"

"You will see, General. You will see."

And despite the fire, despite the warmth of the flames, General Graal realised he was shivering.

● ● ● ●

Dawn broke, the sky filled with grey ice. Pink highlighted the edges of huge, thundering stormclouds. The world looked bleak. To Graal, the world *felt* bleak. A desolation. A world without hope.

They rode from their makeshift camp, and soon could make out the huge, crumbling walls which surrounded the once-majestic and truly ancient city of Old Skulkra. The walls were thick, collapsed in segments, battlements crumbling, and within the city buildings had become slaves to time. Houses were fragments, part collapsed, spires crumbled, domes smashed and deflated, towers detonated as if by some terrible explosion. Those buildings that were intact *were* sometimes skewed, twisted, walls leaning dangerously or gone altogether. Graal observed all this as they rode from Valantrium Moor, and it was exactly as he remembered it. Back when he'd sent the cankers to kill Kell and Saark...

Old Skulkra was haunted, it was said, and as Graal and Skanda grew closer they saw a thin mist creeping through the streets, passing over cracked and buckled paving slabs, ghostly fingers curling around the blackened figures of skeletal trees lining many an avenue. Graal reined in his horse and took a good, hard, long look at this ancient, threatening place.

It was rumoured the city had been built a thousand years ago, but Graal knew this was a misconception. It was probably closer to three thousand years old, maybe even four; it certainly predated the Vampire Warlords and their First Empire of Carnage. It had been a derelict tombstone when Graal first walked the young plains and forests of Falanor. It was simply amazing to Graal that still the city stood, as if defying Nature, as if defying Time and the World.

The city was filled to the brim with a majestic and towering series of vast architectural wonders, immense towers and bridges, spires and temples, domes and parapets, many in black marble shipped from the far east over treacherous marshes. Old Skulkra had once been a fortified city with walls forty feet thick.

Huge, vast engine–houses and factories filled the northeast quarter, and had once been home to massive machines which, scholars claimed, were able to carry out complex tasks but were now silent, rusted iron hulks full of decadent oils and toxins.

A wide central avenue divided Old Skulkra, lined by blackened, twisted trees, arms skeletal and vast and frightening. Beyond this central avenue were enormous private palaces, now crumbled to half-ruins, and huge temples with walls cracked and jigged and displaced, offset and leaning and not entirely natural.

It was said Old Skulkra was haunted.

It was said the city carried plague at its core.

It was said to walk the ancient streets killed a man within days.

It was said dark, slithering, blood–oil creatures lived in the abandoned machinery of the factories, awaiting fresh flesh and pumping blood, and that ghosts walked the streets at dawn and dusk waiting to crawl into souls and disintegrate a person from the inside out...

It was said Old Skulkra, the city itself, was *alive*.

People did not go to Old Skulkra. Through fear, it was a place to be avoided.

Gradually, Graal and Skanda found their way to a breach in the massive walls. Gingerly, their mounts picked their way amongst ancient rubble, and then a coldness hit them and Graal shivered. The mist swirled about the hooves of his charger, and they walked the beasts down a broad, sweeping side-street lined with ancient shops, the fronts now open like gaping wounds, the interiors dark and sterile. They emerged onto the wide central avenue, and now they were closer Graal inspected the twisted and blackened trees – as if each one had been struck by lightning, petrified in an instant. Graal eased his mount closer, and touched the nearest trunk. He looked back at Skanda with a frown.

"It's stone," he said.

"Yes."

"Were they carved?"

"No. They were changed. There was bad magick here, once. Old magick. Come on, follow me."

Skanda led the way, and Graal gazed up at the massive buildings which lined the avenue. They were vast, many of the carvings stunning to behold even after all this time; even the ravages of nature could do nothing to take away their ancient splendour, their once-majesty, their foreboding and intimidating watchfulness.

They are looking at me. Watching me through veils of stone. What is this place? What secrets do the rocks hold? What terrible legends do they hide and protect?

At the far end of the avenue, distant but growing larger with every hoof-strike squatted a giant building of dulled black stone.

It looked almost out of place amongst the majesty of every other building on the avenue, and strangely it seemed less worn, less ravaged; none of the walls leant or were broken, and the roof – a single, sloping slab of black – was unbroken. Pillars lined the front, along with huge steps which, Graal realised as he drew closer, were each as high as a man.

"Was this place populated by giants?" said Graal.

"We found it like this," said Skanda. "The Ankarok. It was our home, but we did not build it. Even we do not know how it was made; what incredible engines, what mighty clockwork must have been used in its untimely creation."

Graal craned his neck, gazing up and up and then across the mighty front facade. Skanda turned his horse to the right, and Graal followed, and there was a ramp, smooth and black. Skanda dismounted and tethered both horses. The beasts were skittish, wide-eyed, ears flat back against their skulls. Graal reached out to calm the beast, not out of any compassion but because he simply didn't want the horse bolting and leaving him stranded... *here.*

They walked up the ramp, Graal's boots echoing dully, Skanda's feet slapping a soft rhythm. They stopped at the apex, and Graal peered in. It was warm in there, uncomfortably warm, surprisingly warm, and for a horrible moment Graal had a feeling he was stepping *inside* a creature, a living entity, into an *orifice*. He cursed himself, and stepped forward into the temple, hand reaching out to steady himself against a smooth wall.

Behind him, Skanda smiled, and started to sing a soft, lilting lullaby, and he followed Graal into the darkness which soon shifted by degrees into a warm, ambient, orange glow. Graal moved down long ramps through a massive, vacant room. At the head there was an altar, and glancing back as if for confirmation, Graal continued down and along the black stone floor until he reached steps. He looked up then, and nearly jumped out of his skin. The high vaulted ceiling was alive with thick black tentacles, that moved ever-so-gently, almost imperceptibly, but they *did* move, and there were thousands of them, and Graal realised his mouth was dry and he felt a strange primal fear course through his blood-oil. He was here, and he felt sleepy, and he was way out of his depth, and he laughed easily, the noise a discordant clash of sound, for he reasoned he'd been duped once more, just like with the Vampire Warlords... only now he thought it might turn out a lot, lot worse. It would seem Kell was not the only pawn in these games...

"Climb the steps," sang Skanda, talking and singing the words at the same time and the small boy followed Graal upwards and the albino vachine stood on the altar and turned and looked out, as if an audience awaited his performance and for an instant, just an *instant*, the ground seemed to squirm as if alive with black maggots. But then the feeling, the *image*, the *essence*, was gone, and Graal tried to speak, but found he could not.

"Over here," said Skanda, and took Graal's hand, and in a bizarre scene led the tall, athletic killer, warrior, soldier, *vachine* to the centre of the stage. They stood there, in the warmth, and Graal felt sweat creeping down his forehead, down his cheeks, trickling under his dull black armour and making him *squirm*.

Skanda's song rose in pitch, and suddenly in intensity and Graal could feel it, feel the magick in the air and he realised the *magick was in the music* and Skanda's song was summoning something, something *bad*, and Graal felt a sudden urge to flee this place, get on his horse and ride for all he was worth. To hell with dominion and ruling the world; some dreams were best left dead.

Skanda's song was a beautiful wail, dropping low into the deepest depths of reverberation, then shrieking high and long like a pig impaled on a spear, but all the time the notes came tumbling and they were beautiful and surreal and they spoke of an ancient time, a time of blood and earth and song, a time before the vachine, a time before the vampires, when Falanor was young and fresh and the Ankarok were good and proud and strong. Graal fell to his knees, choking suddenly, and Skanda was standing above him and he seemed to *stretch* upwards, he was huge, and no longer a boy but savagely ugly, his face the black of carved scorched wood, twisted like the roots of a tree, his face thick with corded knots of muscles and tendon uneven and disjointed and disfigured and this huge face loomed down at Graal and thin tentacles grew from his eyes and his mouth elongated into a beak and his eyes shrunk, became round and circular and still the song went on and on and on and huge powerful hands took Graal, and held him tight, and two more hands moved round only they weren't hands they were *mandibles* and they clamped Graal with sudden ferocious pain and he screamed, screamed as he looked down at the tiny glass disc on the floor before him, glowing black, radiating power and some ancient stench that had nothing to do with even human or vampire; and one of the claws rose, clicking softly, and a smell invaded the place and it was the smell of *insect chitin*. Graal swallowed, an instant before the claw lashed out and cut Graal's throat. He felt his flesh peel apart like soft fruit under a paring knife. Blood vomited from the new hole, his flesh quivering, his body pumping, heart pumping, emptying his blood-oil, his sacred refined *blood-oil* into the glass disc where it bubbled and was sucked down, absorbed. Graal would have screamed, but he could not. He would have fought and thrashed and run; but he could not.

Graal's body twitched and pulsated, and emptied itself onto the altar of the Ankarok.

Still Skanda sang, and looking back he was a boy again and Graal's eyes met Skanda's and Skanda gave a single nod, smiling, and released Graal to slump to the floor where he lay, curled foetal, twitching spasmodically. His fingers lifted, and touched his throat. Touched the gaping wound from whence his blood-oil and blood-magick had been *sucked*...

"Come and watch," whispered Skanda, and without any control of his body Graal climbed to his feet and as he walked, boots thumping clumsily as if he were a puppet on strings, he followed Skanda and a cool breeze blew through the room and into the gaping wound at his throat but he was not dead *was not dead* and he walked across the stone and out into the weak grey daylight –

The city was *squirming*.

Old Skulkra was *alive*, every stone surface a maelstrom of movement as *things* seemed to shift, and move, and push under the surface of the stone, as if the very buildings themselves were fluid, vertical walls of thick oil trapping large desperate creatures within. The whole world seemed to shift and coalesce, and Graal wanted to heave and vomit, but had no control and his open throat was flapping and if he could, he would have screamed with two mouths...

Skanda stood, and watched, and on his hand squatted a tiny scorpion with two tails, two stings, and Graal dragged his unwilling gaze back to the city, back to Old Skulkra, and he watched.

The walls squirmed and pulsed, and now the ground was fluid, heaving and churning as if under the blades of some terrible plough. Paving stones cracked and shifted, and the whole world was alive with movement, with shifting, with coalescing images a blend of reality and the fluid, a mix of sanity and the insane, and Graal watched with lower jaw hung open and his slit throat *forgotten* as from under the earth and from inside the walls they came, they pushed, they heaved, they were *born*.

The Ankarok emerged, and they were children, and their skin was gloss black and shining as if smeared with oil, and their teeth were the black of insect incisors, and many had four arms and claws for feet, some had pincers and mandibles and one young boy crawled forward, and Graal could see he had a thorax. The Ankarok weren't simply children, they were blended with insects, with scorpions and cockroaches and ants and beetles, and they shifted and squirmed and scampered like insects and there were hundreds of them spilling from the walls like ants from a nest, and there were *thousands* of them, surging from under the earth like a flood of beetles from a dunghill, and

we have been imprisoned for thousands of years
and
we have been waiting for this moment, biding our time
and
we were sent here, and trapped here, tricked here, lost here
but
now we are free, now we can work, and that's all we wanted, all we ever dreamed, the joy of the labour, the joy of the slave, the joy of the making, the joy of the killing –

Old Skulkra squirmed and heaved beneath him, and Graal faded away into a realm of impossibility, into a plane of unexistence in which the world was ruled by the Ankarok, and they

were
all-powerful.

TWELVE
Vampire Scouts

Saark was drunk. Saark was allowed to be drunk! After all, it'd been a hell of a day.

He staggered from Grak the Bastard's quarters, set high in the fortress walls and, in times of war or attack, doubling as a storeroom and a place for archers. It also made a good vantage point looking out over the plain to see who approached Black Pike Mines.

Saark, in his drunken state, found another use for the archer's slit in Grak's bedroom wall, and as his urine arced far and long over the snowy field below, Grak patted him heartily on the shoulder and suggested it was time for bed.

Saark staggered across the frozen mud of what was now the "Training Yard", although in all honesty, Saark left most of the training to Grak. Grak was a capable man, and Saark had to admit that he himself was capable of drinking, and enjoying a roll with a woman, and hell even cards or betting on bear fights were high on his agenda; but training men? No sir!

As Saark mounted the steps to his room, he recounted the week's success stories. Kell would be proud, no doubt, when he returned. They (meaning Grak) had whittled the men into a raw but efficient set of fighting units. They weren't an army. Not yet. They (meaning Grak) would need to put in a lot more effort to make sure the men could fight now as a *whole*, that's what Grak kept saying, a bloody *whole* – or was it hole? Saark stopped, and scratched his balls.

Still, they could charge in several formations, and at shouted commands or blasts from a tinny bugle, they could change from square to line to wedge, they could lock shields, they could disengage shields, they could charge and retreat. Because most of the men had worked (and indeed *survived*) the Black Pike Mines for a long period of time, they had great upper body strength and impressive stamina and endurance. Greater than Saark, as today's humiliating race had contested. But then, Saark *had* been drunk the night before. And the night before that. And, what a surprise, the night before that!

He stumbled to his room, and as the world swayed he removed his clothes and stood, hands on hips, naked and proud and desperate for a tankard of water. He moved to a water barrel and dunked his head in, coming up with a splash and lick of his lips. Gods he was hungry! What did he have in the room? Bread, cheese, donkey-meat...

"Saark?"

She sounded sleepy, and sat up in the bed, her dark hair tousled and illuminated by the moonlight easing through a small square window. Saark could make out her upper torso, naked, and he licked his lips again only not, in this case, with the need for water.

"Hello there," he said, and moved towards the bed.

"Have you been drinking?"

"Only a drop, sweetie," he murmured, and crawled onto the bed.

"Good," said Nienna. "I warmed your blankets. I hope you don't mind?"

"Of course not," he said, and she knelt up before him, and her body was perfect, white and pale, gleaming in the moonlight, her small but firm breasts young and pert, her lips slightly parted as her head tilted, and she stared at his face.

"Do you want me to stay?" she said.

"Oh yes," said Saark, reaching out and caressing her breasts. Instantly her nipples hardened and reaching forward, gently, his tongue circled her areola. Nienna murmured, and shuffled closer, and Saark's arms encircled her, and now his hard cock pressed into her, and he kissed her, he kissed her lips and they were warm and sweet from honeycakes and wine, and he kissed her neck, which was warm and soft like silk, and his hands ran down her back and she shivered in anticipation and thrust herself painfully against him, in need, in lust, and his hands came to rest on her buttocks, firm and hard from so much travelling in the wilds. They kissed again, harder this time, with passion and a need that transcended threats and Saark's hand dipped, stroked between Nienna's legs and she squirmed, giggling a little, then moaning and sinking into his embrace as his hand entered her, and he bore her down to the bed, and Saark was lost in wine and lust and memories, and he remembered Alloria; she was his first love and she was his true love and she was before him now, on the soft silk sheets in King Leanoric's chambers, Alloria, with her mane of curled black hair, her flashing dangerous green eyes, her ruby red lips, tall, with her elegant long languorous limbs and her tongue stained from blue karissia, and she smiled up at Saark, and Alloria said, "Make love to me, Saark," and Nienna said, "Make love to me, Saark," and Saark pushed himself into her, all the way, to the hilt, and she groaned and he groaned and they fucked long and hard on the bed, their groans and thrusts rising rising rising to a climax of perfect joy and union, and Saark whispered, "Alloria," but Nienna was too far gone to hear the words and she gave herself to Saark, not caring, not caring about the world and Kell's threats and vachine imperfections... and slowly, they spiralled down into a cold place, a cold world of reality, facing war and mutilation and death.

And in the cold dark hours of the night, they clung tightly to each other like children.

Governor Myrtax could not sleep. He was too hot, sweating and feeling fevered, and so he stepped from his bed and pulled on low, soft-leather boots. His wife murmured in sleep and turned, one arm flinging out, but she did not wake. Myrtax crossed to the next room and looked in on his sleeping babes; he saw their dark shapes, breathing rhythmically in the ink, and he smiled; smiled the happy smile of fatherhood; smiled the smile of innate joy at what a man's child could invest without effort – just simply by *being*.

Too hot. Too damn hot!

Myrtax stepped from his quarters and looked across at the distant fortress walls. Fires burned in braziers on the battlements, and ten guards kept watch across the snowy plains. Damn, but he didn't want to leave this place. Didn't want to go to war. Why would he? His family was here. His wife, who he loved more than life; his children, who he'd die for!

Myrtax jogged down the steps and onto the frozen mud. He was surprised to find he had a knife in his hand, and he slipped it back into the oiled leather sheath. *Strange. I don't remember belting the knife on. Why would I need a knife in my own mine? But of course, after the Governors – the false Governors – took over and threatened my children; well, a man has to protect himself; a man has to look after his own interests.*

Governor Myrtax moved across the ground, seemingly with no destination, until he found himself outside the cell of Sara. Kell's daughter.

How strange to come here. Why would I come here? Kell said she was dangerous, and not to trust her, but I know he's wrong because I have seen into her eyes, and she is a noble creature, a beautiful creature, and anything that stunning must be good...

"Good evening, sir," said the guard, and gurgled and vomited blood as Governor Myrtax's dagger slid under his ribs and up, with a hard jabbing thrust, into his heart. The man sagged into Myrtax's arms, and he frowned, confused at why the man was so heavy, and why the man had been drinking on duty, and why he was now asleep in his arms like a dirty drunkard.

"I'll have you up on a charge," muttered Myrtax, lowering the twitching guard to the ground and taking the keys from his belt. He moved to the cell, the interior of which was a black pool of oil, impenetrable to the naked eye, and Myrtax inserted the key and opened the gate.

Myrtax stood back, his mind flushed with confusion, and he looked up and the stars were bright, bathing him in a surreal glow and he smiled, as he thought about his children. He had been blessed when they were born, and blessed more as they grew into two of the most beautiful things he had ever witnessed in creation –

"Myrtax. You have surpassed yourself," said Sara, stepping from her cage. She smiled, and leant forward, fangs extending towards the dazed Governor of the Black Pike Mines.

"Hey! Hey you!" It was an inner-wall patrol of guards, set up by Grak. Boots pounded stone, and three soldiers wearing new armour and carrying newly forged short swords sprinted forward, and a sword whistled for Sara but she leapt, straight up into the air, the sword slashing beneath her boots. She twisted in the air, back-flipping behind the men. She landed lightly, reached out, and snapped one man's neck. He crumpled instantly. A sword

789

hammered down, and Sara swayed, arm slapping out to break the man's arm in half. His hand and wrist fell twitching to the stone, spewing blood, and he screamed – a scream silenced as Sara punched out, fist entering his mouth and breaking his teeth and exploding from the back of his head... and as it exited, her claws extended with a *flick*, putting out the third soldier's eyes.

Sara withdrew her hand with a squelch and shower of bloody mush, and leaving one soldier sobbing on the floor, holding his ruined face, she reached over and gently kissed Myrtax on the lips. "Until the next time, *lover*," she said, and was gone in a whisper of darkness.

More soldiers arrived, led by Grak, his sword out, his face grim. He stepped up to the man without eyes and only half a face remaining; with a savage downward stab, he put the writhing man out of his misery.

"Check the cell." Grak whirled on Governor Myrtax. "What the hell happened here?" Then he saw the keys still in Myrtax's hands, and the dazed look on the man's face even as he started to drift back into some semblance of understanding.

"What? What... where did all the blood come from? Oh, my... " said Myrtax.

The soldier returned. "Sir. One vampire is gone, the other is... well, it's a husk."

"What do you mean, a husk?"

"It's shrivelled up. Like all the blood has been sucked out."

Grak strode forward, and stared at the skin-bag of bones. "Shit," he snarled, then turned back to Myrtax. "The vampire must have fed from the other one; to keep strong." He pointed at the Governor. "Are you happy with yourself? Eh?" Then back to the soldier, in a tone of disgust. "Go and lock that bastard up, before he does any more damage."

Two soldiers grabbed Myrtax's arms and removed the dagger from his belt. They led him away, tears on his cheeks, protesting confusion and innocence.

Grak looked down at the dead soldiers, then up at the night sky. The stars twinkled. Grak had no time for their cold beauty. "You, lad!"

"Yes, sir?"

"Double the guards."

"Where, sir?"

"Everywhere!" he thundered. "Tell them we have a vampire loose in the fucking mine."

"Yes, sir!"

"And soldier?"

"Yes sir?"

"Go and wake Saark. He needs to know about this."

Kell stared around in disbelief. The Valleys of the Moon was massive, and bisected down the middle of the floor by a huge crevasse from which steam slowly rose, along with a sulphurous stench that made Kell's eyes weep.

His hands were bound tightly behind his back, and Dekkar carried Ilanna in one hand, his own flanged mace in the other. He was grinning madly, and Jagor Mad walked by his side, a kind of strutting arrogance in his step now he had the upper hand.

"I can't believe I trusted you," said Kell, his eyes moving along the rift in the valley floor to the distant huts beyond. They lined the walls, small and made from mud and stone, with slate roofs and hand-carved doors of oak.

"More the fool you," said Jagor, cocky now, too cocky, his eyes shining with a new light. Kell realised what it was. Hatred. It hadn't vanished, only been pushed deep down whilst Jagor brought him here. Kell had been played like a pawn. Like a court jester. And that burned him bad, worse than any poison force fed into his bones by Myriam's invading needle.

"You know the stakes here," said Kell, face filled with thunder. "This is about everybody! This is about Falanor, this is about us all working together to rid the world of a dangerous menace!"

"The only dangerous menace here is *you!*" hissed Jagor, and pressed his sword against Kell's throat. "I *will* have my revenge for all those years spent in that fucking mine! I will spill your blood! But not yet, oh no, not yet!"

"Be silent!" roared Dekkar suddenly, and as they moved across the jagged rocks, filled in places with snow and ice except around the rim of the valley rift, where all snow had melted revealing black rocks veined with red and grey minerals, so Blacklippers streamed from distant huts and moved like a tide to meet their King.

Dekkar.

King of the Blacklippers.

Behind, many of the children followed, bows still aimed at Kell. Nobody trusted him, and he smiled a sour smile. Here, it would appear, he was a dark myth. How now would he convince these people to fight for him? How would he convince them to go to war against the Vampire Warlords? If he attacked them, he would have no chance of convincing them – for he would simply reinforce his status as enemy. And with Jagor Mad ready to stab him in the back, it looked like his luck had come head-to-head with a mountain flank.

"Hear me!" roared Dekkar, halting by the edge of the hot stinking rift in the rocky floor. Fumes hung over the great tear in the earth, and over it, near the centre, Kell squinted. He could see a bridge, a narrow span of brass filled with huge clockwork wheels and gears. Kell frowned. He had never seen anything like it in his life, except in miniature in the workings of a clock. "Here, we have the prisoner Kell! Sworn enemy of the Blacklippers! *Hunter* of the Blacklippers! Raper of our women, murderer of our children, *despoiler* of Blacklipper flesh!"

A hush fell over the Blacklippers.

Kell met their gazes, the men, all armed with spears and swords, faces grim, shoulders stocky and proud. These were a warrior race. These were the outcasts, the criminals, the freaks and deviants of Falanor – who had taken blood-oil to relieve their pain and suffering, to find an inner peace from physical torment, instead finding social torment and a finality as outcasts; names to be revered as evil and unholy, cast away to the dark regions of the mountains where nobody would travel. Kell knew this. He had hunted enough Blacklippers in his time. *Some*, at least, of what they said was true.

He grinned, a sour grin.

Because that's what this came back to, that's what this came round to: his earlier escapades. As a Hunter. A Vachine Hunter, but also a killer of those who smuggled Karakan Red across the mountains; those who stole blood to feed the impure amongst the vachine.

"Shit," he muttered, as full realisation dawned. "They were going to kill him. There was no persuading these people. He had been a fool. An arrogant, trusting, naive fool.

"Kell! The Legend!" roared Dekkar, and an answering roar met him and Kell tried to shout over the noise but it rose like thunder and hundreds of Blacklippers swarmed at him, swamping him, and he went down under a barrage of blows, fists and sticks slamming his head and nose and cheeks and jaw. Kell hit the ground hard, and was kicked, and then the crowd surged back and Kell looked up at Dekkar, who stooped, and *lifted* Kell above his head.

"The Bridge!" somebody shouted.

"Yes! The Trial! The Bridge!"

"Bridge! Bridge! Bridge!" chanted the Blacklippers, and Kell, dazed, felt himself moving as if on a sea of hands and he realised he had been taken, was being carried by many, and Dekkar held Ilanna again and *if only Kell could reach his axe, these bastards, he'd show them who was a fucking Legend, he'd carve himself a path so fucking bloody his name would ring like Death through a thousand fucking years of their mangled fucking history!*

Kell was carried along the edge of the rift. He glanced down, and wished he hadn't.

Fumes welled up, making him choke, and his eyes were met by a pulsing deep glow of red and orange. The heat was incredible. It singed his beard and eyebrows. It made him cough and choke. For the first time in *years* Kell felt panic well in his chest like a striking viper. This was a bad place, an evil place; and he realised instinctively he had been condemned and he would die here. Kell gritted his teeth. If he was to die, then he would take oh so many with him...

As they grew close to the bridge so Kell realised its awesome scope and size. It was a mammoth brass contraption, not just a bridge but a machine. The whole length was a mass of cogs and wheels, gears and levers. In the centre, disappearing down into the glow, was a huge pendulum like Kell had seen in many a clock, only this was the length of twenty men and must have weighed something shocking.

They reached the point where the bridge met the rocky ground – only it didn't. There was a gap too large to jump, and Dekkar reached to a small brass pod and pulled a lever. There came a heavy *clunk*, a spin of cogs which transferred to others cogs and gears stepped up and down like pistons. There was a groan, and the pendulum swung and the bridge shifted, lifted, and eased onto the rocky ground with a crash and grinding of brass on rock. Kell was prodded on, hands tight behind his back, and with a grimace he realised Dekkar had used his own axe, his own damn *Ilanna!*

Kell spat onto the brass grid beneath his boots. Dekkar would pay for that.

They moved across the brass bridge, which continually shifted and moved, rolling like a ship at anchor in a bay. Beneath his boots Kell could feel the spinning cogs, and the shift of gears. It felt like the bridge was *alive*.

Reaching the centre, his eyes streaming with tears from the chemical updraft, Kell saw the swing and the noose of woven brass rope. So, he was to be hanged. *Again*. "Horse shit," he muttered, and glanced back. Now, there was only Dekkar and Jagor Mad. They were both grinning at him, and Dekkar passed Ilanna to his brother.

"Do you want to kill him, brother, or shall I?"

"No, that's my job," said Jagor. "I owe him. Owe him bad."

"Jagor, listen to me!" hissed Kell. "You know the vampires are coming. You know this is insanity! We must all work together, must fight together to remove this menace! If you hang me, the Vampire Warlords – they will not vanish. And slowly, they will hunt down every living creature in Falanor. You might live another month; you might live a year. But they will come for you, and they'll either turn you into a vampire, or they'll burn your fucking soul, lad."

"The Vampire Warlords?" said Dekkar, raising his eyebrows. "I have heard of such creatures. They are part of Blacklipper Legend. Part of *vachine* folklore as scribed within the Oak Testament."

"General Graal of the vachine flooded Silva Valley from the Granite Thrones on Helltop," said Kell. "He sacrificed the vachine in a mass offering of blood, to open the Paths to the Chaos Halls. The Vampire Warlords came back. Now, they are in Jalder, and Gollothrim, and Vor! They will spread, Dekkar. They will kill your people."

Dekkar considered this. Then he smiled. "I care nothing for the people of Falanor. Kill him!"

Jagor prodded Kell with Ilanna, drawing blood across the old warrior's forearm. Kell growled, and stepped up onto the brass ramp. Jagor climbed up behind him, and placed the brass noose about Kell's neck.

"You will die for my suffering," he snarled.

"If you kill me," said Kell, voice perfectly quiet, perfectly calm, "then you condemn yourself. You condemn the people of Falanor to an eternity of slavery. You condemn your entire race of Blacklippers to vampire slavery."

"You think one old man is so important?"

"No. But I know that I can make a difference. If I can get close enough to the Vampire Warlords, I will kill them."

"Ha! I'll do it myself!" snapped Jagor Mad. "Now step off the ramp, old man, lest I use this pretty axe to open your skull!"

Kell turned his back on Jagor, and took a deep breath. A million thoughts rushed through his mind. His misplaced trust in this, a convicted killer. Saark's training of the army. Nienna, sweet Nienna. Sara, snarling and hissing, spitting and cursing. And then back, back through the days and weeks and months, back through Myriam and the Soul Stealers, the fights on Helltop, scrapping on the dangerous ridges of the Black Pike Mountains with snarling cankers and creatures of the dark, the vachine and the vampires, the cursed and the unholy. Back back back, and one face kept returning to his mind and if Kell had to blame one man, then that one man would be Graal. General Graal. He had it coming. He had a hard death coming. But Kell would not be the man to see it through.

Kell thought about Ehlana.

He remembered the Crooked Oak, the sunshine, the flowers in her hair and tears were in his eyes, on his cheeks, in his beard. "You are man and wife. You may kiss her." And he leant forward, and he kissed her, and it had been an incredible moment, a moment of unity and purity and perfection. But how had it gone so bad? How had it all gone wrong? *I'm coming to you, Ehlana, I'm coming just like I said I would, just like I promised. We'll walk the long dark roads together, and I'll bring you to paradise. I can do no more in this place. In this world. In this life.*

"Jump, fucker," snarled Jagor Mad, and Kell turned and smiled at the big man, and saw the shock in his face for to see Kell cry must have been such a rarity; and over the thumping of the bridge and the hiss of the smoke and churning furnace below, Kell heard another sound, like shouting, and Jagor Mad's eyes went wide and Ilanna started to lift in his great brutal fists as an arrow materialised in one eye socket with a savage slap, and Jagor Mad screamed stumbling backwards, falling to the ground, dropping Ilanna with a clatter and reaching up to touch the shaft in his skull – which made him scream again.

Kell squinted through the smoke. A figure was galloping a grey mare along the edge of the valley's rift. Another arrow slashed through the air, but Dekkar was already moving, launching himself sideways and grunting as he hit the bridge walkway.

Kell tugged at his bonds, but they were too tight. He struggled, and dropping his head down and back, got the noose from its promise. Dekkar was crawling across the bridge and he hit a panel against one rail. The clockwork bridge cranked and lifted, as a third arrow sailed over and clattered along the walkway a few feet from Dekkar.

Kell leapt down to Jagor, who was weeping, touching the shaft in his eye tenderly. "Help me!" he wailed at Kell, and Kell drove a knee into his face sending him rolling, embedded arrow slapping the brass bridge and making him scream and scream and scream, and to this backdrop of noise Kell found Ilanna, and sitting and shuffling backwards, he rubbed the bonds across her razor-sharp blades and they parted like simple cotton threads.

Kell took Ilanna, and rose to his feet.

He was Thunder. He was the Storm.

Dekkar was standing, staring at him, his face a fury, the black flanged mace steady in his huge hands.

Dekkar looked down at Jagor, who had passed into unconsciousness. "I am going to crush you for that, worm."

"Show me," snarled Kell through strings of saliva.

With a scream, Dekkar launched an attack. He was huge, mighty, and attacked with such a sudden violent speed it made Kell blink in shock and surprise, stepping back, Ilanna coming up to deflect the mace – which struck in a shower of sparks, and continued onwards forcing Kell down on one knee, teeth gritted, muscles straining and bulging. The mace stopped an inch from his eyes, which flickered up to Dekkar, or rather, Dekkar's boot. The blow sent Kell reeling back across the bridge, rolling, Ilanna gone from his fingers and Dekkar leapt forward, the mace whirring down again. Kell twitched to one side, and the blow left a dent in the brass bridge. It would have crushed Kell's head like a melon. Another blow sent sparks careering from the bridge's rails, and Kell got to his knees, streaked with sweat, panting, anger rising through him in a colossal insane wave. Dekkar was bigger, and stronger, and faster. But Kell was mean. Kell was *fucking* mean. He screamed, spittle lacing his beard, and as the mace whistled over his head in a mighty horizontal stroke he came up from the duck into a lunge, grabbing Dekkar around the midriff and punching the large man backwards, off balance, to hit the ground. The mace flashed up, but Kell caught the shaft against his arm, and it slid from Dekkar's fingers. Kell slammed a right straight down into Dekkar's face, and again, and again, and felt teeth break under impact. Dekkar screamed, and his hand grabbed Kell's balls, the other Kell's throat, and the huge man scrabbled to his knees and hoisted Kell over his head. He threw Kell down the bridge, and Kell rolled over and over, and lay for a moment stunned, his throat and balls on fire and clubbing him with waves of impact pain. Dekkar roared, and ran at Kell who stumbled to his feet. A straight punch jabbed Kell back, a right hook shook him, rocking him on his heels, and Dekkar took Kell's head in his hands and head-butted him, once, twice, three times and let go, grinning, blood and smashed teeth filling his mouth.

Kell stared up at the huge man. "Is that all you've fucking got?" he screamed, groggy, staggering back.

"I'll kill you!" roared Dekkar, and slammed another hook which sent Kell reeling sideways, hitting the bridge's rail and rolling along it, slamming against the panel which controlled the movement of the brass bridge. There came a huge, metallic groan and clockwork started to spin, huge gears pumping, mammoth brass pistons hissing and thrusting. The bridge lurched and suddenly spun, leaving a huge gap to the rocky bank and safety. An arrow sailed through the steam, missing Dekkar by a few inches. He scowled, and Kell realised he had found his mace. Dekkar advanced down the bridge at Kell, who was touching his broken nose and gritting his teeth in anger and frustration.

"Come on!" screamed Kell, as Dekkar broke into a run, but the bridge lurched again, spinning around, a heavy metallic cranking sound echoing through the Valleys of the Moon. Steam hissed from the brass bridge. Along the banks Kell saw hundreds of faces flash past. It was the Blacklippers, and they were watching, motionless, many with mouths open in awe. Kell couldn't see the person who'd saved him. The bridge spun around again. Kell felt sick, and was pitched off balance, landing heavy with a grunt. The bridge tipped, and he was sent skidding down the rough brass ramp, arms and legs kicking, to crash into Dekkar who was pinned against a brass strut. Kell hit him with three straight punches, heavy leaden blows that cracked the man's cheekbone making him howl, then the bridge spun again, lurching and groaning, and Kell was thrown away like a toy doll, down the expanse to hit the rail with such force he thought for a moment he'd broken his back.

"You have to get off the bridge!" a woman was screaming, and Kell nodded at this immutable logic. He got to his knees, a drool of saliva and pain trailing from his beard, mingled with blood from his smashed nose. He ran along the rail, fighting gravity as the bridge rocked back on mammoth pistons and it was all Kell could do to grab a nearby strut and hold on for his life. The bridge rose, near vertical now, and Kell felt his boots and legs slip away from beneath him so he was hanging, gazing down into a distant inferno with clouds of steam and sulphur.

"Holy Mother," he whispered, eyes wide, all thoughts of battle forgotten. Ilanna skated along the metal with a scream, and wedged against a brass strut below. Dekkar was also kicking beneath him, and Kell watched Jagor Mad's unconscious body slip and slide, spinning with arms and legs akimbo, until he bounced from a strut, jigged off at an angle, then soared from the edge of the bridge to be lost in the raging inferno below.

"*Noooo!*" screamed Dekkar.

But Jagor Mad was gone. Gone, into the furnace.

Dekkar looked up at Kell. "This is your fault!" he roared.

Kell said nothing, but looked up, searching for a way to climb from the bridge. The bridge groaned. More clanking came from deep down in the clockwork machine's *bowels*, and then it gave a sudden jerk. Kell nearly lost his grip.

Then –

A noise rent the air, long and ululating, almost like a war cry but far too high-pitched and feminine. Kell stared off across the banks of the valley rift, across black rock and ice beyond. Riders were streaming across the snow, and Kell saw the Blacklippers running for their huts, many drawing weapons and Kell squinted through the fumes, and–

And blinked.

They were vampires. Twenty of them at least, wearing black cloaks and with hair tied back tight. They were riding horses that were… *red?* Kell focused. No, not red. Pure muscle. *Pure muscle,* without the skin. The beasts were panting, snorting, whinnying in pain and fear. Kell could see the heavy muscle fibres working and he suddenly felt very sick, despite his own problems.

"Kell, you've got to reach the control panel," a woman was shouting, and Kell turned back to the rocky embankment. He squinted again, and then shook his head. It was Myriam, bow in hand, face earnest.

"What the hell are *you* doing here?" he yelled.

"Rescuing you, old man! Reach the panel! I can see the core shafts of the bridge, and they're *bending*, you understand? The whole damn thing is tearing itself free! It's going to fall!" Kell felt the sickness in his stomach rise through him. If the bridge fell into the furnace, well, it was Goodnight Sweet Lady.

Kell started to climb down, hand over hand, the brass warm to his touch. He could see Dekkar struggling beneath him, and his gaze moved first to the control panel, then left, to Ilanna. Kell gritted his teeth, and struggled to the axe. He took her. He cradled her to his chest. She was warm to his touch. She was thankful.

"Kell!" screamed Myriam. He glanced up.

The charging vampires hit the massed Blacklippers in a tight wedge, and he saw, *saw* heads sail up into the air and heard the vampires' high-pitched keening, realising with rising gorge that they were laughing, fucking *laughing* as they slaughtered. The swords of battle rang across the Valleys of the Moon. Steel on steel. Steel biting flesh. Steel breaking bone.

Kell scrabbled across the brass strut. The bridge groaned and shuddered beneath him. He stared at the controls, but there were small dials and levers and he did not understand. He started to press and twist things at random, and the bridge groaned, gears clanked, and there came a horrible, booming tearing sound. The bridge shuddered, and dropped – then in an eerie silence, tilted to one side and began to fall.

Kell hung on for his life, wind and sour sulphur fumes blowing through his hair and bloodied beard, and the edge of the bridge clanged against the edge of the valley floor, but behind him it fell away and then snagged with various metallic tearing sounds. Kell looked up, into Myriam's concerned face. "Shit," he snarled. "I can't believe it's you!"

"Come on. We have only seconds!" She glanced behind herself, fearful of the charging vampires who were cutting a path through the Blacklippers. Men, women and children were slaughtered like diseased cattle. Heads were cut from shoulders, arms and legs from torsos. It was a massacre. It was an abattoir.

Kell scrambled up the brass planks and leapt, catching Myriam's outstretched hand. She was strong. She hauled him up onto the rocky ridge, and Kell whirled, eyes narrowed, staring at the vampires. The Blacklippers had retreated, forming themselves into a fighting square surrounded by the corpses of their friends. Those with shields had made a wall at the front, and the vampires coolly dismounted and watched with interest, smiles staining faces as they lifted bright, silver swords.

"Help me up," he croaked.

Kell jumped, and glared down into Dekkar's face. The huge man was in pain, face twisted and battered and streaked with grime. He had climbed as far as he could, but could not traverse the final leap.

"Why?"

"Because they're slaughtering my people!" screamed Dekkar, and held out his hand.

Kell stared at it. The bridge lurched again, dropping another foot. Great tearing sounds echoed through the rift, and the bridge was vibrating as if alive and fitting. Cogs could be seen, spinning slowly. A huge piston went *thunk*.

Kell glanced at Myriam. "Hold my belt." She grabbed him, hands like iron shackles, and he knelt, leaning forward, hand outstretched. His eyes met Dekkar's. "You'll have to jump."

"Can I trust you?"

"No. But you have little choice."

Dekkar growled an ancient curse, and leapt...

Kell leant, and the two men grabbed one another, wrist to wrist and stayed locked there for a moment, Kell staring down into Dekkar's wild eyes, muscles screaming as they took the weight. Then Kell hissed, and hauled Dekkar up the wall as behind him the huge brass bridge squealed like a woman in pain, and slowly tilted, sliding backwards with a *whoosh* to vanish into the abyss.

Kell looked down at his hand, and then up into Dekkar's eyes. He noted the big man carried his mace, and he swallowed. Kell always said he took a lot of killing; well, here was a man hewn from the same granite cast.

Dekkar turned, and stared at the vampires. They had dismounted, and were smiling as they advanced on the retreating Blacklippers. He released Kell's grip, and Kell hoisted Ilanna and glanced at Myriam, who drew her own sword.

"It's time for those bastards to die," said Kell.

"Let's fight," growled Dekkar.

They charged across the rocky ground, and the vampires smiled wider until eyes fell on Ilanna. One pointed, but Kell, Dekkar and Myriam crashed into them and Kell's axe lashed out, opening a throat, and on the return swing cutting a vampire's head free from its body. There was an explosion of flesh, and Kell grabbed the hair and hoisted the head up high. "See!" he screamed "They can fucking die! Die, I tell you!" Everything was chaos. The vampires seemed to suddenly shrink back, staring at Kell, and Ilanna, and the severed vampire head with fangs still gnashing and gnawing. Kell launched the head into the pit, and kicked over the body which spewed out foul stinking black blood. Kell waded into the mass, Ilanna hewing left and right, thumping into flesh, spattering him with gore. The vampires attacked him with their inhuman speed but Kell was a demon, moving smoothly, seeming to shift here, twitch there, and claws and swords sailed past him by a hair's breadth, but always by a hair's breadth, and he had some inhuman instinct, some natural grace as if he was in perfect tune with the killers and always slipping beyond their claws. Dekkar was close behind, feeding in Kell's wake. As Kell moved forward through the vampires, Ilanna slamming left and right, so anything that went past was crushed under Dekkar's mighty mace. Myriam, also, moved with incredible vachine speed, sword slamming out, cutting throats and piercing hearts. Some vampires shrivelled into decayed mush. Some crumbled into ash.

In what seemed an instant, Kell broke through their ranks and high-pitched keening rent the air. Five or six fled, leaping onto horses and galloping away only to find a wall of Blacklippers had gathered, and charged at the remaining vampires with swords and axes, cutting them to pieces. Screams pierced the air. Without mercy, the Blacklippers killed the skinless horses, and threw them into the sulphurous rift.

Kell stood for a moment, panting, then whirled on Dekkar. Ilanna came up. Kell's eyes were bright glowing coals without trust.

Dekkar placed his mace head against the ground, and leant heavily on the weapon. Suddenly he looked old, and tired; boneweary. He smiled weakly at Kell, and rubbed his eyes.

"You did well. For an old man."

"As did you. For a fat bastard."

"Ha! Kell, I think we may have got off to a bad start."

Kell scratched his chin. "You reckon? Maybe I'd have to agree with that one. I came here to warn you about the vampires, about their *army* gathered at Jalder. I have gathered my own army, and I was coming here to ask you to join."

"What, you would have Blacklippers fight alongside the good men of Falanor?" There was a hint of a sneer to Dekkar. Long-held prejudices could not be erased with ease.

Kell shrugged, and gazed at Ilanna's bloodied blades. They were slick with vampire gore. "My army is made up of criminals, freaks, and convicts from the Black Pike Mines."

Dekkar smiled. "That is good, then. My sort of people."

"Will you come with me?" said Kell. "Will you fight with me?"

Dekkar stared hard at Kell, then past him, to the thousands of gathered Blacklippers. His people. His outcast race. Then he nodded, and lifted his mace into the air. "Gather your weapons!" he roared. "We are going to war!"

A cheer rang out, and Kell turned, face a dark sour hole. Myriam grasped his arm and they walked away from the cheering Blacklippers to stare out, past the destroyed bridge and the torn clockwork moorings that were all that remained.

"What is wrong?" she said.

"They cheer because they know they will kill the men and women of Falanor. It is sick."

"You got your army."

"Yes. I got it. But what worries me is once I've unleashed it, and if we win… how do I rein it back again? But that's a problem for another day."

Myriam nodded, and peered down into the depths of the rift. "I'm sorry, Kell. About before. About Saark."

"I should have let you drown him longer. Would have done him good. Cooled him off a little." Kell grinned. "Have you learnt your lesson?"

"So you're not going to cut off my head?"

"You saved my life, didn't you? With that damn fine bow."

"Maybe I was trying to hit you?"

Kell roared with laughter, suddenly, and slapped Myriam on the back. He was battered, his nose broken, his face and clothing covered in gore, vampire blood, strings of flesh. He looked like an animal. He looked worse than an animal. He looked like a Vampire Killer.

Myriam shivered.

"Either way, lass, you saved my hide on that bridge. And in a roundabout way, you have helped save Falanor."

"How so?"

"I think you led the vampires here. They were a tracking unit. I reckon they were after killing themselves a vachine. They know your kind are a threat, and you must be a priority hunt for them."

"Oh," she said, deflating a little. Kell put his arm round her.

"Don't worry, Myriam. You're with me now. And me and Ilanna, we're starting to get quite fond of you vachine. You certainly have your uses in a scrap!"

"Yes, but we're hard to love," said Myriam, and smiled, and looked up at Kell, and he stared at her as if almost seeing her for the first time. When Kell had first met Myriam, back in Vorgeth Forest, and she had poisoned him; she had been a husk of a woman, riddled with cancer, eyes sunken, hair lifeless; now, thanks to her vachine change at the hands of the Soul Stealers, she was tall, powerful, skin pale but radiant, and her hair was long, gently curled, luscious like the glossy pelt of a panther. Her eyes were dark and glittering and intelligent, and if it hadn't been for the brass vachine fangs, she would have been, to Kell's eyes at least, strikingly beautiful.

He remembered her touch. He remembered glimpses of her, little snippets of naked flesh, bathing, dressing. And back in Vorgeth Forest, just before she had injected him with poison, she had pressed close against him, and even now he could remember the musk of her body, and he remembered the rising lust in his loins and cursed himself, now and then, for being weak, for being pitiful, for betraying the memory of his long lost Ehlana. Back in Vorgeth Myriam had kissed him, and it had felt good. It had felt more than good. But he pushed the memory away. Never again, old man, he had told himself. Not in this life.

Kell shuddered.

"No," he said.

"No what?" Myriam was looking at him strangely.

"Just *no*. Come on. Let's take these Blacklippers to Saark and the men. The fight is just beginning."

"Wait." Her hand was on his arm.

Kell stared at her fingers, then lifted his head to look into her face. Again, that curious smile. The tilt of the head. Kell shivered, for he thought he knew what that smile meant. Myriam was weak – she needed to be loved, to be cherished, and to be in control. And she was attracted to power. Attracted to Kell's ferocity, his savagery, his Legend.

"Go on."

"That thing. Back there. With Saark. I didn't mean it."

"What, trying to kill him? Don't worry about that. I love the man, but I, also, want to kill him regular."

"Not killing him, no. The... other thing."

"Ahh."

"It was just... a moment. I am free of him. You see?"

"I see," said Kell, voice low, eyes locked to Myriam. "Come on, lass. We should go."

"Yes."

Kell led the way, and Myriam followed, sheathing her sword.

Dekkar sent a fast rider with three horses within the hour. The mission was simple: to reach Saark at the Black Pike Mines with a letter from Kell. In it, were instructions to assemble the new army and to rendezvous on the plains south of the Black Pike Mines. Then they would take a direct course from the Black Pike Mines to the occupied city of Jalder.

Now Kell, Myriam and Dekkar, King of the Blacklippers, led two thousand armed male and female *Blacklippers* across the ice and snow, and out from the Valleys of the Moon. They moved mostly in silence, hair and furs ruffled by the cold wind from the mountains. It was a bleak day, grey and cold and threatening snow.

"Now, we go to war," said Myriam, voice gentle.

"Now, we fight for Falanor," agreed Kell.

THIRTEEN
The Battle for Jalder

"It's grandfather!" grinned Nienna, shading her eyes from the glare of the snow. From the hilltop across the valley emerged a horde of soldiers, heavily armed, who descended into the valley floor with Kell marching alongside a huge man bearing a mace.

"Looks like a bunch of murderous cutthroats to me," muttered Saark, then gave a sly smile. "As you say. Your grandfather."

"Don't be like that! He's done it! He's brought more soldiers!"

Nienna ran off ahead, boots ploughing through fresh soft snow, an almost childish look on her face which made Saark blush as he remembered the past week and the things they'd done. Nothing fazed Nienna. Saark had to admit, she gave him a run for his money.

Saark watched as Nienna leapt at the old man, throwing her arms about him, and he laughed and hugged her tight, shifting Ilanna to one side out of the way where sunlight gleamed on the dark matt blades.

If he finds out, I'm a dead man. No. More. If he finds out, he'll beat me, then he'll torture me, then he'll cut me up into little pieces! He'll tear off my arms and cut off my balls. Saark clutched his balls with compassion. *And I don't ever want to lose my balls. I like my balls. After all...* He grimaced. *My balls are my best feature.*

Saark moved across the snow, signalling to Grak the Bastard to stand down the men. As Saark approached, Kell grinned at him and cracked his knuckles. "I see you, dandy."

"Somebody hit you?" Saark squinted at the damage.

"People always hit me," said Kell.

"I see somebody broke your nose. You look better for it."

"Yes," said Kell, and gestured to Dekkar, the Blacklipper King. "We had a few, shall we say, disagreements. But then the vampires attacked the Valleys of the Moon, and it all worked out right in the end."

Saark nodded, grinning. "Nice to meet you, Dekkar." Saark held out his hand. Dekkar simply stared at him, as a lion would if presented with a potato. "Ahh, I see, you employ the old school of ignorance just like our big stinking friend here."

Dekkar leaned close to Kell. "Shall I silence this yapping puppy?"

"No, no, he's all right. He's always like this. You get used to him."

"I do not think I will," said Dekkar, scowling and hefting his huge mace.

"Hey," said Saark, scowling, "I'm here, you know, right here in front of you, now I'm used to people talking about me behind my back but this just isn't on. You wouldn't get this sort of thing in the Court of King Leanoric, I can tell you!"

"Did he look after you?" said Kell, to Nienna.

"He looked after me," she said, voice small, but thankfully Kell was looking away, surveying the army of criminals as presented by Saark. So he missed the blush. He missed Nienna's subtle tone of voice. Saark scowled at her, then waved up the slope.

"We trained them. Just like you said. And although I'd like to take all the credit, in fact I *shall* take all the credit, but maybe a little of the credit must go to Grak. He's a bastard, but he knows a thing or two about formations, and training men, and getting the best out of them."

"Stop babbling," said Kell.

"But. We had, er, a couple of problems."

"Such as?"

They watched Grak striding down the slope, dragging with him the unwilling figure of Myrtax. The man was struggling, and his hands were bound before him.

"It wasn't my fault, Kell," said Myrtax, red and sweating.

"Explain."

"He let Sara go," said Saark, voice low. "Killed the guards. Released her into the night."

"Horse shit," snarled Kell, "now the fucking vampires will know what we plan! Why did you do it, Myrtax? Why?"

"I was... I lost control!"

With a snarl, Kell hefted Ilanna and in a sudden stroke cut off Myrtax's head. There came a stunned silence, a pattering of blood, and the body flopped to one side, the head rolling to a stop in crimson snow.

"Why did you do that?" cried Nienna, suddenly, stepping back from Kell, face twisted in horror.

"He was a traitor, with a direct bloody link to the Vampire Warlords," growled the old warrior, and stared hard at Nienna. "I'm sorry. I seem to have *lost control*." He gave a grim smile, and pointed with a stubby, powerful finger. "Now stop asking damn fool questions and get back up the hill to Grak. We have a lot to do, and because of this offal," he spat, "we need to move fast. Saark!"

"Yes sir!" He snapped to attention, then slumped again. He pulled a pained face. "Did I really call you sir? Shit. Something bad must have got into me."

"And indeed," said Kell, voice low, temper now gone, mind drifting into a mood for battle, "something bad *will* get into you if you don't listen. She's called Ilanna, and she takes no prisoners. We will march east on Jalder. It's not a complex plan. You finished all the weapons? And collars?"

"All done," said Saark. "The smiths worked through many a night. Do you think they'll be effective?"

"If they don't, we'll soon be dead," said Kell. "Let's use what remains of the daylight and close down a few leagues; we can talk and plan tonight. GRAK!"

"Sir?" bellowed the bearded warrior.

"Let's move out."

"Yes, General!" bellowed Grak, and leading three thousand armoured convicts, now bearing swords and shields and helms of polished steel, they descended into the valley churning snow to mud.

Kell glanced down at Myrtax. He was touched by sorrow for a moment. The man had a wife. And little ones. But then Kell's heart went hard. For Myrtax would have sold them all out for his own safety. His cowardice had become his undoing... And a lesson had to be shown to the many fighting men around Kell: that traitors would not be tolerated. Dealt with swiftly. Harshly. Without mercy.

"Goodbye, old friend," he said.

Governor Myrtax continued to bleed into the snow.

• • • •

The two new Divisions of Falanor men moved in discrete units. The Black Pike Mine men were grim, it had to be said; but not as grim as the Blacklippers, who considered themselves born to die.

Grak and Saark headed one column, and Kell and Dekkar the other. Nienna rode with Saark, and though this irked Kell, he accepted it. She was upset with him for killing Governor Myrtax, and one day, he knew, she would understand his act. Now was not a time to be planning. Now was a time for action.

After half a day's marching, when they stopped by the edge of a young forest to refill waterskins and eat hurried meals of oats and dried biscuits, Kell strode to Saark. "We'll be joined soon by an old friend," he said, and frowned, feeling like an intruder on Saark and Nienna's conversation. Saark grinned up at him, but Nienna's face remained set in a frown.

"What, old friend?" she said.

"Myriam."

"What?" spluttered Saark, spitting watery biscuit down his pink shirt, "I'll kill the bitch, I'll rip off her head and piss down her neck! The bitch! The back-stabbing *whore!*"

"No," said Kell, and squatted down beside his friend. "In the Valleys of the Moon, I was dead, lad. About to be slaughtered by that huge fucker," he gestured to the mighty figure of Dekkar, who was talking quietly with some of the most senior Blacklippers and examining a steel collar. "Myriam had been following me. She came to my rescue. Without her, Saark, Nienna, I would be *dead.*"

"She betrayed us, grandfather," said Nienna, softly.

Kell shrugged. "Then she rescued me. She redeemed herself."

"Does that mean you'll cut off her head, like poor Myrtax?"

"*Poor* Myrtax stuck a knife through the ribs of a good soldier. That man had a family, Nienna. Little girls, by all accounts. Little girls who will grow up without their father thanks to the betrayal of Myrtax. And down to his big mouth and runny brain, we might all well be walking into a trap at Jalder. This game has not played out yet."

Nienna shrugged, blushing. "Well, why go, then?"

"Because we must!" snapped Kell, feeling his temper boiling once more. He struggled to control himself. "Listen. I'm sorry. I just... I have so many hundreds of things running through my brain! I am a warrior, not a general. A killer, not a damn tactician.

I am out of my world, and trying my damn best. But the only thing I truly know is if we don't make a stand, if we leave the spread of this vampire plague unchecked, then one day, and one day soon, we will all be dead."

Nienna nodded, and Kell rose. He pointed at Saark. "When she arrives, lad, you behave. You hear me?"

"I hear you, Kell. And Kell?"

"Yeah lad?"

"Don't worry. About the battle. We have some good men here. Some tough, hardy, unbreakable warriors, that's for sure."

Kell sighed. "I know we do. The great irony is it's up to the condemned to save the innocent. Still. I'd rather this honour and task had gone to somebody else. I feel uncomfortable wearing a general's helm."

"You'll do grand, Kell. You always do."

Kell snorted, and moved off to talk to Dekkar and Grak.

"Nice to see he's grumpy as ever," laughed Nienna.

Saark smiled, but tension throbbed behind his eyes. Myriam! What a... complication. Now all he needed was a few irate ex-girlfriends to turn up as well, pregnant and waving invoices for food and lodging, and closely followed by their even more irate husbands bearing spears and torture implements.

"Bah," he spat, and rummaged for another biscuit.

Saark watched Myriam arrive at a distance, and she dismounted and walked with Kell for a while, chatting. Saark glanced at her a few times, and Grak slapped him on the back. "She's a looker, eh lad?" he rumbled. "Look at those long legs! Wouldn't mind them wrapped around my back, if you know what I mean."

"Yes, Saark," said Nienna, glancing up at him. "Wouldn't mind them wrapped around your back, eh?"

"You know what?" said Saark, scowling. "I'm starting to hit that point where I've had my fill of women – for a lifetime!"

"Nonsense," boomed Grak, pushing out his chest. "The day I tire of a woman's fine company is the day they bury my casket."

"Not long, then," smiled Nienna, sweetly.

"Little lady," scowled Grak, "that's not a very good thing to say to a man on his way to a battle."

"Well, you talk about women as if they're objects! As if we can't damn well think for ourselves! Let me tell you something, Grak, you bastard, maybe if you'd treated a woman as an equal instead of some cheap slab of meat for the night, *maybe* you'd have a fine warrior wench right here by your side now! As for me, I'm sure I can get some more equitable talk back there with the rapists and killers. I take my leave."

Nienna stalked off.

"She's a lioness, that one, that's for sure," said Grak, grinning.

"Aye," muttered Saark, weakly.

"I pity the man who ends up with *her!*"

"*Aye,*" mumbled Saark.

"And just think, not only have you to get past the sharpened tip of that acid tongue, but if you put a bloody foot wrong, you get Kell's axe in the back of the head!" He roared with laughter. "Not only would you have to be a masochist, you'd have to be as dumb as that mule back there." He gestured with his thumb.

"She's a donkey."

"Eh? Whatever. As dumb as that donkey back there, is what I said. And by the gods, lad, she's a dumb beast if ever I saw one."

"I suggest you leave Mary out of this," said Saark, tetchily, and moved off to walk alone, throwing occasional glances to Myriam – who was laughing at some ribald jest Kell had made.

"Damn them all," he muttered from his psychological pit.

"Saark?"

Saark half-rose from the fire, but Myriam showed both hands as she crept from the darkness, and he slumped back down with a curse.

"What do you want? I thought you wanted me dead last time we met. I *seem* to remember your certain attempt to drown me."

"I'm sorry."

"It's not good enough, Myriam! You can't just roll back into camp, apologise, and get on with your plans for world domination! What is it this time? Take over our army and conquer the Vampire Warlords that way?"

"I'm sorry. Truly. I was… out of hand. I wasn't thinking clearly. It's just, I love you, Saark. I was thrilled by our union. You understand? We are both vachine, and there's not many left now after the devastation of Silva Valley. We have to stick together, you and me." She shuffled closer, and punched him on the arm.

"Ha. Yes. There is that."

"I'm *sorry*, Saark. All right? I promise I won't do it again."

"Which bit?"

"Which bit would you like me to promise?"

"Er, for a start, you can promise not to kill me."

"Sure. I promise not to kill you." She leant in a bit closer. Saark inhaled the musk of her skin. He groaned, as that familiar feeling washed over him and he tried to focus and tried to keep it clear... but could not. *I am cursed. I am deviant. I have a brain like a child and the lust of a platoon. What am I to do with myself? What is the world to do with any man like me?*

Myriam kissed him.

And in the shadows by the edge of the campfire, Nienna stood bearing two cups of honeyed mead, and cried in the darkness, her tears glowing with the colour of the flames.

It was dawn.

Jalder sat below them, sheathed in an early morning mist which made Kell twinge in panic. If the vampires knew they were coming... if they had Harvesters, and blood-oil magick, and ice-smoke... well, the battle would be over before it had begun.

"Thoughts?" said Grak, lifting the heavy sword he had chosen.

They had sat up long into the night, formulating a basic strategy and trying to consider every eventuality. They sought to draw the vampires out onto the plain before Jalder for an open, pitched battle. There, the heavy formation of soldiers with shields and long spears could possibly counteract the vampires' advantage of speed and agility. If their army was drawn into the city itself, however, they lost all the benefits of armed and armoured units.

Kell was convinced they could do it.

"It is their arrogance," he argued. "They *will* come, they'll drift out from the gates and they *will* fight. The stench of our blood will be an overwhelming factor for them! They must have hunted down most of the humans in Jalder now; that means no fresh meat, no fresh blood! And they need fresh blood like a drowning man needs oxygen. When we roll up, it'll be like a plate of succulent beef stuck under the nose of a starving man! Trust me on this."

"I'm not convinced," growled Dekkar. "I think they'll run and hide when faced with a superior force."

"Whatever happens," said Kell, "we must not be drawn into a running street battle. These bastards are cunning. They'll lay traps in the streets, in back-alleys, leap from the rooftops. No. We must get them out here. This is where the battle must be."

And now, the two Divisions descended from low hills. Jalder lay silent, its ancient dark stones steeped in history and lore, its streets and temples and houses and schools silent, slick with ice and mist, echoing with horror from the recent atrocities.

"So far, so good," said Saark; he looked sick.

Kell glanced at him. "You took your happy leaf?"

"I have decided to give up women!"

Kell snorted in laughter, as the five thousand men, ranged fifty men wide and ranked a hundred men deep, a tight fighting square with shields presented to all sides, moved slowly down from the hills.

"An easy claim to make as we head into battle!"

"I mean it! Do not mock me!"

"Well then. I give up whiskey!" grinned Kell.

"And I give up killing generals!" boomed Grak, slapping Kell on the back, and around him many men laughed, helping to ease the fear which was creeping stealthily through their ranks as fluid as any ice-smoke.

They made the plain below. Behind, on the hilltop, Myriam and Nienna sat with another fifty or so women from the Black Pike Mines who had travelled with the army in order to help feed the soldiers and repair clothing and armour. They also carried bows and knives, for none believed this would end well. They were hardy women, stout and tough, with ice in their eyes and fire in their bellies. They frightened Nienna.

"This is it, then," she said, voice almost a whisper as the soldiers spread out on the plain between the hills and Jalder's main western gates.

"Seemed more romantic, back then," agreed Myriam. "Save Falanor! Raise an army and attack the vampires!" She shivered, suddenly, and pointed. "Look. The gates are opening."

Kell halted the army, and the huge bristling mass of soldiers waited. Shields were held tight, and spears stood proud to attention. A cold wind howled across the plain as the gates squealed on rusting hinges. Snow whipped up in little eddies that danced across the bleak place.

A single figure stepped out. It was a man, tall and lean, his face angular and with the blood-red eyes of the vampire. He walked forward with a curious gait, trailing through the compact snow, his eyes fixed on the large body of fighting men without any fear whatsoever.

He halted. He waited.

Kell stepped forward from behind the wall of shields, and approached the tall vampire. And Kell hissed as recognition bit him. This was Xavanath, Principal of Jalder University. Kell had met him once... when the man had been *human*. He was an honourable and respected academic. Now, blood stained his claws, and strips of flesh trailed from his fangs. And... and he *stank*. He stank like a corpse. He stank of death. He stank of murder. The smell washed over Kell and made him want to vomit, and it was something he had never considered before; the *vampires* were trapped in their own filth, their blood coagulated, their flesh necrotic. The longer they remained vampires, the more they began to *rot*.

"You are the leader?" said Xavanath, with all the haughtiness of any true academic superior.

"By all the gods, lad, you stink like a fucking corpse. But then, excuse my manners. You are one."

A ripple of laughter shifted through the ranks, and Xavanath stared hard at Kell. He made a clicking sound, a show of annoyance...

As if dealing with a disobedient child.

As if dealing with a naughty student.

"Kuradek, the great Vampire Warlord, instructs you to immediately lay down your weapons and accompany me into the city. He guarantees your safe passage. He would talk the terms of a truce." Xavanath's blood-red eyes ranged across the soldiers, with their new armour and shields and spears. "There is no need for slaughter on this day," he said, his words soft but carrying to every man on the plain. Then he smiled, and it was a sickly smile, like the smile on the face of a man dying from necrotising fasciitis. "Your slaughter, that is."

"Well, lads," boomed Kell, turning and surveying the five thousand hardened men behind him. "He's come out with fighting talk, that's for sure!" Kell launched himself at Xavanath in a sudden blur of speed, Ilanna slamming up and over, and cutting vertical down deep through the vampire's neck. Xavanath stumbled back, claws flashing up but Kell followed, dragging Ilanna out as the vampire hit the snow; the second blow cut the vampire's head from his shoulders, and the corpse slowly melted into a wide, black, oily puddle.

Kell's head came up, and he glared at Jalder – at the silent city. "Come on, you fucking whoresons!" he screamed. "Don't cower in the dark like little girls, come out and face us! Or is Kuradek truly a coward? Is Kuradek the Vampire Pukelord cowering and whimpering in the corner, sucking his own engorged dick and vomiting up his dinner in rank open fear!"

Kell strode back to the ranks and planted Ilanna's haft between his boots. He waited.

Saark sidled forward.

"I don't mean to be pedantic, old horse," said Saark, "but wasn't that a bit... rash?"

"The only rash here is on your crotch!" snapped Kell.

"Shouldn't we have at least *talked* to him?"

"No. We have to piss them off. We have to draw them out for a fight. If we head into the city now, where they are strong, we lose the advantage of armour and steel. We cannot let them hunt us down. We must do battle."

"Why won't they come?"

"They don't like the light," grinned Kell, his face filled with humour but eyes narrowed, evil almost in the gloom. He glanced up at the clouds, heavy, black and thunderous above. "But there's a storm coming. They'll like that. They like the cold, and they like the gloom. Pray for snow, Saark. That'll bring them to us..."

Even as Kell was speaking, the sky overhead darkened perceptibly. Clouds rushed across the sky and thunder rumbled, deep and ominous. Then the gates to Jalder opened fully to reveal – a woman.

It was Sara. Kell's daughter. And she was smiling.

Kell glanced at Saark. "Go back. I'll deal with this bitch."

"What are you going to do?" said Saark, voice trembling.

"What I have to."

"You *can't*," hissed Saark, grabbing Kell's arm. "Nienna's back there! She's watching!"

Kell took hold of Saark's shirt and dragged the dandy in close. His talk was fuelled with fire and spittle. "I *must!*" he hissed into Saark's face, then threw the ex-Sword Champion back, where he stumbled in the snow and glared at Kell.

Kell strode out to meet Sara. Her hair was dark, her eyes shrouded in gloom, her face beautiful. Kell swallowed. He loved her. Loved her so much. Losing her to bitter internal family feuding had been a hard pill to swallow. Something he tried to put right again, and again, and again. But Sara was a stubborn woman. One of the worst. Kell had laughed at the time; "She gets it from me," he would chuckle, but in reality there was no humour about their situation, and it had to be here, and now, all events spiralling down to this battlefield outside Jalder. Between the castoffs of Falanor, and the vampire converted.

"Father," said Sara, striding forward. She glanced down at the beheaded corpse of Xavanath without compassion. When she looked up, there were tears in her eyes, and this confused Kell. Why was a vampire *crying*?

"Go back to your whining master, girl," snapped Kell. "This is no place for women."

"Spoken like the true woman-hating bastard you are!" she hissed, but still tears trickled down her face and it was this contrast which slowed Kell. He knew he had to kill her. And fast. She was deadly, he could sense it, and the world suddenly went slow, honey treacle, and Ilanna was there in his mind like a ghost...

Talk to her, Kell...

Listen to her, Kell...

You know you must.

Sara leapt, suddenly, claws slashing for Kell's throat. He leaned back, but her fist struck his jaw, rocking him – his boot came up into her groin, and his free hand grabbed her hair and with a grunt, he planted her head against the snow. She struggled violently, but Kell lowered Ilanna so the arc of the left butterfly blade pinned her throat to the ground like a stationary, waiting guillotine.

"Go on!" she snarled, legs still kicking. "Do it, *father*, you always wanted to. You were ever the fucking hero. Well kill me. Kill your own daughter, just like you killed your own fucking *wife!*"

Kell's eyes went hard, and with Sara in place, he pulled free his Svian and rammed it down hard into her heart. She started to kick, and struggle, but Ilanna pinned her in place, held her there like a slaughtered lamb.

Her eyes locked to Kell. And she smiled. And blood bubbled from her mouth.

"You remember the south tunnel?" she said, her teeth crimson, her legs still kicking. Her eyes were locked to Kell now, locked in death, and his teeth were gritted, and tears were on her cheeks, and snow was falling, a gentle drift all around them as huge dark clouds unleashed. Kell gave a single nod. "It is open," she said, on a flood of black blood, "and Kuradek lies at the end."

Then she spasmed, and Sara, Kell's daughter, died.

Saark ran up beside Kell, and the huge old warrior stood, slowly, wearily, and began to clean his Svian whilst staring down at his dead daughter. He remembered holding her as a babe, her mewling sounds, and the incredible love and joy he'd felt surge through him. For the first time in his life, here had been something which truly *meant* something to him. A child. A child for whom he would kill... and for whom he would die. But it had gone wrong. Gone so terribly wrong.

"What happened?" snapped Saark.

"She sacrificed herself," said Kell, gently, his voice cracked.

"What do you mean?"

"She knew I had to kill her. She *allowed* me to kill her. Then she gave me information. On how to reach Kuradek."

"How?"

Kell looked at Saark, then, and the dandy saw the old man crying openly. Tears flowed down his cheeks, and into his beard, and Saark stepped in close, supporting the huge warrior, holding him.

"When she was a child, she came riding with me and King Leanoric. She was so proud, sat on the saddle of a little black pony. We'd found a tunnel, dug by Blacklippers for smuggling, way to the south of Jalder." He waved a hand vaguely. "It led deep into the city, coming up in a building near the Palace. Leanoric had it sealed. Sara has opened the tunnel for me. I know this. I *feel* this."

"To get you inside?"

"To get me to Kuradek," growled Kell.

"It could be a trap."

"This is no trap," said Kell. He took a deep breath, and stepped back. His sorrow passed, and he gazed up at the falling snow. He turned and addressed the army. "They're coming, lads! Be ready! And Saark?"

"Yes... Kell?"

"Thanks, lad."

Saark grinned. "Hey. I love you like a brother, but I still don't want to marry you. So don't get any bloody ideas, you old goat."

"Wouldn't dream of it," said Kell, and turned to face the gates.

And they came.

The vampires came...

In a wide, dark flood, pouring from the city of Jalder with screams and hisses and snarls, red eyes crazy with blood lust, many running, some crawling, some leaping in huge bounds, there were men and women and children, there were bakers and smiths, armourers and greengrocers, teachers and students, and all were snarling and spitting, fangs wide, jaws stretched back, and Kell felt the men behind waver as they realised the *scope* of the battle – for these were not just a few vampires, they *poured* from the gates which bottlenecked their charge. But outside the city they spread, spread wide into huge ranks a hundred across. There were thousands. Kell swallowed, hard. His military-trained eye swept the surging, seething ranks as they halted, and assembled, like rabid dogs pulling at an unseen leash. Kell swallowed again.

"There must be ten thousand!" snapped Grak, who had come up close behind him.

"Fuck," said Kell. "You're right." His hands were slippery on Ilanna. He turned swiftly on Grak. "You know what to do," he said.

Grak nodded, and ran back to the men. "Shield wall!" he screamed. "Long spears at the ready."

"Time for us to move, old horse," said Saark, and there was fear in his face, nestled in his eyes like golden tears.

"Yes. I know. I might be hard," said Kell, "but I ain't stupid."

They turned, and as the vampires let out a mammoth screeching roar that filled the plain from end to end with a terrible decaying sound, and charged at the army of convicts and Blacklippers, so Kell and Saark pounded back to their battle lines and the shield walls opened to allow them in. They took up their positions, each taking a long spear and bracing themselves.

"Hold steady now, lads," growled Grak, and his voice carried through the ranks, strong and steady. "Let 'em come to us! Let 'em fall on us!"

The shield wall held.

Fear washed through the men, like a plague.

Snow fell from winter skies, as dark as twilight.

• • • •

The vampires charged. The front ranks slammed the men of Falanor. Vampires hit the wall of shields, which opened at the last second at a scream from Grak the Bastard, and spears slammed through piercing flesh, throats and necks and groins and hearts and eyes, and the first rank of vampires went down thrashing and screaming, spewing blood and black oil vomit, and the spears withdrew and then struck out again, and again, and again, and waves of vampires went down falling over their brethren, but the wall was wide, too wide, and on both sides the vampire charge swung around like enveloping horns, attacking the men of Falanor from three sides now. The Blacklippers and convicts from the Black Pike Mines were strong, grim men, and although they were not soldiers, they held their ground, and they slaughtered the vampires, and the snow was slippery with blood in minutes, in seconds. A breach appeared to Kell's left, a vampire slashing a man's throat and squeezing into their fighting square of armour and spears, and Kell's Svian was out, slamming into the creature's eye and it fell with a gurgle. "Breach!" screamed Kell, as more vampires poured into the hole in the fighting wall. Short swords stabbed out, but the vampires were fast, and strong, their claws sharp, claws like razors. They fought with tooth and claw. They ripped out throats, and ripped off heads using incredible strength. Snarls echoed through the Falanor men. Screams wailed up from the mud, down amongst tramping boots and the fallen. Kell used his Svian, for Ilanna was strapped to his back, too big and hefty for close-quarters combat. He grabbed a short sword from a fallen man as a vampire leapt, an old woman with yellow eyes. He shoved the sword point into her mouth, and down into lungs and heart, ripping it out in a shower of bone and blood which covered him. Snarls sounded in his ear. Kell whirled about, but Saark skewered the vampire through the back, through its heart. Smoke came out of its ears, and it lay whining in the mud until Kell stabbed it through the spine at the base of its skull. A vampire hit Saark from behind, and Kell cut off its arm. Saark stabbed it through the eye, its punctured eyeball emerging from the back of its head. Blood bubbled and splattered across the struggling men. Kell saw their fighting square was faltering, and with sword and Svian, waded into the breach. A vampire hit him in the chest, and he head-butted it, his broken nose flaring in agony, and his Svian cut up into its groin. He felt a warm flush of blood cascade over his fist and he pushed, heaving deeper. Another two vampires leapt, and coolly Kell sliced a throat and stabbed one in the eye, but there were more, always more, and five had widened the gap, ripping off the heads of convicts with dull cracks and twists and splatters. Kell and Saark launched at them, boots slipping, screaming and shouting as snarls filled their ears, but *these* vampires had swords and metal on metal rang, the discordant clash of steel, a song of battle, a symphony of slaughter, and Kell hacked like mad and a blade whistled in front of his eyes making him step back, as a vampire landed on his shoulders and he reached up, dragging it to the floor and kneeling on its throat to stab out its eyes. Then Dekkar was beside him, had fought his way alongside Kell and there was a space around him and Kell saw why. Dekkar's huge flanged mace whirled with a sullen whine, and caved in the brains of a vampire, crushing its head down into a compact bone platter. Another blow killed a second, then a third, then a fourth and fifth and Kell leapt forward, Ilanna sliding free and together Kell and Dekkar reigned bloody slaughter on the vampires, forcing them back through the breach of the shield wall, back onto the snow-swirling plain. They stepped out beyond their comrades, Dekkar's mace whirling and crushing, Ilanna singing now, a high pitched song like the voice of a woman, a beautiful woman, a sorrowful woman, and Kell felt himself tumbling into that pit, into that dark blood pit and he was back, back there, back in that place, back in the fucking Days of Blood *and it feels good it feels right and they fall before the axe before Ilanna before her blades, and none can stand before me, not man, woman, beast, or fucking vampire* and Kell's axe slammed left, and right, twin decapitations, and heads spun up into the sky on geysers of blood. Ilanna cut one vampire in two from crown to crotch, body peeling apart like halved fruit, necrotic bowel sliding free like diseased oil snakes. She slammed left, smashing ribs and leaving a vampire writhing in the mud where Dekkar's mace crushed the woman's face. In the same swing, Ilanna drove right, removing a vampire's legs. The man floundered, walking for a moment on stumps before being consumed by mud and snow and blood. Dekkar and Kell fought on, oblivious now to the widening circle around them, and although the rest of the vampires fought on, attacking with raw screeching ferocity, they were thinning. A child leapt at Dekkar, and he swayed back but could not kill. It landed on the Blacklipper King's chest, fangs snapping forward for his throat. Ilanna caught the child vampire on one blade, tossing it back into the vampire horde. Dekkar flashed Kell a smile, and Kell, covered from head to boot in vampire blood and gore, gave a nod. There was no smile. In his head, he was in a different place. Then...

A cheer went up.

Kell staggered, and righted himself. He started to breathe, and realised he was panting, and the world slid back into focus and it was a grim place. The vampires retreated, and reformed their ranks, and their dead lay scattered in their *hundreds*, a semi-circle around the fighting square of Falanor men.

"Grak!" screamed Kell.

"I'm on it!"

Grak started reorganising the men, and from behind came stretcher-bearers, removing the wounded. Wails and screams echoed over the battlefield. The vampires watched in silence, like kicked dogs licking their wounds. Licking their balls.

Kell, a gore-coated demon, gathered Dekkar, Grak and Saark to him. "You know what must happen now."

Saark took Kell's hand, wrist to wrist in the warrior's grip. "Be swift, my friend."

Kell nodded, and moved back into the ranks, and removed his bearskin jerkin, handing it to a huge man named Mallabar. The man carried an axe, an axe that looked similar to Ilanna and which had been forged at the Black Pike Mines.

"Fight well," growled Kell.

"Be lucky," growled Mallabar.

"I don't believe in luck," said Kell, and thumped the large man on the arm. "I make my own."

And then Kell was gone, to the rear of the thousands of fighting men where several horses waited. He rode up the hill, towards the women and Myriam and Nienna. He heeled his mount to a stop, and Nienna stared up at him, face hard and white, eyes like stones.

"I had to do it," said Kell.

"You could have taken her prisoner," snapped Nienna.

"One day, you will understand."

"Today, I understand."

"And what do you understand, girl?" growled Kell.

"I finally understand your *Legend*," said Nienna.

Cursing, Kell put heels to flank, and the horse sped away over the hill, and circled to the south, away from the battlefield. Snow fell thickly. Kell rode hard, the stallion snorting and protesting at his weight and abuse. Kell slammed along, knowing that time was of the essence. The army was terribly outnumbered, and although they were fighting bravely, they would only last so long against so many enemies...

Kell entered a snowy forest, and before long could hear the trickle of a frozen stream. Hooves cracked ice, and Kell was across and galloping hard once more. Steam rose from the stallion's flanks, and the beast was labouring hard as they reached the next rise and Kell dismounted. He crouched low, eyes scanning the southern wall of Jalder. His mind was sharp with memories of Sara, the little girl on the black pony, and the laughing face of King Leanoric. In older times. Happier times. Times now gone...

There!

Kell moved through the snow, thinking back to Saark, and Grak, and Dekkar, Nienna and Myriam. Even now, Grak should be organising the women, the archers, to advance to the rear of the fighting square. They had been training hard in previous weeks, and Kell was sure they would inflict a terrible damage on the vampires...

Kell grimaced. He hoped they could hold out.

Kell crouched in a ditch by the tunnel entrance, and scowled. There were thick steel bars, thicker than anything he could ever bend. They had been wrenched open, violently outwards, as if by some terrible, powerful blast. Of one thing Kell was sure: whatever slammed through those bars turning them into splayed-out spikes and giving him a secret opening into Jalder – well, whatever it was, it wasn't human.

Kell squinted into the darkness. "Shit," he muttered, and hefted the solid haft of Ilanna.

I am with you, she said.

"That's what I'm worried about," muttered the old warrior, and touched one of the bars. It felt warm, and warm air drifted from the tunnel. Would it have rats? Or... something more sinister. Kell shrugged, and grinned. "Fuck it." *Whatever's down here, it can't be more terrible than me!*

"Kell! Wait!"

Kell cursed, and turned slowly, glancing up the ice-covered slope. It was Myriam, on foot and holding her longbow in one hand. Kell's eyes dropped to her waist, where a Widowmaker was sheathed. Kell licked his lips. He'd forgotten Myriam used to carry such a weapon, a multi-loading hand-held crossbow, powered by clockwork and packing an awesome punch. It was with such a weapon Nienna's friend, Kat, had been murdered by one of Myriam's former *colleagues*. The memory was fresh in Kell's mind, like a bright stain of crimson against his soul. In some ways, he blamed Myriam. And that weapon. That *dirty* weapon. That *underhand* weapon. Kell hated it with every drop of acid in his soul.

"What do you want?"

"I've come to help."

"You'll get in my way."

"I *need* to help, Kell! All those men dying back there, and a lot of this shit, it's *my fault*."

"Then go and fight in the battle!" hissed Kell, whirling on her. His eyes were flashing like dark jewels. "You'll get in my way! I can carry no baggage."

"Baggage, is it?" she snapped, and was close to him, and her hand slid down his thigh and he groaned, and the blade pressed against Kell's throat. She grinned into his face. "This baggage got close enough to cut your fucking windpipe out."

"I could kill you, you know," said Kell, quietly.

"I know. But what a thrill, yes? It's damn good to be alive!"

Kell looked into her eyes. He saw madness there. He saw a lot of things there. He wasn't sure he fully understood Myriam. She wasn't just complex, but unpredictable and wild. It was this which attracted him to her. This which made him interested in women again... after so long. *One woman*, he corrected himself. One woman.

Once, in the marshes of the east, Kell had been attacked by a wild *kroug* cat, a stinking shaggy beast which roamed the marshes using secret paths. Kell was in the army at the time, and as his regulation short sword slid through its belly, up into lungs and heart, so their eyes had been inches apart, Kell punched onto his back, the dying, bleeding cat above him, foul breath caressing him, entering him, a kiss from the other side of sanity. Myriam's eyes reminded him of that wild cat. Untameable. Living on the edge, dangerous, truly a creature of chaos.

Kell grinned. "You can move your hand off my leg, now."

"Do you want me to?"

"No," sighed Kell, and relaxed, and Myriam stepped back and sheathed her blade. The Widowmaker hung at her belt, longbow on her back. She was tall and fit and athletic. Kell could still taste her breath on his tongue. "Later," he muttered.

"So I can come?"

"I don't believe I have any choice."

"No, old man. You do not. Lead the way!"

"You've not dragged bloody Nienna along as well, have you? Last bloody thing I need is half my family jumping out at inopportune moments. Makes it a bit difficult to hunt vampires."

"And Vampire Warlords."

"Indeed, yes."

They crouched, watching, then eased into the tunnel. The warm air was disconcerting after the cold of the snow and ice. It was quiet in the tunnel, dry as the desert. Kell touched the walls. "What was this place?"

"An escape tunnel for royalty," said Myriam, and when Kell looked at her, she shrugged. "I think it is, although these things are not really publicised. No?"

"I forgot. You fucked your way into all sorts of academic secrets back in Vor. In your quest to survive."

"That's all any of us want," she whispered.

They crept through long, dusty tunnels, thick with grime and smelling stale, with a tangy scent, like raw abused metal. The stonework was ancient, and carved into baroque curves and flutes which made Kell frown. Why make carvings down here? Where nobody could see and enjoy? He got a sense these tunnels had an ancient story to tell; something he would never discover.

After an hour Kell could smell fresh air. The tunnel abruptly ended at an ancient, iron ladder, leading up to far distant daylight. Snow fell down through the aperture, and Kell welcomed it, breathing deep after the confines of the tunnel. He hated tunnels. Hated enclosed spaces. It reminded him too much of the grave…

"Is it safe?" said Myriam.

Kell laughed.

"What?" she said.

"There's three Vampire Warlords on the loose converting thousands into vampires; there's a battle raging on the snowy plains outside Jalder. And you're worried about a ladder?"

"I just don't want to be entombed," she said, quietly.

"Hmm." Kell started to climb, and the ladder shook, but held under his considerable weight. Myriam followed, and they appeared on the roof of a warehouse, emerging and crouching by a low stone wall. Distantly, they could hear the sounds of battle. The vampires were once again assaulting the lines of the new Falanor army.

"Which way?" said Myriam.

Kell pointed. The Blue Palace reared, and in the diffused light of the gentle snowstorm, looked ugly, gothic, ancient and evil. Kell shivered, as if with premonition. Bad things were going to happen here. Very bad things.

"We can go over the rooftops, to... there." She pointed. Kell nodded. "Come on. This is my area of expertise."

They moved, climbing a sloped roof to a ridgeline and then halting. Kell glanced over the walls which surrounded Jalder. He could see the old garrison, once housing one of King Leanoric's Eagle Divisions; now deserted, the cobbles no doubt stained with the blood of the slain.

Kell glanced back, down the hill towards the river, and saw the tiny square of his old house. His heart skipped a beat. *You've come full circle, old man. You're back where you started. Back in Jalder. Back where the Army of Iron invaded. Where the ice-smoke drifted out and took so many lives, froze so many innocent people to be just cattle for the bloodthirsty vachine...*

He glanced at Myriam. Vachine.

He shook his head.

We must go, said Ilanna, her words soft and drifting through his skull. *Kuradek awaits.*

And you want his blood?

I want him to taste the Chaos Halls. To go back to where he belongs...

Kell stood, but Myriam touched his arm. "Wait. Look."

Kell glanced back to the distant battle. The vampires had pulled back. The men of Falanor, no doubt under instruction from Saark, Grak and Dekkar, were reorganising their lines. But then Kell saw something that made his heart leap into his mouth. By the gates of Jalder were Harvesters... a *line* of Harvesters, and their hands were above their heads, eyes fixed on the Falanor men... and around their feet swirled and billowed a huge globe of pulsing ice-smoke.

"Horse shit," snarled Kell, his eyes bleak. And as his gaze drifted, through the falling snow, as if by instinct he looked to the north and saw the army that appeared through the haze. They marched in unity, black armour gleaming under winter sunlight, black helms and black swords proud and Kell's mouth went terribly dry. He could see they were an albino army, very much like the Army of Iron which had first taken Jalder. And they, combined with the summoning ice-smoke at the feet of the Harvesters before Jalder's gates... well, it did not bode well for the men of Falanor.

"Come on!" hissed Myriam.

"Look," said Kell, voice bleak, tears in his eyes. How could they battle such magick? How could they go to war against such evil – and even hope to win?

"They will fight," snarled Myriam. "They will stand strong! Come! We have our own path. *Come on!*"

They hurried across the rooftops, and Myriam signalled a place to climb to the ground. The streets were deserted, most vampires obviously out on the plain already fighting the Blacklippers and criminals of Falanor. Kell stood on the cobbles, and felt foolish. He felt lost. He felt a cold flood of *desolation* through his soul.

Kill Kuradek, said Ilanna. *You must do it! Now!*

Kell grasped the axe, and ground his teeth. They moved to a high iron gate set in a stone wall and grown about with wild white roses. The gate was open. It was almost as if Sara had anticipated their route, and Kell smiled at that.

They moved down paths, and into the cool interior of the palace. High chambers were empty, but showed many signs of destruction. Polished wooden floors were scarred with hundreds of gouges from claws, and furniture lay in smashed heaps, vases shattered, bronze cups twisted and crushed and scattered; everything showed signs of decadence, of destruction, of disrespect.

"I have a bad feeling," said Kell, voice low. He hefted Ilanna, and Myriam cranked her Widowmaker. It gleamed dully in grey light from the high windows.

They moved through endless chambers, empty feasting halls, long high corridors with stone arches, many lined with statues of past kings and queens.

"Where is the bastard?" snarled Kell, eventually, and they arrived at a sweeping set of stairs. They climbed, wary, weapons at the ready, and when they were halfway up there issued snarls…

The vampires leapt from on high, snarling and spitting, and landed lightly before Kell and Myriam. One was a small, narrow-faced man, slim and wiry, his clothing torn, his hands curled into talons, his eyes blood-red and insane. Kell blinked in recognition, and licked his lips. This was *Ferret*, renowned through Jalder as a fighter, a thief, part of the hazy criminal underworld. He had a *reputation*. He was a Syndicate Man. But they'd got to him… the bastard vampires had got to him…

The second vampire was a girl, maybe eleven or twelve years old. She was slim, with dark skin, her eyes shadowed, her face twisted into the bestial. On her fingers were expensive rings set with huge gems, a contrast to her pale vampire flesh, her yellow, crooked vampire claws…

They attacked, in a blur, Ferret launching at Kell who slammed his axe up in a vertical strike, catching Ferret in the chest and lifting him, carrying him, flinging him back down the marble steps and onto the smooth marble floor beyond, where he skidded on all fours like an animal, and came charging straight back at Kell…

"No!" hissed Myriam, but Rose was on her, spitting and snarling and there was a *slam* as the Widowmaker kicked in Myriam's hand, and Rose was lifted vertically into the air, arms and legs paddling, face snarling, blood and strings of flesh drooling from her fangs and Myriam took a step back, aimed, and sent a second bolt hammering into Rose's face. Rose catapulted backwards, her head caved in, face gone, and lay twitching on the steps. Myriam whirled, saw Ferret leap high but Kell ducked, a swift neat movement, Ilanna slamming overhead and hitting Ferret between the legs, cutting straight through his balls and up to wedge in his abdomen. Both Ferret and Ilanna continued the arc, hitting the steps and wrenching the axe from Kell's grasp. He cursed. Ferret squirmed, claws ringing against Ilanna's blades as he tried to drag the axe free from his trapped body. Kell drew his Svian, and moved to Ferret squirming on the steps. Kell smiled, a warm smile of sympathy, and of empathy, and there was compassion in his eyes. "I'm sorry, lad. Really I am," Kell whispered, voice low, and soothing, and he punched the Svian through Ferret's heart. The small man went still, muscles relaxing, and blood pooled under his body, rolling down the steps in a narrow stream, dripping from one to the next until it finally slowed, and all that could be heard in the huge hall was the tiny *drip drip drip*.

Myriam reclaimed her bolts, and reloaded the Widowmaker. She glanced over at Kell.

"You all right?"

"No."

"It's going to get worse."

"I know. Come on. Let's put this fucking Vampire Warlord out of his misery."

Saark was breathing deep, and he touched tenderly at his ribs where a vampire's claws had sliced him down to the bone. But damn, he thought, they were sharp. And fast! Too fast. Faster than him. Suddenly, his vachine status didn't feel so menacing...

"Come on, Kell, come on, Kell," he muttered, watching the vampires retreat. They were hard, and fast, but the stout men of Falanor were standing their ground well and inflicting punishing casualties on the vampires. Long spears for repelling charges, and short stabbing swords for close-quarters combat were a devastating combination. The battlefield was littered with hundreds, even thousands, of dead vampires. Those that didn't disintegrate into oily puddles or smoke.

"How you doing, lad?" said Grak, slapping Saark on the shoulder. Saark groaned. He felt like one huge bruise.

"I feel like a big fat whore sat on my face."

"I thought you would have enjoyed that?"

Saark eyed Grak. The man was oblivious to sarcasm. "Aye," he said. "I suppose I would, at that. How long before they come back?"

"Not long," snapped Grak, peering out from the shield wall. "Shit. What in the name of the Bone Halls are *those?*"

Saark stared, and his mouth went dry. From beyond the gates of Jalder emerged a line of Harvesters. They wore white robes patterned with gold thread. They were tall, with small black eyes and hissing maws, but it was those long fingers of bone which attracted Saark's attention. He had seen up close what they could do. And they frightened him, deep down in a primal place.

"They're Harvesters," said Saark.

"They look mean. Do they fight?"

"They use magick," whispered Saark, and even as he watched, the ground began to blossom with surges of summoned ice-smoke. "Bad magick. Magick that freezes a man, renders him unable to fight. We must retreat, Grak! We must run!"

"Are you crazy?" snapped Grak. "If we run, if we break ranks, the bastards will slaughter us from behind! They'll pick us off like children!"

Saark saw the white clouds starting to billow. The Harvesters became shrouded in ice-smoke.

"They'll freeze us, here, where we stand!" hissed Saark, eyes crazy. "Then suck out our blood. I've seen it done! I've seen this *before*..."

"Sir!" snapped a soldier, slamming to a halt.

"What is it?" frowned Grak.

"Soldiers, sir. Lots of soldiers."

"Where?"

"To the north."

Grak and Saark ran around the fighting square, and stopped, dumbfounded. There, on a low hill, stood at least five thousand albino warriors. They wore black armour, black helms, carried black swords, and their shields were emblazoned with a brass image.

"Holy Mother," said Grak, and drew his sword. "We cannot fight two armies! On two flanks! We will be crushed!"

"We must flee the battlefield," urged Saark.

"No! We must stand! We must fight!"

"We cannot!"

"Archers!" screamed Grak, and turned, glancing to the square of women with bows strung, arrows stuck in the snow by their boots. He glanced back to the Harvesters. Ice-smoke billowed, and started creeping across the ground towards the men of Falanor... and the vampires stood, smiling, watching, claws flexing, blood-red eyes fixed on their prey...

There came a shouted command from the hilltop, and Saark drew his own sword. His mind was blank, mouth dry, bladder full of piss. They were going to die. Frozen. Cut down. Smashed apart like ripe fruit. "Shit shit shit," he muttered. "HORSE SHIT!"

The Army of Brass, led by General Exkavar, drew their swords with eerie precision, with the rhythm of a single machine... and charged down the hill towards the Falanor army in ghostly, flowing silence...

The room was filled with incredible opulence. From carved cherrywood chests, brass and gold urns, rich oil paintings covering huge expanses of wall, thick velvet curtains and drapes, carpets as thick as a man's fist covering the floors; well, it was a room fit for royalty.

At the centre, before the heavy, oak four-poster bed, stood Kuradek.

Kuradek, the Unholy.

"You came," he said, smoke curling around his smoke lips. And he smiled.

Kell and Myriam, who had been in the act of creeping into the room thinking Kuradek was in some kind of fugue, froze. They had waited a good ten minutes, watching him, but the Vampire Warlord had ceased to move, to breathe, apparently, to *live*. But he was alive. Alive and waiting.

"Well, we didn't want to let you down, boy," growled Kell, pushing his shoulders back and hoisting Ilanna.

Be calm, she said.

Until the... Time.

Kell stepped forward, and breathed deeply, and stared up at the towering figure of Kuradek, last seen on Helltop after his summoning from the Chaos Halls by General Graal.

"I thought you'd be bigger," said Kell.

"I knew you would come," said Kuradek. "It is written."

"What, prophecies again?" mocked Kell. "Give it a rest, you smoke-filled bastard. Now then." He pointed. "You know what I want. You know why I'm here. If you don't *fuck off* back to the Chaos Halls, I'm going to give you a damn good spanking and send you home with your tail between your legs."

Kuradek chuckled. "You think to challenge me, mortal? How?" He was genuinely amused. It was a genuine question.

"With *this!*" said Kell, shaking Ilanna at the Vampire Warlord.

The huge figure was silent for some time, as if analysing Kell and his weapon. Myriam, by the door, was of no consequence. Forgotten. Worse than forgotten: dismissed.

"One of the Three," said Kuradek, finally. "Well done. Still, *She* will not be enough."

"She is blood-bond," said Kell, gently, head lowered, eyes glittering dark. "And you know what that means."

"Then show me!" snarled Kuradek, and his huge long arms shot out, claws reaching for Kell who stepped back, and Ilanna smashed out left, then right, striking Kuradek's arms away. But incredibly, as they were slapped away, Ilanna's fearsome blades failed to penetrate the smoke flesh. Kuradek stepped forward, stooping, and behind Kell Myriam's Widowmaker hummed with clockwork and a bolt struck Kuradek straight in the face. The bolt was swallowed. Kuradek laughed. He moved with a hiss, so swift Kell was slammed aside, crashing through vases and a finely carved dressing table, turning them to tinder, hitting the wall and then the floor, winded, mind a blank, stunned by the speed and ferocity of Kuradek. Of the Vampire Warlord. *"You think a fucking mortal could fight me?"* he snarled, and held Myriam by the throat, two feet from the ground, her legs dangling, her face turning purple. *"You think to challenge the might of the Vampire Warlords?"* he shrieked, and threw Myriam who disappeared through the doorway, tumbling and rolling, flapping and slapping stone flags until she came to rest in the distance, useless and broken.

Kell climbed to his feet. He felt like an old man.

He stared at the smoke fangs. He stared hard at those blood-red eyes, glowing like coals.

He tried to summon Ilanna, but she was silent.

He tried to summon the rage from the Days of Blood... but it would not come. It had gone, deserted him, left him here like a lamb to die. To be sucked dry. To be slaughtered...

Kell stood his ground, pushing against the terrible fear which invaded him. "I have killed your kind *before!*" he growled, but his voice came out like a mewl from a frightened kitten.

"Not like me," said Kuradek, and there was a flash, a blur, and he was beside Kell, towering over Kell, looking down with those red eyes and Kell was frozen, could do nothing, and he realised in horror he was *charmed* by the vampire. Charmed, using blood-oil magick, a dirty back-hand trick. Kell snarled, but it was as if he was manacled in prison irons.

Kuradek leaned forward. His eyes were an inch from Kell's.

"You see. I have you in my power. Such an easy thing. Such a simple thing to disable the great Kell. Kell, the Legend?" Kuradek laughed, a low mocking sound, and smoked curled from his mouth, and entered Kell's lungs, and made him choke.

"I would say your time is done."

Kuradek's head lowered, and his fangs sank into Kell's throat...

FOURTEEN
The Days of Blood

Kell stood in the razed city. Around him, corpses burned. He was naked. He was smeared with the blood of a thousand people. Men. Women. Children. He laughed, and there was insanity in his mind, in his heart, in his soul. These were the Days of Blood. This was what Ilanna promised. *Do it*, said the voice, only this voice was not human, it was the voice of the axe, the primal voice of Ilanna – one of the Three. *We must be blood-bond. For the future. For survival.* Kell strode through the streets. When people ran before him, Ilanna cut out, chopping off legs and arms, lopping off heads. Bodies toppled at his feet, dead before they hit the ground. Gore splattered his legs. His toes squelched through pulped flesh. The gutters ran red. The cobbles were slick. Kell walked, and walked, and walked, and it took an eternity, and he wondered if sometimes he were dreaming, or in Hell, in the Bone Halls, in the Chaos Halls. He did not need food, or water, he wanted for nothing. Only constant slaughter. Only constant rampage. And the rage in him was terrible, all-consuming, and he was not human, he was not mortal. His blood flowed like lava. He had become an infection. A plague. A creature created to...

Fight.

The Impure.

To kill the impure, you must become impure. To eradicate evil, you must absorb the essence of evil. You must dance with the devils, Kell, you must be consumed by the Days of Blood, for only that way can you truly understand your greatest enemies, only that way can you become the nemesis

*of clockwork, of vampire, of wolf, of dragon, of all those other dark dreams
which will come to plague Falanor during the following years...*

It is written, Kell.

In the Oak Testament.

It is written you will be a killer, and a saviour.

It is written you must be impure, and pure.

It is written you shall never have redemption.

It is written you shall be a slave for all eternity.

Kell nodded, and walked, and accepted his fate, and reached the house and she was there, his sweet wife Ehlana, slim and naked, lying on the bed, and she glanced up and fear infused her eyes, fear and confusion and horror, and then she recognised him, and started to rise –

"Kell?"

"Shh," he said, and Ilanna slammed down, but the blades did not smash her apart as they would normal flesh and blood and bone, they cut into her spirit, and with a cry, a simple "No!" she was drawn from her body which shrivelled and died, sucked free of fluid, sucked free of fire, sucked free of her terrible dark *magick* and Ehlana, Kell's wife, Kell's love, was taken and *absorbed* into the axe. She melded with steel. Wasn't that the spell she cast? To make Kell immortal. To make Kell a Legend. She had seen the visions. She had seen the following darkness. And they needed a hero. They needed somebody who could fight the demons. But her pact with the *Grellorogan gods* needed *more*. They needed life. They needed blood. They need love. They needed *magick*. Her dark blood. Her dark magick. And so Ehlana, reading the prophecies, casting her spells, creating the ultimate killer, the ultimate champion for King Searlan of Falanor... so she gave her own life, and love, and magick.

Ehlana became a prisoner of Ilanna.

Ehlana became Ilanna.

Kell's eyes flared open, and he understood, and he remembered, and bitterness flooded him and hatred flooded him, and he wanted to scream *Why, Ehlana? Why did you do this to us? I never asked for it? I never fucking asked for any of it!* But Kuradek's fangs were in his neck, biting, sucking his blood in great thirsty gulps and Kell laughed, and breathed deep, and drew his Svian and rammed it hard into Kuradek's groin. Kuradek squealed high and long like a stuck pig and Kell reached up, grasped the smoky skin of Kuradek's head, and dragged the Vampire Warlord's fangs from his flesh with trembling, smoke-stained fingers...

With a heave, Kell sent Kuradek hurtling across the room. He hit the bed, flipped over it, smashed through two of the supports with crashes of splintering timber. Kell rubbed his neck, where blood flowed from twin vampire bites, and the Days of Blood welled free and wild in his mind.

"*I am a pawn no more!*" he growled bitterly and found Ilanna and lifted her. She was cold in his hands. Cold as ice. Her shaft and blades glowed with a deep sable black – not a *real* black, not steel or iron, not burned flesh or the night sky. This black was a *portal*. This black was an absence. An absence of *matter*. A pathway.

"Welcome back, husband," said Ilanna, her voice a soft breeze through his mind.

"Why did you do it? I loved you. I worshipped you. And you left me, sitting here in bitterness, self-loathing, believing I destroyed you in a fit of bloody madness! When all the time it was your own dark magick which brought about your death."

"I am not dead, husband," said Ilanna, "I live on, in this axe, in this symbol of strength and freedom, and together we will send back the Vampire Warlords! Together, we will show them what the Legend can do..."

"I do not want this!" screamed Kell, falling to his knees.

"Want is immaterial," said Ilanna.

Kuradek had gained his feet, towering over Kell, and the Vampire Warlord leapt for the old warrior, huge claws closing around him, lifting him into the air.

"I will tear you apart like a worm!" screamed the Warlord.

Kell looked deep into those blood-red eyes. He smiled, showing his bloody teeth. "My name is Kell," he said, pulling free his arms with ease and lifting Ilanna high above his head. Her blades were a dull black hole in reality. "And it's time you went home, laddie."

Ilanna struck Kuradek between the smoke-filled eyes, splitting the Vampire Warlord's head in two. Smoke poured out, a thick black acrid smoke which filled the room in an instant. Kell stood very still as before him Kuradek stood, top half split wide open and wavering like petals on a stalk in a heavy wind. The world seemed to slow, and *groan*, and a smoke-filled corridor opened up behind Kuradek. It stretched away for a million years. Kell lowered Ilanna to the ground with a *thunk*, and cracked his knuckles, and stared down the pathway, and waited. The corridor led to a chamber of infinity, endlessly black, and from the sky fell corpses, tumbling down down down through nothingness and unto nothingness. Kuradek's glowing red eyes were fixed on Kell.

"What have you done?" snarled the Vampire Warlord, both halves of his severed, smoke-filled mouth working together from two feet apart. "What have you done to me?"

"I've sent you back," said Kell, almost gently, and there came a distant clanking of chains, and something dark and metal, like a huge hook, came easing along the million year corridor of smoke. Clockwork claws fashioned from old iron, pitted and rusted and huge and unbreakable, closed methodically around Kuradek the Unholy. They crushed him with ratchet clicks. Somewhere, there came a heavy, sombre ticking sound. Gears clicked and stepped. Kuradek screamed, and in the blink of an eye was dragged into acceleration down the corridor. Hot air rushed in, and the portal to the Chaos Halls imploded, all smoke being sucked to a tiny black dot, which flashed out with an almost imperceptible *tick*.

Kell breathed, and shivered, and rubbed at the bite marks in his neck. He fell to his knees, then used Ilanna to lever himself up once more. "What a bastard," he muttered, legs shaking, and hurried out into the corridor. Myriam was starting to come round, and the first thing her dazed eyes fixed on was Kell's neck.

"He bit you?"

"Don't worry."

"He bit you! You'll turn, you'll see..."

"He's gone," said Kell. "I can't turn into nothing."

"You killed him?"

"He cannot be killed," said Kell, and hefted Ilanna. "The Vampire Warlords are immortal. But I sent him back to the Chaos Halls. Back to the Keepers. I think *they* were pissed at his escape. I think *they* had a special present waiting for him."

"What about the rest of the vampires?"

"Let's go see."

Kell and Myriam rushed up steps and onto ice-rimed battlements. A cold wind snapped along, slapping them. Below, on the plain, they watched in stunned silence.

The men of Falanor stood in a tight unit behind their shields, spear points twinkling in the ghost light. By the gates stood a massive horde of vampires, waiting behind ten Harvesters engulfed in wreathes of ice-smoke. The ice-smoke was moving towards the Falanor men, creeping eerily across the churned snow, but at the same time an army of albino soldiers charged, in silence, like a dream, and veered at the last moment from the men of Falanor, slamming into the ranks of Harvesters and vampires, crushing the front lines which went down in a scything sea of descending swords...

"I don't understand," said Myriam.

The Army of Brass clove through the Harvesters and vampires, who started to scream and flee. Thousands of albino soldiers slammed through Kuradek's slaves, killing them mercilessly as they turned to run, swords cutting off heads, ramming through hearts. Within minutes, it became a slaughter.

Kell sat back on the battlements, pressing fingers to his punctured neck.

"What happened?" snapped Myriam. "I thought they would turn back? When you killed Kuradek?"

"But I *did not* kill him," explained Kell, patiently. He chuckled, and rested his head wearily against the wall. He closed his eyes. "The Vampire Warlords are immortal. Once they turn you into vampire kind, you stay that way. They are a parasite on all life. That's why they were summoned to the Chaos Halls. That's why the dark gods banished them there."

"What about you?" snapped Myriam. "Should I get my knife ready?"

"Me?" Kell opened his eyes. He laughed again, and shrugged. "Hell, woman, you do what you like. It would appear I am blessed. Dark magick. Or something. From back during the Days of Blood. It would appear I was fucking *made* to fight these creatures. Can you believe that?" He laughed again. A weary laugh. The laugh of the defeated. A laugh of desolation. "Only they did it thirty years too soon. Bloody prophecies. Should have them tattooed on my arse, for all the use they are."

"Prophecies? Blessed? What the hell are you talking about? Who *told you* all this?"

Kell grinned at Myriam. "The wife. Now be a good girl, go and fetch Saark and Grak, will you? They'll be wondering what happened."

"And I suppose you can tell me why the albinos turned on the vampires?"

Kell shrugged. "No idea, lass. I'm as surprised as you. But I do know one thing."

"What's that?"

"Our army is getting bigger," he said, eyes twinkling.

Kell faced General Exkavar from the Army of Brass, and General Zagreel from the Army of Silver. Both men were tall, thin, with long white hair, pale waxen flesh and the crimson eyes of the albino, although Kell knew after his adventures under the Black Pike Mountains, that these warriors were nothing as simple as humans with a difference in pigmentation. These were the White Warriors. These were another *race* entirely.

"Please, explain to me what just happened, gentlemen," said Kell, seating himself at the huge feasting table and placing his hands before him. The two generals removed helms and placed them on the scarred wood. The room had been tidied of destruction, and only these gouge marks from the claws of the vampires were evidence of recent vampire occupancy.

General Exkavar fixed Kell with a hard look. "I thought that was self-evident. We stopped your men from being slaughtered. We killed the Harvesters who brought us through the mountains, and turned on the damn vampires." He gave a glance at Saark, and curled his lip. "We will serve no more. Not vachine, not vampire, not Harvester. It is time the White Warriors took a stand."

"Why help us?" said Kell, softly.

"We share common enemies. For many years the vachine, and indeed vampires, have preyed on both our races. We should stand together. We should rid Falanor of this vermin."

"And then?" said Kell, eyes twinkling. He had twenty men just outside the chamber, swords drawn, waiting for his nod. If Exkavar or Zagreel proved to be a threat, then Kell would exterminate them, and then their men, when they slept that night. Kell could not risk another enemy rioting through his homeland.

"We will leave Falanor, head back to our lair under the Black Pike Mountains."

"Why come out in the first place?"

"We have come for our Army. The Army of Iron. They are currently *slaves* in Vor, under the command of Meshwar, the Violent. There is no way to get a message to them. So we decided a show of *strength* was the order of the day."

Kell nodded, and placed his chin on his fist. He stared at the two generals, and then over to Saark, and Myriam, Grak and Dekkar. All were now bathed, well-groomed, and fed.

After the battle on the previous day, the routing of the Harvesters and the vampires, the Army of Brass had spent the rest of the day hunting down vampires through the streets of Jalder – and putting them out of their misery. Then, slowly, the people had begun to emerge, from sewers and factories, from attics and cellars and hidden tunnels, from warehouses and cottages and holes in walls. They had assembled before the Palace, perhaps two thousand in all, a sorry mess of stamped-on humanity. Kell set Grak to feeding and watering these refugees; to finding them clothes and medicines. Grak happily organised the convicts from the Black Pike Mines, and the men had gone about their work. Only the Blacklippers, sullen and dark in mood, stayed outside the city gates. They said it would be hypocrisy to enter.

With so much organising to do, Kell and Nienna had seen little of each other. Myriam had tended the girl, and reported to Kell that she was angry and hurt about the death of her mother. Myriam tried to explain there was no reversion from the vampire; and that Kell had done her a great service. But Nienna had descended into a world of sullen brooding. Kell shrugged it off. He had more important matters to worry about than a sulking child.

"So you head for Vor," said Kell, and stroked his beard. "You are confident you can wipe out the menace of Meshwar? The Vampire Warlords are terrible indeed. Creatures of the Chaos Halls."

"We have magickers," said Exkavar. "If we cannot kill him, we can open the portal. Once open, believe me, the Keepers will come for Meshwar. They have failed in their duties, you see? They want the Vampire Warlords back as much as we want them gone."

Kell nodded. "I suggest, then, that we head for Port of Gollothrim," he said. "We must cleanse that place of vampires as well, find Bhu Vanesh, and send him home."

"He is the strongest of the three," said Myriam, looking up from a goblet of wine. "The strongest, Kell."

Kell nodded. "Still. We must fight on. Are you with me?"

"I am," rumbled Grak the Bastard, and thumped the table. "By the gods, I am."

"My people will see this through to the end," said Dekkar, and gave Kell a nod. "We are your warriors in this battle, now. We will stand by you. We will fight by you. And we will die by your side, if that is what it takes."

"Good," said Kell, and glanced back at the two albino generals. "How long will you stay?"

"We will head south at dawn. Do not worry yourself, Kell; we have no wish to rule Falanor lands. Once we have our men, and have disposed of Meshwar, we will be gone."

"Have you made an enemy of the Harvesters?" asked Kell.

"Yes. But that is a battle for another day. We have learnt much from their mastery. Now, it is time for the slaves to throw off their shackles, rise up, and smite their masters." Exkavar gave a cruel, brittle smile. "Too long have their injustices been served on us."

Again, Kell nodded, and the two generals stood, donning helms. Kell stood, and reached out to shake their hands. Both generals stared at him, but did not extend their own.

"I am sure we will meet again. One day soon," said Zagreel, his crimson eyes shining.

"Indeed," said Kell, with an easy smile, and watched the two generals leave the hall. He glanced at Grak. "I want triple guards, on every building, every gate, every fucking *latrine*, until they are gone. You understand?"

"Yes, Kell. Can you tell me something?"

"Ask."

"Tell me again why they helped us?"

"Because we have a common enemy. But what worries me, my murdering friend, is what happens when all our common enemies are *dead*. In my experience, many freed slaves are full of bitterness and hate. And that never leads to a pleasant aftermath."

"What about the men? How long do we rest?"

"Two days. They've earned it. Then we march on Gollothrim."

Kell was eating a shank of pork, juice running through his beard, as Saark tottered across the tiles before him. "Oh, such luxury again!" he beamed, and then frowned down at Kell. "What is this? A pig eating a pig?"

"I see you found the perfume again," growled Kell, dropping the shank to his plate and wiping his hands on a cloth.

"You can smell it? Does it smell fine?"

"Smell it, lad? I've smelt *sewers* with more sexual allure."

Saark moved over and seated himself nimbly at the table. Once again, he had managed to find crimson leggings, a pink silk shirt, and some heavy silver beads which were draped about his throat like the finest pearls. Saark leaned forward, and cut a small slice of cheese with his knife. "I say, Kell, one day I really should teach you to eat with a knife and fork."

"And I should teach you some manners."

"Yes, but, I mean, look at your lunch! It looks like... well, like an abortion!"

"Not really the sort of talk I want to hear at the dinner table."

"Well, it has to be better than Grak's boring drivel. Swords and helmets, the feeding of the refugees, talk of repairing the city. Gods, the vampires have only just left and they're talking about fucking *building*. Those who've survived should be out in the damn streets drinking and whoring, dancing and humping! I should say an orgy of some kind is called for."

"They've just survived a terrible ordeal," said Kell through gritted teeth.

"Exactly," smiled Saark, nibbling on his cheese.

Kell stared at him. "Listen lad, don't be thinking you're wearing that *shit* when we march on Gollothrim! Last thing we need is your early warning stench giving away any element of surprise."

"Hah! Really!"

Saark reclined, stretching, and his face was a platter of rapture. "I could always stay here, Kell. Oversee the rebuilding of Jalder. Insinuate myself into the nobility structure here; I'm sure they will have room for one with such refined etiquette as myself."

"You're coming with us, lad," snapped Kell, and continued to eat, gnawing at the joint.

Footsteps echoed, and Saark spun around. "Ah! And here is the most *beautiful* Nienna."

Kell watched the grand entrance, and he licked grease from his lips, and considered his words with care. She wore a long silk gown, silk slippers, and her lips were rouged in the manner he'd seen women employ at Royal Court. And she wore perfume almost as nauseating as Saark's.

"A couple of fine dandies you make together," he growled, at last, and grasped his tankard, drinking his ale and spilling a goodly amount down his jerkin and on the table.

"We're not... together," said Nienna, frowning, then smiled.

Kell placed his tankard down with care, and stared hard at Nienna. Then over to Saark, who grinned, and held his palms outwards in a flourish, shrugging his shoulders. "We're not," he said.

Kell returned to his meal. "Good," he said. And as Saark and Nienna, whispering and giggling, moved towards the arched opening leading from the hall, Kell snapped, "Go pack your stuff. We'll be leaving early in the morning."

"So, just one last night of civility?" said Saark.

Kell glared at him. "Looks that way," he muttered.

Nienna watched Saark undressing. He was a little drunk, but she didn't mind, because she was too. She slid deeper down under the covers luxuriating in their softness, and the firmness of the bed. She wasn't used to such opulent surroundings.

"You still want me, Little One?" whispered Saark, removing his trews in the shadows. Nienna felt a thrill course through her veins. It was like dying. No, it was like being *born*. Born into a different world, at least.

"I want you," she said, husky.

He came to her, sliding under the covers, his flesh warm, soft, and he touched her and she writhed, responding to the delicate caress of his fingers. He was gentle. He was caring. He was skilful. He was kind. He kissed her, and they lay like that for a while, lips connected, tongues darting, his hand between her legs teasing her.

Nienna pulled back.

"Do you love me, Saark?"

"I love you," he said, and the words slid from his mouth like honey from a spoon.

"I bet you say that to all the women," she said.

"Only the ones I love," he said. "And I love you."

"Did you say it to Myriam?"

"No."

"I bet you did."

"I did not. I loved another woman – she was betrothed to another. She was Queen Alloria. She betrayed me. She was Graal's puppet on a string. I felt like a fool, and so the words do not come easy."

"So... you mean it?"

"I mean it, angel."

Nienna drew her to him, and as he entered her she gasped. Her hands raked his hair, cut trenches down his back, grasped his buttocks and pulled him deeper, with lust, with urgency, with open raw desire. "Fuck me, Saark," she whispered in his ear, biting the lobe and feeling him work harder. He liked that, she'd discovered.

"I'm trying," he muttered, biting her neck and then – withdrawing, at the last moment. His brass fangs gleamed under stray strands of moonlight. Saark hissed, but Nienna was too lost to the moment to recognise the danger. Saark shook his head. *How long can I live between worlds? How long can I suppress my vachine instincts?*

Blood. Blood-oil.

The desires increase…

"How long will you love me?" said Nienna.

"Until the day I die," crooned Saark, and the silk under his hands felt fine, the woman beneath his flesh felt succulent, and his perfume filled both their nostrils with its charm and sophistication.

"That might not take very long," came a low, cold voice, and a figure was there and it filled the room, filled the sky and Saark squawked and scrambled from Nienna, falling onto his back and sliding from the silk scattered bed with a *thump*.

"Kell!" he breathed.

Kell filled the space. He was vast, a giant, a titan, a god. His face was bathed in shadows, gloom was his mistress, darkness his master, and Kell stood with Ilanna lifted against his chest and Saark felt fear, knew fear, for this was it, the end, his death come so soon and for what? For the simple pleasure of a girl? *There are worse ways to die… Shit!* The axe glinted, dull in the darkness, moonlight tracing tiny chips in the black iron butterfly blades. Saark could not take his eyes from that axe. It was bigger than Kell. Mightier. It filled the universe. It drank in stars. It *was a pathway to the Chaos Halls and now, NOW Saark understood and he felt the wonder and vast dread and cold hydrogen horror of the weapon, more ancient than time, an eternal devourer in the dark. That was how Kell fought the Vampire Warlords. That was how Kell took on cankers, and vachine, and vampires, and gods. For Ilanna* was not just metal, not even demon-possessed metal. She was a symbol. She was a pathway. She was dark magick made whole. She was Chaos, pure Chaos, in the form of a weapon wielded by Man. And she controlled Kell. Saark felt it. *Knew* it. Here, and now, Kell was not his own person and he always said it was the whiskey which forced him into unreasonable violence. However. It had never been the liquor. No. It had been the *axe*.

"Damn you, do it!" screamed Saark, hands clawing at the thick Ionian rugs. "Get it over with! Cut my bloody head off!"

There came a pause, a slice through the realms of time, and the world ran slow on its shifting axis. Then Kell leant forward, and his face was a writhing mass of war, contorting, a raging inner battle. Through gritted teeth, he growled, long and low and slow, "You've earned it, by all the demon shit that roams the planet, you've earned it, Saark."

"I'm sorry! Sorry, Kell! I love her!"

"He does, grandfather." Nienna was standing, naked, skin pure and soft and white, her eyes glowing as if filled with molten love. She moved to Saark, stood before him protectively, like some faerie creature from dreams come to defend the weak and downtrodden. "I will not let you do this."

Kell stood quivering, torn, huge muscles tense, Ilanna lifted high and ready for combat and slaughter. Then, slowly, he slumped back, seemed to fold in on himself until he was simply a mortal once more. A simple old soldier with a bad back, arthritis, and in need of a simple life.

"I'm sorry, Nienna," he said.

Nienna smiled, and reached out, and touched his arm.

"I'm sorry for being the village idiot. I'm sorry for being stubborn, and rude, and brash, for my bad temper and threats and worst of all, for treating you like a child. You are a woman. I can see that now."

"Yes," she said, voice a lilting rose. "I am a woman."

"Do you know how hard it was?" said Kell, and tears were running down his cheeks, through his beard, making it glisten. "To kill Sara? My own flesh and blood? My own little girl? Shit." Kell shook his head, half turned, then turned back. He glared down at Saark. "You're one lucky bastard's bastard," he said.

"You think I don't realise that?" snapped Saark.

Kell waved Ilanna casually at the popinjay. "Get some pants on. Walk with me."

"But it's freezing out there! It's the bloody middle of... the... fine, fine, I can do that, it's not a problem, if that's what you want, that's what we'll do."

Kell walked fast down the huge hallway. High above, dark towers and pillars glistened. Huge archways and the carvings of ancient demons were hidden in shadows. Saark slapped along, bare-foot beside the huge old warrior. He eyed the axe nervously, not totally convinced this wasn't some secret ruse to get him alone and decapitate him.

Kell halted. Saark stopped, also, but not too close. Never too close.

"You look like pampered donkey shit," said Kell, gesturing Saark's bedraggled appearance, silk shirt hanging out his trews, feet bare, toenails blackened from far too many weeks marching the mountains.

Saark smoothed back his long dark curls. "Hey. We've had a rough few weeks, haven't we, Kell?"

"So we have, lad. So we have."

There came a long pause.

"Is there a purpose to this little chat, Kell? I'm freezing my balls into orange pips and there's a good warm bed, er, waiting for me." He stopped. Kell was glaring. "Er..."

Kell waved his paw. "Don't fret. It's something I'm going to have to get used to. Isn't it?"

"I, er, I suppose so."

"You'll look after her, Saark, won't you?" Kell had turned away, but Saark read the anguish in his words. Here, the mighty Kell was at last relinquishing hold on his precious granddaughter. And, even more frightening, he was passing the mantle to Saark.

Now, it would be Saark's responsibility.

He shivered.

"Of course I will, old horse. I'd kill for her, and I'd die for her."

"I can ask no more than that."

Saark folded his arms, and smiled. A little of his cocky arrogance returned. "Thanks for being so understanding. At last, Kell, you've allowed the girl to flower into a woman! She deserves that, after everything she's been through. She deserves her own life, her own freedom, not your iron shackles."

Kell eyed Saark up and down, nodding. "Aye. I suppose she does. But just be warned." He pointed with one large, stubby finger. "If you disrespect her in any way, I can still come looking. I'll cut your fucking head down the middle with the same thought I'd give to squashing an ant."

Saark shivered and frowned. "Yes. Yes, I know that, old man. I'd not forgotten all our previous... discussions!"

• • • •

Kell sat on his own bed. The night was dark and cool outside the palace windows. Distantly, he could hear song, and smell woodsmoke. He sat, and thought about the past, about the things he had done, and brooded, long and hard. It was all wrong. All bad. This wasn't the way his life was supposed to turn out. Not the way it was supposed to be.

I'm here for you, Kell.

Go to Hell! Ha, I forgot, you're already there! And by your own treacherous dark magick hand, I might add.

I was only trying to do what was right. What was best for Falanor; for the people. For the innocent and weak!

Damn the people, snarled Kell internally. And he felt Ilanna, felt *Ehlana*, shrink back from his rage. It was pure and bright, like a new born star in his soul. *What about us? What about the life we had? The life we should have had? You condemned us, woman! And you condemned me to a life of violence, and here you are, filling the axe with black sorcery in order to help others. WHAT ABOUT US? US! YOU DESTROYED US!*

Ehlana faded, and Kell sat there staring at the weapon. Well, they were blood-bond now. But more. Ilanna contained the soul of the woman he loved, and who, in reality, he would always love...

Until the end of time.

Until the stars flickered out.

Kell curled up on the bed, and slept alone.

"Kell?"

Kell groaned, and sat up. "What is it?"

"It's me. Myriam."

"Ahh. Yes. I could never forget you! That poison sluicing round my veins makes my joints feel on fire *all the fucking time*. So nice of you to call in. Just what I need in the middle of the night. A chat with a riddling mad woman."

"Mad? Maybe I am," said Myriam, and moved in close, sat on the end of the bed, and Kell found himself lost for words. He stared at her, as she whispered, "I am here for you."

Eventually, he said, "What do you mean?"

"You know what I mean. I don't believe you're that fucking naive."

"Myriam, there's something you should know..."

She laughed, and took hold of Kell. She was amazingly strong. She had always been strong, but with her added vachine clockwork she was nearly a match for the mighty warrior...

"Don't tell me. You're married?"

Kell pulled a face. "Well..."

"Shh," she said, and placed a finger against his lips. Then she kissed him, and Kell sat there for a while and let her, and slowly, like a behemoth rising from a slick mud pit, Kell started to respond. They kissed, and Kell placed his large hands on Myriam's shoulders, and pushed her away.

"I cannot do this," he said.

"I think you should," she said.

"No."

"What, I didn't realise you were *that old?*" she mocked. "Old, yes, but not past it."

"I'm not," he said.

"Are your teeth still your own? Do you piss in a bag attached to your leg? Is that really your own hair and beard, or something pasted in place like they do in the decadent theatres of Vor?" She smiled sweetly. "I thought you were a hero. A *Legend*, damn it!"

"Curse all women with sharp tongues," said Kell.

"There's a simple way to make me quiet," she smiled.

Myriam took a step back, and quickly undressed. She stood naked before him, hips swaying a little, her eyes wide and a friendly smile painted on her face.

"Come to me," she said, and distant, like the steady lapping rhythm of the ocean, there came a muffled tick *tick tick tick tick*...

In silence, Kell complied.

The new Falanor army marched in two discrete columns. One column was led by Dekkar, a grim host of Blacklippers in three marching lines. They had lost four hundred men at Jalder to the vampire hordes, and this had made them yet more determined, more hate-filled, and resolute to expel the enemy from their world. The second column, the criminals from Black Pike Mines, had lost nearly six hundred men during the fighting – or at least, six hundred who would never fight again. This now gave Kell a fighting force of just over four thousand. Not exactly the Eagle Divisions of King Leanoric! But at least the Army of Brass and Army of Silver had gone on ahead, to Vor, leaving them a clear path, now, a clear goal: Port of Gollothrim. Where Bhu Vanesh ruled.

Kell marched with a soldier's stride, Ilanna slung across his back, breathing deeply and occasionally whistling an old battle tune, or singing a ribald verse from a battle hymn. He soon had many of the men smiling, and some even joined in, their rolling song echoing out across the valleys and frozen woodlands of Falanor.

Saark sidled up to him. "You're in good form," he said, glancing up at Kell with narrowed eyes. Suspicion riddled his face like a parasite.

Kell stared at the dandy. "What the *fuck* are you wearing now?"

"It's the height of fashion in Vor, I'll have you know."

"Vor is overrun by vampires!"

"Well, I'm pretty sure they'll have better sartorial elegance than *our* army. If nothing else, the vachine have ego. It's what separates men from beasts, you know? Anyway, I was wondering why you were in such a good mood. I thought you were going to chop my head from my shoulders in the night."

"There's still time," said Kell, gruffly.

"Don't be like that, Kell. We're marching to near-certain death! The gods only know how many vampires Meshwar and Bhu Vanesh have turned. The whole damn country might be crawling with the fanged bastards. The last thing we should be doing is squabbling amongst ourselves like buzzards over a corpse scrap."

"Well, they won't miss you, with an orange shirt like that. What a target! Every archer in bloody Falanor will be sighting on you. I thought they taught soldiers to be discreet. You were in the army, Saark, you should know these things."

"Yes, but I was not a common low-life low-ranker, was I? I was bloody commissioned! I was an officer, I was."

Kell shrugged. "Well, a soldier should bloody well know better! Just make sure you stand a good way from me during battle; I don't want to take an arrow destined for your peacock arse."

"You never answered my question, Kell."

"Which was?"

"You're a happy beaver. Why's that? It's not like you to be upbeat. In my experience, you have the happy and joyous nature of a widow mourning five dead sons."

"I'm marching into battle, aren't I?" said Kell, grinning sideways at Saark. "You know how it is. Prospect of a few heads on spikes, a few splintered spines. Brings me out in goosebumps of anticipation, I can tell you, lad. You know me! I'm Kell, nothing gets me hard like a good fight."

"No." Saark shook out his long, oiled curls. "There's something else."

"I'm also looking forward to carving my name on Graal's arse with Ilanna. That's something been a long time coming. After all, it's no good sending these bastard Warlords back to the Chaos Halls if Graal just goes and summons 'em again. Eh, lad?"

"You're quite right. But you forget, Kell, I am a creature of the night. Or more precisely, a creature who hunts in ladies' bedrooms, dances on mosaic ballroom floors, caresses flesh in sculpted flowery gardens, and generally behaves in a way fitting for any would-be member of nobility. You, Kell, you know weapons and warfare. Whereas *I*, well old man, *I* know sex, and you've had you some."

"Eh?"

"You've been playing hide the pickle, haven't you, old man? Well, you cunning, raunchy little squirrel, you. You secret stag, you closet pike, you rampant bull. Go on, who was it? One of the maids? Not that I'm suggesting your low-born lack of nobility excludes you from the finer and more succulent morsels of flesh on offer, I'm aware the city's been desecrated, thousands turned into vampires, and all that stuff. Leaves much leaner pickings for those on the prowl, so to speak." Saark winked. "Go on. Who was she?"

"You are mistaken," said Kell, woodenly.

"Nonsense! When I see fish, I smell fish. And when I see Kell behave like this... well, I can smell fish. Spill the beans old goat, after all, you've done enough laughing at my terrible sexual misfortunes over the last few months. Aye, and judgemental, you've been. About time I got some payback for all those quips about the donkey."

"I notice she's still here," said Kell through gritted teeth.

"Mary is well and fine and carrying a payload of shields. You, however, are changing the subject. Go on, which lucky lass got to play with Kell's Legend? It was that young woman clearing the table, wasn't it? You scamp! She must be thirty years your junior! Have you no shame?"

Saark punched Kell on the arm. Kell stared at the place Saark punched him, then scowled, and glared at the dandy.

"You've got a big mouth. You've got a runny brain. Like a bloody undercooked egg yolk, it is. You need to keep your nose out of other people's business. And *you* need to refine your character if you think you're a fit man to look after my granddaughter for the next thirty years without me hunting you down and crushing you like a beetle under my boot."

"So, it *was* the cook! A fine and stocky lass she turned out to be, and I'm always the first to admit, a woman with a goodly amount of weight and mass to her, a big lass with big bones like that – well, you can't go wrong, can you? I mean, you need a woman who can take a good, hard–"

"It was Myriam."

They walked for a while, in silence, and Saark looked at Kell, opened his mouth to speak several times, then closed it again. He tried again, and again closed his mouth. Finally, he said, "She told me she loved me. She said we would live together, be strong together. That we would never die – thanks to our combined vachine energies. She said we were like royalty! We could achieve anything our hearts desired!"

Kell chuckled. "Just before she tried to drown you, if I remember it rightly?"

"Harsh, Kell, harsh."

"Well, what do you expect? You prance about, trying your amorous expertise on any woman who'll give you the barest sniff. That's what you are, Saark. A bloody sniffer dog. I've never seen a man so damn and permanently *erect!*"

"I thought we were talking about one of my true loves, and how you'd just had your way with her? You seem to have strayed away from our topic, and indeed, the prickly edges of my rapidly breaking heart."

"She seduced me," said Kell, primly.

"*What?* Ha! What arse-rot. I know Myriam, and she is a fine judge of character."

"Maybe *that's* why she tried to kill you?"

"Amusing, Kell. Can you see me laughing?"

Kell chuckled. "No, but I can see Mary laughing. At least your ass finds my comedy a damn sight more amusing than her owner!" The sound of Mary braying could be heard, and various shouts as men tried to stop the unpredictable donkey from kicking and bolting.

"This is hard for me, Kell. You've taken my woman!"

"No," said Kell. "I have taken nothing. She gave me plenty, though."

They walked again, in silence, for quite a while.

"Hey," said Kell, staring at Saark. "You know that little sound she makes?"

"What little sound?"

"Like a bird, chirping."

"I never heard no sound like a bird chirping. What are you talking about, you old fool?"

"Sure, Saark. You must have heard her. She makes it, when she orgasms..." Kell placed his hand over his mouth. "Oh, sorry, Saark. Maybe you didn't hear it after all." Kell's booming laughter ranged across the marching columns on the Great North Road, and Saark trailed along behind him, fists clenched, face like thunder, heart ticking with clockwork.

The albino soldiers from the Army of Brass moved slowly through the valley. It was ringed with trees, and steep rocky flanks led up to Valantrium Moor to the east.

General Exkavar held up his fist, and the army halted. His captains came to him, and he issued orders to set up camp. He ordered scouts out to scan the surrounding country, and various patrols to watch over the troops as they set up base-camp for the night.

After an hour, tents had been erected, fires lit, food was cooking and night descended. Exkavar knew that further south and west the Army of Silver were setting up a similar camp. He smiled to himself. The Army of Silver would check Fawkrin, and Gilrak further south. The Army of Brass would march through Valantrium, and Old Valantrium, and then both armies would convene at Vor and smash the vampires there. The remains of the Army of Iron would join, forming the closing claws of a perfect manoeuvre, and Vor – the capital city of Falanor – would belong to *them*. To the *White Warriors*. And the *Harvesters* with whom they worked...

Exkavar moved to his tent, and slowly removed his armour. Servants brought a bowl of water warmed over the fire, and the old general washed his pale, white limbs, washed sweat and salt from his skin, from his face, from his stinging eyes. And then he sat, in a simple white robe, and ate dried meat and strips of dried fruit – the *eldabarr* fruit, grown far to the north, far past the Black Pike Mountains. In the place where the vachine ruled.

Distant screams reached Exkavar's ears, and frowning, he stood and reached for his black sword. He ran from his tent – and the world smashed down into *chaos*. All around men were fighting, swords slashing, most of the albino soldiers in underwear or simple cotton leggings. There had been no early warning. Not one patrol had sounded a bugle alarm. And the enemy, the enemy were –

General Exkavar *blinked*, hand tightening on the hilt of his sword. They were children, and their skin was gloss black, and they moved fast, some too fast to see until they stopped, for a moment, to chop off a head or arms or legs. They glistened under the moonlight and Exkavar's stomach *churned*, not just with the simple disgust of seeing them, for they were horrible to behold, a blend of child and insect, teeth black and pointed, many with claws instead of hands, and four arms, and taloned feet. They ran and jumped and crawled and squirmed, and some had large pulsing thoraxes dangling between legs like deviant, distorted pregnant bellies. His stomach *churned* because he knew what they were, and fear ate through him as easily as the *Ankarok* ate through his soldiers. They were like a swarm, of locusts, or something more dark and terrible, and there were hundreds of them, *thousands* in fact. They slammed through the Army of Brass, and killed everyone, and all the time there was a background hissing, like a million insects buzzing and croaking and Exkavar stood, and waited to die, but he did not die, it was a miracle, until he saw a boy walking towards him and his eyes were glowing black and he was dressed in rags but Exkavar knew him, he *knew* this was The Skanda. The King.

Exkavar stood to attention as all around him men were decapitated and ground screaming into the snow. White blood splattered tent walls. Limbs flew through the air to impact with sickening crunches.

He could hear them…

we have been imprisoned for thousands of years
we are free now to roam and kill and devour
we are free to take back the land
we are free to kill.

The Skanda halted, and looked up at General Exkavar. "You were heading to Vor?" he said.

Exkavar nodded, and then blinked, for behind The Skanda walked General Graal. The man held his head high, and his blue eyes shone, but his face was riddled with patches of black insect chitin. As if he had started to *blend*. To become a part of the ancient race known as *Ankarok*.

"You have another army, south and west of here."

"I will never divulge military information," snarled Exkavar, and attacked in a blur, sword slamming at Skanda's head. The little boy did not move, but Graal's sword intervened – and slowly, Graal pushed Exkavar's weapon back. With a flick of the wrist, Graal disabled Exkavar, then his head snapped left as if awaiting instruction.

"We have no further need for him. Kill him," said Skanda.

Graal's sword cut Exkavar's head from his shoulders. Graal looked up, and all around the camp had descended into death, and now silence. The several thousand Ankarok warriors stood motionless, eyes glistening, skin glistening. They were perfectly immobile. As if controlled. As if turned to stone.

"Kell comes from the north," said Graal.

"We head south," said Skanda.

"Kell has an army, now," said Graal. "That's what the patrol told us. Maybe five thousand men. Maybe more."

"Our priority is Vor," said Skanda. "Meshwar will be driven back. We *need* that city."

"And what of Kell?"

Skanda smiled, black teeth glistening. He reached out, and patted Graal's arm. "Don't worry. You shall have your time. You shall have your chance. And you shall have revenge."

Skanda turned, and a high-pitched squeal reverberated throughout the valley. The Ankarok turned south, and like a buzzing plague of insects, headed through the forests... and towards the unsuspecting Army of Silver.

FIFTEEN
Bhu Vanesh

It was night. Kell crawled through the snow, which froze his knees and made him wince. Damn, he hated it when his knees seized up. *Getting old*, he thought to himself bitterly. *Old, and weak, and tired, and weary. Weary of the world. Weary of the years. Weary of the fighting. Everything seems so complicated now, why can't it be simple like in the old days? In the old days, Saark would have been hanged from the nearest oak if he'd stepped outside in silk and perfume...*

How decadent we've become.

How decadent...

"It's quiet," said Saark, who was lying next to Kell in the snow. "Maybe too quiet?"

"They're out there," said Kell, and his eyes scanned the huge sprawl of Port of Gollothrim below. On the outskirts were massive yards and factories, silent now, still, motionless, a ghost town within a ghost town. Machines should be grinding and clanking, Kell knew. Gollothrim was a thriving anthill, even at night. But not tonight.

The vampires had taken control...

"You know we'll not get them out for combat," said Grak the Bastard, voice low, stroking his beard. He was a reassuring mass in the darkness. Grak had proved himself to be a more than able soldier. "We'll have to go in after them. I reckon those Warlords speak to each other, up here." He tapped his head. "They'll know right enough what happened to Kuradek. Know how Kell disposed of him. There'll be no sneaking in, this time."

Kell scratched his beard. "I need to get to Bhu Vanesh. I need to bury Ilanna in his skull, open the pathway back to the Chaos Halls. They want him back, that much is for sure."

"Who?" said Saark, looking sideways at Kell.

"The Keepers," said Kell, darkly.

"You know *way* too much for a fat old man," said Saark, and shivered. "And sometimes, you can have too much insight. Me, I'd rather have a plump serving wench sat on my face, ten flagons of ale and a plate of fried pork and eggs in the morning."

Kell stared at Saark. "I have a favour to ask."

"Yes?"

Kell looked down, and seemed to fidget for a moment. He gestured to the vast sprawl of Gollothrim. "It's going to be wild down there, you know that? It's going to be *bad*. Much worse than Jalder."

"You think?"

"I have a sixth sense about these things," said Kell, quietly. "What I wanted to ask you, what I wanted to... *request*, was a promise. Something sworn in blood and honour. Can you do that for me, Saark?"

Saark stared into Kell's dark eyes. There was a glint of desperation there. Saark nodded. "Kell. I fool around a lot. But you know, deep down, I was the Sword Champion of King Leanoric. And yes, I betrayed him, but I do have honour – I have honour for my friends, and for those whom I love. I may wear handsome silks and the finest perfumes – don't comment – but when it really matters, I will kill and die if needed. You *know* that, don't you?"

"I know, laddie." Kell chewed his lip. "If I die down there, Saark, I want you to promise me you'll take care of Nienna. I want you to *swear* on your lifeblood that you will not treat her bad. You will treat her with respect and honour and dignity, help her with the hard choices in life... hell, I don't know. Be like a *guardian* for her. She's a tough girl, I know – she's my granddaughter, after all. But she's still just a babe when held against the warped tapestry of the real world. Of history."

"I will do anything for her, Kell. And for you. So yes. I swear. By every ounce of honour in my blood. By every clockwork wheel that turns and gear that steps. You know this, Kell."

Kell turned his gaze back to Gollothrim, and allowed a long breath to hiss free. He gazed past the factories and yards, storage huts, barracks, houses, schools, temples, narrow twisting streets and broad thoroughfares for the moving of goods from the docks. He could see the dark silhouettes of the ships at anchor in the bay. He could see the skeletons of many more new ships, destined to take the vampires abroad, to spread their plague to other continents in search of global dominion. And Kell knew, this would be the hardest fight of his life. He knew death waited for him down there. It looked quiet, it looked safe, but soon the vampires would come drifting out to play. And Kell had to find his way through the maze. Find Bhu Vanesh, and kill the bastard.

"You know I'm coming with you," said Saark.

"No, laddie. You stay here and look after Nienna. That must be your priority. That must be your mission. If things start to turn bad, then you take her. You get away. You take her some place safe. You understand me?"

"I understand."

"I'm trusting you, Saark, with the greatest treasure of my life. Don't let me down."

"I won't, Kell."

Even as they watched, as Kell had predicted, the vampires started to emerge into the dark quarters of Port of Gollothrim. They wandered the streets mostly in packs, some alone. They howled at the moon like dogs. They laughed and squealed, danced and fought. Kell, and Saark, and Grak watched grimly. They watched, down by the wide yard as a group of vampires cornered a woman. She screamed, and ran. They pursued her cackling like demons, and grabbed her, pulling her apart. Her arms came away spewing blood and she fell over, weeping, still alive. The six vampires descended on her, drinking her blood, laughing and singing and masturbating.

"We must go in," growled Grak, pinching the bridge of his nose. "We must end this depravity."

Kell nodded. "I agree. Go get the men ready. I want archers at the front, and we'll descend real slow. Pick off those we can, then divide into small fighting squares. If we stick to the wide avenues, we'll bring the fuckers out onto our spears. You must warn the men – never chase them into narrow alleys. They'll fall on us from above, and our long spears will be useless."

"How many in each unit?"

"I'd say fighting squares of twenty-five. Shields all round. Couple of archers in the centre of each square. We'll quarter the city, work through it methodically."

"Why don't we wait for daylight?" said Saark. "Most of them sleep."

"We'll never bloody find them," snapped Kell. "We'll waste too much time hunting in sewers and bloody cellars. No. This way we can fight them on reasonably open ground; get some good slaughterin' done. Then in the daylight, we can pick out the rest. Gather those still normal around us, they'll know where some of these vampires are hiding. Sound like a plan?"

Grak stared at where the six vampires chewed on the dead woman. He realised, stomach churning, that she was actually still alive. She was making weak mewling sounds. It was the sickest thing Grak had ever seen.

"Sounds like a solid fucking plan to me. Let's get it done." Grak crawled back, then disappeared into the dark.

Saark looked down on the city. "Kell. There's an *awful* lot of them out, now. Thousands of them."

"Good. We'll have plenty of targets then, won't we?"

"Don't you think the odds are against us?"

"Lad, the odds are always against us. From birth to death, life is just one whole shit of a bitch."

"I meant here, and now."

"I know what you meant." Kell's eyes gleamed. "You remember what I said? About protecting Nienna?"

"In some ways I'm relieved I'm not coming with you," said Saark.

Kell's hand smashed out, and stroked Saark's cheek. He grinned, like a demon in the moonlight. "Look after her, vachine. You're strong, fast, deadly. Nobody else can keep her alive like you."

Saark nodded. "What about Myriam?"

"Myriam? Why, she's coming with me, lad."

The outcast men of Falanor, the Blacklippers and thieves, rapists and murderers, extortionists and freaks, kidnappers and maniacs, the cast out and the depraved and the downright psychotic, assembled in tight military units, eyes gleaming, shields on arms, steel collars fixed around throats, swords oiled and sharpened, boot laces tightened and jaws grim with the prospect of death and mutilation as they considered the enemy – their numbers, and their ferocity.

"Let's move," said Grak, and they marched through the darkness, through the trees and over low hills, boots tramping snow and ice and mud. They found the main arterial route which ran from the Great North Road to Port of Gollothrim, and picked it up like casual syphilis, emerging from the trees like armed and armoured ghosts, eyes hot jewels, lips wet, anticipation and hatred building like a slow-boiled rage.

The armoured units approached Port of Gollothrim.

It began to snow, a heavy snow obscuring their vision.

Boots touched down on slick iced cobbles. Cold hands grasped weapons in readiness.

In the darkness, Kell and Myriam slipped away...

"Steady, lads," said Grak, voice a low rumble. The twenty-four men around him shifted uneasily in their steel cage. Behind, other units were ready. Then the fighting began...

From the gloom and snow the vampires attacked. With squeals of rage they launched at the armoured unit, and spears jabbed out, impaling vampires through hearts and throats. Grak caught a flash of fangs, and claws slid between shields. He slashed down with his sword, cutting off fingers which tumbled below pushing, tramping boots. A fanged face leered at him, hissing, spitting, and in what seemed like slow motion Grak slid his short sword into that mouth, watched the blade cut a wide smile and jab further in, into the brain, killing the vampire dead. Smoke hissed black from nostrils and it thrashed on his blade. Grak pulled back, and heard a clang from above. A vampire, on their roof of shields. He shoved his blade up, skewering a groin. More vampires slammed into the armoured unit, and swords and spears jabbed and slashed and it was chaos, but an organised chaos, madness, but controlled madness. It was a surreal world, a blood-red snow-filled insanity. All around men were fighting, grunting, pushing. Claws slashed through to Grak's left and tore off a man's face with a neat flick of the wrist. Grak saw eyes popping out on stalks, a horror of gristle and spasmodic working jaws. The man screamed blood. Grak cut the vampire's hand clean off with a short hack, then roared in anger and burst from the cage of shields and grabbed the creature, but it was strong, so fucking strong, and they wrestled and Grak was slammed backwards onto the cobbles, and the *thing* with only one hand squirmed like a thick eel above him. A spear suddenly appeared in an explosion of black blood, drenching Grak. The spear point was a hair's breadth from his face. The vampire corpse slid sideways, like an excised cancerous bowel. Dekkar grinned, and held out his hand.

"You fighting it, or fucking it, lad?" he growled.

Grak grinned, and glanced around. The wide street was empty, save for armoured units and vampire corpses. "We beat them off?"

"For now. For a minute."

The units reformed themselves. In Grak's square they had lost four men. Grak stared down at their bodies, mouth a grim line, eyes glittering jewels. He realised, with desolate horror, that they could not win this day. How many were there? How many? They couldn't kill them all.

"I know what you're thinking," rumbled the Blacklipper King, and slapped him on the back. "And the answer is – we must try."

Grak gave a nod.

"The bastards are coming back," snarled a soldier.

And through the darkness, and the falling snow, squeals and cries and giggles reverberated from walls. The noise built and built and built, until it seemed the whole world was full of vampires. Shadows cast across walls, from rooftops above, from alleyways and streets and the darkened interiors of tall regal town houses.

"Holy Mother," whispered Grak, as around him his unit looked up, around, back to back, weapons wavering uncertainly.

And they came, boots thumping in quick succession with a sound like thunder. They came, like a cancerous flood, hundreds and hundreds of vampires sprinting and leaping and cavorting from the darkness...

Command Sergeant Wood sat on the roof of the Green Church, down by the docks, and watched the old soldiers from the Black Barracks creeping into position. Old they might be, but they moved with skill and practice earned over a lifetime of fighting. They may be old, but each would hold his own in a barroom brawl. Each would fight to the death. And Wood could ask for no more.

Fat Bill crouched next to him on one side, and Pettrus on the other. Both men looked grim, faces sour like they were sucking lemons. Wood gripped his sword tight, and blinked. The old soldiers had *disappeared*. Their skills at hiding were second to none.

"There," said Fat Bill, pointing into the darkness. It had started to snow, and everything more than ten feet away was hazy and surreal. A perfect Holy Oak painting. A perfect festival, a time to relax, to put out holly on the doorstep and presents in wooden crates before the fire delivered by Old Crake and his Wraith Keepers. But not now. Not here. Those times were long gone. After all, children had little to laugh about in Port of Gollothrim now the vampires had taken over...

"What am I looking at?" said Wood, careful to keep his voice low.

"The docks."

"So?"

"What's most precious to the vampires? The ships, I reckon. They're beavering away like their lives depend on it. Building a fleet. Take their vermin plague to warmer climates, I reckon."

"But that's good for us," said Wood. "If they clear off and leave us in peace."

"We both know that will never happen," said Pettrus, darkly. "I agree with Fat Bill. We need to torch these bastards. Hit them where it hurts. We haven't enough men to take them on in battle; but by the Bone Lords, we can stick a knife in their ribs whenever we get the chance."

"Most of the lads are carrying oil flasks," said Fat Bill with a fat grin. "I think it's time we turned the night into day."

Wood gave a nod, mouth dry, and stood as Fat Bill and Pettrus stood. There came a *slap* on stone behind them, and Wood turned fast, past a blur which made him blink, stepping back, knocking into Fat Bill as his sword flickered up. The *blur* was a vampire, and her flying kick slammed into Pettrus' chest, making him grunt, stumble back, hit the Green Church's crenallated roof and flip over. There was a hiatus as the vampire hit the ground and rose smoothly.

Then a *slap* and *crack* as Pettrus hit the cobbles far below.

Wood wanted to scream, to rush to the edge and look, but a deep sickly feeling raged through his guts and he knew, knew his friend and mentor was dead and in a moment, he'd be dead too. The female vampire was smiling, and Wood felt a lurch of fear riot through him. It was Lorna, Bhu Vanesh's bitch, the vampire he'd thrown from the high tower roof, watched her break on the ground below, squirming and squealing like a kitten after a hammer blow. But she was here. Alive. And strong.

"Remember me?" she snarled, glossy crimson black eyes bright with hatred. She moved left, and Wood's blade wavered. Then right, and his sword slashed before her face by mere inches.

"I remember watching you break your pretty little spine," he said, eyes fixed on the petite blonde. She was pretty, slim, but she had changed from the woman he had once known. The skin of her face and hands looked stretched, almost fake, as if she wore a mask. Her hair, once a luscious blonde pelt, was now stringy like wire. She exuded death. To Wood, she looked no better than a rotting corpse. "And I knew you were coming. I could smell your dead stink from a hundred paces."

Lorna hissed, claws slashing, then rolled right under Wood's sword, and slashed her claws across Fat Bill's belly. She opened him like a bag of offal, and his bowels spooled out as if from a reel, his hands dropping his sword and paddling at his entrails with mad scooping motions as he tried to hold himself together.

Lorna leapt back as Wood's sword whistled past her throat, and she was smiling, and Fat Bill slammed to the floor of the roof and made panting noises as he slowly died. He waved a bloodied hand at Wood. "Kill her, kill her!" he groaned, "don't fucking bother about me!"

Wood ran at Lorna, her face showing surprise for a moment, but she back-flipped away. His sword slammed at her, cutting a line down her pale arm, and the flesh opened but no blood came out. She grabbed the wound, and the smile fell from her lips.

"You see, you cut like any other bitch," snarled Wood, and anger was firing him into the realms of hatred now. This wasn't just another vampire. This had become personal.

"You didn't kill me last time," taunted Lorna, and they circled. She darted forward, claws slashing for his throat, but his sword flashed up cutting her short. She leapt away, and back-flipped up onto the battlements. She turned, and let out a howl, and below vampires swarmed from still, silent, dark buildings. They began to climb up houses and factories and towers, towards the hidden old soldiers. Faces gleamed like pale ghosts in the moonlight. Snow melted on necrotic flesh, making them shine.

Wood ran at her, but she leapt over him in an amazing high arc, a back-flip but Wood anticipated the move and leapt at the same time, his sword ramming up in a hard vertical strike, entering her body at the core of her spine and emerging from under her breasts in a shower of black blood.

Wood landed, panting, and turned fast. Lorna had continued her somersault, landed, and cradled the point of the blade emerging from her chest. She stood, the sword straight through her to the hilt, and smiled at Wood. There was blood on her lips. On her fangs.

"Bastard," she said, and ran at him, and Wood's hands came up but she grabbed him, and she was awesomely strong, and she pulled him into a bear hug and Wood found the point of his own sword pressing into him, into his chest, and then driving in through flesh and bone, and he gasped and it burned and steel grated on bone. Lorna was close. Close enough to kiss. Her breath stunk like the grave, and her pretty dark eyes were fixed on Wood.

She leant forward. "How does it feel, Command Sergeant Wood? How does it feel, not only to die, *but to see all your old friends die?*"

Wood gasped, and pain swamped him for a moment, the world turning red and hot and unbearable. Then he caught himself from falling into the dark pit, and turned, and saw the vampires stood across the rooftops. There were several hundred. Out of the shadows rose the old soldiers of Falanor, Kelv the Axeman, Old Man Connie, Bulbo the Dull, Weevil and Bad Socks and so many more. So many men. So many soldiers. So many memories. They were surrounded, and outnumbered...

Lorna kissed Wood, first on the lips, then on his ear. Her fangs lowered towards his neck. She jerked him tighter, into her, a metal conjugation of the blade. A hard steel fuck. And her fangs caressed his neck, as she savoured the moment of the hunt. She seemed to sniff him, and taste him, and enjoy a lingering moment.

Below, on the rooftops, the vampires attacked...

Kell and Myriam crept from house to house, from street to street. They kept to shadows and moved with an infinity of care. Their aim wasn't to take on the vampire army. Their aim was to slaughter its Warlord.

"You were right," whispered Myriam, close to Kell's ear, her words tickling. "He's in the tower. How did you know?"

Kell grinned a skeletal grin in the darkness. "Intuition. These vampires. They have some fucking ego, that's for sure. Come on." They moved on through gloom, through falling snow which smelt of a distant, frozen sea. They could hear the sounds of battle now, shouting, screams, the echoing, reverberating cries of attacking vampires and *slap* of steel on flesh. Kell and Myriam did not talk about it. There was nothing to talk about. They simply pushed on, forward, further into the realm of the vampire.

Ilanna was drawn. And ready.

Myriam carried her Widowmaker in one gloved hand, and her vachine fangs were out. They gleamed in the darkness. She was as ready for battle as she could ever be.

They drifted like ghosts. Somewhere, a building burned. Vampires were screaming in the flames, and the roasting of flesh smelled like cooked pig interlaced with something subtly... *human*. Kell nearly puked, so they pulled back, crept down a different alleyway. As they left the black smoke behind they could see the Warlord's Tower.

They crouched and watched it for a while. Around the base were perhaps a hundred vampires, lounging in the snow, some walking, none talking. They seemed lethargic, sleepy, without any focus.

"What's the matter with them?" hissed Kell.

"Lack of fresh blood. They grow tired. Soon, they'll turn on one another. You'll see."

"How do you know this?"

"I feel it in myself," said Myriam, smiling and showing brass fangs. "We're not so different, them and me. No matter what they say, no matter what they think. They believe we are a deviant offspring; the Soul Stealers told me *we* were the more ancient race. We have our clans far to the north, in the cold places where humans don't travel. Me and Saark; we are parts of those vachine clans, now. Part of a distant, clockwork world. Part of an ancient heritage. One day, they will call us. And we will not be able to resist."

Kell stared at her, then shrugged. He got a sudden feeling the vachine of Silva Valley nestled deep within the Black Pike Mountains had been just *a glimpse* of what the vachine really *were*. Of their size, their might, their ferocity. Images flashed dark in his mind. Of huge clockwork vampire armies. Vast, cold and mechanical. Thousands, tens of thousands, hundreds of thousands. And Silva Valley had been an offshoot, rebels almost. And the vampires thought they had birthed the vachine – when in reality, it had been the other way round.

Kell shivered. It was too much to comprehend. Not here. Not now.

"That's a battle for another day," he said, finally, and saw the curious look in Myriam's eye. He held up a finger. "No. Don't even consider trying to convert me to what you have become. You had a good reason for becoming vachine, Myriam. A damn good reason. But I'm happy to die like any other old man."

"You can live forever," she whispered, and kissed him on the cheek.

"Sometimes, I think it's better to die," he said, with an inherent wisdom he did not feel. Then he blinked, and shrugged off her vachine spell. He grinned. "Come on, lass. How do we get in?"

"Up there." She pointed to another tower, and between the two ran twin cables. "It's for passing messages, from the Warlord's Tower to servant quarters. We can climb across that."

Kell looked at the awesome height, with an equally awesome fall to iced cobbles below. "I can't bloody climb across a cable like that!" he scowled. "I'll fall! I'll die!"

"No," smiled Myriam. "You won't. You're Kell, the *Legend*."

"I wish people would stop saying that," muttered the old warrior, and sheathing Ilanna on his back, followed Myriam to the second, smaller tower. It was unguarded, and they entered through a doorway that looked like a broken mouth,

Into the breach, thought Kell, and chuckled. *Somebody up there has a fine sense of humour!*

They climbed a massive circular stone staircase for what seemed an age. Kell's knees complained. His back complained. *He* complained, but in an internal muttering monologue which had served him well for many a decade in the army. Years of running through mud, carrying logs, wading through rivers, staggering under heavy armour, fighting with a heavy shield on one arm, axe in hand, bodies falling before him, beneath him, carved like fine roast beef...

Kell blinked. A chilled wind scoured him.

The view from the tower ledge was incredible, spreading away through a fine haze of snow. Fire burned throughout the Port of Gollothrim. Vampires screamed and shrieked. Again, he could hear the sounds of battle, but could not determine the armoured units of Falanor men, of Blacklippers and criminals he had created. *Here to fight for you. Here to die for you. So get on with it! Kill the Warlord. Then we can go home.*

Is it ever that easy?

It always begins with a small step.

Kell moved to the edge of the precipice, and grabbed the cable. It seemed ridiculously thin, woven from slippery metal, and he scowled and looked down to the distant courtyard. The vampires still lounged. It felt wrong. Like Kell was stumbling easily into a trap like a courtroom jester. Would they *really* leave such an opening unguarded? Or were there vampires with crossbows waiting from him to swing out onto the wire?

"I can't do this," said Kell.

"Why not?" hissed Myriam, who was tying her weapons to herself. "Secure that bloody axe. If you drop anything, the bastards will hear us and they'll look up. Then we're dead."

"This is too easy."

"You call *that* easy?" snapped Myriam, gesturing to the expanse of swaying cable – perhaps five hundred strides in all, and a good height. Good enough to turn the vampires on the ground far below into stick-men.

"We'll be vulnerable."

Myriam shrugged. "That's how us normal mortals feel all the time." She saw Kell's look, and pressed at one of her vachine fangs. "Well. You know what I mean."

Myriam took hold of the cable, and it was cold to the touch. Freezing. She grimaced. "Come on, axe man. We have a job to do."

"One thing."

"Yes?"

Kell grinned. "I like you, Myriam."

Her eyes glinted. "I know you do. You showed me that in oh so many different ways. Just proves what an old man has still got left inside him, if he really tries."

"No. I mean, we've had our differences. And I still don't trust you for spit." He held up a finger to silence her complaint. "But you've come good, Myriam. You may be as unpredictable as a violent raging sea storm, but by the Chaos Halls, I think I like that in a woman."

"What you're saying is, despite what we've been through, if I betray you now, you'll still lop off my head with that bloody axe?"

"You know I will," said Kell. "Now let's move. Before I change my mind."

Myriam took hold of the cable and swung her legs up, crossing them. Then she began to haul herself along the icy length, hand over hand, with smooth effortless strokes.

Kell took hold, Ilanna strapped tight to his back, and hoisted his legs up. The whole cable sagged, and Kell bobbed, and he cursed, and his muscles ached already. It was one thing in battle to be a huge, stocky, iron-muscled warrior – but such mass did not lend itself well to supporting one's own weight from a high cable.

Kell started to haul himself along. Within minutes the tower fell away, and he was far across the expanse. A cold wind whipped him. His muscles screamed. His bones creaked. His knees and back pummelled him with pain. And worse, the worst thing of all, the cable was freezing, and his hands were frozen. They were rigid, like solid brittle steel cast wrong in the forge, and Kell was struggling to move his fingers, struggling to pull himself across the vast drop.

Kell paused for a moment, and glanced down, just like he knew he shouldn't, but perversely revelling in the danger. If he fell now, he'd make a mighty dent in the cobbles. He grinned. Bastard. Bastards! He wanted to scream into the wind, into the snow, but instead he gritted his teeth and forced iron resolve to tear through him and he continued onwards. Onwards.

Half way.

Kell paused. His hands were as numb as they'd ever been. As numb as ice. As numb as Saark's brain.

"Donkey shit."

He clamped his teeth shut, blinking fast. He realised the cold was now numbing his *brain*. He looked up. Myriam was getting close to the portal, and he watched her flip over the lip. She disappeared, and Kell searched for her to reappear with a smile, and an encouraging wave. However, she did not. Kell scowled.

Shit.

He moved, as fast as lethargic muscles would allow, as fast as frozen bear paws would grapple. But the ice was winning. The cold was beating him down, no question.

Three quarters of the way, and Kell could not go on. He could not move and he hung there on a cable, high above vampire hordes and a city at war, and he listened to the wind, and wondered what the hell he was going to do now. And then, worst of all, he heard the sounds of battle from inside the tower. Steel on steel. The clash of blades. Myriam was in trouble!

Kell struggled to move on. To drag himself on. He glanced down. The vampires below had heard the battle as well, and they were looking up at him. One pointed. Several pale faces seemed to be grinning. Some vampires emerged, and they carried bows and Kell groaned. An arrow sailed up, missing him by inches. There came laughter, like a ripple of metal across ice.

Kell tried to force his fingers to move. They would not.

Kell was stuck...

Saark stared at Nienna as if she'd struck him.

"That's the single most incredibly stupid idea I've ever heard in my entire life."

"But you can't stop me," she said, voice low, and purring, and dangerous.

"I *can* stop you," snapped Saark, "and I bloody will!"

"No. You'd have to force me down, sit on me, pin my arms to the icy ground. Because I'm going after them, Saark. I'm going to help them. They need my help, I can feel it in my bones!"

"What a load of old rampant horse shit," snapped Saark, and grabbed Nienna's arm. Her hand flashed up, and it held a blade. The blade touched Saark's throat.

"See? I'm good enough to get past *your* guard."

Saark stepped back, hands out, and shook his head. "Kell told me to keep you here. In the forest. To make sure no harm came to you. He made me *promise*."

"This is unbelievable!" stormed Nienna. "Everybody has gone down to Gollothrim, even the women, to fight! And I'm expected to sit on my hands and play with myself? Well, I won't do it. I'm going after Kell and Myriam. The only way you'll stop me is by killing me."

"The women are trained archers!" wheedled Saark, and Nienna strode off down the forest trail. Saark ran after her. "Wait, wait! At least let me grab my rapier."

"So you're coming with me?"

"Aye, bloody looks like it, doesn't it?"

"Well, a woman should always get what she wants."

"In my experience, she always does. Only most of the time she learns to regret it."

Nienna shrugged. "You know I'm right, Saark. You know we need to be part of this. We can make a difference. We can help Kell."

"Have you heard yourself?" snapped Saark. "*Help* Kell? Have you bloody *seen* him fight? That rancid old lion needs no help from a little girl like you."

"Watch your tongue, lest I cut it out."

"Girl, if Kell learns I allowed you to follow him into *that hell hole*, then he'll cut out more than my damn tongue."

"Well let's make sure we make a difference, then," said Nienna, eyes hard, and by her stance Saark could see she meant trouble. She'd come a long way from the day he'd met her in the tannery in Jalder; then, she'd been soft like a puppy, her eyes gooey and lustful, her skin like virgin's silk. Now, she was hard, and lean, and her eyes were dark. She'd seen too much. Her innocence had been flayed from her, like skin strips under a cat o' nine.

Saark trotted after Nienna through the woods. There seemed little other option.

It did not take long to reach Gollothrim, and they stood in a darkened alley on the outskirts, listening to the sounds of horror reverberating through the streets. Many fights were erupting in the distance. Vampires screamed. Men screamed. Flames roared. The city had erupted into chaos.

"This is a *bad* idea," muttered Saark.

"To the tower, you said?"

"That's what Kell told me," muttered Saark, feeling like a down and dirty traitor, like his tongue would turn black and fall out of his burning mouth. He moved to Nienna, touched her shoulder. "*Please*. Let's turn back. This is not the time for us. Not the place."

"I am a child no longer," said Nienna, eyes hard.

Footsteps padded at the end of the alleyway, and a figure stopped, and turned. It was a woman. A vampire. She hissed, eyes glowing red, and extended her claws.

"Great," muttered Saark, drawing his sword, and turning, watched a second vampire casually close off the end of the alleyway. Two women, two vampires, working together as a small unit. To trap the unwary. To slaughter. To drink fresh blood...

Nienna had drawn her own short sword, and backed towards Saark. "There's two of them," she muttered, glancing up along the rooftops to make sure no more dropped from above.

"You reckon?" he snapped, eyes flickering between the two. They were advancing. Fluid. Too fluid. Graceful, like cats. Saark had seen vampires move like that before. These were the true predators of the pack. Deadly and swift. "Remember," he hissed, "eyes, throat and heart. Strike hard and fast, and keep hitting till the fucker's down," but there was no more time for words as the vampires shifted into a sprint and ran fast down the alley to leap at Saark and Nienna, who stood grim, blades glittering…

Grak shoved his sword into a vampire's open mouth, snapping fangs as claws scrabbled against his breastplate and slashed viciously across the steel band around his throat. But it saved him. The steel saved him.

"There's too many!" screamed Dekkar through the fighting throng. Their units of twenty-five men had been decimated, carved up, and backed together in a disorganised mass. They stood, panting, as vampires circled them on the wide main thoroughfare of Gollothrim. Occasionally, one would dart out but a spear would jab, and it would retreat. Grak looked frantically about. There were maybe twenty of them left, out of fifty. Most had lost shields, now. Most barely carried weapons. Dead vampires surrounded their boots. What happened to the other units? Fighting in their own shit, Grak reckoned. Down streets and alleyways. In buildings. What had he said? Stick to the main wide road, where each unit could help defend the other units. And what had they gone and done? Gone bloody running off in every bloody direction like horny young virgins at the sniff of a brothel! Grak the Bastard hawked and spat. Bloody undisciplined soldiers, was what they were. Bloody untrained, that was their curse! But… of course they were. They were never born for a life in the army.

Dekkar backed to him, and Grak stood side by side next to the Blacklipper giant. Grak glanced up.

"It's been an honour to fight alongside you, brother," he said.

Dekkar looked down. "You too. It's a shame it takes something like *war* to unite us."

Grak nodded. "You see how many there are? You have a slight height advantage over me."

"I reckon three hundred," said Dekkar, voice bitter.

"So, it's time," said Grak, and thought back past all the bad things he'd done. Would he go to the Golden Halls? The Halls of Heroes? He hawked, and spat again. After all the bad things he'd done? This hardly counted. No. He'd go to the Chaos Halls. With the Keepers. But at least one thing was sure and damn well guaranteed… he'd take as many fucking vampires with him as humanly possible…

"COME ON, YOU WHORESONS!" he screamed, and waved his sword, beating it against his breastplate and chanting and snarling.

The others around him did the same, and their noise rolled out over the snarling vampire hordes which jostled and shifted like some huge live thing, some organic vampire snake.

Then a high-pitched squeal rent the air, and the vampires screamed, their noise rising up in waves as their claws extended, their fangs gleamed in the darkness, and with a unity uncharacteristic of their unholy race, they charged the men of Falanor...

Command Sergeant Wood snarled, and his head smashed forward, forehead slamming Lorna's nose and making her squeal, and as her head slapped back so he sank his teeth into *her* throat in a beautiful, ironic reversal. He bit and he chewed, his head thrashing, his teeth gnashing, and he chewed out her windpipe and bit through her skin and muscle and tendon, and Lorna's claws raked at his back but they were pinned together by the sword, and he bit and he chewed, he ripped through her flesh as hard and as fast as he could, and black glistening blood ran down his throat and it tasted foul, like decay, like death, like eternity. They fell to the side, rolled onto the stone flags which lined the circumference of the Green Church roof, and Lorna went suddenly still. Wood, in a crazed panic, in a fit of hatred and loathing, continued to bite and chew, not believing she was dead until his teeth clacked against her *spine*. He had chewed out her entire throat. Wood squeezed his hands between them, and pushed himself from the sword point with a cry of pain which rent the night skies like a lightning strike. Then he lay there, shivering, and with gritted teeth he grabbed the stone crenellations and yanked himself to his feet, bleeding and ragged, pain his total mistress. He gazed out across the old soldiers, but they had out-thought the vampires. Whereas the vampires had surrounded the hidden men of the Black Barracks, so this had simply been a *decoy*... to draw them out, into the open. Hundreds had risen from secondary hiding places, and as the vampires attacked so hundreds of iron-tipped arrows slashed through the night, through the snow, piercing eyes and throats, hearts and groins. Wood watched, saw hundreds of arrows slashing through gloom and darkness, watched vampires pierced and screaming and punctured, rolling down slates and tiles, toppling from rooftops to pile like plague victims in the alleys below.

Then eyes turned, and looked up towards *him*. Wood gave a single wave of his hand as he swayed, wheezing, blood dribbling from his jaws with strings of vampire flesh, and he watched the old soldiers moving across the icy rooftops. Despite their age, they were iron. They were ruthless. They were unstoppable. It filled Wood with a little bit of shame at his own moaning. After all – he was still alive. He gritted his teeth, and ignored the hole in his chest, he regained his sword, tugging it from the vampire corpse. But as he turned to leave… he glanced down at Lorna's face. Her eyes were shining. She was watching him. She was *still alive*…

Her hand moved. Slow, like a white worm in the moonlight. At first Wood thought she was pointing at him, but she made a motion across the gaping hole where her throat had been. It was clear and simple. She wanted him to finish her.

"Not sure you deserve it, girl," he grunted, but lifted the short stout blade anyway. Their eyes met, and there was a curious moment of connection. Strangely, Wood felt like Lorna was thanking him. Thanking him – for removing the plague curse.

The sword slammed down, and cut her head from her torso.

Lorna's eyes closed, and she was at peace.

Wood checked Fat Bill, but he was a fast-cooling corpse on the snowy roof. Wood closed the man's eyes, and wincing like a man with a sword wound in his chest, limped from the roof to join the old soldiers in the alley below.

From there, they headed for the docks…

Saark's sword slammed down. The vampire dodged. "Help me, Saark!" squealed Nienna, and Saark speared his rapier through the vampire's eye and kicked off from her chest, somersaulting backwards to kick the second vampire in the back of the head. She went down on one knee, Saark going down with her and his hand came back – paused for a moment – then scooped out her throat with his *vachine* claws. She thrashed for a while on ice-slick cobbles, then lay still, eyes glassy, blood puke on her chin and soaking her chest and belly.

Saark's head came up. He glared at Nienna. "Now we turn back."

"No. Now we go on." She frowned at him, stubborn as ever.

"You will take us to our doom!"

"Then that's the path I choose," she snapped.

"By all the gods, I can see you carry Kell's blood."

"Better the blood of Kell than the blood of a whining coward!"

"Me? I just saved your life!"

"Yes, that's physical skill! What I'm talking about is *determination*. Now come on!"

Nienna stalked down the cobbles, stepping on a vampire corpse as she passed. Saark followed, head hung a little low, wishing he was back in the Royal Palace like it used to be, dancing to fine tunes, swigging fine wines, fucking fine succulent wenches. Saark had come from the gutters, worked his way swiftly to a place of eminence – and then the damn royal rug had been pulled from under his lacquered boots in an instant!

"I must have been a bad man, in a former life," he muttered.

You've been a pretty lowly shit in this one, too, replied his mocking conscience.

Nienna led the way, almost by intuition. Certainly she seemed linked to her grandfather. As if by a miracle they slid between groups of vampires, eased between units and squads. Many times they heard fighting, and saw glimpses of armoured units, the brave criminals and Blacklippers of Falanor, battling ferociously against groups of screeching vampires. Swords and spears slammed out, piercing hearts and throats. Swords hacked and cut. Men fell to the ice and mud, screaming and gurgling on blood and entrails.

At one point they spied Grak and Dekkar, back to back, from the confines of a narrow alley. Their sorrowful collection of remaining soldiers were surrounded. Saark tugged to move forward, but Nienna grabbed his arm, holding him back.

"No, Saark, *no!*" she hissed. "Kell may need us! We have to focus!"

Saark glared at her, but allowed himself to be drawn along, feeling like a back-stabber all the way but knowing, deep down, bedded in reality, that the greater mission was the destruction of the Vampire Warlords. And Bhu Vanesh, in particular... the leader. The *Prime*.

Through alleys they crept, in gutters filled with corpses. They moved through desecrated houses, across dead people's furniture and belongings, their flesh creeping, their breathing ragged. Closer and closer they got to the Warlord's Tower, and only as they came through a long, low house, and stopped by the smashed doorway filled with the splintered remnants of a battered door, did they peer out onto the courtyard and see the hundred-strong horde of vampires lounging around, lethargic, almost decadent in their casual manner.

"What now?" muttered Saark.

"We have to get past them."

"Using what blood-oil magick, I ask?"

"We must find Kell."

"Well he's not in there," snorted Saark. "He couldn't have got through this hornet's nest without stirring up a whole bucket full of maggot shit. No. He's somewhere close, though. He'll be looking for another way in, I'd wager, the canny old donkey."

Even as they watched, the vampires started to take interest in something above. Something beyond Saark and Nienna's field of vision; a couple fetched bows, and languorously began to fire arrows at some high target...

"That has to be Kell up there," said Nienna, almost desperate with a need to leave their safe confines. "Come on. We must stop them!"

Saark took hold of Nienna, and shook her. He shook her hard. "We die as easy as the next man," he growled. "You need to use your brain, girl, or you'll get us both killed. You hear me?" He let go of her, and caught a glimpse of hatred in her eyes. Saark licked his lips. Suddenly, he realised what was wrong – Nienna was skirting along a razor edge of sanity. She had lost her touch with reality. Maybe it had been losing her mother to the vampires, maybe it was simply the act of growing up way too fast; she'd been through enough horror to last any man or woman a lifetime. But the fact remained – she was fast becoming a danger. To Saark, to Kell, and to herself.

Distantly, there came a sudden, deafening roar. There were more bangs, and clatters, and an undercurrent of strange violent crackling sounds. Saark moved to another window in the ransacked town house and stared off across the wide courtyard. The edges of the city glowed orange. Fire was raging along the docks.

Outside, the vampires had seen the fire as well. Screeches and wails echoed through their ranks, language that was guttural, feral, and definitely inhuman. With Kell forgotten, they moved as a mass of figures, running, leaping, and within seconds were gone, a flood raging out through the night... and leaving the route to the tower entrance undefended.

"They did it!" hissed Saark. "Grak's men must have reached the docks! They've torched the ships!" he beamed, misunderstanding. "The vampires are starting to panic, they need..." He turned, but

Nienna had gone. He peered out of the window, and saw her disappear into the tower across the courtyard. Saark frowned. "You silly, silly little girl," he snapped, and with rapier clasped tight in his sweating fist and vachine fangs gleaming under errant strands of moonlight, Saark surged across the iced cobbles after his entrusted ward.

Wood and a group of old soldiers watched fire dance along the ships, from timber to rigging, from sails to masts. On the docks beside one vessel a store of oil had caught, a hundred barrels of flammable fish oil, and gone up with a terrible, mammoth explosion which Wood felt tremble beneath his boots like an earthquake. Flames shot out, destroying dockside buildings, smashing through four or five ships and spreading streamers of fire high into the night sky. Flames roared. Night turned to an orange, smoke-filled day. Embers fluttered on the wind, igniting yet more ships – many of which were soaked in lantern oil from casks hurled by the old soldiers of the Black Barracks. When the vampires arrived, in a pushing, heaving horde, it was too late to save their new navy, and indeed, their *old* navy. Even ships moored a good way out soon came under fire. Drifting sparks and glowing sections of sail, carried high on heated currents of air, drifted far and wide, igniting yet more sails which spread to masts and rigging, planks and timbers and barrels of oil in storage. More explosions rocked the ocean. The whole dockside became an inferno. After a while, even the ocean itself seemed to burn.

Wood could feel heat scorching his flesh as he leant against the wall. He, and the remainder of the old soldiers, had retreated here after a vicious final battle. But now the ships were burning, the vampires seemed to have more pressing matters on their hands, and the short savage skirmish had been temporarily forgotten. Vampires lined the rooftops in their thousands, eyes glowing in the reflected lights of their burning navy. They simply watched, perhaps too afraid to tackle the flames. But then, Command Sergeant Wood conceded, only the ocean could extinguish such an inferno. He'd never seen anything like it in his life.

Port of Gollothrim glowed like the Furnace in the Chaos Halls.

Slowly, Wood became aware of another group of vampires. There were perhaps a hundred of them, which didn't make Wood feel too good; after all, the old soldiers numbered only thirty or forty, now. Wood nudged his companion, the man's white beard turned black with soot and cinders. His eyes were glowing and wild.

"We fucked them hard, eh, lad?" He grinned at Wood. "It'll take 'em *years* to rebuild all them ships!"

Wood nodded, and gestured to this new unit of vampires taking an unhealthy interest in the old soldiers' predicament. "I think these bastards want a bit of payback," he said, and hefted his battered, chipped, blunted sword.

"Let's make them earn their fucking blood," snarled the old man beside him, rubbing his singed beard, eyes bright and *alive* with the fire-glow from the shipyard inferno.

The group of old men hefted their weapons, and despite being weary, drained, exhausted, they faced the vampires creeping towards them with chins held high, eyes bright, fists clenched, knowing they had done their bit in bringing down the cancerous plague, the fast-spread evil, the total *menace* of the Vampire Warlords...

The old soldiers had helped break their backs.

Now, it would be up to others to finish the story... the song... The Legend.

With snarls and squeals the fire-singed vampires, their pale skin stained with smoke and soot, some bearing savage, bubbling burns and fire-scars, *launched* themselves at the old soldiers, claws slashing, fangs biting, voices ululating triumphant calls across the smoke-filled city...

Swords clashed and cried in the darkness.

And in a few minutes, it was all over.

Kell watched the vampires disappear from down below, taking bows and hateful arrows with them. He watched fire fill the horizon like a flood. He watched the ships burn, his aerial view perfect in witnessing the fast spread of raw destruction. Kell could not believe the fire spread so swiftly; but it did, aided by a good wind and plentiful casks of lantern oil.

Still, he heard sword blows. Then Myriam appeared at the portal. "Come on!" she cried. "I can't fight them on my own!" She disappeared, and Kell grimaced and struggled on, cursing his weight, cursing his age, and vowing never to touch a single drop of whiskey again.

He reached the ledge, panting, sweat dripping in his eyes, his hands like the hands of a cripple with slashed tendons and no *strength*. He jumped down, blinded by the gloomy interior. To his back, silhouetting him against a raging orange archway, the entire naval fleet – old and new – burned.

Myriam was fighting a losing battle against two vampires. She spun and danced, avoiding their slashing claws, her sword darting out and scoring hits – but nothing *fatal*. They were too fast for her.

Kell growled, and hefted Ilanna. Then his hands cramped, and he dropped the axe, almost severing his own toes. "By all the bastards in Chaos," he muttered, scrabbling for the axe as one vampire broke free and charged him. He lifted Ilanna just in time, sparks striking from her butterfly blades and he slashed a fast reverse cut, Ilanna chopping swiftly, neatly, messily into the vampire's face. The man fell with a cry from half-chopped lips, and Kell stood on the vampire's throat, hefted Ilanna, and did a proper job this time, cutting his head and brain in half, just below the nose. Blood splattered the flags. Myriam speared her adversary through the eye, and he fell in a limp heap.

Myriam turned back to Kell. "I thought you were going to fall off!" she snapped.

"Me too."

"Your arse would have made one mighty huge crack in the cobbles."

"I'll lay off the ale and puddings when this is over, that's for sure."

Myriam grinned, and released a long-drawn breath. "Another one's coming. It feels like they were waiting for us!"

"I didn't expect anything less," said Kell.

Division General Dekull stepped from the shadows, a large man with a bull-neck and a hefty scowl. He had thinning brown hair and large hands, each one bearing a sword. He was a formidable opponent, equalling Kell in size and weight, but carrying less fat.

Before Kell could speak, Myriam charged, light, graceful, sword slashing down. Dekull swayed slightly, a precise movement, and back-handed Myriam across the chamber where her head cracked against the wall. It was a sickening noise, and made Kell wince.

"At last, the mighty Kell," said Dekull, voice a rumble. "We've been... *waiting* for you. Let's say your reputation precedes you."

"I won't ask your name," said Kell. "And the only thing that precedes you is the foul, rotten-egg stench."

Dekull's face darkened. "You should learn some respect, feeble, petty, rancid *mortal*."

"Respect? For your kind? I'd rather show you my cock."

"I'm going to teach you a lesson you will never forget, *boy*..." snarled Dekull, vampire fangs ejecting, shoulders hunching, swords glittering.

Kell laughed, an open, genuine sound of humour. "My name is Kell," he rumbled. "Here, let me carve it on your arse, lest you forget."

Kell moved forward, wary, and Dekull charged with a roar which showed his vampire fangs in all their glory, glinting with reflected firelight from the orange glow outside.

Kell felt the killing rage come on him, and it was now and here and the time was *right*. He was no longer an old man. He was no longer a weary, aged, *retired* soldier. Now he was strong and fast and deadly; he was a creature born in the Days of Blood and he *revelled* in his might, prowess, superiority, and although he knew this was a splinter of blood-oil magick, a *dark* magick, a trick and a curse instilled from his dead wife trapped inside his mighty, possessed axe – he locked the information in a tiny cage and tossed away the key with a snort. Now, he needed this energy. No matter how dark. No matter how bad. No matter how inherently *evil*.

Now, he needed the Legend.

Kell needed the *Legend*...

Kell slapped the swords aside, left right, a fast figure-of-eight curving from Ilanna with intricate insane skill, and front-kicked Dekull in the chest. But Dekull came on, crashing into Kell, who grabbed Dekull's ear and with a growl wrenched it off. Dekull screamed, a shocking high-pitched noise as blood erupted, and Kell crashed his fist – still holding the flapping ear – into Dekull's nose, breaking it with a crunch. Then Ilanna lifted high, keening with promise, and slammed down, cutting Dekull from collarbone to mid-chest allowing the huge man to flap open. Dekull staggered back, almost cut in two, his arms a good eight feet apart. Swords clattered to the stone, useless, released by limp twitching fingers.

Kell rolled his shoulders, and stared into Division General Dekull's eyes. They were glazed in disbelief, but he was still alive, still *conscious*. "Damn," muttered Kell, clenching and unclenching his hands. "That cold out there, it spoiled my bloody stroke. Here, lad. Let's have another go, shall we?" The second blow started where the first had ended, cleaving Dekull clean in two. Entrails and internal organs slopped to the floor, along with fat and muscle and skin and neatly severed bones. Kell turned from the dead vampire and stared through the portal.

Myriam had regained her feet, swaying and holding onto the wall. She sensed a change in Kell, and kept well back. He was different. He wasn't just dangerous; he was *deadly*. Deadly to *everyone*. She licked her lips and his terrible raging eyes fell on her. There was insanity there, wriggling, like a corrupt worm at the heart of a corrupt apple.

"Kell?"

"Yes?"

"Bhu Vanesh. Through there." She pointed.

"Stay here," said Kell, with a torn, sickly grimace. "I wouldn't like you to get in the way."

Kell strode forward, through the archway, up several steps and into a huge circular chamber. It was devoid of furniture, but thick rugs covered the walls and windows keeping the room in perpetual darkness. The floor, also, was completely filled with thick embroidered rugs, each showing complex patterns of blood-oil magick invocation, or scenes of rape and mutilation from ancient battles.

Bhu Vanesh sat in the centre of the chamber, cross-legged, long limbs relaxed, his smoky skin squirming with half-formed, drifting scenes of his distilled depravity; the eating of flesh, the biting of throats, acts of decadent arching screaming deathrape, the joy of giggling child murder, the orgasm in the hunt of the innocent, the frail, the stupid...

Bhu Vanesh.

Greatest of the Vampire Warlords.

The *Prime*.

Bhu Vanesh...

The Eater in the Dark.

Kell halted, and Ilanna clunked to the carpeted stone. His eyes burned like molten ore. He smiled a grim smile that had nothing to do with humour, and glanced down at the pile of child corpses, a small pyramid of desolation nestling pitifully beside the Warlord. There were perhaps thirty or forty babes in all, drained to husks, nothing more than bones in mottled flesh sacks.

"Interrupt breakfast, did I, you corrupted deviant fuck?" snarled Kell. His voice was bleak, like breeze over leaden caskets. Like the solitary chime of a funeral bell.

"Welcome to my humble home, Kell, Legend," spoke Bhu Vanesh, and smoke curled from his mouth, around his grey vampire fangs, around his long long claws which reached out towards Kell, as if imploring the old man to lay down his axe.

"Well, I got to say it, this ain't your home, Vanesh. It's time for you to go back. Back to the Chaos Halls. Back to the Keepers. You know this. You know it's time you left my world."

Bhu Vanesh's eyes flashed dark, like jewelled obsidian in smoke pools. He stood, a long, languorous uncurling imbued with restrained *power*. He towered over Kell, and his long legs seemed to sag at knee joints which bent the wrong way, and his arms reached almost to the ground and ended in vicious-looking curved talons. And all the time his smoke skin curled and twisted, depicting scenes of murder and cruelty and evil sex and deathrape and the hunt. The hunting of women. The hunting of children. From Bhu Vanesh's past… His History. His Legacy. Faces flashed in quick succession across his smoke skin. All begging. Pleading. Screaming. Dying.

Darkness, desolation, fear, hate, all emanated from the Vampire Warlord like a bad drug. A stench of hate. An aroma of evil.

Kell swallowed.

Something grabbed him in its fist.

Fear, a rancid ball of fat, filled his belly and throat and mind.

It took him over. It rolled into him, and filled him like a jug to the brim.

Kell wanted to puke. He wanted to scream. He wanted to die…

It was all he could do to meet Bhu Vanesh's piercing gaze.

"You *dare* to come here and challenge me?" snarled the Vampire Warlord. "You, nothing but a smear of shit on the vastness of time and purity, nothing but a wriggling, deformed babe fresh from its mother's stinking syphilitic cunt, *nothing* but a smear of organic pus from the rancid quivering *arsehole* of Chaos?" His voice had risen to a roar. The walls seemed to shake. Brands flickered wild in their brackets, almost extinguishing with Bhu Vanesh's open raw wild fury. He took a step forward, head lowering to Kell's level, and his huge long arms lifted threateningly. "Turn around, you fucking pointlessness, and leave me in peace."

Bhu Vanesh began a slow turn, back to his pile of suckled corpses, his face and *demeanour* filled with disgust, and loathing, and revulsion, and raw pure abhorrence.

"A pointlessness, is it?" growled Kell, and leapt forward with a bestial growl, Ilanna singing a beautiful high song, a song from the dying of worlds, a song plucked from strands of strummed chaos, a song of purity, and Ilanna struck for Bhu Vanesh's head but the Warlord turned fast, long arm slamming out with pile-driver force to strike Kell in the chest. The old warrior grunted, was punched backwards, and hit the wall several feet above the ground. He landed heavy, in a crouch, and his head came up. He rubbed at his chest, and with a wrench pulled out a battered steel breastplate – now a mangled mess of twisted armour. Kell coughed, a harsh hacking cough, and dropped the steel to the ground.

Kell spoke. His words were low, harsh, inhuman, barely more than guttural noises as a fire demon would make... and certainly not the voice of Kell. "Bhu Vanesh. Creature of the Chaos Halls. It is time to come back. The Keepers have decreed it so. I am here as your Guide."

Kell charged again, and Bhu Vanesh turned fast and claws raked against Ilanna's butterfly blades, only now they were not steel – and flames from brands in iron brackets did not reflect from Ilanna's blades but were sucked deep into them like trailing streamers, sucked and spooled and drawn into the eternal portal of the Chaos Halls. Bhu Vanesh fought, and as Myriam staggered to the door and leaned heavily against the frame, watching, it seemed to her that he struck with long, lazy strokes, like a pendulum, a clockwork machine, claws slamming Ilanna left, then right, and curling around Kell to lift him from the floor, accelerating him high up so he nearly touched the vaulted ceiling.

"Petty mortal, I will tear you in two!" he snarled, long smoking drools of saliva pooling from vampire fangs. "You cannot stand against me! I am Bhu Vanesh. The Eater in the Dark. I do not *obey* the Keepers! *I mock them!*"

Kell struck down with Ilanna, crashing her butterfly blades into Bhu Vanesh's skull. "Is that so, you baby-sucking bastard?" he roared. He slammed down again, Ilanna squealing, screaming, wailing like an animal in pain, and again, and again, and sounds of tortured metal reverberated around the chamber, "Well if you don't obey the Keepers, you can fucking obey me!"

Kell struck down a third time. Black light seemed to crackle around the room, igniting the carpets and tapestries, which all burned with black fire. A cold ice wind rushed through the chamber. Bhu Vanesh squealed, and tossed Kell like a piece of tinder. The old warrior hit the wall, clothes setting alight with black fire, and his huge hands patted frantically at his clothing as dark eyes watched the thrashing figure of Bhu Vanesh. But it wasn't enough, it still wasn't enough, and Kell charged back at the Vampire Warlord who was thrashing and squealing, claws flailing wide and flashing like scythes through the air, and a deep groaning chimed through the chamber, making the very stones vibrate. Through this chaos came Nienna, face pale, lips drawn back in horror, and Myriam grabbed for her, brushed against her arm, but Nienna slapped her away and stumbled into the chamber, sword held high, her eyes glowing triumphant as she faced *that* which she feared the most, Bhu Vanesh, the Eater in the Dark, and Haunter of Dreams, Desecrater of Flesh. "I defy you!" she screamed, "I banish you back to the Chaos Halls!" and Bhu Vanesh's laughter rolled out like terrible thunder, like the crushing of tectonic plates, and Kell was battling in fury in the midst of the storm, Ilanna rising and falling, the black fire inside him, his bearskin jerkin aflame, sparks dancing through his beard and grey hair, Ilanna slamming left, and right, and left and right, striking away the Warlord's claws, sinking into smoky flesh only to pull back and the flesh seal like hot wax as faces screamed at Kell from beneath the smoke surface. A claw struck Kell a mighty blow, sending him whirling through the chaos, Ilanna still singing, and his tumbling, spinning body careered into Nienna, crashing her to the ground, Ilanna's blades cleaving through her chest, straight down to bone, straight into her heart.

The storm ended, with a *click*.

The black fire died.

Kell, kneeling, his jerkin drifting smoke, an old man again, looked up slowly and in horror. Saliva pooled from his silently working jaws. His face and hands were lacerated. His blood dripped to the thick burnt carpets. Nienna was lying at his feet, gasping, a huge wound from her shoulder to ribs. Blood bubbled at her chin, on her tongue and lips. Blood pulsed easily from the wound. Her eyes were glazed, confused, tears lying on her cheeks like spilt mercury. Kell dropped to her side, threw Ilanna to the floor, and grabbed at the huge slice through Nienna's flesh. With trembling fingers he tried to hold Nienna together. With force of will, he tried to meld her body back into one piece. Blood pulsed up, ran over his hands with the beating of her damaged, irregular heart. "No," whispered Kell, staring down into his sweet grand-daughter's face, "no, not here, not now, not this way…"

"Grandfather?" she said, although it was barely audible. "*Why?*"

And then her lips went pale, and her eyes closed, and she convulsed, and although Kell's hands tried to hold her back together, she died there on the floor at the bequest of the great Ilanna – at the command of the Vampire Warlord.

"NO!" screamed Kell, and shook Nienna, but she was dead, and gone, gone to another realm, and Kell stood and took up Ilanna, and he gazed at her butterfly blades where Nienna's blood, her life-force, her essence, her *soul* stained those portals into the Chaos Halls… and a wild wind slammed through the chamber, both hot, and cold, and bitter and sweet. Smoke poured out from Ilanna, a thick black acrid smoke which stank of Nienna's blood, her summoning, and which filled the room in an instant. The world went slow, filled with black sparks, and a *groan* rent the air, *the groan of the world torn asunder* as a smoke-filled corridor opened up behind Bhu Vanesh. It stretched away for a million years. It led to a chamber of infinity, endlessly black, and from the sky fell corpses tumbling down down down through nothingness into lakes of blood and rivers of death and oceans of evil weeping souls. Kell hefted Ilanna, and glared at Bhu Vanesh, who lifted his hands in supplication, eyes glowing red, smoke curling from his slick wet mouth.

"Get thee back to Chaos," snarled Kell, and strode forward, and there came a deafening clanking of chains and deep within the vaults Kell could see figures, tall and thin, like grey skeletons, their eyes pools of liquid silver that *glowed*. They came forward, walking oddly, and Kell blinked for he was on the roadway, on the path to the Chaos Halls, and thick pitted iron chains slammed past him, wrapping around Bhu Vanesh who was weeping, smoke oozing from every orifice like drifting blood-mist, and Kell strode forward and slammed Ilanna between his eyes, splitting Bhu Vanesh's head in two but still the Vampire Warlord wept, and still the smoke spilled from his mouth, for Kell could not kill Bhu Vanesh. Nobody could kill Bhu Vanesh. He was *immortal*.

"That's for Nienna," he spat.

"Not the Halls," Bhu Vanesh wept. "Not the Halls!"

The chains rattled, and Bhu Vanesh hurtled off along the infinite road all the while chanting his mantra, and now Kell saw the roadway was made of bones, of skulls, a wide flowing road of skulls and Kell dropped to one knee and wept, and the tall bony figures strode towards him and stood, five of them, watching him with their silver eyes, in complete silence.

Finally, Kell ceased his crying. He stood, breathing deeply, and lifted Ilanna in both hands still stained with Nienna's blood. Only then did a chill breeze caress his soul. He turned, wind ruffling his scorched bearskin jerkin, but the portal to the World of Men was gone.

All that remained was that infinite roadway of skulls, an obsidian sky, and a world stretching off to a distant horizon of eternally falling corpses, of fallen souls…

Kell was trapped in the Chaos Halls.

Kell was lost to Chaos.

SIXTEEN
Kell's Legend

Grak the Bastard knelt amidst a hundred vampire corpses, sword lashing out, and Dekkar was behind him, a few remaining men beside. As fires roared along the dockside, so other units from the new army of Falanor had found Grak, and they fought vicious short battles until they were together, clashed together, united, the last few hundred survivors. But still they were losing. Still they were being massacred...

Then, the vampires fell back.

The dawn was coming.

Still fires raged, flames crackling, and Grak couldn't tell where the snow ended and the ash began. The world was in chaos. A living nightmare madness. Grak watched the ring of vampires, their snarling faces, their blood-red eyes.

"What are they waiting for?" rumbled Dekkar.

"Beats me," said Grak, sword before him, eyes lost to *the horror*. There was no way out of this. If Kell had killed Bhu Vanesh, then it would have been done a long time ago. If Kell had killed the Vampire Warlord, then his creatures would have turned to dust, to slime, to oil. But here they stood. The dawn had come.

Kell was dead, Grak knew it in his heart, in his bones, in his soul. Kell wasn't coming back.

"Shit," he said, hawked, and spat.

"What are they waiting for?" snapped Vilias, words edged with pain. He had a long, ragged slash down his face, from one eye to his chin. He'd been moaning about how no woman would ever look at him again. Grak supposed it didn't really mattered any longer... soon, they would all be corrupt. Either that, or dead.

"Maybe they know they're outnumbered?" suggested Grak. "They know they're beaten! After all, we're what? Three hundred? And they've..." his eyes scanned the rooftops, the roadways, the distant rubble, the edges of inferno. "Three, four thousand blood-sucking scum? We can take 'em, eh lads? We'll give 'em a damn good kicking!" Chuckles ran up and down the ranks, and exhausted men, wounded men, hoisted their weapons and waited grimly for the end.

"Come on!" screamed Grak. "Show us what you're made of! Fucking cowards! FUCKING VAMPIRE PLAGUE COWARDS! COME ON!"

"Hey." Vilias nudged Grak in the ribs. "Somebody's coming."

"Who is it? Dake the Axeman?" He roared with laughter. "Shall I show him my arse?"

"Better than that," grinned Vilias. "It's Kell."

"No!"

"It is, I swear it!"

From the distance, and as the dawn broke like a soft ruptured egg, Kell strode. Beams of yellow winter sunlight traced lines over the horizon, and Kell was blocked for a moment by the huge edifice of the Warlord's Tower. Then he moved through the rubble, strode past corpses, past fallen shields and fallen men, and stopped before Grak with boots crunching. Eerily, the vampires had parted to let him through. Their snarling subsided. They stared at him.

Everything was focused on Kell.

On Kell, the Legend.

Kell hefted Ilanna, and Grak could see the old warrior had tears in his beard. He lifted Ilanna, and his mouth opened, and he looked out at the vampire horde.

When he spoke, his voice was soft. Gentle, almost. Like mist creeping over a battlefield of corpses.

"Time to go home," he said, and each vampire lifted its head and smoke poured from its mouth, and flowed like lines of silver into Ilanna, into Kell's axe, in the Portal of the Chaos Halls. Kell stood, shuddering as each vampire was cleansed, each vampire purified. And now, as people, they fell to their hands and knees weeping in horror as they remembered what they had done.

It seemed to take an age.

One, by one, by one, the vampires' corruption was drawn into Ilanna. Their evil exorcised.

A cold winter wind blew over the slain, bringing ice, and making those watching shiver.

When it was over, Kell sank to the ground, rolling gently to his side and closing his eyes. Vilias moved tenderly to the old warrior, the old man, the old soldier. No longer did he look like Kell the Legend. Now, he just looked old and withdrawn and lost.

"Well?" snapped Grak, frowning.

Vilias looked up. "Holy Mother! He's dead, Grak! Kell's dead!"

Kell stood before the Keepers of the Chaos Halls. He scowled and clutched Ilanna tight, and looked from one, to the next, to the next, and they surveyed him with eyes of silver, unspeaking, unmoving, uncaring.

Is this it, then? Is this where I die? Is this where the game ends? Is this my new eternity?

No. It was Ilanna. Her voice was honey in his brain, and she was weaving her dark magick once more. *This is not punishment, Kell. This is reward. This is not where you die. This is where you choose to live!*

Choose to live?

So there's a bloody *choice?*

Kell braced himself, staring up at the five Keepers. They exuded a lack of emotion. A neutrality. They were neither good, nor evil. They simply *were.* Kell scowled.

"Can I do something for you sorry-looking fuckers? Eh, lads? Or maybe you'd like a good kick to get you started?"

"You are to be congratulated," said one of the Keepers. Its voice was low but musical, and without threat. "Without your help, we would not have all the Vampire Warlords back in our custody."

"What about Meshwar? He's in Vor…"

"He is with us, now," said the Keeper. "You are not the only creature with the power to open a portal to the Chaos Halls. Although, it would seem, you are the most… *efficient.*"

Kell considered this, then gave a single nod. Then he seemed to deflate. He remembered Nienna. Bitterness washed through him like a fast-flood of liquid cancer.

"Why am I here?"

"We have one last task for you."

"And suppose I don't want to accept your task? Suppose I'm sick of these games? Suppose I'm just a bitter and lonely old man, who wants nothing more than to die?"

The Keeper moved close, and bent down until its face was a finger's breadth from Kell's face. Those silver eyes drilled into him and in those swirling silver depths Kell saw something impossible, something eternal, something truly godlike. The voice was a gentle breath across his face, and he inhaled the words, sucked them straight down into his soul... "You are lost at the moment, Kell, lost to the sadness and for that I still grant you life for foolish words and foolish thoughts. But do not think to test us, for we are the Keepers and we hold the Key to All Life. The Vampire Warlords should never have broken free – and one day, there will a reckoning for that abomination. But still, in Gollothrim, the vampires roam, the spawn of Bhu Vanesh... you can go there, we will give you the tools to take it back. You can save thousands, Kell. Either that..." The Keeper pulled back, silver orbs still fixed on Kell who coughed, and dropped to one knee, choking as if on heavy woodsmoke. "Either that, or you can stay here and be our guest for an eternity."

The sky went dark, struck through with huge zig-zags of crimson. The falling corpses fell faster, and screams rent the sky, screams of pure anguish like nothing Kell had ever heard. Nor would want to hear again.

"There is always a reckoning," said the Keeper. "Nothing goes unseen. Nothing goes unpunished. Remember that, Kell, the Legend, when you finally seek our forgiveness."

Kell nodded, but could not speak. The world tilted, the Chaos Halls spun away into a tiny black dot and Kell fell through light and opened his eyes, lying on his back, next to the fast-cooling corpse of Nienna.

Three horses picked their way across a pastel landscape of white, greys and subtle cold blues. The beasts entered a sprawling forest of pine, and it was half a day before they emerged again on the flanks of a hill, climbing, following old farmers' trails high into the hills east of the Gantarak Marshes. From here, the glittering, ancient sprawl of Vor could be spied far, far to the south, and Kell reined his mount and sat for a while, staring at the distant city; staring at the new home of the Ankarok.

Saark watched him for a while, then glanced at Myriam, who shrugged, pushing out her lower lip.

"You want to visit?" asked Saark, eventually.

"No."

"Do you trust Skanda?"

"No."

"He claims all the Ankarok want is that one, single city. He delivered Meshwar to the Vampire Warlords, turned the vampire slaves back into people, and set them gently outside the city gates. He did everything he promised. More. He gave them food, supplies, money. It's a small price to pay, I think, for saving so many lives."

Kell said nothing, continuing to scowl. Eventually he coughed, rubbed his beard, then his weary eyes, and said, "Only bad things will come of this, you mark my words. This is not the last we've heard of Skanda, nor the damned Ankarok. I have a bad feeling in my bones, Saark. A bad feeling that runs right down into the sour roots of Falanor."

"We could ride down," said Saark, eyes glittering. "Take the city! Single-handed! Just like the old days, eh, Myriam? Eh?"

Kell shook his head. "The battle for Vor. It is a battle for another day. I'm tired, Saark. Too tired. Too old. I saw my daughter die, and I saw my granddaughter die." He turned, and there were tears in the old soldier's eyes. "It shouldn't be like this. You should never outlive your children. Sometimes, Saark, I fear I will never laugh again."

"At least the scourge of the Vampire Warlords has ended, Kell. Nienna died defending the land she loved. She did it for the good of Falanor, for its people, its history, its honour."

"Doesn't make it any easier to swallow," growled Kell, still staring at the haze of Vor.

"We are free of oppression," said Saark, forcing a false brightness into his voice. As ever, he was dressed in silk; bright green, this time, in an attempt to "blend with forest hues".

"Yeah," snarled Kell, curling his lips into an evil grimace. "But for how long? The Keepers, down in the Chaos Halls, told me that a war is coming. The vachine from Silva Valley – they were just the beginning. There are more, many more, far to the north, far beyond the Black Pike Mountains where no man has trodden for ten thousand years. They have a vast, corrupt, vachine empire built in the ice. And they want revenge, for what happened to the vachine of Silva Valley."

"You think a war is coming?" said Saark, quietly.

"There is always a war coming," said Kell, impassively.

"What shall we do?"

"What can we do?" said Kell, voice and eyes bleak, tears running down his cheeks as he thought about Nienna for the hundredth time, thought about the terrible axe blades of Ilanna and tried to persuade himself *tried to convince himself* that the axe had nothing to do with the young woman's death. After all, Ilanna was just steel. Cold black steel. Nothing more, nothing less.

"Time to leave," said Myriam, glancing up at the sky. "There's a storm coming."

Kell nodded, and dug heels to the flanks of his mount, cantering ahead of the small group.

Myriam glanced at Saark. "Do you think he'll be all right?" she said. "I mean. We thought he was dead, back there."

Saark gave a single nod. "Maybe he did die. A little bit. Lost a part of his soul."

"But will he be all right?"

"Of course he will. He's Kell. Kell, the Legend."

Spring was coming to Falanor. The cold winds from the north grew mild, and snow and ice began a long melt, gradually freeing up the Great North Road for easier passage; of both people and supplies.

Over the coming months, slowly, the cities of Falanor rebuilt themselves, and the thousands of people who'd fled the horrors, first of the albino Army of Iron, the Harvesters, and later the Vampire Warlords, the refugees, the outcasts, slowly they drifted back and populations began once again to grow, to build, to prosper.

As the first daffodils scattered brightness across the hills and valleys of Falanor, a new King was crowned. He had been found sheltered in the forest city of Vorgeth close to the Autumn Palace along with his brother, Oliver. His name was Alexander, son of Leanoric, and proud grandson of Searlan the Battle King. And although he was only just sixteen years old, he was wise, and stern, and honest, and promised to make a fine new leader. Immediately, he appointed a new General of his infant Eagle Divisions. The General's name was Grak, who earned his rank through sterling service to the Land of Falanor.

In time, Alexander's eyes turned south. South, to the city of Vor, once the capital of Falanor, once his *father's* city, his father's *pride*. And Alexander brooded on the secrecy of the occupying race known as the Ankarok.

Since Vor closed its great iron gates, nobody had entered nor left the much-altered city.

A year after the banishment of the Vampire Warlords to the Chaos Halls, Alexander, Oliver, Grak and twenty soldiers reined in their armoured mounts far to the west of Vor, and gazed with a mixture of wonder and horror at what had once been the oldest city in the country.

Whereas once huge white towers, temples and palaces dominated the skyline, and the city had been surrounded by white stone walls, now everything had been... *encompassed* by what looked, at first glance, like a giant, matt black beetle shell.

"Holy Mother," said Oliver, rubbing his chin and placing his hand on his sword hilt. "The city! It's gone!"

"Not gone," said Alexander, who now sported a small scar under one eye from duelling, from *training*, "but *buried*. What have those bastards done to our father's city? What have they done to *our heritage?*"

Grak kicked his horse forward, and placed a warning hand on Alexander's arm. "Majesty. I suggest caution. We must not approach the city. That was the pact made, the agreement between the leaders of Falanor and the... Ankarok."

Alexander nodded, but his eyes gleamed, and secretly he thought, *that was not my agreement*. Later, as he pored over maps in his tent, drinking watered wine from a gold goblet and eating cheese and black bread, so Alexander doodled a *hypothetical* retaking of the city of Vor.

For the honour of his father's memory, of course.

For the honour of Falanor.

A cold, fresh mountain wind blew.

Kell stood on a crag, exercising with slow, easy movements, swinging Ilanna left and right, running through manoeuvres so long used in battle they were now an instinct. He breathed deep, drinking in the vast pastel vision of mountains and hills and forests, valleys and rivers and lakes. It was a mammoth, natural vista, a painting more beautiful than anything ever captured on canvas. And it was there, there for Kell, there for his simple honest pleasure.

Kell finally ended his routine, and stood for a while, holding Ilanna to his chest, a violent internal war raging through his skull and heart. Part of him wanted to cast the axe away, far out from the mountain plateau, to be lost in the wilderness of crags and rocky slopes and scree below. But he did not. Could not. Even though he blamed Ilanna, to some extent, for the death of Nienna.

Nienna.

She haunted him.

Haunted him, with her innocence and the unfairness of it all.

"How are you feeling, old horse?" Saark grinned up at Kell, then deftly climbed up the ridge and sat, staring out over the early morning view. "By all the gods, this is a throne for a prince!"

"What are you doing here?"

"A simple *good morning* would have been a far more pleasant and agreeable salutation."

"Ha. I'm not here to be pleasant."

"I noticed. Here." Saark unwrapped a cloth sack and handed Kell a chunk of cheese and grain bread. Saark bit himself a lump of cheese and began to chew.

Kell, also, broke his fast, and the two men sat in companionable silence for a while. Until Kell winced, and clutched his stomach, tears springing to his eyes. He coughed, then rubbed at his head.

"The poison?"

"Aye, lad. It's gotten worse."

"You know what this means?"

Kell stared into Saark's eyes, and gave a nod. He sighed. "Aye. I must travel west. Find the antidote. Find the cure. I am reluctant to leave Falanor, but – well, I think after what happened with Nienna, maybe it would do me good. To see new countries, meet new people. To put my mark on a new place. A new world."

"'Different cultures, different customs'," quoted Saark, chewing on his bread. "You would of course need to travel far across the Salarl Ocean, my friend, out towards the lands of Kaydos. It is told the place is a vast, hot continent. Thousands and thousands of leagues of forest, hot, humid, damp, uncomfortable, where insects fight to make a merry meal of a man, and it is claimed in hushed whispers around strange fires that men and wolves walk together under the full yellow moon."

Kell eyed Saark thoughtfully. "Sounds like a harsh land, laddie."

"Only a fool would travel there," Saark agreed.

"I've already packed my things. I believe a ship leaves from Garramandos in a week. It should not be hard to acquire passage. As I said, it would do me good. And of course, this damn poison still courses through my veins. Some days, I curse Myriam her lusts."

"And some days you thank her," grinned Saark.

"Aye. That I do."

They sat in silence for a while. Eventually, Saark said, "I, also, have taken the liberty of packing. It would, of course, be highly foolish to let such a moaning old goat as yourself travel alone. Imagine the trouble you would get yourself into, with your ignorant peasant ways, base stupidity and crude manners! Whereas I, I with my noble breeding, sense of natural etiquette, and *love* of everything honourable, well, I would surely keep one such as you out of terrible mischief."

Kell looked sideways at Saark. "I suppose you've packed a huge wardrobe? Silver goblets? Silk shirts? A perfume of subtly mingled horse shit?"

"Of course. But thankfully, I have Mary, my donkey, to help shoulder my burden."

Kell groaned. "You're *not* bringing that stinking and cantankerous beast."

Saark frowned. "But *Kell*, how else will I journey with an extensive wardrobe? Just because I travel with peasants, doesn't mean I have to look like one. I must protest..."

"Wait, wait." Kell held up a huge hand. "What do you mean, *'peasants'*? Plural? You told Myriam?"

"Well," Saark shifted uncomfortably, "I couldn't have you sneaking off in the night without her, could I? I couldn't allow you to do the dishonourable thing."

"*Dishonourable thing!*" spluttered Kell, turning bright red. "You! *You!* You dare to come out with that whining bloody gibberish? After all the things you've done to the poor women of Falanor! After all the hearts you broke? After all the children you sired? After all the chastity locks you picked?"

"Hey," frowned Saark. "I never said I was perfect. Only that you should show some morals."

"Morals?" screeched Kell, but they were rudely interrupted. Myriam appeared, climbing deftly up the rocky ridgeline. She was dressed for travel, and had her bow strapped to her back. She smiled at the two men.

"I'm ready," she said.

Kell scowled. "So I need to book passage for three travellers, do I?" he snapped.

"And a donkey," said Saark.

"And a donkey," growled Kell, through gritted teeth. "Well, we better be going, I reckon. It's a long trek to Garramandos, that's for sure. Over some treacherous terrain."

All three stared across the western flanks of the Black Pike Mountains, vast and black, towering and defiant, and their gazes drifted down towards the Salarl Ocean, which glittered like molten silver in the early morning sunlight.

"Men and wolves," said Kell, distantly.

Saark grinned and slapped him on the back. "Aye. Men and wolves. Come on."

Against a sparkling horizon of ocean and a rearing backdrop of savage mountains, the three travellers began a long, careful descent from the mountain plateau to the breathless, waiting world below.

ABOUT THE AUTHOR

Andy Remic is a British writer with a love of ancient warfare, mountain climbing and sword fighting. Married with two children, he works as a writer in the fields of Fantasy and SF, and in his spare time is a smuggler of rare Dog Gems, a drinker of distilled liquor and hunter of rogue vachine. He also dabbles in filmmaking.

www.andyremic.com

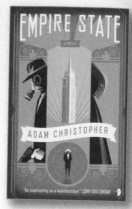

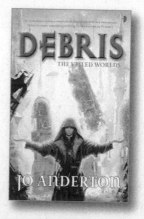

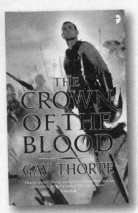

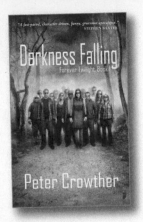

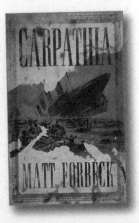

ANGRY ROBOT

FILL YOUR BOOTS
Snag the complete Angry Robot catalog

DAN ABNETT
- [ ] Embedded
- [ ] Triumff: Her Majesty's Hero

GUY ADAMS
- [ ] The World House
- [ ] Restoration

JO ANDERTON
- [ ] Debris

LAUREN BEUKES
- [ ] Moxyland
- [ ] Zoo City

THOMAS BLACKTHORNE
(aka John Meaney)
- [ ] Edge
- [ ] Point

MAURICE BROADDUS
- [ ] King Maker
- [ ] King's Justice
- [ ] King's War

ADAM CHRISTOPHER
- [ ] Empire State

PETER CROWTHER
- [ ] Darkness Falling

ALIETTE DE BODARD
- [ ] Servant of the Underworld
- [ ] Harbinger of the Storm
- [ ] Master of the House of Darts

MATT FORBECK
- [ ] Amortals
- [ ] Vegas Knights

JUSTIN GUSTAINIS
- [ ] Hard Spell

GUY HALEY
- [ ] Reality 36

COLIN HARVEY
- [ ] Damage Time
- [ ] Winter Song

MATTHEW HUGHES
- [ ] The Damned Busters

TRENT JAMIESON
- [ ] Roil

K W JETER
- [ ] Infernal Devices
- [ ] Morlock Night

J ROBERT KING
- [ ] Angel of Death
- [ ] Death's Disciples

GARY McMAHON
- [ ] Pretty Little Dead Things
- [ ] Dead Bad Things

ANDY REMIC
- [ ] Kell's Legend
- [ ] Soul Stealers
- [ ] Vampire Warlords

CHRIS ROBERSON
- [ ] Book of Secrets

MIKE SHEVDON
- [ ] Sixty-One Nails
- [ ] The Road to Bedlam

DAVID TALLERMAN
- [ ] Giant Thief

GAV THORPE
- [ ] The Crown of the Blood
- [ ] The Crown of the Conqueror

LAVIE TIDHAR
- [ ] The Bookman
- [ ] Camera Obscura

TIM WAGGONER
- [ ] Nekropolis
- [ ] Dead Streets
- [ ] Dark War

KAARON WARREN
- [ ] Mistification
- [ ] Slights
- [ ] Walking the Tree

IAN WHATES
- [ ] City of Dreams & Nightmare
- [ ] City of Hope & Despair
- [ ] City of Light & Shadow